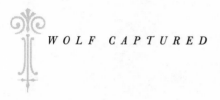 *WOLF CAPTURED*

TOR BOOKS BY JANE LINDSKOLD

THROUGH WOLF'S EYES

WOLF'S HEAD, WOLF'S HEART

THE DRAGON OF DESPAIR

WOLF CAPTURED

THE BURIED PYRAMID

WOLF
CAPTURED

JANE LINDSKOLD

A TOM DOHERTY ASSOCIATES BOOK

NEW YORK

WOLF CAPTURED

Copyright © 2004 by Jane Lindskold

This book is printed on acid-free paper.

Edited by Teresa Nielsen Hayden

Map by Mark Stein Studios based on an original drawing by James Moore

A Tor Book
Published by Tom Doherty Associates, LLC
175 Fifth Avenue
New York, NY 10010

www.tor.com

Tor® is a registered trademark of Tom Doherty Associates, LLC.

Library of Congress Cataloging-in-Publication Data

Lindskold, Jane M.
　　Wolf captured / Jane Lindskold.—1st ed.
　　　p　　cm.
　　"A Tom Doherty Associates book."
　　ISBN 0-765-30936-X (alk. paper)
　　EAN 978-0765-30936-5
　　1. Wild women—Fiction.　　2. Human-animal relationships—Fiction.　　3. Human-animal
communication—Fiction.　　4. Wolves—Fiction.　　I. Title.

PS3562.I51248W64 2004
813'.54—dc22

　　　　　　　　　　　　　　　　　　　　　　　　　　　　　　　　　　　　　2004051685

First Edition: November 2004

Printed in the United States of America

0　9　8　7　6　5　　4　3　2　1

＊

For Jim —
who listens when I
talk, and notices
when I don't

＊

ACKNOWLEDGMENTS

As always, I must thank my husband, Jim Moore, for providing a sounding board, responding with incredible patience to questions that often began with "I don't want to go into all the details but, if . . . " Jim's services as my first reader are also valuable beyond compare.

Thanks also to Bobbi Wolf and Mort Kahl for their comments on the manuscript.

My editors, Teresa Nielsen Hayden and Patrick Nielsen Hayden, were, as usual, a great help. My agent, Kay McCauley, provides me with encouragement as well as sound professional advice.

Finally, I'd like to thank all the readers who have taken the time to contact me and let me know they're enjoying the Firekeeper books. You can find information about these and other projects on my Web site: www.janelindskold.com.

DETAIL MAP OF THE LAND OF LIGLIM

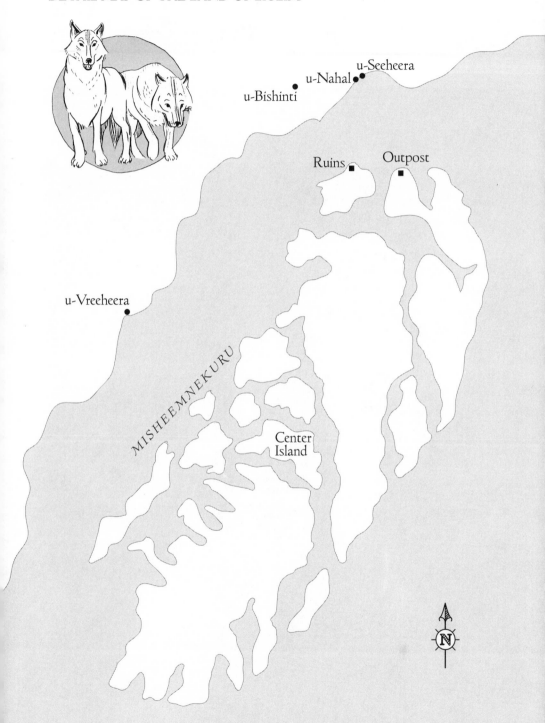

u-Seeheera

u-Nahal

u-Bishinti

Ruins

Outpost

u-Vreeheera

MISHEEMNEKURU

Center
Island

N

I

DERIAN CARTER AWOKE WITH HIS SHIRTFRONT wet with blood and his head pounding. The floor on which he lay was damp and reeked so strongly of piss and vomit that his stomach roiled. The rough board planks also seemed to be rising and falling—an impression he was willing to dismiss given how the rest of him felt.

Derian had experienced his share of hangovers, but this one was the worst by far. His last coherent memory was of dancing with that pretty girl from Bright Bay. She'd suggested they go for a walk along the riverbank. Something in how she phrased her invitation hinted that she had activities in mind more interesting than merely strolling on the spring-thick sward. She'd been very pretty, the neckline of her gown cut very deep. Derian had followed with slightly tipsy alacrity.

How had he gotten here?

A husky voice broke into Derian's efforts to sort fragmented impressions into order. "Fox Hair? You wake?"

The voice came from a short distance away, and for the first time Derian registered the dimness of the room. There was enough light for him to see his hands and the dark stain on the front of his shirt, but the light was diffuse, leaking into a chamber imperfectly sealed rather than being shed by sunlight or lantern.

Where was he?

The voice, forgotten almost as soon as heard, came again.

"Fox Hair! Derian! I hear you move. Talk."

The words were gruff, urgent, words spoken from a mouth struggling to give shape to the sounds, struggling against panic that would drive away the words and leave nothing but whimpers and howls.

A deeply ingrained sense of responsibility for the person who used that voice gave Derian his first breath of stability. He clung to it, grabbing his aching head between the curved fingers of his hands, forcing himself to remember. He found a word.

"Firekeeper?"

The sigh of relief that answered held a soft whimper, but when the voice spoke again there was no hint of tears.

"Firekeeper. Is."

A remembered image came with the voice, a woman, a few years younger than he. Dark brown hair slightly curly, cut unevenly, as from necessity rather than with any sense of style. Eyes very dark, figure slim, but no longer starvation skinny. Neither tall nor short, but somewhere in between.

Firekeeper, the woman who thought herself a wolf rather than a human. Firekeeper, whom he had taught to use the words she was in danger of losing. Firekeeper.

Memory almost sucked him from reality. The voice brought him back again.

"Fox Hair. You bleed. How bad?"

Derian touched his shirtfront, registering cold dampness there, stinging pain, but no fresh flow of blood. He'd already forgotten the wound until Firekeeper had reminded him. He wanted to forget it again now, but he forced himself to focus.

"I've been cut," he said, and heard the surprise in his voice. "Several times. Long, shallow slices. With a . . . knife?"

Despite himself, the last word came out as a question.

Firekeeper answered from somewhere in the gloom. Derian wondered a little that she didn't come closer now that she knew he was awake, but then Firekeeper saw far better in the dark than he did—than any human he'd ever heard of did.

"Yes. A knife. They cut you to bring me here. To bring me and Blind Seer."

"Blind Seer?"

Impressions were flooding back into Derian's mind now, competing with the ache, making the space behind his eyes feel crowded.

Blind Seer, an enormous grey wolf with blue eyes—named for those eyes, which his parents had thought meant he was blind until the staggering explorations of the pup had proven them wrong. A wolf with parents, not merely sire and dam. Born of beasts with sufficient intelligence to worry about a damaged pup, beasts possessed of the inhuman resignation to accept the handicap and the early death it promised for a pup Derian knew meant as much to them as did any child to human parents.

"Blind Seer," Firekeeper's voice repeated. "He sleeps. They give us all to drink."

Derian processed this, enlightened by his throbbing head.

"We were drugged?"

Firekeeper snorted. Derian could almost see her toss her dark brown hair from even darker eyes. She was rarely patient with the human tendency to repeat what to her was obvious.

"Firekeeper," Derian said, and made his voice as stern as he could. "I feel like shit. My head wants to split open down the middle. Tell me what happened. Tell me slowly and carefully."

He heard a soft laugh.

"My head hurt, too," Firekeeper admitted. "I try to tell what happened, but keep voice down. We not want them come."

"Them? Who?"

"Not know."

"Why don't you come sit next to me?" Derian felt almost frantic for physical contact.

"I no can. They have me in . . ." The pause came that meant the wolf-woman was struggling for a specific word. "A cage. Blind Seer in cage, too. Not you, I think. Can you move?"

Derian tried, felt something tug at his ankle, tested and found a length of chain cuffed around it. By now he was hardly surprised.

"I'm chained," he reported. "What's going on?"

"I tell what I know," Firekeeper promised, her voice soothing. "We were at the night dancing. A man come to me in the dance. He say 'Derian needs you.' I am not sure, but think maybe it is a king thing so I follow even when the man takes us from the bright spaces to the fields by the river."

Mentally, Derian fleshed out Firekeeper's words. She and Blind Seer had been participating in one of the large public dances being held to celebrate the naming of the firstborn son of Crown Princess Sapphire and Crown Prince Shad. The celebrations had been extensive, for not only was young Sun the first child born to the royal family of Hawk Haven for many years, but through his parents he was destined to unite Hawk Haven and Bright Bay, sibling kingdoms that had been rivals for over a century.

Sun of Bright Haven, a name filled with promise and hope.

Normally, Firekeeper would have shied from such loud and noisy gatherings, but among all human achievements she loved music and dancing best—and at the royal celebrations where she was welcomed, the finest of both were to be found. So she had joined in the festivities at the castle, and when these had spilled out into the square in front, doubtless she—like Derian—had followed.

Blind Seer would have paced her, unseen in the torchlit darkness, never far from his human pack mate.

"I wonder some at the man," Firekeeper went on, "for he is not one I know and he stink of fear, but," she added a touch complacently, "many is feared of me and Blind Seer."

Derian grunted. Bragging she undoubtedly was, but it was a brag rooted in truth. It was commonly known that Firekeeper had been raised by the wolves west of the Iron Mountains. In the two years since she had come east to learn about her human heritage the only thing more incredible than the stories told about her was, quite possibly, the truth.

"And," Firekeeper added, and Derian heard the sorrow that roughened her voice, "I was happy and thought good of everyone."

After a long pause during which Derian knew Firekeeper was swallowing her bitterness at this error, the wolf-woman went on.

"The man take us to place on river where is not so easy to see water, the bank goes down sharply. We see a boat of the river type, hiding in branches. There is no other boat near and this boat is not such as king would have, so I am about to run and Blind Seer with me.

"Then the man who leads us raises his arm. He points and I see you. You are on the boat, a big man holding you against the wall, but you are not standing strong. I think maybe they have tied you there. As I look, the big man takes a knife and cuts you, long, across the chest. Blood comes, so I know you live, but I am not happy."

It took a moment for Derian's aching head to follow this last. Then he realized that what Firekeeper meant was that his blood flowing had confirmed he was alive. Dead things don't bleed, but certainly she could not have been happy to find him alive in such a circumstance.

Firekeeper went on, "Then the man with me say, 'You come and the wolf, too, or we'll let out all of Derian Carter's blood, and we'll do it slowly and make sure he's awake to feel it.' "

Derian rubbed his face with his hands again, trying to waken a memory of any of this, but there was none. He must have been well and truly drunk—or drugged.

"And you came?" he said, hearing the disbelief in his own voice. "You came?"

"We come," the husky voice replied. "They would do what they say, and though after we kill them all there would be no saving you. And I remember what you tell me when first I come from my pack—how Earl Kestrel use Blind Seer to make me do as he wish—and I think these men know that trick, too, and if not you, then maybe Elise or Doc or some other. I would not buy my running free for your blood."

"Horse . . ." Derian swore softly. He understood Firekeeper's reasoning, but it angered him to have been the hostage used to force her actions. She had come to him without any ties, unable to understand the concept of hostages until he had explained it. Now she was bound, and he hated being one of the ropes that bound her.

Firekeeper seemed to sense his anger, but misunderstood it. Her rough voice was almost tender when she next spoke.

"I think they want you for you," she said, "not just to use me. I hear them call you my keeper, and I think it good if they think this."

Derian nodded.

"Firekeeper," he said softly. "Do you think we can get away?"

"I not know," came the frank reply. "But I know no one of mine will look for us."

Derian's memory was returning now with such dismaying clarity that he almost wished for the headache to dominate again.

"No," he said, forcing the words. "We were leaving tomorrow morning, first west, then on a buying trip. No one will miss me for a moonspan or more, and even then they'll just think I was delayed."

He cursed the ill luck that made this possible. How many other people could travel through isolated areas so completely alone? He might be the only man in Hawk Haven who could—and that was because Firekeeper would be with him.

King Tedric had wanted them to take a look at the new fortifications going up in the gap in the Iron Mountains—to make the kind of report only they could manage, for

Firekeeper could ask her people if the measures were acceptable, while Derian could explain more clearly than anyone else just what was going on.

Most expeditions of this sort would involve pack trains and armed guards. The one Earl Kestrel had led two years before had done so. However, horses and mules were less than relaxed around Firekeeper and Blind Seer, so if she was to be involved, the fewer pack animals they used the better. Derian had access to a handful of horses and mules that had learned to tolerate the wolves, and after very little discussion had convinced the king to let them travel alone.

Derian suspected that Tedric had been easily convinced because the two of them arriving without fuss could more easily inspect—"spy upon" was a more honest term— the garrison before the garrison put on its best manners for the counselor of the king.

Derian felt a guarded flicker of hope.

"Firekeeper, we may be missed. True, we'd already said our good-byes, but there's Roanne and my pack horse, my camping gear, too. I left them west of Eagle's Nest."

Usually, he would have stabled at his parents' facilities, but Prancing Steed Stables was filled to overflowing. Its buildings were mostly grouped to the east of the city, and Derian hadn't wanted to guide Roanne and the pack horse through the streets that would be crowded with departing festivalgoers the next morning.

Far easier to move them the day before, taking them to a farm owned by friends of the Carter family who were more than happy to offer space in a back pasture.

"I forget this," Firekeeper said, and Derian was absurdly pleased to hear relief in her voice. "Then someone see we not take them and ask questions. Did any see you leave dancing?"

Derian shook his head, regretted the motion, and massaged his temples as he answered.

"Lots of people, but no one in particular. There was a young woman . . ."

Firekeeper snorted again, the soft gust mingled exasperation and amusement. She seemed immune to sexual impulses, even though regular nourishment had filled her once slat-sided figure into small rounded breasts and gently curving hips. It wasn't a matter Derian felt comfortable discussing with anyone. He grew pink even thinking about it.

Doc, Earl Kestrel's cousin, was less shy—at least where Firekeeper was concerned—and had once commented that prolonged starvation might have slowed Firekeeper's development. Sometimes, though, Derian wondered if there was something more involved, if Firekeeper really didn't think of herself as human and so human sexual impulses—and the things they led humans to do—really were alien to her.

Certainly, while the wolf-woman understood perfectly well why his mention of a young woman meant that Derian hadn't been anxious to draw attention to his departure, Firekeeper did not understand at all why he should be so eager to be alone with that same young woman.

Firekeeper snorted again, more laughter in the sound this time.

"You not the only one who want to be alone together," she said. "There were many leaving the dancing with that scent about them. But this not help us, only tell us that if there is help, we must make it."

Derian couldn't but agree.

ALTHOUGH SHE DIDN'T WANT TO say anything to Derian, Firekeeper was very worried—and worry was not an emotion with which she was at all comfortable.

Firekeeper was accustomed to the urgency of a hunt. Indeed, Derian had called her obsessive and irresponsible when she was after something. She preferred to think of herself as undistracted.

Humans were so good at worrying about what might happen that often they did nothing rather than risk a wrong action. Firekeeper never forgot what she was after and went directly for it. At least that was how Firekeeper preferred to think of herself, lightly dismissing the times she had worried about the consequences of her actions but acted nonetheless.

Now, trapped in a metal-barred cage in a smelly boat heading who knew where, she was worried. To make matters worse, all of these worries conspired to keep her from doing what she wanted to do, which was break out of the cage—if possible—and get out of this boat. She'd rather take her risks with the river than with these strangers.

However, there was no way she could do this. Derian had lapsed back into semi-consciousness, before, she thought, he realized just how serious their situation was. For one thing, he hadn't seemed to register that they were aboard a boat, and that the boat was moving. She had little idea of how swiftly they were traveling, but the sound of water against the sides suggested a fair amount of speed.

The Flin River was in spate, channeling runoff from the spring snowmelt, and the current was swift. It did not take an experienced sailor to realize that they were probably moving far more rapidly than anything ashore. Moreover, no one would notice one more boat among so many. Spring brought a return to river traffic, and with a new season nothing would be unusual—or rather, everything would be. Moons would wax and wane before the riverside dwellers would register which boats ran usual routes and so notice those that did not.

To make matters worse, she had no idea where they were headed. Maps were something Firekeeper understood, though she tended to struggle a bit with them. She had seen maps of the local waterways, rivers drawn as bright blue curves that to her eyes bore little resemblance to the broad, powerful reality. From Eagle's Nest, the capital city of Hawk Haven, the Flin ran southeast before encountering the Barren River. The Barren then continued northeast before emptying into the ocean at Hawk Haven's one harbor, Port Haven.

Then we are being taken, she thought, *either to Bright Bay or to the ocean.*

But this train of thought led her to no constructive conclusions about their captors. Bright Bay was officially friendly to Hawk Haven, but unlike in a wolf pack there were those who grumbled about the rulers, even when those rulers led strongly. She had heard few complaints about King Allister of the Pledge from those who had come from Bright Bay to celebrate the birth of his grandson, but then she would not have. She was known as Allister's friend, and in any case his enemies would not have made the long journey to celebrate the child's birth.

What if the boat was carrying them out onto the ocean? Firekeeper had seen the ocean, understood that somewhere across impossibly vast stretches of water were the Isles where Queen Valora—no friend to Firekeeper or those she valued—ruled. Firekeeper understood, too, that humans used the ocean as deer might a forest trail. Reaching the ocean might not be journey's end, but rather journey's beginning.

No. Thinking where they were going was useless. Only humans spent time planning hunts when the game had yet to be sighted. She would concentrate on what she did know.

That forced her to face uncomfortable facts she had been avoiding—that Blind Seer was sleeping very deeply, showing no sign of waking. The wolf's breathing was steady and regular. Indeed, whereas Derian had vomited as he was waking, Blind Seer showed no distress at all. Although it should have reassured her, that lack of distress bothered Firekeeper. Were their captors using some sort of magic to keep the wolf asleep? In the past she had witnessed the use of magics both great and small, but although the possibility of magic being used against them was disturbing, there was another possibility that bothered her even more.

There had been one among their captors, a slim, dark man with the highest cheekbones she had ever seen, who had made Firekeeper very uneasy. He had seemed unusually . . . She struggled to find the right word for the man's attitude. "Comfortable" didn't quite cover the idea, neither did "matter of fact," but there had been something of both in the man's actions as he gave orders. This bothered her. She had yet to meet any human whose initial encounter with Blind Seer had not been colored by fear. They might not show it, but Firekeeper knew the signs, knew the scent.

This man had not been afraid. Cautious, yes, but not afraid. He had emerged from inside the boat after Firekeeper and Blind Seer had come aboard. He had been the one who had measured out the drinks for her and Blind Seer.

The wolf's had been poured into a bowl of beef stock and set down on the deck. Firekeeper had been told to make certain Blind Seer drank it all before she drank her own. The man had watched with something of the same manner she had seen about Doc when the physician was dosing one of his patients—an air of analytical curiosity.

But no fear. No doubt. He had acted as if he knew what he was doing and had no question that what he planned would work. Was this merely confidence or was it something else?

It was a question Firekeeper knew she would not ask, even if opportunity presented itself. From the little she had overheard before the drug took her into sleep, she gathered that their captors might not be aware how clever she had become in understanding human ways. Best that they continue to think so. It might provide her a means of escape.

As much as Firekeeper disliked the possibility that magic had been used against them, she dreaded more the confidence she had perceived in the dark man. It had not been without cause. She had slept. Blind Seer still slept. Derian had slept, and though he had awakened sick, this could be because of the other things he had drunk earlier in the evening's entertainment rather than from whatever the dark man had done.

The dark man had reason for his confidence, and Firekeeper was wise enough to dread that confidence—and to wonder at its source.

Firekeeper had a wolf's patience when necessary, but she also had a wild animal's aversion to being trapped. Just because she couldn't see any way to escape now didn't mean she didn't want to be prepared in case the opportunity presented itself.

The square cage in which she was held was generously proportioned—if you were feeling charitable. She could lie down fully stretched out, even stand without stooping. The base and top were wood, the bars iron. A faint odor clung to the floor, but it wasn't one she could place. She'd ask Blind Seer about it when he woke. Compared with the wolf, she was nose-dead, just as compared with most humans she was astonishingly sensitive.

The reminder of her companions' drugged state gave a fresh urgency to her desire to break free. One by one she tested the bars. Each was solid in itself, but a few moved promisingly within the sockets that held them in the wood. If she had her Fang, she could have enlarged the hole, but the knife, along with the small pouch in which she carried flint and steel, had been taken from her.

She patted herself down to see what remained to her. She wore a long-sleeved cotton dress, certainly soiled by now. Originally, it had been pale blue with red trim, the colors of House Kestrel, the Great House into which she had been adopted. She had refused the matching slippers, but accepted a strand of coordinated glass beads. These had gone the way of her knife. The little cap that had started the evening pinned to her hair had been missing long before she'd been lured from the dancing.

Not much to work with. She was wondering if Derian had been as thoroughly disarmed when she heard footsteps on the deck directly above. These stopped and a moment later a square of light appeared off to one side. Almost as soon as it appeared, it was occluded by the shape of a man climbing down the angled steps of a ladder. He was followed by an arm that handed down a lantern, and then the owner of the arm also climbed down. Finally, a third man descended. With a chill, Firekeeper recognized the dark man.

Blind Seer and Derian were well and truly out of it, and she decided it would be to her advantage to appear at least somewhat disoriented. She debated pretending unconsciousness, but decided against that immediately. Although she had been doing her best to ignore it, she was very thirsty, and if the men did not offer her water, she must ask.

Another advantage of not pretending to be asleep was that she could see everything they did. So when the circle of lantern light came over by the cages Firekeeper was sitting up, her arms wrapped around her knees, her chin resting on her folded arms.

"Rarby, hang the lantern up," the dark man said. He spoke Pellish, the language common to Bright Bay and Hawk Haven, but with an accent Firekeeper had never heard before. "I may need your assistance."

"Right, Harjeedian," Rarby said.

Rarby was a big man, both tall and broad. The bright blue-and-white-striped sweater he wore emphasized that breadth. His accent was familiar, though with more of the sound of Bright Bay to it, Firekeeper thought. Not surprising, since he and his companion were both obviously sailors and Bright Bay traditionally followed the sea.

The other man resembled Rarby closely enough that Firekeeper guessed they were brothers. This second man was a touch taller, but not as broad as Rarby. He wore a knit cap in the same blue and white, pulled tight to his ears. His chin seemed both pale and reddish. Firekeeper realized after a moment's thought that he must have very recently shaved off a heavy beard.

Then she recognized him. The newly shorn man was the one who had lured her from the dancing. Rarby was the man who had cut Derian. She swallowed a growl. They must think her weak.

Harjeedian saw Firekeeper move and crossed to stand in front of her cage. Firekeeper noticed that he stopped an arm's length away. She didn't think this was accidental. In the lantern light, she got a far better look at him than she had at their first encounter.

He was of medium height, his build slim, though lithe and muscular. His jet black hair was very straight, parted in the center, left to hang loose to just above his shoulders. The blunt weight of it emphasized the sharp angle of his cheekbones and the tilt of his eyes, so that the eyes seemed squashed to slits between cheekbone and eyebrow. His skin was a deep, warm brown, without the extensive weathering evident on both the sailors, so she thought the darker color must be natural.

"How do you feel?" Harjeedian asked in his precise Pellish.

Firekeeper paused before answering. Let them think her slow.

"Not good," she said. "They worse, though. Fox Hair stink and Blind Seer no wake."

"Put your arm through the bars where I can reach it," Harjeedian said. "I need to feel the pulses."

Firekeeper had seen Doc do this, and knew degrees of health could be read through the art. She had tried to learn it, but never was certain she felt any pulse but her own. Reluctantly, she thrust her arm through the bars, determined to seem cowed.

Harjeedian grasped her wrist in one long-fingered, lightly callused hand, positioned his fingers, and stared at nothing.

"Somewhat fast," he said, "but nothing to worry about. Does your head hurt?"

"Much," Firekeeper lied.

"Hmm. I thought I judged the dose better than that. I understood that you did not drink alcohol. I must have misjudged the relative ratio of muscle to fat."

Firekeeper stared at him. The words were Pellish, but made little sense to her. All she was certain of was that Harjeedian didn't think she should have a headache.

"I'm thirsty," she whined.

"That could account for the headache," Harjeedian said. "Shelby, draw water for Lady Blysse—while you're at it, draw enough for all of our guests."

The man in the knit cap nodded and left. His steps were quick, and Firekeeper was certain he was glad to be away.

What is he afraid of? she thought. *Me? I am locked. Perhaps he fears Harjeedian. Harjeedian gives the orders.*

Harjeedian let her hand drop and stepped back from the cage.

"Has Derian Counselor or the wolf awakened?"

"Derian did, for a little. Blind Seer, no."

She heard the worry in her own voice. Harjeedian looked pleased.

"The wolf still sleeps? Very good. I will look to him last. First, the king's counselor."

He walked to where Derian lay sprawled on the deck, knelt, and lifted the young man's head. As before, Harjeedian spoke his conclusions aloud, though Firekeeper was uncertain just who was intended to be his audience. Rarby never responded to anything said, nor did Harjeedian seem to expect a response.

"Breathing. That's good. A bit shallow. Vomit on mouth and face, but not sufficient to choke him. The purge worked as planned then, but there must have been too much alcohol already in his blood."

Derian moaned, stirred, and tried to sit up. Harjeedian did not restrain him, and Derian succeeded in propping himself onto one elbow. The chain securing his ankle clanked as he moved.

"Who the . . . What?" Derian managed rather incoherently. "Firekeeper?"

He blinked and his hazel eyes focused on Harjeedian. He paused as he registered the unfamiliar face, Rarby standing a few paces beyond, and Shelby coming from above with waterskins slung over his shoulders and a bucket in one hand.

"Who are you?" Derian asked, sounding more angry than afraid.

"Harjeedian will do," the man said, leaning forward to grasp Derian's free wrist. "I am your escort."

"Escort?" Derian wrested his wrist free and pulled himself into a sitting position. "Kidnapper is more like it! Escort where? To whom? Did you ever think about issuing more usual invitations?"

"The ones who sent me do not think that way. They desire something, and what they desire will be acquired for them. You will learn more of this in time."

Harjeedian smiled and Firekeeper was uneasily aware that this man was dangerous.

She was also unhappily aware that Harjeedian had spoken of whoever it was he served as "they." In the back of her mind she had thought that their enemy was somehow connected to Queen Valora of the Isles, but Valora would never be mistaken for more than one. Her husband was most definitely not a power who could be spoken of in one breath with her as one might Princess Sapphire and her consort, Prince Shad.

Harjeedian extended his hand for Derian's wrist.

"Cooperate with me and I will do what I can to eliminate any physical discomfort you are feeling. The dosage of the drug my agent administered to you could only be estimated. I could not account accurately for the alcohol in your system and though I took measures to ascertain that you would not be harmed, I could not . . ."

"Who are you!" Derian roared, surging to his feet. "I want answers."

"You want something for your headache," Harjeedian said, rising with effortless grace. "You want a bath and clean clothing. I can obtain these things for you, but only if you cooperate."

Derian stared down at Harjeedian, but for all the difference in their heights—Derian was a very tall man—to Firekeeper it seemed that Harjeedian was the larger. Perhaps Derian too felt the force of the dark man's personality. Perhaps he simply became aware of Rarby standing ready a few paces away, or felt the weight of the chain around his ankle, but Derian suddenly held very still.

He thrust out his arm, wrist turned upward. Harjeedian smiled slightly and took it.

"Quick and erratic," he commented. "No great surprise there."

He raised a hand to Derian's forehead.

"Damp. Fever broken, though. You are a strong young man. I think even without my assistance you would soon be in good form. Shelby, did you bring sufficient water for washing?"

"Yes, sir."

"Good. Pour a little into this cup, then give a wet rag to Counselor Derian. You can handle the deck."

For Firekeeper, the next few minutes were almost dreamlike in their ordered practicality. Derian washed, then was given a change of clothes, and a cup into which Harjeedian had mixed some powder. Shelby thoroughly scrubbed the stinking deck; then the damp area was covered with a heap of clean straw. A blanket was placed over that, and Derian was invited to sit. He did so without comment, his movements so contained that Firekeeper wondered if he were feeling ill once more.

"There is a covered pail for waste behind you," Harjeedian concluded. "I suggest you use it, if at all possible. Now I shall look to the wolf."

From inside his shirt, Harjeedian pulled a chain that glittered gold in the lantern light. He removed one key from a small assortment that hung upon a ring and tucked the rest away again.

"Rarby, Shelby, ready the crossbows. Rarby, orient yours on Lady Blysse, Shelby, on the wolf."

As much as Firekeeper hated Harjeedian for his foresight, she also had to admire him. There was a distinct possibility that if Blind Seer attacked their captors he could take out all three men before any injuries he took significantly slowed him—and although she hated to admit it, his devotion to her was such that he might well risk his own life to win her freedom.

Rarby moved to where any shot from his bow would be instantly fatal for Firekeeper.

"Ready, Harjeedian."

Shelby grunted his own readiness.

Harjeedian turned to Firekeeper before stepping close to Blind Seer's locked cage. "I think he is still asleep, but if he is not, I suggest you tell him of my arrangements."

Firekeeper did not say a word. She had resolved some time before that her early attempts to convince humans of the intelligence of her Royal Beast companions had been an error. What she would not admit to in the company of allies she would not do in front of enemies.

Harjeedian's thin lips shaped a small, humorless smile. Without further comment, he opened the cage and went inside.

Almost without volition, Firekeeper found herself drawn close to the bars of her own cage, as close as she could get to the wolf. She heard Derian gasp, and knew that her movement must have startled Rarby as well, but the crossbow remained unfired.

Harjeedian placed his hand on Blind Seer's head, peeled the lid back from the wolf's eye and inspected the pupil, grunted something, then inspected the gum, pressing the skin above the shining white fangs. He pushed back fur to expose the skin below and pinched there, then lifted the bushy weight of the tail and inspected beneath. Examination completed, he rose to his feet and left the cage.

After Harjeedian had locked the door behind him, he said, "The wolf is somewhat dehydrated, not surprisingly, given the amount of time he has slept. It will be to your advantage if you convince him to drink when he awakens."

"You not," Firekeeper asked, "make him sleep again?"

"Not yet, at least," Harjeedian replied. "There would be no advantage in that. You will be fed and given fresh water to drink for the duration of our voyage. Later, there will be opportunities for exercise as well. However, let me make clear here and now that the quality of the food and the quantity of the exercise will be awarded in proportion to your good behavior."

Firekeeper blinked, tilting her head to one side in confusion.

Derian gave a dry cough of a laugh. "You'll get fed better if you don't give them any trouble."

Harjeedian gave him a nod of thanks.

"We will be going now. Food will be brought later. You have sufficient water."

Rarby raised a hand to take down the lantern.

"Wait!" Derian said. "Surely you can leave us some light."

Harjeedian paused, considering.

"I think not. Fire is a dangerous thing to leave untended, especially on a wooden vessel with all this straw about. Your eyes will adjust to what daylight comes from above."

With that the three men departed, lowering the trapdoor above and shooting home the bolt.

II

"FIREKEEPER?" DERIAN SAID into the grey darkness.

He started to ask, "Are you there?" but stopped himself in time. Of course she was there. Where could she go? Articulating the question would only emphasize their captivity.

"How do you feel?" he asked instead.

"Not so bad as you," she replied. The slightest hint of a chuckle underlay her words, so Derian suspected she knew what he had been about to ask. "How feel you?"

"Better than when I came around the first time," Derian replied. "Whatever else he is, that Harjeedian knows his doctoring. The powder he gave me has pushed back most of the headache."

"You hear what he say?" Firekeeper asked. "We are on boat. Where do we go? Who is this man? The other two could be Bright Bay or maybe Isles, but him is strange."

The speech was a long one for the wolf-woman, and for once Derian felt no reflex impulse to correct her grammar.

"I have no idea who Harjeedian is," Derian said, "except that he's in charge of this operation. I've never met anyone who looks quite like him. His eyes remind me somewhat of a Stoneholder's—one of their Alkyab—but I don't think I've ever seen skin that color."

Stonehold, a kingdom to the south of Bright Bay, was populated by two groups with wildly different physical appearances, the big, fair Tavetch and the petite, dark-haired, ivory-skinned Alkyab.

"Skin not stained, as in New Kelvin," Firekeeper added. "I look when Harjeedian is close. Is his own color."

"I may have seen a few people like him at a horse fair once, years ago," Derian said, "but I can't be sure. To tell the truth, my attention was all for the horses. I didn't spare much for the people."

The Carter family ran a successful livery stable in Eagle's Nest, with affiliated stables in several other Hawk Haven cities. Until a few years ago, Derian had imagined he would inherit the family business and had been quite content with the prospect. Like all his relations, he had a sense for good horses, and enjoyed their company. He hoped that the farmer had found Roanne by now and sent the mare back to his parents.

"I wonder," Derian said to distract himself, "what day it is? How long do you think we were out? It was late evening when we were taken and the sun's bright now, but is it the next day or later?"

"Not know," Firekeeper admitted. "I would say next day, but my belly is rumbling so it may be longer. Derian, do you think they take us east?"

"That seems most likely. I'm not a sailor, but if we were going west I think we'd hear more motion from above, sails being set to go against the current, that kind of thing."

His eyes had adjusted to the gloom and he could see Firekeeper's nod.

"And more back-and-forthing, I think," she added. "Down we just go like a leaf, with some keeping from rocks."

"They could use a sail going downstream," Derian said, "and probably are. I don't remember where the winds come from this time of year, but I know I've seen sailing boats out on the Flin."

They sat for a moment, Derian pondering his ignorance, Firekeeper perhaps doing the same.

The Flin River eventually emptied into the Barren, which provided the boundary between Hawk Haven and Bright Bay. The confluence of those rivers was fairly densely populated. Only a year or so before, any boat coming through that point might have faced customs inspections from either or both of the kingdoms. Indeed, the cities of Rock Fort and Broadview had maintained garrisons expressly for that purpose. Now the two kingdoms were so eager to avoid any appearance of friction that anything other than an obvious warship would probably make it through unchallenged. The garrisons remained, focusing their attention on easing the economic merging of the two former rivals.

All right, Derian thought, *then unless we've been missed, we can't count on any random search finding us. I wonder if we have been missed? I wonder what day it is? I wonder how far from Eagle's Nest we are? Did they risk sailing by night? Smugglers do. Could Rarby and Shelby be smugglers? And who is Harjeedian?*

Derian longed to articulate his questions, but knew Firekeeper would be frustrated by empty conjecture. He looked over and saw that Firekeeper had moved in her cage, crossing to the side nearest to the cage holding the wolf.

"Is Blind Seer awake yet?"

"Waking. I think. Yes."

Derian moved as close as his ankle chain would permit. The enormous grey wolf was indeed stirring, and with that awakening he seemed to gain in size as well as in mobility.

Blind Seer belonged to a type of animal that Firekeeper, struggling for an appropriate term in those days when her command of Pellish had been limited, had dubbed "royal." As Derian understood it, the Royal Beasts were at least as intelligent as humans, and were possessed of their own laws, customs, and legends. If Firekeeper was to be believed, the Royal Beasts—or at least the wolves who had reared her after the death of her human parents—were also possessed of far greater integrity and far less indecision than the mass of humanity.

The Royal Beasts had been the sole inhabitants of the land before explorers from the Old World nations had established the colonies that had evolved into Hawk Haven, Bright Bay, and their neighboring nations. The Old World nations had used very powerful magic to force the Royal Beasts into retreat across the mountains to the west. They had also used it to control their own colonists, teaching the key elements of magical lore only to those who traveled to the homeland. When plague had driven the rulers back across the ocean, knowledge of greater magic had vanished as well—a forgetting hastened along by the colonists themselves, who had no desire to find themselves under some homegrown version of that particular yoke.

Even after the Old World rulers had departed, the Royal Beasts had not returned from their exile across the mountains, and until recently—at least as far as Derian knew—humans had stayed to their lands in the east. An unconscious truce existed, helped by the fact that until Firekeeper had been found, most humans had believed the tales of gigantic, intelligent beasts were just legend. It was more comfortable to believe the legend—even when faced with the evidence.

Blind Seer was the size of a pony, though leaner in build. His fur was predominantly grey, touched with brown and white. His eyes were a startling blue. Derian had learned to read some of the moods in those eyes, though perhaps the tilt of ears and the amount of exposure given to gleaming white fangs told more about the wolf's feelings. In turn, Blind Seer had developed a limited ability to communicate with humans, nodding and shaking his head for "yes" and "no," refining these gestures with growls, whines, and tail motion—whatever served to get his point across.

But Derian was certain that Firekeeper's ability to communicate with the wolf was far less limited. Indeed, he thought she might speak "wolf," if there was such a language, far more easily than she spoke Pellish.

What the relationship was between Blind Seer and Firekeeper Derian couldn't quite tell. Sometimes Firekeeper referred to the wolf as her brother, always referring to the heads of their pack as "their" parents. Other times the two seemed like best friends or sworn companions, recalling the tales of warriors from Old Country ballads.

Of one thing Derian was absolutely certain. Blind Seer was not Firekeeper's pet, and though she had ceased to object when such a reference was made, Derian knew that the easiest way to offend her was to refer to the wolf as such.

Firekeeper was intent on the wolf, watching as Blind Seer tested his footing, shook the straw and chaff from his fur, otherwise ascertained just how much damage remained from the drug. Doubtless Firekeeper was also informing the wolf what had happened while he had been asleep, for at one point Blind Seer looked toward the deck above and gave a deep, rumbling growl.

"Derian," Firekeeper asked, "how deep into boat is bottom of chain?"

Derian was puzzling through this odd question when footsteps on the deck above signaled someone approaching the trapdoor to the upper deck. Woman, wolf, and man each froze, eyes turning in the direction of the hatchway, all questions forgotten but for the essential one: Who was coming and what were his intentions?

They heard the solid metallic thud of a bolt being shot back, then a rectangle of light announced a lantern being lowered. Shelby followed the light, waterskins flung over his shoulders. While he was hanging the lantern from the ceiling, Rarby descended, carrying a covered pot.

"Supper," Rarby said with mocking cheerfulness. "Harjeedian said the wolf would be awake by now, and I see he was correct. We have a different menu for him. Go get it, Shel."

Shelby grunted assent and mounted the ladder. Rarby set his pot down on a shelf built into one side of the hold, then rummaged in a cabinet snugged below the shelf, coming out with wooden bowls and spoons.

"Now," Rarby said, still with that tone of assumed geniality. "Let me explain the rules. I give each of you two a bowl of this stew. Fish stew. Fresh. Same as we had ourselves. I give you bread and fresh water. You enjoy. Any messing about, trying to grab me or attack or such, and I stop waiting on you and you go hungry. Same goes for the wolf when Shelby comes down with his grub. Understand?"

Derian nodded. His mouth was watering at the scent of the savory stuff, but he wondered if he should trust the contents. He didn't much want to be knocked out again.

Rarby seemed to divine his thoughts.

"This stuff is good. No drugs. I'll even demonstrate." He dipped a ladle into the pot and drank from it. "Harjeedian says too many drugs aren't good for a person—especially one like you who has mucked up his system with too many nights out on the town. So you can eat what we offer and keep your strength. That's what Harjeedian wants."

Shelby came down the ladder carrying a loose canvas sack. Damp bloodstains leaked through the fabric at several points. He stepped toward Blind Seer's cage, then hesitated. Standing, the wolf looked very big. Rarby gave Shelby a crooked half-grin.

"I've explained the terms," he said, "and I think our guests are smart enough to accept them. Anyhow, you don't have to open the wolf's cage to put that sack in there, just squash it through the bars."

Shelby did as he'd been told, but Derian could tell he was nervous. Blind Seer didn't make the sailor's job any easier by standing in the center of the cage, his jaws parted so that his teeth showed. Derian thought the wolf might be laughing, but to anyone unfamiliar with the animal, the pose looked watchful and dangerous—indeed, humor or not, it *was* watchful and dangerous.

After shoving the sack of meat through the bars, Shelby stood back and squeezed water from one of the large leather bottles into the deep bowl inside the cage. While he was doing this, Rarby served Derian a bowl of what proved to be very good seafood stew and cut him a thick slab of dark brown bread.

"Butter or soft cheese?"

"Butter," Derian replied automatically. "Thanks."

"My pleasure." Rarby turned to Firekeeper. "You're not going to try anything, are you? I have to open the cage to hand you your bowl. Give me any trouble, and you'll get raw meat."

"No problem," Firekeeper said, her voice sounding strained, "and I like meat."

"Well, you're not going to see much this trip. We're saving what we can keep fresh for the wolf. After that, he eats fish, if we can catch it."

Firekeeper did not reply, only stepped back in her cage when Rarby approached with the bowl of fish stew. She let him put the bowl on the deck and close the door between them before claiming her meal. She tested the temperature, then tilted the bowl to her mouth, drinking messily, slurping out the chunky bits with evident satisfaction.

Rarby watched her with disgust for a few moments before slicing a chunk off of the loaf of bread.

"Butter or cheese?"

"Butter," came the wolf-woman's reply, muttered around a spine bone from a large fish. She spat the bone out, "Please."

Rarby shook his head. Derian heard him say softly to Shelby, "And they call that 'Lady'?" Shelby, who had been trying not to watch Blind Seer efficiently ripping open the bag of meat and tearing into the contents, didn't comment.

The two men stayed until their captives had eaten, then retrieved bowls and spoons. Smaller leather water bottles were filled and distributed, and the captives were reminded to use the waste buckets.

"We'll make arrangements for cleaning up after the wolf," Rarby said. "Nice if he'd shit near where we can get to it without opening the cage."

Firekeeper didn't reply, and Derian wondered if she'd even take the hint. Lately she'd been as reluctant to do anything that would confirm rumors about the wolf's intelligence as she had once been to prove it. He didn't much like the idea of being imprisoned in a small area reeking of wolf shit, though, and hoped Firekeeper wouldn't press the point.

For now she was lying on her back, as close as possible to Blind Seer. Her eyes were shut, and Derian couldn't tell if she was sleeping. He did know she was in no mood for conversation, so reluctantly he settled himself onto his straw pallet, wrapped his fear and loneliness around him, and tried to sleep.

"FIREKEEPER," Blind Seer's words went unheeded by Derian or the other two humans. Indeed, they were not words as humans used them but a combination of sounds and body cues. Firekeeper understood them automatically, not even thinking about how she managed. For her, the language of the wolves was her birth tongue and Pellish a clumsy second.

"What?" she grunted.

The fish stew had tasted good, but to Firekeeper's surprise her stomach did not seem happy with it. It was all she could do to choke the thick stuff down. Even after being swallowed, the viscous mass moved uneasily in her belly. She left the slab of bread half-eaten, tucking it under the straw for later.

"My meat," the wolf said, trailing off.

"Is it tainted? Did they lie about the drugs?"

Blind Seer shoved a piece near where she could see it.

"Can you catch the scent from there, Little Two-legs? The hide is still attached."

The use of her childhood name indicated that Blind Seer was uneasy, feeling protective. Firekeeper ignored her unhappy belly and moved closer to the edge of the cage. Blind Seer had shoved a large chunk of meat cut from a haunch, leg bones still attached, to where she could see it. She sniffed.

"Only blood scent," she replied apologetically. *"Horse blood?"*

"Horse," Blind Seer replied. *"A horse I know. Derian's Roanne."*

Firekeeper froze, weighing the implications of this and not liking them at all. She took a closer look. The long white stocking that had flashed so proudly in contrast to the gleaming chestnut coat was there, though bloodied, the chestnut hair dimmed with dirt and handling.

"Didn't you say," Blind Seer asked, *"that Derian hoped the finding of the horses would lead to our disappearance being noted? I think someone else had that thought and took steps to make certain all would think we had left by usual routes. Roanne was a showy beast, though, and could not be easily sold or disguised. Then, too, they would need feed for me. Slaughtering her and possibly the pack horse as well would solve two problems."*

Firekeeper nodded stiffly, a variety of emotions warring within her. She, too, had known Roanne, and had come to something of a truce with the chestnut mare. The mare was Cousin-kind, not Royal, but she had been smart enough to know that neither Firekeeper nor Blind Seer offered a real threat. Roanne's awareness had communicated itself to other horses, and they had been moderately content to follow the herd mare's lead.

For that reason, if no other, Firekeeper had reason to regret the mare's death. However, she had other reason. Derian had loved the mare as humans did their valued pets. Roanne had not merely been an elegant and reliable means of transportation, she had been a friend and ally. Derian had known her moods, good and bad, treasured her beauty and laughed over her little vanities. Learning that Roanne was dead would have been hard at any time. To find that she had been slaughtered and turned into wolf-feed would . . .

Firekeeper wasn't sure exactly what Derian's reaction would be. Anger, certainly.

Revulsion, probably, along with self-hatred for his inability to prevent the act. Then, too, there would be the loss of hope, for if Roanne was dead, so was any hope it would be realized they were missing. Doubtless their gear had been carried away as well. With no trace of them remaining, everyone who knew them would assume they had begun their journey west.

"*Do you tell Derian?*" Blind Seer asked, cracking into the leg bone and licking out the marrow. He had gone hungry often enough to not pass up a meal, not when his fasting would do no good for Roanne.

"*I think we must,*" Firekeeper said, "*but not until he has a chance to digest the food within him. He was very ill and might vomit up what he has eaten if we upset him now.*"

Blind Seer grunted agreement and went back to his meal. Firekeeper made herself a bed on the side of her cage closest to the wolf. She couldn't touch him, not even if she stretched her arm to its full length. However, there was a reason other than proximity for putting her bed here. When she had tested the bars of the cage, several in this area had rattled a little. While she thought how to tell Derian about Roanne, she could loosen them.

Firekeeper had concluded one thing about their captors. They—or at least Harjeedian, and the other men followed their master's lead—were fairly certain Blind Seer could understand more than the usual wolf. However, either they had not heard tales of her own abilities or they had discounted them as the exaggerations of traveling minstrels.

She must take advantage of this. They must attempt to escape before the boat reached the ocean. If she could break out of her cage, then she thought she could break Blind Seer out of his. Derian was chained around his ankle, and Firekeeper was not strong enough to break an iron chain. However, if the chain was anchored in wood it might be worked free.

"Derian," she said, breaking the silence.

"What?"

"I ask before. What is your chain tied in?"

There was a clanking noise as Derian traced the iron links down to their base.

"It's set in a big timber, screwed into the wood."

"Is at all loose?"

More clanking.

"I don't think so. I gave it a good tug and it didn't budge."

"Ah . . ." Firekeeper thought. "Can unscrew?"

Clank. Silence except for grunting.

"Maybe a little. It's pretty snug."

"Can you reach cabinet? I not see butter knife go up."

Derian dragged his chain behind him, stretched to his full limit, the long, lean length of his body extended along the floor. A moment later he made a satisfied noise.

"It's here. Not much of a weapon, but it might hack loose where the iron anchor is set in the wood."

Firekeeper returned to working on the bars of her cage, patiently wiggling the hard iron against the wooden socket so that friction wore away the wood. Her captors had taken her knife, but not her strength. After a long while she was able to rub one area thinner than the surrounding socket. Impatiently, she tugged, trying to break through that thinner edge. Nothing.

Firekeeper continued her methodical rubbing of iron against wood, grateful for her callused hands. Finally, she sufficiently thinned the wood so that a single, focused jerk broke through. A bit of twisting, and the bar came loose from the upper socket and could be drawn out. Now she had both weapon and tool.

"Derian," Firekeeper called softly, her voice holding a touch of a musical wolf's howl. "Look." When he turned from his labors she showed him the gap in the bars of her cage, hefted the bar triumphantly.

"I push through," she said, demonstrating, glad she wasn't more thickly built, "and put the bar back if must hide what I have done."

Derian grinned at her, his first cheerful expression since he had awakened. Firekeeper hated the idea of taking his rising morale from him, so resolved to hold the news about Roanne a bit longer.

"Now," she said. "I come and see your work."

Given that all he had to work with was an old butter knife, Derian had done very well. The bolt had been driven into the wood fairly recently, and the timber had not been of the finest or driest, even before Derian had begun his ministrations.

Firekeeper hunkered down next to Derian, focusing lest the persistent queasiness in her gut get the better of her. She grasped the anchor bolt where the chain ran through the loop at the end and twisted. The bolt moved, just a little. She wrenched again and this time the bolt emerged slightly from the wood, leaving a faint haze of sawdust in its wake.

Behind her, Derian cheered under his breath.

"Now," Firekeeper said, "you keep working it loose. I go see what I do for Blind Seer."

"Firekeeper, do you mean to try and escape?"

Derian did not sound upset. He was only doing as humans always did, confirming what common sense should have told him.

"We must," Firekeeper replied. "I think we must try first time they come to look at us after we are free of chains and cages. This food time they not bring bows. They not lock door. Food time will be our time."

But perhaps I will not eat, she thought. *I do not think eating will make me strong. I do not like how my gut feels.*

"But someone may rescue us," Derian said.

She could tell from the man's tone that he didn't believe this was likely, but felt he must make the prudent suggestion, so she only grunted in response.

Firekeeper knelt alongside Blind Seer's cage now, testing the bars, seeking out the loosest ones. With the iron bar as a tool, breaking away the wood should prove easier.

The ship itself made so many noises—timbers popping and creaking, sails snapping—that as long as she didn't pound too loudly or too rhythmically, her working should pass undetected.

The wolf-woman decided that the best place for Blind Seer to emerge from his cage would be the open side away from her cage. The backs of both cages were bolted to the side of the ship. If she concentrated her efforts on the side with the door the sailors might see evidence of the damage she had done. Besides, the alley between their cages was wide enough to separate them, but not so wide that the wolf could maneuver easily. Straw bedding could be shoved over the base of the cage bars in an emergency, and so hide what she had done.

Firekeeper got to work before resuming her conversation with Derian.

"Derian, no one come looking for us. No one worry we is gone for many moons turning." She took a deep breath. "Roanne is dead. The meat they bring Blind Seer is her."

Derian made a sound somewhere between a choke and a sob.

"No," he said in a voice full of pain, but Firekeeper knew he wasn't accusing her of lying, only trying to deny for a few minutes longer.

"Yes," she said, crossing to him, putting her hands on his bent shoulders. "Blind Seer know and tells me."

Had she been human, she would have made up some comforting lie about the wolf being sorry, but she knew Derian wouldn't believe her. She settled for letting him hear her own sorrow and anger, hoping that would be enough. Beneath her hands she felt Derian shaking, not only with tears, she thought, but with rage.

"Put anger-strength into the bolt," she said, "and we will be free."

She left to her own task before Derian could reply, knowing he would not want her to see his tears, and knowing as certainly as she now heard rain falling on the exposed upper side of the deck that he was weeping.

DERIAN SHOVED THE BUTTER knife into the wood, gouging out a chunk and exposing a bit more of the bolt's base. He blinked back tears. Somehow, he didn't think Firekeeper would think the less of him for crying, but she was being so strong in the face of their shared adversity that he didn't want to seem less.

He grasped the bolt and felt it turn, took a new hold and made slightly more progress. A third attempt did nothing, and he returned to hacking away with the butter knife. Tears blurred what vision was permitted by the dim light that seeped through the decking, so he stopped, forcing himself to face his grief.

Roanne had been among his first really good purchases. He'd spotted her potential when she was a newly weaned foal, hardly more than long legs made to seem longer by the snow white stockings that reached to just below her knees. Her dam was unremarkable, and her sire could have been any of several studs kept by the sloppy breeder, but Derian had known Roanne was special. He'd purchased her from his earnings as a hand at his parents' stables, trained her himself, and refused several good offers for her. Roanne was going to be his mount, proof that the Carter talent for judging horseflesh had been passed to the new generation.

Over time, Roanne had become more than a pride piece. During the journey west over the Iron Mountains Roanne had been Derian's confidant, his friend when he felt out of place among Earl Kestrel's men. When he went north to the Norwood estate, Roanne had been a touch of home. When their travels had taken them into New Kelvin, Roanne had been someone reliable in increasingly unpredictable surroundings.

Now she was dead, slaughtered for dog food. Colby Carter, Derian's father, had tried repeatedly to convince his son to breed Roanne and begin a line of gleaming chestnut foals. Putting her image on the sign for the newly rechristened Prancing Steed Stables had been a bribe to get Derian to see things his father's way. Derian had refused, wanting his horse with him. Colby's most recent try had been last season, but had Roanne been bred then, she would have foaled this spring, and Derian, who had already suspected he'd be traveling again, had not wanted to relinquish his favorite mount.

Now there would be no copper-bright chestnut foals, no dynasty claiming proud foundation in Roanne. All that would remain would be her image, swinging from the iron support in front of his father's office.

Derian ground his teeth together, finding anger easier to admit to than grief. He grabbed the bolt and twisted. This time it turned so easily he was surprised. He twisted again and the length of metal worked free from the wood.

"Firekeeper," he called softly, hearing the surprise in his own voice. "I got it loose."

"Good," Firekeeper said. "I almost have one of these free. Two and Blind Seer can push through. Can you get the chain from your ankle? I can give you iron bar to help."

Derian inspected the chain. It was fastened to an iron cuff. The cuff fit loosely enough on the outside of his trousers to prevent chafing, but not so loosely that he could slide his foot free. The first link of the chain was attached to a loop in the cuff, and with the use of the iron bar, Derian thought he might be able to force apart that link or one close to it.

Firekeeper handed him an iron bar, reminding him that she would need it back if the sailors returned before she had finished freeing Blind Seer.

"Light's going," Derian said. "Either they'll be back soon or we may not be fed until morning."

Firekeeper grunted.

"Is raining, too," she commented. "Maybe they not want to get wet."

The sailors did not return that night, and when Derian complained of hunger, Firekeeper offered him a piece of stale and straw-adorned buttered bread.

"I not hungry," she said in a curt fashion that forbore disagreement. "Wolfs not eat so as humans."

Derian, who had seen Firekeeper tuck in as if every meal might be her last, wondered at this, but didn't comment. He ate the bread, picking off the straw as best he could and washing the whole down with water.

He was adjusting to the idea of Roanne's death, determined to somehow get revenge for her. He didn't know just how he'd manage, since, if they escaped, relocating Harjeedian and his allies would not be easy. Nonetheless, Derian made his promise that Roanne's death would not go unrevenged to the Horse, his society patron and the guardian of all equines.

The vow was an empty gesture, but it made him feel better.

Derian was just swallowing the last of the bread when Firekeeper gave a grunt of satisfaction.

"There!" she said softly. "Blind Seer is now free. Let me do what I can with your chain. Have you had luck?"

"I managed to separate it a little," Derian said. "Not the link closest to the cuff—that was too near to my foot—but the next one. I kept hitting myself after the light failed. Can you see anything?"

"Not much," Firekeeper admitted. "I see better when is at least a little light. Still, if you trust, I go by touch."

"I'll trust," Derian said. "I want out of here."

He felt Firekeeper warm next to him, then the bigger, furrier warmth that was Blind Seer.

"You'll both be able to get back into the cages if we hear them coming?" he asked.

"Blind Seer hear better than we," Firekeeper said. "He warn."

Derian knew this was true, but he grew edgy waiting there in the darkness, feeling Firekeeper tugging at the chain, dreading that any moment the sharp tap of feet on the deck above would announce the sailors.

What if Blind Seer dozed off? What if the wolf didn't hear the sailors coming because of the rain? The storm was picking up, thunder crashing and rain trickling through the boards where light had come before. The straw on which he sat was damp and the air smelled of wet human and wetter wolf.

The boat tossed in the storm and Derian felt a cessation in Firekeeper's efforts and heard her groan.

"What's wrong?" he asked.

"My gut," she managed, then he heard her retching.

After what seemed like a long time, she stopped.

"Water?" she asked in a weak voice.

Derian handed her his bottle.

"Drink slowly," he said, "or you'll have it up again."

He heard her swallowing and simultaneously a lapping sound. When he realized what it was, he wanted to retch himself. Blind Seer was cleaning up after his pack mate.

"Did Harjeedian drug you after all?" Derian asked when Firekeeper put the water-skin back into his hands.

"I not taste it," she said, "Blind Seer not either. I think it is how the boat moves."

"Seasick," Derian said in revelation. "High Stepping Horse, you're seasick!"

Firekeeper groaned. "If giving word makes so, then is. When sea moves, I am sick."

Derian felt cautiously down his chain. Firekeeper had increased the gap, but not enough for him to slip the link free from the whole.

"Does this mean our escape plan is off?" he asked.

"No," Firekeeper replied sternly. "Now that gut is empty, I am a little better. I can finish chain."

She did, though the effort took her much of the night and she vomited more than once. The last time nothing more than sour bile came up, and Derian held her head and eased a bit of water into her. Her breath smelled foul and he almost wished Harjeedian would come. The man was strange and uncomfortable to be around, but there was no doubt he knew the medical arts. He might well know some trick to ease seasickness.

The worst of the storm ceased by morning. Though the boat still moved enough to make Firekeeper uncomfortable, she was clearheaded enough to offer a plan.

"Blind Seer's cage is closest to trapdoor. They see you, too. Me not so easily. We bundle straw and clothing into me and put in cage. You say I feel sick."

Derian manufactured a grin, knowing Firekeeper would see it in the traces of dawn light.

"That will be easy enough to make them believe. Even with Blind Seer's ministrations this compartment stinks."

"Blind Seer agree," Firekeeper replied, not sounding amused. "Now, I take bar from my cage. We hope they not notice. From where they hang lantern, light not reach good there. You take chain. They not think odd if you clank."

"And where will you be?" Derian asked. "Since your clothing will be standing in for you in your cage, I assume you plan to be elsewhere."

He caught the wolfish flash of Firekeeper's teeth in the grey light. It was not a friendly expression.

"I stand in shadow behind ladder. I watch before. They not look there. Busy with carrying things, they face other way. When they are down and lantern hung, I strike."

"And if you don't get that much time?"

"I strike," came the simple reply.

Derian nodded. "While I do my part from this side. What about Blind Seer?"

"His bars only look like they is in. We check and he can take out not too hardly."

"Without too much difficulty?"

"So I say."

Firekeeper's voice was tight and underscored with a growl. Derian realized the wolf-woman must still be fighting nausea and was in no mood to be teased.

"Let's be about it, then," Derian said. "Hand me your clothing and I'll stuff it. Good thing you were wearing a gown. It'll be easier to make look like a sick woman lying on her stomach."

Firekeeper stripped, still as completely shameless about nudity as she had been when Derian had first met her. She liked clothing, but as protection and sometimes ornamentation, not because she was uncomfortable in her skin.

Derian tried to match her ease with her nudity, but even in his current condition it was tough. Firekeeper was a whole lot more filled out than she had been two years before, and even the plethora of scars that adorned her every limb couldn't detract from his awareness of her small, firm breasts, topped by dark nipples, erect from the chill in the compartment.

Firekeeper handed him her underwear along with her gown, and he forced himself to look away from her slim torso, the hips slightly curving, the legs long and muscular.

"Use these clothes to make something to seem like head, maybe?" she said. "I rub boat dirt into skin so I not so bright."

She meant the grime from the boards, none of which were new or in the best condition. Derian had already guessed that the sailors had bought or stolen an older riverboat for their venture, probably the former since they wouldn't want anyone looking for the missing vessel. The condition of what he could see of the boat argued against it being taken out very far into the rougher waters of the ocean.

If this escape doesn't work, Derian thought, *maybe we can try again then. They'll probably work the switch some night at Port Haven.*

But he knew this attempt had better work. They were not likely to get another chance.

Firekeeper had just finished arranging the straw-stuffed gown into some semblance of a woman sleeping with one arm thrown up around her head when they heard the now familiar sound of feet on the deck above.

Firekeeper lifted the iron bar from where she had left it. Derian adjusted the length of chain, keeping his hands in the straw bedding, hoping if either Shelby or Rarby noticed, they would think he was easing the weight on his ankle.

As she glided into the shadows behind the ladder, Firekeeper's seasickness seemed gone. Derian almost fancied he could see the gleam of her eyes, dark stars amid greater darkness. Then the hatchway was unbolted and swung back, and he had attention for nothing but their bid for freedom.

III

FIREKEEPER TRIED TO IGNORE THE COLD air against her skin, but with her innards still shaking from repeated bouts of vomiting, she didn't find this at all easy. She distracted herself by testing the weight of the iron bar in her hands and mentally reviewing her plan.

Let both of the men down—all three if Harjeedian is with them. Hit the last one in line. Hope Derian can handle the one in front. Head for the upper deck, leaving the others to clear up below.

The first scent the wind carried down to her was that of horseflesh slightly spoiling, mingled with more of the seafood stew. Her gut twisted, and she had to fight the urge to vomit. This wasn't good.

Next she saw heavy boots on the ladder, facing forward. She admired the agility of the sailors on these narrow steps. It was as if their feet had eyes. A ring of light accompanied the booted feet, and she knew that Rarby carried the lantern with him. Two more sets of feet waited above.

So Harjeedian come, too, she thought.

Rarby carried not only the lantern, but two full water bottles slung over his shoulders. He sniffed as soon as his head was fully in the compartment.

"Whew!" he said. "What a reek!"

"Lady Blysse," Derian replied. "Seasick as a squirrel on a mill wheel. Where were you last night?"

Derian sounded indignant, not scared, and Firekeeper felt a warm surge of admiration for him.

"Storm was bad enough we didn't want to risk being swept over the side," Rarby said, glancing over at Firekeeper's cage as he hung up the lantern. "Didn't figure you'd want a great wash of water down here either."

Another set of boots were on the ladder now, the scent of horse meat and fish stew was stronger. Shelby, carrying the meat in a sack over one shoulder, the stew in a bucket.

Firekeeper listened. Yes. One more set of feet moved above. Rarby called back.

"Harjeedian, got anything in your bag for seasickness? Appears that Lady Blysse didn't take well to last night's storm."

"I have something," came the precisely enunciated words. "Don't give her anything to eat until I look at her."

Derian laughed dryly, a fairly natural sound except to one who knew him as well as did Firekeeper.

"I don't think she'd eat anything anyhow."

Firekeeper paused, reconsidering her plans. If she killed Harjeedian, she would also be killing the one person who might help her. Well, she hadn't planned on killing Harjeedian—one of the first lessons Derian had drilled into her was that she must not kill humans except in times of great need—only disabling him. She must be careful how much force she put behind the iron bar.

Shelby was down now, setting the bucket on the shelf, looking over to Rarby.

"Shall I give this to the wolf?"

Rarby glanced over, noted that Blind Seer was standing away from the front of the cage.

"Sure. He seems to know the drill."

Harjeedian's feet, clad in neat shoes of a design somehow unfamiliar—though perfectly practical—were on the ladder now. Unlike the sailors, he did not trust his feet, but came down facing the ladder, both his hands on the rails, unbalanced slightly by a bag hanging from a loop at his waist.

Firekeeper made herself motionless, even to her breathing. Harjeedian's attention was mostly for his feet, but if he looked through the treads, he might see her. She knew that motion rather than any actual image was what gave away one hidden in shadows, and Harjeedian's eyes would be adjusted to the bright sunlight above, not the dim light shed by the single lantern. Still, best not to take chances.

Rarby had pulled out the wooden bowls. He glanced over at Firekeeper's cage before beginning to ladle out the servings.

"She's awfully quiet over there," he said uneasily. "Could she have died? People sometimes choke."

Derian shook his head.

"I don't think so. I can't believe the wolf would be so calm."

"I'm going to take a look," Rarby said. "Shel, take over dishing out the stew. When Harjeedian is off the ladder, go back up and get the bread."

Harjeedian was three-quarters of the way down the ladder, and stopped at this implied criticism of his speed. He stared into nothing, apparently seeking to compose his expression, and looked directly into Firekeeper's eyes.

He made a small sound of surprise, and Firekeeper lunged. Her free hand snaked through the steps of the ladder, pushing Harjeedian back and off balance. He fell heavily to the floor and she was around the ladder, prepared to hit him with the iron bar.

Derian had two potential targets, for both Shelby and Rarby were close to him.

With an almost wolf-like sense of priorities, he went for Rarby, swinging the heavy weight of the iron chain at the other man's ankles. Rarby went reeling, crashing into the bars of Firekeeper's cage.

Shelby froze for a moment, ladle in hand, then went for Derian. The heavy metal bowl of the utensil glanced off Derian's shoulder, making the redhead stagger and drop the end of the chain.

Off to one side, Firekeeper heard Blind Seer removing the loose bars from his own cage.

"This one!" she howled. *"Let no one else down."*

The grey wolf howled in reply, and Firekeeper left Harjeedian and leapt at Shelby. Her iron bar caught him across the middle and he bent around the solid length, gasping for air. She jerked the bar free and brought the weight of it across Shelby's upper back. With a yell of pain and surprise, he went down.

Derian had recovered from Shelby's blow and was moving to secure Rarby. Rarby, however, had recovered from his shock and came around, catching Derian a solid fist into the gut. Derian came up from this, head-butting the other man in the hollow between his ribs. They grappled with each other, neither gaining ground, the heavy chain clanking beneath their feet.

Blind Seer had secured Harjeedian by the simple expedient of sitting on him and panting into his face. He didn't need language to make the threat any more clear. The man lay still and when a clatter of boots on the upper deck announced that others had heard the commotions, Harjeedian shouted:

"Don't come near the hatch. We'll handle it."

This hostage taking works both ways, Firekeeper thought grimly, securing Shelby's hands with a scrap of canvas torn from a meat sack. *I wonder how they like it?*

Rarby had paused when Harjeedian had yelled, and in that moment Derian knocked him cold with a blow that left him shaking his hand and blowing on the fingers. Firekeeper noted that Derian had a loose link from the iron chain in his fist and smiled at her friend's initiative. He must have worked it loose while she removed the bars from Blind Seer's cage.

"We have you," she said to the two who remained conscious. "Shelby, give me shirt."

Shelby's protest faded into silence when Blind Seer growled. His shirt was cotton with a long tail, and covered Firekeeper to the middle of her thighs. She borrowed Shelby's belt so the fabric wouldn't flap about, noting the sheathed knife with satisfaction. She had hated to be unarmed.

"Now we go above and take others. Derian, tie Rarby. I go up with Shelby and show the others we win."

"And Harjeedian?" Derian asked.

"Blind Seer watch for now. Then you tie."

Shelby cursed as she shoved him toward the ladder, but it was empty defiance. Whether Rarby was his brother or some other relation, they had him, and Harjeedian was clearly master of this expedition.

"Tell them," Firekeeper said as they climbed, "to put down all weapons or we kill others."

Shelby did so, adding of his own initiative, "They're right mad and the wolf is loose. Back off, mates."

There were three other sailors there, and they did as they were told. At Firekeeper's command, they tossed the weapons they held into a heap on the deck and stood over near the wheel.

"Make sure boat sail right," she said. "Or else."

Even though she was out of the stifling hold, her head was swimming. It was easier to fight the nausea if she kept her focus close and didn't look about. She longed for Derian to come up and take over the onerous task of communication. Blind Seer first, though. He would make most words unnecessary.

She called down, *"Can you come to me, sweet hunter? Has Derian secured the men?"*

"I come," the wolf replied. *"Give me room."*

Had the ladder not been at an angle, Blind Seer might have had some difficulty, but they had used such things before and he had practiced until all but the most acute angles were within his ability.

When his enormous grey head emerged above the deck, the three sailors took an involuntary step back. Firekeeper realized that they might not have seen the wolf conscious—if at all. Only Harjeedian, Rarby, and Shelby had been evident when they were captured.

"Check, sweet hunter," Firekeeper said, allowing her hand to trail through the wolf's thick fur. *"See if there are others still hiding and that these have put away all their weapons."*

The wolf reported back shortly.

"No others to sight or scent," he said. *"Those men still carry knives, but they are sheathed."*

Firekeeper looked at the three huddled sailors.

"You have knives. Drop them, too."

They did, and Blind Seer brought her one.

"It is not your Fang," he said, *"but it will bite nearly as deep."*

Firekeeper stuck the knife into her belt alongside Shelby's, then called down to Derian.

"Bring Harjeedian. His turn to be hostage."

Derian called back. "I've tied Rarby to the bars of your cage. No need for him to get frisky."

Firekeeper agreed. Her real reason for wanting Harjeedian above decks was to see if he could do anything for her nausea, but she didn't want to admit that until Derian was there to manage the other men.

Harjeedian came up, his expression angry, his eyes narrowed. Derian was right behind him, holding a long knife, doubtless taken from Rarby, to the other man's back.

Harjeedian gave a thin-lipped smile when he saw the other sailors subdued.

"I am impressed. I thought the cages would hold you. I admit to underestimating your capacities."

Firekeeper bared her teeth at him. The expression was not a smile, but closer to a snarl. Harjeedian remained calm.

"You have escaped," Harjeedian went on. He made a wide gesture with his arm. "But where will you go?"

Firekeeper followed the gesture, registering for the first time that the only land in sight was a distant shape of green. They were as trapped as they had ever been in the compartment belowdecks. Her head swam with renewed seasickness.

"I see sails," Derian said defiantly. "We will get that ship's attention and be taken to shore."

Harjeedian laughed.

"That ship is coming to meet us," he said. "We could not make a long voyage in this tub, nor could you—even if you had the skill. This boat is leaking in a dozen places already, for it was never intended for rougher waters. You have done well—and I promise not to underestimate you again. Will you surrender, or must the crew of *Child of Water* subdue you?"

"If I promise to kill you," Firekeeper said, trying to keep her voice steady, "then maybe they think and take us home."

"That only works," Harjeedian said, sounding amused, "if the other party cares if I live or die. Frankly, I do not think the ship's captain would weigh any of our lives very highly if the prize to be won was taking you. I must also warn you that my teachers, who are not on that vessel, but whom you will meet someday, will care very deeply if I am killed."

This flood of words was too much for Firekeeper. She looked blankly at Derian.

Derian hissed out his breath between his teeth.

"Firekeeper, we may have no choice but to surrender."

DERIAN KNEW FIREKEEPER felt betrayed, but he believed Harjeedian. The man was not merely blustering. He spoke with the confidence of one who knew he had the upper hand.

"Can you explain more clearly?" Derian said. "Firekeeper confused is not a safe person. What puzzles me is why you want us. You've gone to a great deal of trouble to keep us alive. Who are you working for? Queen Valora? The pirates?"

"Neither," Harjeedian said. "Though you might say that your actions against both those parties played their role in bringing you here. Nor is this the time for you to know my teachers' wishes."

Firekeeper growled, the sound echoed by Blind Seer's deeper rumble.

Derian felt a bit frantic. He knew the pair could easily take out their captors, but he didn't see how that would do them any good—and it could do a great deal of harm.

"Harjeedian, you can't care so little for your life. I beg you, explain."

Harjeedian seemed to reassess the situation.

"I can tell you this much," he said. "One of whom you made an enemy brought word of Firekeeper and Blind Seer to my teachers."

Derian could tell that, short of torture, he would learn nothing more.

"Firekeeper really was seasick," he said. "If you don't want her wasting away, you're going to need to help her."

Harjeedian considered. "After the transfer. I see no advantage to having her strong and clearheaded now."

Derian could see his point.

"What next?" he said.

"You surrender and the transfer takes place as planned," Harjeedian replied, "or you kill us and deal with this ship sinking and the oncoming vessel. That is all."

Derian looked at Firekeeper.

"Your call," he said.

Firekeeper looked at Harjeedian.

"First to hurt us dies. I have enough hostages."

Harjeedian met her gaze.

"I can see how you might. Very well. I understand. Men, I warn you, no getting back a bit of your own. I won't answer for the consequences."

Derian shivered, trying to believe it was caused by the sudden wind that had whipped up, but knowing that the real source was the chilly glint in Firekeeper's dark eyes.

EVEN FIREKEEPER COULD TELL that considerable preparation had been done with the specific intent of moving Blind Seer from the riverboat to the larger ocean vessel. There was a cage, big enough to hold the wolf, small enough to keep him from sliding around and possibly doing himself injury. It was strongly built, but light enough that it could be hauled up through a complicated web of ropes.

What she hadn't expected was that the same cage would be used to move her. Harjeedian and Derian had been taken aboard via a strange chair-like contraption, but when it came time for her to go aboard it was the cage, not the chair, that was lowered.

"Get inside," Rarby ordered. Obviously, the ease with which he and Shelby had been overcome still stung, but equally obviously, he had been told not to lay a hand on her unless she refused to cooperate.

"Why this?" Firekeeper asked, gesturing toward the cage with a toss of her head. "Why not chair?"

Rarby shook his head.

"Don't know. Don't care. What I do know is that's what they've sent. Now, are you going to get in it, or am I going to have to beat the crap out of you first?"

He looked as if he'd welcome the opportunity, and it pleased Firekeeper to deny him. She crept into the cage, musing over what they had won in their effort to escape. There had been three victories as she saw them.

The first was confirmation that all three of them were wanted, alive and in at least fair condition. She had suspected this, but hadn't known for certain. However, the fact that Harjeedian had not harmed Derian to punish Firekeeper made her fairly sure that Derian had not been kidnapped merely as a hostage against her good behavior.

The second victory was that she thought she had convinced Harjeedian that merely threatening either Blind Seer or Derian would not be enough to keep her in line. Deep inside, she wasn't sure if this was true, but she thought that Harjeedian would be more careful. Whether this care would take the form of courtesy or more intensive imprisonment she couldn't be certain. However, she felt she had regained some status, and wolf-like, she felt this was important.

The third victory was both the smallest and the largest. Only one of the two knives she had acquired in the scuffle had been taken from her. Shelby had demanded the return of his knife, but the blade Blind Seer had given her had not been noticed. At first opportunity, Firekeeper had slipped it inside the loose folds of the shirt she now wore. When Harjeedian had insisted she don trousers and a heavier shirt over the first as protection against the sharp spring winds, she had readily agreed.

Now the knife nestled between the baggy folds of the outer and inner shirts, hopefully undetectable. Firekeeper thought that Derian might also be armed. He had returned Rarby's knife, but the butter knife, jagged-edged from working the chain, and the solid link of chain he had hidden in his fist had not been taken from him.

Of course, these victories would be lost if they were stripped and searched, but for now Firekeeper felt more secure. Her fangs were not drawn, only hidden.

Privately, she mourned the loss of her own Fang, the garnet-hilted knife that had been given to her by the first One Male of her memory, a knife that had belonged to Prince Barden, leader of the settlers who had crossed the Iron Mountains in the hope of building a life for themselves. Her human parents had been among those settlers—some said her father had been Prince Barden himself—and Firekeeper treasured the knife both as a valuable tool, and as a tie to that forgotten time in her life.

However, as she allowed herself to be secured in the transport cage, she was glad for any knife at all.

Once Rarby had closed the door and snapped home the lock, he gave a shrill whistle, waving his arm broadly over his head. Almost immediately, Firekeeper felt the cage jerk and rise swaying over the deck. It rose regularly after that, the stops—presumably so those hauling the rope could adjust their grips—coming smoothly. Nonetheless, her traitor stomach wanted to rebel and she fought hard to keep from vomiting. She had no desire to arrive at the next stage in this unplanned-for journey bent over and spewing.

She managed, though only just barely, and from the look Derian gave her when the cage was lowered onto the deck she suspected she didn't look very healthy. Blind Seer licked her face through the bars.

"Be ill if you must, dear heart," he said. *"There's been talk enough of your ailment. That's the reason they brought you up in this fashion. They feared otherwise you might fall."*

Derian opened the door of the transport cage for her; Firekeeper saw that all three of them were within a larger cage. It was not so solid that she didn't think she couldn't break out of it, given time, but even as she crawled out of the littler cage she saw a roof being lowered and lashed into place.

No, the cage would not stop her or Blind Seer, but it would slow them. If they were guarded, that would be enough.

Derian helped her stand, putting a supportive arm around her—a gesture she was grateful for, even as she found the need galling.

"How do you feel?" he asked.

"Maybe better now," she replied cautiously testing her footing. "This boat not move so much, I think."

Firekeeper glanced around, taking in the tall tree trunks that, shorn of their bark, held webs of rope and wide canvas sails. There were three such trees, as far as she could tell, and she thought that this made for a very big boat indeed. It had stood as high over the riverboat as the castle at Eagle's Nest stood over the city below. As so often when confronted with human achievements, the wolf-woman was reluctantly impressed.

The last of the sailors who had crewed the riverboat came over the side now, climbing like squirrels rather than resorting to the clumsy lifts. Rarby snapped a salute to a woman who stood to one side, her skin the same tone as Harjeedian's, her aura one of calm authority.

"The riverboat is going down now, ma'am," Rarby said. "We took an axe to the hold and the ocean was rushing in."

"Very good," the woman said. As with Harjeedian, her voice contained an unfamiliar music. "Report to my first mate. He will show you where to sling your hammocks."

Rarby seemed pleased with the arrangement—indeed, to expect it. Gesturing to Shelby and the other sailors, he led them hurriedly away. Firekeeper wanted to think that Rarby moved quickly from fear of her, but knew this was only puppy dreams. Beside her, Blind Seer was sniffing the wind.

"What?" she asked.

"For a moment, a scent teased my whiskers," the wolf said, *"but the wind carried it away."*

"Do you see any Royal-kind among the seagulls?" Firekeeper asked, trying not to seem too hopeful.

"None," the wolf replied, *"and I would tell you if I did."*

This last was an important reassurance, for once there had been a time when Blind Seer would have hidden such knowledge from her.

DERIAN OFFERED FIREKEEPER a leather water bottle, wondering how much of her unease was from lingering seasickness and how much from their new situation.

"Have you noticed," he said quietly, "that most of the crew of this ship is like Harjeedian—the same color skin and tilting eyes, the same dark hair. They aren't Stoneholders, either. I've heard a bit of their language, and I'd swear it isn't the same."

"These are browner," Firekeeper agreed, struggling a bit for comparison. "The Alkyab of Stonehold have skin like winter grass, golden as much as brown. These have skin like clean mud."

Derian forced a laugh. "There's many a housekeeper who would say that 'clean' and 'mud' don't go together, but I know what you mean. I thought of toasted bread, or—even better—the crust on a smooth loaf. It looks tanned, but you can tell they started that way."

"Not too bad to look at," Firekeeper commented, "and better for sun than your pink skin."

Firekeeper rarely sunburned, possibly because her skin had given up protesting the abuses she put it through, but Derian always suffered as the summer sun grew stronger.

"You must ask them for hat," she added, "if we is outside all day and night."

Derian nodded, but he was only half listening. He looked side to side, then up to where a small flock of seagulls quarreled around the tallest of the tree trunks.

"Any of . . . your people there?" he asked softly.

"Blind Seer say no," Firekeeper replied. "Maybe one will come. We know they look at boats."

"Ships," Derian correct automatically. "When a boat is this big and goes on the ocean it's called a ship."

Firekeeper opened her mouth to reply, but then she caught motion from where Blind Seer had been resting on the deck. The wolf had risen to his feet, and now stood very still and suddenly intent.

Firekeeper swung in the direction from which the wind was coming, and Derian followed her motion. He gasped as a man he had hoped never to encounter again emerged from one of the hatchways.

The newcomer was a big man, both in height and breadth, though less fleshy than when last Derian had seen him. His light brown hair was covered with a billed cap, but beneath this cover Derian recalled his hair was thinning. The man's skin was weathered and his walk held a sailor's roll.

"Waln Endbrook!" Firekeeper said, tugging on Derian's sleeve.

Derian nodded, swallowing a gasp of surprise.

"I guess it's true that rotten things always float to the top," he said softly.

Firekeeper sniffed indignantly, "He seem to do well since his queen chase him from his pack."

At first glance, Derian would have agreed, but now he noted how Waln's skin showed signs of having been out in the weather fairly recently. Waln walked with a slight limp, and the jowls beneath his neck hung loose, as if he had lost a great deal of weight through something other than healthy exercise.

"I think," Derian said, still keeping his voice low, "that he took time to rise."

"Him here," Firekeeper said, "tell a lot."

Derian nodded. Waln Endbrook's presence did explain a great deal. How the kidnappers had known how to prepare for them, perhaps even how to capture them in the first place. They had been enemies, and enemies learn a great deal about each other.

Derian strove to remember what they knew about Waln Endbrook. Waln was from the Isles, the group of five larger and many smaller islands east of both Hawk Haven and Bright Bay. Until the settlement at the end of King Allister's War, the Isles had belonged to Bright Bay, but Bright Bay had granted them to the woman once known as Queen Gustin IV of Bright Bay, now called Queen Valora of the Isles.

Valora had accepted her demotion only because she had been given no choice, for her self-serving policies had turned the majority of her own subjects against her. The people of Bright Bay had welcomed Duke Allister Seagleam as king in her place, and Valora had gone to the Isles. There she had courted the wealthiest and most powerful of the local residents. Among these had been Waln Endbrook, whom she had made her diplomatic liaison.

Derian had heard that Valora had not forgiven Waln when he had failed her. Instead she had exiled him, disavowing any knowledge of his claims that he had acted in her interests, seizing his fortune and assets to augment her slender treasury. What had happened to the wife and children Waln had left behind had not been said.

In all fairness to the queen, Derian had no doubt that some of Waln's actions had exceeded his ruler's orders, but there was no question at all that Valora had set Waln on his eventually disastrous course. Such would have been perfectly in keeping with her previous actions.

Over a year had passed since the last time Derian had seen Waln, and he wondered what course had brought the Islander from the Smuggler's Light to the deck of this ship. One thing was certain. Whatever had brought Waln to this point had not made him love those who had thwarted him.

Now Waln crossed the deck and stood just outside of arm's reach of the three within the cage. He smiled—a slow, greasy expression full of self-satisfaction. The satisfaction faded somewhat when his smile met only blank expressions in return.

"Surely you remember me," Waln said. "Don't you have a greeting for an old acquaintance?"

Derian eschewed the easy pretense that he did not remember Waln. To do so would be to flatter the man that he was improved beyond recognition. Instead he met Waln's gaze with direct intensity.

"I remember you," he said, "but I hardly believe the situation of that meeting merits the claim of acquaintance."

I sound like Lady Luella, he thought, recalling Earl Kestrel's socially conscious wife.

Firekeeper didn't even bother to say so much, and Blind Seer turned away and started washing under his tail.

To Derian's satisfaction, Waln flushed a deep scarlet, his color deepening when Harjeedian didn't bother to hide his amusement.

Waln's discomfiture did not last. His smile became sly.

"Fine words for a rat in a trap," he said.

"Does that make you the rat catcher?" Derian replied, his flippancy earning another smile from Harjeedian.

"That makes me the general who coordinated your capture from the very doorstep of King Tedric's castle!" Waln retorted.

Privately, Derian had to admit that if Waln had indeed been the mastermind behind their capture, he did have reason for pride, but Derian wasn't going to let the other man know that.

"'General,' is it," Derian replied. "I suppose that's a nice way to put the matter when in reality you didn't dare come into Hawk Haven, or probably get too close to the Isles. 'General' might not be the word I'd use for a man who lets others take the risks."

Derian knew he wouldn't be so bold if the protection offered by the cage didn't work both ways—and if he wasn't fairly certain that whatever use Harjeedian had for them was not restricted to Firekeeper and Blind Seer. As it was, he saw Waln ball his fist and knew that had they stood face-to-face, the other man would have hit him.

"So," Derian said, "how are the wife and children? Is business going well?"

Waln flushed again, and Derian knew he needed to take care.

"Business is going very well," Waln replied, the words clipped, "and in the not too distant future I expect to find myself in a diplomatic capacity once more."

"Lovely," Derian replied. "I admit to being curious. What brought you to this point?"

He knew from various sources that Waln Endbrook was a bully and a braggart, and suspected that the other man would like nothing more than a chance to boast about his rise in fortune. Perhaps in telling that tale he would give some hint as to their own fate.

Waln rocked back, leaning against the nearby mast, all his self-satisfaction returning. As he did this, Derian had his first clear look at the man's left hand. It was gloved in black, and the two smallest fingers jutted unnaturally stiff.

So he wants others to overlook his mutilation, Derian thought, *though it is such as could be excused by many accidents that would be routine in a sailor's trade. Interesting, if not immediately useful.*

"As you may recall," Waln began, "I was in possession of important information that caused Crown Princess Sapphire to grant my life."

Derian suppressed a grimace. He supposed that was one way to relate the shameful circumstances surrounding Waln's defeat.

"Upon my release, I returned to the Isles, but the queen I had so faithfully served betrayed me. She could not execute me lest my father-in-law, a powerful man in the Isles, argue that my estates must pass to my legal heirs. Instead, she named me traitor, stripped me of the titles she had given me, and sent me into exile.

"Exile included very little that would assure my comfort: passage to the port of my choice and what few goods I could carry in a pack. I was permitted to take nothing of great value. All that could not be proven to have been brought into our marriage by my wife or what had been earned because of her actions was forfeit to the queen. My wife and children went into her family's care. I have not heard from them since."

Derian felt a momentary flash of pity for the man until he recalled what Waln had done to earn that exile. Then pity melted from him, leaving him cold as the ocean depths. He found himself involuntarily taking a step back.

Waln was so caught up in his own tale that Derian doubted he had noticed, but Harjeedian did and his eyebrows rose in silent comment. Waln went on.

"I was barred from the ports of both Hawk Haven and Bright Bay, and had no wish to try my luck in Waterland."

Derian knew perfectly well why this would be so. Not only did Waterland share a border with New Kelvin—a nation which, at that time, harbored others whose enmity Waln had earned—but Waterland judged the worth of its residents by their fortunes. One such as Waln, coming with no fortune, might well have found himself enslaved.

"Therefore I took passage on a ship heading into southern waters. I had voyaged in these some in my younger days, and thought I might find some curiosities or at least those who, unallied with those who had wronged me, would be willing to give me honest employment."

As far as Derian knew, nothing much was known about the lands to the south. Stonehold, the nation to the south of Bright Bay, was a land power, but their southern border was variously reported as densely forested or swampy. Dangerous shoals and fever-ridden swamps to the east kept the majority of Stoneholders on land. However, he supposed that the sailors of the Isles must have ventured south out of curiosity if nothing more. He admired their daring. Navigation out of sight of land had been among the arts the Old World rulers had kept to themselves.

"Luck seemed not to be with me in this venture either," Waln continued. "Some days after we had navigated the Shipwreck Shoals and were trying to discover whether we had also found the end of land, a storm came out of nowhere. We were driven far off course. When the storm abated, we were left with tattered sails and less than half our crew. Happily, the winds had also taken us close enough to land that we were intercepted by a local vessel—this very vessel, in fact.

"Her name is *Fayonejunjal*. That translates as *Child of Water*," Waln said, proudly, as if he had named the ship himself. "She originates from a land called Liglim. They are a curious people, claiming origin in an Old Country nation I had never heard of before. As with our own land, when the Plague came, their rulers left, and the remaining colonists established their own country."

"Do they have contact with their Old Country?" Derian asked.

"No," Waln said. "Nor do they wish it—even if they could locate them. I think there must have been a pact of some sort among the Old Country rulers to keep all the colonies in ignorance of those things that would let them challenge their masters. The consistency is otherwise impossible to explain."

Derian agreed.

"So that storm proved to be a fortunate wind," Derian said, prompting Waln to continue, feeling that the answer to why he, Firekeeper, and Blind Seer had been kidnapped must lie in the next part of the story.

"Fortunate for me," Waln agreed, his smile arrogant and greasy once more, the taunting smile of a bully who knows he holds the upper hand. "However, I wonder if you will think it is so fortunate for you?"

Derian refused to be goaded, though he heard Firekeeper shifting slightly behind him and knew she was growing impatient. Waln's accent was an Islander's and doubtless the wolf-woman did not understand everything he had said—or worse, she understood and was growing impatient with Waln's account, wanting to know precisely how it applied to their situation.

Waln couldn't resist continuing to gloat.

"Yes," he said. "My good fortune—and perhaps your own. The captain and senior officers had given their lives in keeping the ship afloat during the storm. I assumed command of the survivors."

Of those who, like you, cowered belowdecks while others risked wind and waves, Derian thought. *I'm sure that the few who survived the loss of their officers were too exhausted to deal with your relative strength.*

"In that capacity, I worked with our rescuers. My first task, of course, was to learn something of their language, and in return grant some knowledge of our own. When we arrived at their capital city, this kept me quite busy, as did answering questions about from where we had come. In turn, I learned something about their culture.

"I gathered that the Liglimom have no king or equivalent. Instead, they are led by a small group of religious leaders. I cannot say I understand the intricacies of their belief system, but it bears some small resemblance to our societies in that various animals are held to represent certain traits. However, they have a great respect for the elements as well."

Waln shrugged, dismissively. "Their beliefs are not important. What is important is that I soon learned that this priesthood keeps a collection of animals—a menagerie. Whether they are for worship, sacrifice, or inspiration, I could not quite understand. It seems they are chary of sharing their secrets with a foreigner."

Derian was beginning to dread where this thread was heading, and from Firekeeper's soft intake of breath he thought she was on a similar track.

Waln rubbed at the stiffened fingers of his gloved left hand.

"As soon as I could speak the language well enough, I told my new friends that I knew where they could find a fine representative of at least one of their sacred animals—an enormous wolf."

Blind Seer growled, raising his head from where it had rested on his paws through much of this account. Beside him, Firekeeper—who had eschewed her usual nonchalant seat beside the wolf to stand—took a step forward.

"I told them about Lady Blysse as well," Waln went on unctuously, "how some say she can speak to the beast. And I told them about you, Derian Counselor, the keeper of wolf and woman—the only one known to make her obey anything but her own bestial urges. The rulers of Liglim were very excited by this, but thought you might not accept their invitation for an extended visit."

"Extended?" Derian repeated.

"As in for the rest of your life."

IV

"EASY, DEAR HEART," Blind Seer cautioned when Firekeeper would have reached for the knife hidden within her shirt. *"Killing him would be satisfying, but it would pull your one fang."*

Firekeeper froze almost before her hand moved, knowing Blind Seer was right. Her only chance of hitting Waln was if she threw the knife. Whether or not she could hit him through the intervening bars and using an unfamiliar weapon hardly mattered in the light that she would only have that one throw. Instead she stepped to Derian's side and spoke for the first time since Waln had approached the cage.

"What you mean? Our kin *will* miss us."

Harjeedian also joined the conversation for the first time.

"Not really, Lady Blysse—or should I call you 'Firekeeper'?"

"Firekeeper is wolf name, for friends," she spat, "and a word will not change how I feel."

"Lady Blysse then," Harjeedian said, "though the time will come when you may be glad to have me as a friend."

Firekeeper dreaded that Harjeedian might be right and so swallowed her impulse to deny that any such thing could happen. Instead she stood, her hand resting on Blind Seer's shoulder. The wolf had risen to his feet and now stood pressed protectively close to her left side.

Harjeedian studied them for a moment, then returned to his original question.

"Your kin will not miss you, Lady Blysse. We ascertained in advance that none of your avian companions seemed to be accompanying you at this time. You are known for disappearing from human ken. Although you are apparently of some importance to the wolves, I do not think you are in constant contact with them. If you do not arrive when they expect you—if they expect you—they will assume there is good reason."

He shifted his gaze to Derian.

"Derian Counselor offers a greater problem. However, it is not one we will need to solve for several moonspans. I will tell you this, Counselor. The time will come when you will be offered opportunity to communicate with your family. It will be up to you whether you will agree to communicate a somewhat edited version of events or leave your family grieving, assuming you dead."

Firekeeper could tell that, for Derian, this last was like a blow to the gut. Fox Hair might have spent much of the last two years away from his family, but whenever possible he had written them, often scribbling away even when the letters could not be sent and then sending a large package all at once. Given the choice of lying or of leaving his family to grieve, she knew Derian would lie.

Harjeedian knew this, too. She could tell by the satisfied set of his shoulders, the confident tilt of his chin. He might speak another language with his lips, but the language of his body was not too different from the one that she had already learned. That reminded her of another question.

"How you speak Pellish so well?" she asked, aware of her own deficiencies in that area. "Did you know before?"

Harjeedian shook his head.

"In Waln's account of events, he trimmed a few details. One of these is that among those traveling with him on the ill-fated ship was a minstrel. Barnet had hoped to gather new tales with which to make his fame and perhaps win the favor of Queen Valora's court. He was already multilingual, speaking the tongue of Waterland and something of that of New Kelvin. He found learning our language and teaching yours fairly easy. Although you were not introduced at that time, Barnet was one of the other sailors who accompanied me into Hawk Haven. There, when not serving as local liaison, I had him tutor me. I am, however, a quick learner."

"Very," Firekeeper said with grudging admiration. She hadn't understood much of the long speech, but the very flow of words was proof of Harjeedian's boast.

"You will meet this minstrel before long," Harjeedian said. "He and I will be teaching both of you—but especially Derian Counselor—my language."

Derian shook his head.

"I'll try, but if you had wanted skill with languages, you would have done better to bring Elise or Wendee."

"Goody Wendee remains in the North Woods," Harjeedian said, "and this Elise of whom you speak would be Lady Archer. That title alone is reason why we would not lay hands on her. The baron, her father, has become protective of his chick since her last venture abroad, fearful, I think, that Lady Archer's interest in foreign lands and ways will draw her away from her inheritance."

"How do you know so much?" Derian asked almost angrily.

Harjeedian smiled. "That selfsame minstrel has collected numerous tales. He added to his knowledge while we waited for fit opportunity to take you."

Firekeeper wondered why the minstrel hadn't taken advantage of what had apparently been ample shore time to escape. What hostage had Harjeedian held over the minstrel's actions? Perhaps they could learn, and so turn this stranger into an ally.

Obviously frustrated by his loss of dominance, Waln had been trying to insert himself into the conversation. He managed to do so at this point.

"The immediate question is," Waln sneered, "whether you want to spend the rest of what will be a rather long voyage locked in that cage or whether you will give your parole."

Firekeeper looked at Derian, waiting for translation of this unfamiliar concept. She had heard of parole in another context—Doc had once made her promise not to leave the house when she had been recovering from injuries—but this didn't sound quite the same.

"Waln wants us to promise we won't try to escape or offer harm to any on this vessel," Derian translated, glancing at Harjeedian to see if he had understood correctly. "If we will do so, they'll let us out of this cage."

"That is correct," Harjeedian said. "If you offer your parole, we will give all three of you freedom of the ship. You will share a cabin abovedecks and be fed as well as any member of the crew."

He gave Firekeeper a sly grin.

"I will even see if I can help you with your seasickness. You may adjust on your own, but I do have drugs that may help during the transition."

Firekeeper considered. "This may be good. If we do this parole, we are free to move about. What else?"

"What else?" Waln retorted indignantly. "What more could you want?"

Firekeeper fastened her gaze on Harjeedian.

"To know what he want."

Harjeedian met her gaze.

"I cannot tell you everything now. My teachers reserve that right for themselves. For now, I want you to learn my language so that you can speak for yourself when we arrive. Is that too much?"

Firekeeper shook her head, though inwardly she sighed. Another language! Why couldn't humans speak as simply and directly as wolves?

ALTHOUGH *FAYONEJUNJAL* SAILED WITHIN SIGHT of the coastline, Derian knew that as far as any watchers ashore were concerned, they were invisible. It was all a matter of size. *Fayonejunjal* might be large as far as seagoing vessels went, but compared with the wasteland of water surrounding them the ship was minuscule.

Harjeedian and Waln had been as good as their word. Now that parole had been given and accepted, the cage had been disassembled, the pieces stored in one of the holds. The cabin they had been assigned seemed small when filled with two humans and a wolf, but Derian suspected that Firekeeper wouldn't spend much time in those cramped confines. She was experimenting with what minimized her seasickness, and for now preferred to be out in the open air.

Derian leaned against the rail, watching the boat race through the waves. He had no idea how fast they were traveling or how far they had come. The sailors seemed to be doing a good deal of setting sails, and the boat kept jigging back and forth.

There must have been landmarks that meant something to the captain, for she appeared placid and content. All Derian could make of the activity was that their course was carrying them more or less to the south. Soon enough, they would be away from friendly coastline, and then the vessel was likely to come in closer to the shore. As far as their situation was concerned, proximity to the shoreline didn't matter. Whether they were a mile or a half-mile or even a quarter of a mile out, the three of them couldn't swim the distance without being recaptured. Even if they stole one of the shore boats, they couldn't sail it.

Derian had grown up near the Flin River, but his family had been distinctly land-oriented. He could paddle a bit, but the lore of sails was a mystery to him. As far as he knew, Firekeeper had been on a boat only once, during their visit to Revelation Point Castle in Bright Bay, and that had been just messing about. Now that he thought about it, she'd been eager to get ashore fairly quickly. He wondered if she'd felt seasick even then.

It was a moot point. Firekeeper was certainly seasick now, and *Fayonejunjal* made as good a prison as any he had ever imagined.

Derian turned his concentration to considering what he could do that might be turned to their advantage. Learning Harjeedian's language would be a good start. He knew how much they had relied on Elise and Wendee in New Kelvin—enough that his own command of New Kelvinese had never progressed beyond the very basic words and simple grammar necessary to buy market goods or ask directions.

In this situation, he would need to fill both Elise's and Wendee's roles. If Firekeeper's willingness to learn Pellish was any indication, she would make her own rules as to what elements and how much of the language was necessary to her needs, then progress no further.

Derian glanced over to where Firekeeper was stretched out near Blind Seer, both apparently asleep. He wondered just how much Pellish the wolf understood—that he understood some, Derian had no doubt. Could it be that Firekeeper understood more than she was letting on—that her fractured grammar and simplistic vocabulary were an elaborate ploy?

Derian had no idea, but he resolved to do his best not to give away everything he was learning. He knew that there were times when he and Elise had spoken deliberately quickly and using more complicated words in order to talk over Firekeeper's head. Their captors might resort to some similar ploy—and then Derian would have the upper hand.

Derian grinned to himself and wiped spray off his face. Of course, all of that rested on his ability to learn something of the language. He might never get beyond the basics. They might never teach him more than what they wanted him to know. For the first time, Derian understood—really understood—the Old Country rulers' policy of withholding training in key skills from their colonists. Lack of knowledge could be a prison far more unbreakable than any walled dungeon.

He was still considering this when he heard footsteps on the deck. Turning, he confronted a man he vaguely recognized as one of the three sailors Firekeeper had subdued during their failed escape attempt.

The newcomer was shorter than Derian, but that didn't make him short; Derian was taller than average. He was clean-shaven, and as his wispy, straw-colored hair didn't look to be the type that would make a thick beard, this was certainly a good choice. It also gave a clear view of features that were just a trace too bland to be handsome—that was, until the man smiled. Then his face lit up from within.

Derian felt a surge of instantaneous liking, and warned himself to guard against it. The man clearly knew his power—and if he had this effect on another man he probably had an even easier time with women.

He won't have an easy time with Firekeeper, though, Derian thought. *She thinks smiles are a way of showing how sharp your teeth are.*

"Barnet," the man said, offering a slight bow. "Harjeedian said he had mentioned me to you."

"You're the minstrel," Derian said. "The one who taught Harjeedian Pellish."

"And the one who is going to teach you Liglimosh—that's my term for their language," Barnet agreed. "They just change the inflection on 'Liglimo' and I find that too confusing."

Barnet leaned his forearms against the railing and looked down over the side. The pose looked natural, as if he had spent a lot of time on ships. After a moment, Derian joined him.

"I thought," Barnet said after a moment, "we should get acquainted, given that we're going to spend a lot of time together."

Derian nodded. Barnet's attire was similar to that worn by the rest of the ship's crew, so it didn't give away much about him. He wore his hair long and tied back—the style most usual in Hawk Haven—but as most of the sailors did the same, and they most certainly were not from Hawk Haven, it didn't tell anything about him.

Barnet's accent sounded more like Bright Bay than Hawk Haven, though Derian supposed he could be from the Isles. Derian hadn't met enough of the people from there to be sure just how much their accents differed from that of their parent country.

"You first," Derian suggested. "Tell me about yourself. From what Harjeedian said, you already know more than enough about all of us."

"Stories," Barnet said, shaking his head as if to dismiss his information. "Gossip. Doubtless exaggeration. Useful, as your being here proves, but probably not the first things you would tell about yourself."

Derian grinned, admiring the man's way of setting him at ease. He'd guess that Barnet was older than him, maybe in his mid-thirties, but he had the weathered skin common to seagoing peoples, and that made it hard to judge. He might be five years younger.

"I'd like to know more about you," Derian persisted, "to put us on more even footing."

Barnet gave a slightly theatrical sigh.

"Very well. I was born a Lobster, cadet branch, no prospects for inheritance. Does that tell you anything?"

It did, and Derian had to hide his own reaction. Lobster was one of the Great Houses of Bright Bay, not the highest ranking, but until recently very prestigious. Queen Gustin IV—now Queen Valora of the Isles—was married to Harwill Lobster. Almost to a one, the Lobsters had followed their queen and her husband into exile.

Derian was determined not to say too much.

"So did you move to the Islands after King Allister's War?" he asked.

"I did," Barnet said. "I had nothing against Allister Seagleam, but my entire family was going and I had to choose which I would never see again—my parents and siblings, or my birth land. In any case, I spend much of my time at sea. That's my real home."

"You're a sailor then?" Derian asked. "Harjeedian named you a minstrel."

"Minstrel is a valid post in the Bright Bay Navy. Minstrels haul line with the rest of the crew, but during the long voyages it is our duty to keep up morale. Think of us as doctors, except we treat the spirit rather than the body."

"I think I understand," Derian said, remembering how much good having Wendee Jay and her wealth of stories had done for their group during the long treks from the Norwood Grant to Dragon's Breath.

"Probably the only hard part of being a minstrel," Barnet went on, "is keeping your hands supple. It's hard to play a stringed instrument, but then again, it's hard to keep one in tune, so at sea most minstrels play flutes or pipes. I get so I'll hardly touch one on land."

"Oh."

"And being a minstrel cuts you out of command, most of the time," Barnet went on. "The navy, and most ship owners, don't think the crew will obey someone they think of as a singer or piper—someone they've seen doing tumbling or acting out bits from a play."

A trace of bitterness there, Derian thought. *Or does he only want me to think that?*

"Are the rules the same in the Isles?" Derian asked.

"The rules in the Isles are still pretty much in flux," Barnet admitted. "Until less than two years ago, the Isles' navy was Bright Bay's navy. Now neither is as large as it once was, and merchant ships owned by people like Waln Endbrook are finding themselves required to take care of themselves."

"How about the pirates?" Derian asked.

"You've met some of them," Barnet countered. "What do you think?"

"I think they'd be looking out for themselves and trying to see what their own best interests would be," Derian said. "On the one hand, cooperating with Queen Valora gives a certain degree of validity to ventures that otherwise might be wholly illegal. On the other hand, that same cooperation might mean giving up some freedom."

"And profit," Barnet added. "Don't forget profit. And cooperating with forces who until a short time ago existed in large part to curtail your actions. No, nothing's settled yet."

Derian nodded.

"We're seeing a lot of changes in Hawk Haven, too," he said, hoping to ease Barnet into telling more. "There are those who made their living from the conflict between Bright Bay and Hawk Haven—and I don't just mean the soldiers. Smugglers. Guild liaisons. Tariff collectors. They're all finding new places for themselves, and not all of them are doing as well as before."

"Same for minstrels," Barnet said, "especially minstrels within a smaller navy. That's why I jumped at the chance to go on the *Explorer*. Exploring to the south might give me new stories—and some respect at court."

Derian turned to look at Barnet and found the other man's grey-blue eyes studying him. Barnet grinned, unashamed at being caught in his scrutiny.

"Tell me about yourself," Barnet suggested.

Derian deliberately framed his own reply to match Barnet's initial "revelations."

"I was born to a merchant family. We own Prancing Steed Stables in the city of Eagle's Nest. I'm the eldest, and that makes me the heir, but my folks are ambitious. When Earl Kestrel came looking to rent mounts for an expedition he planned west, they insisted I go along—to look after their property, they said."

"But also in the hope you'd catch the earl's attention," Barnet said, his tone suggesting he'd been the subject of similar maneuvering.

"That's about it," Derian agreed, "except that I didn't catch the earl's eye as a horse handler—at least not so anyone would have noticed. I caught it after Firekeeper came to us."

"And you ended up her handler," Barnet said.

"That's right," Derian said. "She seemed willing to trust me. Somehow, one way or another, I'm still working more as her handler than as anything else."

He tried to put a trace of bitterness into his tone, but found it difficult. There had been a time he resented his role, feared that he might find himself nothing more than a glorified valet. Now, he was proud of the trust Firekeeper put in him. Still, if Barnet really did resent the light in which minstrels were held in the navy, he might respond to what he perceived as Derian's dissatisfaction.

"She relies on you," Barnet said. "I was watching earlier. Whenever Harjeedian got too high-flown, she'd glance at you and settle into waiting, like she knew you'd make it clear later."

"That's been my job for two years now," Derian said, "making things clear for her. I don't think anyone can do it better."

He wasn't precisely boasting, but he also suspected that he had been kept alive to this point because of the perception that he somehow controlled Firekeeper. He wasn't about to discount his own importance.

"How'd you become a minstrel?" he asked. "Was that your role on the ship that got wrecked, the *Explorer,* I think you called her?"

Barnet considered.

"I became a minstrel almost in spite of myself," he said. "I wanted to be a naval officer. Thing was, I kept finding it easier to persuade people than to order them around. Then, honestly, I might not have been the best battle commander. Even when other people were giving the orders I kept thinking about the people on the other ship— wondering if they were frightened or angry or just doing their job. I'd imagine their stories: the sweethearts they'd left behind, children or elderly parents who depended on them. Got so I realized I might have trouble giving the orders to attack."

Barnet gave a twisted grin.

"Never had any trouble when my own life or the life of one of my mates was on the line. Just with the abstract. Does that make any sense?"

"It does," Derian admitted. "I wonder if Tavis Seagleam—Prince Tavis, now— would have ended up a minstrel if things had been different."

"Hard to tell," Barnet said. "I heard he is artistic, but it takes more than artistic talent to be a minstrel. You have to like people, and people have to like you."

Derian nodded.

"It's like that with handling horses," he said. "You can teach someone to ride and to judge a good beast, but to do what my father does—what I do—you need to really like them, almost be able to get into their heads. Not everyone can do it. I remember how surprised I was the first time I realized that."

"And handling wolf-women?" Barnet asked. "Does that take liking them?"

"Respecting first," Derian replied honestly. "Wolves are really hierarchical. They make us look like chickens running after feed. Firekeeper doesn't care if you like her, but you'd better respect her—or give her reason to respect you. Otherwise, she'll pay you no mind at all."

Barnet looked over to where Firekeeper slept sprawled against Blind Seer. She looked almost fragile, wrung out from sickness and defeat, not at all like the fierce, indeed dangerous, creature Derian knew she was.

"Respect . . ." Barnet mused aloud. "There's different sorts of respect. There's respect born from admiration and respect born from fear."

"And Firekeeper recognizes both," Derian said.

He was about to say "And I pity those who try to make her fear them," but held his tongue. That came to close to showing one of Firekeeper's vulnerabilities. He couldn't quite figure out her reaction to fear. She clearly valued the warning it gave, but resented it as well.

Barnet continued his thoughtful inspection.

"She was dancing when Shelby lured her away. I've heard she likes music."

"Music and dancing," Derian said. "She told me once that music was her first indication that humans had something to offer that wolves did not."

Barnet nodded.

"Well, I need to convince her to work with me. Waln Endbrook may like to believe otherwise, but all of us who were wrecked a year ago are living at the sufferance of Harjeedian's people. I'm useful, but I'm going to be a whole lot less so if I don't manage to teach you two at least some Liglimosh. If music is the way to Lady Blysse's respect, then I'll use music."

Derian cleared his throat awkwardly.

"What do they want with us?" he asked.

"I don't know," Barnet said. He must have seen the doubt in Derian's eyes. "Honestly, I don't. We were ashore for moonspans after the wreck, but kept close to our quarters—really semi-imprisoned to be honest. I've learned a little about the culture from talking to the sailors here on *Fayonejunjal,* but I'm still sorting reality from tall tales. One thing I'm sure of is that Waln's wrong when he thinks they want Firekeeper and Blind Seer as some sort of curiosity. There's something else they want, but Harjeedian won't drop even a hint."

Derian drew in a deep breath.

"If you don't know, you don't know," he said. "But I'd appreciate your passing it on if you find out."

"I will indeed," Barnet said, his smile warm and engaging. "I need your help, too, after all."

Derian wished he believed him.

HAVING THE FREEDOM TO ROAM the ship didn't do Firekeeper much good for several days. Even with the rather noxious-tasting brews Harjeedian provided for her, the deck still seemed to move unpredictably under her feet, and if she rose from a seated position too rapidly, her stomach rebelled.

Eventually, Firekeeper either developed some tolerance for the motion or Harjeedian's potions took effect. Either way, as long as she took care not to do anything that drew her attention to the ship's progress through the waters, she did better.

Her early explorations were restricted to the area at the rear of the ship, where they had been told to sleep. That was when she learned that Harjeedian kept snakes in his cabin.

Blind Seer was the first to notice.

"Do you smell that?" he asked.

Firekeeper sighed. Her usually poor sense of smell—at least by wolf standards—had not been improved either by her illness or by the plethora of new scents aboard the ship. In reply, she simply glared at Blind Seer. He panted laughter at her.

"I smell something reptilian from Harjeedian's sleeping place. I can't be quite certain what. It isn't a scent I've smelled before, but my nose says 'snake.'"

Firekeeper tilted her head in inquiry.

"You're not teasing me, are you? Most humans I've met are afraid of snakes—a good thing, as I see it. It's too hard to tell by sight alone the poisonous ones from those who lack venom, at least until you're right next to them."

"Snake," Blind Seer insisted. He snuffled. *"I don't think poisonous, but I can't be certain."*

Firekeeper wasn't inclined to question further, but with the return of stability to her head, her curiosity was also returning.

"Let's look," she suggested. *"Harjeedian is on the upper part in the front, talking to Barnet."*

Blind Seer wagged his tail in a slow arc, indicating that he thought this was a good idea. Harjeedian's cabin door was closed, but not locked. Firekeeper lifted the latch, and they went inside. It was dark within, but her eyes readily adjusted to the available light.

The cabin was much like the one she was supposed to share with Derian and Blind Seer. It was small and cramped. A narrow sleeping shelf was built into one wall. Boxes for storage were built into the opposite wall. In between was a narrow place for standing.

What caught Firekeeper's attention immediately was the glow from the squat, covered brazier anchored on top of the storage box. The brazier was rounded, tapering at the top and bottom rather like an acorn. Slits to admit air had been cut in the top and a thin trickle of smoke worked its way out.

The brazier had been very carefully set on an iron plate, and the iron plate nailed to the cabinet. All these arrangements, Firekeeper supposed, were so the brazier wouldn't slide with the motion of the ship. From the amount of heat the brazier gave off, Firekeeper guessed there couldn't be more than one or two coals inside. However, this was enough for the snakes nestled in its vicinity.

The snakes didn't touch the hot metal, but coiled around stones placed nearby. Their scales were intricately patterned, the shine of the green, yellow, and black that dominated proof that they were well fed. They were torpid, hardly moving, even when she came close to look at them. Clearly, even with the artificial heat, a spring voyage was not to their liking.

Firekeeper wondered why Harjeedian had brought the snakes with him. She counted three, and a fourth stone suggested the existence of another. They were large snakes, larger than most she had encountered, even in the wild lands west of the Iron Mountains. Their brilliant colors suggested the need to camouflage in environments other than the brown, green, blacks of the woodlands she knew.

She was puzzling over this when Blind Seer gave a warning huff of breath.

"Harjeedian comes. From how he moves, I think he sees his door is open."

Firekeeper made no attempt to flee. She was interested, and Harjeedian was the one who could answer her questions. He, however, started talking before she could voice even one.

"What are you doing in my cabin?" he asked sharply, his tone holding both anger and anxiety.

Firekeeper looked steadily at him.

"I am parole. I go anywhere on ship."

Harjeedian pushed past her, and his anxiety faded as he saw the three snakes were untouched.

"Didn't anyone tell you it is rude to go into someone's private space?"

Firekeeper tilted her head.

"I am parole," she repeated patiently.

Harjeedian sighed. Derian had appeared from somewhere, and Harjeedian addressed his next remarks to him.

"Explain to her, when you have time, that parole does not include the right to invade other people's quarters. I do not care to think how the captain would react if she found Lady Blysse in her cabin. Seafaring folk have so little private space that they are quite protective of what they do have."

Derian glanced at Firekeeper, amusement and exasperation blended on his face.

"You know about this," he said. "It's the same as in Hawk Haven or Bright Bay or anywhere else."

Firekeeper repeated stubbornly.

"I am parole."

Derian looked at Harjeedian.

"I'll work on it," he promised. "It's a wolf thing. She tends to interpret very literally, especially where rights and privileges are concerned. It isn't just redefining a term. It's taking something away—and wolves are very protective of what they think of as belonging to them."

Harjeedian shook his head.

"I will remember this. You will explain how she thinks to Barnet and the captain— as well as explaining our customs to Lady Blysse."

"Right," Derian said.

He was turning away when Firekeeper asked, "Harjeedian, why do you have snakes in cabin? Where is snake four? What kind are they?"

For the first time, Derian seemed to notice the odd arrangement atop the cabinet. Firekeeper had to remind herself that he saw far less well in poor light than she did— and his eyes had been sunblinded from the glare of light against water.

"Snakes?" Derian repeated. "Here?"

Harjeedian grew momentarily defensive; then his usual arrogant amusement returned.

"Snakes here, here, and here," he said, pointing at the three rocks, "and here."

With the last he opened the folds of his shirt to show a fourth snake coiling close to the brown skin of his body. This one was less torpid than its kin, warmed by contact with the man. It raised its head and studied them, detached interest in its cold, flat gaze.

"Snakes?" Derian repeated. "Why are you wearing a snake?"

Harjeedian drew in a deep breath.

"Why shouldn't I? The air is colder than is comfortable for snakes, even with the heat from the brazier. It helps if I let them warm themselves against me. I would take them out on deck, but the chill from the wind would undo whatever good the sunlight would do. Also, I do not wish them to get lost."

One of Firekeeper's questions had been answered, but not in a fashion that answered the others.

"Why you bring them? Are they from where you come?"

Harjeedian closed his shirt over the snake.

"I brought them because I wished to do so," he said. "Does not your culture have societies affiliated with various animals?"

"Derian's does," Firekeeper said. "He is Horse."

Harjeedian gave a half-smile at her reply.

"My culture has something similar," he said, "although the only ones who choose a specific totem are those in direct service of the deities."

"Deities?" Firekeeper said. "Snakes are deities?"

She was still having trouble with the concept of deities. Her first explanation had been from Derian, triggered by her discovery of the societies to which every human in Hawk Haven—and later she learned, in Bright Bay as well—belonged. Young children were dedicated to one of the societies soon after they were born. Each society was named for an animal. Humans regularly called on their society patron in times of stress, but apparently they didn't expect these patrons to do much of anything. When humans wanted something done, they talked to their ancestors.

Every home had its own ancestor shrine, which celebrated past generations. It also celebrated the deeds of the living. Wedding pouches were hung in family shrines, as were items commemorating other important events. When Derian had been made king's counselor, his mother had a miniature replica of his counselor's ring made to keep in the family shrine. As Firekeeper understood it, she would have liked the real ring, but Derian was too often away from home for this to be practical.

Shrine or not, Firekeeper couldn't see that the ancestors did much for their descendants, but she guessed it made the humans feel better to have someone to ask for help and advice. It also seemed to soothe them to feel that when they died some part of them stayed on.

Ancestors as deities or counselors or whatever made more sense to Firekeeper than some of the other religions about which she had heard. Apparently, in Waterland they thought the stars gave advice. She had no idea what the New Kelvinese worshipped—though it was doubtless related to magic. One of the cultures in Stonehold worshipped their ancestors, but the other had developed some complicated system having to do with the sun and the moon and any number of other things. She had glimpsed an entire tent stocked with the paraphernalia related to this latter religion when spying on the Stonehold army during King Allister's War.

What puzzled Firekeeper most of all was that the humans didn't seem to be able to agree on their deities. Certainly, if there were deities then there would be no doubt about them.

Wolves had too much to do just to stay alive and raise their pups to worry about such things. She'd never heard them howl to anyone to stop the rain or save a dying pup. They hunkered down and took what came. They didn't like it, but they took it. What else was there to do?

Now here she was confronting yet another approach to deities, and this one seemed to have something to do with snakes.

"Direct service of the deities?" she repeated, leaving the question of totems for later.

Harjeedian straightened, leaving no doubt that he was very pleased with himself.

"That's right," he said. "I was selected for service, though my family had never before had the honor. My teachers have been pleased with me, and I have been a member of the initiated—our word is 'disdum'—for many years."

Firekeeper didn't understand any of this, so she decided to try totems.

"Totems?" she asked.

Harjeedian partially closed his eyes, looking very snaky himself for a moment.

"I suppose it does no harm to explain a little, though my teachers have reserved the right to tutor you themselves. All the deities are receptive to the prayers of all worshippers, but there are some worshippers who understand the will of the deities more clearly than do others. These become members of the elect. We have two orders within the disdum. The aridisdum, to whom I belong, concentrate mostly on interpreting the omens and offering guidance based on these. The kidisdum are special servants of the deities, keepers of the sacred beasts."

Firekeeper nodded encouragement, though she still wasn't at all certain what Harjeedian was talking about.

"Among the disdum," Harjeedian went on, "there are divisions according to who seems to understand the ways and will of certain deities more clearly. These are then initiated into the lore of those particular deities and take the deities' totems for their own."

"And your deity is snake?" Firekeeper asked, hoping she understood correctly.

"No. My totem is the snake. I serve all the deities," Harjeedian said.

"And so you take snakes with you when you travel?" Firekeeper persisted. "Why? If you like snakes, why take them where it is not good for them?"

Harjeedian glowered at her, obviously offended. Then his expression became merely nasty. He looked over at Blind Seer, who lay on the floor next to her, close enough that his fur brushed her leg.

"You might ask yourself the same question," he said.

Then he asked them to leave his cabin and closed the door, effectively ending the conversation.

V

FIREKEEPER GREW ALTERNATELY ANGRY and moody following her discussion with Harjeedian regarding snakes and deities, and Derian decided that a distraction was in order. He couldn't get anyone to tell him how long the voyage was likely to take. He wondered if even the captain knew, since the voyage to Hawk Haven was apparently the first time a ship from Liglim had sailed so far north—at least in post-Plague history.

He had already lost count of the days, having failed to start a record early enough, and by the time the idea occurred to him, it hardly seemed to matter. What did matter was that Firekeeper was in a snit, and Firekeeper in a bad mood was dangerous not only to herself but to others.

Barnet had been tutoring Derian on the basic elements of Liglimosh, starting with nouns, promising to move on to verbs, and warning Derian that the linguistic structure was not as simple as Pellish.

"In Pellish," Barnet said, "a noun usually has two forms: singular and plural. In formal Liglimosh, a noun has six forms, according to how it is being used. To make matters worse, as I hinted earlier, sometimes the only difference between forms is in the stress given to a particular syllable. I'm going to start by teaching you the informal form—nominative singular and plural—and leave it at that. To those with an educated ear, you'll sound like Lady Blysse speaking Pellish, but it's faster than making you memorize six different forms for each word. You'd use them wrong anyhow."

Barnet gave one of his engaging grins when Derian stiffened.

"I did."

Derian found himself grinning in return. If he was honest with himself, he was rather glad he didn't need to learn all those forms just to make himself understood.

It was Barnet's easy charm that made Derian decide that Firekeeper needed to start her own language lessons. He'd let her sulk on her own—or rather with Blind

Seer, since the wolf never left her—and that hadn't worked. Time to pull her out of herself.

He suspected he knew exactly what had her so upset. Harjeedian's parting comment had hit a nerve. In the two years since Blind Seer had crossed the Iron Mountains with Firekeeper, the wolf had come close to death twice. People feared him. Feared what he might do to their children, pets, and homes.

Firekeeper clearly loved the wolf. There was no doubt Blind Seer was the one person she completely trusted. Yet, by keeping him near her, she was endangering his life on a daily basis. Threats to him could control her, which also had to make her wonder about the wisdom of keeping him near.

However, Derian could do nothing about this. Moreover, he suspected that any attempt to discuss the matter with Firekeeper would simply upset her further, since there was no way that—even had she wanted to—she could send Blind Seer into safety. Therefore, a distraction, and an intensive one at that, seemed to be in order.

Derian didn't bother to explain any of this to Barnet. The minstrel hadn't been present for the entire encounter between Harjeedian and Firekeeper, but he had drifted into the group at some point during it, and had heard what Harjeedian had said. If he made the connection between that comment and Firekeeper's current mood, fine. If he didn't, well, he could think whatever he wanted. Maybe Barnet thought she was having female troubles or something.

That brought Derian up short. Did Firekeeper have cycles? If she did, he hadn't observed the evidence. Wendee and Elise had both been discreet during their various journeys, but Derian had both mother and sister and was pretty good at guessing what certain signs meant. He hadn't seen the like with Firekeeper.

Another mystery, and though Harjeedian might be as knowledgeable as Doc about medical matters, it wasn't something about which Derian was going to question him. Nor was he going to ask Firekeeper. Even civilized women didn't welcome such queries when offered as an explanation of their moods. He'd learned that the hard way. It was quite possible that the wolf-woman would be angered further at the suggestion that she had a purely human weakness.

So Derian stored that new question away, and went off to bring Barnet and Firekeeper together.

He expected Firekeeper to fight the notion of learning Liglimosh, since it was something that Harjeedian wanted and the snake carrier was currently out of her favor—the little favor he'd been able to obtain by treating her seasickness. However, Firekeeper proved eager to learn the new language, fastening on nouns and committing them to memory with an eagerness that reminded Derian of her early efforts to learn Pellish.

She demanded other parts of speech as well, saying that nouns were little use when you couldn't say what you wanted to do with them.

"Like 'cut throat'?" Barnet suggested after a lesson on various parts of the body. "I can see your point. While I'm at it, I'd better include the words for asking 'what is.' As far as I can tell, it's your favorite phrase."

Derian felt himself growing jealous when he saw the comparatively easy time Barnet was having teaching Firekeeper this new language. Barnet noticed, and went right to the point one afternoon after Firekeeper had fallen asleep.

"Don't let how quickly she's learning bother you," Barnet said. "She's working from the foundation you put in place. You had to teach her the idea of a wholly spoken language, and that word order and all the rest mattered."

Derian forced a smile.

"Not that she pays much attention," he said.

"More than you think," Barnet said seriously. "I've noticed that she tends to drop words—especially articles—and mangle sentences only when it doesn't alter the meaning too severely. She's very, very careful when the meaning might be altered—at least when she cares about the issue—and that's pretty much whenever she bothers to speak. She isn't much for small talk."

"No, she isn't," Derian agreed, feeling better.

Barnet glanced at Firekeeper and confirmed she was really asleep, not just dozing.

"I'll make you a bet," he said.

Derian cocked an eyebrow.

"I'll bet you that Firekeeper refuses to refine her knowledge of Liglimosh any more than she did her Pellish."

"No bet," Derian said with a laugh. "If you can convince her of the need for proper grammar, you're a better instructor than I am."

Days melted into each other. For a time, the only indication that they were traveling at all was the varied shapes of the distant land. Then the weather became noticeably warmer, more so than could be explained by the mere passage of time.

"We're getting further south," Barnet confirmed. "I've talked to the sailors, and most of them have never seen snow—and what they have seen has been the result of a rare storm, the kind that's talked about for years afterwards. They've different plants in Liglim, and different animals, too. You think Harjeedian's snakes are big? I get the impression those are considered moderately sized specimens."

"How long until we come into port?" Derian asked.

Rarby happened to be passing by. On the whole, except for Barnet, the ship-wrecked Islanders avoided the three captives. Now he gave Derian a tight-lipped smile that said he hadn't forgotten their fight in the hold of the riverboat.

"The captain says we're coming into port for fresh provisions tomorrow. You'll be kept on board, of course, but don't worry. We'll be at our destination by the end of the moonspan."

Derian fought a sudden desire to run. The moon had been on the wane last night. They didn't have long to wait.

A BARELY SUPPRESSED AIR OF EXCITEMENT told more clearly than any announcement when *Fayonejunjal* drew near to her final port of call, but Firekeeper didn't need this to awaken her spirits from the final clinging wisps of despondency.

The air was filled with wonderful, heady, gloriously strange scents, the most dominant of which was rotting vegetation. Strange bird cries tantalized her ears, mingling with the more familiar shrill screams of the gulls. And there, close enough that she could see individual pebbles on the beach, was land—real, solid, unrocking land.

It hardly mattered that she would still be a captive once they were ashore. What mattered was that she would no longer be aboard this pitching, sliding, shifting, unpredictable ship.

Derian came and stood beside her.

"Harjeedian asked me to tell you that we would be taken ashore."

Firekeeper heard the odd inflection in his voice.

"Taken?"

"Remember how the New Kelvinese got around the city?"

"Carried by other people," Firekeeper replied, "on boxes between poles."

"They'll be using something similar for all of us," Derian said. "I expect that we'll be in—well—cages."

Firekeeper heard the tension and unhappiness in his voice, and knew it was not solely on her behalf. Derian didn't like the idea of being put in a box.

"Can we promise parole?" Firekeeper asked. "We have kept on ship."

Derian frowned. "I offered, but Harjeedian didn't want to take any risks—and he seems to be taking your threat not to be swayed by hostages pretty seriously. He's nervous now that we're close to those 'teachers' he keeps mentioning."

Derian had talked enough with both Harjeedian and Barnet by now to be fairly certain that the word Harjeedian translated as "teacher" meant something more, a concept that included "commander" or "superior," along with that of instructor.

"I talk to him," Firekeeper said. "Wait."

Derian might think she had paid no mind to Harjeedian since the day of the snakes, but in reality she had watched him closely. A wolf always paid attention to the will of the Ones, and in this situation, Harjeedian was very clearly a One.

She found Harjeedian in his cabin, settling his snakes into boxes that even her eye could see were beautifully made. Each snake had its own box, the interior padded with straw so the snake's scales would not be damaged.

"Harjeedian," Firekeeper said, pausing in the doorway. She hadn't violated his territory since he had warned her away, though privately she felt wronged.

The man turned, and she saw that he was dressed differently than he had been during the voyage. He wore fabric trousers, loose over hips and leg, but buttoned at the ankle. Over these was an equally loose shirt, the bindings heavy with embroidery in which the snake motif was frequently repeated. On his head was a small conical hat adorned with a sculpted snake. This coiled around the brim before making its way in lazy loops to rest its head on the top.

Even if Firekeeper had been inclined to be fooled by the loose tailoring—so unlike either the long robes of New Kelvin or the breeches, waistcoat, and jacket worn by men in Hawk Haven and Bright Bay—she would have noticed the sumptuous fabrics and come to the correct deduction.

"He is in formal dress," Firekeeper said to Blind Seer.

"Yes, and if your dead nose is not warning you, he is as nervous as a new mother when her litter first emerges from the den. Take care."

Firekeeper did catch a whiff of Harjeedian's tension in his sweat, but even more she saw it in the tightness of his skin over his high cheekbones, in the way he narrowed his eyes at her, daring her to give him any trouble.

"Yes, Lady Blysse?"

The words were perfectly courteous in tone, but not in the least cordial. There was a guarded element as well, as if Harjeedian sensed the impending challenge of his will.

Firekeeper did not lock eyes with him, but looked humbly at his shoes. "Derian say you put us on land in cages."

"That is so," Harjeedian replied, not bothering to correct her wording as Derian—or even Barnet—would have done.

"We ask no."

"And I say it will be so."

"Why?"

"Why do I say so or why must it be so?"

"Why second thing."

"Because I do not wish anything to happen to you."

"Happen?"

"Like your getting lost or thinking you might escape."

Firekeeper tilted her head to one side.

"We give parole."

"I do not wish to find that this is the time you choose to violate that parole," Harjeedian said.

"I can promise again," she said, still doing her best to look humble.

"True," Harjeedian said, "but I also have no wish for any to see you before my teachers do. The cages will be covered for this reason."

Firekeeper frowned. She didn't like this at all, but she could see there would be no convincing Harjeedian without further persuasion. She made a move as if leaving, then paused.

"You be important for bringing us here?" she asked.

Harjeedian gave a thin-lipped smile.

"Yes."

"I think you be more important if we walk with you," Firekeeper said, "than if we in cages. If in cages, some say, 'I can do this thing. How hard is it to put wolf in box?' If we give you parole and we walk with you, then they think you have power."

Harjeedian's hands kept moving about their chores, but Firekeeper could tell she had given him a thought worth considering.

"And you would renew your parole?"

"Unless life is threatened," Firekeeper said, "by you or yours. Parole until we reach this place of teachers."

Harjeedian finished settling his last snake into its box and began tightening down the lids.

"Can I believe you?"

Firekeeper looked at him levelly.

"We give parole on ship. Land is not so different. We not know where we are, where to go. But choice is yours. We only ask."

She padded away then without another word, for though she was willing to ask Harjeedian to change his mind, she was not willing to beg. However, she was not surprised when shortly before *Fayonejunjal* docked, Harjeedian came and said they would be permitted to walk to their destination rather than be carried in the cages.

He recited a long list of rules for how they must behave, but Firekeeper only listened to these with half an ear. Her heart was singing at her victory, and beside her, Blind Seer panted with openmouthed approval.

The *Fayonejunjal* was so large that they were taken to shore in smaller boats rather than the ship coming in to the dock. Derian went with Barnet in one boat, while Firekeeper and Blind Seer traveled in another. The sailors in their vessel were all of Harjeedian's race, silent and unspeaking, the ease they had acquired with wolf and woman vanished now that they were restricted to a comparatively small boat.

Firekeeper, however, intended no trouble. What she had said to Harjeedian was true. What use would it be to run before she learned something of the lay of the land? Of course she knew in what direction was north, but that meant nothing if a large river or ravine blocked their way. For now she was actually content to be a captive, if seeming such would enable her to ultimately plan an effective escape.

The small boats grounded themselves directly on the sandy shore, grating against the bottom and coming to a rather jarring halt. Firekeeper was grateful for an end to the rowing, for though the rowers had been skilled, the motion of the smaller boat had brought a return of her nausea. She had no wish to have these new people's first vision of her to be of her on her hands and knees, vomiting up whatever remained in her stomach.

She leapt to shore as soon as the boat was grounded, only to make another unpleasant discovery. The ground would not stop moving. It pitched and dropped, much as the deck of the ship had done. She stood very still, bracing herself, biting back a wail of frustration and fear. Had the very land rejected her?

Nor was Blind Seer immune to this sensation, as he had been to the seasickness. He took a tentative step, and it was as if his foreleg buckled beneath him. He sat, then dropped to a lying position, and gave a slight whine.

"It will pass," Barnet said, sounding amused. The boat on which he and Derian had traveled was grounded a short distance down the beach. "Wait just a few minutes."

Barnet stood squarely on his booted feet, giving no impression that the ground was moving. Firekeeper looked over at him.

"Sure?" she asked.

"I promise," Barnet said. "It's not uncommon, even for veteran sailors, to feel the land moving after long voyages. It's just that your body is a bit slow to adjust. I promise that by the time the rest of the vessel is unloaded, you'll be yourself again."

Firekeeper wanted to ask who else could she be, but she thought she understood his meaning. She certainly didn't feel much like herself with her feet unsteady and her head swimming.

Harjeedian joined them. He had come ashore on the first boat, along with his snakes and Waln. The Islander now stood some distance down the beach, recording crates of goods as they were unloaded, every line in his body screaming his need to be thought important.

In truth, although Waln had worked his passage along with his fellows, his status had been different. He had often worked alongside the captain, and Firekeeper had heard them arguing the merits of hull designs, sail shapes, and navigational techniques. At first she had listened, trying to gather information that would help in an escape, but listening to them was like listening to wolves discussing subtleties of a scent trail. She simply lacked the means to even begin understanding.

Harjeedian took inventory of his captives, but not even the slightest smile twitched his lips when he saw how Firekeeper was struggling to adjust to being on land. For this she was grateful. Had he been in the least mocking, she might well have tried to rip his throat out, and piss on the consequences.

"We're here," Derian said. "Do we have much farther to go?"

Harjeedian pointed. "Do you see that building? The tall one?"

Firekeeper turned to follow his directions and noticed for the first time a strange edifice rising over the confused mass of foliage and stone that must be yet another variation on a human city. This building was like nothing she had seen, even in New Kelvin, a place that gloried in strange architecture. It rose in steps or layers, each somewhat smaller than the one below, so that the outer surface looked like an enormous, rather steep set of stairs.

"That building stands at the heart of our destination," Harjeedian said. "It is a long walk, but my teachers have arranged to have the thoroughfares cleared before us."

Firekeeper understood almost nothing of this, but she heard the pride in Harjeedian's voice. It was the pride of one who shared in a powerful pack and and—perhaps truly, perhaps mistakenly—believed this made him powerful himself.

"We can walk," she said, taking a step and discovering to her surprise that this was true. "Blind Seer and I."

"Me, too," Derian said. "The ground has almost stopped moving."

"Then we go," Harjeedian said. "An escort is meeting us, and I remind you of your parole. You are not to threaten them, nor are you to go outside of the perimeter they set."

Firekeeper shook her head and gave him a wolfish grin.

"Big words, like a young wolf's howl, but I understand. Lead. We walk with you."

❀

DERIAN SAW HARJEEDIAN'S SCOWL and knew that Firekeeper had regained whatever ground she'd lost over Harjeedian's gibe about Blind Seer's safety. The wolfwoman knew it, too, and he thought that if she had a tail it would be held as proudly as Blind Seers's was at this moment, a jaunty plume rather than merely a trailing appendage.

However, whatever satisfaction he felt over his friend's victory simply intensified the emotions he felt at his first sight of u-Seeheera, the First City.

As far as architectural flourishes and fancies, u-Seeheera was far less overwhelming and astonishing than Dragon's Breath, the capital of New Kelvin. Indeed, u-Seeheera was less impressive than even a small New Kelvinese town. Yet, while the Liglimom seemed to lack the New Kelvinese taste for the fantastic, neither were they given over to the sense for practicality and comfort that dominated the majority of buildings in Hawk Haven and Bright Bay. Instead the buildings of u-Seeheera seemed designed to proclaim monolithic stability.

Overall the buildings were constructed from glazed bricks. The exteriors were sharply angular, but contrasted and softened by the curve of arched doorways and windows. These were often built from bricks glazed in a contrasting shade, so a pale grey building might have doorways of bright blue or shining yellow.

Even had the bricks all been the more usual red, the buildings would have been kept from severity by the riot of growth that contrasted with the underlying brick. Vines surged up the sides of buildings, showering the stone with foliage and brilliant flowers. Planters held yet more flowers, and even slender trees. In many cases, the foliage was unfamiliar to Derian, but then he'd never been much for plants, other than noticing what could and couldn't be eaten—and enjoying the beauty of an occasional flower.

The road Harjeedian directed their escort to follow had been cleared of routine traffic, making its breadth even more impressive. The road had two sides, divided by a wide walkway that Harjeedian explained was meant for pedestrian traffic. The pedestrian walk alone was wider than most of the city streets in Eagle's Nest and was ornamented with planters. Sections of the walkway were constructed of brightly colored mosaic, often counterpointing similar designs on planters or nearby walls.

To this point in his experience, all of the cities Derian had visited had evolved—in some cases to the point of self-strangulation. This one had clearly been designed, and designed with either growth or an existing large population in mind.

Streets crossed each other at precise intervals, their surfaces paved with stone or brick. The paving stones showed deep grooves worn by carts. Where pavers had been replaced, the newer stones had been grooved in turn. Gutters ran alongside the curbs, testifying that at some times rain must fall very heavily in this area. The lack of filth in the gutters argued for good sewers or a well-managed street-cleaning system.

The roofs of the surrounding buildings were peaked, but lacked the sharp angle Derian had seen in regions where snow was a regular occurrence and must be encouraged to slide off lest its weight collapse the building onto itself. In u-Seeheera, the slope of the roofs was more gentle. The architectural motif of each unit of buildings was maintained in the materials used for shingling and even to the pattern in which those shingles were cut and layered. Slate dominated some sections, in others tiles rounded to further channel water were the favored choice.

Down near the harbor, the buildings had a sturdy, practical appearance that mutely reminded Derian how violent hurricanes could be. The city streets sloped uphill, and where the chance of flooding was reduced, the buildings became more elaborately decorated. The brickwork trim was set in regularly repeating geometric designs. The closer they drew to the towering step pyramid, the more often animal-inspired designs began to be seen. These were not merely painted onto the brick, but molded, so that twenty or more bricks were needed to complete a design.

The creatures represented were not always ones Derian recognized, though there were the familiar, if stylized, forms of horses, dogs, snakes, and large cats. Fanciful renditions of many of these same animals, but with wings or strangely patterned coats, were also depicted. Once Derian would have dismissed these monsters as whimsy— creatures from Old Country tales told to amuse children on cold winter nights. Now he had seen too much to do so, and he found himself wondering if there really were creatures with human heads, the bodies of bulls, and the wings of eagles.

From the way Barnet was looking around, Derian guessed that the other man had not come so far into the city on his earlier visit. Barnet confirmed his guess.

"Last time they kept us in one of the buildings down by the harbor. We were treated well, even had a nice interior courtyard in which we could take the air, but our hosts seemed eager not to expose us to the bulk of the population."

"Like now," Derian said, dropping his voice, though he really didn't care if anyone overheard. "I've been looking, but unless the locals can look out the windows without being seen, we might as well be marching along the bottom of the ocean for all we're being noticed."

"Less so," Barnet agreed. "I'd guess on the seabottom the fish might drop down to take a look."

"Is it just that by local standards we're weird-looking and they don't want to start a riot?" Derian asked.

"I don't think so," Barnet replied. "The sailors on *Fayonejunjal* didn't seem unduly impressed or frightened by our differences. They seemed to feel superior rather than otherwise, especially when they learned how easily some of us sunburn."

Then I guess we're a state secret of some sort, Derian thought, but he didn't say it aloud. He figured Barnet was along to continue as a language teacher, more for Harjeedian than for Derian. They were reaching the point where Derian would need a local to help him along. Barnet was still ahead of him, but the minstrel often needed to ask Harjeedian to explain why some part of speech worked the way it did.

However, there was another possible reason Barnet had been included in their party—as a spy. His easygoing manner and affability made it easy to confide in him, but Derian hadn't forgotten that Barnet had gathered much of the information that had been used to capture them. The minstrel might be doing a related job now, except his goal would be to keep them from escaping without warning.

Unaccustomed as their time at sea had made him to walking long distances, Derian was beginning to regret not letting himself be carried to his destination, even if the conveyance in question would have been a cage, when he heard a soft gasp of wonder from Firekeeper.

He looked up—for a long while now his gaze had been on his own plodding boot toes—and saw that they had reached the end of the road. "Culmination" might be a better word. Derian knew without explanation that this entire grand progression was meant to inspire just such a gasp of wonder.

Before them stood a towering gate, the midpoint between walls that swept away side to side, their upper edge shaped to evoke the rise and fall of ocean waves. The walls were made of bricks glazed a shining blue-green, but the gate was a brilliant golden yellow. Something glittery—mica fragments, Derian thought—had been set in the glaze, so that the bricks sparkled. They must be magnificent at sunrise. Even now, at midday, the effect was remarkable.

Both gate and walls were set with molded designs. Those on the walls showed sea creatures, both fanciful and real. The gate depicted animals, but here Derian noticed a marked difference. Every animal represented was real. There were peculiar shades and textures to coats, but in no instance did he see wings on a creature that shouldn't have them, or that unsettling melding of human and animal characteristics.

"This," Harjeedian said with what Derian felt was perfectly excusable pride, "is Heeranenahalm, the City of Temples. It is where the elect live, and the deities are honored. Walk with respect, for many of even our own citizens are restricted from coming here except for special feasts."

Derian glanced at Firekeeper.

"Got that?" he asked.

Firekeeper nodded with more solemnity than he expected.

"This is a formal dress place," she said.

Harjeedian led them through the gate into a plaza walled with buildings several stories high. Crossing the plaza, he turned left. The walls surrounding them might have been oppressive but for the omnipresent greenery and the width of the road. Again

Derian was made strongly aware of the planning that had gone into this city.

Harjeedian was setting a rapid enough pace that Derian couldn't look around as much as he'd like, but he had the impression of more gleaming bricks and even more incredible flowers. Unlike along the road through the city, here he saw they were watched, but the watchers looked out from over walls or from balconies, and made no sound or comment. The uniform silence was more disturbing than any shouting or jeering could have been, and soon Derian focused his eyes directly in front of him rather than risk catching someone's gaze.

Their escort stopped before a building made from bricks glazed an unnaturally bright and shining green. Harjeedian motioned for them to wait, and went forward to a gate trimmed in golden yellow. He said something in his own language and received a measured reply. Then he spoke again.

This had to be ritual of some sort, Derian decided. There was no way they weren't expected. He wondered that they hadn't been cleaned up more, then wondered if the contrast of their own workday grubbiness was meant to make them feel humbled. Well, he'd lived several moonspans in Dragon's Breath, the capital of New Kelvin, and though u-Seeheera was impressive, he was beyond being awed by tall buildings and intricate architecture.

Barnet looked a bit pale, though, and Derian felt a completely unkind surge of satisfaction. It was good to know the Islander wasn't always on top of the situation.

Stepping back a pace and craning his neck, Derian looked around with assumed nonchalance. He guessed that this green wall was not part of a building, but rather the wall of a compound of related buildings. A smaller step pyramid rose from the center of the complex, its apex topped with a statue of a coiled snake, mouth gaping and ready to strike. The exterior walls continued this serpentine motif. The arched doorway, in which Harjeedian stood conversing with several men dressed much like himself, was carved in the shape of a large snake, coiled around and holding its tail in its mouth.

The carved snake atop the pyramid looked slightly cross-eyed, and Derian had to fight back what he was certain was a very unwise urge to laugh. Firekeeper seemed to have no such impulse. Indeed, her dark eyes were wide and unguardedly frightened as she inspected what was obviously their destination.

"This place smell of poison," she said. "We no go in?"

She spoke not as one who plans to defy, but as one who knows that defiance is not an option and hopes against hope that what one dreads will not happen.

"I think this is our destination," Derian said, putting a hand on her arm. "You won't cause trouble, will you?"

"I give parole," Firekeeper said firmly, but when he touched her arm, Derian couldn't help but notice that she was shaking.

VI

FOR ALL THE CEREMONY at the gateway between Harjeedian and the ones who stood within, the three captives and their escort passed into the compound with hardly any recognition at all of their coming.

"You will be greeted by all the great teachers," Harjeedian said, "at one time and in one place. For now you are to wash and rest, and pray to whomever you make offerings. So it is said."

Firekeeper noticed a new rhythm had entered Harjeedian's speech, and the strange, precise accent with which he spoke his excellent Pellish had become stronger.

She also sensed he was a bit miffed.

"So the welcome by his Ones did not happen as he dreamed," she said to Blind Seer. *"I wish my ears were more keen."*

"Mine are sharp enough," the wolf boasted, as was his way. Modesty was not considered a virtue among the wolves. *"But though I have been studying this new language as have you, I did not understand enough to account for his unhappiness. All I could gather was that Harjeedian's teachers were not having things their own way and that student shared his masters' unhappiness."*

Firekeeper thought about this.

"I noticed that after we passed through the golden gate we passed other compounds like this one. I wonder if each one houses a hive of these teachers. It would explain much. We are but one flower, and they are many bees."

"Many bees and many hives," Blind Seer agreed, *"though this hive into which Harjeedian has taken us has about it the reek of a nest of snakes rather than honey."*

Firekeeper nodded her agreement.

Unspeaking, Harjeedian led them through a maze of cool shaded walkways to a twisted, wrought-iron gate. Harjeedian unlocked the gate, waving them before him into a flower- and vine-adorned courtyard. There was a small pool at the courtyard's center. Alongside the pool were a low table and several chairs. Flowering plants grew both from the soil and from ornate, mosaic-adorned pots, perfuming the air so heavily that Blind Seer sneezed.

The back edge of the courtyard was flanked with two arched doorways. These proved to lead into large rooms with cool, tiled floors, furnished with heavy pieces worked from intricately carved wood: beds, clothes chests, and tables overhung with framed mirrors. The beds were covered with embroidered quilts that seemed too heavy for the warm air, and overhung with fine mesh nets.

Harjeedian turned to the three.

"Here is where you will stay," he said. "Decide how you will divide up the sleeping rooms as best suits you."

He turned to Firekeeper and looked at her very sternly.

"Your parole does not give you leave to roam outside of this courtyard and these rooms. Do you understand?"

Firekeeper nodded, amused and pleased by the care Harjeedian took to set her limits. It spoke of respect for her cleverness.

"Food will be brought to you," Harjeedian went on more generally, "and drink, and a change of clothing."

With that, he hurried away, and they were left to contemplate their new situation.

Blind Seer padded over to the pool and drank deeply. He raised his head and sneezed, backing away from the water, shaking as if he were wet all over.

"What's with him?" Derian asked. "Get a fish up his nose?"

The pool was home to many small, brightly scaled carp, but these were not the source of the wolf's distress. Blind Seer sneezed again, and Firekeeper crossed and knelt beside him.

"*Beware the pool, sweet Firekeeper,*" the wolf said. "*The water is not as fresh as its sparkle seems to show—though I have drank worse without becoming ill. Snakes lair within its waters.*"

Firekeeper leaned over the water to inspect the edges of the pool and saw several sleek greenish black forms coiled about the rocks and water plants. One had half consumed a small fish, and the carcass hung from its gaping mouth. She wrinkled her nose in disgust and looked at Derian and Barnet.

"Snakes in the pool," she said. "Water is tainted."

Derian gagged. "And to think I was considering taking a dip. I hope they bring us wash water along with the fresh clothing."

As if in reply, a clanking sound announced the iron gate being opened. A young woman stepped through, holding the gate open while dropping a key back into the folds of her blouse. She was clad in a similar fashion to Harjeedian's formal attire—though without demonstrating his obsession with snakes and lacking the conical hat. Her skin was the color of toasted bread, and the hair that fell past the middle of her back was the precise shade of wet ink. There was something of wet ink as well in her hair's silkiness, and in the liquid way it fell from the loose clip that gathered it at the nape of her neck.

The young woman smiled shyly at them, and in that smile Firekeeper recognized something of Harjeedian, but a younger Harjeedian, gentler and more curious. The same high cheekbones that distorted his face and made his eyes seem slitted were as elegant as sculpture on her, and the same brown eyes were warm and inquisitive.

Firekeeper heard twin intakes of breath from Derian and Barnet and knew that what she guessed was indeed true. This was a young woman of surpassing beauty.

Clapping her hands twice in a signal that Firekeeper already knew from shipboard meant "come," the young woman motioned to some who stood outside the gate. Three large men answered her command. They were all simply clad in loose breeches and smocks, and had the air of servants about them. One wheeled a cart on which was a metal container that radiated much heat. One carried a tray on which was an array of good-smelling food. The last carried a tightly woven basket.

The tray of food was set on the low table near the pool before the servant hurried away, his hard-soled sandals tapping on the bricks of the courtyard floor. The man with the cart wheeled his burden into the nearest of the sleeping rooms. He exited empty-handed, said something to the woman, and hurried away. The third man paused, indecisive, and asked a question of the woman.

Firekeeper caught a few words of what he said, and wasn't at all surprised when Barnet turned to ask her, "Which room do you two want, or do you plan to sleep out here with the snakes?"

Normally, Firekeeper would have declined the offer of a sleeping chamber, but the snakes made her reconsider. She didn't think these snakes were poisonous, but snakes were known to nestle near any source of warmth, and the idea of waking to find one of the pool dwellers wrapped around her in the same fashion that Harjeedian carried his pets was unpleasant.

She recalled that one of the rooms had held a single large bed, the other two smaller ones.

"I take room with one bed," she said.

Barnet relayed this information, and the man with the basket went first into Firekeeper's chosen room, then into the other. When he returned, he carried the basket as if it was much lighter and Firekeeper guessed that it had been his task to deliver fresh clothing.

Meanwhile the young woman motioned them toward the tray of food.

"Eat," she said in her own language. "It is very good."

Firekeeper was hungry, but what she'd tasted of local cooking on the ship hadn't pleased her. The Liglimom had a liking for heavily flavored sauces that seemed to serve mostly to hide when the food underneath was near spoiling.

To her pleasure, she saw that among the sauced dishes there was also a selection of clean grilled meats and lightly cooked vegetables quite suited to her tastes. For Blind Seer, the tray carrier returned a moment later with a haunch of some type of deer, raw and butchered no later than that morning.

"I am Rahniseeta," the woman said, still in her own language, but speaking very carefully. "I am Harjeedian's sister, and will assist him in making you welcome."

Derian was looking very stiff and awkward and couldn't seem to find his voice. Barnet was not so discommoded, but smiled warmly, awakening an answering smile from Rahniseeta.

"Thank you," Barnet said in Liglimosh. "We are grateful."

Rahniseeta sank gracefully onto one of the low chairs placed near the table and picked up a metal pitcher that was sweating from the coolness of whatever was inside.

"This is a fruit drink," she said. "Very good. This," she lifted another pitcher, "is fresh water."

Firekeeper reached for the water. No bowl had been put on the tray for Blind Seer, so she supplied one by pouring apricots out onto the food tray. Then she set the bowl on the brick floor of the courtyard and filled it with water.

Rahniseeta watched without either comment or complaint. When Firekeeper set the water pitcher back on the tray, she said, "We remembered food for your companion, but thought he would drink from the pool."

Firekeeper struggled to answer in Liglimosh.

"It taste like snake shit," she managed. She knew when she saw Derian color that she was using cruder language than was proper, but the sailors' terms she had heard dozens of times a day came more readily to mind.

Rahniseeta nodded.

"How do you know this?"

Firekeeper answered guardedly, not certain whether or not she was being insulted.

"He not like."

Rahniseeta's grin was unguarded and friendly.

"I would not care to drink tainted water either. You will be pleased to know that your bathwater is not taken from this pool or any like it. Hot water has been brought. Cool is being brought, along with a tub."

Derian found his voice for two words.

"Thank you."

Rahniseeta robbed him of his voice with another of her smiles before continuing.

"There are baths here in the compound with running water, both hot and cold, but we thought you would like privacy."

Firekeeper said to Blind Seer, *"And to let us go there and bathe would make it difficult to keep us in hiding."*

Blind Seer laughed, beating his tail on the floor. His powerful jaws cracked the deer bone at its thickest point and he grunted in satisfaction as he licked out the marrow. Firekeeper noticed with some satisfaction that Rahniseeta was impressed.

But not afraid. Like Harjeedian, she did not fear Blind Seer. Did these people think them tamed? Controlled? She swallowed a growl, not liking the thought at all, and resolving that as soon as possible she would make sure these Liglimom knew that captive and tame were not at all the same thing.

ONCE THE COOL WATER HAD BEEN DELIVERED, and Rahniseeta had made certain they knew how to operate the tank for adding hot, Harjeedian's sister left. Derian found it very difficult not to stare after her as she walked out through the iron gate. Her hips swayed ever so slightly as she walked, a gait with music in every step, very different from what he had observed elsewhere—and Derian was an enthusiastic observer of feminine charms.

He wondered if the loose trouser costume she wore accounted for it, the gentle fall of folded fabric accentuating her movements, or whether it had more to do with Rahniseeta's own perfect grace. He was willing to place money on the credit being Rahniseeta's own, for certainly neither Harjeedian nor their escort—both of whom had worn variations on the same costume—had so captured his eye.

Suddenly, Derian became aware that Barnet had asked him a question. Judging by the mild amusement in his tone, Barnet was repeating himself.

"Excuse me, I wasn't listening," Derian said honestly.

"I asked if you were going to finish that stew," Barnet said. "I acquired something of a taste for it during my last stay."

"Oh, no, please, go ahead. It's nice, but I'm quite full."

Derian paused long enough that he hoped his interest wouldn't seem too obvious, then asked: "Did you meet Harjeedian's sister when you were here before?"

Barnet shook his head, but his full mouth couldn't quite hide his amusement.

"No. Of those you have met, only Harjeedian and, later, the captain of *Fayonejunjal*. There were many others who came by to learn a bit of Pellish or gape at us, but I don't think Rahniseeta was among them. I would have remembered her if she had been."

Derian felt irrationally jealous.

"She is pretty, isn't she?" he commented, deciding honest admission was better than evasion.

"Pretty doesn't say it," the minstrel concurred. "She's lovely. Graceful as a swaying tree limb or perhaps a single flower in a field of wheat."

Derian despaired. He hadn't been able to do more than gulp out a few words. Barnet was already composing poetry—and the minstrel had the jump on him as far as speaking the local language went, too.

Oh, well, he thought, *at least I have another incentive to improve my Liglimosh.*

Firekeeper had slipped away at some point, and now she returned. She was freshly washed and still damp, hands busy adjusting the clean clothing that had been set out for her. As the style—a version of the ubiquitous loose trousers and blouse—was not overly different from what they had been given aboard ship, she had done fairly well. However, she was having trouble with the trousers.

The trousers they had been given shipboard had been tapered, cut to slightly below the knee, then laced to whatever snugness the wearer preferred. Since Firekeeper preferred freedom of motion, she had kept hers laced very loosely, sometimes not bothering to tie the laces at all. The trousers in her new outfit, however, were cut to ankle length, and the excess fabric in the legs was sufficient that if she didn't tighten the lacing, the legs bunched and dragged on the ground.

"Is there knife on that eating plate?" she asked. "I think these need cutting off."

Derian glanced at the tray, noticing for the first time that the only utensils were spoons. The meal had been so cleverly arranged that he had not noticed the lack. Even Firekeeper's rarer meat had been cut into neat chunks in advance.

"No knife," he said, "but I think there's something we can do about those trouser legs. Come over here."

Firekeeper did so, hauling up at the waistband of her trousers so as to not tread on the hem. Derian investigated, admiring the tight weave of the dark green fabric as he did so. Whatever else about their situation, they were not being dressed as prisoners.

"Look here," he said. "There's a drawstring at the bottom, different from lacing, but not too much so. You work the fabric around the lace until it's as snug as you'd like. Then the fabric stays above your ankle, rather than tangling your foot."

"Untangle one foot," Firekeeper suggested. "I watch, do other."

Derian complied.

"How does that feel?" he asked.

"Not so bad," Firekeeper replied, propping her foot on one of the vacant chairs and tying the other leg to match. "Though my legs feel odd with so much cloth around. Shirt in or out?"

Derian inspected the blouse, which was woven of a similar fabric, dyed a slightly lighter shade of green and trimmed with a darker green ribbon that could be used to adjust the fit of the neckline. Firekeeper had left her blouse unlaced and untucked. Comparing the wolf-woman's appearance to his all too vivid memory of Rahniseeta, Derian passed judgment.

"Tuck it in, I think," he said, "but not too snug, leave a little extra untucked and the shirt will flow. That's right. Now, lace the neck just a bit. Hanging open like that looks slatternly."

Firekeeper obeyed, and when she had finished, she looked so cool and clean that Derian couldn't wait for his own turn at the bath.

"Flip a coin for the bath?" he asked Barnet.

"Don't have a coin," Barnet replied laconically, pouring the last of the fruit juice into his glass and swirling it to examine the color. "You go on ahead."

Derian's initial gratitude was moderated slightly when he realized that this meant his would be the awkward task of rolling the tub into the room he would share with

Barnet, then bringing the hot-water cart after. Firekeeper helped him, and they managed without too much sloshing.

The clothing that had been left for him—it was obvious which was his by the length of the trousers—was in shades of rusty brown. As with Firekeeper's outfit, the trousers were darker than the shirt. His shirt, however, lacked the lacing at the neck, but was cut instead in a keyhole pattern that left a narrow line open midway down his chest. His full-length trousers were not as full either, and he supposed the differences were meant to accommodate male and female anatomical variations.

Even so, compared with the tailored knee britches he'd worn in Hawk Haven, the trousers did feel very full—almost uncomfortably so. The shirt reminded him of the smocks he wore when doing heavy work. However, compared with his few ventures out in New Kelvinese robes, he was comfortable, and he had to admit that the loose cut was perfect for the damp warmth of the local weather.

And it is still yet spring, he thought. *What will the weather be like when summer comes?*

Firekeeper, as was her wont, had not bothered with shoes, but Derian found that footwear had been supplied. There were both a pair of full-foot-covering leather slippers and a pair of sandals of the simple type that are held on with a thong through the two largest toes. A dark brown ribbon had been supplied for binding back his hair, set on the table before the mirror along with both comb and brush.

Derian chose the thong sandals and combed his hair, and though the reflection in the mirror looked very strange to him, he thought he looked a great deal better than he had in salt-stained, not too frequently washed, sailor's togs.

Barnet seemed to agree, for he hurried to take advantage of the bath immediately after Derian came out, emerging some time later in an outfit identical to Derian's, but that shirt and trousers were dyed in shades of blue that went very well with his fair hair.

"Tailors must not make too good a living here," Barnet commented, slinging himself down into a chair again. "These shirts and trousers could be made in advance and all one would need to do is choose the length trousers that would best suit. Even those have some leeway because of the extra fabric."

Derian nodded. "The weaving is excellent, though, and they must have some trade for silk—or the ability to grow it themselves. This fabric is cotton, I'm pretty sure, but Harjeedian had silk in his clothing."

"Or something like it," Barnet agreed. "I wonder if some enterprising Waterlanders have made it this far south?"

Derian hoped so. Waterland was neither friend nor enemy of Hawk Haven, and a Waterlander ship might be willing to take them home on promise of future reward.

Home, he thought, wondering why the word wasn't as sweet as it had been. Unbidden, Rahniseeta's image came to mind. He shook his head violently to clear it away. Surely he must have been charmed!

From where she lounged on the floor next to Blind Seer, Firekeeper looked at him curiously.

"Fly in my ear," Derian said, a trace lamely.

The wolf-woman nodded.

"Now what?" she asked simply.

Derian glanced at Barnet, but the minstrel only shrugged.

"Now," Derian said, taking a deep breath, "we wait."

BUT TELLING FIREKEEPER TO WAIT and making her do so were two completely different propositions. A full day away from the pitching of the ship's decks, a few meals that didn't threaten to come up almost as soon as they went down, and she wanted out of the confines of the courtyard. Derian realized how awkward their position was becoming the second night after their arrival.

Barnet snored, loudly and robustly, as befitted a man of good lungs and voice. Even the insect netting and the rich carpets scattered on the tiled floors could not keep the sound from reverberating. The first night after their arrival, Derian could have slept through anything. On this second night, a day of relative inactivity combined with the memory of Rahniseeta's dark, liquid eyes made sleeping through Barnet's snoring impossible.

Rising, Derian pulled the light coverlet off his bed, tossed it over his shoulder, and headed out into the courtyard, deciding that snakes were a far better option than sharing a room with a thunderstorm.

He found Firekeeper there before him. She had climbed up onto the biggest planter and was testing whether the ornamental fruit tree planted within would bear her weight. Blind Seer stood below, looking up intently, no doubt calculating his own chances if he were to leap from that raised platform onto the roof tiles.

The blue-eyed wolf greeted Derian with a lazy sweep of his tail, and Firekeeper looked down almost immediately.

"Hey, Fox Hair," she said softly. "No sleep with thunder? You can use my room. The snakes are little fish eaters."

He understood the leap between the sentences. Having assured herself that the snakes were not dangerous, Firekeeper didn't mind, in fact probably preferred, sleeping under the open sky. He ignored her generous offer.

"What are you doing up there?"

"Wanted to go on roof. It is not too slant, and Harjeedian did not say we could not go top of the rooms."

Her teeth flashed in the moonlight, her smile seeming quite like Blind Seer's at that moment.

"The gate," she added, seemingly without connection, "has metal thorns on top, and at the end of the hall—walkway—just happen to be guards standing. Blind Seer sniffed them, but I heard Rahniseeta talk to them when she went last."

Derian was glad the wolf-woman couldn't hear how his heartbeat quickened at the mention of Rahniseeta's name.

Horse in a windstorm! Sure he'd been celibate shipboard, but Eagle's Nest had been home ground and several women he knew had been in a holiday mood. What was his problem? You didn't fall in love with a woman after a couple of meetings. That was just the meat and bread of minstrels' tales, the kind of stories Elise would have mooned over back when they first met. Look where that kind of thinking had gotten her—engaged to a complete scoundrel. Only luck had saved her from a very bad marriage.

Derian saw Firekeeper grinning at him, and wondered if he'd somehow given himself away.

"Well, come down from there," he said sternly. "No matter how you want to interpret your parole, I don't think Harjeedian included the rooftops in his definition of limits."

Firekeeper leapt down, springing lightly as a cat—though given some of the things he'd seen Blind Seer do, Derian thought she was also probably moving as lightly as a wolf. She was serious now, and hunkered down in the attitude that meant she wanted to talk.

"Fox Hair, I not like this parole. It is all Harjeedian's way, none mine. I promise to not escape and still I am locked up in here. I not like it at all."

Derian slid into one of the chairs near the table. Barnet's continued snoring was ample testimony that they had some sort of privacy—in many ways, the first privacy that they had been given since their escape attempt. Parole or not, Derian had noticed how one or more of the sailors just happened to be working near them when they were out on deck. If the sailors weren't near, one or more of the captain's small children always seemed to be playing nearby. Barnet might have been pleasant and interesting company, the language lessons a good way to fill the empty days on the seemingly endless ocean, but he, too, had been a guard of sorts.

"I don't like it either, Firekeeper, but I don't know what other option we have. We're in an unfamiliar city, unknown distances from Hawk Haven. If we ran north, the first country that we'd know would be Stonehold, and I don't think we could expect much help there."

Firekeeper shook the dark tangle of her hair.

"If we go other side of mountains, then we is in my people's land. Different packs, yes, but they could cry the call north and they would help us."

Derian wished he was so confident. Local wolves—if there were local wolves—might help Blind Seer and Firekeeper, but he couldn't resist the feeling they might think he was to be numbered among the enemy. He'd heard tales of what the Royal Beasts could do to those they declared against, and he didn't wish to invite any opportunity.

"I think," Firekeeper went on, "that from roof I might see where mountains are."

She looked suddenly forlorn, and Derian wished he could comfort her, but comfort—and encouragement—were the last things she needed.

"Firekeeper, from what Rahniseeta said today . . ."

There, the thought underlay his spoken words, *I said her name as casually as I would Elise's or Dami's.*

"Tomorrow is going to bring a change. Harjeedian has been making some sort of report to his teachers. That's why we haven't seen him. Rahniseeta says he is coming to see us tomorrow soon after breakfast. Listen to what he has to say. Then, if you must, ask him about changing the terms of our parole. All I ask is that you let him have his say first. He may give you what you want without asking."

"Not unless he let us go free," Firekeeper said, "is he letting us have what we want. Still, I listen."

Derian had to be content with that, and since Firekeeper didn't show any inclination to climb back up on the roof, he gave a mental shrug.

"Were you serious about letting me have your room?"

"Of course."

"Good night, then."

"Sweet dreams," she replied, and Derian blushed, for he heard the laughter in her voice.

WHAT DERIAN APPARENTLY HADN'T GUESSED was that Firekeeper had already been up on the roof. What he had caught her about was trying to find a good route by which Blind Seer could join her. She hadn't intended to try and escape—certainly not while Derian slept—but she thought that checking her options was a good idea.

Now as Derian went into her room and closed the door, Firekeeper pillowed her head on Blind Seer's flank and tried to sleep, but sleep did not wish to come. Two years of associating with humans and the fact that Firekeeper had done much of her own hunting by daylight even before coming to humans had not changed the fact that for her, night was no less usual a time to be abroad and active than day. The need for action, not the height of the sun, was what made her choices, and the very darkness seemed to cry that night would be the time to slip away.

She sighed and Blind Seer bent his head to lap her face.

"Rest, dear heart," he said. "You need your wits about you. For all your boldness, you have hardly recovered the strength the sea sucked from you."

Firekeeper puffed her agreement, made her eyes stop watching the stars, and, eventually, lulled by the wolf's even breathing, she fell asleep.

Warm, aware of the beating of her mother's heart, the rise and fall of her breathing, the baby drowses. This is the best place to be, cuddled against Mother's softness, almost asleep, awake only enough to savor the pleasure of a full belly and warm closeness.

Mother goes about her routine, stooping and bending, but the baby is not disturbed. The swaying of Mother's motion is what a rocking cradle poorly counterfeits, lacking as it does the soothing accompaniment of heartbeat, and the rise and fall of breath.

The baby might have slept then, her dreams intertwined with growing plants and the scent of warm leaf mold, but a voice breaks through the tranquil music of heartbeat and breath.

"Serena? Where are you?"

A man's voice. Familiar enough that the baby relaxes some.

"In the garden."

Mother raises her voice and the vibrations carry through her flesh into the baby's ear, dimming the comforting lullaby. The baby whimpers slightly. A hand pats her, and she quiets.

The man's voice again.

"Serena, you'll never believe what happened to me."

"Hush," *Mother says.* "I've just gotten the baby to sleep."

The man's voice immediately softens. "Sorry. I didn't see her there. Want me to hold her? She's getting heavy for the backpack."

"I have her," *Mother says.* "Yes. She's getting heavy, but she wouldn't settle and I had to get these seeds in. I've a feeling it's going to rain tonight."

"Ah, well, let me help while I talk." *The man's voice remains soft, but the note of excitement returns.* "I've got to tell you what happened when I was out checking my snares. I happened on a cherry tree where the fruit was just beginning to ripen. Little things, and tart even when ripe, but they'd be a welcome change from dried apple slices. Figured I'd get what I could before the birds ruined the rest.

"After I'd picked what I could reach from the ground, I noticed there was a good ripe batch up higher, and went after them. I'd nearly finished picking when I caught some motion from the corner of my eye. There was a hole in the surrounding tree cover—probably why the cherries had ripened at that point and not elsewhere. A big maple had gone down and, like I said, left a hole."

His voice has risen now, but the baby isn't disturbed. Mother has resumed her gentle motions. The sun is warm. The birds, startled to silence when the man first arrived, have now resumed their songs.

"You'll never believe what I saw," *the man says.*

"Probably not," *Mother says, and there is soft laughter under her words.* "Why don't you tell me, Donal?"

"It was a deer the size of a moose—or maybe just an elk, but a white-tail buck in every other way, right down to a rack that would be the envy of any trophy room in the kingdom."

"If you say so," *Mother agrees.* "But how could you tell the size at such a distance?"

"I'd been out to that very spot," *the man says,* "just a few days before. There's a couple of boulders and I wanted to see what was denning there. I could guess the size of the buck from how he dwarfed those boulders. But, Serena, wait—the size of the buck isn't the best thing."

"Go on."

"While I was watching, the brush moved and out stepped a wolf—a timber wolf nearly the size of a pony. What do you think the buck did?"

"I won't even try to guess. Hand me the seed sack, will you? I'm out. And go on with your story. Somehow I don't think it's going to end with venison hanging in the larder."

"Here. Let me pour some seed into your basket."

A sound with a hiss like falling rain intervenes. The baby squirms, but Mother resumes her motion and the man his speech.

"I thought to see the buck bolt, though how it had let the wolf get so close I couldn't imagine, but I can't say I was thinking much, just watching. The buck didn't bolt, though, nor did the wolf spring. They stood for a moment, sniffing each other, then they stood for all the world like two men gossiping over a fence while resting from the plowing."

"You're not making this up?" Mother asks.

"On my honor," the man says. "It's too early in the season for fireside tales. Buck and wolf stood there, then a bear lumbered out of the cover and joined them, and the three stood there. By now if it hadn't been for the tree branch digging into my knees I would have thought I was dreaming.

"All of a sudden, there was a harsh croaking call and black wings flashed over where I was. Buck, wolf, and bear all froze, but they didn't flee as animals should when the raven calls warning. Instead, as one, they turned their heads and looked right where I was in my tree. I don't know if they could see me, but it was like they knew what the raven said."

"Don't animals always take warning from a raven's cry?"

"In a general way," the man said. "Not like this. Not looking right where the trouble's sitting. They looked at me one long moment. Then the wolf turned his head and looked in the direction of our settlement. Then, just like they'd finished a conference, they melted back into the brush. I was too scared to move for the longest time, but then I got down and came straight here."

"You're not teasing?" Mother's voice sounds tense and the baby whimpers in response.

"No, Sarena," the man says. "I don't want to say anything yet—not to anyone but the prince, maybe—but I keep thinking of the fireside tales my grandfather would tell, and, I wonder if we might have neighbors."

The baby stirred again, and this time mother's arms drew her close, rocking her. The baby snuggled close into the softness of comforting fur, and fell soundly asleep.

FIREKEEPER AWOKE SHORTLY AFTER DAWN, and occupied herself attempting to work some of the tangles—she hadn't cared much for grooming aboard ship—from her hair. She was reaching the unpleasant conclusion that she might need to cut some of the hair off as the only solution, when Barnet emerged from his room.

He glanced over at the other closed door and grinned.

"Did I snore last night?"

"Summer thunder is more quiet."

"I thought about warning Derian I snore," Barnet admitted, slouching into one of the chairs alongside the pool and yawning mightily, "but he didn't seem to notice the first night."

"First night," Firekeeper said, "everyone too tired. How you do on ship?"

"Well," Barnet laughed, "it wasn't just my way with words and charming smile that got me a nice private place to sleep in the sail locker. I think my mates wanted a door between me and them."

Firekeeper nodded.

"Breakfast come soon. Maybe I should wake Derian."

"Not going to give me a chance at Rahniseeta without the competition?"

Firekeeper tilted her head, acting more puzzled than she was. She'd seen that both men liked Harjeedian's sister, and thought that they were fools, but then she was coming to learn that humans took a different view of choosing a mate than did wolves. In a small pack, only the Ones would mate. In a larger pack—so she had heard, though her pack had never been so—there would be a second pairing. Humans seemed to pair for many reasons, pleasure being an important reason, with the alliances that meant so much to wolves meaning something only to those humans who had more to protect.

She shook her head, for she was confusing herself, and gave an easier answer.

"I think that Rahniseeta say Harjeedian come after breakfast," she said. "Derian not wish to be sleep-tossed then."

"True," Barnet agreed.

He didn't say anything more about Rahniseeta, but now that Firekeeper considered it, he was very neatly groomed, making more effort than he had on shipboard. Was this because he wished to impress Rahniseeta or because he also had not forgotten Harjeedian's coming?

Firekeeper woke Derian and took advantage of his waking to fill the tub with tepid water and scrub the evidence of her roof-climbing ventures from her hands. The dark green fabric of her trousers hid the slight soiling well enough, especially since her preference for sitting on the ground left her trousers less than pristine rather quickly.

Breakfast was delivered by Rahniseeta and the usual servitors. The woman was clearly excited—more, Firekeeper thought, than her brother's coming could explain. However, as Rahniseeta did not volunteer anything and neither Barnet nor Derian appeared to notice her mood, Firekeeper kept her reflections to herself.

As if he had been awaiting a signal, Harjeedian arrived immediately after they had finished eating. He was clad in snake-embroidered garments and had one of his pets coiled loosely about his shoulders. It was a pretty creature—pale golden brown with darker brown angular patterns—and much more alert here in the warmth than it had been shipboard. Still, it was Cousin-kind, not Royal, and Firekeeper paid it scant heed.

Harjeedian seated himself in the chair Firekeeper was not using, and motioned for Rahniseeta to leave. If he noticed how Derian's gaze rather fixedly did not follow the young woman's graceful departure, he did not choose to comment.

"I hope you have been comfortable," he said.

Derian nodded. Barnet murmured something genial. Firekeeper snorted.

"Comfortable, yes, like birds in cage are comfortable. We eat, we drink, we wash, but we cannot fly."

Belatedly, she remembered how Derian had asked her to hold her complaints until after Harjeedian had his say, so she swallowed all else she wanted to add and said rather lamely.

"The clothes are good. Very comfortable."

Harjeedian gave a thin smile.

"I am pleased they suit you. Today you will be receiving more clothing, a great deal more."

"And to what do we owe this honor?" Barnet said.

"There is an upcoming reception to which the three of you are invited. My teachers have agreed to assure that you will be clad in honor of the occasion."

"Reception?" Derian asked. He managed without being rude to put a note of doubt into the word, implying that they were not so much being received as displayed. Firekeeper admired his skill.

"Reception," Harjeedian repeated solidly, ignoring Derian's tone. "This will be an opportunity for you to meet u-Liall, as well as many important aridisdum and kidisdum. It is to be a formal occasion, but not a solemn one. There will be no rituals, simply introductions."

"But why?" Firekeeper pressed. "Sure they come here. We not go anywhere."

Harjeedian's smile was tight and thin-lipped. Firekeeper knew she had annoyed him, but she didn't care.

"As I have told you," Harjeedian said, "we wish you to remain in Liglim as our guests. If you are to be guests, then you must meet your hosts."

Derian was about to say something—probably to moderate any anger Firekeeper might have aroused—but Barnet cut him off.

"I was given to understand," the minstrel said sharply, "that after helping you meet with Lady Blysse and Derian Counselor, I would be permitted to return to sea—to return to my travels, and eventually go back to the Isles. My mates and I have been from home a year or more by now."

"We have not said otherwise," Harjeedian answered smoothly. "Indeed, I believe we also discussed the possibility that you would act as our ambassador to these Isles— Baron Endbrook being less than welcome there at this time."

"You promised Baron Endbrook help reestablishing himself," Barnet said, his tone flat and guarded. "He had hoped for that ambassadorial position himself, and I heard you indicate that he was not hoping in vain."

"We did say as much," Harjeedian agreed, "and we have not said otherwise. However, it is up to us who will be our ambassador and at what time. We do not think it would be in Liglim's best interests at this time to send as emissary one such as Baron Endbrook who has been exiled by the very queen with whom we are hoping to open negotiations."

"Waln had hoped that your favor would help him reunite with his family," Barnet said, his tone becoming harsh.

"So it still may do," Harjeedian said. "Baron Endbrook's desire for a dramatic confrontation with Queen Valora is his own fantasy. It is no business of our own."

Barnet's glower said more clearly than words that he felt the Liglimom had led Waln Endbrook into believing his hopes were more than fantasy. Harjeedian ignored the minstrel's expression and continued on blandly.

"You have no such blot on your reputation. However, you also know too little about us to serve as a proper emissary. We propose to detain you here in u-Seeheera until you are better prepared, and until you can teach your language to those who will accompany you. You are by far the most talented language teacher among those we rescued from the wrecked ship."

Blind Seer beat his tail on the ground.

"So the hunter finds himself the prey!" he laughed. *"Barnet does not look pleased."*

Firekeeper scratched him between his ears.

"Still your tail, dear heart. I do not like how Harjeedian looks at it with his eyes thinning. It is almost as if he knows that you laugh, and why."

Barnet sputtered a few more protests, but he knew as surely as if Harjeedian stated so baldly that he had no real choice but to comply.

Derian looked quietly pleased at the minstrel's discomfiture, but oddly Firekeeper found herself pitying the minstrel. Barnet had been smug at times, but hardly unkind, and she was not so reconciled to imprisonment that she didn't feel sorrow for one who suddenly realized he had dug himself a pit too deep to jump out of.

"This reception is very important?" Firekeeper asked.

"Very," Harjeedian agreed. His next words held a silky, threatening note. "I would be very displeased if you refused to attend. I might need to take unpleasant actions."

Firekeeper met the oddly snakelike eyes over those high cheekbones.

"I tell you once before," she said. "No hostage games anymore."

"Are you saying you would let Derian be harmed?"

Firekeeper nodded. "I would. I am wolf."

Harjeedian frowned deeply and Firekeeper struggled to find the words to explain.

"I love Derian and Blind Seer, but all wolves love pack mates and still hunt the big game with them. In a hunt, a head may be stove in, a leg broken, but still we hunt the big game. In winter cold time little rabbits will not fill empty gut."

She drew in a deep breath, as this was a long speech for her. Harjeedian did not seem to understand. Derian offered his own explanation, a certain softness in his voice showing Firekeeper how shaken he was at what he must see as her abandonment. It stung her, but there was no other way.

"Harjeedian, what I believe Firekeeper is saying is that although wolves care for each other, the risks they must take in order to survive mean that they weigh those risks against the potential gain and then take the risks. Firekeeper clearly feels that her need for freedom is 'big game' for which she would risk even those she loves."

Firekeeper nodded, adding, "Without big game the pack cannot survive the winter. It is worth dying and maiming."

Harjeedian looked very upset. Clearly he had not taken very seriously Firekeeper's warning about the effectiveness of using hostages to control her actions. Why should he have? He had seen the ploy work before.

"And what is it you insist upon?" he said. "Will you starve yourself unless we let you free?"

Firekeeper had no real desire to fast and she did not trust these people to take her to familiar lands. She remembered, too, how she and Derian had discussed the need to plan an escape if they were to actually get away.

"You say 'guest,'" she replied, ignoring Harjeedian's question. "I say we are not treated like guest. Where is my Fang? Where is Derian's ring? Why must we stay in this small place?"

Harjeedian immediately looked relieved.

"We could renegotiate the terms of your parole," he said.

"But parole," Firekeeper was quick to interrupt, "parole is for prisoners. I think you say we is guest. Which?"

Harjeedian spread his hands.

"Very well. Prisoners, but honored prisoners—ones we would like to convince to remain as our guests."

Firekeeper nodded.

Blind Seer commented, *"Now we bite hard and hold the prey by the throat. I think Barnet wishes he had done such hunting. His sweat chills his skin even as he sits so calmly. As it is said, 'A wise wolf scouts the prey, knows when to hunt, when to run away.'"*

Firekeeper only half listened. She was waiting, forcing Harjeedian to further explain himself. One thing she had learned from her time with humans: There were few who could keep silent when caught in the wrong. They must justify themselves. Harjeedian did not disappoint her.

"We have things that might interest you enough to make you stay among us willingly, Lady Blysse."

"Not magic things!" Firekeeper retorted. She'd had enough of these to last her forever.

"No," Harjeedian said, "not, at least in the sense you mean. I have heard the tales of what Queen Valora stole."

Again Firekeeper held silence and, again, Harjeedian broke into it.

"From what Barnet Lobster tells me, until your coming from the west the yarimaimalom, the Wise Beasts, were only known in legend, legends only half believed in. Would it interest you, Lady Blysse, if I told you we of Liglim have had knowledge of the yarimaimalom for a long time—and that some of those Beasts are our guests?"

Firekeeper stared at him. Then, almost against her will, she threw back her head and howled in astonishment and disbelief.

VII

TRUTH WAS CLEAN-LIMBED, lean-limbed, and she smelt omens in the wind as she smelled the hot blood of the deer they brought her to kill. Not for nothing was she born of a long line of diviners.

Omens—for good and for ill—were what she had been bred to hunt, so her surprise was great when this new scent told her nothing more than that something portentous was about to occur. It was as if an ocean wind had switchbacked when it struck the hard limestone of the cliffs, taking on the stone's scent and the scents of all who grew upon them or lived among them, thus subtly altering the salt and fish-rank character of the wind until it seemed land-born.

Omens good or ill. Truth did not know, and the not knowing troubled her in every line of her body and made her tail twitch with irritation. She bent her head and rasped at the fur between the toes of one paw, noticing how the claws had slipped loose from their sheaths and wondering if perhaps, after all, this meant the portents were of ill things to come.

She took another deep breath, opening her mouth and wrinkling back her lips to taste the wind as she might a male's scent, and faintly caught the note of a wolf's howl raised in anger and in protest.

"HOW DO THEY EXPLAIN the existence of magic in your land?" asked Rahniseeta.

She had come as always to serve the meals to their guests, but this time Harjeedian had asked her to remain and visit with their guests. He was greatly upset by the outcome of his interview that morning, and felt the guests needed to be better understood.

"I made a mistake in judging Lady Blysse," he said to her. "I had thought I had taken her measure aboard *Fayonejunjal*, but now I see how much seasickness had weakened her. Go to them. Stay with them as long as you think you are welcome. Meanwhile, I shall speak with the teachers."

Rahniseeta needed little urging to follow her brother's request. She was fascinated by the newcomers, not only by the Lady Blysse but by her two male companions. Appearance was only part of it, though she could hardly keep herself from staring. Except for the color of her skin and her strangely rounded eyes, Lady Blysse did not look too different from normal, but the men! One had hair the color of dry corn silk, the other the warm red of flame—and she could hardly believe they could see out of eyes so light. Even the wolf had blue eyes. It was all very odd and very strange, and nothing like it in all her twenty-one years had ever caught her attention.

She nursed the idea that they were maimalodalum, beast-souled, just like in the stories. That would explain their odd-colored hair—though perhaps not their eyes. Lady Blysse might be a wolf or bear. The redhead a fox, perhaps. What of the corn-silk man? A puma, maybe. Maybe a jaguar, though he lacked the rich golden color of their pelts and showed no sign of spots. There were horses with coats that color, but Rahniseeta didn't sense anything else horsy about him. Then there was his singing. Could he be a bird of some sort? He possessed the lightness of build.

No, Rahniseeta did not have any difficulty doing as Harjeedian requested. It certainly was more interesting than the jobs he usually set her, and even better did not involve snakes. Rahniseeta did not dislike snakes—after all, they were among the most common residents of the temple—but she lacked her brother's fascination with them, and being constantly surrounded by them was one of the trials of living in the Temple of the Cold Bloods.

It was highly preferable to poverty, though, and Rahniseeta was grateful to Harjeedian for his loyalty to her. So now she sat with the guests even after they had finished their midday meal, and she thought the men were pleased. It was hard to tell with Lady Blysse. She was lying on the ground, her head on the Wise Wolf's flank, dozing.

"How do they explain the existence of magic in your land?" she asked, hoping through their answer of this question to get some hint as to whether they were indeed maimalodalum. She did not expect the expression of dislike that came over both of the men's faces almost as one.

Derian Counselor, the red-haired one, was—rather surprisingly, for he was not usually talkative—the first one to answer.

"We don't usually talk about magic, Rahniseeta," he said a bit stiffly. "It is not considered a good thing."

Barnet, the minstrel, seemed eager to make certain she was not insulted.

"Derian is right," he said, "but I love a good story and it's going to be another long afternoon. How do they explain the existence of magic in your land?"

"It is not the existence of magic in my land," Rahniseeta said, taking care to make certain she had understood. This conversing when she understood little of their language, and they only a bit more of hers was challenging. "It is the existence of magic in all the great wide world."

She made the gesture that indicated the surrounding Earth and Earth as mother. The two men looked startled, and the Lady Blysse, who had sat up and was now openly listening, drew back as if fearing she would be struck.

Rahniseeta repeated the gesture, slowly, so it would not be misinterpreted, bringing her hands up from directly below her navel, straight up so her arms formed a graceful curve a hand's breadth above her head, then hands and arms parting, rounding down to meet again near the navel, like a mother cradling a child.

"The great wide world?" asked Barnet, trying the gesture and not doing too badly. "Do you always have to do that when you say those words?"

Rahniseeta giggled.

"Not always, but it is always good to remember the Earth who holds us and feeds us, for she is our mother, as the Air that rounds out our lungs is our father."

She made the Air-as-father gesture beginning with hands flat and tips of forefinger and middle finger meeting over her head, pulling out to draw an imaginary line between them, then falling in the gentle curve that indicated the horizon, before closing the line in front of her. This time both Derian and Barnet imitated her.

"You know," Derian said, turning to Barnet, "I saw some of the sailors do that one a few times, especially right after that nasty storm. They did another one, too."

He colored as he looked at Rahniseeta, doubtless because he feared to make a mistake.

"It was like this."

He put his hands in front of himself at navel height, then parted them with a wavy gesture before carrying them up in a straight line, and bringing the hands down with fingers stiff.

"That is very good," Rahniseeta said. "That is the sign of the waters. The first is the ocean waves, then the mists that rise and the rain that falls. Sailors acknowledge the power of Water frequently and they are wise to do so."

Barnet looked a little nonplussed, doubtless because he had not shown his own knowledge of the sign first.

"Let me guess," he said, making fists in front of his navel, then bursting them apart with stiff fingers while his hands rose. "This one must be fire."

Rahniseeta nodded, but she felt a trace uneasy. The men were doing the signs as if they were steps in a dance or some other secular act. They apparently had no idea of their sacred significance.

"That is right," she said, "but how do your people acknowledge the elements? How do you praise Earth our mother and Air our father?"

The two men looked at each other, and at the Lady Blysse, who was watching with great amusement. Finally, his tone holding a mixture of embarrassment and awkwardness, Barnet replied.

"We don't, Rahniseeta. We've never heard anything like it."

Rahniseeta was appalled, but maybe they were testing her. The maimalodalum were kin to the yarimaimalom, after all.

"You must know. It is something every child knows."

Derian cleared his throat. "If that's the case, maybe you had better tell us."

Rahniseeta was certain now this was a test, and she felt proud that her brother was an aridisdu and had made certain she knew the teachings in the best and most comprehensive form.

"I will tell you then how nothing became something," she said, "and of the creation of Earth and Air, of the birth of their three children, and of the creation of all living things."

The three guests nodded. Rahniseeta thought that the Wise Wolf nodded slightly as well, and settled themselves as for a long telling. Rahniseeta began, trying to keep the words simple, since the guests did not seem to know the speech of the Liglimom very well—though now she was wondering if they were pretending.

"Once there was only a great swirling with no shape nor form nor height nor depth nor breadth, but within the swirling were the seeds of potential. As the swirling slowed, the potential separated. Part was heavy and falling became the earth. Part was light and rising became the air that surrounds the earth. Earth and Air knew themselves as separated from the swirling. This knowing was the beginning of life.

"Earth and Air never forgot how they had once been one thing. They reached for each other and tried to rejoin the swirling where they could again be one, but this could not be done. All they succeeded in doing was to throw off parts of themselves. These parts became their first two children: Water and Fire.

"Water loved his parents and wanted them to be happy. He ran between them, carrying messages. These messages are the rains and mists and all other ways the waters seek to rise and to fall. So many messages have been sent between Earth and Air that Earth holds many rivers, lakes, streams, and oceans, while the sky is filled with clouds.

"Fire was jealous of the love of Earth and Air. At first he held himself apart, and this holding apart is what we call the sun, which to this day is the home of Fire. Earth and Air wished for Fire to be happy, but Fire remained a sulky child. This is why some days the sun is warm and pleasant, while other days the sun is too hot. This is why Fire remains the least trustworthy of the elements. However, unpredictable Fire is directly responsible for the coming of other types of life.

"Fire thought, 'If Air had something to distract him from Earth, then Earth could pay more attention to me. When Air becomes offended, then I will say sweet things to him, and he, too, will pay more attention to me.'

"So Fire coughed out bits of himself and shaped them into the first birds. Air was at first a little afraid to find these things in himself. After a time, as Fire had predicted, he became interested. However, Fire was wrong in how Earth would react. Instead of paying more attention to Fire, she made of herself pleasant roosts for the birds: cliffsides and trees and tiny little shrubs. The birds came to Earth, and Air's attention was drawn hence, and they laughed together, for these living things seemed to make them closer.

"Air said, 'Earth, you are more lovely so adorned. Let us make more creatures for you.' Together they made many more animals to live in the forests and deserts and hills. They made more birds and insects to fly between and to color the Air. They made fish and whales and crabs and boneless things to amuse Water, but because Fire was sulking, unhappy with how his plan had come to pass, he would not join them. Thus, to this day there are no creatures who live within Fire, and most creatures fear Fire more than anything in Air or Earth.

"Fire remained unhappy, and seeing him sulk, Earth and Air said, 'We will make you a creature who will need you in order to live.' So they made humanity, which naked and blunt-toothed does indeed need Fire to thrive. For the first time since he was born, Fire was happy.

"However, now Water grew envious, for though many creatures filled him, he felt that his fidelity to his parents had not been sufficiently rewarded. Fish are well and good, and they cannot live outside of water, but jealousy does not lead to clear thought. Moreover, Fire constantly kept reminding everyone how he had created the first birds and thus started the coming of living things.

"Water said to himself, 'I will make a creature myself, even as Fire made the birds. It will be a wonderful creature, different from those that swim or fly or walk or creep or in any way adorn Earth or Air or Water. It will not be a mere bird, but a force to compare favorably with us First Four.

"Water drew from himself a ball of water and concentrated that water into itself. He envisioned a creature with the power to create and to change, like himself, but different, so it is no great surprise that the creature he created was female. Water's creation rose from the depths of the deepest ocean and into the skies above. Just as she was about to take her place among Earth, Air, Water, and Fire as one of the great creations, she burst.

"Little parts of her flew everywhere, some sticking in the sky where they became stars, others falling to the Earth even as we still see them do today. Where the pieces landed, whatever they touched became imbued with magic—for Magic was what this daughter of Water was to be. That is why there are Wise Beasts and humans with magical talents. That is why some rocks and plants and waters hold the ability to enhance magic. That is why magic is scattered among us, and not all of us understand it equally.

"Magic did not completely fragment. The greater part of her remained in the sky, where her injuries are visible on any clear night. We here living on Earth name the shattered remnants of Magic the Moon. To this day, Moon calls to her father Water, asking him to make her whole, and when he pities her most, then the oceans ebb, for Water is attempting to rebuild his daughter once again."

Rahniseeta drew in a deep breath, concluding with the ritual storyteller's words, "So it was told to me, so I tell it to you," only then did she emerge from the story and look at her audience.

Their reactions were very different. Barnet's brow was slightly furrowed, not in anger, but as if he had been trying to commit the tale to memory. Derian looked simultaneously uneasy and fascinated. Lady Blysse's dark eyes were dreamy, as if she still dwelled in the time of the story and that time was more real to her than the present moment.

Despite Lady Blysse's mood and her usual uncommunicativeness, she was the one who spoke first.

"I like. Explains all so close—so neat. Is it true?"

Rahniseeta blinked. "Of course it is true. This is the way the story has been told forever and always. Have your people lost the tale?"

The Lady Blysse did not answer directly, but looked to Derian.

"Actually," he said awkwardly, "we don't have any story like that. It isn't that we have lost it, I don't think, we just don't have it. How about in Bright Bay, Barnet?"

Barnet shook his head. "It's a wonderful story, but I've never heard the like. The Tavetch of Stonehold have their own story about how the sun and moon are associated with the creation of the world in their stories, but it isn't at all the same."

Rahniseeta couldn't believe him.

"But how do you explain the way the world came to be?"

Derian slid the empty cup from which he had been drinking fruit juice around the table, drawing damp snail trails with the base.

"Actually, we don't worry about it much," he admitted. "There are levels of mystery, and we leave such things to the ancestors."

"I do not understand."

Derian's hand shifted from the pottery tumbler to the small bag he wore at his waist. Harjeedian had told Rahniseeta that these had been inspected while the guests were unconscious, but they held nothing that could help the guests to leave prematurely, and seemed to be religious in nature, so they had been permitted to retain them.

"In each of our houses," Derian said, "there is a shrine to the ancestors of our family. In some cases, they go back for generations, but in most households, they are concerned only with the nearest ancestors—one's own parents, or grandparents if they have died, the generation before if not. Then as one grows older, one adds to the array. Eventually, the family shrine is passed to the eldest child in the family. There are deep secrets associated with this passing on, but—well—I am not old enough to have been initiated into them. There are stages in the initiation, and the first comes when one becomes a parent—and thus a potential ancestor oneself."

"It's much the same in Bright Bay—or the Isles," Barnet agreed. "We call on our ancestors to intercede for us with the powers beyond, but we don't really discuss what those powers are. We just know they are there, but we don't give them names or shapes."

He looked apologetic, but went on, "It would seem to reduce them—as if they were mere society emblems."

Rahniseeta couldn't believe she was hearing this. It must be the fault of the abbreviated language they were forced to use. She decided that further pressing the matter would only create unhappiness for them all—and Harjeedian had wanted her to enter-tain their guests.

"What is a society?" she asked. The word Barnet had used in the language of Liglim meant something like "friendly group," but she felt he meant more.

"Societies?" Barnet paused, visibly relaxing, his delay in speaking a matter of lin-guistics and nothing more. "Well, in Bright Bay we have fourteen—one for each moon of the year and the last associated with the royal family. They're named for animals. I think our countries vary a bit there, don't they, Derian?"

Derian nodded. "You have a Gull Society, instead of our Elk, I remember that, and Fox instead of Dog. I don't recall the rest."

"Whale instead of Bull," Barnet said, "and, of course, our royal family wouldn't associate with the Eagle. Their society patron is the Osprey—or at least Queen Val-ora's is. I don't know what King Allister has done."

Rahniseeta fought down a mingling of rising excitement and confusion. Despite their odd discussion of changing names of these societies, it did seem to hint that these were indeed maimalodalum.

Very carefully, she asked, "So each of you has an animal with which you are associ-ated?"

Derian nodded. "My society patron is the Horse."

"Mine's the Whale," Barnet said. "That's why I remember the difference from Hawk Haven."

Rahniseeta glanced over at Lady Blysse, but the answer was obvious even before she spoke.

"I am wolf."

Rahniseeta considered these associations. That the woman was a wolf gave her no problems at all. She still thought Derian's coloring was more that of a fox, but horses did often manifest in shining chestnut. Barnet was so slim and sleek that there seemed nothing of the whale about him, but who knew what wonders Water held in his depths?

She could hardly wait to tell Harjeedian her conclusions, but stayed a while longer, letting the conversation drift to more general topics. Barnet and Derian vied in recounting the festivals their various societies had sponsored, while Lady Blysse and her companion drifted off to sleep.

At last Rahniseeta felt she could glance up at the rising glow of Fire's Home and say without awkwardness:

"I must leave now if you are to have a proper midday meal."

Both men rose courteously to see her to the gate, acting as if they were hosts seeing away a guest rather than what they were—not really guests, no matter what Rahniseeta wanted to think.

She asked one of the guards at the end of the passage where she might find Harjee-dian.

"I saw him coming from a meeting not long ago," the guard replied. "He went toward the residences."

Rahniseeta thanked the guard and hurried off to the apartment she shared with Harjeedian and his snakes. It was a small enough space, but since they took their meals communally and used the temple baths, it was quite sufficient for their needs.

She found Harjeedian dropping live mice to his snakes and murmuring the appropriate prayers. He turned from these rather more rapidly than was his wont. Rahniseeta had often felt he lingered over these rites when she was near precisely to impress his importance on her, but that was probably foolish. He was truly devout, or he never would have been chosen to join the ranks of the aridisdum.

"Your eyes sparkle like Magic's brightest stars," he said. "What have you learned?"

Without sparing detail, Rahniseeta told him everything, including her conjecture that their guests might be maimalodalum. She had expected Harjeedian to be pleased, so she was startled to see him grow paler and paler. He did not interrupt until she had finished, and then his words were not at all what she expected.

"You say that Derian Counselor claimed affiliation with the Horse Society?"

"Yes?"

Harjeedian groaned and pressed his face into his hands.

"Harjeedian, what is wrong?"

"I may have committed a great wrong." He took a deep breath and continued, "We knew of the association of Lady Blysse with the blue-eyed wolf and took care to secure both without injury. However, we knew nothing of Derian Counselor and the horse."

"What horse?"

"You must understand that in order to secure our guests we had to make certain that no one would believe they were not about their usual business."

"Yes. That is why you were gone so long. You had to wait for the propitious time."

"We also had to erase any indications that they had not gone on their planned journey. For that reason we secured their mounts and baggage."

He paused for so long that Rahniseeta was forced to prompt him once more.

"Yes?"

"There were two animals they planned to take with them. One was clearly a pack animal, well built, but not exceptional. The other was a chestnut mare with white stockings, and even to my eyes—and I know little of horses beyond what any aridisdu must—she was a beautiful creature, elegant and high-spirited. It came near to breaking my heart to . . ."

"To what?"

"To order her slain."

"No!"

"What else was I to do? I had no idea she might be the man's associate. Barnet told me nothing of these societies. I simply saw a horse too notable to be sold, a creature who would be difficult to ship, even if I had been so inclined. Also her death meant solution to another problem—how to feed the wolf without drawing attention to ourselves by purchasing quantities of meat or livestock."

Rahniseeta was now as horrified as her brother, but loyally she tried to soothe him. "I am sure you did the right thing."

"I am not," Harjeedian said bluntly. "After the wolf was first fed from the mare's flesh, Derian looked at me with great hatred, though he said nothing. I thought nothing of it, for after all, he was adjusting to the idea of being taken from his place—and that we had used Lady's Blysse's friendship toward him to lure both her and the wolf. Now I think the hatred may have been for other reasons."

He looked over toward the lovely carved boxes in which he kept his snakes, and Rahniseeta knew he was thinking how he would feel if someone slew any of his snakes and used them for animal feed—and that the matter would be worse if Derian Counselor was indeed a maimalodalu, for then the horse (a chestnut horse, she could not forget) would have been not merely associate but kin.

"The omens have been bad," Harjeedian said, "so bad that although there are many among the disdum who wish to meet Lady Blysse and to begin with her, we have not been able to get an agreement as to the propitious time and day. Now I may know why the omens have been so dark, and I must admit my actions may be the cause."

He straightened, glanced toward the snake boxes, remembered that the snakes had just been fed and so should not be disturbed, and then turned toward the door.

"Rahniseeta, I hope the teachers will be merciful and the omens will not call for me to atone for my error in the final way—but this is a jaguar year. If anything happens to me, you will find I have set by something for you."

"Harjeedian!" She flew to his side and embraced him. "Surely it will not be so terrible. I was foolish, romanticizing these foreign visitors. If they were really maimalodalum would they not have fled? Barnet, at least, could have called on the whales, yet he did so neither when his first ship was storm-wrecked nor on the return."

"Barnet thought he had an agreement with us that was to his liking," Harjeedian reminded her, "and who knows that he did not call on the whales and that is why he survived when so many who voyaged with him died. Or perhaps he is not a maimalodalu—as you said, there is little whale-like about him—but the other two may be. In any case, conclusions must be left to those who read the omens. I would be less than honest if I did not report what you have told me—and if they call upon you to tell your tale, do not change it on my account. Do you understand?"

"Yes, Harjeedian."

Rahniseeta kept her eyes on him as he left, her back straight and confident, but when he was out of sight, she ran from their rooms and went to the central Temple of the Cold Bloods. There she knelt before the towering enameled statue, praying with all her heart that her brother, who had served the elements so faithfully, would not be forgotten in this, his time of dire need.

FIREKEEPER WAS THINKING ABOUT the story Rahniseeta had told earlier that day. It certainly made sense, explained a good many things about which she herself had occasionally wondered during these last two years, when merely finding enough to eat had not occupied her mind so fully.

The metallic jangle of the gate at the end of the corridor being opened broke her from her reverie, and she sprang to her feet. Derian and Barnet, who had been making an attempt to move the language lessons forward, turned to see who the new arrival would be. Contrary to their expectations, Rahniseeta had not escorted the servants who had brought the midday meal, nor could those servants say where she had gone.

When Harjeedian opened the gate into the courtyard, Firekeeper noticed that Derian's hazel eyes lost some of their animation, that Barnet leaned back into his chair. Neither man was rude, but it was clear that Harjeedian was not welcomed as his sister would have been.

Observing her human companions as she was, it took Firekeeper a moment to notice a change in Harjeedian's bearing. Always he had been confident, even on the day when they had nearly managed their escape. Today some of that confidence was missing. He looked, she thought, like a young wolf who has made a try for the One, but has been soundly beaten—like a wolf who has been forced to reassess his importance within his pack.

Firekeeper saw that Barnet and Derian were also aware that something had changed, but they did not see as deeply as did she and so were made edgy while she felt her own confidence rising.

"Lady Blysse, Blind Seer, Counselor Derian, Barnet Lobster." Harjeedian's greetings were punctilious and correct. Firekeeper noted that she and Blind Seer came first and was pleased. "Not long ago, you asked me to reconsider the conditions of your residence among us."

"He takes refuge in the big words," Firekeeper said to Blind Seer. *"what does he fear?"*

"I would like to say 'us,'" the wolf replied, *"but he has not feared us thus far. I would say his Ones have thrashed him—but why?"*

Harjeedian produced a rabbit-sized bundle of finely woven grey-blue fabric from within the folds of his shirt. He unwound the fabric, producing Firekeeper's Fang and the worn pouch in which she carried her fire-making stones. Derian's ruby counselor's ring rolled from the last fold and settled upright and glittering on the table.

"You," he said, bowing slightly to Firekeeper, "requested the return of your treasured belongings. Here they are. Am I correct in believing that you do not care unduly for the clothing you were wearing when you were taken?"

Firekeeper nodded. She cared little for any particular item of clothing, though having discovered the usefulness of attire for protecting one from thorns and scrapes she preferred having it to not.

Derian also nodded. He reached for his ring slowly, as if fearing its return might be a trap. Firekeeper had no such concern. She nearly pounced on her belongings and was pleased to see that knife belt and sheath were within the tangle of cloth as well.

She strapped them into place, feeling very pleased, not so much that she was armed again—for she knew well how little one blade could do against an armed force—but for the respect represented by the returning of her weapons.

"And you have the second knife as well," Blind Seer reminded her. *"I would keep it hidden, as snakes hide their poison."*

"You have snakes in your brain," she teased, though she agreed with him.

"Who would not in this place?" the wolf replied. *"Ask him when we will be let out of this place. I must run or go mad with chasing my own tail."*

Firekeeper did as requested.

"Do this mean we go from here?" she asked. "I would run more than a few paces, and Blind Seer with me."

Harjeedian looked uncomfortable.

"Yes, you will go from here, but not quite yet. My teachers have asked that your first coming forth be to the reception I mentioned earlier. There is . . ."

He frowned, not because he didn't know the word, Firekeeper was certain, but because he did not like telling them his thoughts.

"There is great interest in meeting you," Harjeedian finally said, "and rivalry that no one be given advantage over the others. Already the heads of other temples are less than pleased that you dwell within these walls, but they trust our word that you have not been seen by any but me, my sister, and a few servants."

"And I think Rahniseeta is not considered of much more account than those servants," Firekeeper said to Blind Seer.

To Harjeedian she said, "How long until this reception?"

"Omens indicate that tomorrow at midmorning would serve," he replied. "Will you wait until then?"

"Yes," Firekeeper said.

"But only," Blind Seer added, *"until then."*

VIII

.

TRUTH LOUNGED ON HER LEDGE ABOVE the gathering crowd, amusing herself by thinking about how easy it would be to break necks and get away with it.

It wasn't that she hated humans. There were several she rather liked, but it was a heady thing being invited into their presence, being what she was, knowing what she could do. With this a jaguar year, she could get away with even more than usual.

Yes. Such thoughts were amusing, but an amusement Truth did not plan to pursue beyond the realm of thought. The omens were against it, after all, and who should know better than she?

So she lay on the wide ledge, paws hanging over the edge, watching the eddy of the human herd. They were interesting in their dynamics, bouncing off of each other like ripples in a pond. Wise Jaguars were more social than their Cousin-kind, but even so, most adults ranged alone for moonspans on end without missing companionship at all. Humans were more like deer or fish, gathering in succulent groups, vying for domination within their group, never seeming to realize that their very grouping showed how expendable the individual was. This was not the way of her people.

Yes, like deer or fish . . .

Motion in the crowd at the far end of the vast assembly chamber indicated the entrance of important new arrivals. Truth caught their scent as they came through the large double doors. Two humans, two wolves. Omen scent mingled with actual scent, muddying the impressions in Truth's highly sensitized mind. She sniffed again, forcing away the omen scent so she could concentrate on the odors riding the currents of the air.

Three humans, one wolf, the last large enough and confident enough that Truth did not need to further isolate his scent to know he was of the yarimaimalom, but she did not think he was among the yarimaimalom she knew.

Scent again. No. Definitely not.

She focused in on the newcomers, isolating the one whose scent had been so confusing. It was the smallest of the three, a dark-haired, dark-eyed female. Despite her size, she walked with quiet treading confidence, her hand resting lightly on the wolf's back.

This wolf-woman was afraid, Truth decided, but hid that fear admirably well. Truth did not disdain her for her reaction. It made good sense to dislike being so surrounded by strangers. This one bore watching. Around her swirled those uncomfortable omen scents that had so disquieted Truth some days before. They still refused to isolate themselves into omens for good or ill, and Truth growled and rasped her tongue between her toes.

But she did not stop watching.

The crowd parted to admit the newcomers. Individuals Truth recognized as important within the human community—individuals who had bowed and scraped before her just a few moonspans before, when she had been selected as the representative of this year—now made themselves known to the four newcomers. They did not bow or scrape, but they were hotly interested.

Truth scented again as she watched these interactions, so very different from her own regal isolation. These newcomers were more of the herd: deer or fish or . . .

She twitched her tail in amusement as she thought how most certainly offended the newcomers would be by her assessment, but they really were all one, all the same: deer or fish . . . or wolves.

DERIAN WISHED THE ELABORATE COSTUME with which he had been provided made him feel less like he'd been attired to play a role in a society pageant. It didn't help his feeling that he was dressing up that his entire ensemble was liberally embroidered with horses. He wished with all his heart for decent trousers and waistcoat, for brass-buckled shoes and fine knit stockings, and, lastly, a sharply creased tricorn hat.

However, wishing would not do him any good. It had been hard enough to convince Rahniseeta to let him tie his hair back into its accustomed queue. Apparently, men might do so for work, but left their hair loose for formal occasions.

Loose and bejeweled was the style for men's hair, it seemed, at least if the hair was very long and might interfere with sight. If not held back from the face with a neat clip, then longer tresses were adorned with a hat. Some of these would have been considered outrageous for either gender at home. Derian suspected they were meant to indicate the wearer held some particular office—at least he hoped so.

To Derian's right, Barnet wore his own whale-adorned costume with apparent aplomb. He'd even left his hair loose, and his pale blue eyes darted from face to face, outfit to outfit.

Collecting story material, Derian guessed sourly. *Barnet Lobster hasn't resigned himself to staying here, not one bit. I wonder if he thinks he has something to barter for his freedom—or if he's already writing the ballad about his daring escape.*

Derian grinned to himself, knowing he was being sour in order to cover his apprehension regarding this reception. Not only was he unnerved to be at the center of so much attention, but he had Firekeeper to worry about. The wolf-woman was much better about crowds than she had been when they first met, but he couldn't help but notice how one hand never strayed far from her knife, while the other rested on Blind Seer—both sure signs that she was ill at ease.

He watched her noting the exits. There were four, massive double doors, one to each side of the huge step pyramid within whose base the large room was built. Following Firekeeper's gaze, Derian noted that the building only had the appearance of a pyramid. The room they were within was clearly built along more conventional lines. The steps must be a cosmetic shell without.

Probably a great way to save on weight, Derian thought, *though I wonder what they made the outer shell out of?*

He shrugged the thought off. Architecture only interested him to the extent that it was either useful or particularly beautiful. What did interest him was how the huge room was decorated. Elaborate mosaics covered the lower walls, catching and giving back the light from both lanterns and openings higher up the tiers. High, wide shelves, many with ramps leading up to them, held vases, statues, and other items, probably of symbolic value.

Derian recognized depictions of the four elements done in gold, silver, and precious stones. Two other shelves set in places of similar prominence held items whose significance he could not work out on his own. One held a large lumpy rock—or maybe it was a chunk of partially melted metal. It was hard to tell at a distance. The other shelf held an amazingly realistic statue of a feline with a golden-yellow coat adorned with spots, like but unlike the spots on a young puma's coat. The feline was quite large and surveyed the gathering below with regal indifference.

Derian didn't have much more time to continue his inspection, for his line of sight was being interrupted by an orderly throng of elaborately costumed men and women, all of whom were clearly people of importance.

Harjeedian acted as translator, handling the introductions with more humility than Derian had glimpsed from him thus far. Names and titles flowed and blurred into each other: This One of the Temple of Flyers. That One of the Temple of Felines. There were kidisdum for just about any animal of which Derian could think: bears, deer, rabbits, horses, raccoons, deer, owls, mice.

Derian lost track rather quickly, just nodded, smiled, and exchanged bows. Barnet did the same. Firekeeper and Blind Seer merely stared. Even the man who introduced himself as the keeper of wolves did not press for acknowledgment.

Gradually it came to Derian that all of this was somehow associated with deified elements that had been mentioned in Rahniseeta's story. He wished he'd had time to hear other stories. The more names and titles he heard, the more elaborate costumes, each with their hint of meaning he viewed, the more confused he became.

Snakes, it appeared, were very important in the worship of Earth, though they had some secondary association with Water. The Temple of Flyers was interested in divining the will of Air. For some reason felines were associated with Fire. Nor were these divisions absolute. Derian's head began to spin as he tried to keep it all straight. Birds were associated with Air, unless they were water birds, like ducks or egrets. Horses were apparently associated with both Earth and Air.

It was as he was trying to figure out why the woman he'd just been introduced to was carrying a snake, though her clothing was embroidered with bears and wolves, that he made a startling discovery.

The enormous spotted feline he had seen lying on a ledge a few feet above the heads of the crowd was now sitting upright, licking its shoulder. Derian froze, forgetting to even pretend to acknowledge the person to whom he was being introduced. His eyesight was good, and he was certain this was no dog dressed up in an elaborate costume as he had seen in New Kelvin. Nor was it a puma, dyed and painted. This feline had a stockier build, more compact. Its head was rounder, the shape of the ears different.

Moreover, there was something in how it seemed to notice his gaze, how its golden-orange eyes met his own, direct and appraising. He'd met such eyes before, though they were blue.

He tapped Firekeeper's shoulder and whispered into her ear, "Did you see the cat up there?"

Her soft snort meant "of course," but what she replied was "Yes. And, yes, as you think, it is Royal. Harjeedian did not lie. They keep some of my people captive as they keep me."

Derian was about to respond when a hand was laid on his shoulder. He turned and found a man of almost his own height standing to one side.

"Derian Counselor? I am Varjuna," the man said, "senior keeper of the Horse. I understand you have an interest in horses."

Derian blinked. He remembered thinking there was something familiar about the man when they had been first introduced. Now he realized that coloring and clothing aside, Varjuna reminded him somewhat of his father, Colby Carter. There was the same strength and stillness, the same broad shoulders and powerful legs. Varjuna might even be about the same age as Colby, maybe a little older, but about that Derian was not certain.

Derian gave a neat bow.

"You named me Derian Counselor," he said, searching for the words, "but that name is still new to me. For most of my life, I was called 'Carter'—a word that in my language indicates working with horses and the things they pull."

It wasn't a very good translation, but Varjuna seemed to understand. His expression brightened, and Derian had the sudden unshakable conviction that someone had suggested Varjuna come and talk with Derian—and that Varjuna had feared they would have little in common.

Derian glanced over at Firekeeper, but the wolf-woman seemed in control of both herself and the situation. She was handling the efforts at small talk directed toward her by giving either short answers or none at all, taking refuge in her presumed ignorance of the language.

He returned his attention to Varjuna.

"What does the keeper of the Horse do, exactly?" Derian asked, aware he was mangling the phrase.

Varjuna put one finger to his chin, and closed his eyes for a moment in thought.

Trying to find easy words to explain a complicated job, Derian thought. *I can be patient.*

Again he glanced over to check on Firekeeper. She had now moved to where she could look more closely at the big spotted cat lying on the ledge. Her interest was attracting a fair amount of attention from those gathered in the huge room, but no one was moving to interfere.

"A kidisdu, what I have heard translated as a 'keeper,' " Varjuna said with a childlike pride in his few words of Pellish, "is one who is specially dedicated to the well-being of a particular type of animal."

"Like Harjeedian and his snakes?" Derian asked.

"Yes and no," Varjuna said. "Harjeedian has been honored with snakes, but he has been anointed an aridisdu, as well as a snake holder."

Derian didn't understand, but he nodded encouragement.

"I," Varjuna went on, "wish to be nothing but a kidisdu, though the divine will has ordained that I shall be ikidisdu—that is 'senior keeper.' All kidisdu, no matter their rank, deal more with our specific animals than with omens or the wills of the deities. In this way, we become close to the deities."

"I don't quite understand," Derian admitted.

Varjuna didn't look offended.

"It is hard to explain with so few words between us. Also, I have heard it said that you know nothing of the deities. Is this true?"

Remembering Rahniseeta's shocked reaction to a similar question, Derian was careful with his answer.

"Perhaps we know them differently," he said. "I do not quite understand how the deities and the animals are related."

Varjuna nodded. "It is a long story."

"Tell me," Derian urged, trading on his impression that for some reason or other Varjuna was supposed to be talking to him. Rahniseeta had seemed to enjoy telling them a story about the deities; perhaps Varjuna would as well. It beat standing around worrying what Firekeeper would do next, and obviously these stories of the gods were as essential to understanding the Liglimom as the New Kelvinese's peculiar history had been to understanding them.

Derian glanced around. Firekeeper was still over by the big cat, Harjeedian hovering near and apparently shielding her somewhat. Barnet was over talking with a woman Derian recognized at second glance as the captain of *Fayonejunjal*.

I wonder if he's trying to wrangle a berth? he thought.

Varjuna seemed to have overcome his indecision as to whether this was an appropriate time to tell a long story. He motioned Derian over to one of the tables set up along the edges of the room.

"Be comfortable," he said. "I will begin."

Derian accepted the seat and poured himself a drink from the pitcher of chilled water set there.

"I think you have been told," Varjuna began, "how the deities came to be, and also the living things on the Earth?"

"Yes," Derian replied, feeling a little like a student, "right up through how Water attempted to create a daughter and Magic was born and broken almost all at once."

Varjuna smiled. "This will make my telling easy. You have the beginning of the story."

"Good," Derian said. He noticed that several other people had drifted close. A few of the bolder ones had even taken seats.

Well, no wonder, boy, he thought. *You're one of the key attractions. If Varjuna doesn't want them here he'll send them off. Doesn't look like he talks to a crowd, often, though. I guess kidisdum really do focus on the animals.*

Varjuna seemed momentarily taken aback, but recovered with good grace.

He said to his compatriots, "I am about to tell Derian Counselor about the special relationship between the deities and the animals."

"A good tale," approved a fat woman, her outfit embroidered with both bears and raccoons, their forms so stylized that Derian had to study awhile to be sure what the figures were intended to represent. "One that is too often forgotten."

Others nodded their agreement, and so Varjuna, with every appearance of mild nervousness, began his story.

"You have heard how upon her creation Magic fragmented. Where the parts of her landed, that which they touched became . . ." He used a word that meant nothing to Derian and quickly struggled to use simpler words. "That is, they became somehow filled with magic. This is why there are both yarimaimalom—the Wise Beasts—and their lesser kin."

"Cousins," Derian said without thinking, interested only in helping Varjuna along.

"What?"

Derian colored, but struggled on. Relationship terms had been included in their lessons, because many of the sailors, it had turned out, were kin to each other.

"Cousins," he repeated. "That is the word Firekeeper—Lady Blysse—uses for the beasts who are not Wise Beasts."

There was a murmur of discussion about this, and Derian had the feeling that what he had said was thought to be somehow very important. Varjuna did not participate in the general discussion, only smiled.

"I like that way of putting it," he said, then returned to his story, while Derian resolved to keep his mouth shut. "Now although both the yarimaimalom and humans were blessed with the gifts of Magic, humans did not remain content.

"Some say that this is because humans were created to take comfort from Fire, and so they took from him along with his heat and brightness some of his eternally hungry and dissatisfied nature. Whatever the reason, humans began to strive for magical gifts beyond those they had been given."

Varjuna's tone made quite clear that he did not approve of this, and Derian felt a touch of kindred spirit for the otherwise alien Liglimom culture. One of the most unsettling things about his time in New Kelvin had been how the New Kelvinese sought after magic—a force anyone raised in the traditions of Hawk Haven knew was dangerous.

As dangerous as a fire unchecked, Derian thought.

Varjuna went on, "Humans were successful in gathering and building magical power. What they did with that power belongs to other stories—many other stories. Suffice to say, the deities were not pleased and ceased to speak directly to those who practiced magic beyond those talents with which some are born, and for which they cannot be faulted.

"The animals—both Wise and lesser—continued to hear the will of the deities. Eventually, humans learned humility and looked to the animals to interpret divine will. Thus humans once again drew close to the deities. To this day, we honor the beasts for their role in assisting us to know the will of the deities."

Varjuna's tone made clear that he had finished his tale. The nods of approval from the small crowd surrounding them told Derian that the listeners thought he had made a good job of it.

Derian concentrated on Varjuna, willing himself to forget all the other ears that would hear his question.

"So as a kidisdu you are somehow associated with the animals you ask to help you understand what the deities want?"

Varjuna gave a short, approving jerk of his head.

"That is so. Not all animals have the same degree of—call it 'hearing.' We check for it when promising young ones are born, and if the omens are good, they join those kept for divination."

The fat woman leaned forward, eager to participate.

"There are many forms of divination," she said. "Not all techniques work with all animals—or not even with all animals within a species. It is demanding work, and a kidisdu has much to do assisting the aridisdum."

Derian held up his hand, smiling broadly and hoping he would not give offense.

"Not too much at once, Kidisdu," Derian begged, hoping she would not take offense. "My head is alive with new ideas."

The fat woman did not take offense, but smiled warmly at him.

"It is difficult even for our own acolytes," she said. The word she used had been translated for Derian as "apprentice," but he had the feeling that in this context it had a more complex meaning, specific to the priesthood. "There will be time for you to learn."

Varjuna nodded.

"I have been told you are skilled with horses," he said, returning to his initial point. "Perhaps you would care to visit the herds I keep. This reception has served its purpose."

Derian nodded, feeling a sudden, almost violent urge for something as familiar as a stable. The emotion was mingled with anger and sorrow for Roanne, but he felt certain that had Varjuna been sent in Harjeedian's stead the mare would not have been so lightly killed.

"I would enjoy seeing your horses," Derian said honestly. "Let me tell Firekeeper."

He rose to his feet, tall enough to look over most heads and all but the most elaborate headgear. He shifted his perspective and looked again, but there was no doubt about it.

Firekeeper was nowhere to be seen.

DOING HER BEST to ignore the people who crowded close to her, Firekeeper edged closer to where the great cat lounged with such provocative indolence above the human throng. She knew the great cat was aware of her intent, but other than the slow closing and opening of captivatingly round golden-orange eyes, the cat gave no sign it knew she was coming.

Firekeeper hardly knew what she found more annoying, the way the cat ignored her or the way the humans pressed close to her. Both underlined something that troubled her. She had not realized how much she relied on being thought different—someone for whom exceptions were made.

In all the human lands the wolf-woman had visited, that difference had held a note of fear—if not of her specifically, then of her apparent control of Blind Seer. Among the wolves, she was the weak one, but with a few notable exceptions that weakness had been reason to protect and care for her.

Here in Liglim, she was accorded neither fear nor protection, yet she knew these strange people wanted something of her. Thus far none of the humans would tell her what this was. Perhaps the great cat would tell her. In the woodlands where she had been raised, the hunting grounds of the pumas and the wolves overlapped, but on the whole they were not rivals.

Pumas hunted much the same prey that the wolves did, but they were solitary hunters, taking much smaller quantities than would interest a pack—and any lone wolf who tried to steal a puma's kill rapidly learned the punishing force and lightning-quick power contained in the cat's forepaws. A wolf would be cut to bloody strips before she could close for a deadly bite at throat or flank.

So Firekeeper approached the great cat with appropriate humility, but also with joyful anticipation that at long last she was meeting one of her own kind.

A few snaps from Blind Seer, wearied of how the humans pressed close and that a few even dared stroke his fur, gave the pair breathing space, and within that space, Firekeeper dared address the great cat.

"What are you?" she asked. *"In all my life I have never seen a great cat with a coat the rich yellow of a field of summer flowers, nor one so elegantly marked with spots."*

Those spots had initially puzzled her, for most of the creatures she knew about lost their spots once they grew from infancy. However, by now she was certain this was a fully mature representative of whatever species it belonged to, and she took care to accord it appropriate respect.

"And what are you?" drawled the great cat. *"What type of creature speaks after the manner of the Wise Wolves, but walks as a human, reeking of human scent?"*

"I am Firekeeper," the wolf-woman replied, keeping her tone respectful though anger flared inside her at the cat's arrogant rudeness. *"The wolves are my people, though I was born human. Beside me stands my pack mate, Blind Seer."*

"Firekeeper," the great cat replied. *"Do you then worship that god?"*

Firekeeper blinked, confused to hear a Beast speaking so like a human.

"My name comes from my mastery of fire," she replied, *"a mastery without which I would not have lived many winters."*

"So you claim to be Fire's master, not merely his keeper. Interesting. There will be those who will think that claim questionable."

Firekeeper shook her head as if clearing gnats from her ears.

"I do not understand," Firekeeper said.

She was aware that Blind Seer's hackles had risen slightly, aware as she was that this strange cat was toying with them. It was too soon to tell whether this attitude represented active hostility or merely the cruel playfulness in which she had heard all cats indulged. No matter which, she no longer felt any joy in this meeting.

Firekeeper would have turned away and gone looking for Derian, but the great cat was speaking.

"My people are called jaguars," she said. *"My name, divined for me at birth, is Truth."*

Firekeeper tried hard not to show her disbelief that anyone—even a cat—could claim such a name, but the lashing of the spotted tail told her that her reaction had been noticed.

"It is a good name," the jaguar said, *"one that has been in my family many times. My mother's father's sire was called Truth. It is said that, though I am female, I am he come again."*

Firekeeper couldn't help it—this time she did blink. The wolves named for some physical characteristic or trait. Sometimes a name was changed to commemorate a great deed, but this handing on of names one to another seemed strange—as did this talking of dead ones come again. But then she had never known any great cat well. Perhaps insanity was usual among them.

"*My talent,*" Truth continued, "*is divination. I scented your arrival before ever you stepped from boat onto land and have been smelling you since. I will admit that my gift is considered powerful, but there is that about you which muddies the air.*"

Petulant indeed, then, Firekeeper thought. *How interesting—and how strange.*

"What is this divination?" she asked aloud. "Surely I have never heard of it."

Truth's eyes narrowed. "*Is it a talent unknown to your people?*"

Blind Seer, whose hackles had not yet lain flat, growled slightly.

"*It is known to us,*" he said, "*but has not emerged within our pack, so there is no wonder Firekeeper has not heard of it. The stories were related on great hunts, so she may have missed them.*"

"What is this divination?" Firekeeper repeated.

Blind Seer answered, "*It is the ability to find something but not by seeing or smelling or any of the usual senses, but by means of a talent. There are those who can divine where water can be found, though that water may be hidden deep under earth or rock. There are those who can divine where game may be found, though the herds may not yet have migrated to that place. There are those who can divine where certain minerals are buried.*"

"Which is your gift?" Firekeeper asked Truth with genuine interest.

"*I can divine the future,*" the jaguar replied, the rumbling purr that underlay the announcement making clear how pleased she was with her gift. "*I can divine whether an action will have good consequences or bad. I can divine which name is propitious, or on what day a festival should be held. I am the source of many omens and this is my year.*"

Firekeeper stared, trying to take all of this in, and settling for breaking her questions into small parts.

"*You can tell what the future will be? For how far ahead?*"

Truth licked a paw. "*The future is like a stream breaking into many rivulets as it passes over rocks. The farther away an event is, the less accurately I am able to tell, but if an event is sufficiently momentous, then it cuts a deep course and I can read it truly.*"

Firekeeper was impressed and she let the jaguar see this. In all her experience of both beasts and humans, she had never found it hurt to reveal honest appreciation. Truth's purr deepened as she continued her explanation.

"*I was asked whether the* Fayonejunjal *would safely return if she sailed to the north under the direction of Endbrook and the others who had been shipwrecked. I was able to reply that yes she would. Sometimes I can even see clearly enough that were the entire crew paraded before me in different combinations I could indicate which crew would best insure success. This, however, is very wearying for me, so such is not usually done.*"

Firekeeper thought how using his healing talent wearied Doc, and understood. It seemed to her that intensive use of a talent was rather like focusing any other sense. One did not get eyestrain from merely looking about oneself, but if one strove to see a great distance or to concentrate on something small for a long time, then indeed did the head throb.

Blind Seer asked the jaguar, *"I can understand why it would be useful to know what day was best for a hunt—or a festival—but what is all this about names?"*

Truth's ears slicked back and she hissed.

"You—you who are given a name weighty with omens—you claim not to understand this?"

Blind Seer would not grovel for the jaguar as he might have had a One turned such anger on him, but he rocked the heavy weight of his tail slowly side to side, indicating he had not meant any offense. Truth apparently considered this sufficient apology, for her rounded ears rose from her skull.

"Names," she said, *"can simply be tags by which one is known from the next. Then there are titles. These are earned or awarded for skill or deed."*

Firekeeper thought about the names she had carried. She had no idea what her human parents had called her, but Earl Kestrel, who had first brought her from the forests, had called her "Blysse" in the belief that she was a child who had been given that name. Later, when she had been adopted into his family, she had been given the title "Lady" to indicate she belonged to a noble house.

The wolves had first called her Little Two-legs, and her elders still did so sometimes, as a sign of affection. Firekeeper, though, was a name that revealed something about her achievements and abilities, much as the young wolf who had been called the Whiner in her youngest years was now called Sharp Fang in recognition for her growing abilities as a hunter.

For the first time, Firekeeper realized that Blind Seer still bore his puppy name, and she wondered if that troubled him. He was some five years old now, and had traveled farther than most wolves and had seen things of which they could not even dream. Still, many wolves never changed their puppy name—especially if there was nothing derogatory about it. Moreover, Truth seemed impressed by the name, so Firekeeper allowed herself to be comforted.

Truth was going on, *"But there are those who at their first showing before the priests and teachers reveal themselves to be possessed of merit. For these do we seek a name that will indicate the path which they might do best to follow. In other cases, the merit does not manifest until later and, again, when this happens, a change of name may be in order. Always, though, always, the name must be right or the deities may not realize who it is who prays to them for aid. The deities, you see, know each one by the real and truest name."*

Firekeeper wanted to rub her head, feeling an ache coming on, almost as if they were back on the ocean, but she restrained herself.

"It is not unlike," she hazarded, *"how Derian's people change their names and titles throughout their lives."*

"*They do this?*" the jaguar said, interested. "*Then perhaps they are closer to an awareness of the deities than I had been told. It does sound as if they are reaching for communication with the divine.*"

Wisely Firekeeper kept her thoughts sealed behind her teeth. Blind Seer did not even pant the faintest breath of laughter. She thought she knew now why Truth had called herself the source of many omens, for it seemed likely that the jaguar somehow communicated the results of her divinations to the humans. However, Firekeeper was still puzzled by the final thing the jaguar had said.

"*How is this your year?*" Firekeeper asked.

"*This is a jaguar year,*" Truth said, clearly proud, "*and I am selected from all my kind to represent the year in this city, which is among the greatest of Liglimom cities, though some argue that u-Vreeheera in the south is greater.*"

"Oh," Firekeeper said. "*I think I understand. Derian's people—and the people of Bright Bay as well, for they are kin—name the moonspans in cycles. Do your people do the same with years?*"

Truth's ears flattened, and Firekeeper knew that once again she had somehow erred.

"*I beg forgiveness,*" she said quickly, having none of a human's embarrassment about apologizing when ignorance was the cause. "*I misunderstood. I am a pup before your tremendous wisdom. Make the sun chase away that darkness.*"

"*Whatever else,*" the jaguar replied, "*your parents taught you to speak prettily. I can see that you are sincere.*"

Firekeeper felt a faint chill at this last, for it seemed possible that the jaguar could divine when lies were spoken. She was glad she was a wolf, for wolves do not often lie, but for humans, who seemed to exist on shades of half truth, the jaguar's gift could be very dangerous.

Truth licked her paw and washed thoroughly behind one ear, an action that created a mild ripple of excitement among the humans, who thus far had watched the interaction of wolves and jaguar from a distance far more polite than they had accorded the wolves alone.

"*What year belongs to what beast is divined,*" Truth explained at last. "*Such divination is a complicated matter that courses over several days before the closing of the previous year. Different beasts are associated with one or more of the deities, so not only does the divination arrive at which beast will represent the year, but also arrives at some understanding of which of the deities will be taking an active hand in events.*"

"*And which deity is associated with the jaguar?*" Firekeeper asked, sorry now she hadn't paid more attention to Rahniseeta's discussions of these matters.

"*Fire,*" purred Truth, "*so you can see why the coming of one who styles herself the fire keeper should be seen as of such importance.*"

Firekeeper could indeed, and the awareness gave her no great comfort at all. What gave her even less was the feeling that the jaguar didn't find her important.

IX

UNTIL HARJEEDIAN RETURNED, Rahniseeta didn't realize that he had been gone.

"The u-Liall are ready to speak with Lady Blysse," he said. "I must go ahead and prepare them."

The sour expression on Harjeedian's face told Rahniseeta how little he was looking forward to the upcoming interview—and why should he? Who would have expected that a woman so obviously blessed by the deities would be so unpleasant?

"Bring her," Harjeedian said, "as soon as you can separate her from Truth without awakening undue omens."

Rahniseeta nodded, understanding. There were those in the group that had gathered to watch Lady Blysse in conversation with the jaguar who were reading omens into every flex of the great cat's ears, every twitch of her tail. As the jaguar seemed restless, those omens were not good.

Happily, not long after Harjeedian departed, Lady Blysse and Blind Seer turned away from the jaguar. The woman's face was a study in impassivity, but Rahniseeta thought Lady Blysse was both unhappy and disgruntled.

Rahniseeta glided forward to intercept Lady Blysse before any of those close by could create a distraction.

"Lady Blysse?" she pitched her voice low, having already learned that the other woman's hearing was extraordinarily acute. "Please come with me. U-Liall are ready to meet with you."

Lady Blysse's dark head tilted slightly to one side, as if she was preparing to ask a question, but her reply was a simple statement.

"We follow."

Rahniseeta said nothing further, but led the way to where a curving ramp ran along the interior wall, mounting to the next highest level of the building. Although the enormous ground-floor chamber and the step pyramid above were both used for major religious ceremonies honoring all the deities, the honest truth was that most of u-Nahal was an administrative center rather than a place of worship. Contained within base and apex were the rooms in which u-Liall met in full conclave, the scriptorium where documents pertaining to the business of the five rulers were kept and copied, and a variety of other rooms dedicated to routine business.

Seeing where Rahniseeta was taking their guests, none of the very important people gathered in the reception hall made any attempt to slow her. Rahniseeta felt a thrill of pride, though she reminded herself that she was little more than a servant of the great.

They mounted the ramp—aware that all but those clustered around the table where Varjuna spoke with Derian Counselor were watching. Rahniseeta led them through a doorway, then mounted a second ramp, this one walled on all sides.

She noted that Lady Blysse paused, eyeing the enclosed space warily.

"It becomes wider above," Rahniseeta said. "We go to a place above the reception hall."

Lady Blysse nodded, but Rahniseeta did not fail to notice that her hand rested on the hilt of her knife.

"You will be safe," Rahniseeta said soothingly. "U-Liall will be honored to entertain you. My brother has gone to make your way smooth."

This last was rewarded with a small smile that twitched one side of Lady's Blysse's mouth. So she was aware of at least some of the discomfort she was causing. Rahniseeta didn't know whether to feel annoyance or admiration.

The ramp had been constructed so that even horses or deer might mount to the upper levels of the temple, but Lady Blysse and Blind Seer followed Rahniseeta in single file.

In case they must fight, Rahniseeta realized with a thrill, her feeling that Lady Blysse must indeed be one of the maimaladalu intensifying. Perhaps Blind Seer was one, too, only he had chosen to remain in his animal form.

At the next turning of the ramp, Rahniseeta led the guests down a short corridor that terminated in an elaborately carved door. She tugged on the heavy, twisted rope that would announce her desire for admittance. There was no verbal acknowledgment of her signal, nor did the doorkeeper open the hatch to check who was outside. Instead, the double doors were pulled inward, granting the three admission.

Rahniseeta had been in this chamber many times before, but familiarity had not removed the awe with which she viewed the room, especially when u-Liall, the conclave of the five supreme representatives of the deified elements, was in session.

Although smaller than the vast chamber below, the conclave room still was spacious. The walls were adorned with painted tiles displaying events in the origin story and the important events that followed—a visual text of the faith that influenced all of their lives.

Five high-backed thrones were arrayed at perfect intervals along an imaginary curve at the far end of the room. Each throne was a marvel of costly workmanship: the woodwork encased in gold or silver foil, brilliantly faceted gemstones adorning the arms, legs, and—though it was not visible at this point—the backs as well. The cushioned portions along the back and seat were of tapestrywork, constantly repaired and restuffed so that the least wear never showed.

The thrones were arranged and rearranged according to the omens. Today Fire's representative sat in the center, flanked at her right and left by Earth and Air. Water sat to Earth's right, Magic to Air's left. Harjeedian stood in the center, slightly to one side of Fire's throne, so as not to block the ahmyndisdu's view of the new arrivals.

Two muscular male servants, deaf and dumb, stood to either side of the double doors. When Rahniseeta and those she escorted had passed through, the servants closed the doors behind them, then turned to face the wall where the bobbing of a bell would let them know if another rang for admittance—not that any would dare interrupt such an important meeting for anything less than a life-threatening situation.

Rahniseeta saw Lady Blysse tense as they were closed in, but there was nothing she could do to reassure the wolf-woman, not even point to where other doors were cleverly concealed among the ornamental tiles. At this point, Rahniseeta must act as if deaf or dumb, or risk—so it was rumored—becoming so in fact.

"Welcome, Lady Blysse," said the ahmyndisdu.

Lady Blysse said nothing in reply, and well she might be struck silent. The most senior representative of divine Fire in this temple was a woman younger than Rahniseeta herself. Tiridanti had marked the passage of her seventeenth year of life only two moonspans ago. Her elevation to her high position had occurred three years before that—when she was barely fourteen.

Members of u-Liall held their position for life, and Tiridanti's predecessor had been seventy-three when a winter chill had stolen into his bones and hastened him to a warm seat in Fire's hall.

In theory, successors were selected from all who gave service to the deities. In practice, they usually came from the higher ranks of the aridisdum and kidisdum, most especially those whose service was in some way closely related to the appropriate element. Tiridanti's predecessor had been ikidisdu of fifty-one years when he had been elevated from keeper of ravens.

Tiridanti herself had been an underkeeper of pumas when confusing omen after blank reading had led to the rejection of all of those senior to herself, right until the day that the four remaining members of u-Liall had followed a trembling doe (for it had been the year of the deer) along to where Tiridanti was bottle-feeding an orphaned puma kitten.

Even then there had been protests from a few that the doe had been somehow influenced, but these had quieted with the stern reminder that Fire was well known to be the least predictable of all the elements. If he wanted his ahmyndisdu to be a barely educated child, then they must follow his will.

Later, so Rahniseeta had heard, the seniors in Fire had become reconciled to Tiridanti's elevation when they realized that in her they had the potential for a reigning member of the conclave who might well serve for seventy or eighty years. This was not to be lightly dismissed, for though the deities were, of course, consulted on matters of great importance, there were many matters of routine that were handled by much more mundane political maneuvering. Many favors could be accumulated in fifty or sixty years. Soon Tiridanti was as treasured as she had once been scorned.

There had been no further changes to the conclave since Tiridanti's elevation, though with old Bibimalenu of Air in his eighty-first year it seemed quite likely that there would be another soon. Nor was much beloved Dantarahma of Water very young. At seventy, he had officiated at the beyond-sendings of several colleagues.

The remaining two members, Feeshaguyu of Earth and Noonafaruma of Magic, were of robust middle years, their elevations having followed the more usual course. Both had held their seats for a decade or more and were well respected, if not always well liked. Since her brother was aridisdu himself, these internal rivalries did not shock Rahniseeta. Every so often she'd say something to some market acquaintance who did not have a brother who was an aridisdu or who was not an intimate of Heeranenahalm, the City of Temples, and the shocked look she received would remind Rahniseeta how very different her life was from the usual.

Today, watching Lady Blysse study the members of u-Liall while they studied her in return, Rahniseeta thought that here was one who would not be overwhelmed by the height of their diadems or the history represented in their embroidered stoles. Here was one who took things as she saw them and as nothing more.

And that, thought Rahniseeta, *will be a mistake.*

Since it was a jaguar year and Fire was senior, Tiridanti took charge of the meeting. When Lady Blysse did not respond at all to her formal speech of welcome, Tiridanti's smooth brow creased in the faintest line of irritation, but otherwise she did not comment. Instead, she moved to other matters.

"Have you been made comfortable since your arrival in u-Seeheera?" she asked.

Lady Blysse looked as if she might not reply, but then she said, "We have food and water. Shelter, too."

"Then you are comfortable," Tiridanti said, obviously wanting a straight answer and perhaps a bit of the praise that usually accompanied anything said to any of u-Liall.

Technically, the praise was addressed to the deities u-Liall represented, but the disdum would have been less than human if they didn't feel a little rubbed off onto themselves.

Lady Blysse gave no such balm.

"We are not hungry or thirsty, but that is not comfort. We are taken from our own places and kept from returning. This is not comfort."

Rahniseeta knew this was a long speech for Lady Blysse, but to u-Liall it must have seemed short and overly critical. After all, there were prisons and dungeons. Where was the flowery praise given to thank the deities for sparing the speaker from such a fate?

There was a very tense silence. Then Tiridanti apparently decided she must adapt to the situation.

"Water and Air brought hence the ship that first gave us word of your existence," she began.

Lady Blysse tilted her head to one side and looked at Harjeedian. In Pellish she asked, "What say?" Rahniseeta knew that phrase well by now.

Harjeedian bowed low before the thrones.

"Lady Blysse does not understand any but the most elementary of the wise statements and incisive questions that fall from your heaven-blessed lips, O Fire's Chosen. May I have your permission to translate?"

"You may," Tiridanti replied with a gracious inclination of her head, "now and in the future. We know the subtle swiftness of the snake's tongue, and trust you to serve wisely."

Harjeedian thanked Tiridanti appropriately, then said, "If perhaps the great ahmyndisdu would deign begin again, I might garner your thoughts and translate them appropriately."

Tiridanti nodded and returned her attention to Lady Blysse.

"Water and Air brought hence the ship that first gave us word of your existence. We were intrigued, for it seemed to us that in your person was embodied a gift we had thought never given to humankind."

Tiridanti paused to give Harjeedian opportunity to translate. It was notable that he needed to use far fewer words. Tiridanti then continued:

"The artists in travel by means of Air and Water from the foreign lands noted our reverence for animals and how we turned to them again and again for guidance. One said to us, 'Would it suit your gracious person to have among you one who speaks with the animals more easily than I speak to you?' We said that this would be up to the deities. The omens were consulted and the deities said that we should bring you before us. This was done and now we ask you to confirm the truth of these rumors. Can you indeed speak to animals more clearly than I speak to you?"

There was a slight smile on Tiridanti's lips as she made this last statement, as if she was well aware that communication even between humans was not an easy or reliable thing.

Lady Blysse listened to Harjeedian's translation, then said in the language of Liglim, "Wolves raised me. I understand my kin."

The members of u-Liall all looked very interested at this confirmation of rumor.

"And do you understand other than your kin?" Tiridanti asked, leaning forward slightly so that the gold chains on her headdress swayed. The little rubies and bits of diamond sparkled as if the metal and stone were imbued with Fire. "It was said that you went over to Truth, the jaguar of this year, and that you stood a long while as if in conversation."

Lady Blysse looked as if she would refuse to answer, but at last she said very heavily, "I understood jaguar."

Tiridanti turned and smiled brilliantly at her fellows in u-Liall. They each nodded, though their expressions were more guarded.

But then this will be Fire's coup, Rahniseeta thought. *They would be less than perfectly pleased.*

"And can you speak with other animals as well?" Tiridanti pressed.

Lady Blysse glanced at Blind Seer, then shrugged.

"Beasts you call Wise Beasts," she said, "those I can speak with. Cousins I understand only a little."

There was a longish pause while Harjeedian explained what Lady Blysse meant by "cousins." Some further discussion followed as to what this might mean on a theological level. Through it all, Lady Blysse waited with well-concealed impatience, one hand resting on Blind Seer's shoulder, the other near to her knife.

At last Tiridanti asked with unaccustomed bluntness, "Can you teach us how to speak to the Wise Beasts?"

Lady Blysse looked genuinely surprised.

"I not know," she said in the language of Liglim. "I have not tried."

Then the wolf-woman switched to Pellish, which Harjeedian translated without flourishes, "Why should I teach you? You claim to respect the Wise Beasts and go to them for omens, but you keep them captive as you keep me captive."

Tiridanti looked offended, jerking back so suddenly the metal on her costume clashed unmusically.

"What do you mean? We do not keep the yarimaimalom captive! Did Truth tell you this?"

Lady Blysse looked honestly confused and Harjeedian had to race to translate her words. In his haste, something of the choppy fashion in which Lady Blysse spoke came through.

"Truth say nothing. Why else would yarimaimalom stay in such crowded places when the whole world is there—at least to the west where humans are not."

The faces of each member of u-Liall blossomed with expressions of horror and astonishment, but before they could address this point the bells above the door began to jangle violently.

Something had happened, something so dire that a messenger dared to interrupt this most private conclave.

Tiridanti glanced at the other u-Liall, then raised one hand to the slave and made the sign that said, "Admit them."

DERIAN TUGGED AT THE BELL-ROPE, trying to decide which thing surprised him more—that he actually had the gall to interrupt what was apparently a ruling council meeting, or that he was doing so based on permission granted by an extremely large spotted cat.

As soon as he'd noticed that Firekeeper was missing from the reception area, Derian had started looking for her. Almost immediately he had confirmed two things. One, Firekeeper had not left the building, and, two, she and Blind Seer had been escorted to an upper level by Rahniseeta.

Trouble started when Derian started to follow her. Varjuna—among others—had explained that the upper levels were restricted. Someone else had said that Firekeeper had been brought before u-Liall.

"That means 'the five,' doesn't it?" Derian asked. "Five what?"

Varjuna looked momentarily confused, then struggled to explain, mingling Liglimosh and Pellish.

"The five most senior servants of the deities," he said, "one for each of the deities. They are selected from within the ranks of the aridisdum and kidisdum, and serve for life."

Thinking about how blunt the wolf-woman could be, how poor was her command of Pellish—not to mention her Liglimosh—Derian started getting frightened on her behalf. Firekeeper was perfectly capable of saying something wrong simply out of her habit of cutting verbal corners. If she got offended—and he knew her well enough to know that she'd been on a low boil ever since she'd realized the big spotted cat was a Royal Beast—she didn't much care what she said.

It was the definitive downside of Firekeeper's wolfish sense of hierarchy. Until someone earned her respect, they could be the acknowledged ruler of the land and it simply didn't matter. To make matters worse, ever since her freedom had been taken from her, Firekeeper had become increasingly volatile. There had always been restrictions she had to accept since she came east of the Iron Mountains with Earl Kestrel, but the choice to associate with humans had been the wolf-woman's own. Derian was only now realizing just how much that element of choice had led her to moderate her actions.

Derian was growing both angry and frustrated that no one would even agree to deliver a message containing his request that he be permitted to join the meeting when a hush fell over the room. The great spotted cat—a jaguar, he had heard it called—had risen to its feet.

It leapt down from the ledge on which it had perched, landing as lightly as if it had jumped a handsbreadth rather than from higher than Derian's head. Then it stalked toward Derian, the crowd parting around it as tall grass might have in a more usual jungle. The tip of its tail twitched slightly, but Derian had a sudden odd feeling that the jaguar was amused rather than angered. The tail twitch was a reminder of what it could do, rather than a threat to do something.

Murmuring rippled through the gathering: "Truth takes a part." "What is the will of Truth?" "Will Truth punish him for his arrogance?"

Derian realized that Truth must be the jaguar's name. He struggled to remember that, as with Blind Seer or the few other Royal Beasts he had encountered, this jaguar was no well-trained pet, but a person, as intelligent as Derian was himself—and certainly, in this place, more respected.

Truth paused in front of Derian and looked him up and down; then it touched him lightly on the back of one hand with the tip of its nose. After glancing up at him from those unsettlingly focused burnt-orange eyes within which flecks of gold glittered, Truth started walking toward a ramp that led to the upper floor.

Derian stood, uncertain what he was supposed to do, until Varjuna shoved him gently between the shoulder blades.

"Follow her," Varjuna hissed. "Truth has heard your petition and will take you to u-Liall. Go quickly lest she become offended."

Derian did so, the dull impact of his sandals against the polished stone floor seeming the only sound in all that vast hall. He fought down an urge toward nervous laughter. "Petition." Was that what the Liglimo called a raging fit of temper? Useful to know.

But Derian knew that in this very mannered society his loss of temper had been just as impolite as it would have been at home. Only the jaguar's decision to honor his request had saved Derian from—at the very least—a major social misstep.

Derian saw this when, as the ramp turned in its rising, he looked down and saw Barnet endeavoring to follow him. Hands, some gentle, some less so, grasped the minstrel and held him back. A few guards moved purposefully across the hall, the mostly ceremonial spears they had held now easing to the ready.

Derian thought about calling down to Barnet to relax, to stand easy, but something of the awful dignity of the jaguar pacing in front of him stilled his lips. In any case, Barnet needed no such warning. The minstrel stopped well before the guards reached him, but his gaze continued to track them, his expression alive with concern.

Is he worried about Firekeeper, too? Derian thought. *Or about me? Or is he just afraid he'll miss something important?*

He didn't know, nor did he have time to consider the matter further, for the jaguar had halted before an ornately carved double door. The great cat stretched, reaching easily to a bell-rope hanging down. She didn't pull it, though Derian had no doubt that she could easily do so. It was, after all, an action well within the abilities of any house cat—if a house cat had been able to reach effortlessly four feet from the ground.

Derian took the hint and pulled the bell-rope, pulling hard a second time for good measure. The door was so thick he couldn't hear whether what he had done had any effect, but Truth seemed content, settling onto her haunches and staring calmly at the door, so Derian waited as well.

Not too long thereafter, he heard the door being unfastened. Then, as smoothly and evenly as if they had been yoked together, the heavy doors were pulled open, admitting them into the conclave chamber.

Truth walked in front of Derian, and at her approach the quiet in the room became stillness. Derian followed, noting to his relief that Firekeeper and Blind Seer did not seem harmed. Then he kept his gaze centered on the five figures enthroned in a curve at the far end of the room. Their costumes were so elaborate, their diadems so high and elegantly constructed that he had trouble at first concentrating on the people inside the attire.

One thing he knew for certain. These had not joined the general reception below. They were too aware of the dignity of their positions to be introduced as part of a general crowd. Derian also didn't doubt that they counted on their thrones and costumes to add to their general impressiveness. He swallowed a completely inappropriate grin. That, at least, would have been lost on Firekeeper.

Derian had just noticed that the figure on the central throne was so young she seemed overweighted by her elaborate attire when she spoke.

"Truth has brought you before us," said the young woman, moving so the gold and fiery gemstones in her diadem flashed in the light. "Therefore, we admit you. What is your purpose for interrupting our conclave?"

Derian felt a sudden shiver of cold at what his reception might have been had not the jaguar taken it into her mind to escort him. Then he gave a mental shrug and replied politely:

"I noticed that Lady Blysse was missing. I heard she was here, so I came."

"Are you then her keeper?" this question came from an incredibly old man seated to the young woman's left.

His costume was in silvers and pale blues, set all over with crystal and diamonds and other translucent stones. It contrasted strongly with the golds, red, yellows, and oranges worn by the young woman. Derian remembered what Varjuna had told him and understood. This old man must represent Air, the girl, Fire.

Derian answered very carefully, "I am not her keeper. She keeps herself. I have known her since she first came from the forests, and I know she often has trouble understanding human ways."

An older woman whose browns and greens were touched with every color ever known on Earth frowned and spoke.

"We have Harjeedian of the Temple of the Cold Bloods here to translate. Is his command of your language less adept than we have been told?"

"No, ma'am," Derian said, certain he was grossly demoting her by employing the polite address he had used when speaking to *Fayonejunjal*'s captain, but not knowing what was the correct form, he made do. "Harjeedian speaks our language with incredible aptitude. However, Lady Blysse does not only need translation for language—she often needs it for custom. I admit that Harjeedian knows your culture far better than I do myself, but I can serve as a bridge between your world and my own."

The Fire member of u-Liall now took over again.

"Truth has brought you before us," she repeated, "so we will take her advice and admit you. Indeed, Truth may have divined our need and brought you on that accord."

The jaguar licked her right paw and looked impossibly smug.

Divined or not, Derian thought, *you're not above taking the credit, are you?*

The young woman continued, "Lady Blysse had just made a very startling statement, one that I think must be clarified before we can progress further. Harjeedian, repeat her words."

Harjeedian straightened, and with his attention on the figures seated in the five thrones still managed to give the impression that he was checking with Firekeeper as to the accuracy of his report.

"As Ahmyndisdu Tiridanti requires," Harjeedian said, bowing almost to the floor. Then he quoted, " 'Truth say nothing, but why else would Beasts stay in such terrible places when the whole world is there—at least to the west where humans are not.' "

"We had been asking," Tiridanti said, seeing Derian still looked puzzled, "if Lady Blysse could indeed speak to animals. She admitted she could speak to the yarimaimalom, but when we asked her if she would teach us she grew angry and stated that we did not respect the animals, for we kept them captive. We thought she might have misunderstood something Truth had said—for we had heard they shared converse—but she replied as Harjeedian has reported."

Derian glanced at Firekeeper and saw that she was not about to speak on her own behalf.

"I can only guess, Ahmyndisdu Tiridanti," he said, attempting the honorific Harjeedian had used and mangling it only slightly. "In our lands the Wise Beasts live to the west of the mountains. Humans stay to the east."

He thought quickly and decided that he could not violate those secrets Firekeeper had confided in him last spring when they had returned from a journey west. Instead he offered the human version of the tale.

"When our colonists first came from the Old Country," he said, carefully picking his words, "the yarimaimalom lived all over this land."

"So it was with us," Tiridanti said encouragingly when he stopped.

Derian had been trying to think of the right words and realized he didn't have half what he needed. Harjeedian looked at him, not kindly, but not unkindly either.

"Use what you know of our language," he said, "so u-Liall may hear your tale in your own words as much as possible. However, if you must use a word from your own language, do so, and I will translate."

Derian nodded his thanks, trying not to be embarrassed. After all, Harjeedian not only had the sort of gift for languages that Elise did, he'd also had a lot longer to study. A flicker of sapphire blue from where the disdu of Water sat reminded Derian that for all their finery his audience was only human, so he hurried to continue.

"At first the beasts and the humans didn't crowd each other, but as farms grew and flocks were set out to graze, well, there was competition. I don't really know how it happened, but long before the Plague . . ."

He paused again and saw that these people also knew of the Plague.

"Long before the Plague the Wise Beasts were little more than legends. In fact, by the time we found Lady Blysse, I don't think most of us even believed in them. I certainly didn't."

Tiridanti looked side to side at her associates, and Derian could tell they were experiencing a mixture of shock and understanding.

"So your founders drove the yarimaimalom away?" Tiridanti asked.

"I think they must have," Derian said. "I don't know. The Wise Beasts aren't telling and no one today is alive who remembers. It makes sense, though. Their magic was said to be terribly powerful."

"So was the magic of those who founded this colony," Tiridanti said, "but our tale is somewhat different. Will you and Lady Blysse listen? I think it may explain a few things about which she is clearly misled."

Derian was quite interested in listening, but his feet and legs were getting tired. He shifted, trying to ease where the straps of his new sandals were wearing blisters. Apparently, Firekeeper wasn't interested in standing much longer either, but she didn't wait to be given permission to sit. She simply dropped to the floor alongside Blind Seer. The wolf sat next to her, close enough so that she could fling an arm around him.

Harjeedian started to protest, but Tiridanti waved him down.

"Lady Blysse knows her will, even if her manners are not of the best. Still, as the question has been raised as to whether she and her countrymen are guests or prisoners and we wish them to feel themselves guests, let chairs be brought."

This was done. When the chairs were brought out from somewhere behind the thrones, Derian became aware for the first time that Rahniseeta was also present. She had waited alongside the wall, so silent and still that if he had seen her at all he had taken her for one of the life-sized figures depicted in the murals that adorned the walls. Now she accepted the chair she was given with equal silence, placing it back where she would not be obvious.

Out of sight, out of mind? Derian thought, and reminded himself that for all Tiridanti and her associates were being very polite to him and Firekeeper, they were rulers accustomed to being treated as well above the common herd.

More certain of themselves, Derian thought, *than our own nobles because these u-Liall don't hold their place just from right of inheritance, but because their people believe the deities have chosen them.*

Predictably, Firekeeper refused a chair, but Truth leapt gracefully onto a low dais covered with thick lamb's wool and obviously intended for this purpose.

When all were settled, Tiridanti turned to the representative of Air.

"Bibimalenu, you are the most senior of us all," she said with formal politeness, "and know the story best. Will you tell it?"

Bibimalenu smiled, showing what had to be artificial teeth, and peered over his glasses.

"I thank you for the honor," he said, "but my old voice is not strong. In any case," and here he actually twinkled at his much younger associate, "I am old indeed, but not old enough to recall the Plague years."

Tiridanti then took a deep breath and Derian realized with sudden insight that she wasn't completely sure of the details of the story. He wondered how she had come to hold such a high office and what rivalries might there be among u-Liall. It was not a comforting thought, for Tiridanti clearly wanted some sort of alliance with Firekeeper. Who might be seeking to undermine the wolf-woman for no other reason than that the Ahmyndisdu was a rival for power? Might it even be that old man who had seemed to feel kindly toward her?

Tiridanti said, "Then I will tell the tale, and try to keep my words simple so that it need not be translated. Harjeedian, you are to step in for me as you did for Derian Counselor."

"I would be honored to so serve," Harjeedian said. Without further delay, Tiridanti began.

"You have already been told the story of how the world was created. It was brought with us from our Old Country, and so from the Old Country also came the custom of consulting the animals as to the will of the deities. However, in all the Old Country— indeed, so we are told, in all the Old World—there was nothing like the yarimaimalom."

Derian fought down an irreverent desire to ask then how it was that part of the story about Water's creation of Magic included fragments falling onto the animals and creating the yarimaimalom. He had a feeling he would be stumbling into something far more dangerous than the debate over whether Fox or Dog was the original society— and blood had been spilled over that one for sure.

Tiridanti went on, "Since there were nothing like the yarimaimalom in the Old Country, consulting the animals was done through watching for signs and omens. Good or bad luck for a venture might be read in how a dove pecked at grain or whether a stallion mounted a mare. There were many ways, and we still use them today. However, one way that we no longer use is reading the will of the deities in the sacrifice of living creatures. This change came directly from the discovery of the yarimaimalom.

"When they were first encountered, the yarimaimalom were thought to be nothing other than exceptionally fine, exceptionally strong examples of their kind. The Old Country masters hunted them for sacrifice, thinking the deities would be pleased by this. Time passed, however, and it was learned that not only were the yarimaimalom at least as clever as humans, but that they also possessed talents. Thus they were shown to be our equals.

"Some then argued that as we did not sacrifice humans, so we should not sacrifice the yarimaimalom. Others, however, especially those who delighted in the chase, argued that the deities would be more pleased with such sacrifices since the effort that must be made in the hunt was so tremendous. The argument split the population. Those who had been born here tended to favor respect for the yarimaimalom. Those who had come from the Old Country or who had returned there for training argued in favor of sacrifice.

"This might have led to war among us, even though all the power was on the side of those with Old Country ties, but for that the deities themselves spoke their will. They brought down fever and death on those who had become so corrupted that even the gifts of divine Magic were used against the yarimaimalom. Those with Old Country ties fled to the Old World in an effort to avoid this divine retribution, but as they have not returned, we know the punishment meted out by the deities followed them even there."

Derian saw a slight frown crease the face of Earth's representative, and guessed that Tiridanti had oversimplified some point of theology, but the frown melted instantly away, as soon as she noted Derian's gaze upon her.

Tiridanti went on, "Now, unlike in your own land, the yarimaimalom had never retreated from the territory which our colony claimed. Perhaps this is because although they were hunted, there was never an attempt to exterminate them. Indeed, in many small towns and villages they were revered alongside the resident disdum. When the plague had driven the Old Country masters away, representatives of the yarimaimalom came to the disdum who remained. They spoke as follows:

" 'Let the sacrifice of all animals end, for it is not pleasing to the deities. Moreover, give over the hunting of the yarimaimalom even for food, for we truly speak to you for the deities. Long before your coming did we regulate our own growth, so we shall continue to do.'

" 'In return for your promise to do this, some of our number will come and live among you. Give us the fine islands out in the bay for our own and make other preserves in areas we will divine as being within the deities' will. We shall come peacefully among you then, and speak to you for the deities. Never will we raise paw or hoof or horn against you or your children unless harm be offered first. There will be peace among us, and the deities will smile upon you and you will prosper.'

"As you can imagine," Tiridanti said, "the people were happy to make such a pact, for they could see how it would be pleasing to the deities. Moreover, as if to show their hearts were one with ours in this matter, the yarimaimalom offered one other promise.

" 'We will also keep watch for you against the return of those who have fled. Truly the deities have punished them, but someday survivors may seek to return. From our place on the islands in the bay we will watch. We will speak to our lesser kin and learn what they see as well. Thus we will have warning well before our old enemies return. Then they will find you have prepared and are ready to resist them. The deities will be pleased, as they have ever been pleased to see their worshipers standing up for themselves, asking only for guidance, not to be forever treated as children.'

"And the people were also happy to do this, and to this day a small gathering of disdum lives on the islands in the bay—we call them Misheemnekuru, the Sanctuary Islands—and to them the yarimaimalom will bring warning if ever our common enemy return."

Tiridanti folded her hands, and when she spoke again her voice was less formal, so it was clear that she spoke now for herself, rather than as a repository of sacred lore.

"So you see," she said, looking directly at Firekeeper, "why we were astonished when you claimed we kept the yarimaimalom captive. They associate with us by their own desire."

Derian thought it was a pretty good story, but Firekeeper was obviously not ready to believe it.

"In story you say the Beasts say this, Beasts say that," she said, "but you tell me you not can talk to Beasts. How is it then?"

Tiridanti replied a trace stiffly, "It is a short way of explaining that the yarimaimalom communicated their will to us through the methods of divination we were accustomed to use. They are laborious, but communication is possible."

Firekeeper nodded, her gaze resting on Truth so that Derian suspected that the jaguar had added some collaboration or further information.

"But the yarimaimalom are on islands, mostly," Firekeeper said, her dislike of traveling over water quite evident. "To me this seems like big cage."

Tiridanti spread her hands. "I can offer no answer to that but to remind you that Truth sits there calmly and she wears no collar, no chain, no restraint upon her actions."

"That I see," Firekeeper growled. "I give parole to Harjeedian or he hurt me and mine. How I know it not the same here?"

"You can ask," Tiridanti said mildly. She looked at her associates and then went on, "Apparently, Lady Blysse needs more reassurance than we can give. What if we let her go to the wolves who live on the islands in the bay? She can speak with them, and learn that we have done them no harm. Then, perhaps, she will feel clear of mind about sharing her knowledge with us."

Magic's member of u-Liall, Noonafaruma, nodded approval.

"There is inspired wisdom in that suggestion, Tiridanti," she said. "However, I know that Varjuna, senior keeper of the Horse, has heard that Derian Counselor is knowledgeable in the way of horses. He had hoped to consult with him. May Derian Counselor remain on the mainland?"

Firekeeper looked at Magic's representative with unguarded anger.

"I have said, no hostage, no more, not even Blind Seer who is dear to me from my home."

Noonafaruma spread her hands in what Derian knew was a gesture of apology—a great concession, he suspected, on the part of one of her rank.

"We do not intend for Derian Counselor to be kept hostage. We sincerely honor his knowledge."

Derian saw that Firekeeper was still unconvinced. He rose and gave his best bow.

"U-Liall, may Lady Blysse and I withdraw and discuss this matter in private? As I explained, I interpret human ways for Lady Blysse and she will be more comfortable if we speak alone."

"Go where you will," Tiridanti said immediately, "but only within the bounds of the temple city."

Firekeeper gave a very thin smile, one that said without words that she knew herself a prisoner still, no matter what polite words were spoken.

Derian bowed. "Thank you. When will u-Liall give us audience again?"

Tiridanti glanced—not at her associates, but at Truth. The jaguar rose from its lambskin pad and crossed to one of the sections of mosaic on the walls. After careful consideration, she reared onto her hind legs and indicated a particular symbol.

"Noon tomorrow," Tiridanti said, "is the time for which the omens are propitious. That gives you nearly a full day to consider."

"Thank you," Derian said.

Noonafaruma added, "Speak not only among yourselves, but also with Varjuna. It would be good if you were to know what we offer you, Derian."

Derian bowed again, but though Firekeeper rose to her feet she remained stiff and straight.

Tiridanti looked at her, and Derian thought he saw the Ahmyndisdu swallow a sigh.

"You are dismissed. Harjeedian, you and your sister shall announce what u-Liall has decreed. Let none trouble our guests unless our guests first approach them. You are to remain available to them in case they have questions."

Harjeedian's expression left no doubt that this was a tremendous honor.

"I will do as the Blessed Five command."

Firekeeper snorted and turned. Without further comment, she headed toward the double doors, moving so swiftly that the two servants barely had time to pull them open.

Derian, fearing the worst, eschewed courtesy and hurried after her. He hoped his rudeness would be forgiven.

X

"*FIREKEEPER,*" BLIND SEER SAID as he ran alongside her down the ramp, "*you are being rude. Whatever you think of them, those five humans are the Ones in this land—and surely even you have learned that human Ones hold power beyond that of personal fang and claw. That younger one in the center even seemed to be trying to help us.*"

Firekeeper couldn't listen—didn't want to listen might be more honest. The tale Tiridanti had related had shaken her as perhaps only one other story had shaken her. Even being forced to acknowledge her own human heritage had not bothered her as much. What troubled her was once again learning that her knowledge of her own people was far less than complete.

"*It does not seem to trouble you,*" she said heatedly, "*to find our own captives of these humans—to find Royal Beasts so turned from themselves that they think it an honor to live among humans as their vassals.*"

"*One does not judge an entire herd from a single fawn,*" Blind Seer replied from his seemingly endless store of wolf proverbs, "*nor a pack from a solitary hunter.*"

Spinning to a halt in the walled garden that surrounded the step pyramid, Firekeeper glowered at the wolf.

"*Sometimes I think you make those up,*" she said accusingly.

"*Flat folded ears do not hear as clearly as those carried alert,*" Blind Seer replied. "*Neither anger nor fear make for good judgment. What has you so upset, Firekeeper?*"

Firekeeper walked a few steps to where a cluster of shrubs gave at least the illusion of privacy. None of the humans still gathered in the reception hall had followed them outside. She almost wished someone would. It would feel good to have someone to snarl at—someone other than Blind Seer, who was only being reasonable.

She plopped down onto the soft dirt, and patted the earth next to her. Blind Seer came over and put his head in her lap, but his question remained in the air between them.

"*I am upset,*" Firekeeper replied after taking time to think, "*because I cannot believe that wolves would make themselves dogs to these humans. Maybe the jaguar would. Jaguars are cats and cats are lazy, but wolves?"*

She sighed and in that sigh was all her belief that a pack of wolves would take what it wanted without the need for truces with anyone. It also contained her memory of how when she had come east with Earl Kestrel and his companions there had been a long time when she had been content to be fed and cared for, to not make any effort for herself. The memory was made no sweeter by the fact that Firekeeper could not forget how only the mocking comments of the peregrine falcon Elation had shaken her into action.

"*I am very confused,*" she admitted.

" '*Crossed game trails must be backtracked,*' " Blind Seer quoted, " '*if one is to find the truest scent.*' *How then do we untangle these?*"

"*We go and talk with these yarimaimalom wolves,*" Firekeeper said without hesitation. "*Relying on the word of humans and cats is not enough.*"

"*And our return home?*" the wolf asked.

"*We do not know enough to go,*" Firekeeper replied, "*at least not if we are to take Derian with us. You and I might manage, but I could not leave him here, not when I think his being in this place has much to do with me.*"

"*Well said,*" Blind Seer agreed, "*but do you think going and talking to these island wolves will help us find our trail home?*"

"*No,*" Firekeeper said bluntly. "*However, I do not like the thought of slinking away with this question left unanswered. These humans have learned the sea road north. How long before they meet with the people of Bright Bay or Waterland and mingle their strange ideas? I can think of many terrible things that could come from this. Better we know first, so we can prepare our people.*"

Blind Seer thumped his tail in agreement, then he panted laughter.

"*Besides, you are curious.*"

"*I am,*" Firekeeper admitted, "*and angry. Perhaps Harjeedian's people think that their agreement with these tame yarimaimalom mean they can rule all Beasts. I wish to show them differently.*"

"*And,*" she continued, stroking the wolf between his ears, "*if there are captives here as we are captives, I wish to do what I can to help them go free.*"

ALTHOUGH HE INTENDED TO follow Firekeeper as quickly as possible, Derian found himself delayed by the crush of people still assembled in the reception hall. Without Truth to clear his way, Derian found himself trapped. In the babble of many voices, he had difficulty making out what was being said.

Barnet came to his rescue.

"Lady Blysse came through here a few moments ago," the minstrel explained in Pellish. Oddly, the crowd quieted, as if in silence they could better understand the foreign tongue. "She was so intense no one thought to stop her—though Blind Seer may have had as much to do with that as anything. They're outside now, just a few running steps from the door, but these . . . people . . ."

Derian had the distinct impression Barnet had been about to say "idiots," but had remembered in time that there were a few present who spoke at least some Pellish.

"These people are seeing omens in everything from the number of steps she took once she left the temple to the color of the flowers on the shrubs near where she is sitting. What is going on?"

Derian tried to decide what could and could not be said in such a public place.

"During Lady Blysse's audience with u-Liall, she learned a great deal about local history, some of which she found unsettling. She also doesn't like being closed in, and though the conclave chamber was large, I think she felt cramped."

That'll do, Derian thought. *Better than the truth, at least.*

"Someone will be down to explain u-Liall's ruling," he continued. "Meanwhile, I'm going out to Lady Blysse."

Barnet nodded. "I'll stay here and field questions."

"Thanks."

As Barnet began translating Derian's explanation into Liglimosh, Derian found his path no longer obstructed. He hurried outside, feeling almost unwilling kinship with the minstrel. Here in the foreign land the differences that had separated them—including the political enmity between their countries—didn't seem to matter as much as the similarity of language and culture.

I wonder if I'll start feeling friendly toward Waln Endbrook next? Derian thought, but remembering what Waln had done, he didn't think this likely.

He found Firekeeper sitting with Blind Seer next to a clump of highly scented white flowers. He entertained a fleeting thought that to something as nose-oriented as a wolf, this might seem like hiding, but dismissed the conjecture as ridiculous. Firekeeper was the first person to call herself "nose-dead."

He dropped onto the grass next to them.

"So, what do you think about Ahmyndisdu Tiridanti's offer?"

Firekeeper bit into her lip.

"I think," she said, "I must see with these eyes what the wolves are like."

Derian nodded.

"Do you want me to come with you?"

Firekeeper blinked.

"Tiridanti, Varjuna wish you here."

"Firekeeper, I may remember my social graces, but that doesn't mean I'm going to do everything someone else tells me they think is best. You are my friend. If you want me with you, that's where I'll be. If you think it is best I stay here . . ."

He shrugged.

"I think," Firekeeper said slowly, "you must make this decision for you. Why not go and see what this Varjuna offer? Then we consider together, best each for each."

Derian nodded.

"You have something there." He got up, brushed grass off his trousers. "Varjuna's still in the reception hall. I'll go talk to him. Where can I find you?"

"Tiridanti say we can go anywhere in temple places," Firekeeper replied. "These gardens seem better than snake place. I will be here, or if not, somehow I will let you know where I am."

Derian grinned at her.

"It would be a whole lot easier to leave a note if you'd learn to write."

"Paah . . ." Firekeeper said, but he knew she agreed with him. From how Blind Seer thumped his tail on the grass, Derian suspected the wolf did, too.

FINDING VARJUNA WAS EASY, and in a very brief time they had separated themselves from the surrounding group and were headed toward what Varjuna called u-Bishinti, or the Stable. It was easy to tell the place must be important because the word shared the same "u" prefix that changed "liall" from the mere number five to a title of respect, so Derian did not expect to be taken to any usual housing for horses. However, he was certainly not prepared for their destination.

First Varjuna took them to a very nice little carriage with two seats before and a higher seat behind. The ikidisdu must have sent word ahead, for a handsome bay gelding was being set between the shafts as they arrived. The stableboy made numerous gestures indicative of deep respect as he handed the reins to Varjuna, but these didn't distract him from sneaking several long, curious looks at Derian himself.

"I'll drive," Varjuna said, as the stableboy climbed up behind. "Do you mind sitting alongside me?"

"Not at all," Derian replied, quite happy not to be relegated to the passenger seat. "Easier to talk this way."

"We have a bit of a drive ahead of us," Varjuna said. "U-Bishinti is outside of the main city, so there is ample pasturage."

"My parents' business is outside of Eagle's Nest for the same reason," Derian said. "That's the name of our city," he added when Varjuna looked puzzled.

They talked about the difficulties of maintaining a large horse facility in an urban center while Varjuna took them out of the temple district. Then Varjuna shifted to affable tour guide, pointing out buildings of interest and mentioning historical events that meant nothing to Derian. He tried to take note of everything though, in case, as with Rahniseeta's story about the origin of the gods there proved to be something of importance buried in the rambling tales.

Before leaving the city proper, Varjuna drove to a point from which they had a clear view of the bay.

"Those are Misheemnekuru, the islands where the yarimaimalom dwell," he said, pointing with the butt of his driving whip.

Derian would have had no trouble finding them, even without Varjuna's pointer.

"They're huge!" he said, looking at the curving green outlined by sparkling blue waters.

"Of course," Varjuna said. "They must be to support the populations there—not only the wolves, but great cats and small foxes, bear, raccoons, deer, elk, and more. There are several islands, most close enough that the larger animals can swim between them. Most of the islands possess high ground as well, so that the animals can get to safety in storm season."

Derian nodded, noticing that no matter how close the islands were to each other, they were still far enough from land that he wondered if anything without wings could leave them. Otters and beavers might, but wolves?

He held his thoughts, moving to a safer topic.

"How about horses? Are there wild herds?"

Varjuna shook his head. "Not there, though there are some in a preserve near u-Bishinti. We do not let our domestic horses roam, of course. The farmers complain enough about the deer and rabbits."

"Sounds like home," Derian chuckled.

But u-Bishinti, when he saw it spread out in the green vale outside the city, was nothing like home.

Prancing Steed Stables was a good working stable, but its stables and storage barns were built for function, not beauty. Even the building where Colby Carter had his offices had begun life as a hay barn, and over half of it still served as a tack room. Probably the most ornamental thing about it was the portrait of Roanne that decorated the wooden sign that swung outside of Colby's office.

Derian felt a familiar tightness in his chest as he thought of the chestnut mare and his absent family, and concentrated on the complex rather than remember. Varjuna had chosen to approach via a road that provided an overlook, and Derian knew from the expectant quiet with which the other drove that Varjuna was waiting for him to comment.

"It's incredible," Derian said, glad that Barnet's language lessons had included a few superlatives.

"Begun in the days when the Old Country rulers were still here," Varjuna said, "but we've added to it and maintained it. Frankly, I think even they'd be impressed."

"No doubt," Derian agreed.

He guessed that the small step-pyramid temple roughly central to the complex was one of the original buildings. Its surface tiles were silvery white and grass green, colors he had learned were associated with Air and Earth—even as horses were.

However, the elaborate exterior ornamentation was not reserved for the temple. Buildings that just had to be stables, judging from what he could see through the doors and windows now opened to the pleasant warmth of the spring day, also came in for a fair share of tile or enameled brick. Even the trim on the hay barns and sheds was carved with ornamental complexity.

"We have our own smithy," Varjuna was saying complacently. "Two, actually, one devoted almost exclusively to shoeing, another for work on tack. We have a leather shop, though not a tannery. The smell upsets the horses—people, too."

He grinned and, clucking to the bay, started the descent.

"How many horses do you have here?" Derian asked.

"Hundreds," Varjuna said casually, "if one counts new foals, young horses being trained, brood mares, and the like. There are those which have been brought in to be tested. They stay in that pale grey stable to the right."

He pointed with his driving whip.

"Tested?" was all Derian could think to say.

"For special gifts," Varjuna explained. "The Wise Horses have the gods' ear. That goes without saying, but many a lesser animal is gifted as well. Then, too, we keep an eye open for good prospects for breeding or for such mundane uses as riding and driving. Of all the temples, we are probably the only one that earns far more than it takes in taxes."

He paused, then added in the tone of one who is doing his best to be fair, "The Temple of the Cold Bloods does very well in earnings, too, as does the Temple of Sea Beasts."

Derian would have liked to ask about this, but they had dropped closer to the pastures, and his mouth was all but hanging open at the wide selection of magnificent horseflesh idly grazing. Any one of the horses would have been the prize of a noble's stable, and yet from how they were set in this outlying pasture Derian had the feeling that these were the least prized of the animals.

For the first time, Derian found himself really thinking about meeting a horse who was to other horses what Blind Seer was to the usual wolf. At first he felt exhilarated, then, suddenly, very shy.

"We also have quarters here," Varjuna was saying, "for those of us who are kidisdum of the horses. Happily, the living areas are set where the winds from the bay keep off most of the flies. There comes many a hot day in summer where I give thanks to whoever laid out the general lines of this complex. If you look up there . . ."

Again the whip pointed.

"You'll see them. Dormitory arrangements in most cases with communal dining— as you must have learned in the Temple of the Cold Bloods that's pretty typical—but since I am ikidisdu I get a nice place all for myself and my family. Can't see it from this angle, but our house overlooks the entirety of u-Bishinti and even offers a glimpse of the sea."

"It's a city," Derian said, awed, "a city dedicated to horses."

"A town at least," Varjuna said, obviously pleased with Derian's reaction.

"Is there something like this for each type of animal?" Derian asked.

"Oh, no!" Varjuna laughed. "Only for the horses. There has been talk from time to time about setting up facilities for cattle and sheep, but the dominant theological opinion is that the gods are more inclined to speak their will to the wild varieties of animals. Horses have always been viewed as an exception, though. Maybe it's because we don't raise them in order to eat them."

"Maybe," Derian echoed, completely overwhelmed. "You're going to have to explain to me which animals talk to the gods and which don't."

Varjuna nodded. "There will be time for that, especially if you choose to stay with us. I hope you realize that part of the reason for taking you here is that I'm going to do my best to try to persuade you."

"That's fine," Derian said, and for a long moment he didn't really care if Varjuna meant for life or just for as long as Firekeeper was out visiting the wolves. "That's just fine."

As they drove into the complex, Derian lost his overview, but it hardly mattered. There were more horses to look at, and he could hardly decide in which direction to turn his head. There were mares with spindly-legged foals at their sides; herds of last year's colts and fillies, not yet seriously into their training; mixed herds of more mature animals. Here and there were horses evidently well past their prime, but still well cared-for. This last warmed Derian's heart toward Varjuna and his people. Derian well knew how expensive horses were to feed, and most of the time his parents sold the older animals—but one or two were given honorable retirement.

In arenas and on tracks, horses were being trained for both riding and driving. Derian swallowed a grin when he saw how carefully the grooms and trainers didn't stop work. Only a few of the older men and women waved, and these most casually. None stopped to gape at the red-haired stranger.

"So they knew I was coming," he said to Varjuna, and Varjuna had the grace to look mildly embarrassed.

"Perhaps you have no idea how important your arrival is," the ikidisdu said.

Derian decided to tackle this directly.

"I don't have any idea at all," he said. "Harjeedian says little and until this morning's reception we saw only him, his sister, and a few servants. The servants weren't talking, and Harjeedian and Rahniseeta seemed mostly interested in preparing us for today."

"You heard nothing on the ship?"

"Nothing."

Varjuna shrugged. "I am ikidisdu of horses, but I don't make policy. It is a jaguar year, too, so we are very much out of the loop."

Derian nodded, though he didn't quite understand why this should be. Didn't Fire need Air and Earth or whatever it was the horses represented? He didn't know how to ask that in his limited Liglimosh, so he kept silent.

At last Varjuna drew the carriage to a halt in front of the temple. The stableboy, who had been riding nearly forgotten in the back, leapt down and took charge of the pretty little bay and the vehicle. Varjuna took charge of Derian.

The sun had dropped appreciably lower by the time Varjuna had finished showing fountains from which water was piped directly to the various barns, box stalls with walls padded so that the horses would not damage their coats, barns piled high with choice grain, hay, and bedding. And, of course, a sampling of the magnificent horses. With a sudden shock of guilt, Derian recalled Firekeeper, waiting back at the main temple in Heeranenahalm.

He realized he had better get back to her before full dark had fallen and she was inspired to prowl.

"I need to go back to the city," he said to Varjuna.

Varjuna looked instantly disappointed.

"I had hoped you would dine with my family."

Derian looked apologetic.

"I really must return to Lady Blysse. She will be expecting me."

Varjuna spoke almost as if reciting a proverb, "Wolves are difficult to keep waiting."

Derian grinned. "Impossible."

"There is so much more I'd like to show you," Varjuna said. "If I promise to return you by a more rapid road than before, can you tarry a bit longer?"

"Only a bit," Derian said. "I really should be back before twilight."

Varjuna nodded crisply. "I can do that without even raising a sweat on the horses. I don't want to send you away without introducing you to at least a few of the Wise Horses."

The sensation of nervous anticipation came back in full force.

"Lead on," Derian said. He swallowed an urge to say, "You mean we haven't seen them already?," because he knew they hadn't.

"The Wise Horses are free to use any of the pastures," Varjuna said, "and some enjoy mingling with the lesser horses. Actually, they're a great help in keeping order among the young uncut males. They seem to be able to control them—talk sense to them, as we like to put it. However, they like their privacy as well, so we have facilities . . ."

Derian didn't hear another word he spoke. He had seen his first Wise Horse, and the sight took every bit of attention he had to spare.

He had expected the Wise Horses to be outsized, as Blind Seer was to the more usual wolves, but though the Wise Horse that was walking across the smooth stretch of spring pasturage toward them stood easily as tall as a warhorse, it was no larger. What was incredible about it was the delicacy of its lines.

The nostrils that flared to catch Derian's scent were almost dainty, the ears sharp and perky, the bone structure—while amply strong to carry the muscles that rippled over it—was without the least trace of heaviness. In the arch of the neck, the straightness of the leg, in every line of the horse's frame there was raw power, but no clumsiness.

No wonder, Derian thought, *these people think that the horse is some sort of wedding of Air and Earth.*

Only after his horseman's eye had finished drinking in the horse's incredibly perfect lines did Derian notice what another person would have noted from the start. The horse's markings were a mixture of black and white. These were not the orderly pattern of stockings against a solid coat that Roanne had borne, nor yet the splashing of blaze or star or stripe as adorned so many ordinary horses, nor even the occasional splash of white across the belly that might mark an otherwise solid coat.

The Wise Horse was colored with a wild defiance of what humans would have called order. His coat was more black than white, the head solid black but for a thin white blaze. Behind the ears, running along the mane, was a patch of white nearly half the length of the neck. It mixed snow into the long flowing hairs of the mane. There was white patched along the horse's flanks as well, including four white stockings, each well over the horse's knees, the hind set going right onto the rump. Thus the horse's tail was particolored as well, and the mixture of white and black somehow made it seem longer and fuller.

"High Stepping Horse!" Derian swore softly in Pellish. "Your image before me!"

He dashed sudden tears from his eyes, feeling as if he was being disloyal to Roanne's memory, but aware that he had never seen a more beautiful horse in all his life.

"This is Eshinarvash," Varjuna said, and Derian mentally translated the name as meaning something like "Wind Runner." "He is the chosen ambassador of his people to us this moonspan."

"Ambassador?" Derian said, speaking the first word that came to his mouth.

"Go-between," Varjuna said, obviously not certain Derian had understood him. "We can't expect the entire herd to come when we have a question. The designated ambassador keeps watch, and if another must be summoned, takes care of the matter."

Varjuna lowered his voice slightly. "It gives the younger stallions something to make them feel important. There are only so many mares, after all, and not all of them care to breed."

Derian wanted to press his hands to his ears, unable to grasp any more. Instead he laid his hand flat so Eshinarvash could sniff it. He felt the lips, curiously dry, move over his hand, and the horse blow softly.

"Don't have any carrots or sugar," Derian said, reverting to Pellish.

He leaned forward and blew gently into the horse's nostrils, giving him his scent as Colby had taught him to do. Eshinarvash breathed back, and then pulled away, but only far enough to lip Derian's hair with apparent curiosity.

"He likes you," Varjuna said, not as a man would about a pet, but as a man might translate for a friend with laryngitis, "and he's never seen hair the color of Fire before."

Derian pulled his hair away, but reached up to scratch the horse behind his ears. Even with his height, he had to stretch.

"And I have never seen a horse so magnificently colored," Derian replied. "I've seen the occasional patched or piebald, but usually they're poor creatures, from wild stock. They lack the shine—the elegance."

"And what stock do you think these are?" Varjuna said with a laugh. "No human puts stud to mare among the Wise Horses. They work these matters out for themselves. I'll tell you something strange, though. Time and again someone decides to put a Wise Horse in with the mares, hoping, you know, to improve the strain, but never has the stud leapt the mare—not even when she presented and flirted. They're aware of the differences between them, and the Wise Horses won't breed the lesser."

"I'll believe you," Derian said, "though it's more the pity. What foals this one would throw!"

"Much like his sire," Varjuna agreed. "The black and white patterning runs true in that family."

"Then all the Wise Horses aren't black and white?" Derian asked.

"Oh, no. Chestnuts, greys, bays, but almost always mixed with white. The patterning differs, too. Eshinarvash comes from a line that does these wonderful patches, like clouds against the night sky, but there are those who are more spotted than patched. Then again, there are occasionally solid ones—duns and greys—but even these aren't solid, not really. They have the heavy barring along the spine and usually darker points."

"I'd love to see a herd of the Wise Horses," Derian said dreamily.

"You can," Varjuna said, "but only if you stay with us. We don't have time if you're to get back to the city on time."

Derian reluctantly let his hand drop from Eshinarvash's crest.

"You're right. Thank you, Eshinarvash, for letting me make your acquaintance."

His knowledge of Blind Seer kept Derian from being completely astonished when Eshinarvash dipped his head in evident acknowledgment. Varjuna was definitely pleased. However, the pleasure on his face shifted to mild astonishment when Eshinarvash reached up and tugged on a heavy piece of rope set on the edge of the fence. This opened the gate, and the Wise Horse walked through.

Eshinarvash came over to Derian and stomped his forehoof lightly against the turf.

Derian glanced at Varjuna, certain that something more than another neck scratch was being requested.

"He's offering," Varjuna said with a certain amount of awe, "to take you back to the city himself."

Derian shared the other man's awe and took a step back. Varjuna misinterpreted this as uncertainty.

"Can you ride bareback?" he asked. "The Wise Horses suffer a saddle from time to time—it protects their back and our behinds—but we do not keep such here."

Derian nodded. "I can ride bareback. I just wanted to make sure it was acceptable that I ride one of them."

"Whatever is acceptable to the horse," Varjuna said, "is acceptable to their keeper. Use the fence rails as a mounting block, or I can give you a hand-up."

But Eshinarvash already had the matter under control. He knelt with contained grace, bringing himself close enough to the ground that Derian could get astride with ease. There was nothing humbling about the gesture—it was more like a parent bending to take up a child.

Without further delay, Derian accepted the invitation, glad that he had not restricted his riding to relatively smaller horses like Roanne, but in his employ for Earl Kestrel had ridden warhorses as well.

"Tell Eshinarvash where you wish to go," Varjuna said, "and he will take you there. He knows the city well enough to find any of the temples."

Derian was careful to speak Liglimosh, though he wondered if the horse might actually understand all languages.

"I need to go to u-Nahal," he said, "in Heeranenahalm."

Eshinarvash blew out through his nose in acknowledgment and began to walk.

Varjuna called hastily, "I hope we will see you again."

"Me, too," Derian replied, setting himself more firmly and hoping Eshinarvash wouldn't mind his rider gripping his mane.

Then the Wise Horse moved from a walk into the smoothest canter Derian had ever had the pleasure to experience and carried him across the mellowing green of the late-afternoon fields.

Their route took them to the west of the main city, through farmland, orchards, and forests that showed ample evidence in their cleared riding trails and well-maintained bridges that they were anything but wild lands.

Game parks, Derian thought, *maybe for hunting.*

He remembered the jaguar, Truth, and the thought that her kind might hunt here unsettled him and made him scan the tree limbs wherever they extended over the trail. He reminded himself that his mount was a Wise Horse. Even a more usual horse would shy at the scent of predators—a thing that had made Firekeeper's association with horses difficult. Certainly a Wise Horse would be at least as sensitive.

But what if the yarimaimalom don't want us here? he thought, remembering how the Royal Beasts had reacted to the efforts at settling the lands west of Hawk Haven's portion of the Iron Mountains. *What if we're upsetting their orderly existence? Certainly Firekeeper is finding her ideas upset. What if these yarimaimalom are finding their own ideas upset?*

The more Derian let his thoughts run down those courses, the less delight he took in Eshinarvash's smooth gait and the speed at which they traveled. He found himself eyeing the side of the trail, wondering if he would be safer if he jumped off and made his own way.

Then, of course, he would be a strange red-haired man out in countryside where the dark-haired inhabitants might not have heard of his coming. They might be afraid, or hostile. Then, too, Derian had no idea how long it would take him to reach the city on foot, and he didn't fancy making the journey after dark.

So despite his trepidations, Derian remained astride Eshinarvash. In the end, nothing jumped from the tree branches, nor did Eshinarvash throw him and leave him to the wolves. Instead, the Wise Horse slowed as the blocky heights of u-Nahal came to dominate the horizon, came to a walk along what must be the hindmost wall of those temple gardens, came to a halt next to a door in that wall.

Eshinarvash bent his head and blew, shaking his skin as he might to dislodge a fly. Derian took the hint and slid to the ground.

"Thank you for bringing me back," Derian said in Liglimosh. "I hope I'll see you again."

Eshinarvash blew again and lipped at Derian's hair, then without further delay turned away, heading back from where he had come.

Derian watched the receding figure for a long moment, then turned to the gate. He was not surprised to find that the latch rose at his touch. A doorman within pulled the door open and motioned Derian inside.

In the garden the heady aroma of flowers combined with the sleepy sounds of birds settling into the boughs, for the night gave dimension to the gathering dusk. Derian accepted the small candle lantern the doorman gave him, and with its light to illuminate the path, went off to find Firekeeper.

XI

AFTER DERIAN LEFT WITH VARJUNA, Firekeeper and Blind Seer inspected the whole of u-Nahal's gardens. They were more extensive than they had seemed from outside the walls. Claw marks on trees and sprays of acrid scent showed that the jaguar had claimed them for her own, but this did not trouble Firekeeper. Wolf sign would have given her reason to feel concern, but all she found was so very faint as to be nearly gone. Wolf or wolves had been here then, but probably not for a moonspan or more.

Firekeeper and Blind Seer had a good run before finding a quiet grotto on some soft grass alongside a burbling spring and falling asleep. They awoke as the light was fading, alerted by the sound of someone coming along one of the paths.

There had been others who had walked in the garden while they rested, but if they had seen the pair they had not offered any threat, so wolf and woman had settled back into sleep. This time it was not threat that brought them fully awake, but the awareness that they knew those footsteps, even before they heard Derian call softly, "Firekeeper? Blind Seer?"

"Here," Firekeeper replied.

Derian stopped and she realized his eyes were having difficulty finding them amid the dusk and shadow. His dependence on the light from the candle he carried didn't help his night vision, but she couldn't seem to get him to understand that. His reply was always the same.

"But when there is no light, my eyes cannot make any."

Firekeeper stepped forward so that the edge of the pale circle of candlelight touched her, and Derian smiled.

"So you did stay in the gardens," he said. "I was imagining going door-to-door looking for you."

"You smell like horse," she said, her nostrils flaring as she tried to analyze a subtle difference in the scent. "You see many horses."

"Many," Derian said, coming to them. "Is this a good place for us to talk? Private, I mean. Even if we're speaking Pellish, I'd prefer not to be overheard."

Firekeeper glanced at Blind Seer and the wolf panted laughter.

"Tell Fox Hair that even through the reek of horse and the scent of burning wax I can tell that no one larger than a rabbit is near."

Derian accepted this, and settled cross-legged on the grass.

"Hungry?" Firekeeper asked.

"Not really," Derian said. "Varjuna gave me bread and cheese. He was showing off the bakery. Firekeeper, you should see the place! It's an entire city—well, maybe town would be more accurate—devoted to horses."

"You like then?"

"It was amazing."

Derian started telling about u-Bishinti, and even as he told about barns and pastures, stalls and blacksmiths, Firekeeper could tell he was keeping the best for last.

"And Firekeeper," he concluded, "I met a Royal Horse. He was called Eshinarvash, that means 'Wind Runner,' and he was black and white in the most astonishing patches—like he was a black horse on whom someone splashed whitewash. And his gaits—I've never ridden any horse with such power who also carried himself so smoothly."

Firekeeper listened, taking pleasure in her friend's enthusiasm, and feeling some relief that Derian's genuine interest in Varjuna's domain would make it easier for her to do what she had decided she must. Finally, Derian's rhapsodies ebbed to contented silence.

"I would like to meet this horse," Firekeeper began. "His kind might not even fear Blind Seer."

The wolf beat his tail on the ground, chuckling at the idea.

"If a Wise Horse would carry you," Derian agreed, "you might actually have a decent mount, but they're not just any horse, just like Blind Seer isn't just any wolf."

"I know," Firekeeper said, a bit annoyed that Derian would think she could forget the difference between the Royal Beasts and any other. "But I not want to ride a horse. I want to go see island wolves. I have thinked . . ."

"Thought."

"And I think it not be as good for seeing them if you come with. Is going to be hard to make them know me wolf. Harder if I am watching for another human."

"Makes sense," Derian replied. "And I have to admit I'm not really enthusiastic about going to an island where the animals apparently dictate policy. What if they decide I'm trouble and tell their pet humans to get rid of me? I don't like all this talk of omens and the way no one seems to question them."

"Not me either," Firekeeper agreed. "But will you be safe without me?"

"I could ask the same thing," Derian countered. "Neither of us has been safe since we stepped aboard that boat back at Eagle's Nest. Whatever we do, we're taking risks, but this way you can learn something about these wolves—and the other Royal Beasts kept on those islands. I know you. Even if someone offered to put us on a ship for home this minute you wouldn't go now, not until you understand more."

Firekeeper grimaced at the thought of getting on any ship at any time, but Derian's words made her remember something.

"True," she said, "and if you are here, you can try to learn what is to north of Liglim and how we might go home by land. Ship is not how I want to go, but even if I do, we cannot sail ship, not even with Barnet's help—if he would help."

"I think he would," Derian replied thoughtfully. "I think he resents not being permitted to leave, and he's no Waln Endbrook to be lulled with sweet words about ambassadorial appointments."

"You keep eye on Barnet?" Firekeeper asked, "even if you is not in city?"

"I can try," Derian agreed. "I suspect it will be fairly easy. I don't think I'll escape being a language tutor. I rather suspect access to Varjuna's stables is being offered as a bribe to keep me happy. What I can't figure out is why my happiness should matter."

"I notice, too," Firekeeper said, thinking how Harjeedian's body language toward Derian had altered over the last day or so. "Is almost like Harjeedian is almost to grovel, and all the rest wait to see if you grow great fangs. Use this, I think."

"I will," Derian agreed, "though it would be easier if I knew what I was using."

"Yes," Firekeeper said. "So while I go see my people, you stay here. I think you have too much to do, not too little. I only wish we could howl to each other across the waters."

"Me, too. I don't suppose," Derian paused, obviously not certain how she was going to take his question, "that you've seen any of the wingéd folk since we've been here. One of them could carry messages—simple picture ones, like an 'x' "—he drew one in the air with his finger—"for all is well and a circle for all is not."

Firekeeper knew that Derian was aware how she felt about the Royal Beasts becoming slaves to humans. Doubtless that was why he hadn't teased her again about her unwillingness to learn to read and write. She concentrated on the first part of his question to play down her nagging sense that he was perfectly right about the need for her to learn to write.

"I have not seen so far," she said, "and have wondered. I will look while I am at islands. If I can find a wingéd folk who will help, then I will send as you say."

"And," Blind Seer said, feeling no desire to spare Firekeeper, *"It would really make things easier if you would learn to read and write."*

Firekeeper kicked him gently, covering the action by leaping to her feet.

"Then we is settled," she said. "Tonight is too dark, I think, by how humans are, and I have no wish to go back to snake place. Will you go there or sleep here?"

Derian rose and dusted grass off his trousers.

"I'll go back to the Temple of the Cold Bloods," he said. "That way I can tell Harjeedian what we have decided. After all, they're going to have to arrange a boat to take you two to the islands."

Firekeeper sighed. She'd been trying hard not to think about boats. "I know. I know."

RAHNISEETA WAS WATCHING UNOBTRUSIVELY from the main gate into the u-Nahal compound, hoping to see any of the three who had vanished earlier that day. A note had come from Varjuna saying that Derian should have reached the city before dusk. A doorkeeper had reported letting Derian into the gardens, but the redhead had not come forward. Tiridanti had insisted he be given his privacy. Of Lady Blysse and Blind Seer, nothing had been seen for hours.

Rahniseeta filled her time by musing over the possible implications of the other information in Varjuna's letter—that Derian had been carried back to the city by Eshinarvash, one of the Wise Horses—when the young man who so occupied her thoughts came down the path.

The candle lantern he carried was sparking and guttering, and he paused to blow it out when he came into the outer ring of light shed by the temple's lanterns. Rahniseeta stepped forward then, taking care not to startle him.

"I am here," she said, "to see if there is anything you want, and to guide you if you wish to be taken somewhere."

Harjeedian had told her she must be very careful to avoid saying something that would make it seem as if the parole extended by Ahmyndisdu Tiridanti was being rescinded. They had already learned from Barnet's anger at having his return to sea delayed that these northern people had a curious idea of what was due to any living creature. Rahniseeta supposed it must have something to do with their having no real gods to give them omens.

Derian smiled at her, for once not seeming in the least distracted or awkward.

"I would not mind something to eat," he said politely in his awkward but understandable rendition of the language of the Liglimo, "but I think that can wait until I tell someone what courses of action Lady Blysse and I have decided to follow. Would Harjeedian be the one to tell, or should I ask to speak with Ahmyndisdu Tiridanti?"

Since Rahniseeta had no immediate knowledge where Tiridanti was to be found, and since she thought Harjeedian would benefit from bearing the news to u-Liall, she worded her reply accordingly.

"Let me take you to Harjeedian. He is wiser than I in the ways of the disdum."

Derian Counselor fell into step beside her without comment, though she wondered if the twinkle in his eye was an indication that he suspected what game she played, or just a trick of firelight on those unsettlingly light eyes of his. Her people's eyes ran to shades of brown, but never had she seen eyes like these, in which the brown mixed in equal parts with green so that the color changed according to the light.

Is this another sign he is a maimalodalu? she thought. *They are supposed to be able to change their shapes. Perhaps their eyes do not remain the same color.*

But then she thought of Lady Blysse, who was beast-souled if anyone living was beast-souled. Lady Blysse's eyes always remained a brown so dark as to be almost black, so then maybe eyes offered no indication of nature.

"Did you have a good visit to u-Bishinti?" she asked.

"Very. I have never seen such a facility before—never even imagined that one could exist. I understand that some horse breeders in Stonehold have large establishments, but I am certain that they do not spend time adorning their stables with enameled brick and tile, nor do they have such beautiful horses."

Rahniseeta felt pleased, though she had nothing to do with u-Bishinti. She wondered if Derian would be equally impressed with the inner portions of the Temple of the Cold Bloods. The nesting areas were wonderful, as were some of the gardens where the oracular snakes dwelled.

Then again, Derian might not be as pleased. Horses did not usually care for snakes, and if Derian was a maimalodalu of the horse persuasion, well, no wonder he had not been happy residing in their temple!

But Derian showed no resistance to returning to the Temple of the Cold Bloods. Indeed, he smiled slightly when he glanced up at the magnificent statue of the coiled rattlesnake that adorned the top of the step pyramid. As with all the totemic representations, it was illuminated at night, an effect best appreciated from outside the walls of the temple quarter, for then it was as if the various animals moved in the flickering firelight.

Rahniseeta resolved to take the outlanders to see the display some night. Even small children with no sense of the complexities of religion liked the sight, so they should, too, and it would be something in the way of an apology for how they had been kept—she considered the best way to word it—"quarantined" from the general population.

Finding Harjeedian was not difficult, as he was waiting in the main area of the Temple of the Cold Bloods complex on the chance that either Derian or Firekeeper might return there on their own. Barnet had done so, his attitude (according to the note Harjeedian had sent Rahniseeta) somewhat forlorn, like that of a child who has run away only to find that the world outside his parents' house is not as inviting as he had imagined.

Rahniseeta did not doubt that other temples would have been glad to take Barnet in, but he would have rapidly realized that they wanted him for much the same reason as did the Temple of the Cold Bloods, and at least within the Temple of the Cold Bloods there were a few people who spoke his language.

Now Harjeedian stepped forward to greet Derian with very real warmth.

"You have returned to us," he said. "May I offer you anything in the way of hospitality?"

"I wouldn't mind a meal," Derian replied, "and unless you have a problem with talking business while we eat, I can fill you in then."

Harjeedian most emphatically did not have a problem with this, and he turned to Rahniseeta.

"Could we eat in our suite?"

"Definitely," she said.

She knew her brother was wondering if the suite was neat enough for entertaining. He could never keep track of what day the maids came.

"Do you mind eating in our rooms?" Harjeedian asked Derian. "My sister and I share a small suite. Otherwise, we must go to the dining halls. Given your celebrity, I think we would be frequently interrupted."

"That would be fine," Derian replied.

"Rahniseeta," Harjeedian said, "would you take care of ordering our meal? You have some idea of what foods our northern guest prefers."

Rahniseeta forced a smile and hurried away, fuming a little. She had been at her vigil for many hours and Harjeedian's only thanks was to send her on another errand. However, now was not the time to raise the matter.

Placing the order and arranging for it to be carried to their suite did not take long, and she returned just as Harjeedian was completing what had evidently been a short tour.

"So you see," he concluded with a smile, "we did not accommodate you any differently than we do ourselves."

Derian looked around the suite, which, with its two sleeping rooms, covered common area, and small courtyard, was indeed much like the quarters he shared with Barnet and Lady Blysse.

"I suppose so," he replied, "but I think it makes a great deal of difference whether the doors open to your command or only to another's."

"Omens," Harjeedian said, using the universally accepted excuse. Rahniseeta could see that Derian did not accept it. "Now the omens have changed and you will find yourself free to come and go as you wish."

"I am glad to know that," Derian said politely, "and I hope your welcome will not alter if I tell you that I have decided to stay at least some of the time with Varjuna at u-Bishinti."

"Of course not," Harjeedian said. "Creatures of Earth and Water and those of Earth and Air are closely related. We are very happy to share you."

"Does this mean," Derian asked, looking perhaps more puzzled than the incisiveness of his question indicated, "that were I to say I was going to reside within the Temple of Felines—I understand they are considered more creatures of Fire than anything else—that I would be less welcome?"

Rahniseeta was proud of her brother's composure, for though Derian might not have realized it, he was prying into matters that led to long and angry debate among the theologians. Among the common folk, the calmer elements were often thanked for the good things in life, while the unpredictable elements were blamed for the evil. Fire's disdum in particular resented this, reminding over and over again how much humanity owed to Fire and how humanity had been created specifically to acknowledge Fire's good gifts.

But Harjeedian's reply stayed away from troublesome matters of theology.

"You will always be welcome here. No element is greater than the rest, nor is there enmity between us."

The arrival of the servants with trays of food saved them from further awkward discussion. Rahniseeta had learned that Derian liked mildly spicy food, especially if there was beer with which to wash it down. Thus far he had not drunk more than was wise, but if he chose to do so, and if that choosing loosened his tongue, was she to blame?

Harjeedian did not dismiss Rahniseeta, as she had half expected, but instead motioned for her to take a seat at the table. He had the servants set the platters in the center of the table where they could all easily reach, then dismissed them. The pitcher of beer was set near Derian, the pitcher of cool water between Rahniseeta and Harjeedian.

"I thought we would eat informally," Harjeedian said, filling Derian's beer glass, then his own and Rahniseeta's. "Our quarters are not really the place to stand on ceremony."

"Fine with me," Derian said. He ladled himself a portion of spiced chicken and raisins mixed with rice. "I am not a very ceremonial person."

They briefly discussed the different dishes, just as if this were a more typical dinner party, and then Derian himself turned the conversation to business.

"I hope you don't mind," he began, "but I don't know how long it will take you to make arrangements."

"Arrangements?" Harjeedian asked.

"Lady Blysse has decided she wants to go to the islands and see the wolves. I didn't know whether you need to . . ." He looked rather uncomfortable. "I don't know, see if they're receiving visitors or something?"

Rahniseeta lost part of what came next because they switched to Pellish, but afterward she gathered that Derian wasn't certain how one went about visiting yarimaimalom. Apparently, his culture had all sorts of different rules for making visits based on the social rank of those involved, and he wasn't certain where the yarimaimalom were placed—not surprisingly, since his first introduction to the local yarimaimalom had been Truth, and the great cats were notoriously haughty. He might have had a different impression if it had been a bear year.

After he understood why Derian was concerned, Harjeedian explained that there was no established protocol.

"It varies from type to type," he said. "I am certain that Lady Blysse knows what is proper among wolves."

"I hope so," Derian said. "Having seen what passes for play between Firekeeper and Blind Seer, I worry about her if someone wants to fight."

Harjeedian frowned. Rahniseeta thought he might enjoy seeing the wolf-woman humbled, but he definitely did not want her killed.

"Is there anything I should offer her in the way of equipment?"

Derian considered. "Bow and arrows might be nice, in case she needs to hunt. Whetstone and oil for her knife. You returned her flint and steel, so that's fine. And she might want tougher clothing. You'd need to ask her."

Harjeedian nodded. "And when am I likely to have an opportunity?"

"Tonight, if you want," Derian said. "I think she's staying in the u-Nahal gardens. She never has been much for sleeping indoors. We could walk over after dinner."

"That would be fine," Harjeedian said. "Will you be sleeping here?"

"I would prefer that," Derian said. He gave a half-grin. "Now that I know the doors will open, I imagine I'll be pretty comfortable. Is Barnet still here?"

"He is," Harjeedian said.

Derian's expression was so noncommittal that Rahniseeta guessed that despite Barnet's charm and the ease with which the two men had conversed in her presence, there was still some resentment on Derian's part regarding Barnet's role in their invitation to u-Seeheera.

Realizing that Derian was not going to say anything more, Harjeedian filled the silence before it could become awkward.

"In the morning, I can arrange for a boat to take Lady Blysse to Misheemnekuru. There are several of appropriate size always available to the temples. The only thing that could alter our plans is the weather, and the omens are that it will continue fair."

Derian nodded, and the conversation shifted to a general discussion of how the local message service worked. Since he would be staying in various temple facilities, he could simply use the established courier system.

"Transportation is easily arranged as well," Harjeedian concluded, "and, of course, your needs in the way of food and clothing will be met as a small thanks for the knowledge you will share with us."

Derian nodded. "It seems fair that I teach Pellish to those who can put up with me as a teacher. Be warned, I do not have Barnet's facility for instruction."

"I shall keep that in mind," Harjeedian assured him.

"One more thing," Derian said, and all the awkwardness that had left him earlier returned. "There was a time when you said I might be permitted to write my parents so they wouldn't worry."

"Yes?"

"We've been gone awhile. I don't know exactly how long a message sent from here will take to reach them. They're not worrying now, but I'd prefer they didn't have reason to start."

Harjeedian smiled, as well he might, for this was the strongest indication they had been given that the northerners were coming to view themselves as guests rather than captives.

"Arrangements can be made," he said. "All I ask is that you not mention where you are—even to direction—or as to how you came here."

"I can do that."

"I believe there are already writing implements in your quarters."

"There are," Derian said. "Then you'll send a letter if I write one?"

"With great pleasure." Harjeedian looked at the nearly empty trays spread before them. "Are you finished eating?"

Derian nodded. "The meal was very excellent."

"Then I think it would be wise if we located Lady Blysse. That way she will know what arrangements will be made, and I will have opportunity to acquire what equipment she desires."

"Sounds good," Derian agreed.

He rose and offered Rahniseeta a bow after the fashion of his own country, following it with a fairly good rendition of the pulled-hands gesture used for polite leavetakings between those who were not kin or close friends.

Rahniseeta offered him the same, and a delighted smile.

"You are learning so much, so quickly," she said.

"Thank you, miss," Derian replied. "I hope I'll have opportunity to visit with you again."

"Frequently, I am sure. Harjeedian wishes me to learn Pellish so I may better assist him."

Derian nodded, and the two men departed, Harjeedian promising he would be back before long.

"Wait up for me," he suggested to Rahniseeta in a low voice. "I have something to say to you."

Rahniseeta agreed without difficulty. The day had been very full, and she was glad to have the opportunity to reflect. There was also a little poem she had been working on, and this would certainly keep her occupied. She was seated at the now clean table, puzzling over how to make the meter of line work without forcing the meaning, when Harjeedian returned.

She had expected his step to be lighter, but it remained measured, a sign that he was deep in thought. Therefore, she said nothing, continuing with her composition as if she were alone. Beneath her calm exterior, her temper was rising. She was getting a bit tired of how her brother treated her as nothing more than an extension of his own will.

"Rahniseeta," Harjeedian said after a long pause, "I think it would be wise if you went out of your way to be pleasant to Derian Counselor."

Rahniseeta put on her most neutral expression. "I apologize, brother, if I have been less than pleasant."

"Don't be impossible, Rahni," Harjeedian replied. "I wasn't criticizing you."

"Than what were you doing?"

He looked completely astonished. "Simply making a request that you be pleasant to our guest."

"Very well," Rahniseeta said. "I have been and I shall continue to be so."

She rose and began to gather up her papers.

"Rahni . . ."

There was a warning note in Harjeedian's voice, but she kept on as if she hadn't noticed.

"Rahniseeta."

"Yes."

"What is wrong with you?"

She set her papers down and leaned both arms on the table, pressing down with all the anger she could not otherwise express. Nor did she raise her voice when she spoke. The walls within the Temple of the Cold Bloods were thick, but the weather was warm. Too many doors and windows were open for her to be sure her voice wouldn't carry. However, the tightness in her voice made quite clear she was less than happy.

"What is wrong? Perhaps the fact that for the last several days I have been watching over the strangers—arranging for their meals, clothing, and entertainment—and you have yet to say anything other than 'Rahniseeta, I think you should . . . ' Perhaps it is that I have repeatedly placed myself at tremendous risk, allowing myself to be shut in with two men, a crazy woman, and a wolf, and you don't seem to realize my danger? Perhaps it is that today I attended a meeting of u-Liall—a highly important meeting of the type one of my rank does not usually attend, unless deaf and dumb."

Harjeedian interrupted her, "Rahniseeta, don't be ridiculous. You have never been in any real danger. U-Liall's meeting was private, yes, but nothing sensitive was discussed."

"But what if it had been?" she retorted.

Harjeedian shook his head dismissively. "What it could have been is not worth discussing. I am certain you would have been sent away if anything serious had arisen."

"If any had remembered I was there," Rahniseeta muttered, aware she was sulking, but unwilling to withdraw her protest now that it had been made.

Harjeedian pretended not to hear her, but moved on to another aspect of her complaint.

"As for the time you have spent with our guests, I dwelled quite closely with them for a long while on board the ship and studied them carefully. They are well enough aware of their vulnerability to treat all of us with care."

"I wish I was so certain," Rahniseeta retorted. "Every time I was alone with them I found myself remembering how you captured them by playing off Lady Blysse's fondness for Derian Counselor. What if it occurred to them to try the same? Remember, Lady Blysse was ill aboard ship. She is no longer ill and might act quite differently."

Harjeedian was trying to speak, but Rahniseeta spoke through his words.

"And do you know what bothered me the most? The knowledge that they might just overestimate my importance to you or anyone else, and that I might find myself a hostage without redemption value."

Rahniseeta sealed her lips shut, though all the pent-up worry and fear she had felt urged her to say more. Besides, she wanted to hear what Harjeedian would say in his defense. His first words were not the apology she craved, but more in the lines of an accusation.

"Rahniseeta, why didn't you say something sooner?"

"What?"

"You could have explained that you felt at risk."

"Would you have changed anything?"

"I could have reassured you that I do not think our guests would react in the fashion you feared."

"What about Lady Blysse?" Rahniseeta persisted.

"Rahni, she did not do any of the things you feared. Tomorrow she will go to Misheemnekuru. Why must you harp on things that did not happen and now are unlikely to happen?"

"Because," Rahniseeta snapped, getting to the root of her unhappiness, "I am tired of being treated as an extension of your will. Feed this one. Clothe that one. Wait here outside this temple—no matter that you have been up since dawn and had an exhausting day. Now what is it you ask? Be pleasant to this Derian—and since I have been perfectly pleasant to him, to Barnet, to everyone who so much as looks my way, I think that you want something more than mere pleasantry. Why not say precisely what you want? Do you want me to seduce him? To make him love me? To steal his secrets?"

Harjeedian thumped his fist on the table.

"Have I ever asked any such thing of you?"

"Not yet," Rahniseeta hissed, "but how long will it be? The higher you have risen within the temple, the less you have seen me as your equal. Oh, I am grateful to you, Harjeedian—you brought me with you as you rose in status. Many brothers would not have done the same. However, I am not going to pay for my comfortable room and good clothing by becoming your obedient lackey. Better that I return to the town where we were born and take up residence in our mother's hut!"

"I will not have it," Harjeedian said sternly.

"Why?" Rahniseeta replied, her emotions too high now to be stilled. "Because having a weaver of grass mats for a sister would shame the rising aridisdu? Because I am too useful to lose? Because you have other plans for me?"

"Because," Harjeedian said, rising and pulling her hands from the table so he might hold them in his, "I love you, little sister. We have been each other's support since those days of poverty. Our mother's last request was that I watch over you, but I would have done so without those words. If I have been an overweening, overly ambitious garbage-eating dog I apologize."

He raised her hands and beat his forehead against them in the second-most-humble gesture of apology—and the one that was certain to touch her heart, for it was the one used between equals.

"Will you forgive me?" he asked with true sincerity.

Rahniseeta looked at him and smiled. "Maybe. If you start explaining yourself and stop giving orders without offering thanks."

"I can manage that," Harjeedian said with a matching smile. "The short explanation now, for as you have so aptly noted, we have had a long day."

"Short then," Rahniseeta agreed, resuming her place at the table. "What did Lady Blysse want?"

"Very little," Harjeedian replied. "Offer of a hunting bow was accepted with pleasure. I also convinced her to take a few items of camping gear—though she refused my offer of a tent with real scorn. She did thank me prettily when I offered to make her up a small medical kit, and even asked me to include some of the powder I gave her for seasickness."

"So she doesn't think you wish to poison her," Rahniseeta said. "That's good."

"She knows perfectly well that I hope she will agree to teach the art of speaking with Beasts, and she cannot do that if she is dead. However, we are taking a great gamble letting her go to Misheemnekuru. They are large enough that if she does not wish to return, and sways the yarimaimalom to her way of thinking, then we will never see her again."

"Not all the yarimaimalom will agree," Rahniseeta reassured him. "I am no aridisdu nor kidisdu, but I am perfectly certain that unanimity between them is as rare as between humans."

"True. Still, if only the wolves agree to protect her, we would be hard-pressed to force her back against her will."

"Is this why we need to be pleasant to Derian Counselor?" Rahniseeta asked.

"Partially," Harjeedian said, "but not wholly. Varjuna's news that the Wise Horse carried Derian back to the city has aroused considerable conjecture as to Derian's own worth, above and beyond what he offers as a means of swaying Lady Blysse. Many will court him now. I only wish that our temple's voice not be overwhelmed—and he does not like me."

"He has little reason to do so," Rahniseeta said bluntly. "You kidnapped him and used him to manipulate his friend. I have wondered this ever since I met them. Why did you not simply issue an invitation?"

Harjeedian's face grew very still and from this Rahniseeta knew he was debating whether or not to confide matters of the disdum.

"The omens were against it," he began, and she thought she was going to have to settle for that unarguable point, but he continued, "and u-Liall and their highest counselors thought it unwise that word of our land reach the rulers of the northern realms. So far the gods have kept us out of contact with them, and after hearing what warlike people they are, I say the gods' wisdom is unchallengeable."

"And both Lady Blysse and Derian Counselor would not depart without telling more than is wished known."

"Precisely," Harjeedian said. "The letter Derian wrote to his parents is a model of conformity to our wishes in this matter. He reassures his parents as to his safety and suggests that any questions as to where he is and what he is doing be answered with misdirection."

"And how," Rahniseeta asked with genuine curiosity, "is this letter to be delivered? I did not know another vessel was going north."

"One is not," Harjeedian said. "Derian has created a problem for us by asking to write home earlier than we had imagined he would. However, when we spoke, I realized that he expected that one of the wingéd yarimaimalo would be carrying the letter. I simply did not discourage this belief."

"Clever," Rahniseeta said. "Though I am surprised he would think such a thing."

"Apparently, Lady Blysse has friends who have done her similar favors in the past."

"Then she is honored by her own land's yarimaimalom."

"So it seems," Harjeedian replied. "Now, we must both sleep. We can talk more later—and I promise I will remember that you are my sister, not my servant."

"And I," Rahniseeta said, making her own apology, "certainly will go out of my way to be pleasant to our foreign guests."

XII

SO THE WOLFLING WAS GOING to Misheemnekuru. Truth licked a paw and considered the implications of this action. She had given up trying to read the future where Firekeeper was concerned. Not only was it impossible to get a clear resolution on something that should be as clear as whether good or ill would come from this action, it was impossible to get any resolution at all. And trying to force one gave her a blinding headache.

Truth's tail snapped in annoyance as she contemplated the fact that Firekeeper seemed to exist in the deities' blind spot. It wasn't really that incredible when one considered the young woman's given name. Who could keep Fire, after all? Only someone incredibly lucky—or incredibly ignorant of the risks she took.

Then there was the wolf who accompanied her—his own name overweighed with omens and contradictions—and yet neither of the pair seemed to be able to see beyond their own immediate concerns.

Didn't they see that the fate of everything they held dear might rest upon what they did—or did not do?

⚘

"THAT GREAT LAND IS AN ISLAND?" Firekeeper asked. She tried to keep the doubt and wonder out of her voice, but from the amusement in Harjeedian's voice when he replied, she knew she had failed.

"Mostly, yes," Harjeedian said. He was seated near to where she and Blind Seer were, in the bow of the sailing vessel that was taking them to the islands. Ostensibly, he, like them, was getting out of the way of those who must run the ship. In reality, Firekeeper was sure the aridisdu was keeping watch over his two not-quite captives.

"If one wishes to be perfectly accurate," Harjeedian continued, "there are several islands situated very close to each other. However, from here it does rather look like one large island, doesn't it?"

"Island' means land surrounded on all sides by water," Firekeeper said, wanting to make absolutely certain that she understood.

"That is correct," Harjeedian said. "Our ships have sailed all around these lands—proving that they are indeed surrounded by water. However, the amount of land is large enough that such sailing is not an undertaking for an afternoon's pleasure."

Firekeeper acknowledged the truth of his statement with a wondering shake of her head. Prior to this, her knowledge of islands had been restricted to those in rivers or lakes. She knew intellectually that there must be other types of islands that were much larger. After all, hadn't Queen Valora settled for a kingdom consisting entirely of islands? However, Firekeeper now knew that she had imagined that haughty woman perched with her ousted court on something like an overgrown sandbar.

Beside her, his paws up on the side of the boat so his great head cleared the railing, Blind Seer sniffed the wind. He trusted what the odors it carried told him much more than what he saw, to accurately inform him about what was ahead. He sneezed and sniffed again.

"There must be creatures who live and die for countless generations and never see half of these islands," he commented, *"and never realize that they are cut off from true land."*

Firekeeper agreed and didn't know whether to feel happy about this or upset. Certainly her image of Royal Wolves cooped up on a small lump of dirt, imprisoned by surrounding waters, was undergoing rapid revision. The long green stretch of land that was drawing closer as the sailors adjusted the sails so the boat could move against the wind was large enough to support many wolf packs—if the hunting was good.

The wolf-woman could imagine no reason why the hunting would not be good. The wind brought the scent of plants that could not survive without ample fresh water. Birds erupted from the shoreline as the sailing boat drew closer. She thought she glimpsed the head of some swimming mammal—otter, perhaps, or beaver or muskrat. Not the game for a wolf pack, but again evidence of a thriving and healthy land.

Firekeeper gripped the rail tightly, wondering if she had been too impetuous in insisting on coming here. Perhaps she should have taken the words of the humans as spoken in honesty. Now she was about to thrust herself not among weak and miserable wolves, but among wolves who would have every right to view themselves and their territory with pride.

Her own wolves had protected her from other packs when she was small, but events of the spring before had brought ample reminder that not all of the Royal Beasts, not even all of the Royal Wolves, welcomed her. They saw her as all too human, even as many humans saw her as all too much wolf.

What would these Wise Wolves think her? More important, what could she do, surrounded on all sides by water as she would be, if they decided she was an enemy? All paths of flight would end in water, and she could not escape that way.

Blind Seer licked her hand.

"Is the motion of the boat making you feel ill?" he asked.

"No," Firekeeper said. *"A bit. What Harjeedian gave me does help."*

Firekeeper felt a bit queasy even thinking about the boat's motion. Blind Seer didn't tease her, so she guessed that maybe she was looking a little sick. She resolved to pull herself together. Wolves had no respect for weakness in strangers, especially strangers whose very arrival would be seen as a challenge.

"I wonder," she said to Blind Seer, *"if the local packs will know of our coming? Do these yarimaimalom send messages between the land and the islands?"*

"We will know soon enough," Blind Seer said with his usual wolfish practicality. *"The boat is turning again. I think we are heading toward that cluster of buildings on the point."*

Firekeeper looked and saw what he had indicated, a selection of square stone structures constructed on a high ridge overlooking the water. There was no wall around them, but lower down the slope there were several fenced areas. Some held cattle or goats. Others were fenced high and tight, and Firekeeper thought they might be garden plots. Certainly, there was no reason for a fence that snug unless you were trying to keep rabbits out.

The boat swung, orienting on one of the several long docks that stretched out from the sheltered sandy beach. Firekeeper felt her stomach lurch. To distract herself, she scanned the tree line with frantic intensity. She had expected to see only greenery, but her gaze caught an interruption that was not natural.

"There," she said to Harjeedian, raising her hand and pointing, "what is?"

Harjeedian turned his head in the direction indicated, but Firekeeper felt convinced he knew exactly what she meant. How could he have missed it? The solid blocks of squared-off stone rose taller than many of the trees around them, and there was no doubt that they were not part of a natural formation.

"That," Harjeedian said, "is part of a castle built in the times before the Divine Retribution. The ones from the Old Country made these islands their first base for colonization. They liked the security of being surrounded by water. Later, when they felt safer, the majority moved to the mainland, but some remained here. Our histories relate that even with the inconvenience involved, the islands were considered very prestigious places to live. Many of the old buildings remain, though I would think they are gone to ruin by now."

Firekeeper nodded. She wondered if those first colonists had been looking for security from the Royal Beasts or from their own kind or from something else entirely. That they had gone to the trouble to build castles, structures she now understood were constructed for defense as much as for residence, said that their fears had been strong.

Harjeedian rose from his seat.

"I hope you will permit me to introduce you to those who staff the outpost here. It is the only settlement of humans on all Misheemnekuru. If you wish to send a message to the mainland, or request a boat, they will be the ones for you to contact."

Firekeeper nodded.

"I meet them. Are they many?"

"About twenty," Harjeedian said. "Over the years we have found that many more become cumbersome to provision and intrusive on what the yarimaimalom have claimed as their own. Too many fewer and boredom or arguing arise. Now we use the post as a training ground for particularly promising disdum. Even with the hope of promotion as a reward for doing well, they still often find it a very trying time."

He spoke with what Firekeeper was coming to recognize as a hint of nostalgia in his voice. Harjeedian, then, had almost certainly been dispersed to this strange place to train.

"How boring?" she asked. "It is a beautiful place."

"It is indeed," Harjeedian agreed, "but the humans never go any further than this point. There is ample fresh water from springs in the rock. Gardens and domestic animals supply fresh food. One can fish or swim in this immediate area. However, leaving the outpost area is strictly forbidden. Violators are always caught. The yarimaimalom are jealous of their privilege."

"But I can leave the point," Firekeeper stated, making certain that she had understood the terms on which she was coming to the islands.

"Oh, yes," Harjeedian said. "Truth has said you are to be permitted to venture beyond the usual human limits—but she did not precisely say you would be welcome."

Firekeeper hid the fear this bland statement awoke in her.

"Wolves," she said with a calm she did not feel, "do not welcome on the word of a great cat. I am not afraid."

"Liar," Blind Seer said, dropping to all fours onto the deck as the sailors came forward to make the boat fast. *"And, in this, I would not have you any other way."*

Once the vessel was secured, Firekeeper climbed out onto the dock, ready for her knees to play tricks on her. They did, but only a little, and by the time Harjeedian had finished speaking with the sailing vessel's captain about when the boat would have unloaded provisions and be ready to head back to the mainland, she felt quite steady.

"If you change your mind about staying," Harjeedian said as he directed for them to come with him to where a handful of people were now descending from the ridge, "the boat will be leaving shortly after noon."

"I not change my mind," Firekeeper said.

"Somehow, I didn't think you would," Harjeedian replied.

"Even if the local pack beats us bloody," Blind Seer added, *"you would not have us return so soon—this would mean seeming weak before these humans."*

Firekeeper only snorted in reply, but she knew Blind Seer was correct. She had made her brag, now she must make it good—or at least seem to do so.

Out of touch with the mainland as they were, the residents of Misheemnekuru outpost were initially only mildly interested in the new arrivals. However, as soon as they got a closer look and realized that Blind Seer and Firekeeper were no one that they knew, letters from home and supplies alike were forgotten.

Their reaction once again forced Firekeeper to modify her assumptions. She had grown so accustomed to the very sight of Blind Seer awakening interest that this calm acceptance that Royal Beasts might interact with humans was hard to take. For the first time she considered what this might mean for her reception by the local wolves. They were accustomed to humans—but to these Liglimom humans, not to a human who was a wolf at heart.

Firekeeper reminded herself to take care that her own subconscious assurance that these Wise Wolves would find her strange and interesting did not make her careless. A social flub among humans was merely embarrassing. Among wolves it could well be fatal.

With what she considered very good grace indeed, Firekeeper attended while Harjeedian introduced her to the old man who was in charge of the outpost, to his assistant, and to several other humans. She pretended to understand less of the local language than she did in order to avoid having to stand answering questions any longer than absolutely necessary.

At last Harjeedian said in Pellish, "I can see that you are impatient to be off, Lady Blysse, and I have done my duty to you by making all the correct introductions. Do you have any idea when we might expect to see you again?"

Firekeeper started to shake her head, not liking the idea of being even slightly required to report to humans. Then she reconsidered. Derian would worry about her, and though she hoped to find one of the wingéd folk to carry messages to him, she was not certain she could do so. Better, too, for Derian's sake, that these people remember she cared for his well-being.

"The moon is waning into her last quarter," she said thoughtfully. "I will try to come at each quarter. If I have not come with the turning of two quarters more then maybe something is not well with me."

Though she kept her expression perfectly neutral, Firekeeper couldn't resist a sly dig. "But you can check omens and learn how it is with me, true?"

To her surprise, Harjeedian didn't seem to know he was being teased.

"Precisely," he said, "and we would certainly do that before interrupting the yarimaimalom. You are learning our ways quite well."

Firekeeper didn't know what to think of this. Indeed, she wasn't certain that Harjeedian wasn't getting in a gibe of his own. She decided to call them even.

"I go then," she said, then remembered her manners. She might not like Harjeedian, but he had done her a service. "Thank you for treating seasickness. You have wisdom."

Then, before Harjeedian could win through his mingled surprise and pleasure, Firekeeper began trotting toward the green veil of the forest edge.

She had not thought she and Blind Seer would go far without being noticed, and she was not disappointed. Almost as soon as they left the fringes where to their eyes there was evidence of human activity—wood cutting, berry picking, some small foraging—a low growl warned them against going any farther.

Firekeeper stopped immediately. Blind Seer took a position that would put him slightly in front of her, guarding her from any sudden onrush, then also froze.

"Wolf," said the growl, "why have you brought this human here in violation of our treaty?"

Blind Seer, as the one addressed, took the burden of reply upon himself.

"Wolf," he said, "I am an outlier, come not from the mainland you know, but from lands to the north and west. My birth pack lives west of the mountains."

Listening silence met this declaration, so Blind Seer continued, "This one you call a human is only so in shape. She was born to humans, true, but from the time she was very small she has lived among us.

Firekeeper was aware that their scent was being taken and tried not to reveal either fear or the almost overwhelming desire to draw her Fang and stand ready to defend herself.

The answering growl sounded as if it would turn into a bark of laughter, but gave way neither to humor nor mockery.

"Your scent is not one known to me," the yet unseen wolf said, "but I am still young and have not yet met all the packs—certainly not those that dwell on the mainland. Still, you are not Cousin-kind and your manners are good. Wait and I will call my parents to inspect you. Know that if you move forward, I will fight you—and I am not alone."

"We wait," Blind Seer replied, "but tell your parents this. We may be outliers, but we are no low-ranking wolves to be beaten about. Attack us and we will fight, and you may find that our fangs are sharp."

Blind Seer did not say all of this in words as a human might, but in how he held himself, in his refusal to cringe even the slightest amount, in how he cupped his ears forward rather than holding them to the side.

Fresh from hearing u-Liall's request that she teach their people how to speak to the yarimaimalom, Firekeeper considered with new confusion how she managed to communicate with the Royal Beasts though she lacked ears and tail and the acute sense of smell that meant so much to them. In the next moment she heard the stranger wolf howling news of their coming, and she shook conjecture from her. It would do her no good at this time, and like anything that weakened her confidence in herself, it could well do her harm.

"Strangers! Strangers! Strangers! Strange!" rose the howl.

Firekeeper stiffened as she realized this was the very call that had announced the coming of Earl Kestrel and his party into her pack's lands two years before. This time she was the "strange" the call announced, and she did not like it. The loneliness of being neither wolf nor human flooded her, and she coiled her hand in Blind Seer's fur for comfort.

Even that contact, as familiar as it was, underlined her predicament, for she couldn't help but notice that her own skin was bare.

AT FIREKEEPER'S REQUEST, Derian did not rise to see her off. Instead, he slept past sunrise, worn out from the accumulated events of the previous day. They invaded his dreams: the jaguar escorting him to the council meeting; the ornate mosaic adorning the walls in the temple; that amazing horse with its wild coat and intelligent eyes; Firekeeper's voice, husky in the darkness, explaining why she must go to Misheemnekuru.

Images blended and mingled until the jaguar explicated the meaning of the stories told in the mosaics, and the horse spoke with Firekeeper's voice, explaining why u-Liall must let themselves be carried.

Eshinarvash is cantering, and Derian clings to his mane, the long hairs biting into his fingers, his knees slipping as he tries to stay astride. Something is interfering with how his knees clench into the rise and fall of the horse's body. He glances down to see what is impeding him.

How odd. Instead of his usual trousers and riding boots, he is wearing something completely strange. Then he remembers the elaborate attire he had worn to the reception that morning. Certainly this is the same. There are horses embroidered on the trouser leg, beautiful horses in all the hues Derian has ever imagined and a few he had only dreamed.

But no, these are not the same. The horses are not the only creatures. There are jaguars with their spots of living flame. Lumbering bears, rising from the earth mold, mushrooms growing on the broad area between their ears. Seagulls with feathers edged in living crystal air-dancing over otters that glide half-dissolved into the waves.

Derian leans forward to try and get a closer look at the elaborate diorama, then realizes that he has unbalanced, that he is falling, falling into the picture, and that his own image is appearing there, edged in vibrant lines of thread.

Derian shook himself awake with a start, finding himself sliding headfirst half in, half out of the bed. He pulled himself back onto the level and lay for a while, staring at the fine netting that surrounded his bed.

Although he had been assured that the season for insects had not yet arrived, Derian thought he must have misunderstood, for even by the pale daylight that filtered through the windows he could see dark flecks where the little creatures had become tangled in the mesh and died. He stared at them for a long while, trying to make out what exactly they were, and felt himself drifting again into nightmare.

He swung his legs over the edge of the bed, reassuring himself of the solidness of reality in the cool tile under his feet. Pushing the netting aside, he stood, stretching and rubbing his eyes until the last vestiges of his disturbing dream were forgotten.

Sufficient daylight was filtering in through the window—these screened and curtained with finely woven fabric—that he didn't bother to light a candle. His stomach grumbled, and he realized that the day must be well advanced. He hoped the servants hadn't cleared all the breakfast away.

As Derian washed, he became aware of voices out in the courtyard: Barnet and Rahniseeta. He couldn't make out precisely what was being said, but he heard Barnet sing a few bars of something and Rahniseeta's gentle laughter followed by the melodious notes of some wind instrument. There was a rude twang, then Rahniseeta laughed again.

Derian flushed and scrubbed at the back of his neck with rather more vigor than necessary. He had enjoyed the time he had spent with Rahniseeta and Harjeedian yesterday evening—and for more reason than that he had finally had some questions answered. Derian still didn't much care for Harjeedian, but almost against his will he was coming to understand something of how the other man thought.

Derian still didn't have much idea how Rahniseeta thought—except that she obeyed her brother with admirable loyalty—but long, intellectual conversation wasn't the first thing that came to mind when he was with her. His lips curved in an inadvertent smile as he thought of her beauty, of curves both rounded and slender, of the graceful way in which she walked.

After shaving, Derian pulled on clean shirt and trousers, made sure his hair was neat, and with something of the same feeling he'd had before walking onstage to take part in a Horse Festival pageant, opened the door connecting his room to the courtyard.

At the sound, Rahniseeta and Barnet turned to look his way. They were seated, Derian noted with almost absurd pleasure, across from each other at the low table, not side by side as he had imagined. Barnet held his guitar—one of the several instruments he played—in the position Derian had come to associate with tuning or otherwise working on the strings. It seemed that the damp played havoc with their ability to hold a note.

Rahniseeta also held a musical instrument—in her case a long flute or recorder-like instrument. In front of her on the table was a broad, flat, covered basket of the type Derian already had learned was made for carrying snakes.

"Good morning," Derian greeted them. "Any food about?"

"Plenty," Barnet assured him, indicating one of the wheeled carts the servants used with a toss of his head. "We set your share over there so Rahniseeta could show me a trick. Hope you don't mind."

Derian didn't mind that the food had been set aside, but he wondered how he felt about Rahniseeta showing Barnet anything, even—or maybe especially—a trick. Keeping his composure, Derian motioned for Rahniseeta to remain seated when she would have moved—whether to serve him or to make room at the table, he wasn't sure.

"Stay put," he said. "Plenty of room for me."

He found that the tea had cooled, but the fruit juice in its double carafe remained pleasantly chilled. He helped himself to a slice of bread thick with raisins, smearing on some lightly salted butter before carrying the lot over to a chair on Barnet's side of the table. The seat had the advantage of giving him a good view of Rahniseeta and putting him at a comfortable distance from whatever she had in her basket.

Rahniseeta was obviously waiting for him to get settled before going on with whatever stunt she had been about to perform, and Derian felt oddly welcomed. He knew all too well how easily a young woman could make a newcomer feel he should be anywhere but in the same room where she was flirting.

"This I will show you is a type of performance still done in our temples," Rahniseeta explained, lifting her flute and inspecting the mouthpiece. "However, the disdum say it is not sacrilegious to show it at other times and places. Indeed, some encourage it, for they say it dispels some of the fear so many feel for snakes."

Without further explanation, she began to play a melody on her pipe, beginning with low notes that Derian imagined he could feel as much as hear. After a short phrase of this music, motion occurred within the basket and a snake's head rose above the rim. Its tongue flickered in and out, tasting the air, as if it were scenting the location of the sound. Moment by moment, it uncoiled further, holding its body unright, orienting on the pipe, and following the rise and fall of the musical notes in a swaying dance that was perfect accompaniment to the melody.

The concord between the slender dark woman and the jewel-toned snake was uncanny, and Derian realized that he had frozen in place, the slice of bread halfway to his mouth. He made himself take a bite, but he had to remind himself to chew.

Her gaze fastened on the snake, Rahniseeta played on and on, her music complex and intricate despite the limitations of the instrument. The snake emerged so that its upper length rose a forearm's length above the basket. Its tongue flickered as it attended to the music, adapting its swaying to every variation.

At last, Rahniseeta drew the piece to a close. With the fading of the music, the snake lowered itself into the basket once more, coiling with a sinuous motion that was as captivating as its dance. When it was settled, Rahniseeta covered the basket with a matching woven lid. Then she leaned back in her seat, her eyelids lowering over the dark beauty of her eyes as if she were very weary.

Derian found himself thinking that the performance had seemed somehow sad, with a sorrow that stilled all compliments in his throat. Barnet, however, was enthusiastic. Arms filled with guitar, he settled for thumping his open palm against his leg by way of applause.

"That was marvelous!" the minstrel exclaimed. "How do you train the creatures? Do all snakes do that or only certain types? Could I learn?"

Rahniseeta opened her eyes and smiled gently, then set her flute down next to the basket.

"I am glad you liked it," she said. Derian noticed she didn't answer a single one of Barnet's questions. "Did you like it, Derian?"

"It was captivating," he said, "and a little sad, too. Maybe it was just the music you played."

She smiled a trace wistfully.

"It was a sad song, perhaps, one about the parting of friends. It seemed appropriate for today." She brightened then, "But it is not an entirely sad song, for it also speaks of friends coming together again. So I hope it will be."

Derian wanted to say something, to find out whether she meant his leaving for u-Bishinti or perhaps was referring to Firekeeper's departure for the islands, but his tongue got all tangled. Barnet's slightly quizzical smile, as if he was trying to decide how best to take advantage of Rahniseeta's evident melancholy, didn't help the redhead's composure.

"Well, um, yes," Derian managed after a moment. "It was really a very astonishing thing you did there, making the snake dance and all. Tell me, was that a Wise Snake, or a more usual one?"

Rahniseeta put her instrument down next to the snake's basket.

"This snake is what you would call a more usual one. Indeed, there may be no Wise Snakes. Certainly, we do not think any have come to us."

"Then are there no Wise cold bloods?" Derian asked.

"There are," Rahniseeta said, "but they are more likely to be among the large creatures—the alligators and larger lizards. I will show you later."

"That's quite all right," Derian said. He'd seen a statue of an alligator and wasn't sure he wanted to see the real thing.

Rahniseeta smiled as if she had guessed his thought, but didn't press her invitation. Instead she changed the subject slightly.

"Very few of the yarimaimalom dwell within the temples as does the jaguar Truth. Mostly the aridisdum and kidisdum must work through the lesser, or Simple, beasts. Some say they provide truer omens in any case."

"Oh?" Barnet stopped twisting the pegs on the neck of his guitar, his eyebrows raised in question.

Rahniseeta put her fingers to her lips as if physically stopping words from coming out. Then she went on more slowly, "This is a matter for aridisdum, not for sisters of aridisdum. I do not think I should discuss it."

In an obvious move to change the conversation, she looked at Derian, "Are you going to u-Bishinti today?"

"I'll need to know if Varjuna wants me," Derian replied. "I left things rather indefinite when I departed yesterday."

"Oh, he will want you," Rahniseeta said. "He sent a message telling of how the Wise Horse carried you back to the city, and saying that as he read it this was an omen favoring your staying. Of course, he is a kidisdu, not an aridisdu, but ikidisdu are very wise in the ways of those they keep."

"So," Derian said, a little confused, "I can go along there any time, then?"

"That is right," Rahniseeta said. "I had looked forward to showing you something of our city . . ."

She trailed off, obviously uncertain whether urban charms could compare to those of u-Bishinti.

"I'd love to see the city," Derian assured her, "and I promised Harjeedian that I'd continue with what I can do to teach our language. Perhaps we can combine the two?"

"That would be very fine," Rahniseeta said. She was about to say something else when Barnet interrupted.

"What about me?" he asked, trying to sound jovial but sounding, to Derian's ear at least, a trace petulant. "I hope you haven't forgotten that I'll still be here. At least I don't think anyone has invited me to stay elsewhere."

"Stay elsewhere?" Rahniseeta replied, and Derian was dismayed to hear her sounding rather indignant. "I should think not. Your knowledge is a gem and we hope that this temple will be a fit setting for it."

Barnet was momentarily mollified, but then worry shaded his pleasure.

"I am still free to come and go," he said, "just like the others?"

"Just like the others," Rahniseeta assured him, "although if you choose to go to Misheemnekuru you will be restricted to the human compound. I think you would be much happier here."

"So do I," Barnet said with a warm smile. "So do I."

Derian wished he hadn't been so quick to state his intention of going to u-Bishinti, but there was nothing much he could do about it. Harjeedian had told him how the local post service worked, so after Rahniseeta had left—saying she had to settle the dancing snake into more comfortable quarters—he penned a note to Varjuna asking when he might come to u-Bishinti.

Before the midday meal was served he had his reply. Varjuna himself came, driving the same light carriage, though a dapple grey had replaced the bay between the shafts. Harjeedian had not yet returned from Misheemnekuru, and Rahniseeta was not in the immediate vicinity.

Derian decided he'd feel rather odd hunting her out—after all, hadn't he said he'd be coming back fairly frequently? Nor did he have the Liglimosh to write her other than the most simplistic note. Finally, he settled for the unsatisfactory solution of leaving his thanks with Barnet.

The minstrel looked honestly sorry to see Derian depart and even walked to the gates of the Temple of the Cold Bloods complex to see them off.

"I hope I can come visit you," Barnet said. "It gets rather dull when there's no one to talk to."

Does he mean when Rahniseeta's not around? Derian thought jealously.

He let no trace of his jealous thought color his voice, though, and only motioned toward Varjuna.

"He's the man to ask, not me. I'm visiting on his sufferance."

Varjuna gave one of his amiable smiles as he mounted to the driver's seat.

"Of course Barnet is welcome to visit," he said, "but I think he is wrong if he thinks he will lack those with whom he can talk. When I stopped by u-Nahal on my way here, who would get access to him was the matter of heated debate."

"Me?" Barnet said, apprehensively. "Whale's flukes, I hadn't thought about that. . . ."

They left Barnet on that note. Looking back to wave his farewells, Derian couldn't decide whether he felt at all sorry for the fellow—or just satisfaction in knowing that Barnet wouldn't have time for too many long talks, one on one, with Rahniseeta.

XIII

THEY CAME OUT OF THE FOREST'S FRINGE, all with eyes the color of old pine-tree tears and fur in which silver-grey dominated the browns, blacks, and whites that usually intermingled within a wolf's coat. By this likeness, Firekeeper guessed them to all be members not only of the same pack, but of the same family as well.

There were six present. From the sharp angle at which they held their ears and the attitude in which they carried their tails, Firekeeper immediately identified the One Male and One Female. She guessed that the slender female off to one side, deferring to just about everyone but a male of about the same age and build, was the wolf who had addressed them from the shrub. This one and her brother still had the darker outlines around mouth and eyes, so were probably two of last year's pups grown, but not yet dispersed.

The remaining two were older. One was quite old, and, judging from his ragged fur, infirm as well. The other was an elegant female whose thick coat and abundant ruff made quite clear that she was a hunter who ranked just below the Ones in the order in which she claimed her share of the kill.

Firekeeper guessed that there was at least one other adult member of the pack, probably attending to nursemaid duties with this year's litter. That there was a litter, Firekeeper knew without a doubt. The One Female's teats had not yet grown small after nursing, though probably by now the pups were almost—if not entirely—weaned.

A healthy pack, then. Mother, father, children from earlier litters not yet dispersed, and one elder, possibly a previous One Male. Contrary to what Firekeeper had discovered most humans thought, defeated Ones were not slain by their rivals, nor always driven off. Usually, they accepted their demotion with grace, glad to remain part of the pack, sometimes moving into another pack where the loss of their former status might not sting as intensely.

In a few cases, especially those where a One had been displaced owing to an injury that had healed or a sickness that had passed, the former One might regain his or her place, but this was not common. At least among the Royal Wolves Firekeeper had known, the choice to fight to take over heading the pack was made after a certain amount of deliberation, rarely on impulse.

All these things flew through her thoughts during the long breaths during which the local pack examined the newcomers. Firekeeper did her best to stand tall during this examination, but she felt very vulnerable indeed. Blind Seer was a magnificent wolf, but the One Male in this pack matched him point for point where height and mass were concerned. She was all too aware that while Blind Seer would have only one human on his side if it came to a fight, this One would have five other adults to back him.

The One Female was the first to step forward, and she did so stiff-legged and with her hackles slightly raised, but with her tail moving slightly to indicate that while she was not offering welcome, she was not offering threat either. Blind Seer stepped forward in the same attitude, and Firekeeper realized with a thrill of pride that he was greeting this stranger as One to One, not pressing her on her own turf, but not deferring either. It was an attitude that went well with how he had spoken with the scout and Firekeeper felt very proud of him.

"You told my daughter," the One Female said without any of the preamble about the weather or titles or suchlike as in human conversation, "that you were not in violation of our treaty with the two-legs because the human who stands beside you is not human but, somehow, wolf. I see hairless, fangless, standing on two-legs. How is this not human?"

Blind Seer replied with perfect courtesy, as if the One Female had not just called him a liar.

"She has run with the pack into which I was born since she was a small child. Just as a wolf who disperses from his birth pack and forms another is no longer considered a member of his original pack, so it is with Firekeeper. She may have been born to human shape and human ways, but she has been a wolf far longer and claims us . . . as we claim her."

The growl that underlay Blind Seer's final statement was almost inaudible, the lowest of rumbles, not threatening, but warning nonetheless.

"She claims you?" asked the One Female. The flaring of her ears and nostrils indicated a degree of astonishment.

Firekeeper decided it was time she spoke for herself.

"I do claim the wolves as my people. Moreover, others among the Royal Beasts have acknowledged my allegiance. Even the jaguar called Truth with whom we spoke on the mainland sensed there was something of the wolf about me."

Boasting is not bad form among wolves—not, at least, if the one making the boast can make it good. However, the One Female froze, torn between sitting in astonishment and going on defense against something truly strange.

"It talks!" she said in amazement. "Fire burn off my fur and make me naked as a baby possum. The human talks!"

The rest of her pack was less astonished and more guarded. The two younger wolves slunk back, tails between their legs. The magnificent female hunter seemed to double in size as her hackles raised. The One Male stepped forward, ready to back his mate if it came to a fight.

Only the old male seemed more amused than afraid. His tail moved in a slow arc, and he commented to the air in general: "Well, she could hardly have grown up with wolves without learning to understand them somehow, though I must admit, this goes beyond imagination."

Blind Seer decided to address this one nonhostile member of the group, giving the others a chance to recover without feeling challenged.

"So I have always thought," he agreed with some of the loose jointed amiability that he had learned put humans at their ease, "but then Firekeeper was there from my first emergence, so I have never really thought that her ability to speak to us was peculiar. That she lacks fur and fangs . . ."

Firekeeper punched Blind Seer in the shoulder and he grinned at her, but neither completely dropped their guard.

The One Female shook herself thoroughly. When she stopped her hackles were lowered. Her gait as she stepped forward to sniff tails with Blind Seer had lost most of its stiffness.

Firekeeper had never indulged in tail-sniffing. She got little from it other than odor, but she had learned to let any wolves get a good sniff of her scent. Now, though she was still uncertain just how safe she and Blind Seer were among these strangers, she crouched and let the One Female poke her nose here and there, finishing with a lick across Firekeeper's face.

"You smell something like a two-legs," came the assessment, "but there is no doubt there is something of the wolf about you, too. Your manners are good, a credit to those who reared you. Is there a name by which you prefer to be called?"

"My pack calls me Firekeeper," the woman replied, well aware that there was a measure of respect implied in the name.

"And I am called Blind Seer," the blue-eyed wolf said, asserting his rights One to One by not waiting to be asked. "Are we welcome in your hunting grounds, or would you have us go elsewhere?"

The One Female glanced over at her mate, and though Firekeeper couldn't tell how, in the fashion of married couples of all types, he communicated his answer to his mate.

"We will let you hunt among us," the One Female said. "Better with us than with one of the other packs. We have some familiarity with the two-legs, and you are interesting."

Firekeeper stiffened at this implication that she was being lumped in with humanity. The One Female guessed the meaning of the wolf-woman's reaction and panted laughter.

"Lay down your hackles, Firekeeper. What I mean is that as our hunting grounds border on the place where the humans have their lair, we are more accustomed to seeing them. Thus we are better able to see how you are not entirely like them."

The female hunter broke the silence the pack had held until their Ones had decided how to deal with the strangers.

"Not entirely like," she said softly, her upper lip curling as she scented the air.

All the wolves were closing now, and much sniffing was going on. Firekeeper braced herself to be welcoming, for in all honesty—other than the times her pack had met with others for hunting of larger game and the pleasure of shared company and new voices in the songs—this was her first encounter with so many wolves who were not her family. During all those other times, her parents had been present to assert their authority in her favor.

The wolf pack introduced themselves in order of rank. The One Male and Female were Tangler and Hard Biter. The female hunter was Moon Frost, a descriptive name that told little about her personality. The young two-year-olds still had puppy names. The female was Nipper and the male High Howler. The old male was Neck Breaker, doubtless in memory of some long-ago achievement.

Having decided to let the newcomers hunt among them, the Wise Wolf pack took Firekeeper and Blind Seer back to where this year's pups were denned. There were five pups, three females and two males. Their nursemaid was a sibling of Nipper and Howler, a skinny wolf with a playful attitude. He was called Rascal when his fellows were pleased with him and all manner of insults when they were not.

It was a good-sized pack, though not overwhelmingly so. They could support themselves off of the local deer and small game, with occasional forays for larger game like moose and elk. Indeed, it was not a pack all that different from that in which Firekeeper had been reared, but she couldn't help but feel that these wolves—she decided to continue thinking of them as Wise Wolves, to differentiate them from the Royal Wolves who had raised her—were strange still.

The pack went hunting in the early evening when the day creatures were stupid with sleep and the night creatures not yet fully awake. Firekeeper with her bow acquitted herself well, but the Wise Wolves had lived in proximity to humans for generations. They knew how bows worked, and while mildly pleased to have one on their side, they were not impressed.

Nor were they particularly impressed with her ability to strike fire from flint and steel. Moon Frost sneered at Firekeeper's need to cook her food, but Firekeeper had dealt with several seasons of strong young hunters who needed to prove themselves by mocking those weaker. She bit her tongue and kept silence, though she longed to challenge the other.

And could you win? she asked herself, and had to admit that she was far from certain.

After eating was done, the pack settled in to gossip and nap, interested in what Blind Seer could tell them about the lands to the north. Firekeeper resolved to listen more than speak, determined to learn everything she could, and knowing that the novelty of her would take time to wear off. Better to let them forget that she was there and concentrate on Blind Seer.

Watching the One Male effortlessly crack a bone, Firekeeper wondered at her own arrogance in thrusting herself into this company—especially as she had done so with every intent of telling them she was there to free them from an alien and terrible imprisonment. If these wolves were imprisoned, they certainly felt no shame.

You have been too much among two-legs, Firekeeper thought, *and have forgotten how dangerous wolves can be.*

It was an unsettling thought to carry with her into sleep.

VARJUNA KEPT THE TALK FOCUSED ON horses as they drove to u-Bishinti. He asked when Derian had received his first pony and what type it had been, what had been the first horse he had selected for himself, what his family tended to do with horses past the prime age for work. As the ikidisdu learned more, he asked about the purchasing Derian had been doing for House Kestrel's depleted stables, about the trips Derian had made to horse fairs with his father. Varjuna wanted to know if Derian could drive—as if with a name like "Carter" Derian could not—and what style vehicle he preferred.

At first, Derian thought Varjuna was just making conversation. Then he began to wonder. Varjuna wasn't a subtle man as the politically astute Earl Kestrel was subtle, but he wasn't just a monomaniacal horse fancier either. His reaction to learning about Roanne's death had been indignant and quietly angry, but not shocked, so that Derian began to believe Varjuna had been told in advance.

Who would have told him? Only a small number of people knew: Harjeedian, Barnet, and the sailors who had been on the small ship. Waln might have known, and perhaps the ship's captain, but would they have attached any importance to the event? Waln had been a phantasm after whom Derian and his companions had chased for long moonspans, but they had actually spent very little time in his company. The only way Waln would have learned how fond Derian was of his chestnut mare would have been for someone to tell him.

Harjeedian seemed the most likely source of the information, but try as he might, Derian could not think why he would confess what he had ordered done to Roanne and the pack pony to Varjuna of all people.

Derian filed this away as one of those mysteries for which he lacked sufficient information to find a solution but resolved—as he still resolved to get revenge for Roanne—to somehow learn why Roanne's death should have come to matter enough that Harjeedian had let word of it get to the ears of this most horse-loving of humans.

When they arrived at u-Bishinti, the atmosphere was markedly different. Whereas upon Derian's first visit all but the most senior hands had kept studiously to their work, now everyone turned to look—many to wave a cheerful greeting. Derian suddenly realized that the attentiveness to duty had not been for Varjuna's benefit as he had thought, but had been meant to impress him.

And now I've decided to come for a stay, he thought, *and they're happy about it. Is it just because this means that the horse keepers have scored some sort of coup over their fellows or is it something else?*

Derian decided he'd learn soon enough. Meanwhile he basked in the warmth of the welcome and luxuriated, as before, in the sight of so much magnificent horseflesh.

Varjuna's house—the residence of the ikidisdu, to be more correct—was a splendid place. It was built, as seemed to be the case for the best buildings in this land, of brick ornamented with mosaic reliefs in enameled brick. These, of course, depicted horses.

One thing immediately caught Derian's eye as Varjuna took him on a quick tour. The entire structure was built on one level, which Derian had already learned was not the rule, and each room either had doorways large enough to admit a horse or was equipped with broad windows clearly intended to permit a horse to poke its head into the room.

"My mother," Derian laughed, "would be horrified. She was always reminding us to close the doors after ourselves. 'You're not down at the stables' is what she'd say."

"I say the same thing," came a calm, level, feminine voice, "but it doesn't make any difference."

Varjuna turned and, with an abbreviated form of the hand gesture that served as the local version of a polite bow, indicated the woman who stood framed in one of the doorways.

"My wife, Zira," he said with evident affection.

Zira was, at first meeting, incredibly plain. Her dark hair was a bit coarse, her teeth stained to the ivory-brown of old bone. Her figure showed the effects of bearing three children and a fondness for nuts dipped in honey. Her skin showed that she spent lots of time out-of-doors. Even in her first bloom she had probably never been pretty. Now there were the hints that in old age she would be ugly.

Yet, as Zira joined them for the rest of the house tour, Derian began to be captivated by her personality. She was incredibly vital. She noticed things, whether a butterfly on a flower or the detail in a wall mosaic. Her teeth were stained from a tea she loved, but though she must have drunk thousands of cups of the brew, her expression as she took her first sip held a childlike bliss. Within a short time, Derian was comparing Zira favorably with his own mother—and Vernita Carter still gave ample evidence of why she had been one of the great beauties of her day.

Derian didn't immediately meet Varjuna and Zira's three sons. Two were still living with their parents, but were out at school. The third had graduated to living in the dormitories with the other younger kidisdum and was busy with his duties.

"Are all your children involved with horses?" Derian asked.

"They are, thank goodness," Zira replied, leaning her elbows on the table in order to select just the perfect honeyed nut from the bowl in front of her. "This is not to say that all of them will follow us into keeping or even into the disdum, but they all share our enthusiasm. It would be deadly otherwise."

She went on to tell a story about a family much like their own but associated with bears. The daughter of that family had no empathy with the animals and they in turn sensed her indifference. It led to a great deal of unpleasantness for all concerned.

"However, happily the girl was quite pretty and clever—though not with bears. She married a wool merchant and does very well with the lambs. No use trying to force rain to fall upwards. Water will always follow his own way."

The use of the personal pronoun for what—had Derian's mother said something similar—would have been a purely neutral element with no store of legends associated with it made Derian feel a stranger again. Varjuna might have noticed, for he jumped to his feet.

"Well, we've ample time to inspect at least some of the horses, if you'd be interested."

"Interested!" Derian said, setting down his cup so that it rattled in the saucer. "I can hardly wait."

Zira came with them. She was a kidisdu in her own right, associated with the brood mares.

"It doesn't take another mother to understand what they're going through, the dears," she said, stuffing her feet into very well-used boots, "but it does help. If I won't be in the way, I'll trot along with you."

Varjuna glanced at Derian to make sure Derian didn't mind. Derian felt odd as he realized that he merited some element of respect here. He was used to being a servant—or at least a commoner—and the horse people were treating him more like a noble.

"Please do come," he said. "I'll bet you've seen a good number of the horses we're going to look at into the world."

"I have," Zira agreed placidly, "and their sires and dams as well."

Because Zira was along, Derian had expected that the tour would include the new foals. After all, foals were the hope of every operation, and their antics were—at least in Derian's opinion—the most delightful of any young animal. Since Prancing Steed Stables rarely bred horses, preferring to buy promising young animals already beginning their training, Derian particularly enjoyed seeing other people's foals. Indeed, he had already resolved that, no matter how expensive it was to carry brood mares and foals, he would have at least a few when he founded his own stables.

That was his new idea. During Derian's last trip home, his parents had again gently indicated their hope that he would not stand in the way of his younger brother and sister taking over the family business that should go—were simple legalities followed—to Derian. There were two ways a first born could be disinherited. The first was through legal appeal on the part of his parents—an appeal usually only resorted to in cases of abandonment or criminal behavior. The second was by agreement with the older members of the family. These were scrutinized even more carefully than the first, for it was not unheard of for a parent to try and disinherit an elder child in preference for a favored or more tractable younger child.

Colby and Vernita Carter, however, did not favor their younger children over their elder. Rather, Derian had already exceeded their wildest hopes for his advancement. He was a counselor to the king, had been consulted by the heirs apparent, and had the patronage of Earl Kestrel. As Colby and Vernita saw things, Derian was certain to do as well or better through these connections than he could through the stables.

Derian felt a sudden, familiar pang of homesickness as he remembered his family. He knew it was a normal part of reaching adulthood to discover that the orderly world known since childhood is changing, but that made the sensation no less disturbing.

And, he thought wryly, leaning over a fence rail and concentrating to understand as Varjuna discussed the merits of a particular stud's get, *I've had rather a few more changes to my orderly world than is usual, more, I think, than most people experience in a lifetime.*

This made him think of Firekeeper. The wolf-woman had been through as much as had Derian—and more. He wondered how she was doing out there on Misheem-nekuru, and whether the wolves were anything like what she had expected.

"Hey, Derian!"

A laughing voice brought him back to himself. Derian started, finding Zira waving her hand in his face.

"Sorry," he apologized, feeling himself color. "I must be a bit tired. I was up late last night, making arrangements."

"Would you like to go back to your rooms?" Varjuna asked, beginning to turn that way.

"No, please," Derian said. "If I nap now, I won't sleep later. I'd prefer to keep looking at the horses. I can honestly say I've never seen so many fine animals in one place."

"They are good," Varjuna said. "I've been here sixty-five years and I can honestly say I've never seen finer."

"You say that every year," Zira said fondly.

Derian halted in his tracks.

"Sixty-five?"

"I cheated a little," Varjuna admitted with a chuckle. "I was born here. My parents were aridisdu and kidisdu, so I have a head start on my residency."

"He does look good, doesn't he?" Zira said. "I thought so when I met him twenty-nine years ago when I came to u-Bishinti from a little village to the south. There was Varjuna, without a thought in his head for anything but horses. I said to myself, 'There's the man for you, Zira, my girl—if you can just get him to notice you exist.'"

Varjuna chuckled again. This was clearly an old story and one he liked as much as she did.

"So," Derian said, fumbling for something to say, "I thought you were younger than Varjuna."

"Seventeen years," Zira replied without hesitation. "He's well preserved and I am not so, but we get along like many a stallion and his reliable herd mare."

Later, Derian was to learn that the Liglimom did not grey as quickly as did his people and that their oilier skin kept them from showing lines as early. However, at the time he felt as if he had stumbled into one of those tales of Old World magic wherein sorcerers remained comparatively youthful while those around them aged and died.

"Here's a group you may be particularly interested in," Varjuna said, gesturing to a pasture where a small bachelor herd was grazing in apparent amity. "We haven't cut any of these, waiting to see which show real promise."

Derian immediately knew why Varjuna had indicated this particular group. Superficially, they greatly resembled the Wise Horse who had let him have a ride the evening before. He wondered why he immediately knew that these were not Wise Horses. Unlike Elation and Blind Seer, who had been noticeably larger than the "cousins" of their type, the Wise Horse had not been unduly larger than many domestic horses Derian had known. The answer came to him as quickly.

Although a horse or two raised his head and examined the newcomers—and indeed a couple whickered with recognition and came trotting over—the eyes that examined the humans were bright, inquisitive, and yet lacking that extra penetrating intelligence that Derian had found in Eshinarvash's eyes—and in those of the Royal Beasts he had been fortunate enough to know.

"We call this coloration type 'paint' for rather obvious reasons," Varjuna said, "and to save you from asking, yes, we're breeding for it in imitation of—one might even say homage to—the Wise Horses. They are widely admired, but not one rider in ten thousand can make the claim you now can—to have ridden a Wise Horse."

"I was honored," Derian said sincerely. Then, because he felt vaguely embarrassed—what had he done to deserve the honor, anyhow?—he changed the subject. "I see that these paints are not all black and white, like the gentleman I met last night. There are brown and white, some greys, and even what has to be called a bay."

Varjuna nodded. "It's rare to have more than three colors mixed in. Usually, it's just white and one other. We've tried but never managed to eliminate the white."

Zira sighed. "One time I was at the delivery of a foal and we thought we'd pulled it off. Chestnut coat with darker patches, but there was the white—a big splash of it across the belly and a star on her forehead. Still, she was a good horse nonetheless."

"There's enough variety in the paints to satisfy anyone," Varjuna went on. "They've been an interest of mine since I was a boy."

"I'm not surprised," Derian murmured, for he had heard a note of obsession in the other's voice. "These seem to have mostly blots—for lack of a better word. What else do you get?"

"Spots," Varjuna said, pointing in case the word wasn't in Derian's vocabulary to a handsome stallion grazing at the far side of the pasture. "Sometimes all over like a jaguar, other times clustered. We also get ones with speckles—irregularly shaped spots. Those can be really striking."

Derian touched his own forearm. "I'd call those 'freckles' and I agree, they're quite spectacular."

"Would you like to try that one?" Varjuna asked. "I can have him brought in and saddled up in a heartbeat. One shouldn't choose a horse just on our say-so. So much depends on how the horse and rider relate."

And that was how Derian realized that they planned to give him a horse. He realized immediately that the gift was meant as compensation—for there could be no replacement—for dead Roanne, but nonetheless, he was deeply touched. There had been no reluctance in Varjuna's voice, only eagerness and enthusiasm.

Zira looked a bit more thoughtful, but that was only—as Derian learned a few moments later—because she thought Derian might be a bit too tired to ride well, and that he should wait until tomorrow to start testing possible mounts.

"After all," she said, "you don't need to rush. There are plenty of horses than can be loaned to you if you need to ride to the city. You want to make sure you're perfectly happy."

"And if you're not," Varjuna interjected, "as sometimes happens, we can let you exchange."

"But we don't want him disappointed," Zira objected, "nothing is worse than choosing a horse and having to trade. I remember when I outgrew my first horse. I had expected to keep riding her for years to come, then I shot up like a weed and we just weren't right for each other."

"I think I can manage a ride or two," Derian said, almost overwhelmed, "and I certainly won't be deciding anything today."

That satisfied both his hosts, and the next several hours passed quite pleasantly for all of them—and for the small group of grooms, trainers, and kidisdum who drifted over to offer comment and advice. They chatted about teeth (no one was in the least insulted when Derian checked the teeth of a horse he was interested in) and hooves and the merits of various types of saddles and stirrups.

It was during this fine muddle that Derian met Poshtuvanu, Varjuna and Zira's eldest, though introductions waited until they were well into a friendly argument over which types of hay were best. Later, the younger two sons—both near Derian's age—arrived. Everybody had their own opinion, and in the end Derian was rather relieved when the rattling of an iron rod against the sides of a wrought-iron triangle signaled that the time had come for horses to be brought in from pasture, for feed to be hauled to those who were remaining out for the night, and for any of the dozens of jobs that are repeated daily at a working stable.

Dinner that evening was a small, family affair, for though many people wanted to meet the foreign visitor, Varjuna had commanded that Derian be given a chance to settle in first.

"We wouldn't ask a new horse to run a race on his first day, would we?" he said, and everyone agreed with such immediacy that Derian wouldn't have been surprised if he'd been fed hot mash and had his ankles wrapped before being put to bed.

Dinner, however, was an excellent seafood stew served over a tiny white grain Derian had not encountered before coming to Liglim, but which apparently grew well where the weather was both hot and wet. A pale beer was served with dinner, and

Derian had to remind himself to keep an eye on the unobtrusive way his mug was filled whenever its level dropped below half. There was fruit to follow, and, of course, honeyed nuts.

He tumbled into bed that night, still subconsciously weighing the merits of various horses he had ridden, and wondering whether he should choose a mare or a stallion. He knew he wanted a breeding animal. While a stallion could be set to several mares, mares were generally more even-tempered. He wasn't looking to found his own stable quite yet. He needed an animal to ride. On the other hand, Varjuna assured him that on the whole their stallions were tractable and some were even mild. One simply didn't force them into proximity with other stallions, especially around a mare in heat . . .

Somewhere in the midst of this, Derian fell asleep, and dreamed, unsurprisingly, of horses.

DERIAN DIDN'T MAKE HIS DECISION the next day or even the next after that. He found this gained him respect rather than making the others think him difficult to please or picky.

"Only a child or someone in great need chooses a horse quickly," Varjuna said. "After all, horses can live for many years. It is not a relationship into which one enters lightly."

Reviewing his options gave Derian ample opportunity to get to know the denizens of u-Bishinti. Since Varjuna and Zira had duties, that kept them from being Derian's guide all the time, Poshtuvanu was given the job. At first, Derian thought this was simply because of who his father was, but within a short while he realized that Poshtuvanu was knowledgeable beyond his contemporaries.

"It was either learn fast," Poshtuvanu confided in Derian as they sat on a fence rail surveying the same paint bachelor herd as the day before, "or disappoint both myself and my parents. As it is, I keep needing to prove myself over and over again."

"Do you want to be a kidisdu or an aridisdu?" Derian asked, knowing that specialization often came after a candidate had tried both courses.

"Kidisdu," Poshtuvanu replied promptly. "I'm more interested in the horses themselves than in the books of lore. Don't get me wrong. I'm very glad that animals can help us understand the best way to live in accordance with the divine will. It's just that my mind doesn't seize on all that stuff. Now, my youngest brother is another matter. I think he'll be an aridisdu."

One thing they did not do was haunt the pastures where the Wise Horses could be found.

"Everyone goes sneaking off to look at them when they're kids," Poshtuvanu said. "It's a rite of passage, almost, and the Wise Horses are pretty patient about it. However, once you're older, you realize it would be rude, like peeking in the windows of someone's house. The Wise Horses set a young stallion or two on watch, and messages are given to them."

"Your father took me up there pretty confidently," Derian said, kicking at the rail with his heel and wondering how much of his inability to settle on a new horse was due to the memory of Roanne—and how much to the memory of that one wonderful ride. After all, he'd had to make choices much more quickly at horse fairs and had never had any difficulty.

"Father probably had been granted an omen," Poshtuvanu said with the breezy unconcern that Derian was coming to accept on this matter. "In any case, if the watch stallion hadn't wanted to acknowledge your coming, the ikidisdu would not have pressed further."

"But," Poshtuvanu went on, giving Derian a strange, sidelong glance, "you probably know more about this than any of us."

Derian blinked.

"How could I? I'd never seen one of these Wise Horses until last night."

Poshtuvanu looked a bit nervous, like he'd said something he shouldn't have.

"Never mind," he said. "Forget I said anything. It's just that you're so good with horses I forget sometimes you're a stranger."

Derian didn't think that anyone looking at him—the one red head among all these dark ones—could forget for a moment that he was a stranger, but he accepted the apology in the spirit it had been offered, and politely changed the subject.

"So," he said, returning to well-trodden ground, "what would you pick, if all things were the same, a mare or a stallion?"

XIV

"I HAD ASKED TO SEE Ahmyndisdu Tiridanti," Waln said stiffly to Harjeedian.

"She is not available," Harjeedian replied, smoothly. Although Waln did not invite him, he glided into the two-room suite Waln had occupied since the return of the *Fayonejunjal*. "Word of your request was given to me, and I am here to see what I may do to assist you."

Waln swallowed a snarl, covering his agitation by moving over to the tidy liquor cabinet and pouring himself a glass of the sharp white wine he was learning to enjoy.

"I understand that there was a reception a few days ago," Waln said, deliberately not offering Harjeedian a glass of wine. "A reception for those we brought from the north. I had thought I would be invited to such an event. After all, without my intervention, you would not have learned of their existence."

"The omens," Harjeedian said, "did not indicate that you were to be included among those entertained."

"Omens," Waln said, almost sneering. "Right. When will I see the ahmyndisdu again?"

"I am not privileged with such information," Harjeedian replied.

"What about the other members of u-Liall?" Waln said, drinking half his wine in one deliciously cool swallow, and filling the glass again. "They were glad enough to meet with me when the voyage was being planned."

"Then the omens indicated that such pleased the deities," Harjeedian said. He crossed to where water chilled in a sweating pottery jar and dipped himself a cup. "The omens apparently have not indicated that visiting with you is how u-Liall is to spend their time. Perhaps you might tell me what you would discuss with u-Liall, and I could seek solutions."

Waln didn't want to put his questions to Harjeedian, but since the alternative seemed to be not putting them to anyone, he began, though reluctantly.

"First, I want to know how long we're expected to stay in this place."

Harjeedian looked around the spacious room.

"Are you not comfortable?"

Waln swallowed a rude retort, for in truth, he was comfortable. Along with Shelby, Rarby, and the other survivors of the shipwrecked *Explorer*, Waln now resided in a large building down near the harbor. Each man had his own suite of rooms. Servants brought meals and handled the cleaning. The men had been provided with a wardrobe in the local style. Last night there had even been entertainment—minstrels singing after the local fashion. However, the relative luxury of their situation could not change two things.

One, they were expected to work as tutors in return for their keep. Two, for all the mannerly words the Liglimom used to avoid discussing the matter directly, they were prisoners.

"The quarters are quite adequate," Waln said, careful to offer praise lest his jailers put him in a worse place, "but I find that I am not permitted to leave the building. None of us are."

"That is for your own safety," Harjeedian said. "The residents of u-Seeheera are not familiar with foreigners, and we have some legends that feature evil creatures that quite resemble you northerners. Perhaps these legends are remnants from the days before the deities blew the breath of Divine Retribution upon the land, when perhaps our founding nations were less than friends. Whatever the source, we do not think it would be safe for you to walk the streets."

Waln hadn't noticed any xenophobia on the part of *Fayonejunjal*'s sailors, but then that venture would have been crewed with open-minded types—as had the *Explorer*. He put this aside for further consideration.

"Also, I find we are expected to work as teachers. I, myself, had at least three different men here today—all disdum. At first I thought they were making a social call, but I soon realized that they expected me to teach them Pellish."

Waln let creep into his voice a hint of his indignation that he, the anticipated new ambassador, had been reduced to the role of language tutor. Harjeedian seemed to miss the point entirely.

"Then you are not capable of teaching Pellish?" The aridisdu looked mildly puzzled. "I thought you quite passable—not equivalent to the minstrel, certainly, but then your training is different."

Waln swallowed a mouthful of bile at this insult so casually offered.

"That's another thing," he said. "Where is Barnet Lobster? Where, for that matter, are Lady Blysse and Derian Carter?"

Harjeedian's annoyance showed momentarily, but there was no trace of it in his reply.

"Of course you would be concerned for your fellow northerners, especially after you did so much to help bring them here." Again there was an implied insult in the silky words, a reminder that neither Lady Blysse nor Derian Carter would view Waln with any fondness at all. "They have been staying in Heeranenahalm, although all but Barnet have recently relocated."

Heeranenahalm translated as "City of Temples" and was, as Waln knew from earlier meetings, the district surrounding the towering step pyramid, a very exclusive area. His resentment burned brighter at hearing this, but not sufficiently to make him abandon his search for information.

"You said, 'until recently,'" Waln prompted. "Where are they now?"

Harjeedian apparently decided to humor him.

"Derian Counselor has been taken to u-Bishinti. Lady Blysse has gone to Misheemnekuru. Barnet Lobster remains a guest of the Temple of the Cold Bloods in Heeranenahalm."

Earlier, the fact that the name of the place where Derian had been taken literally translated as "the stable" might have fooled Waln into believing that the proud young king's counselor had been demoted to a mere a stablehand. However, Waln had been speaking Liglimosh long enough to know that while the "u" prefix literally translated as "the," it meant something more like "top" or "best" or "model." So u-Bishinti must be the most important stable, if not in the nation, at least in this area.

Waln felt a certain sour satisfaction when he learned that Barnet Lobster remained in Heeranenahalm, but his command of Liglimosh was not adequate for him to figure out where Lady Blysse had gone. Doubtless, he realized sourly, precisely what Harjeedian had intended.

Another little reminder to keep me in my place, Waln thought, and though his first impulse was to pretend that he had understood perfectly, he knew this was what Harjeedian would expect.

"I know that 'mishem' means 'islands,'" he said. "After all, I am an islander myself. 'Ne' indicates possession, but 'kuru' is beyond me."

Harjeedian's slight smile accorded Waln a point in this little battle of wills.

"It is a difficult concept to translate," Harjeedian said, "not knowing your culture. In a limited sense, it means 'safety,' but it implies more than mere physical safety. It means a safety that is defended by the will of the deities."

"We have something like that," Waln said. "It isn't precisely the same, but if a fugitive chooses to take refuge in the society chapter house, that refuge is granted and the society must be appealed to before the fugitive is turned over to authority."

"Is the society then more powerful than the law?" Harjeedian asked.

"No," Waln said bluntly. "If say a thief is fleeing the law, then he's going to find the society turns him over pretty quickly. A servant fleeing an abusive master, or a wife from a husband who beats her—even a child from his parents—can appeal to the society to help resolve the matter. There's law involved in those cases, too, but sometimes a person needs to hide first, then call on the law."

"Interesting," Harjeedian said. "Your societies then have real power. They are not simply social entities."

"I never thought about it much," Waln said. "Everyone thinks about the festivals first. Those are the most fun, but the societies do have power."

Harjeedian nodded as if making a note of this for later reflection.

"Your explanation of the society as refuge does help me," the aridisdu said. "The term 'kuru' is closer to this refuge as granted by a society than to mere safety, but in this case, the safety is granted—even assured—by the deities. If any trespass against kuru then the deities will punish that person."

"A sanctuary on an island doesn't seem like much good," Waln said. "How would a person who needs help get there?"

Harjeedian made an apologetic gesture.

"I forget that you do not know the history of those islands. The sanctuary is not given to fugitives, rather, the land is reserved for the sole use of the yarimaimalom. It is their sanctuary, and any human who violates it will suffer divine punishment—if the yarimaimalom do not resolve the matter first."

Waln had already figured out that the Liglimom were nuts about their animals, but he had to keep from gaping at the idea of giving over entire pieces of land to them. He might have asked more, but then he remembered why the situation had come up in the first place.

"But Lady Blysse went there. Isn't she violating that restriction?"

"Lady Blysse claims herself yarimaimalo rather than human," Harjeedian replied. "Blind Seer has accompanied her. The rest is up to the divine will."

Waln had the feeling that Harjeedian wasn't as comfortable about all of this as he pretended, but he was an astute enough trader to know when not to push his point.

"So both Derian and Lady Blysse have left u-Seeheera," he said, politely providing Harjeedian with an escape from this awkward topic. "Barnet's still here. Maybe we can visit."

"I shall speak with him about the matter," Harjeedian said. "He, too, is very busy teaching."

Waln felt a little better about his own work if this was the task that Barnet—who after all was blood kin to King Harwill—had been set. Maybe it wasn't a demotion after all. In any case, he had a lot to think about now, and he was willing to bet that Harjeedian had told him a whole lot more than that pretentious twit Tiridanti ever would have.

"I appreciate your offering to ask Barnet," Waln said. "Those of us who survived the shipwreck are like brothers after what we went through. I've worried about Barnet."

"I am sure," Harjeedian replied ambivalently. "I must return to my own duties. Is there any message I can bring to Ahmyndisdu Tiridanti?"

"Only that I wish to continue to be of service to her and to the rest of u-Liall," Waln replied. "You have been a great deal of help in answering my questions."

"I am pleased to have been of service," Harjeedian said.

After Harjeedian had left, Waln moved to one of the outer windows. All the windows on the exterior of the building—as opposed to those that overlooked the interior courtyard—were small and narrow, meant to permit the circulation of air, but to shield the interior from the violence of the weather—or so one of the servants had said when Waln had asked. Waln still thought these small windows meant the building was intended as a sort of glorified prison, but he had decided not to say so.

Although the exterior window wouldn't permit even a child, much less a man of Waln's bulk, to climb out, it was sufficient for him to view the bay. He had remembered islands in the bay, but as they had not been much in use he had dismissed them from consideration, thinking they must be swampy or disease-infested.

Now he viewed the green masses with new interest, noting for the first time what seemed to be the ruins of buildings thrusting up here and there. Harjeedian had spoken of history. The buildings implied that before the islands had been turned into a preserve for the yarimaimalom, they had been used by humans. That meant there was probably fresh water, game, timber . . .

Waln didn't know to what use he could turn these conjectures, but he knew that he wanted to learn more about Misheemnekuru. He wouldn't ask Harjeedian. No good would come from giving that snaky-eyed aridisdu whatever he would deduce from Waln's questions. No, Waln would be a devoted little language tutor, and while he was teaching his students, he figured they'd be teaching him, too.

ONLY A FEW DAYS HAD PASSED since their arrival on Misheemnekuru and Firekeeper already was certain of two things. One, she did not like how Moon Frost was sniffing around Blind Seer. Two, she was certain that the Wise Wolves were hiding something from them.

Firekeeper could hardly blame them for the latter. After all, she and Blind Seer were strangers, not only from another pack, but from another land as well. Although the Wise Wolf Ones tried to present their proximity to the human outpost as merely a coincidence of territories, Firekeeper had recently grown more aware of the delicacy of such matters.

Her own birth pack held territory near the easiest path through the Iron Mountains from Hawk Haven into the western lands. Once Firekeeper might have thought this just coincidence, since someone must hunt those lands. During the last summer, she had realized that the territory was considered a place of honor—and great danger. After all, as far as taking advantage of the deer and other woodland creatures that lived in those lands, Cousins could have hunted there as easily as Royal.

Thinking over the choice made by the Royal Wolves to keep some of their own near that critical area, Firekeeper couldn't believe that these Wise Wolves, for all their apparently amity with humanity, were not aware that this borderland was sensitive territory. There were many decisions to be made by those who held it.

How far would the Wise Wolves let humans penetrate—say, after a strayed cow—without warning them back? What action would they take if some adventurous or ambitious young aridisdu decided to make a name for himself by claiming exploration rights? What would they do if the humans decided to visit some of the ruins left by their ancestors?

Once Firekeeper would have believed that killing the interloper was the simple, and obvious, solution, but now she knew that such killing was far from simple, and that humans—for all their own territoriality—tended to get very offended when asked to respect the rights of others. Would these Liglimom humans be in any way different? Firekeeper wasn't at all certain they would be.

However, these were all things about which she hoped to learn more over the course of her stay—part of her desire to find out whether the Wise Wolves were indeed prisoners of the humans, no matter what each group wished to pretend to itself. Pups were less reserved than adults, and Firekeeper could already sense that the adults of the pack were inclined to view her as a peculiar sort of pup—a youngling like Rascal at best. This annoyed Firekeeper, but as she thought she could turn the misconception to her own advantage, she didn't fight against it.

Watching Moon Frost play up to Blind Seer, Firekeeper felt an urge to fight rising from deep inside her—but it was a confusing urge. Shouldn't she be glad for Blind Seer? Moon Frost was a very powerful hunter. Firekeeper had never liked the idea that her beloved pack mate be limited to the lower-ranking, nonbreeder role. She had been proud when she saw him asserting himself One to One when introductions were made to this new pack. Was that the reason for her anger? Fear that Blind Seer would be demoted to a lesser place within this larger pack if he bonded with Moon Frost?

Honesty forced Firekeeper to deny this at once. This pack was not large enough to support two breeding couples. Were Moon Frost to find a mate, she would split off and found her own pack. Far from being demoted, Blind Seer would be elevated, and next spring would find him father of his own litter.

A litter that would, inevitably, tie him to this land, to these wolves.

Firekeeper felt her heart sink within her at the thought. She knew without knowing why that she had long footsore wanderings in front of her before she settled in any one place. She might join with a pack for a while, might return to her birth pack for a visit, but there were too many questions she wanted answered, questions that could not be answered if she contented herself with the round of hunting, sleeping, romping, and hunting again that defined the lives of even Royal Wolves.

She had always imagined Blind Seer at her side in these wanderings, but now, as the days passed and she saw how he seemed to welcome Moon Frost's playful overtures, the wolf-woman wondered if he might have found a place to stay.

Had Firekeeper possessed a tail, it would have drooped. Had she possessed proper ears, she would have found it difficult to keep them pricked forward and alert. As it was, she struggled to display appropriate confidence when she and Blind Seer were invited to relocate with the pack to some distant meadows near a river through which ocean fish were making a spawning run.

"When the fish are running," Tangler explained, "there is ample food for many wolves. We often join up with other packs so our children will know each other. This season, many are interested in coming and making your acquaintance."

Although meeting the Wise Wolves was precisely why they had come to Misheemnekuru, Firekeeper wondered if the alacrity with which Blind Seer accepted the invitation for them both had anything to do with the fact that it would keep him close to Moon Frost. Had they not chosen to travel with the borderland pack, she and Blind Seer would have more reasonably gone exploring on their own, asking first for introductions to the neighboring packs. This trip would eliminate the need for such introductions—and for leaving the borderland pack behind.

Firekeeper shook from her head what would be the main outcome of such socializing, and went to find Blind Seer.

"So," she said, "we go to these meeting meadows. I don't mind, but have you thought about how we will keep our promise to Harjeedian—the one that said we would tell the outpost humans that we still live and breathe?"

"It was only a small promise," Blind Seer said lazily. He was still drowsy from the afternoon heat. "You didn't say that you would do it, only that you would try."

"I had intended," Firekeeper said a bit sharply, "to use such as a means of reassuring Derian that we still live and breathe. Not so long ago, you were the one telling me not to run off without letting friends know. Has this changed so much?"

Blind Seer had the grace to look a little ashamed, but not very much.

"It has changed," he protested. "We are here among our own people. We intend to do nothing more dangerous than hunt elk."

"The One Male before your father was killed when hunting elk," Firekeeper reminded acidly. There were times she hated remembering how many more years she had seen than Blind Seer. It made her acutely feel her lack of achievement. "Hunting elk is more dangerous than hunting deer or rabbits, even with a large pack. I am not convinced that what we do is so safe."

She meant more than merely accompanying what was—for all their welcome—a strange pack, but Blind Seer was either too sleepy to think or being deliberately dense.

"We will be fine," he said, adjusting himself into deeper shade. "If you worry so, run off to the humans and tell them where we go and that we will speak with them again when we come back."

For all its good sense, Firekeeper didn't like this suggestion. It seemed too much like admitting these humans had a hold on her, but Blind Seer's comments made her remember a course of action she had considered when first contemplating coming to Misheemnekuru.

Leaving Blind Seer slumbering, she went looking for a representative of the local wingéd folk. Like most wolves, Firekeeper felt a certain affinity for ravens. Even the Cousin wolves and ravens banded together, the big, black birds tolerated in denning areas and at rendezvous points. She had even seen a raven perch on a wolf's head, pecking gently for attention, inviting a chase. In return for scavenging rights, the ravens acted as invaluable scouts. They saw the approach of potential predators, and were not above calling when they noted an injured animal, hoping to bring a hunter who might pull it down and open it up for all to enjoy.

Among the Royal Wolves and Ravens, the relationship was more sophisticated. Here, too, the ravens served as scouts and relayed information regarding possible prey. They also acted as liaisons between other members of the Royal Beasts and the landbound carnivores. Although something of a truce existed between herbivores and carnivores, the herbivores preferred not to have to deal with the carnivores directly. Ravens, with their bossy, social ways, liked the importance of serving as diplomats.

Now Firekeeper went seeking the ravens who associated with this pack. As was common with their Cousin-kind, it was a juvenile band, for the mated pairs held territory and would not care to rove as a wolf pack did once the pups were past their youngest days. However, as was not usual with their Cousins, the group of young rowdies was accompanied by a few senior members. These did not precisely rule their juniors, but they did provide a moderating influence. They were the ones with whom Firekeeper should do her negotiating.

She found the ravens easily, tracking them by the croaks and yells they made as they scavenged the remains of a putrefying carcass dragged into a tree by one of the local jaguars and now too far gone for even a cat to enjoy.

For once, Firekeeper was glad that her sense of smell was less acute than was that of a wolf. Even from where she paused a short distance away, politely waiting to be noticed, the thing—had it once been a fawn?—reeked.

Nor did she have long to wait. Ravens were inquisitive creatures, and Firekeeper created an excuse for investigating her presence by taking her Fang from its sheath and tilting it back and forth slowly so that the sunlight glinted from the large cabochon-cut garnet set in the hilt.

Two ravens broke from the squabbling mass of their juniors and came toward her. One swooped from tree limb to tree limb, perching between glides to study her. The other walked along the ground with a rolling gait that, after her time at sea, inevitably reminded Firekeeper of a sailor. Like many Royal Beasts, the ravens were large for their kind. Like all ravens Firekeeper had met, they mingled arrogance and playfulness in a fashion a human might have found contradictory.

These were beautiful birds, the glossy black of their features showing such iridescent green, purple, and blue when the sun angled across it that Firekeeper thought them more colorful than the robin who, after all, wore his color only on his breast.

Firekeeper waited, giving the ravens opportunity to inspect her, rocking the garnet back and forth in the sunlight so that its deep red was added to the ravens' own iridescent glow.

"Can I have it?" asked the slightly smaller of the two ravens. "I like it. It is like frozen blood."

"More shiny than frozen blood," the other commented. "It is only a rock and would not taste as good."

"I would still like it," the first raven commented. "I would put it in a hidden place in a tree that only I know. I have other treasures there, but this would be the prettiest."

Firekeeper decided she had better speak before they decided her Fang was being offered.

"I cannot give you this," she said, "but I could hunt for you."

"The wolves do that!" the second raven said, sounding rather as if providing meals for ravens was the primary reason wolves had been put on the earth. "And if they eat too much, there are always other hunters who will feed us."

"It is kind of you to offer," said the first raven, hopping sideways in a fashion that told Firekeeper that it had not given up on the knife. "The wolves do not offer. They bolt down their kills as fast as they can. We let them, of course, because we cannot have them going hungry. They need so much to keep themselves strong."

Firekeeper found herself smiling at this new way of seeing the world. The raven's egotism reminded her of newly weaned puppies for whom every hunt clearly existed only so they could be fed, never mind that their begging emptied the stomach of every adult within hearing.

"You are thoughtful," she said. "As I knew you would be."

"You knew of us?" asked the first raven. "Of course you did. We knew of you. You are the wolf who looks like a human. The human who thinks she is a wolf. We have been watching you."

"For how long?" Firekeeper asked. "Since before I came to these islands?"

"Some have," said the first raven evasively. Firekeeper had identified it as a male, and thought it was somewhat older than its female companion.

"Since you know me," Firekeeper said, "offering my name is only a formality, but I give it to you in any case—so that if you wish me to hunt for you, you can call me. I am called Firekeeper."

The ravens—who she was perfectly certain had already heard the name—made a great show of repeating it.

"I," said the first raven, "am called Bitter."

"And I am called Lovable," said the second one. "I am pleased to meet you."

Lovable—who was the one who had walked over—now swooped a short distance so that she perched on the lower branch of a tree. She leaned precariously so that she could get a better look at the garnet, and Firekeeper took a step back, well respecting the power in the raven's horned bill.

"Do you ever fly to the mainland?" Firekeeper asked the ravens. "Because if you do, I had hoped to ask you a favor."

"Favor?" asked Bitter guardedly.

"Would you give me the stone if I did you a favor?" asked Lovable.

Firekeeper smiled. "I told you. I cannot give you this stone. It is attached to my knife and I need the knife in one piece. However, I could find you other things that shine, since you have the wolves to hunt for you."

Lovable was clearly interested in that offer, but Bitter remained guarded.

"What is this favor?" he asked.

Firekeeper sighed. "I have a friend in the city on the mainland. He is a tall human with hair the same color as the fur of a fox. He is staying at a place called u-Bishinti."

She wasn't certain how, but instantly she was certain the ravens had heard of Derian. No wonder, really, given that gossip flew.

"I see you do know of him," she went on boldly. "The favor I would ask is that you carry messages to him from me."

"Does he speak our language as you do?" Lovable asked.

"No," Firekeeper admitted. "He does not. I had thought I would ask the humans to give me some paper on which I could write."

She decided to overlook for now that she was going to depend on a skill that she had disdained to learn properly.

"We might do this," Bitter agreed. "And you would hunt for us in return?"

"And give us bright things?" Lovable added. "There are many bright things here, especially in the places where the first humans built their nests. I have taken some away already, but I would like more."

"I could do this," Firekeeper agreed. "My need is to make certain that my fox-haired friend does not worry, for I go with the wolves when they leave for the meeting meadows."

Bitter considered, raising and lowering his feathers so that he created the illusion that he had long ears or, again, that his head was a fluffy ball twice its usual size. Lovable seemed quite impressed.

"We can do this," Bitter said at last. "I would like to see your fox-haired friend for myself. Can you tell him to give us presents, too?"

"I can try," Firekeeper said hesitantly. "I am a wolf and writing does not come easily to me."

A new thought occurred to her. Could these ravens—or their kin—carry messages farther than to the mainland? Could they carry a message as far as to her own birth pack or to Hawk Haven?

She put the question to the ravens, and Bitter looked distinctly upset.

"We do not leave our territories here in the south," he said. "Across the big inlet to the north, what you call the Royal Beasts do not like us. They say we follow strange ways, associate too closely with humans, and have adopted their customs. If we go there, we are attacked on sight, and so none of our kind, not raven, nor gull, nor any other goes further north than the edge of the northern point before the inlet. A few who have gone, whether by eagerness to see if attitudes have changed or by the chance humor of Air, have carried back terrible stories. We will carry your messages to the fox-haired friend you left on the mainland, but we will never fly north."

Firekeeper hastened to soothe Bitter, so enraged did he seem, and she wondered at the prejudice shown by the Royal Beasts. What had these yarimaimalom done to deserve it? Was it only that they intimately associated with humans? That might be enough. She knew to her deep sorrow how many of the Royal Beasts still hated and feared humans, blaming them for what had been done in the days of the Old Country rulers.

Acquiring paper and a waxed hide tube in which to keep it was easy. The humans showed her how to use a bit of charcoal or a stick and berry juice to make marks. Firekeeper found herself thinking how much they would like the colored writing sticks the New Kelvinese made if this was the best ink they had. One of the aridisdu insisted on showing her the marks that meant "all is well," "help is needed," and a few others. The Liglimom apparently had single signs for these, less complex than the series of characters used to write Pellish, and Firekeeper found them no more difficult to commit to memory than animal tracks.

The outpost humans were very interested in her, and asked many questions. Firekeeper answered only a few, enough to keep the humans sweet. She needed them to tell Harjeedian and Derian where she was going so that they would not worry, and their worry create problems for her with the yarimaimalom.

The outpost humans agreed to pass along her message. So Firekeeper felt reassured—at least as reassured as one can who is going into unknown wilds in the company of barely known wolves, with uncertainty regarding the loyalty of one's best friend to speed the trail.

XV

"SO, HAS DERIAN COUNSELOR BEEN to see you yet?" asked Harjeedian, stalking into the common room of their suite and glowering down at Rahniseeta.

She looked up from the letters she was copying for the iaridisdu of the Temple of Cold Bloods. Being neither of the temple nor not of it, she came by lots of this type of labor. It didn't hurt that her handwriting was excellent—easy to read, yet elegant.

Rahniseeta finished the line she was transcribing before looking up.

"You know perfectly well that he has not. The temple would be buzzing like a rattlesnake's tail if Derian had been here. He left three days ago, and as far as I know he has not yet returned to the city—nor has Lady Blysse."

Harjeedian dropped his annoyance, and shifted into worry.

"I know. Lady Blysse has not been so much as glimpsed since she walked into the forest three days ago. The residents of the outpost report a greater frequency of wolf howls, but nothing else. Truth refuses to comment on anything related to Lady Blysse. Her refusal has u-Liall quite perturbed. Even the lesser beast auguries are inconclusive. All anyone is willing to commit to is that Lady Blysse is probably still alive."

Rahniseeta understood now why her brother was so agitated. He had staked a great deal on his mission to bring Lady Blysse here from her northern home. Now not only hadn't she proven tractable to their requests that she teach them how to speak directly to the yarimaimalom, she had completely disappeared. Probably no one was blaming Harjeedian, but that didn't keep him from blaming himself.

"And have the residents of u-Bishinti confirmed or denied whether Derian is a maimalodalu?"

Harjeedian didn't exactly brighten, but he did marginally relax at the reminder that he was not alone in finding it difficult to extract information from the foreigners.

"No. Although from what I have heard, Derian Counselor has demonstrated incredible skill with horses. Varjuna is quite taken with him—and so is Zira."

Rahniseeta understood the significance of this immediately. Varjuna tended to bond with the most troublesome people imaginable—as long as they shared his interest in things equine. Zira's vivid appreciation of the good things in life was matched with a complete intolerance for the bad. This intolerance had cut off what otherwise might have been a solid political career, for Zira had undeniable charisma that made people overlook her physical unattractiveness.

"So what has Derian been doing there?" Rahniseeta asked. "Has he been visiting with the Wise Horses?"

Harjeedian shook his head.

"As far as I can learn, he has not visited the Wise Horses at all. Varjuna offered to give Derian a horse, and for the last several days Derian seems to have been quite contentedly visiting every pasture and stable on the place. The denizens of u-Bishinti think this is wonderful, of course, but it tells us nothing about his true nature."

"Has anyone asked him directly if he is maimalodalu?"

Harjeedian gave her a sideways look.

"Odd you should ask that. Someone has tried. Poshtuvanu, Varjuna and Zira's eldest and an initiated kidisdu, did drop a few hints, but Derian looked at him so oddly that he said nothing more. Apparently, the general opinion is split. Half say Derian must be maimalodalu to have such a rapport with horses. Others say that his ability with the animals is nothing we haven't seen among our own most talented, and that his eyes are the wrong color."

"Wrong color?"

Harjeedian sighed. "Apparently it's pretty rare for normally sighted horses to have anything but brown eyes. Occasionally there are horses with blue or amber eyes, but Derian's are hazel—the brown-green mix. This has been held against him, though others argue the color of his coat—excuse me, hair—is equally telling."

"In other words, we don't know much more than we did before," Rahniseeta said. "And you would really like me to find something out."

Harjeedian nodded. "As I said before, Derian doesn't like me. He does seem to like you."

Rahniseeta considered. She was not going to prostitute herself to her brother's ambitions or even to his curiosity, but there might be another way. . . .

"Barnet is growing restless," she said. "The number of people eager to learn Pellish is quite astonishing. I think he is about to go off his feed. What if I offered to take Barnet to u-Bishinti for a change of air and a chance to see his countryman?"

"And, perhaps to agitate for Derian to return and assist with the teaching?" Harjeedian said with a grin. "That could work. We have tried using the other rescued sailors as language teachers, but they lack patience or even interest. The only one who has applied himself at all diligently is Waln Endbrook—though I don't think we should mention that to Derian."

"No," Rahniseeta said. "Derian and Lady Blysse despise Waln—hate him, I think is not too strong a way to put it. It would be best if we do not remind them that Waln, too, is here in u-Seeheera."

"Of course, of course," Harjeedian said in that annoyingly absentminded way he had that meant that he was thinking about what was important to him and not at all about what she had said.

Rahniseeta was used to Harjeedian's manner, and had also learned that he actually remembered what was said to him at such times. Very well; she had warned him, and it was up to him to remember to act on her warnings.

"You will go down to u-Bishinti, then?" Harjeedian asked. "Barnet does give you a good excuse. I will see when he can be freed from his tutorial duties and check back with you."

Harjeedian departed with a brisk, purposeful step. With a sigh Rahniseeta returned to her copying. She found she was having difficulty concentrating. Her mind kept straying to the two foreigners and the problem of proving whether or not they—or Lady Blysse, the most likely candidate—were beast-souled. In her opinion, the aridisdum and kidisdum were being too cautious. She would try her own methods.

Rahniseeta stared down at the letter and noticed that she had narrowly avoided an error that would have meant recopying the entire thing. She forced herself to concentrate, but even as she did, her lips curved in a smile of quiet self-satisfaction. She would succeed where the others had failed. She would venture where they had not dared. She would learn the truth.

BITTER THE RAVEN PERCHED IN a flowering bush in the garden surrounding the step pyramid in Heeranenahalm and told the jaguar Truth of his interview with Firekeeper.

The jaguar was not pleased, but Bitter had chosen his perch well. The branch that would hold his weight would not hold that of the jaguar, so Truth was saved from giving improper vent to her indignation.

"You told her that much?"

"She will learn in time," the raven croaked. "I may not have your gifts, Truth, but that Firekeeper has a wolf's nose for game trail and a human's curiosity. It is a dangerous combination—at least for those who would keep secrets."

"And as she would keep Fire, so we must keep secrets," the jaguar replied, her tail twitching back and forth. "So say the omens, but I agree with you, Bitter, I do not foresee that we shall keep our secrets for long."

"And then?" The raven leaned forward, every feather of his body drawn tight. "What do you foresee?"

"It is as with everything related to that wolf-child," Truth replied. "There is no one tight, clean line. She knows so little that almost anything could happen."

"Perhaps then . . ." said Bitter, righting himself and plucking a half-spent flower from the shrub, tilting his head to one side as he contemplated the withered thing. "Perhaps then we should see that Firekeeper learns more. Already she and her pack mate move deeper into the islands. It would be possible for one of them to find something . . ."

Truth hung limp on the bough, freeing her mind to wander, but no images came, only disturbing fragments. Still, she was more than a diviner. Truth knew, if no one else did, that over half the omens she provided for the humans were based on her own good sense and knowledge. The same should serve in this circumstance.

"Yes. Let them be given opportunities to learn, but under no account let either Blind Seer or Firekeeper suspect we have beak or claw in this. Knowing we are interested in their reactions will color those reactions and further muddy a picture we hope to make clear."

"Wise," agreed Bitter. "Surely I can arrange something. Many wolves are gathering. It has been my observation that though the greater pack is strong, it is not always as intelligent as one with fewer heads."

"If so you say," Truth replied with the disdain of the solitary for those who herd or flock or gather in packs.

"I do," Bitter said, and without farewell or further discussion he launched into the air.

Truth watched him beating his heavy-winged way out toward Misheemnekuru. She knew that many humans would have observed the raven's coming and wondered at their conversation. Doubtless before long someone would be coming to beg that Truth enlighten u-Liall at least as to whether Firekeeper continued alive and well.

It took no diviner to know this. The same question had been asked of her daily since the wolves had left for Misheemnekuru. Truth had been honest, indicating that the omens were unclear, but today she could give an answer.

For a long moment, Truth contemplated going to u-Liall of her own initiative, but she dismissed the idea with a sharp jerk of her tail. It would have been one thing if the five members had been scattered and her summons would have brought them running, but they were already in the step pyramid.

Truth settled herself higher in the branches where she was both better hidden, and in a better position to see when a messenger would leave the pyramid. Then she turned her face to the glow of the sun, letting the warmth wash away the uncertainty that, cat-like, she refused to show to anyone in all the world, no matter what the consequences might be.

TO WALN'S SURPRISE, he was the only one among the *Explorer*'s survivors bothered by their situation.

"Why kick up a fuss?" Rarby replied in response to Waln's question. "We're barely back from a long voyage. I, for one, am grateful that all they want out of me is talking. It's a shitload easier than hauling line."

"Think about it," Shelby, Rarby's brother, added. "If we'd fallen into Waterlander hands, we'd have been sold unless we could come up with a ransom. Only you might have had ransom money—and maybe not even you."

It was a cruel cut, but even crueler was Waln's realization that he was in no position to object. Not so long ago, if a common sailor had spoken to him like that, Waln would have backhanded him right off his feet. When Waln had been a younger man, his strength and size would have kept all but the foolhardy from intervening. Later, his wealth and social standing were more potent protections.

Shelby's comment forced Waln to face that he had neither his youthful strength—though he wasn't beyond improving on what he had left—nor money nor position. In the hardest analysis, he had very little left other than his knowledge of northern lands. As soon as more of these intellectually voracious Liglimom soaked up what he had to tell, and they had made a few voyages on their own, he wouldn't even have that.

Rarby, seeing something he didn't like in Waln's expression, quickly moderated his brother's imprudent comment.

"Maybe even if we had ransom we'd have been sold anyhow," Rarby added. "I heard tell of a man who . . ."

As the sailor rambled through a version of a tale Waln had heard in a dozen variations since putting to sea when he was boy, Waln thought about what made him different from the other survivors.

Except for Barnet, these are harbor scum. What do they have to go back to? I seem to recall that those chosen for the exploratory expedition couldn't have either wife or dependent children. Sure, they might have parents or siblings, but if they're like too many of the sailors I've known, they're accustomed to being away from their kinfolk.

It's different for me. I am a gentleman, wrongly accused of betraying my queen and nation, stripped of title and property. Not only do I have name and property to redeem, I must hope my father-in-law is taking care of my wife and children. I thought the Liglimom would help me, as I have helped them, but once again, I am betrayed.

Waln liked the shape of this reflection and didn't look too closely at it for truth. This interpretation of the facts gave him back his sense of self-respect and purpose. However, he was not the type to indulge in self-pity for long. Revenge was a meat more to his taste, and he immediately began considering how he might win his freedom and get the upper hand over those who had wronged him. These two things must come before he could even hope to head back home.

The first step Waln knew he must take was perhaps the most galling. Aware that he was being slighted, that his achievements were being overlooked, he still forced himself to smile and be as cooperative as possible. His altered attitude did him more good than he had dared imagine.

Eight men had survived the wreck. Among these, without a doubt Barnet was the most verbally acute. Waln came second, in his opinion not far behind the minstrel. The remaining six were good sailors, but not terribly brilliant outside of their limited sphere. They could tell how to trim a sail or stone a deck, how to predict the weather with fair accuracy, how to load a variety of cargoes. Beyond things having to do with ships and the sea, their knowledge was peculiar and limited.

Nolan knew more about rope than any one man should, but then that had been his family trade. He also was fond of part-singing, especially when he carried the melody. Tedgewinn knew how to carve in wood, ivory, and soft stone. He had been carpenter's mate aboard the doomed vessel.

Wiatt knew fish: what kinds swam in what waters, which were good to eat, which only showed at certain times of the year. He knew how to cook them, too, and how to make even salt fish taste good. Elwyn said that Wiatt had survived the wreck by being lifted up from drowning on the backs of schools of minnows, but then everyone knew that Elwyn was addled in the head.

Elwyn, a former deckhand, had little going for him but luck. Luck he had by the bushel, so though he was heavy-footed, tactless, and given to gas, he was welcome aboard any ship in the hope that his luck might rub off on the venture.

And, Waln thought, *I suppose it did in a way—at least some of us survived, though the ship herself went down.*

Having resolved that the end of his usefulness as a language instructor would not be the end of his comforts—or even of his existence—Waln began searching after information, any information that he could turn to his use. His initial interest in Misheemnekuru remained with him. In one of the aridisdum who came to him for daily lessons, Waln found someone who could tell him more about those mysterious islands.

Shivadtmon was associated in some way with the Temple of the Sea Beasts. Waln gathered that Shivadtmon preferred seals and otters, but that the temple also kept dolphins, muskrats, and even water rats. Although most of the temples were built in the vicinity of the step pyramid, Shivadtmon's was located down near the harbor.

Waln didn't know exactly what Shivadtmon said that made him aware that the other man did not precisely favor the giving over of Misheemnekuru exclusively to the use of the yarimaimalom. Perhaps it was the manner in which he spoke of the noise and bustle of the harbor area or the way he mentioned his fears for the safety of his more adventurous charges. Whatever the reason, in Shivadtmon Waln found someone who was willing to talk about the islands as something more than places both restricted and sanctified.

"I was permitted to do some of my training at the outpost there," Shivadtmon said proudly. "It is an honor granted to very few."

"Then humans do reside there?" Waln asked. "Or are my shortcomings in your language misleading me?"

Shivadtmon smiled. "Your command of the language is quite adequate to this understanding. The yarimaimalom permit us to maintain an outpost there for our mutual convenience. Otherwise, all messages would need to be relayed by birds or sea creatures, and my understanding is that this was not satisfactory to either those who would carry the messages or those who must send them."

"Interesting," Waln said. "Then the yarimaimalom who live there continue to interact with humanity?"

"Certainly," Shivadtmon said, a little surprised. "Many of those who now reside in temples came from the islands and will return there when the omens are appropriate."

"I understand," Waln said. "So Misheemnekuru is not nearly as isolated as Harjeedian led me to believe."

"Oh, the majority of the islands are no longer known to us," Shivadtmon hastened to correct. "We may sail around the outer perimeter, but even the inner waterways are forbidden to us."

"Inner waterways? Do you mean rivers and streams?"

"Those, yes, and also the inlets where water flows between individual islands. The yarimaimalom are jealous of their privacy—as well they should be," Shivadtmon added hastily. "They build neither walls nor houses. The elements themselves provide their homes."

Waln thought fleetingly of wolf dens and rabbit burrows, but there was something more interesting he wished to pursue.

"But I am certain I glimpsed buildings there," he said. "These are then not in use?"

"Perhaps as aeries for fish eagles or haunts for bats," Shivadtmon said with what Waln was sure was envy in his tone, "but not as proper residences. I doubt if a human has walked within them since the last of our corrupt rulers fell beneath the Divine Retribution."

"Until now, of course," said Waln, not certain why, but trusting the impulse that guided him.

"Now?" Shivadtmon looked genuinely confused.

"Lady Blysse has been permitted to explore Misheemnekuru," Waln reminded him, "and for all her claims otherwise, surely she is human enough."

Shivadtmon's expression went from confusion to understanding and then to anger. He took his leave soon thereafter, and Waln felt well pleased. Time enough to ask more about the islands, time after his new friend had absorbed the injustice that was being done to him and his fellows.

Plenty of time.

Waln rubbed his hands together as he might have after finalizing some deal of a more routine type, then returned to his studies. It would not do for him to be unable to communicate with the Liglimom—not when so much was coming to depend on at least some of them coming to learn to see the world as he did, rather than through the veils of superstition that had held them back.

It wouldn't do at all.

❧

ONCE THE PACKS HAD MOVED to the meadows where the elk herds had gathered, Firekeeper had to struggle to keep her spirits up. Even the praise old Neck Breaker gave her when her straight-shot arrows brought down a panicked elk cow and so spared young High Howler from a nasty kick did little to lighten her mood.

From a silent watch post high in the boughs of a new-leafed apple tree, Firekeeper had seen Blind Seer and Moon Frost running side by side, singing to drive an elk, moving at speeds her human legs could never reach, much less sustain. She had seen them dive almost as a pair into the carcass after the elk had fallen, snapping back at the Ones—who usually took the first and best parts of any kill as their right.

The Ones' own growls and snaps had been perfunctory at best. Indeed, they had permitted themselves to be driven back. This was hardly a great sacrifice on their part. Between the elk brought down by the Ones themselves and the elk Firekeeper had finished with her arrows, there was plenty of meat for everyone without the Ones invading Blind Seer's kill. Even High Howler, Rascal, and Nipper came in for chunks of liver—a delicacy usually claimed by the Ones alone.

Yet Firekeeper could not help but feel that the Ones had not growled Moon Frost and Blind Seer away for a reason other than the quantities of good meat available. She thought Tangler and Hard Biter were pleased at the accord growing between these two strong hunters. Well they should be. Mating season would not come until late winter, and until the snappish tempers of that time arrived, Moon Frost and Blind Seer would use their skills to support the existing pack. With two such fine hunters working as a pair, the pack would claim a high number of kills without paying in blood and broken bones.

What would it matter if by late winter Moon Frost and Blind Seer were splitting off? By then Nipper, High Howler, and even Rascal would have had time to grow into another two seasons' strength. Even with the loss of Moon Frost, the pack would be more powerful than it had been the previous spring.

Firekeeper tried not to brood over the pattern she saw developing, but she didn't feel any more friendly to Moon Frost when the female sneered at her for cooking her share of the meat or needing her knife to remove the hide. The fact that Moon Frost's pack mates—all but Neck Breaker, who was perhaps wiser, perhaps merely more prudent—joined the game caused anger and resentment to blend in Firekeeper's belly.

The wolf-woman wanted to leap at Moon Frost, to make the other wolf take back the gibe by force, but memories of Moon Frost's lean, graceful silver-grey form ripping in through the grass-swollen roundness of the elk's flank stayed her. Firekeeper knew herself beaten without battle ever being joined, and the elk flesh, just beginning to be marbled with grazing fat after the thin days of winter and early spring, tasted flat and stringy in her mouth.

Yet for all of this, there were things to distract Firekeeper from her unhappiness. At the meeting meadows, she and Blind Seer met their second pack of Wise Wolves, these from lands slightly to the west of the meeting meadows.

The west pack was slightly larger than the borderland pack that had taken Firekeeper and Blind Seer with them to the meeting meadows. In addition to Grey Thunder, the pack's One Male, and, Half-Snarl, its One Female, the west pack boasted three hunters roughly equivalent to Moon Frost. Only two younger cubs from previous litters remained with the pack—a male a year old and a female two years old. They also had an older wolf among their numbers, a female called Cricket, and a small litter of this spring's puppies.

Soon after the west pack's arrival there came another pack, this one from hunting grounds some distance inland. By now Firekeeper was having trouble keeping track of which wolf was with which pack. She had no idea how many wolves there were now gathered around the meadows, making any prey animal nervous, and the nights ring with their boastful songs.

With private shame, Firekeeper felt how her refusal to bother to learn how to commit larger numbers to memory was a handicap. She knew that Derian would have had no difficulty assessing and categorizing the swirling mass of lean, grey-furred bodies. Nor, she realized, did the wolves. Their keener noses permitted them to "see" differences between individuals that Firekeeper could not. Only Firekeeper, who had refused to learn the human way of accounting and who lacked the ability to learn the wolfish way, was limited.

However, she had no trouble telling the next arrival from the rest. He was a magnificent male who belonged to none of the three packs already arrived, but was an outlier, dispersed from his birth pack but not yet bonded to another.

The newcomer shared the silver-grey coloration so common among the wolves of Misheemnekuru. He was as large as any of the One Males present, with big feet that seemed to promise further growth, though from other signs he had achieved at least four or five winters. Yet neither size nor any other physical trait was what set him apart from the others in Firekeeper's eyes, but a commanding presence that as much as declared him One Male, although his pack had yet to be formed.

"My divined name is Dark Death," the outlier introduced himself after proving his worth by flinging himself into a hunt in progress and bringing down the twisting, leaping buck that had eluded the others thus far. "I was born to the center-island pack. By swimming and running I have made my way here, drawn by songs old and new heard rising from this place."

It was a good boast. By now Firekeeper had gathered something of the relationship of the different islands to each other, and Dark Death must have heard those songs in relay from a long way off. She understood his claim as the wolves did—proof of Dark Death's prowess as a solitary hunter.

Firekeeper watched as the wolves went about their usual rounds of tail-sniffing, fascinated by how the dynamics of the packs were adjusting in response to this outlier. Two of the young hunters in the west pack were females: Beachcomber and Freckles. They sniffed tails repeatedly with Dark Death; then Beachcomber snapped at Freckles when she came too close. Young as she was, Nipper also showed interest in the handsome male, as did the females from the latest-come pack. Indeed, only Moon Frost acted indifferent, almost as if she already had a mate.

The dynamic among the males changed as well. The unmated males grew definitely defensive. Blind Seer put up his hackles and growled softly. Another male, Smoke Jumper, snapped at the tip of Dark Death's tail. Dark Death ignored him—a greater insult than if he had snapped in return. There would definitely be fighting before the males established who outranked whom—and as the females competed to show off their better qualities.

Perched up in her apple tree, Firekeeper found herself fascinated by Dark Death. The outlier wolf walked with an arrogant swagger as if he were a One of Ones, not a packless, isolated male. Indeed, Dark Death's arrogance put the One Males, each of whom had claimed mate and territory, on edge before long.

Firekeeper wondered if Dark Death was wise to behave in this manner, then realized the outlier was wise indeed. He was declaring himself competition for any and all mated males—or males who might hope to find a mate—and this meant that any battles would be between him and his opponent. The packs would not take part as they would against an invader into their territory.

After introductions were completed, Dark Death pretended to notice Firekeeper for the first time.

Firekeeper knew this noticing was pretense because she knew how easily a wolf scented anything unfamiliar. Doubtless Dark Death had been aware of her presence even before he had walked from the forest fringe into the meadows. However, as the other wolves had paid Firekeeper no heed, manners and prudence had dictated that Dark Death must account himself to them before commenting on the anomalous human in their midst.

Now the outlier wolf trotted over to the apple tree in which Firekeeper had taken her perch. He stood on his hind legs and stretched up toward her. Dark Death was tall enough that he easily reached within touching distance—but then Firekeeper hadn't been trying to get out of range. It was simply her habit when in unfamiliar places to claim a place from which she could see her surroundings. Otherwise, especially within a swarming, jostling mass of wolves, she was likely to become overwhelmed.

If she had chosen this perch because she knew that Blind Seer could easily join her if he so chose, Firekeeper didn't admit this, even to herself.

Now she looked down at the rudely sniffing nose and resisted an urge to bring her heel solidly down onto the damp, black leather.

"I thought we had a treaty that forbade humans from coming into Misheemnekuru," Dark Death growled, "but perhaps that does not apply on this island."

The outlier's attitude was faintly insulting, implying that the wolves he knew would never have permitted such a thing.

Blind Seer responded.

"She is a member of my birth pack, my sister, and so not a human at all, but a wolf."

Firekeeper's response upon hearing Blind Seer defend her mixed pleasure and discomfort. She was glad that Blind Seer had spoken up for her and named her a wolf, but she felt unsettled that he referred to her as his sister. It had been a long time since he had called her "sister" or she him "brother." Yet that was the basis for their relationship. Why did the renewal of the term make her so uncomfortable?

The wolf-woman knew full well, but she could avoid thinking about it with an enormous wolf sniffing around her knees. The discomfort she felt flared out in her response.

"Wolf I am and wolf I will be, no matter who denies it," Firekeeper snapped. "Would you still be wolf if some mischance cut off your tail? If you were missing an ear? If you were missing an eye? My shape may be wrong, but my heart is a wolf's and I'll fight any who deny it."

Dark Death dropped lightly down onto all four paws and looked up at Firekeeper, his head tilted quizzically. Then he turned and surveyed the gathered wolves, where indeed there was one with a missing ear, another with a blinded eye, another whose tail had met with some misfortune.

The outlier's reply was somber—not angry, as Firekeeper had expected. The seriousness of it touched her heart.

"True," Dark Death rumbled. "Shape does not make a wolf, nor scent, nor anything we can touch. I am sorry, wolf. May I have your name?"

Firekeeper was so astonished she found herself sliding to the ground almost without volition.

"I am called Firekeeper," she said. "As with Blind Seer, I am from lands very far to the north and west."

Dark Death sniffed her, "You are very brave, Firekeeper, but then your name promises you would be so. I am pleased to have the opportunity to hunt with you."

Firekeeper blinked and to her surprise realized that she was blushing. She hoped that none but Blind Seer would recognize the sign.

Then the moment passed and Dark Death once again concentrated on meeting and re-meeting the local wolves. Firekeeper, forgotten, found her gaze following him as he moved about. For the first time since their arrival, she even forgot to worry about Moon Frost, even when the other female crowded close to Blind Seer.

AS NECK BREAKER HAD EXPLAINED, the meeting meadows were neutral territory, bordered by lands hunted by several different wolf packs. In the winter, when the fish were not running, the elk clustered here, taking advantage both of the remnants of lush grass that remained under the snow and the proximity of so many of their number to keep their calves safe. Where the elk gathered, so gathered the wolves.

"It is an odd cycle," Firekeeper said to Neck Breaker one afternoon when she was trying very hard not to notice that Blind Seer was involved in some rough-and-tumble with Moon Frost and Freckles. "We follow the elk, but the elk cluster because we follow, and in turn more of us come because there are so many elk."

"And in time," Neck Breaker agreed, "there will be too many elk and the surviving calves will grow too strong for the hunting to be good any longer. Then, too, there will be pups to be taught hunting on more manageable prey. So we will leave, and the elk, no longer feeling threatened, will also break into small groups, and eventually bear their new young. In the absence of both hunters and grazers, the meadows, well fertilized by shit and piss and blood, will recover to be hunted upon when the next winter year comes."

"Are there rules?" Firekeeper asked. (Blind Seer had Moon Frost's scruff in his mouth and was rattling her back and forth while she snapped and growled in ineffectual protest.) "Rules for who can hunt here and how many to take? I noticed that the latest-come pack even swam across the water to join in the hunting, but no one challenged their right."

"There is no rule but that of having enough to eat," Neck Breaker said. "Sometimes—sad as it is to admit—even Wise Wolves can behave like Cousins and kill more than they need, but such greed is unusual even for Cousins. It would be a violation of divine Earth's goodness."

Firekeeper fell silent, caught between the discomfort she always felt when the Wise Wolves employed the terms of what she felt should be a purely human thing—this religion that spoke of deities who somehow shaped events—and her unhappiness at Blind Seer's play. Then, too, Dark Death had trotted out from the forest where he had gone earlier—presumably on one of the solo hunts that were not uncommon for a wolf who belonged to no one pack. She watched as ripples of awareness played over the gathered wolves at his arrival, finding it the easiest thing to accept.

The hierarchy of non-mated males was working itself out, readjusting with every new pack or outlier drawn to the meadows. Both Dark Death and Blind Seer remained at or near the top. Smoke Jumper had fallen some, though not to the bottom. Puma Killer, a male who would have been handsome but for the ear he had lost in the fight that had won him his name, was another high-ranking contender.

Firekeeper had paid less attention to the dynamics among the females, but she knew that Moon Frost's standoffishness had done her no harm in the eyes of the males. Although—at least to Firekeeper—Moon Frost seemed to favor Blind Seer, she had bonded with no male. The males, with the contrariness Firekeeper had observed in both humans and wolves, were all the more interested in Moon Frost because she refused to fawn over them. Freckles and Beachcomber vied between trying to imitate her indifference and making themselves noticeable through their antics.

Though Firekeeper could not help but be aware of this unfolding drama, the wolf-woman strove to concentrate on the original reason she had come to Misheemnekuru. She still was not certain whether the wolves remained on the islands by choice or by some odd coercion. One thing of which she was certain was that this was a sensitive topic. Even the two oldest wolves, Neck Breaker and Cricket, drew back from questions on the matter. From the answers she received, Firekeeper pieced together that the wolves were pleased with their lands on Misheemnekuru, that they would fight to keep them, but that there were problems, problems of which they would not speak to a relative stranger.

Firekeeper kept seeking information, worrying at the problem like a teething pup on a strip of rawhide. However, as rawhide resists puppy teeth, so the problem resisted solution.

I wish I could talk to Derian about this, she thought, *but Derian is far away across the waters, and we are a good day's run even from where the humans have their outpost. Perhaps I could get one of the ravens to carry him a message, but how would I draw a picture of a problem? Certainly the few characters the aridisdu insisted on showing me will not serve. All is not well, but all is not wrong either.*

But even as she thought such things, Firekeeper knew it was not Derian to whom she wished to speak—no matter that his human perspective might be useful. The one she wished to speak with was Blind Seer. He, however, sprawled in the sunlight, wrestling with Moon Frost as if there were neither problem nor mystery in all the world.

XVI

SHORTLY AFTER NOON three days following Rahniseeta's talk with Harjeedian, Barnet and Rahniseeta drove along the coast road toward u-Bishinti. She had chosen this route deliberately. Not only did it take them through some beautiful countryside, but some of that scenery would provide her with the opening she sought.

"You handle the reins well," Barnet said.

Rahniseeta smiled her thanks. The somewhat chubby black gelding between the shafts was so well behaved that the young woman suspected a child could handle him in anything except an emergency.

"Do you drive?" she asked.

"No," came the laconic reply. "Sail, row, paddle, and ride—the last barely passably. The land on which I grew up was so wet we moved everything we could by water. I don't think there was a wheel on the place bigger than those on a child's toy."

By now Rahniseeta knew that Barnet was inclined to exaggeration. She also knew that though his family name was a high-ranking one in his birth land, his branch of the family had not owned one of the great estates. That was one reason Barnet had decided to risk the voyage of exploration which had ended so disastrously.

Really, she thought, *his prospects are little better than my own.*

She couldn't decide if this similarity made her warm to him or despise him a little. She might not have many prospects, but she could ride, drive, write a good hand, make a snake dance to flute music, and do many other things that would advance her as surely as Harjeedian was advancing through the ranks in the Temple of the Cold Bloods.

And Barnet? He could tell stories—and sail, but it was clear that his heart was not in the handling of boats.

In our land he might have followed the same path as Harjeedian, but his people are ignorant of the deities. They go their way blindly, trusting to ancestor spirits to guide them—as if such would be wiser after death than they were in life!

Rahniseeta realized she had fallen too quiet. Barnet, tired no doubt from hours of trying to teach Pellish when he himself spoke the language of the Liglimom only passably, was drowsing beside her.

"See there?" Rahniseeta said, pointing out into the bay with a tilt of her head.

"Where? What?"

Barnet had indeed been drowsing. Rahniseeta pointed again.

"There, out in the waters. See the land? Those are Misheemnekuru."

Barnet expressed none of the surprise about the size of the islands that Harjeedian had reported from Lady Blysse.

"Nice looking," he said. "Do I see buildings there?"

Rahniseeta nodded, well pleased. She had waited her comments until they had reached this point precisely for this reason.

"Yes. Those on the high point belong to the outpost maintained there by some of the disdum. However, the ones you see toward the end closer to us . . . You see there?"

"Yes. It looks like the top of a ruined tower, maybe a bit of wall."

"You have sharp eyes," Rahniseeta complimented him. "Those are ruins from the days when the Old Country rulers first came here. They made their first settlement on the island, and some continued to live there even after they had a foothold on the mainland."

"No one lives there now?" Barnet asked. He sounded a bit disappointed.

"No one but the yarimaimalom," Rahniseeta said, then dropped her bait, "except if there are the maimalodalum—the beast-souled."

She had to translate the term for him, and when Barnet understood he still looked puzzled.

"I thought that was what the word must mean, but it doesn't tell me anything. Do you mean someone like your kidisdum, someone who has a rapport with the beasts?"

Rahniseeta shook her head. "Don't you have tales of the beast-souled?"

"Didn't I just tell you I have no idea what you're talking about?"

He sounded annoyed now, not merely interested, so Rahinseeta hastened to explain.

"Maimalodalum are supposed to be able to be both human and animal," she explained. "There are all sorts of stories about them."

The road was good here, so Rahniseeta turned to look at the minstrel. He looked interested and faintly puzzled—but not at all like she had surprised a secret out of him.

"Some stories," she went on, "tell that they were friends of the yarimaimalom. Others make it sound as if they were allies of the Old World sorcerers and fought against the yarimaimalom. But all the stories agree on one thing. The maimalodalum could take the shape of a given animal—always one animal only. They had an enchanted skin they used in order to do this. When they were in human shape they either wore the skin as a cloak or hid it away so they could pass undetected."

Barnet was listening intently. "We have a few stories like that, but they always belong to the lore from the Old World, and never from our Old Country—always from another land. I wonder if the land mentioned was your Old Country. Do you know what it was called?"

" 'Homeland,' usually," Rahniseeta said. "It has a name of its own, but we never use it. Harjeedian could look it up for you."

"That would be marvelous," Barnet said. "Tell me more about these maimalo-dalum."

Rahniseeta considered. She was fairly certain that Barnet was not pretending his interest. That meant he was probably not one of the maimalodalum himself, but then in her mind Barnet had always been considered the least likely candidate.

"Well, in addition to the skins they sometimes wore," she said, "another way you could tell someone was a maimalodalu was that they bore some resemblance to the animal, even in human form. Sometimes they had an animal companion and, it was said, even animal families."

Barnet laughed. "It sounds like you're describing Lady Blysse. Is that what your masters think they have caught, a maimalodalu?"

Rahniseeta was indignant at hearing herself described as having masters.

"I do not have masters," she said.

Barnet reached over and patted her arm, letting his hand linger almost a little too much for propriety.

"I'm sorry. Put it down to my lack of ability in your language. I haven't quite figured out where you fit in the Temple of the Cold Bloods. You're not training to be an aridisdu or a kidisdu—right?"

She nodded.

"But you live there and do work for them. . . . Can you see why I would be confused?"

He was so pleasant, almost sweet, that Rahniseeta couldn't hold on to her anger.

"I understand. It is this way. My brother and I were without parents when he was accepted into the temple for his education. He wished to bring me with him so I would be cared for, and the temple—eager to have one of his abilities—agreed. Now I have reached my majority, but I have not left. I make myself useful, and since Harjeedian has not married and we occupy quarters that would be his right if he did . . ."

She trailed off with a sigh.

"I am neither one thing or another. From time to time I consider what I could do elsewhere, but then something happens—there is an illness and hands are needed for nursing, or a conclave is happening and there are letters to be written, or a great festival is coming and . . ."

"And," Barnet said gently, "someone says, 'Let Rahniseeta help. She's very good at many things.' "

"That's right," she said, "and I look into the sky and see the moon has changed her face or even the seasons their colors, and I am still there, sharing a suite with Harjeedian."

"Don't be so despondent," Barnet said, suddenly laughing. "This can't have been going on for too long. You're young yet."

"I am twenty-one," she said stiffly.

"In my land," Barnet replied, "you would have only been considered an adult for a year. What is the age of majority here?"

"Seventeen for women and men both," Rahniseeta said, "but if the girl wishes to marry and her parents agree she can be granted her majority at a younger age. Both men and women must be twenty in order to be ordained either kidisdu or aridisdu, but the training begins at a much younger age."

They had reached the road where they must turn inland to reach u-Bishinti while they were talking, and at the next turn the complex became visible before them. After that, Rahniseeta was kept busy telling what she could about the place, but she did so with some satisfaction. Barnet had not heard of the maimalodalum, but he had not rejected the idea that Lady Blysse might be one—that was someplace to start.

Now, for Rahniseeta to win the acclaim she so desired, she must find how best to continue.

"HOW ARE YOU DOING with Waln Endbrook?" the master asked Shivadtmon.

He would have preferred to handle this matter without employing Shivadtmon, but given the situation, that was impossible, so Shivadtmon was who it must be.

There was much good about Shivadtmon. The aridisdu was smart enough to keep silence when ordered to do so, unimaginative enough not to think too hard about why he was given the orders he received.

Indeed, if anything puzzled Shivadtmon, he was likely to think that his own lack of understanding indicated that he was being given some sort of test. Shivadtmon was the kind of man who secretly, probably even unconsciously, longed for a return to the classroom, to days when tests were given and value judged on knowledge of theory, not performance in reality.

So Shivadtmon only asked those questions he thought would lead him to deducing the larger picture. He never asked directly: "Why are we doing this? What purpose will it serve?"

That reticence suited the master perfectly.

"Fairly well," Shivadtmon replied. "At an early meeting I made certain Waln Endbrook knew that Lady Blysse had been permitted to go to Misheemnekuru. I also attempted to indicate that I did not completely approve either of this or of the islands' continued isolation from the mainland."

"Very good."

"I am pleased and proud to be of service, Master."

"It is very important," the master said, "that Waln not realize that he is being guided. You do realize this?"

Shivadtmon nodded and, with a trace of the inflection of a student reciting for a teacher, said, "Waln Endbrook has been used for other people's gain at least twice before—that we know. In each case, his personal ambitions were employed to steer him. Therefore, it is reasonable to believe that we can steer him a third time."

The master raised an admonitory finger, but he kept his tones gentle and kind.

"However," he said, "it is very important that Waln Endbrook not realize he is being steered. He is a clever man, and his past failures in the service of others will certainly make him hesitant about being used again. Therefore, you must do your best to make certain that Waln believes he is manipulating you, rather than the truth."

Shivadtmon nodded. "I understand. I will let myself be led. I will grant him favors—but only after he asks me for them. I will make certain information comes his way through various channels, so he does not realize how interested I am in his actions."

"Very good," the master repeated. "Very, very good."

IN THE END, DERIAN HAD DECIDED on a mare—a magnificent three-year-old bay paint. Her markings reminded him somewhat of the exuberance of Eshinarvash, the Wise Horse, though in reality she was nothing like him. She was mostly brown on her head, neck, and lower body, with long dark points on each leg. Her left foreleg was dark to the hoof, but the right was marked with a white pastern. Her hind legs had nearly matching white stockings. White spread rather like an uneven blanket across her middle and rear quarters. Her face bore a long white blaze that shaded into a white muzzle. Her mane and tail were a striking blend of both black and white, and on the right side of her neck was an uneven patch that reminded Derian of an island.

The name that had been divined for the mare when she was a year old was Prahini, which meant "Rainbow" in Liglimosh. Derian liked the sound of it well enough in both languages that he decided not to change it, though he decided that in deference to her birth land the mare would be called Prahini rather than Rainbow.

Prahini appeared delicately boned at first glance, but she showed considerable endurance when Derian took her out for a day trip. Despite her apparent delicacy, Prahini had height enough to carry Derian without seeming dwarfed, and good endurance. Her flaws were those of a young horse, recently trained, and Derian looked forward to working with her.

She wasn't Roanne. No other horse would ever be Roanne. As Prahini shied at blown leaves in genuine astonishment, rather than in temperamental play as Roanne would have done, Derian felt his loss deep inside. Prahini was going to be fun, but not even the gift of her would make him forget Harjeedian's callous slaying of Roanne and the pack pony. He reminded himself daily that for all the pleasant welcome he had been given, at least some of the Liglimom were capable of very practical brutality.

Derian was putting Prahini through her paces in a largely uninhabited pasture, imagining how it would be when he rode his new mount to the doorway of the Temple of the Cold Bloods, when he saw a light carriage with two passengers coming down the sea road from the city. At first his attention was mostly for the slightly dumpy black gelding who pulled the rig; then his heart skipped a beat as he recognized the driver.

"Rahniseeta!" he said aloud, drawing rein. He didn't shout, but Prahini swiveled an ear around in his direction as if wondering what this new command might be.

Derian nudged the mare into a walk and cut across toward the road. His initial delight that Rahniseeta had come to visit was quelled when he saw that her passenger was Barnet, but seeing Barnet's face light in welcome as Derian drew near made Derian realize he was glad to see the minstrel, too.

He opened the gate from the saddle, Prahini standing perfectly still as she had been trained, then waiting while Derian leaned down to close it. The black gelding gave a rather bored look their way as he continued plodding down the road toward u-Bishinti, but the humans were much more communicative.

"Derian!" Rahniseeta said, her Liglimosh accent giving the three syllables unwonted music. "We have come to see you, and now you come to see us. Is that your horse?"

Derian patted Prahini on the neck as he drew the mare into a walk alongside the still-moving carriage.

"Yes. This is Prahini. I chose her yesterday and planned to come up to the city to see you—and fulfill my promise to act as teacher—as soon as we knew each other a little better."

Barnet gave a gusty sigh. "And you wouldn't be a moment too soon. Rahniseeta rescued me today. It seems that learning Pellish is the fashion of the moment. I'm not quite sure why, since no one seems particularly eager to talk about the practical side of things—trade goods or markets or even the dangers of piracy."

"It is a way," Rahniseeta said seriously, "of demonstrating agreement with Fire's daring in sending *Fayonejunjal* north earlier this season. In learning Pellish, the disdum are in effect saying 'This was good. We are preparing for the next step.'"

"What they are saying," Barnet said with a broad grin, "is, 'Hello, Your Majesty. How are you? My name is Whatever, and I am a servant of the deities.' Over and over again with very little sense for anything but memorizing the sounds. When I try to explain that learning the language involves more than memorizing a few phrases, most of them don't want to hear it. More and more I appreciate what a good student Harjeedian was."

"My brother does have a gift for languages," Rahniseeta said, rather smugly.

Derian felt nettled.

"How would you know about languages?" he asked. "From what I've been told, you folks are pretty isolated here. There's that inlet to the north that cuts you off from there, the ocean to the east, and I haven't heard much mention of neighbors on your other flanks."

"True," Rahniseeta replied. "It seems that we did once have a neighboring nation, or colony, to the south, but that they did not survive the aftereffects of the Divine Retribution—not in any systematic fashion. There are small, independent settlements there, not even necessarily allied with each other, much less with us. I believe there is some trade, but on a small scale."

"So," Derian persisted, cutting in before Barnet could ask about these southern peoples, "how do you know Harjeedian is good with languages?"

"Well," Rahniseeta replied tartly, "there is the evidence of his experience with Pellish."

"You spoke," Derian persisted, "as if you had prior experience."

Rahniseeta looked at him as if wondering why he was belaboring such a minor point. Derian couldn't tell her that Prahini's warmth beneath him was creating a guilty surge of anger at Harjeedian—and with that anger an unwillingness to hear the aridisdu praised.

"Well," Rahniseeta said, "although we are one people, we have two languages. The documents related to the disdum—holy stories, guidelines for auguries, ceremonial incantations—are all kept in the older form of our language. The two have diverged a great deal over time."

Barnet leaned forward to get her attention.

"Had the languages begun to separate before the Divine Retribution or is this something that has occurred since?"

Rahniseeta pursed her lips thoughtfully, an expression that made Derian think irresistibly about kissing her.

"The separation began a long time ago," she said, "but Harjeedian says that the language we speak now is becoming different than what was spoken at the time of the Divine Retribution. He says that it is likely we would have no problem communicating with peoples of the Plague time, but that we would tell ourselves apart by how we used words and structured sentences. My understanding is that the old form of the language is markedly different, and that even at the time of the Divine Retribution it took a scholar to be able to speak and read it."

"Well, that explains something that had been bothering me," Barnet said. "I've been trying to learn to read your language, and some texts were pretty simple to piece through—especially after one of my more diligent students made me a copy of the dictionary he'd been keeping for himself. Other texts might as well have been written in New Kelvinese for all I could make out."

They had come up to the central hub where visitors customarily left their carriages and checked in with the resident officials regarding their business. Derian gave Prahini to one of the stable girls, promising to come check on the mare later.

"I don't really have a place of my own," he said. "I'm staying up the hill with Varjuna and his family, and it's a fair walk. There is a public eating house where even at this hour I think we could get something to drink."

He looked at Barnet, offering a bit more explanation. "It isn't quite a pub, more like a guild house or a society meeting hall—members are welcome without a fee, but I'm not sure how they handle guests."

Rahniseeta smiled. "If it is anything like the Temple of the Cold Bloods, no one will begrudge us a cup of something, but they might question if we ordered a banquet. May we go there? I would very much like to rinse the dust of the road out of my mouth."

Again she worked those lovely full lips and Derian found himself imagining taking the road dust out of her mouth in an entirely different fashion. Shaking himself slightly, he led the way to what he couldn't help but think of as the local tavern.

At this point in the day, it was nearly deserted, but Derian managed to secure drinks for them all without having to ask either Rahniseeta or Barnet to translate. The woman who had been drowsing in the kitchen area supplied a chunk of soft cheese and some bread of her own accord. She didn't ask for money, and Derian simply resolved to check the correct procedure with Varjuna or Zira. Meanwhile, his red hair proclaimed who and what he was, and he hoped any slips would be forgiven.

Derian looked over at Barnet.

"So, minstrel, how goes your turn as teacher?"

"Not so bad," Barnet said, "though I could do with a smaller class or a bit more pay."

This last was a sore point with him—one he'd already mentioned to Derian. Initially, like all his shipwrecked mates, Barnet had been glad enough simply to be alive and among kind—if odd—people. Now, however, with a voyage behind him, as well as countless hours of language lesson, Barnet was growing impatient.

Rahniseeta looked puzzled.

"Pay? For what do you need pay? Haven't the temples answered your least need?"

"Least?" Barnet considered. "I admit I've been kept fed and clothed, and that Harjeedian was generosity itself when we were in Hawk Haven and I wanted to replace my musical instruments, but sometimes it's nice to feel the weight of unspent credits heavy in your pocket."

Rahniseeta continued to look confused.

"But is there anything you desire that you have not been given? Indeed, there are those among the younger aridisdum and kidisdum who feel you have been tended to more like one of the fully anointed than as a guest who owes even for his life."

Derian caught his breath at the anger that flared in Barnet's eyes.

"I thought your people didn't practice slavery," he said, his tones hard and chill as iced steel.

"We do not," Rahniseeta said proudly. "I was appalled when Harjeedian explained the practice to me, and I knew that being enslaved was one of the risks he took in going into northern waters."

"Seems to me," Barnet pressed, his tones still cold, "that expecting someone to work for no reward is pretty much the same as slavery. Don't get me wrong, Rahniseeta, I'm grateful to be alive and all the rest, but the horses here"—he gave a broad-armed gesture that encompassed all of u-Bishinti's elaborate complex—"have more freedom than I do."

Rahniseeta looked genuinely shocked.

"Have you ever been truly hungry, Barnet Lobster?" she asked, and her voice was fire to melt his ice.

"A few times at sea," the other replied levelly, "when something happened to spoil the provisions. I've been thirsty, too, so starved for water that drinking pee seemed like a good idea."

Derian shuddered at the image that evoked, but Rahniseeta remained angry. He gazed at her, uncertain how he felt at seeing the seething temper that must have always lain beneath the sweet, kind exterior he had admired. It frightened him a little, but excited him. After all, the best horses were those who were brought into line without losing their fire. It seemed to him that it must be the same with women, too.

Rahniseeta glowered at Barnet.

"Well, I know something about hunger. My father died when I was very small. My mother took care of Harjeedian and me as she could, and in what time she could spare, she plaited mats from reeds and leaves. The money from selling these—or more often what she could trade for them—was all we had. Otherwise we ate what we could scrounge: fish caught in the canal, eggs when our hens were laying, and sometimes the huge oval insects that creep out into the light at night. They aren't too bad if you're hungry enough."

Rahniseeta surged on without giving Barnet an opportunity to voice what Derian was certain had to be an apology.

"You make my stomach twist more than those bugs ever did," she said. "You have shelter, fine food, good clothing, and if you would but ask, you would be given more. Yet you whine because you don't have money weighing your pockets?"

Derian would have been stammering apologies and seeking to placate the angry woman, but Barnet was made of stronger—or at least different—stuff.

"And if," the minstrel said, all silky sweet, "I wanted to buy a present for a lady, what would I do? Would I go to Harjeedian or the doorkeeper or Ahmyndisdu Tiridanti and say 'Give this to me'? What if I didn't wish to remain a lackey in the temple all my life? How do I earn what I need to build my own house or boat? Do I sing on street corners with my hat at my feet?"

The woman who had been napping in the kitchen had come to the doorway to eavesdrop, but Derian doubted that she had heard much. The argument had taken place without voices being raised. Even at her angriest, Rahniseeta had never spoken above a fierce, hissing snarl.

Rahniseeta suddenly reminded Derian of the jaguar, all sleepy indolence one moment, but revealing masses of muscular power when it moved. Varjuna had told him that even a lesser jaguar could haul a deer as heavy as itself into the treetops, where it would cache it against scavengers. Derian thought his earlier comparison of the young woman to a horse seemed as foolish as mistaking Firekeeper for a cottontail rabbit.

Rahniseeta had cooled as quickly as she had flared up, and was studying Barnet with a return to puzzlement—and perhaps with a touch of wistful sorrow.

"I have considered," she said softly, "much the same thing sometimes."

Derian wondered if she was speaking of Barnet, then realized with a sudden illumination that Rahniseeta was speaking about herself.

RAHNISEETA WAS ASHAMED OF HER OUTBURST of temper. It was a flaw she had thought she had conquered, but hearing Barnet whine after privileges as she had listened to other children whine for a sugared roll with jam inside when she would have given anything for a chunk of dry bread had infuriated her. Now she remembered too little, too late that it was her job to placate these strangers so they would do what the temple needed.

Now she swallowed cool tea as if by doing so she could put out the fire in her belly and focused on Derian. The red-haired man was staring at her in fascination—but not in disgust. This relieved her. Her one chance at marriage to someone prosperous had been ruined shortly before the shipwreck victims had arrived in u-Seeheera. What had ruined it was her prospective husband realizing the force of her personality. What had attracted him had been beauty, soft voice, and graceful movement—and her brother's connections within the disdum. None of these were enough to hold him after he realized that she had opinions of her own and ability to express them.

Since then, a few men had come courting, but as they were all within the temples Rahniseeta had found it easy to resist them. If she was going to live the temple life, she might as well do so with Harjeedian. He, at least, had few illusions about her and little belief that he could change her—use her, yes, but not change her.

"I have washed the dust from my throat, and the cobwebs from my mind," she said, rising and punctuating the phrase by giving Barnet a friendly smile. "Shall we walk about and see how well Derian can show us his new domain?"

The men rose with her, and she thought Derian had looked a little nonplussed when she had smiled at Barnet. To ease him, she slipped her hand into the crook of his arm, then her other into Barnet's. Seemingly escorted by the two fair foreigners, she guided them out into the sunshine.

How to raise the question of the maimalodalum? she thought. *Perhaps Barnet can be made to do it for me. . . .*

It was easy to find a horse with the same red-brown coloring as Derian's own hair, and she indicated it with a toss of her head.

"That one's pretty." She lowered her voice and let her own very real discomfort show. "Is it much like the one . . . the one . . ."

"The one your brother had killed?" Derian's reply was clipped, and she felt his anger in how the muscles of his arm tensed beneath her hand. "No. Roanne was bright as new copper and had white stockings on her legs. This one lacks the white and is a shade or two darker."

"More like your hair," she said, laughing nervously with no pretense at all. Derian usually expressed his displeasure in sarcasm. Now she was aware that he was capable of a more direct response. She had forgotten what Harjeedian had told her about the violence Derian had shown aboard the ship.

Barnet, Water wash away his woes, took the bait.

"I bet Rahniseeta is wondering if you're really a horse in disguise," the minstrel said with a laugh.

Derian's arm didn't tense beneath her fingers, and his expression of puzzlement seemed genuine.

"What are you talking about, Barnet?"

"Rahniseeta was telling me a local legend while we were driving here." Barnet shifted to the voice he usually used for storytelling. "Magical creatures, were the maimalodalum, sometimes taking the form of humans, sometimes that of animals. Some legends said they used talismans to make the change, such as the skin of the animal whose form they took or a bone from the rib closest to the heart. Even when these beast-souled took human form, they carried this talisman with them, so that it was one way to know the truth about them. Yet, even when they did not, a skilled observer might see upon them the mark of their animal self. The mark might be in the line of the face or their preference for certain foods or even their coloring. It might merely be their uncanny rapport with the animal of whom they were kin. Often they traveled with one of their own, and drew power from the relationship."

Barnet trailed off dramatically, and Rahniseeta couldn't help but be impressed by how he had embellished the slight details she had given him, turning the whole thing into something much more interesting.

Derian said nothing at first, only stopped in his tracks and looked down at her, his expression blending both hurt and amusement—and what might have been a hint that he felt flattered by her assumption.

"Are you saying that I look like a horse?" he asked, starting to walk again down a long tree-shaded path between two pastures.

"You do not look like a horse," Rahniseeta said quickly, "yet your coloring, you must admit . . ."

"Firekeeper—Lady Blysse—calls me Fox Hair for that same coloring," Derian said. "My dad teases my mother—from whom I got the hair—by calling her vixen, sometimes. No one ever called my hair 'chestnut.' "

Rahniseeta persisted. "But you are so good with horses. Everyone says so. One of the Wise Horses let you ride him at a first meeting. I thought it might be because you were somehow related."

"Eshinarvash's condescension to me surprised me as much as it did Varjuna, I assure you," Derian said. "As for my being good with horses, well, I've been around them all my life. So they could tend the animals when I was little, my parents would put me in a saddlebag with just my head poking out—they had a smaller operation then and Mother helped in the stables as well as in the office. Yes, I'm good with horses, but that only makes sense. I could no more not be good with horses than Barnet could fail to learn to swim and handle a boat."

"Still," Rahniseeta said, vaguely disappointed, "there was your familiar."

"Familiar?" Derian looked puzzled for a moment. Then his face stiffened as she had seen it do before when he was trying to hide his anger. "Oh, you mean Roanne. She was nothing more than a much treasured riding animal. We'd been a good many places together—across the Iron Mountains, about Hawk Haven and Bright Bay, even over the White Water River into New Kelvin. I'd thought to have her for many more years, and to breed fine foals from her. To have her killed as dog meat . . ."

His voice softened to a rough growl and Rahniseeta felt truly frightened. Derian might be excited about acquiring Prahini, but he had in no way forgiven Harjeedian for the death of Roanne.

When she didn't say anything, Derian went on.

"You're not telling me that Harjeedian wouldn't be upset if something happened to those snakes of his, are you?"

Rahniseeta chose her words carefully.

"He would be upset, yes, but part of the upset would be because the snakes are connected to his role as aridisdu. We keep a few in our quarters—everyone in the temple does, because that is the best way for the snakes to become accustomed to human handling—but they are not pets. They are divine contacts."

Barnet, perhaps to save her from the barely banked intensity in Derian's gaze, cut in.

"Is that why Harjeedian brought them on the sea voyage with him?"

"Yes," Rahniseeta said quickly. "On that voyage he served as kidisdu as well as aridisdu. It was a considerable honor."

Derian interrupted as if he had not heard this last exchange.

"So that's why everyone got so nice all of a sudden," he said stiffly. "Who was it who first got the idea that I might be one of these maimalodalum? I'm sure they suspected it of Lady Blysse all along."

Rahniseeta heard her voice come out much smaller than she had intended.

"It was I," she said. "When we were talking about the societies your culture has in place of temples. You mentioned you were given into the Horse Society. I thought of that, and what Harjeedian had said, and . . ."

"Well, I'm sorry, lady," Derian said brusquely, "but there's nothing special about me. I'm just a man who likes horses and is good with them. That's all."

"Hardly 'all,' " Rahniseeta said weakly, but she knew she had erred badly, and if she alienated Derian, how could she ever find out about Lady Blysse?

She was still struggling for something to say, when Barnet smiled one of his impossible-to-resist smiles.

"Hardly 'all,' " he said, echoing her. "Didn't you promise to help me teach Pellish?"

Derian gave the minstrel an obviously forced grin.

"You mean I can't go into a snit and avoid the lessons?"

"Sorry," Barnet said. "I simply won't have it."

Derian's smile was more genuine this time.

"Then I surrender to the inevitable."

They walked along. When Derian next spoke it was to comment on the superior structure of the fence rails. He sounded casual, but Rahniseeta knew without a doubt that she had lost a great deal of ground with him. To her surprise, she realized that she felt not only worried, but also somehow rather sad.

XVII

TO HER SURPRISE Firekeeper discovered that the Wise Wolves were reluctant to let her nursemaid their pups. She found this reluctance very odd, for no one seemed to question either her or Blind Seer's assertion that she had watched over litter after litter for their own pack. Nor were the pups so young that they should need the constant attendance of a nursing female.

Firekeeper noticed other strange things as well. Whereas the first pack of Wise Wolves with whom she and Blind Seer had joined had practiced puppy care in ways familiar to her from childhood, as packs joined and the puppies were lumped together for greater ease of care, differences became apparent.

As far as Firekeeper knew, it was usual that when puppies were weaned or nearly weaned more and more of their care was given over to a young wolf. This nursemaid wolf was usually considered in some way or another to be less than an ideal hunter. Sometimes youth was the factor, other times ineptitude, temperament, or injury. In a few cases, the nursemaid was an older wolf, but in all cases, the nursemaid was one who was a lesser hunter.

The borderland pack followed this tradition. Young Rascal was temperamentally ill suited for the hunt. He was also smaller than his littermates. Neck Breaker also served as nursemaid, and Firekeeper suspected that Rascal and the younger puppies both benefitted from exposure to the old wolf's wisdom.

When the nursery was expanded to incorporate the puppies of more than one pack, this pattern began to change. It did not change with the first pack who joined them, but with the second and thereafter the difference was marked. The less suitable hunters were still often given the care of the pups, but now one or more very strong hunters also assumed the duty.

"Do they fear some predator other than ourselves?" Firekeeper asked Blind Seer one afternoon when, bellyful and tired of even Moon Frost's overtures, the blue-eyed wolf had come to rest in the shade of her favorite apple tree. "Do the jaguars and pumas come to hunt the young wolves as we do the fawns and calves? Are the bears here so mad that they would challenge a wolf pack?"

Blind Seer rolled lazily, exposing his stomach to the wind's caress.

"I have scented no sign of any large predators other than ourselves, except possibly at tangled edges of the meadow fringes where the tree limbs hang low. Nor are the bears mad. In any case, why would these dine on wolf pups when spring is here, bringing plentiful game along with the warm weather?"

"It doesn't make sense," Firekeeper agreed, "but neither does robbing the hunt of strong hunters when there are ample others to watch. Have you noticed that these guardians are always drawn from the packs which brought the pups? Outliers like Dark Death are never asked, and my offers have been most coldly rejected."

"Odd," Blind Seer agreed drowsily. "I could ask Moon Frost if she knows the reason for this."

Firekeeper felt a ice fist hard around her heart at this suggestion.

"Best not," she said, hoping Blind Seer would not scent the reason for her evasion. "It is not Moon Frost's pack which made the rule, and I notice that she also is not asked to take a turn as nursemaid—though both the Ones in her pack have done so."

Blind Seer rolled over and turned his blue-eyed gaze on her.

"You have been watching very carefully," he said.

"I have had little else to do," Firekeeper said bitterly. "There is no need for me to hunt. The Ones will not let me mind the pups. Neck Breaker and Cricket seem to enjoy speaking with me, but to the rest I am as strange as a white doe in a herd of brown—they do not quite reject me, but they shy away lest my odd color bring some danger upon them."

The blue-eyed wolf rose and pressed his head against her, nearly tilting her backward with his weight.

"Are you lonely then, sweet Firekeeper, though in the heart of this mighty pack?"

The wolf-woman buried her hands in the scruff of his neck and felt a touch of anger when she felt the rough corrugations where Moon Frost had mouthed him. These were not true bites, but a wolf's jaws are strong and Moon Frost's teeth were sharp, even in play.

"I am lonely," Firekeeper said, holding back much more that she would like to say.

"Come and run with me then," Blind Seer suggested, rising and stretching out his spine in a long bow. "Lately, when running in the forest I have seen things I would have liked to show you, but somehow night comes and I have forgotten—and these are things better seen in daylight."

Firekeeper embraced the wolf with rough enthusiasm. Then she pushed back, leaping to her feet.

"I will gladly go," she said, "wherever you will lead. What manner of things are these?"

"Heaps of stone," Blind Seer said, "ruins, so I am told, of places where humans once lived. You and I have seen their like in the Gildcrest lands and again in New Kelvin, but the forms of the buildings seem different again here. I have been wondering whether the ruins might have been lairs to yet another pack of humans than those of which we have already heard. None of these Wise Wolves . . ." Blind Seer's inflection held a trace of arrogant dismissal. . . . "know anything of lands other than their own."

Firekeeper's heart surged full with the warmth of renewed happiness. She might not be able to spar with Blind Seer as the other wolves could, nor could she keep up with a running wolf in the course of the hunt, but there were things she and Blind Seer had seen and done together that none of these island-isolated, so-called Wise Wolves could begin to dream of.

There was no rule that Firekeeper and Blind Seer—outliers as they were not only from any pack, but from these lands—must report their comings and goings, but Firekeeper's bow and arrows were near to where Neck Breaker slept. The old wolf roused at her approach.

"Hunting, Firekeeper?"

"Not for game," she said, bending to slide her bow from the dry shelter of the rock where she had cached it, "but Blind Seer wishes to show me some things he has found in his wanderings."

"Be wary," the old wolf replied, beating his tail slightly at the pleasure in her voice. "Many of those who would hunt in the meadow but for fear of our packs circle on the fringes. Wise respects Wise, but many of the lesser beasts will only see you as warm meat."

"I am warned, grandfather," she said, slinging her quiver over her shoulder and adjusting its balance.

As Firekeeper ran to meet Blind Seer, quiver bouncing lightly against her shoulder, knife at hip, unstrung bow in hand, she fought down the fear that Moon Frost would be waiting beside the blue-eyed wolf. She imagined the two wolves standing shoulder-to-shoulder, Moon Frost perhaps biting playfully at one of Blind Seer's ears or grabbing at his ruff. The image was so vivid that Firekeeper's feet started to slow, reluctant to bring her face-to-face with what it seemed she must find.

But Blind Seer waited alone for her, the dappling of light falling through the leaves making him almost invisible. He started for the deeper forest before Firekeeper had caught up with him.

"We go inland, first," Blind Seer said when she was trotting beside him in the easy mile-eating jog both could effortlessly maintain for hours. "There is a place where the stone comes above the soil, and the humans built on that rise. I would never have found it, but for ravens calling. I never learned what had them so agitated, but I did find something worth the climb."

In the heart of the forest where they now traveled, summer was well established. The leaves had darkened and lost the tenderness of springtime. Oaks, maples, hazels, and gum spread their leaves to catch the sunlight. Somewhat lower down, scrubby pine and holly mingled with fruiting shrubs. Briar, blackberry, raspberry, and honey-suckle laced tightly in the interstitial areas. Moss carpeted the damp clay where the duff had not settled. Lichen grew on fallen tree limbs, and mushrooms paraded in the shadows.

This was a damper, younger forest than the ones Firekeeper knew best, a forest that had filled in after the trees had been cut away by human hands or leveled by the violence of storms. This forest's understory was thicker, its odors headily enhanced by the carrying wetness, every evocative scent underscored with the bite of salt.

Here and there were the signs that once humans had claimed this territory for their own. It might be shrubs growing in too straight a line or a cluster of mature fruit trees struggling to maintain their rights against the crowding of exuberant sapling oaks. There were no open fields, but crowds of younger trees—some now growing to dominate kin sprouted the same year—told the skilled eye where once a clearing might have been.

Noticing more and more of such signs, Firekeeper was not surprised when Blind Seer slowed and began to cast around as after an elusive scent.

"Near here, I think," said his ears and tail. "Yes!"

Ears perking, the blue-eyed wolf slightly changed his course. Soon they had intersected a wide path and began to climb. Initially, Firekeeper thought this must be a well-used game trail and wondered at its width. Two deer could walk side by side on this trail and their shoulders would hardly brush.

Could it be a trail cut by Wise Deer? Firekeeper knew there must be such, but she thought that yarimaimalom would not mark their ways so clearly. The Royal Deer she had known before did not. What purpose did this wide way serve?

Firekeeper had her first clue as to the true nature of this trail when she and Blind Seer came to a place where runoff from one of the frequent rainshowers had cut away the duff. Her bare foot encountered not the sticky coldness of clay, but rock. Moreover, this rock was smoothed and polished, as one would expect to find in a streambed but not on the side of a hill.

"Blind Seer," she called softly, "hold up a moment."

The wolf waited, then came to watch as Firekeeper scraped away the surface vegetation. His tail wagged slowly when he saw what she had found.

"This was once a roadway," Firekeeper said, "one paved with stones such as we have seen in cities. Was there a city here once?"

"Not a city," Blind Seer said. "At least, I do not think so. Come along and see."

Firekeeper motioned for him to wait while she checked the extent of the road more carefully.

"Maybe not a city," she agreed, "but this road was no small one. Even with the paving broken and pushed apart by young growing things I can guess that carriage or cart could have used this trail with ease. Lead on. I would see who these were who were grand enough to need such a road."

Blind Seer bumped his head into her arm.

"I thought you would be interested. I don't know why I took so long to bring you here."

Moon Frost's doing, Firekeeper thought sourly, but she said nothing—not even to tease as she would once have done so easily. She wanted to do nothing to remind Blind Seer of the she-wolf they had left behind.

They mounted the trail swiftly, for the incline was easy, curving to go around the occasional large rock that interrupted the hillside like an island in a sea of green. As they walked, Firekeeper was reminded of the Norwood Grant, where she and Blind Seer had spent some time. There, too, the rocks had claimed their part of the woodlands, and she had often sought them out as comfortable places from which to watch the stars. The memory made her feel friendly toward these otherwise strange forests.

At last they emerged onto a less thickly wooded hilltop. The reason there were fewer trees was immediately obvious.

"Here the winds do not like those who thrust themselves up too tall," Firekeeper said, looking to where the shattered length of more than one such woodland giant was giving itself back to the forest in mold and loam.

"But their children do not learn," Blind Seer agreed. "They rise, free now from the shade of their parents, to defy the power of the wind."

"Until the next storm comes," Firekeeper said. "Then those who have forgotten how to bend will fall. Still, it is nice to be out in the sunlight again, no matter how it comes to touch the ground."

She began to seat herself on an upthrust bit of rock, but stopped in midmotion. Her automatic inspection for anything that might be dangerous—whether as large as a sunning rattlesnake or a small as a biting ant—had shown her that this rock was no more placed by natural forces than the trail had been.

"What is this?" she said, kneeling to better inspect her find. "A bit of wall, and I do not think it was just set here to border a garden patch. Look at how wide it is at the base. It was meant to hold weight."

Blind Seer scratched vigorously behind one ear.

"If you say so, dear heart," he replied. "Humans pile rock on rock to make their lairs as no other creatures do. However, I have not made a study of how they manage to keep them from tumbling over."

"I have, a little," Firekeeper admitted. "When last spring brought us to New Bardenville there was much talk of the best ways to build both in rock and in wood. I listened because I thought such lore might someday be useful for making some small lair of my own."

"Females and nest-building," Blind Seer laughed. "Why not just dig into the earth as our mothers do?"

"Perhaps because I lack strong front claws," Firekeeper retorted, feeling very strange at the turn the talk was taking. "In any case, my fires cannot breathe well beneath the earth. I thought more to build a house for them than for myself."

Blind Seer rose and shook, scattering bits of leaf and dirt to all sides.

"Clever," he acknowledged. "Come, let me show you some of the places where these humans built lairs to house their fires. The weather has done much to wear them away, but interesting scraps remain."

"Lead," Firekeeper replied. "This has been a good hunt so far."

She followed the tip of Blind Seer's tail as he moved with silent sinuosity over the broken ground, slipping between heaps of rock that were now clearly identifiable as broken building material. Most was the local rock, broken to size and often showing remnants of the mortar that had held it in place. Occasionally, however, there were scraps of enameled brick such as that which was common on the mainland. There were also remnants of stone carved into elaborate borders, often found with polished—if mostly broken—tiles.

Firekeeper wanted to stop and look more closely at these things, perhaps collect a few more shining scraps as bribes for the ravens, but Blind Seer urged her on.

"Come. This is nothing to what lies ahead. This is mouthing at a hank of rabbit's fur hanging on a bit of bramble when you might have its hot meat."

Firekeeper laughed at the image, quickening her pace to match Blind Seer's, nor was she disappointed when he led her through a tangle of honeysuckle and wild rose into the remnants of what must have once been a beautiful room.

The roof was entirely gone, but the angle of the two walls that still stood had protected the interior from all but the most direct precipitation. Honeysuckle and rose made such a solid barrier on the sides where the walls had almost completely collapsed that for a moment Firekeeper entertained the idea that the wild flowers were somehow protecting the shell of the room. Then she saw without fancy.

Far from protecting the remaining room, the honeysuckle and wild rose had contributed to the collapse of the stonework walls. Perhaps some day long, long ago the humans who had built this place had planted the flowering vines along the outside of the wall. Firekeeper had seen this done in many places, the flowering vines treasured for their scent, for the shade they cast, and even for the birds they attracted near.

Had this room then been a lady's bower? The quiet retreat wherein the lady of the house came when the summer heat grew too intense? Had it been a study or an eating room? Firekeeper felt fairly certain it had not been a kitchen or laundry room, for the two walls that remained were designed for beauty, not mere practicality. Grease stains were surely never meant to accumulate here, nor steam and soap scum to dim the elaborate borders.

Firekeeper raised the lower edge of her shirt and used the fabric to rub away the dirt that clung to the walls. Blind Seer watched with curiosity.

"What do you see there, Firekeeper?"

Firekeeper continued her cleaning, wishing for a bigger piece of cloth and a bucket of warm water.

"The wall is decorated with pictures made from small bits of stone or glass or tile," she said. "We saw the like in New Kelvin. Such work is very time-consuming to do, or so I understand, and not so common in buildings unless the owner is very rich."

"What is pictured?" Blind Seer asked.

"I can't quite tell," Firekeeper admitted. "Here are flowers, certainly, though as with many of the things humans draw, I cannot tell for certain what type of flower. Birds, too, though I am not sure about the type of bird—a robin, maybe, though the red may simply be mold."

The wolf came closer so that he might look, and bumped his head against her arm.

"Do you like it?" he asked, and Firekeeper thought he sounded a bit tentative, even shy.

"This place is very interesting," she assured him, reaching so she might embrace him. "I am learning slowly to understand the fashions in which humans do their decorations, and I think you are right. There is something here that does not seem like what we have seen in New Kelvin. It is harder to say whether or not the artists favor the style of those who founded Hawk Haven and Bright Bay, for much of those people's work was destroyed in the days following the Plague. Still, I think you may be right. This seems more like what we saw in u-Seeheera than what we have seen elsewhere."

"I did not make a hasty judgment," Blind Seer said. "There are other places like this one—though I think these walls are two of the best for holding pictures. My eyes must still sometimes struggle to tell what the humans have drawn, but, do you know what, Firekeeper?"

"What?"

"The wolves I was here with—Moon Frost, Freckles, and some of the others—they could not see either a flower or a bird or a cloud in the sky until I showed them how to look."

Firekeeper must fight down a touch of jealousy at this reminder of how Blind Seer had first come here before she could think clearly about his comment.

"That is interesting. You would think that these Wise Wolves would have learned something of human ways, living in such harmony with humans as they do. Instead it seems that they have kept some blindness while you, dear heart, have learned to see a little with human eyes."

"Even as you see with wolf's eyes," Blind Seer said.

"I wish I could show Derian this," Firekeeper said. "I think there must be things I am missing. I wonder if there is writing here among the pictures."

"Writing?"

Blind Seer tilted his head and stared at the wall, his brow furrowing in what some would have called a most human manner.

"Yes," Firekeeper went on. "We know that the people of Hawk Haven and Bright Bay make their words in one way, but those of New Kelvin make them in an entirely different way. The Liglimom use yet a third form. I think I might see traces of it here, but I cannot be certain it is not simply an ornamental border."

"Could Derian?" Blind Seer asked doubtfully.

"I don't know," Firekeeper said, "but surely as the Ones get the best bites from the kill, so Derian has by now seen how these Liglimom humans write their language."

Firekeeper glanced up and noticed that the sun was beginning to set. It would be many hours, though, before full darkness came.

"You said there are other places," she said. "Can you take me to another?"

Blind Seer tugged her hand in his jaw, as gently as a snake carrying eggs.

"Follow," he suggested, and so Firekeeper did, her heart lighter than it had been for many days—perhaps since that evil night when Harjeedian had taken them from the banks of the Flin River.

SHIVADTMON DIDN'T SHOW ANY TRACE of his prior agitation when he arrived a few days later for his next Pellish lesson with Waln. Indeed, he focused so intensely on reviewing the routine phrases that Waln thought he might need to start his efforts at subversion over again, maybe even with another person entirely.

If Shivadtmon had said something inappropriate to one of his supervisors and been slapped back into line, especially if powerful concepts like "deity" or "omen" had been used in the reprimand, there might be no bringing the aridisdu over to Waln's way of thinking.

Waln knew perfectly well the power of abstract ideas. Even if residents of his native islands didn't worship deities as these people did, there wasn't a sailor alive who didn't know deep down in his heart that the ocean was a potent and capricious force. And though Waln didn't like to accept this, he knew that Queen Valora had bought him with nothing other than words, words like "lord" and "baron," words that had transformed a whore's bastard son into a peer of the realm through a medium no more potent than breath.

When he thought about it, Waln realized that Valora's rulership of the Isles was another thing based on little more than words. Valora called herself "queen" and expected people to respect that word and the lineage it represented, never mind her own lack of deeds. Could she and her little fleet have held the Isles if the residents had decided to resist her? Waln didn't think so.

Words were very powerful indeed, and Waln would not overlook their power here among the Liglimom. Best to begin with this lesson.

"Slowly, aridisdu," Waln said. "You are running the words together. Separate them more distinctly from each other. There is a pause between 'good' and 'afternoon,' another between 'Your' and 'Majesty.' "

Shivadtmon pursed his lips as if he might object, but obeyed.

"Good afternoon, Your Majesty," he said, this time exaggerating the syllables too much, so that "Majesty" became "Ma-jes-tee."

Waln swallowed a sigh. Accurate instruction and flattery did not go hand in hand.

However, as much as he would rather move to flattery, Waln could not have his student poorly taught, or his efforts at winning Shivadtmon to his side would be undone the moment Barnet or someone else corrected the aridisdu's diction.

Then Waln realized how he could combine fishing for information as to Shivadtmon's mood with the lesson.

"That is too great a separation," Waln said, "especially in the phrase 'Your Majesty.' Pellish does not break between each syllable any more than your own language does. Like you, we pause between words. The difference is that where both of our languages have compound words . . ."

Waln felt a flash of pride that he remembered the technical term he had heard Barnet use.

". . . Pellish has far fewer compounds than does your own language."

Waln saw Shivadtmon frowning, so quickly seized chalk and wrote an example on a slate. Waln was far from literate in Liglimosh, but two sea voyages with little to do had given him ample time to practice a limited vocabulary.

"Let us look at your own title, 'aridisdu,' " Waln said, writing the word. "It breaks into two parts. 'Disdu' is the root that means 'one who has been initiated into the service of the deities.' Am I correct?"

Shivadtmon nodded, and Waln was pleased to see him relaxing slightly. He'd thought choosing this word with its implied acknowledgment of his student's special status would be a good idea.

" 'Ari' indicates that you belong to the elite group which has intensively studied the great wealth of knowledge handed down through divination of the divine will."

Shivadtmon relaxed even more.

"That is so," he said, nodding regally. "Not only must the aridisdum study prior divinations, we must study the interpretations written by our forebears, especially as to what these past messages indicate about the code of behavior pleasing to the divinities."

"Not only that," Waln said, figuring it couldn't hurt to rub in a little more oil, "you aridisdum must also study how to interpret omens yourselves. There is a great deal of responsibility included in the small syllable 'ari.' "

Shivadtmon smiled, and Waln returned his focus to linguistics.

"In Pellish, however, we would probably use two separate words for the concept, rather than combining the two. We speak of a 'head gardener,' not 'headgardener.' Indeed, the latter might imply one who gardens upon heads, rather than one who is in the highest authority regarding garden lore."

Shivadtmon frowned. "Pellish is not a strong language if it is so open to misinterpretation. Why say 'head' when you have a perfectly good word in 'chief'?"

That last was beyond Waln's ability to answer, so he ignored the question, rightly guessing that Shivadtmon was less interested in learning the evolution of Pellish than he was in asserting the superiority of his native language.

"I agree that Pellish is sloppy," Waln said. "I suspect that when commerce is established between our lands, your language will come to dominate. However, in order to establish such commerce, we must be able to speak with each other. Here the Liglimom have the advantage. You have the opportunity to learn Pellish, whereas the residents of the lands where that language is spoken remain ignorant even of the existence of this great nation to the south."

Shivadtmon was all but purring now, so Waln decided to try introducing a more sensitive topic.

"Before we return to the phrase book, let us examine another word in your language—a more complex one. I believe this exercise will give you insight into how Pellish works."

Shivadtmon was no different from any other student in inviting a change from routine. He leaned slightly forward as Waln wrote the characters for "misheemnekuru" on the slate. Waln thought he heard a faint intake of breath, but didn't turn to look. It was very important that Shivadtmon not realize the intensity of Waln's curiosity regarding the place.

Waln had spent lots of time over the last several days thinking about the effects of the Plague in his own land, about things that had been left behind when the Old Country rulers left. Much had been destroyed in the antimagic fervor that followed, but fortunes had been established on the more mundane loot. If he understood what Shivadtmon had told him, the situation had been different here. He needed to find out just what those differences were, but if his conjectures were correct . . .

Waln forced his attention back to the lesson, rapidly drawing straight lines between the segments of the word, lecturing as he did so.

"Your people probably think of 'misheemnekuru' as being able to be broken into two words—isn't that so?"

Shivadtmon frowned, but gamely went along. "That is so, 'misheemne' and 'kuru.' "

"Well, a Pellish speaker like myself," Waln said with a self-deprecatory smile, "would see it broken into three words—and maybe even four. 'Kuru' is the easy one. Harjeedian told me that means a sanctuary, a place to which access is restricted by command of the divine will.

" 'Misheemne' is where we would get tripped up. In our language, possession is indicated by the use of a separate word: 'of.' So we see that part as two words: 'islands' and 'of.' You make it even harder for us in that your language tends to imply the . . ."

Waln struggled to remember the word Barnet had used for that part of speech, but he couldn't remember it.

He shrugged. "The word that goes in front, like 'the' if there isn't any other possibility than the one you're referring to, and 'a' if there's more than one possibility."

Waln saw Shivadtmon getting confused, and grinned.

"See why your language is so hard for us? What I mean is that if the only way you can say it is '*the* Sanctuary Islands,' you leave off the 'the.' It's only when there's a choice, like 'the wolf' or 'a wolf,' that you bother to state it."

"And Pellish," Shivadtmon said, nodding as if a mystery had been clarified, "always states this part of speech, even if there could be no other option?"

"Pretty much," Waln said. "That's what makes Lady Blysse such a sloppy speaker. She doesn't bother with any word she doesn't find immediately necessary, and so she comes across as what she is—uneducated and rather stupid."

Waln suppressed a smile. From watching Shivadtmon's expression change both when Waln had used the word "wolf" and again when he mentioned Lady Blysse by name, Waln was pretty sure now that whatever had happened after Shivadtmon had left the other day, the aridisdu was still offended by Lady Blysse being permitted to go to Misheemnekuru. Waln was tempted to ask if anything had been heard about the little bitch, but knew he'd do better if Shivadtmon brought up the matter himself.

As if he had no other interest in all the world, Waln returned to parsing the word "misheemnekuru."

"Let's get back to 'misheemne,'" Waln said. "'Mishee' means 'island.' 'M' is your most common way of forming a plural, the way 's' is in Pellish. 'Ne' is a possessive ending. Do I have it right?"

"You do."

"So where we would say 'the islands of sanctuary,' you folks say one compound word, 'misheemnekuru.'"

"But you have a possessive ending as well," Shivadtmon protested. "I have it in some of the phrases I have written down here."

He looked quickly down his list, then read off slowly, "'Your Majesty's good health.' It is here again, 'Waln's hat. Waln's shirt.'"

Waln nodded. "I didn't ever think about it before this teaching started, but from what Barnet Lobster says, our language used to have a lot of endings that have fallen out of use over time. That ending you mentioned is one of those."

Shivadtmon was no more eager than Waln himself to go into the reasons for this particular linguistic evolution. They had already discussed how languages evolve. As practicality ruled both of their natures, the matter of lost endings was left behind. However, to Waln's delight, the matter of Misheemnekuru was not.

"As you had expressed interest in Misheemnekuru," Shivadtmon said with forced casualness, "I thought you would like to know that Lady Blysse sent a message some days ago via the aridisdu currently in charge of the outpost there. She not only has been accepted by the Wise Wolves she encountered, but she and her companion, Blind Seer, were invited to travel inland with these wolves."

"Why that's amazing," Waln said. "That would make Lady Blysse the first human to walk those lands in well over a hundred years—that is, if the Divine Retribution struck here at about the same time as it did in my homeland."

"Close enough," Shivadtmon said, dismissing past history with a wave of one narrow, long-fingered hand. "There is much debate in the temples as to whether Lady Blysse being on Misheemnekuru counts as a human intrusion or whether, since the wolves have accepted her, she is indeed, as some claim, maimalodalu, and therefore not intruding at all."

"Maimalodalu" was a new word for Waln, but he broke it down easily: "beast soul."

Not "a soul of the beasts." That would be more like "dalunemaimalo." What Shivadt-mon was definitely saying was that some people were claiming that Lady Blysse was legally possessed of an animal's soul. In Bright Bay that would have been a demotion, but here, where the yarimaimalom were accorded rights equivalent to—or even supe-rior to—those of humans, that meant that Lady Blysse could be rising in status.

Indeed, from what little Waln had grasped, the yarimaimalom were considered to have a clearer understanding of the divine will than any human—even than the dis-dum. The beasts were the sources of omens, not mere interpreters. If this transforma-tion of Lady Blysse from human to animal was pushed to its logical conclusion, that would mean that Lady Blysse could end up at least the equivalent of a disdu—though Waln wasn't sure whether a kidisdu or an aridisdu—or even a member of both orders.

Only the members of u-Liall were considered members of both orders, initiated into membership in the kindred order upon elevation. Would this then mean that u-Liall would no longer be "the Five" but become "the Six"?

Until this moment, Waln had intended to capture Shivadtmon's interest in working with Waln by appealing to either greed or curiosity. Now he saw another route, and one that could bring them additional allies when such were needed.

Shivadtmon was very proud of his place as aridisdu. He'd worked long and hard to gain initiation into his order. Maybe he even dreamed of being iaridisdu, the head of his temple, someday. Now forces were in motion to promote a newly arrived stranger to a rank senior to his own—senior, perhaps, to any to which Shivadtmon could ever aspire.

Waln reached for the flask of chilled white wine. He hadn't been drinking as much these last few days, but now it certainly seemed like a time for a celebration. He poured glasses for himself and Shivadtmon. From the eagerness with which the other man drank, Waln thought he had deduced the other's thoughts fairly accurately.

"Well, this is grand for Lady Blysse," Waln said. "She has the best luck. Earl Kestrel found her living on carrion in the wilds, hauled her back and stuffed her in a dress. In no time, she becomes a member of the peerage, as well as a favorite of Hawk Haven's dotard king. Now she stands to take rank and title in your own land as well. I wish I had her luck."

"So," Shivadtmon said, his voice very soft, but the level gaze that met Waln's full of yet unspoken meaning, "do I."

XVIII

WHEN THE PAIR OF ENORMOUS RAVENS dropped out of the sky and circled them, Prahini started. Derian swore ferociously as he struggled to keep her from bolting. The footing was none too good, and he didn't like to think of the consequences if the mare's panic won out.

Only after he had the bay paint under control could Derian spare energy for the source of the distraction. He located the ravens immediately, sitting on each of the largest branches flanking the slender trunk of one of the few trees on the hilltop. They didn't look in the least ashamed of themselves, but he didn't expect them to. It wasn't only their size and perfection that marked them as yarimaimalom, but also the directness of their gaze as they looked him over.

"I don't care what anyone has told you," he said, speaking in Liglimosh as the most likely human language the ravens would understand, "but a horseman is only as good as his horse. Prahini is a young creature, and easily frightened."

The raven on the left gave a faint, hoarse croak that just might have been an apology—at least, Derian chose to take it as such. The one on the right merely puffed out its feathers.

Hearing the conversational note in Derian's voice, Prahini let her head drop and began lipping at the grass. Derian scratched with one hand at the base of her mane and felt her skin ripple with pleasure, but he didn't allow himself to be distracted from the ravens. He didn't know why they were here, but of one thing he was perfectly certain, it wasn't by chance.

Derian suspected they were looking for him specifically, not simply for any human. For one thing, especially hatless, he looked very little like a Liglimo. For another, he was the only person around.

Instructing in Pellish took up a fair amount of Derian's time, but as there were ample potential students in u-Bishinti and its vicinity, Derian still had not yet returned to u-Seeheera. However, Varjuna had ordained that not all Derian's time would be occupied with teaching.

"It has been said you are a guest," Varjuna said, "and a guest does not work from dawn to dark. Moreover, I want your opinion on our establishment. We are proud of what we have achieved, but not too proud to learn from another."

Derian doubted that he could teach the disdum of u-Bishinti a thing about caring for or raising horses, but he was grateful to have a reason to escape the otherwise uninterrupted stream of students. Barnet had been right when he said that learning Pellish was something of the fashion right now, and while Derian was certain the interest would level in time, he felt sure it had yet to peak.

He took advantage of the fact that most of his students had early-morning chores about the facility to take Prahini out for an early ride. The weather was growing increasingly hot and humid as summer advanced, and although the winds off the bay ameliorated the effect somewhat, by midmorning Derian was just as happy to be inside the shady reaches of some thick-walled courtyard.

There was another reason for his early-morning rides. Although Derian did not want to admit it, he was obsessed with the Wise Horses. His one ride on Eshinarvash had lit a fire that was far from burning low. He felt like he'd fallen in love with some unattainable royal beauty, and while every glimpse of the wild herds fed his awareness of the hopelessness of his situation, he could not go without at least trying to see them.

Poshtuvanu's comments about how the children often crept to look at the Wise Horses, combined with Derian's own recollection of the direction in which Varjuna had taken him when they had gone to meet Eshinarvash, gave Derian hope that there might be some place from which he could see the herds. A few days' trial and error had led him to this hilltop, and now every morning he rode over.

Sometimes he caught a glimpse of the grazing herds. Sometimes his only reward was mist rising off the ground and obscuring what lay below. Sometimes the air was as clear as polished glass, but the horses were nowhere in sight. Never did he see one of the Wise Horses as any more than a shape in the distance, small as a child's wooden toy. Even so, even knowing that his obsession must be obvious to everyone in u-Bishinti, Derian continued to make his pilgrimage.

Today's had not been rewarding, and he had been turning Prahini for the ride back to the field where she would be turned out for the day when the ravens had landed.

Derian remembered the reverence with which the yarimaimalom were usually regarded and thought his initial comments might have given offense—especially as the ravens had done nothing but stare at him since.

"May I be of service to you?" he asked, using the most formal phrase he knew—the one more typically used in temple meetings than in daily encounters.

Immediately, the raven on the left perked up. It ducked its head down into the feathers and came up holding in its beak a slender cord from which a small capsule depended.

"For me?" Derian asked, and the raven emitted a hoarse, satisfied noise.

Derian slid from the saddle. Usually, he'd trust Prahini to stay drop-tied, but with these ravens about he thought he'd better secure her. A fat shrub supplied a hitching post. Then he crossed to where the raven still held the capsule dangling from her beak.

"Is this for me?" he asked.

In reply, the raven bent slightly and dropped the capsule into his hand. The capsule was still attached to the cord. Now that he was close enough, Derian could see that the cord looped around the raven's neck. He could also see how large the raven's beak was and thought uncomfortably that it could easily take off a finger.

Derian loosened the capsule from the cord, then, despite the proximity of that formidable beak, asked, "Would you like me to remove that cord? It can't be comfortable."

He gently tugged the end of the cord to make clear what he meant. The raven didn't nod as Derian had half expected—both Blind Seer and Elation had learned the gesture as a means of speeding their communication with humans. Instead it ducked its head and the cord dropped loose.

Derian laughed in appreciation, and the raven seemed to understand, bobbing up and down and puffing its feathers in a fashion that transformed its head into a variety of grotesque shapes. Through all of this, the other raven—the one seated on the right side of the trunk—had remained still and watchful. Now it darted its beak toward the capsule in Derian's hand.

"You want me to open this," Derian said. "Right."

The capsule was interesting in itself. The body of it was made from a length of lightweight bone from which the marrow had been meticulously cleaned. The ends were capped with beeswax, this tamped neatly into place and still holding the fragmented whorls of a human fingerprint.

Derian hadn't doubted that this was somehow from Firekeeper, but somehow this mark of human involvement unexpectedly reassured him. He might converse with the ravens as if they understood him, but deep inside, he wondered.

He slid the wax from one end of the bone tube and found inside a tightly rolled spiral of paper. He didn't know what he'd expected. They'd discussed various ways they might communicate, but hadn't settled on anything. Now he looked down on what appeared to be Liglimosh written characters. There were several in a line, all unintelligible to him, though he was beginning to read simple words. Only when he came to the end did he find something he understood: a rough drawing of a handprint side by side with a sketch of a wolf's paw. Firekeeper had "signed" one other message this way and Derian shuddered involuntarily when he remembered what that had presaged.

"This is from Firekeeper," he said aloud, looking at the ravens for reassurance. "But who did the writing?"

For answer, the ravens chortled, then dropped off the tree branches and launched into the air. It was notable that they did so without making nearly as much fuss as they had upon arrival, so Derian decided not to feel insulted.

"Well, Prahini," he said as he unhitched the mare. "We have a new mystery. Who is with Firekeeper who knows how to write? Whatever the answer is, I know where I can find someone who reads this stuff."

Swinging into the saddle, Derian took one more long look down the slope to where the Wise Horses sometimes could be seen. The field was empty, but he hardly noticed, his mind already on the message in the bone tube.

WHEN HE ARRIVED at the ikidisdu's residence, Varjuna hadn't yet arrived from his morning tour of the facility, but Zira was already at the breakfast table drinking tea and frowning over a written report. Two empty bowls, not yet cleared away, testified that the two younger sons had already eaten and left.

Derian took his seat and smiled his thanks to a servant who set in front of him a cup of hot mint tea and a bowl of cereal that mixed toasted oats, raisins, and a variety of nuts. It was very good, even without the rich cream supplied to pour over it.

Zira looked up from her reading as Derian finished taking the edge off his hunger.

"Good ride?" she asked.

"Prahini moves like a dream," he assured her, "but something rather odd happened."

He told her about the two ravens and the message capsule, finishing by pulling out the capsule itself.

"Can you read this?" he asked. "It looks like your language, but it's nothing I've learned."

Zira weighted down the top of the rolled paper with a little bowl of honey-toasted nuts.

"No wonder you couldn't read this," she said. "It's in an abbreviated script used pretty routinely by both temples and businesses. Thing is, each character has to be separately memorized, so I doubt anyone has taught you it. Enough for you to memorize now."

"That's true," Derian said. "What does it say?"

Zira placed a finger under each character in turn as she elaborated its meaning.

"'All is well.' 'Must talk.' 'Keep out.' Then there are the rather odd final characters. They aren't ours."

"They're Firekeeper's—I mean Lady Blysse's—idea of a signature. The hand is her; the paw is Blind Seer. What a weird message! And I wonder who wrote it?"

"Couldn't she have done so?" Zira asked.

"Never before," Derian replied, "but it's not impossible. I'll have to ask Harjeedian if he taught her the characters when he dropped her off."

"Or maybe one of the disdum at the outpost did," Zira said. "Didn't you get a message a few days back saying that she'd told them she was going somewhere with the Wise Wolves and you weren't to worry."

"That's true." Derian mulled over this for a moment, and then the humor of the situation hit him. "Trust Firekeeper to learn to speak one language and write in another."

He stared down at the written characters. "I wonder what she meant by this? I'm glad all is well, but this 'must talk' doesn't seem to fit either with that or with 'stay away.'"

"Seems to me like she's saying that she's well. There are things she wants to talk to you about, but she doesn't want you to go to Misheemnekuru."

"Sounds right," Derian agreed. "I sure wish that if she's decided to learn to write, she would have learned more than a few cryptic symbols."

"It's a start," Zira said soothingly, in much the same tone she used when one of the foals was being fractious. "It's a start."

Varjuna entered, smelling strongly of horses, hot damp, and the soap he'd obviously just used to scrub his hands.

"What's a start?" he asked.

Between them, Derian and Zira explained. Varjuna listened without interrupting, a trait that reminded Derian of King Tedric.

"Interesting," he said, "and pleased as I am to hear the young woman is well, I hope she is not planning to return to the mainland too soon."

"What do you mean, sir?" Derian asked sharply. The cream over his cereal suddenly seemed soured.

For a moment, Varjuna looked all of his sixty-five years.

"Complications," he said briefly, "are arising regarding your visit—or, to be completely blunt, that of Lady Blysse. Had it been other than a jaguar year, and had the ahmyndisdu been older, maybe they would have been foreseen. On the other hand, Tiridanti had plenty of older heads to advise her and no one raised any questions. Perhaps no one really believed that Lady Blysse could do what Waln Endbrook claimed. I know I had my doubts."

"You are talking," Zira said, "in riddles and are making our guest quite anxious. Have our guests been traced? Has someone come looking for them?"

"No," Varjuna said.

Derian didn't know whether to be relieved or disappointed. Now that he actually knew the Liglimom a bit better, he'd thought a great deal about what a rescue mission would mean and had come to the reluctant conclusion that it would be a very bad way for their two cultures to make contact. He thought that with Barnet's skill at spinning stories and a few preparatory letters, the eventual embassy could be handled peacefully. Only a few people need know the full truth.

Still, the sick sensation deep within him told him that no matter how much his mind knew differently, his heart wanted very much to go home. He resolved to start another letter to his family as soon as possible, but for now he needed to concentrate on what Varjuna was saying.

"The problem is theological in nature," Varjuna said. "As you know by now, Derian, our entire culture is structured around endeavoring to serve the deities and live as they see best. Even in the homeland, we relied on auguries from various animals to know the divine will. When we came here, we met the yarimaimalom and our lives were enriched. Although no one seems to have thought about it before now, the coming of Lady Blysse and her ability to speak to the animals directly is a revolution on the same scale."

Derian frowned. "I don't understand. I'm sorry, but don't you already talk with your yarimaimalom?"

"After a fashion," Varjuna said. "Tell me, have you ever had laryngitis so severely that you lost your voice?"

Derian blinked. "Last winter, in fact. I underestimated how cold winters in the Northwoods could be."

"How did you communicate?"

"By hand gestures mostly," Derian said. "Sometimes I wrote notes. Sometimes Wendee—Wendee Jay looked out for me mostly—could guess based on a few words."

Varjuna smiled, "And were you happy to get your voice back?"

"Immensely! It was so much easier to talk rather than write. Sometimes I wouldn't even ask for something because it was just too much trouble . . ."

Derian paused. "I see your point, Varjuna, at least part of it. You think that if your people could learn to talk to the yarimaimalom a whole lot more communicating would go on. What's wrong with that?"

"Just hold the idea for a moment," Varjuna said. "Ease of communication is only part of it, nor if Lady Blysse can teach us to speak to the yarimaimalom are we assured of easy communication. Don't you still prefer Pellish to our language?"

Derian grinned. "I speak your language really well when we're discussing horses and a few other things, but just now, when you asked about laryngitis, I had to guess what you meant. It helped that you touched your throat and mentioned losing my voice."

"So you see," Varjuna said, "and you have been forced to immerse yourself in our language and ways. But this is a sideline to the main issue. When does your next appointment come?"

Derian frowned. "Actually, fairly soon."

"Then let us talk again later, when we will not be interrupted. This is too serious a matter to go over quickly. In the end, we may need your help to arrive at the best decision."

Derian didn't like the implications of that. He already knew that government and religion were one and the same in this land. He found himself wishing he could send Firekeeper a message.

And what would I write? he thought with a wry smile. *"All's well. Must talk. Keep out."*

THE RUINS PROVED A CONTINUING fascination to both Firekeeper and Blind Seer, and they made several trips together to various interesting locations. One was a tower, its exterior shell still three-quarters intact, though a fire had gutted the interior, burning the wooden floors to cinder and taking out the roof as well.

Rubble was heaped inside the base. Vines intertwined throughout, and small animals had built their dens. Although there were recognizable human artifacts mixed with the heavy pieces of burned wood and heat-shattered stone, Firekeeper didn't linger here long. The scent of old burned things made her uncomfortable, and for many nights thereafter her sleep was filled with nightmares she couldn't quite remember, but which cast shadows over her days.

Far better were places fire hadn't touched, where the agents of decay were wind, water, and good, honest rot. Firekeeper studied mosaics and sculptures, identified what was almost certainly writing, and carried away bits of broken glass and fragments of jewelry as gifts for Bitter and Lovable.

Best of all was that Firekeeper now had something she was doing with Blind Seer, an interest they shared as none of the Wise Wolves did. Indeed, Firekeeper was astonished by the Wise Wolves' lack of interest. It was almost as if they deliberately avoided these places. Her own Royal Beasts had hated and despised the Old Country rulers, but she had not had this same sense of avoidance. She tucked the impression away in a corner of her mind so that she might gnaw over it during some slow time.

With clear honesty, she admitted to herself that she was glad for this avoidance. Not only did it leave her free to investigate as she wished, without taking too many others into consideration, but also she had something she could share with Blind Seer and Blind Seer alone. This gave her a good feeling that remained with her as they returned from each of their daily jaunts, buoying her up above the continued slights that came from many of the Wise Wolves.

On one particular day, Firekeeper was rejoicing over a particularly good find—a pendant with small, faceted sapphires set in gold. It had cleaned up nicely, and Firekeeper knew that Lovable would adore it. She had grown rather fond of the female raven, and enjoyed Lovable's childlike delight in pretty things.

The raven had taken to appearing from time to time when Firekeeper and Blind Seer headed out on one of these expeditions, sometimes dropping riddling hints where they might find something interesting. Firekeeper suspected Lovable's motivation was greed, because the ruins that the deciphered riddles guided them to were invariably better preserved and contained more interesting—and shiny—objects.

Almost as soon as they emerged from the thick tangle at the edge of the forest into the scrub growth and grass, Firekeeper's mood darkened. Moon Frost came loping over to meet them—or rather, to meet Blind Seer. Firekeeper was pointedly ignored.

"Dark Death is arranging a hunt," Moon Frost said, wriggling with delight. "We were hoping you would be back in time to join us."

"Dark Death?" Blind Seer asked. "He isn't among the Ones."

"No," Moon Frost replied, snapping at a fly, "but the Ones aren't the only wolves who can hunt. Since they get the first go at the kill, none of the Ones are hungry, but a few of us were thinking it would be nice to have firsts—and I, for one, am tired of eating fish."

Blind Seer hadn't paused at Moon Frost's approach, but continued padding to where the joined packs were stirring from the late-afternoon drowse that saved them from the worst of the heat. Dark Death was gathered with a small pack of the strong hunters. Much tussling was going on, bumping of shoulders, biting at the thick fur of neck ruff and shoulder scruff, small snatches of howling—all indications that they were indeed planning a hunt.

Firekeeper walked next to Blind Seer, saying nothing, acutely aware of Moon Frost's presence—and of how she herself was being ignored. After the day's closeness with Blind Seer, Firekeeper found it very hard to be reminded that in the end she was not one with this pack—perhaps would never be one with any pack.

Sorrow and anger warred within the wolf-woman. She wanted to howl as she had heard human children cry "It's not fair!," but no one knew better than a wild creature that the course of one's life was not governed by fairness. Only death was fair, for in time death came for everyone.

"I'm not hungry," Blind Seer replied mildly. "Firekeeper and I ate while we were out."

Moon Frost sniffed.

"Rabbits," she announced contemptuously. "Hardly food for a hunter."

"It fills the belly," Blind Seer replied.

"You and I are such a good team," Moon Frost wheedled. "We're sure to pull down the kill and get the liver. A big strong male like you could work up an appetite for that, couldn't you?"

"There are other strong males," Blind Seer replied. "I see several of them already set for the hunt."

"But I hunt best with you," Moon Frost said, "and I think you do very well with me. Don't you?"

What Blind Seer might have replied remained unknown, for Firekeeper felt her long-stretched temper give way as a bowstring might after being kept strung for too long.

"Blind Seer said he isn't hungry," Firekeeper snapped, staring at Moon Frost. "Are you too deaf to hear?"

"My ears are sharper than yours, fool pup," Moon Frost snarled, flattening those ears against her skull. "Stay out of matters better suited to wolves than to humans."

"Human? Perhaps," Firekeeper said, narrowing her eyes, her hand drifting to her Fang, "but at least I'm not so unnatural as to be pressing my suit out of season. What's wrong with you?"

Moon Frost peeled her lips back from gleaming ivory fangs. "You calling me unnatural? That's like an eel telling a fish it is covered in slime. I am not unnatural, whelp. It is you, clinging to ways and peoples that are not your own, who are unnatural. You mouth our talk, mimic our ways, but smell yourself. You are human!"

Firekeeper snarled in turn, her bow staff dropping from her hand, her Fang moving into the best position for cutting. She and Blind Seer had sparred any number of times, and she knew that at this proximity the bow would be useless, but that with her knife she had a fair chance against one wolf—especially one who had never seen her fight and was likely to underestimate her skill.

However, although Moon Frost might be inclined to underestimate Firekeeper, she remained a Wise Wolf, possessed of all a Wise Wolf's size and strength and intelligence. Moonspans of hunting had left Moon Frost lean and muscular. Good eating had erased any trace of winter weakness. Moon Frost easily outweighed Firekeeper and could put that weight to good use—and from how she was eyeing the knife, she had not forgotten that Firekeeper's bite would come from deceptive places.

Moreover, Moon Frost had napped through all the lazy afternoon, while Firekeeper had traveled long distances, climbing and digging to see what the ruins held. The advantage was definitely with Moon Frost there, as in so many other ways, but Firekeeper was not about to surrender without a fight. She was tired of being treated as not quite wolf by most, and by those who did acknowledge her as a wolf, as a very stupid pup. One way or another, this fight would change her status. Firekeeper tried hard not to think how final that change could be.

Scenting the impending fight, Blind Seer had stepped from between them and now stood a few paces away. As was proper, he neither interfered nor encouraged one or the other. Many of the other wolves were drifting over to watch, the planned hunt delayed, the evening games postponed.

Yet, although Firekeeper was peripherally aware of all of this, she did not take these watchers into account. She knew that this was a fight not between pack and pack, but between individual and individual. In such a case, no one would interfere.

Or at least so she hoped. Did the Wise Wolves follow the same rules as those who had raised her? Would they accept her as a wolf or would this challenge between a wolf they knew and a relative stranger make them alter their already tentative acceptance of Firekeeper as a wolf rather than a human? In that case, then Firekeeper would be transformed into an invader—a human who had violated the truce between wolves and humans. As such, her life would be forfeit.

These questions slid through Firekeeper's mind, but did not interfere with her focus on Moon Frost. They slowly circled each other, pivoting around the empty space between them, each feinting, testing to see who would be first to attack, who to defend.

Their battleground was a piece of open meadow, thus robbing Firekeeper of whatever advantage she might have gained among the trees or scrub. The grass was well grazed, well trampled. The footing reliable. Darkness was falling with gradual grace, leaving neither Firekeeper nor Moon Frost at any particular disadvantage.

At last, as Firekeeper had thought she would, Moon Frost sprang. It was a compact leap, meant to bring her weight into Firekeeper's upper torso and so knock her flat. From there Moon Frost would doubtlessly go for the throat—for the throat was among the most favored targets of a hunting wolf.

But Firekeeper was not there when Moon Frost landed. As quickly as the wolf had leapt, Firekeeper had been quicker. She had recognized the signs contained in bunching of muscle and shifting of weight. Holding her place until Moon Frost was committed to action, Firekeeper had immediately darted to one side. Then, when Moon Frost landed, momentarily nonplussed at not finding her prey where it should have been, Firekeeper swung behind her and launched herself astride.

It was a daring move, for it brought Firekeeper into intimate proximity with her opponent, but it also robbed Moon Frost—at least temporarily—of the ability to easily bring her fangs into play. Firekeeper gripped hard with her knees, holding as Derian had taught her to do when astride a horse—a thing quite possible, for Moon Frost was the size of a pony. Firekeeper was very strong, and the pressure she could bring to bear with her legs was considerable. Moreover, the sensation was unfamiliar to Moon Frost and momentarily disconcerted her.

Wolves mount and clasp each other when wrestling, but never had a wolf possessed a set of bony knees with which to grasp and hold. A Cousin wolf might have sunk beneath Firekeeper's weight, but Moon Frost was a Royal Wolf, large for her size, and would not give way, especially when giving way was so like surrendering.

Firekeeper knew her advantage would not last more than a moment, and readied herself. With her left hand, the wolf-woman grabbed hard onto Moon Frost's neck scruff. With her right, she held her Fang ready. She did not particularly want to kill Moon Frost, but she knew she must be prepared to do so.

For a single trembling moment, Moon Frost stood holding Firekeeper on her back. Then she twisted, bending her neck to bring her fangs into play, aiming for the leg so annoyingly pressing into her midsection. She was so fast that her teeth ripped through the fabric of Firekeeper's right trouser leg, tearing it apart and grazing the skin beneath.

Firekeeper ignored the flash of pain and brought her Fang down onto Moon Frost's skull. Gone were thoughts of not killing the other. The sharpness of those teeth reminded her how easily she could be the one who was killed.

The blade of the hunting knife sliced through fur and hide, but skidded when it met solid bone. Firekeeper regained her grip before the blade could do her any injury. In that moment of correction, Moon Frost adapted her tactics. She no longer held Firekeeper clear of the ground, restricting her own motion with the wolf-woman's weight, but dropped almost limp.

Firekeeper corrected her balance quickly enough so that Moon Frost did not succeed in rolling on top of her as she had intended. Even so, Moon Frost's fangs nipped her heel as she pulled herself free. Now Firekeeper was bloodied in two places, but neither wound was severe. Moon Frost's cut scalp ran blood into her fur, matting the silvery-grey dark. Doubtless her head would ache come morning—but morning was far away.

The two opponents reoriented on each other, circling as before. Moon Frost was not likely to make another dramatic leap. Wolves had many tactics for bringing down their prey, and Firekeeper's bleeding heel and the slight limp that resulted from it had reminded Moon Frost of another.

Belly flat to the ground, Moon Frost rushed forward, intent on hamstringing Firekeeper. Firekeeper had expected this—indeed, she had exaggerated the damage to her foot in order to encourage it. When the wolf's long snout was near, Firekeeper kicked up, catching Moon Frost beneath the jaw. The impact hurt, but as Moon Frost had been close to the ground, Firekeeper was not unbalanced.

As Moon Frost snapped air and bowled back from the sudden pain, Firekeeper crouched and brought her bunched fist, hardened by the hilt of her fang, into the wolf's throat. The impact knocked the wind from Moon Frost, and her tail dropped for a moment.

Firekeeper didn't let her alertness falter, but she knew she had given away some valuable information to her opponent, if Moon Frost was able to analyze what she had learned. The hilt of her knife had given Firekeeper's blow a solidity it would not have had alone, but the blade could have opened Moon Frost's breath to the wind. Would Moon Frost realize this? And would she take the information as Firekeeper intended?

There was no time for further assessment. Moon Frost had recovered and with less calculation than before had lunged forward. Firekeeper was ready for this and rolled to one side, coming up and slashing Moon Frost a long cut on one flank. This hit no vital organs, but it clearly hurt. Blood sprayed, gluing hair and blood onto the knife, forcing Firekeeper to adjust her grip.

The wolf-woman did not press her attack, but waited, knees slightly bent, for Moon Frost's next move. The other shook as if the blood on her head and side were rain that could be shaken off at will, but the pain from both injuries reminded her that it could not. For a long moment Moon Frost stared at Firekeeper, her golden-brown eyes wide with a mingling of astonishment and pain. Then very deliberately, she crumpled onto her uninjured side and rolled onto her back, exposing vulnerable throat and belly.

Firekeeper saw fear in Moon Frost's eyes, and heard a whimper that would not have been expressed were Moon Frost surrendering to a wolf of her own pack. The fear was that, after all, Firekeeper was not a wolf and would not honor surrender.

Firekeeper approached and let the bleeding wolf lick her hands and feet.

"Up with you," she said gruffly to the quivering Moon Frost. "You'll get elk shit in your cuts and the pack will be deprived of a fine hunter."

Moon Frost rose trembling, her head low, her gaze downcast.

"I know something of mending bites as well as of making them," Firekeeper said. "Come with me and I will make sure you do not take lasting harm."

Together the former combatants limped off to the nearby stream, and no one, not even Blind Seer, followed.

XIX

HARJEEDIAN GREW VERY TENSE and sharp-tempered in the days following Rahniseeta's less than conclusive visit to u-Bishinti. She was secure enough in her knowledge that she had done everything that could have been expected of her not to worry that his current mood was somehow her fault.

However, after several days, she was quite tired of being snapped at for the slightest reason. That the outburst was almost immediately followed by an apology did not help, and so when Rahniseeta reached the point that she realized she was making excuses to leave for her room almost as soon as Harjeedian arrived in their suite, she grasped the snake firmly behind the head.

"Harjeedian, what is wrong with you?"

"Nothing," he said.

He had been about to take a seat in his chair at their dining table, but now he made as if to rise and leave. Rahniseeta moved behind her brother and pressed him down into the chair.

"Nothing, nonsense," she said. "You're as edgy as a snake with pre-shedding blindness. Wash the liquid from your scales and take a look."

Harjeedian sagged into the chair, and Rahniseeta realized that he was actually relieved to have her confront him. Oddly, this worried her more than if he had continued to assert that nothing was wrong. Harjeedian was so much the older brother, so confident—and protective—that even this mute admission of need was disturbing.

Harjeedian reached for the pitcher of peach nectar set on the table and poured himself a tumbler. Rahniseeta took her hands from his shoulders and moved to her own seat. She had cadged some fresh blueberry muffins from the kitchens when on an errand there for one of the kidisdum, and now slid the plate over to her brother.

Harjeedian took a muffin, but didn't bite into it. Instead, he sat staring at the pastry as if he might read omens from the way the blue fruit bled into the surrounding cake. Rahniseeta didn't press him. He had stayed, and would speak when his thoughts were in order.

"Nothing," Harjeedian said at last, setting down the muffin untasted, "has gone right since the day we took Lady Blysse and Derian Counselor aboard the riverboat."

Rahniseeta made an encouraging sound.

"They were not at all the type of people Waln Endbrook led me to believe they would be," Harjeedian continued. "In some ways they were far better. Waln's report had made them out to be connivers and scoundrels. Although I distrusted him sufficiently not to take his opinion at face value, still my three captives had more honor than I expected. They were angry, yes, but they kept the terms of their parole, and Derian, at least, made a serious effort to learn our language.

"I am beginning to think that very parole is the wellspring of our difficulties. In showing them that we valued them and were willing to treat with them as equals, we permitted them to keep some sense of self-worth. Had I kept them belowdecks, fed and exercised them only when they performed as I wished . . ."

His voice trailed off, and Rahniseeta knew that these thoughts were not his own. Harjeedian was ambitious, but he was not cruel. He would never have answered obedience with harshness. It was her place to remind him how he had seen the situation then rather than how he saw it now, through the distorting glass of later events.

"Harjeedian, you were the teacher who taught me that one does not train a snake to dance by making it fear the swaying of the flute," Rahniseeta said. "Why would you have done differently with these humans you wished to train? Moreover, Lady Blysse companioned a Wise Wolf. Could you have harmed her without offending the wolf, and so offending the deities? Your behavior was perfectly in keeping with the teachings of both the temples and the gods."

Harjeedian picked a blueberry from his muffin, but didn't raise it to his lips.

"Perhaps," he said, "but the fact is that when we arrived here, my captives—no matter how prettily u-Liall names them 'guests,' they were captives—were prepared not to serve, but to negotiate. Negotiate is what they have done, and the only gain we have taken in these negotiations is a greater knowledge of their language and country—things we could have learned from the northerners already in our keeping."

"You are too harsh with yourself," Rahniseeta replied. "First, you speak as if that knowledge is useless. It is not. Second, I do not think even Barnet Lobster knew as much of Hawk Haven as do the other two. They also have traveled to this other land, this New Kelvin, and have told us something about that place and its customs. Barnet knew little more than fireside stories about New Kelvin. I know this for certain, for he has told me how eager he is to learn more."

Harjeedian squashed the blueberry into his plate.

"But that is not why they were brought here!" he said. "They were brought here specifically so that Lady Blysse might teach us the language of the yarimaimalom. Not only has she failed to do that, now there is even talk that our learning such would be sacrilege—an offense to the deities and the beasts alike."

"I don't understand," Rahniseeta said.

Harjeedian drew in a deep breath and finally took a drink. He seemed vaguely surprised to find the nectar warm—as it would be, after being left so long outside of the cooling thickness of the pitcher.

"What is strangest," he said, "is that while there are several factions willing to argue that our learning to speak directly to the yarimaimalom would be sacrilege, they do not all agree why our learning to do so would be sacrilege. Indeed, some of the objections verge on being sacrilegious themselves."

"I think," Rahniseeta said, "that before you explain further, you had better tell me what some of these objections are. Why, by the way, didn't anyone make them before *Fayonejunjal* was sent north?"

"Who knows?" Harjeedian said. "It is a jaguar year and everyone is insane."

Then he grinned. "Actually, I think no one bothered with any objections because no one really believed we would find Lady Blysse or that if we did find her we would be able to bring her back with us. The fact that we succeeded has unsettled those who were ready to protest the cost and wasted resources of such an ill-thought expedition."

"And now they look for other ways to protest?" Rahniseeta guessed.

"That," Harjeedian said, "and a hand of other reasons. As I said, it is a jaguar year. The ahmyndisdu is very young and has enemies."

Rahniseeta put this aside. "Tell me how learning to speak to the yarimaimalom could possibly be thought sacrilege. We can go from there."

Harjeedian sighed, but he actually ate half of his muffin before beginning, and Rahniseeta felt relieved.

"When Waln first told us of Lady Blysse and her ability to speak with the yarimaimalom, most of us thought that this would be a wonderful thing to do. It would almost be as good as speaking directly to the deities themselves. As things are now, we must rely on signs and portents. Even the wheels and charts we use are limited in the range of meanings they can convey."

Rahniseeta nodded. She knew this, but like most who have spent a great deal of time in teaching and being taught, Harjeedian had a very orderly way of presenting information.

"One of the first objections raised to our learning to speak the language of the yarimaimalom was that it would further lower the lesser beasts in our estimation, for who would go through the more laborious divinations if they could simply ask a question and get a clear answer?"

Rahniseeta nodded again. "I can see this. It would further intensify the debates that have been going on since our people first encountered the yarimaimalom. Aren't there those who have never trusted the Wise Beast auguries?"

"They are reactionaries," Harjeedian said rather angrily, though Rahniseeta knew the anger wasn't directed at her. "If we followed their ideas to their logical conclusion, we would be pushed back to the days of animal sacrifice."

"True," Rahniseeta replied. "Though how many of those would like the reinstitution of the ancient rite wherein one of every beast that crawled or swam or walked or flew—including human beings—were sacrificed I am not certain."

"A few of them probably would like it," Harjeedian said darkly. "If you read between the lines in some of the older histories, it is implied that this was a great way to get rid of enemies."

Rahniseeta smiled. "But none of those who currently sit as u-Liall will let the yari-maimalom be rejected, so we need not worry. Is the only objection to our learning the language of the yarimaimalom that the lesser beasts would be discounted?"

"That is only the slightest ripple that heralds the windstorm," Harjeedian said. "Related to the first objection is another. These say that the achievement of free speech between humans and yarimaimalom would encourage the yarimaimalom to turn the auguries to their own advantage. Some have always argued that the yarimaimalom gave less true auguries than the lesser beasts because the yarimaimalom might have their own agendas and seek to promote them. This argument has always been countered by reminding that the yarimaimalom 'speak' to us within the context of holy traditions—that the deities have provided a balance in this way."

"But," Rahniseeta said, "if we could talk to the yarimaimalom directly, there would be no need for these traditions and rituals."

She felt a chill touch the back of her neck, though the weather remained hot and sultry.

"I can see," she said, speaking honestly, "why some fear we verge on sacrilege. This begins to frighten me."

Harjeedian gave her a crooked smile. "If it frightens you, sister mine, imagine how it frightens the aridisdum. You and I have spent enough years in the temple precincts that I know I can speak honestly. I think all who rise high in the divine service have some respect for the deities, but though I may be verging on yet another sacrilege, I do not think that all those initiated believe with the same depth. Indeed, I suspect our mat-weaving mother believed in Earth, Air, Fire, Water, and Magic more devoutly than do many who dwell within the temples and daily walk before the altars."

Rahniseeta felt a little sad, but she knew what Harjeedian said was true—even of herself. She thought how she had felt when u-Liall had met and she had been expected to remain. She had not feared because they represented the divine, but because she knew they were all too human.

An extension of this was that she no longer felt awe of them as if they were near to the deities. Her mother would have been nearly as impressed to meet the ahmyndisdu as to meet Fire. However, it had never occurred to Rahniseeta that the aridisdu who spent so much time and energy studying the holy writings and traditions might lose some of their own simple faith.

She looked at Harjeedian and wondered if he still believed in the deities he had striven so hard to learn how to serve. She also knew she would never ask.

Harjeedian went on, "Leaving faith and depth of faith aside, let us take this new course to its logical extension. Let us say that we learn to speak directly to the yari-maimalom. Next, let us say that it happens that the yarimaimalom come to be favored over the lesser for auguries. Perhaps except in the temples where the lesser beasts give other service—as in our own and in the Temple of the Horse—the lesser beasts are all released, or at least their populations are not replenished. In a human lifetime, we would reach a point where many would think the aridisdum would no longer be necessary."

"No!" Rahniseeta said, but Harjeedian was shaking his head and looking sour.

"Yes, sister mine," he said. "The primary role of the aridisdum is to interpret auguries. If we spoke directly to the yarimaimalom, then there would be no longer any need to interpret auguries."

"Are you so certain?" Rahniseeta asked, but she knew her own argument was weak. "I have talked some with Lady Blysse. I admit she's a foreigner, but it is quite clear she does not see the world as you and I do. Who is to say that a wolf or jaguar or snake would speak without need of interpretation?"

Harjeedian reached across and squeezed her hand.

"I'll remember that argument the next time someone talks of our becoming obsolete, but I fear the quick answer—the one that immediately came to my mind—is that the kidisdum would be as good interpreters in that case, for all that would be needed would be an understanding of animal nature, not an understanding of hundreds of years of divine will."

Rahniseeta refused to argue the point further, for she could tell it would do little good. She settled for feeling satisfied that she had made Harjeedian think.

"So far we have three possible ways that learning to speak directly to the yarimaimalom could lead us into sacrilege," she said. "Are there any more?"

"Isn't that enough?" Harjeedian said. "There are many. There is the question of where Lady Blysse fits into the hierarchy."

"Does she fit at all?" Rahniseeta asked, astonished. "How could she?"

"How couldn't she?" Harjeedian countered. "We have let her go to Misheem-nekuru and the yarimaimalom have let her go among them. That means we must accept her as a Wise Beast—as she herself has always claimed."

"And the yarimaimalom are accepted as conduits of divine wisdom . . ." Rahniseeta said. She pressed her clenched fists into her temples. "My head hurts!"

"Mine hurts worse," Harjeedian said. "What I have told you are only a few of the arguments raised to suggest we verge on heresy. I have spared you those based on divine texts. I have spared you those that argue we must set aside the current u-Liall and appoint another. I have spared you those that are not religious at all, but only based on fear of finding that we disdum will be flung out into the world on the heels of the lesser beasts—or even before."

"Before?" Rahniseeta felt a panicked fear for the same peaceful productive life that a few days earlier had felt like a trap.

"Certainly before," Harjeedian said bitterly. "After all, we owe the lesser beasts care and shelter since many of those we keep for divination have become dependent on us. However, if they are not going to be used for auguries any longer—and, remember, this assumes that the ability to speak directly with the yarimaimalom would replace those auguries—then why would we need aridisdum to interpret the auguries?"

Rahniseeta laughed, but there was no humor in the sound.

"No wonder there is such eagerness among the aridisdum to learn Pellish. They wonder if they might need a new way to earn their keep."

Harjeedian didn't laugh in response. "You speak closer to the truth than you realize. One place that it has been thought that lesser beast auguries would continue to be useful are in outlying areas where the yarimaimalom might not care to live. If we begin trade to the north, we would need aridisdum aboard."

Rahniseeta did not need to reassure her brother that he would continue to be useful, even if every other aridisdu in the land was rendered obsolete. She realized that his anxiety was not for himself, but for what he might have released into their land.

"Maybe Lady Blysse will not teach us how to speak to the yarimaimalom," Rahniseeta said, but she didn't feel a great deal of hope.

It seemed too much that what had been started could be solved so easily. Even if Lady Blysse refused to teach them the language of the yarimaimalom, she herself would continue to exist. If only she didn't exist. If only the yarimaimalom would reject her. If only she would die.

Rahniseeta felt horrified, for she had almost liked the strange feral woman, but the idea wouldn't go away.

If only Lady Blysse would die. Then everything would go back to normal. If only she would die . . . or something would kill her.

WALN KNEW WHAT HE WANTED. He wanted what the Liglimom had promised him—to go home to the Isles in such a position that he could reclaim his family and fortune. He realized that the Liglimom hadn't given him a promise in any form he could insist be enforced. It wasn't as though any vows had been spoken or contracts exchanged. They hadn't even shaken hands on the deal, but Waln knew what had been implied in the silky words and long speeches: You give us what we want. We'll give you what you want.

He'd given the Liglimom what they wanted. They had Lady Blysse, her wolf, and her keeper. That he'd gotten the satisfaction of seeing a few of those who had wronged him get their comeuppance wasn't the point. The Liglimom owed him a triumphal return to the Isles, the type of return that would make Queen Valora not only rescind his exile, but shower him with new and higher titles. He wanted a return that would make her realize how she had wronged him, a return that would make her fear him, and the threat he offered to her crown. Whatever it took, Waln was going to get what was coming to him.

Waln had thought he would make his return home in some sort of ambassadorial role, protected by his importance to the Liglimom. That would have been marvelous. The Isles needed a trading partner who would neither enslave them or dominate them.

The Liglimom needed a solid contact point in the north. Waln could have negotiated both—and while doing so negotiated his return to power as well.

Now he realized that unless he could get some leverage over the Liglimom themselves, this wasn't likely to happen. For one thing, his plans had been based on a quick return and himself as one of the sole speakers of both languages. Barnet would have been his only threat, and the minstrel could have been paid off—literally—for a song or two.

However, although Waln now understood that the Liglimom were refusing to honor their bargain, he was far from giving up hope. The last few days had revealed several very interesting possibilities. One was the instability with the seemingly monolithic theocracy that ruled the land. Another were the promising hints as to what might still be found on Misheemnekuru.

As much as Waln longed to race ahead with his plans, the Liglimom's deliberate nature forced him to act in much the same fashion. Shivadtmon—and any others Waln might win over with the aridisdu's assistance—would go as limp as a sail in a dead calm if pressed too quickly. Because of the unpredictability of these foreigners, Waln also realized that he needed to win the few Islanders over to his way of thinking. They must be ready—eager, even—to follow when he led, even if it meant abandoning their comfortable situation.

Waln wasn't sure he could win over Barnet. Up there in Heeranenahalm, the minstrel was pretty much out of his reach. He was also probably getting access to a far richer wealth of stories than Waln could offer. Winning over Barnet would have to wait, though Waln did hope to eventually gain him as an ally. As a cousin, no matter how many removes were involved, of King Harwill, Barnet would bring a degree of legitimacy to any action Waln took.

However, the other six should be easier to convince. They might not be feeling cooped-up yet, but while no minstrel, Waln was a merchant. A merchant's job—especially one collecting support for a chancy sea voyage—was to sell people an idea, rather than a solid item like a barrel of wine or length of rope. He didn't see how this would be much different. What he needed to sell first was an idea that things could be better. When he had done that, the move to making them take action against their current situation should be easy.

Waln considered where he should start. Rarby and Shelby had said only a few days before that they were enjoying their current situation. Very well, they could continue enjoying it. If they started wondering what they could be missing, they might start enjoying it less.

Nolan the ropemaker was a touch under the weather, and was feeling grateful to the Liglimom for the nursing he was getting. He wouldn't be a good target quite yet, though Waln thought he might eventually hint that the Liglimom's food or climate or clothing or something was responsible for Nolan's illness.

Elwyn was too stupid to be a real asset. In any case, he'd follow the herd. Hopefully his luck would come with him.

That left Wiatt, the cook, and Tedgewinn, the carpenter's mate. Each presented certain advantages. Wiatt was well liked and affable, possibly the most popular of the survivors. His popularity had only grown during the past year, for whenever he had the opportunity he would use his skills to create meals more after the northern style. In a sense, he had literally become the taste of home.

However, Waln wasn't quite certain what argument would best sway Wiatt. He had left no one important back in the Isles, and like Rarby and Shelby, he seemed to have no particular hankering for a greater degree of freedom. He seemed to have adopted the building in which they had been given quarters as his current vessel—a vessel rather better supplied than most, and therefore not stirring him to a desire for shore leave.

Tedgewinn had also fallen into this shipboard frame of mind, but unlike Wiatt, Waln knew Tedgewinn had left behind a younger sister of whom he was very fond. His parents were alive, too, but Waln had a vague memory that Tedgewinn didn't particularly care for at least one of them . . . his father, perhaps. Best to avoid mentioning parents.

Waln deliberately approached Tedgewinn just after the carpenter had finished giving a lesson to a middle-aged kidisdu who rather resembled the bears with which she worked. This kidisdu had a rather bearish temperament as well, playful one moment, growly and irritable the next. Whichever temper she was in, she was intensely focused, and Waln knew Tedgewinn found her exhausting.

Announcing himself with a tap on the doorframe, Waln strolled into the outer section of Tedgewinn's suite. It was similar in size and shape to Waln's own suite, but Tedgewinn's art made it unique. Lithe, vaguely feminine shapes adorned the legs of tables and chairs. Carved figurines stood on most flat surfaces. An elaborate scene of a ship at sea was being worked onto the top of a clothes chest. Tedgewinn knelt in front of it, a narrow rasp in one hand, apparently about to deepen the curl of a wave.

Waln waited in respectful silence while Tedgewinn finished, then hefted the pitcher he held in one hand.

"I brought some beer," he said. "Thought the bear lady had probably dried you out."

Tedgewinn rose and thanked Waln with a lopsided grin. He was an odd contrast of traits: broad and muscular above, lean and sturdy below. He wore a coarse black mustache and beard trimmed to a finger's width below the line of his jaw, and a long braid that touched the top of his belt.

"Talking with her's dry work," the carpenter admitted, taking two tankards from a scrollwork cabinet. "I wish I'd never taught her how to ask questions. It was easier when all she did was repeat stuff and see if I understood her."

Waln filled the tankards and then sat uninvited in one of the comfortable high-backed chairs. Looking at the room from the point of a common sailor, he had to admit that life here must seem an improvement. Shipboard, even a skilled hand like the carpenter's mate would be lucky to get a portion of a narrow berth. These two rooms with all their attendant furnishings—even to private dishware—must seem like astonishing luxury.

Very well, Waln thought. *My job is to make him long for more. Shouldn't be hard. Greed's as natural as sucking down mother's milk.*

"You've been doing nice work here," Waln said, picking up the nearest carving—one of a seal sprawled asleep on a rock. "I'd buy this for one of my better students but . . ."

He shrugged. None of them had been paid for their work. It wasn't much of a sore point . . . yet.

"Take it," Tedgewinn said, waving his hand. "I can make more. Once the servants found I liked carving, they made sure I was kept in wood." He laughed. "Probably wanted to save the furniture. Gave me some nice tools, too, far better than my knife."

"Give them any of the carvings in return?" Waln asked, sensing an opening.

"Not so much in return," Tedgewinn replied, "but if they like a piece, I usually give it to them. I like the making more than looking at stuff afterwards. After, it seems all I can see are the places where I could have done better. Look at that seal, for example. I'm sure I could have done a better job around the eyes."

Before the conversation could get sidetracked into the niceties of carving, Waln cut in.

"You used to sell some of your carvings, didn't you?"

"Sell or trade," Tedgewinn agreed.

"Got a good price?"

"Fair, fair . . ." Tedgewinn sounded complacent. "Did better with commissioned pieces. Did a little study from the waist up of a girl Shelby was taken with once. I swear he kept it with him everywhere he went that trip. Didn't do him much good. He got home and found she'd married an apothecary who didn't go off to sea. I think he took the berth on the *Explorer* to soothe an aching heart."

Waln had heard something about his, and thought that Shelby's emotion had been less tender. Shelby had wanted to make the girl sorry for not waiting for him. He'd have to remember that. It could come in handy later.

"I bet the servants are getting a good price for your carvings," Waln said, masking a pretended yawn behind the heel of his hand. "Not only are they wonderfully lifelike, but they've novelty value as well. 'Get a carving of your special animal, made by the demon from the north!'"

"You think so?" Tedgewinn seemed genuinely astonished.

"Sure," Waln said. "Your animals do everything but eat and shit. These people are nuts about animals. Add in the novelty value that the carvings are made by one of the northern demons and I'd bet the servants are getting their weight in gold for them."

"Naw . . ." Tedgewinn sounded so uncertain that Waln knew he had pushed too hard. "These people don't have money like that."

"Well," Waln said, "maybe I exaggerate. I bet some of them are keeping them and are the envy of all the neighbors. What happens when a neighbor says 'Can you get me one of a cat?' or a bear or something? Just wait."

Tedgewinn's expression held a mixture of pleasure and annoyance, just as Waln had hoped it would.

"Think I can sell them?" Tedgewinn asked. "I can't quite get whether these people even use money or if everything's barter. There's not much I need to barter for, but it would be nice to have a nest egg for when we go home."

Waln swallowed a whoop of triumph.

Carefully . . . carefully, he reminded himself. *Reel him in slowly or he'll snap the line. You don't want him swimming off to go into business as a small-time carver. You want him yearning to go home with his duffel filled with gold.*

"They use money," Waln said. "I asked one of my students about it—trying to hint we should be getting paid for our time."

Tedgewinn nodded, his gaze focused.

"Well," Waln continued, "they told me that within the temples, money isn't much used. The temples take care of their own and no one gets paid for working for the temples. Apparently, we're considered part of the temple system."

Tedgewinn snorted. Like all the survivors, he found the Liglimom religious system—especially its reliance on omens—questionable, even laughable.

"That's how he told me it works," Waln said. "Outside of the temples, though, they use money. The system's different, but not too different. They value gold, silver, and gems, as well as paying honestly for honest labor."

"I wonder how much they'd pay for one of my carvings?" Tedgewinn mused aloud. "I'm not much good at pricing things when I can't even stroll in the market square and see what's the going rate."

Waln nodded. "I know what you mean. For all they call us guests and treat us nicely—very nicely—we're prisoners. Not until I have the key to the front door in my pocket and can come and go as I choose will I believe I'm a guest. Until then I'm just a dancing bear wearing a pretty collar."

He knew that his big, burly frame reminded many of a bear, so the comparison wasn't inopportune, but he also hoped to remind Tedgewinn of his most annoying student. Judging from the scowl that knit the other man's brow as he scanned the room, he had succeeded.

"I hadn't thought of it that way, Waln," Tedgewinn said slowly, "but you're right. Even at sea we have our chests and the right to kick the crap out of anyone who goes in without our leave. What do we have here? Pretty rooms, good clothes, but not the privacy or freedom a man would give his five-year-old son."

Waln didn't argue with the logic of this. What mattered was that Tedgewinn was suitably annoyed.

"We could try for freedom of the marketplace," he said. "I'd be happy to help you get a fair price for your carvings—and charge no commission at all. It would be a pleasure to use my skills for a countryman rather than slave for these foreigners."

Tedgewinn grunted shy thanks. Waln leaned forward and lowered his voice. Tedgewinn leaned forward to match his posture and Waln knew the conspiratorial closeness would do as much as any words to sway the other.

"I think," Waln said, "I know a better way to build that nest egg you were mentioning. We'd need to get out of here, first, but once we were out. I think I know where we'd find treasure heaped up for the taking—and better yet, not one of these Liglimom would dare follow us and interfere."

"What are you talking about?" Tedgewinn asked. There was doubt in his voice, but he didn't pull away.

"Have you heard talk of Misheemnekuru?"

"The Sanctuary Islands?" Tedgewinn nodded. "A little from the sailors on *Fayone-junjal* when we were outfitting her. They said it was a holy place, that only a few of their disdum lived there."

"That's true as far as it goes, but there's more." Waln glanced with affected nervousness toward the door. "How long until your next student comes?"

"Bear-lady was my last for the day," Tedgewinn said eagerly. "How about you?"

"I'm done for the day, too."

Waln rose and closed the door into the suite, an unnecessary gesture, since the only ones likely to understand their conversation—which was in Pellish, after all—were those he eventually hoped to bring into the scheme. If the servants understood anything, he'd just be relating a local legend. Still, the motions toward secrecy would convince Tedgewinn this was important.

"Misheemnekuru was where their Old Country rulers made their first base, and where they continued to have palaces even after u-Seeheera was built," Waln began.

Choosing his words as carefully as if he were a ship's minstrel with a crew about to mutiny, Waln spun out the tale of Misheemnekuru, emphasizing that it had remained without human inhabitants since the Plague, while playing down that the beasts to which it had been given were yarimaimalom.

It wasn't hard to make Tedgewinn discount the yarimaimalom's importance. Even in Liglim, none of the northerners had seen more than one or two of the supposedly intelligent animals. The only Wise Beast they'd had extensive acquaintance with was the wolf Blind Seer. That had been shipboard, where he had done nothing more extraordinary than hang close to his pathetically seasick mistress.

When Waln finished, Tedgewinn looked at him, his eyes bright with conjecture.

"You thinking what I'm thinking?" Tedgewinn said. "You're thinking that if their Old Country rulers dropped dead or ran away, that they left all their good stuff behind?"

"That's a thought," Waln agreed, acting as if the man had originated the idea, rather than been led to it. "In our own land, the palaces and castles were looted, the wealth the rulers didn't take with them was used to found fortunes. Here the islands were made into an animal preserve. Sure stuff will be buried under leaves and fallen trees, but it should all be there."

"For the taking," Tedgewinn breathed, "just for the taking. And since these people are crazy superstitious about their omens, they won't dare chase us. We'll be like kids in a berry patch."

Waln didn't think it would be quite that easy, but he didn't see any advantage to dissuading Tedgewinn now. Enough time later, when they were planning, to speak of the difficulties.

"As I see it," Waln said, "we have two things we have to do to get ourselves over there."

"What?"

"We need to get the others on our side," Waln said. "We aren't going to be able to sail out of here without help, and anyhow, they're our buddies. I wouldn't leave them impoverished slaves when they can go home wealthy as lords."

Tedgewinn nodded, though his lips thinned momentarily at the idea of sharing. Doubtless, though, like Waln he realized that getting home without help would be impossible—and what good would their wealth do them here?

"What's the other thing?" Tedgewinn asked.

"We're going to need a few locals on our side," Waln said. "We need out of this prison and some freedom to move about if we're to get to Misheemnekuru."

"Right," Tedgewinn said, "we can't swim over. We'll need a boat and, more importantly, someone to cover for us. I don't think we can tell any locals what we plan, though."

"Absolutely not," Waln agreed. "They'll get all superstitious on us. I think I can bring them around without letting on just what we're doing. One of my aridisdum isn't really happy with how things are going, and I think he'd be glad of an opportunity to challenge his bosses."

"Sounds good," Tedgewinn said. "You want my help talking to the others from the ship?"

"Not all at once," Waln said, "but you get along well with Wiatt. Can you work on him?"

"Consider it done," Tedgewinn said. "He's often talked about wanting to start an inn with a fine dining hall back on his home island—the kind of place nobles would be proud to visit. I'll work him up on that, then hint that I might know a way to make it possible."

If Tedgewinn felt any resentment at being worked on himself in a similar way, he didn't show it. Doubtless, Waln thought, he was flattered to have been the first chosen.

"I'll take Shelby," Waln said, "and he'll probably bring Rarby around. Remember, though, we've got to take this slowly and carefully. We need to have a ship ready for our escape even before we go to Misheemnekuru and collect our goods."

Tedgewinn nodded. "Maybe one of those local allies you mentioned can help you set that up."

"Good idea," Waln said, adding a touch of flattery, "though I'd want you to check its soundness."

"No problem," Tedgewinn promised. "I'll do anything you'd like if it will get me out of here and make me rich."

"Even continuing to teach the bear-lady," Waln said with a laugh. "We're going to need to continue teaching, you know, otherwise they'll get suspicious."

"Even teaching the bear-lady," Tedgewinn promised.

XX

SINCE THIS WAS ONLY THE SECOND TIME in her life that Firekeeper had beaten an adult wolf in a serious fight, her pride in her accomplishment was pardonable. However, she quickly came to realize that it was not so much that she had beaten Moon Frost that counted with the Wise Wolves, but something far more subtle.

"We had no doubt," Neck Breaker explained, "that you were deadly. How could you have survived among wolves otherwise, with your soft human claws and blunt teeth? No. It was not that you defeated Moon Frost that proved to us that you are an adult, not a pup. It was how you did so."

Firekeeper tilted her head in inquiry, thinking she understood, but preferring to hear the lesson from the old wolf's jaws.

"Not only did you accept Moon Frost's surrender when it was offered," Neck Breaker went on, "but you gave her many hints that you would accept surrender if it was offered. That took courage, for to do so you forced yourself to hold back from a killing blow."

"And," added Blind Seer, wuffing out air through his nose, "that was very stupid. Moon Frost was near crazed. In her own pack she is second only to the Ones, but here in the greater pack she has repeatedly had to reassess herself. There are many among the females as strong or stronger than Moon Frost. I believe this is why she spent so much time with me. We are not in competition with each other."

If this is what you wish to believe, Firekeeper thought dryly. Then a new thought came to her, *Or is it what you wish me to believe—that there was nothing there other than the insecure companioning the outlier?*

Firekeeper had no wish to press the issue of Moon Frost's courtship of Blind Seer—or his apparent interest in her attentions. Ever since the fight, Moon Frost had politely deferred to Firekeeper and pretended as if Blind Seer did not exist.

Firekeeper felt uncomfortable about this last. Had she been a wolf in form as well as heart, the fight would have gone a good way to declaring her interest in Blind Seer as a potential mate. That mating being impossible, it seemed that all Firekeeper's anger had done was rob Blind Seer of a friend and possible partner. However, the blue-eyed wolf did not seem to mind Moon Frost's new attitude toward him. Indeed, he was luxuriating in the status Firekeeper had gained through her victory.

The change was marked. No one treated Firekeeper as if she were some peculiarly shaped pup any longer. She had stepped into the ranks of the adults—the lower ranks, perhaps, but clearly those of the adults. Many of the yearlings deferred to her as a matter of course. The remainder of the gathered packs treated her with easy courtesy and open curiosity. As long as Firekeeper did not start acting like she thought herself above all of them, the informality of the joined packs would reign.

While overall wolves were governed more by caution than curiosity, now that the Wise Wolves had seen Firekeeper fight, they were fascinated by her technique.

"It is not like a wolf fighting," Freckles commented, swishing her tail low so that Firekeeper would not take this as an insult. "You leapt like a jaguar onto a deer, then used your feet to kick and pummel as might an elk. Yet for all of these other tactics, you didn't forget your Fang, not for a moment."

Firekeeper did not deny the truth of this, but did not pursue the matter. Blind Seer didn't feel nearly as shy.

"It takes skill to fight a two-legs," he bragged, "even a lesser one. When that two-legs is a wolf as well, the combination is as potent as a rattlesnake's venom. I have frequently practiced fighting with Firekeeper and have learned much that keeps me alive when I must fight humans."

After Blind Seer made his brag, Firekeeper received many invitations to wrestle, but she accepted few. She knew all too well how roughly a wolf could play. Even Blind Seer, who knew her vulnerabilities and took them into account, had repeatedly left her scored and scraped. Firekeeper made certain her refusals were expressed humbly, so that rather than seeming too proud to tussle, she showed proper awareness of her relatively junior status in the packs.

Firekeeper worried that her refusal to wrestle, no matter how carefully presented, would rob her of hard-earned status. Among wolf packs, mock battles were the most elementary way that the complicated status hierarchy was established. However, a few days after her fight with Moon Frost, Cricket provided Firekeeper with all the reassurance she needed that her place as adult was secure.

The old wolf came over to where Firekeeper and Blind Seer were drowsing against the heat of the day. They had spent the cooler morning investigating one of the nearby ruins, where they had found a new area, full of mosaic pictures. Even as she drowsed, Firekeeper's mind played with the troubling images and tried to make sense of them. She wished so many pieces had not been missing or that she knew some way to make sense of the bits of tile, glass, and stone scattered on the ground so she might gather them up and return them to their places.

"Firekeeper, you have expressed interest," Cricket said, when all the tail-sniffing and other greetings were concluded, "in taking a turn as nursemaid to the pups. We are planning a great hunt tonight, and wonder if you are still willing to watch the pups."

Firekeeper nodded, then remembered that this human gesture might not be commonly understood here.

"I would be interested," she said. "However, I haven't met most of the pups. Will they accept me?"

"Pups are more accepting than are adults," Cricket replied, "and though you have not met them, they have watched you from the shelter of the nursery, as they do all the adults. You will not be a complete stranger to them."

Firekeeper felt warmed by this automatic acceptance of her adult status, and leapt to her feet, signaling her willingness to follow.

Blind Seer thumped his tail against the dirt.

"Although I will join the chase tonight," he said, "I, too, would like to meet the pups. Is this permitted?"

Cricket's ears flickered back and forth, but then she huffed agreement.

"Do come. What your pack mate sees would come to your ears in any case."

Firekeeper felt a thrill of foreboding in her gut. Something was not right here. Wolves doted on their pups, but Cricket's posture did not hold the smug pride that would be common in such a situation.

Blind Seer had sensed Cricket's hesitation as well, but he was too interested to turn back now that he had permission to accompany them. No matter how often he chided Firekeeper for her curiosity, he had his share as well.

They crossed the elk meadow to a hollow that had been chosen as nursery. It was a good place. Even from a distance Firekeeper could tell that it had probably served this purpose for generations. Large rock outcroppings offered a barrier against the puppies wandering too far, while providing ample shade. The rocks also offered raised perches from which adult wolves could watch both the surrounding countryside and the pups below.

The few scattered saplings and small shrubs within the nursery area itself gave additional shade, but were not large enough to have limbs sufficiently sturdy to support a predator. Long grass had been trampled down into a comfortable mat, and provided concealment in which the puppies could play stalking games. There was even a small spring, slightly muddied from enthusiastic use, but sufficient to need.

At the edge of the nursery area, the trio were met by Grey Thunder, One Male of Cricket's own pack.

"Grey Thunder will be in charge tonight," Cricket said. "As you may know, he sliced open the pad of his foot a few nights ago. The damage is not quite healed."

"I could run on it if I must," Grey Thunder said gruffly, "but there are hunters here aplenty so I will take my ease."

"I will be watching the pups as well," Cricket continued, "along with another wolf you have met—young Rascal."

Firekeeper didn't think it coincidence that her first night on nursemaid duty would be shared by two with whom she was already comfortable. It was a little courtesy, one meant to make her feel at home, and she made certain they saw her pleasure.

"How many pups are there?" Firekeeper asked. "I have lost track of which packs arrived with litters."

Firekeeper's wolves had always been careless about larger numbers, and the Wise Wolves proved no different.

"A good many," Grey Thunder replied. "At least five packs came, and most brought pups born this spring. All of the pups are weaned—not that some don't still try to nurse. Hit them if they start on you."

Firekeeper needed no warning on this point. She knew how puppies could forget they had teeth when they grew eager to suck. In her case, fingers were what usually were damaged, but male wolves had even more delicate parts that were vulnerable. From how Blind Seer rose momentarily onto his toes, she could tell he had not forgotten either.

Cricket snorted, and led the way into the hollow. Immediately, they were the center of a whining, fawning mass of grey-furred puppies. The adults responded to the whined pleas by regurgitating part of their earlier meal. Firekeeper contributed by picking up a few fluffy pups from one scrabbling mess and depositing them near a yet unnoticed heap of semidigested meat.

It was then that she noticed that there was something wrong with one of the pups she held. It was a young male and his otherwise chubby robustness was foreshortened. Simply put, half of his tail was missing. As Firekeeper set him down, she tried to see what injury had taken the tail, but there was no sign of injury. The tail simply was not there.

She glanced at the pups and noticed another with a deformity, a thickening to the skull that made the pup heavy and awkward. A third pup limped—a thing she had overlooked, for puppy games were rough, but now she saw that his foreleg was twisted like the trunk of a tree that had grown in high wind.

Firekeeper heard a low growl from Blind Seer and felt him press against her leg, whether in apprehension or protectiveness she couldn't tell. In some situations, there really wasn't a great deal of difference between the two impulses.

Firekeeper looked for Cricket and Grey Thunder. The two Wise Wolves were studying them, and Firekeeper felt very sharply how she and Blind Seer were outsiders.

"What is this?" she asked. "What illness has come to these little ones?"

Cricket studied her for a long moment, then she sighed.

"Since you insist on acting like a breeder intent on staking out a mate, you are old enough to know, but it is not a pretty story. Come outside the hearing of the little ones."

Firekeeper and Blind Seer did so, and when they were all comfortable on a rock-shaded area overlooking the nursery, Cricket turned to Grey Thunder.

"Some are your children," she said. "The story is best begun by you."

Grey Thunder's hackles rose as if he scented something dangerous, but he did not refuse—though his silence was so prolonged that Firekeeper thought he might be about to do so.

"Does nothing like this happen among your own pack?" Grey Thunder said rather cryptically. Then he looked more directly at Blind Seer, "Are you one of many blue-eyed wolves in your line?"

"I am the only one I have ever met," Blind Seer replied. "My father says that occasionally a blue-eyed wolf is born into his birth pack, but this happens so infrequently that he had never seen one until my eyes did not turn when those of my littermates did."

"But the seeds for those blue eyes are planted in your family line," Grey Thunder said. "Were you to father pups there is a chance one of your get would also have blue eyes."

Blind Seer chewed the edge of his paw for a moment, considering this.

"I suppose so."

Grey Thunder huffed indignantly. "Do you know anything of how father and mother both contribute to the characteristics of their young?"

Firekeeper interrupted. "This matter was never discussed in our family, at least not in my hearing. All that was said was that it was good for the strongest in the pack to parent the pups because then the pups would be strong."

"And is that all you know?" Grey Thunder asked.

"That is all I heard when I was only with wolves," Firekeeper replied. "When I came to humans I learned more. One human of the family that adopted me kept dogs. Do you know what dogs are?"

"I do."

"Well, Edlin was forever trying to get his bitches to bear pups with qualities that were considered useful. His dogs were especially skilled at hunting birds and small game. Edlin was always talking about matching some bitch possessed of some quality—say, good hearing—to a dog with good 'bird sense.' I found this very confusing, but Edlin talked about it enough that I got some idea of what was involved."

"This Edlin must have talked a great deal," Grey Thunder said, seeming impressed, "to teach a reluctant learner."

"Edlin is, if nothing else," Firekeeper said with fondness, "enthusiastic. But what does this have to do with these hurt pups and Blind Seer's eyes?"

"Walk with me through an idea," Grey Thunder said. "It will be easier. Let us say Blind Seer wished to assure that his pups would have blue eyes. How might he do this?"

Firekeeper didn't like the trail along which this question led her, but she followed it, thinking of how she had heard Edlin discuss breeding pups or Derian the breeding of horses.

"Might he seek a bitch with blue eyes? That would be a poor way to choose a mate."

"I agree," Grey Thunder said, "but we are not saying this would be done. We are walking a trail."

"Lead then," Firekeeper said. She found her hand drifting to bury itself in Blind Seer's fur, as it often did when she was uneasy, but though she knew she gave herself away, she did not move her hand.

"Blue-eyes and blue-eyes would not necessarily have blue-eyed pups," Grey Thunder went on. "Trust me on this."

"Easy to do," Firekeeper said. "Our mother, Shining Coat, rarely has a pup to match her own unblemished silver. More often the pups look like their father. Sometimes they look nothing at all like either parent."

"This is because all of us carry many forebears in our blood," Grey Thunder explained, "and when we mingle ourselves in mating, the most common forebears come forth. Now if blue-eyes and blue-eyes mated, there is a greater chance that they would find a common blue-eyed forebear and that forebear would come forth in the color of a puppy's eyes."

"So you are saying that though neither Rip nor Shining Coat had blue eyes," Blind Seer said, "that both must have had a forebear with blue eyes."

"Yes. However, that forebear probably lived a long time ago."

Firekeeper leaned forward, thinking of things she had heard humans discuss when they talked of religious matters.

"Are you saying all of us are our forebears reborn?"

"No," Grey Thunder said. "I am saying that what we were given by our forebears remains within us, even when we do not see it, as the blue eyes were not seen in Rip and Shining Coat. Even unseen, a trait is there, and may come forth."

And how does this apply to the pups? Firekeeper wanted to ask, but she could tell that even now Grey Thunder was tense. His hackles had not smoothed all the way, but remained ruffled like the quills of a feeding porcupine.

"Now," Grey Thunder went on, "I agree with you that it would be foolish to seek a mate merely to attempt to breed pups with blue eyes. However, you did not think it foolish to encourage mating between those who would have strong pups, true?"

"True," agreed his listeners with thump of tail and nod of head.

"Do you think the only strengths are those of running and biting?"

Looking at Cricket, whose days of being a strong runner and sharp-fanged biter were over, but who still had so much to give, Firekeeper replied:

"No. There are other strengths. Knowledge. Courage. Even humor."

Grey Thunder thumped his tail in approval, though his hackles did not quite lie smooth.

"Do talents arise in your people? Not the usual ones like sharp sight or a keen sense of smell, but the odd ones?"

"Like never getting lost?" Blind Seer said. "Or being able to hasten healing? Or finding game? Yes. We have these, and others. They are not very common, though. In all our pack, we had none who were talented. A pack we often mingled with during winters had one member who could always find his way home, no matter how far he wandered—or even if things were done to muddle his trail."

"Blind Seer and I have seen talents among humans, too," Firekeeper said. "We know one who can enhance healing—a talent I have found useful more than once."

"Useful, yes," Grey Thunder said. "Keep that close to you as we walk this trail."

He licked his foreleg thoughtfully for a moment, his golden-brown eyes focused on the three puppies who were playing below with Rascal. The one with the big head was clumsy, the one with the mutilated leg slow; the one with the missing segment of his tail shouldn't have been affected at all, but Firekeeper noticed that he often darted in the wrong direction. She wondered if his eyesight had somehow been injured.

Cricket stirred, and her motion prompted Grey Thunder to continue his tale—as doubtless she had intended it to do.

"Now we walk a long road back into the past," he said. "To the days when a great sickness came among the humans and drove many of them away—you know of this?"

Firekeeper felt as if she were a pup being catechized, but answered politely enough.

"Both our birth pack and the humans had stories of those days. We have even heard a little of how it was here—though only from the human perspective."

"Forgive me if I repeat a little," Grey Thunder said. "Perhaps you have heard how in those days the yarimaimalom made a treaty with the humans. We had long noticed their respect for animal-kind, and felt the true heart in their tales of how the deities were formed and how humanity had drawn away from them."

He must have seen how both Firekeeper and Blind Seer dropped their gazes at these words, for when he continued, a slight growl shaded his speech.

"I shall not trouble you with any long tales, but Blind Seer has bragged to many ears that this journey south is not the first long trip you two have taken. Surely then you have heard about the Old World rulers—about their casual cruelty and disregard for life?"

Firekeeper shifted uneasily, but raised her dark eyes to meet the golden-brown of the wolf.

"Yes. We have heard such tales, both in the former Gildcrest colonies and in New Kelvin. Even allowing for the distortion that comes with years, the Old World rulers were worse than the usual walk of humanity."

Grey Thunder's response startled her.

"I think they were not worse than the mass of humanity—not in the bone—but in order to practice the magical arts they relied upon as a wolf relies upon a strong body and quick mind, they needed to dull themselves to what they were doing. Much of their high magic drew power from death—or rather, from the extinguishing of life. Did you know this?"

Much of what Firekeeper had seen, but had not been able to grasp, in the fragmented artwork she and Blind Seer had uncovered in the ruins now came clearer to her. She also recalled the actions of the sorceress Melina and found them of one piece.

"Yes. I think I did, but not clearly."

Blind Seer tilted his ears back slightly. "I, too, have made myself blinder than I should have been."

"Now follow that trail," Grey Thunder said, "and realize that in order to do the things they must to gain the great powers, the Old World sorcerers had to distance themselves from the natural world into which they had been born. They even had to distance themselves from other humans, to view themselves as somehow superior to the mass of humanity, and to the ethical order that governed these people."

Firekeeper, again thinking of things she had seen, of humans—and wolves—she had known, grunted acknowledgment of the truth in what Grey Thunder said.

"If you learn more of the religion practiced by the Liglimom," Grey Thunder went on, his ears angling back slightly as if he anticipated physical, not intellectual, protest, "you will hear how after the first birds were created as a gift from Fire to Air, the deities decided they must take responsibility for these little lives. They guided mortals through omens and auguries. However, with the coming of great sorcery, humans grew deaf to divine guidance."

"We have been told something of this," Firekeeper said, "and how the humans turned to animals for guidance."

Grey Thunder's attitude was now clearly one of defense.

"Would you listen if I told you that we yarimaimalom have experienced the speech of the deities? That we have indeed felt ourselves conduits for communications from beyond ourselves?"

"We listen," Firekeeper replied, and Blind Seer thumped his tail in concurrence.

Grey Thunder relaxed a trace.

"Not all of us hear as clearly as some. You met the jaguar Truth?"

"We did."

"She comes from a long line of diviners," Grey Thunder said. "Her hearing is very sharp. However, such hearing is not restricted to any one type of beast—or even to yarimaimalom. It is found in Wise and lesser, and in all species. The one advantage Wise have over lesser is that we can better interpret the divine will and better communicate it to humankind."

Cricket interrupted for the first time since she had eased Grey Thunder back into speech.

"I think you walk off the trail, son."

"Not so far," Grey Thunder protested. "For these two to understand what we have done, they must understand why."

Cricket neither agreed nor argued, but Firekeeper noticed that Grey Thunder did return to his original point.

"Now when we made our treaty with humanity, we insisted that these islands be given to us for our land and that no humans be permitted to come here."

"Except for those who reside at the outpost," Blind Seer added, his attitude that of a youngling who wishes to prove he has learned to pounce and so now can be taught to bite.

"Except for the outpost," Grey Thunder repeated. "We chose this place for many reasons. Having been subjected to the cruelty of the Old Country rulers, we did not wish to live among their subjects until we were certain the change of heart was sincere. A more important reason was that from here we could better watch the sea.

"You see, for all their magic, the Old Country rulers have always come from across the ocean. Perhaps large bodies of water interfere with the power they command. Perhaps the sorcerers lacked the ability to use magic to transport themselves over long distances. Whatever the reason, in all our tales the ones from the Old Country have only come from the east, from over the water."

"So," Firekeeper said, "it is told in the northern lands as well. I once asked my parents if any tales remained of humans coming from the west, and they replied that there were none such they knew that did not include the sorcerers traveling from east to west first."

Grey Thunder relaxed even more at this agreement, and continued, "The yarimaimalom took for themselves these lands farthest to the east, where we could keep watch. To this day, the wingéd folk send representatives out a day's flight to the east each day. The water beasts also keep watch."

Firekeeper wanted to ask about these water beasts. She knew there were Royal Otters, but she had glimpsed seals during their voyage south and had wondered if there might be Royal ones among these creatures as well. She wondered, too, about the huge sea creatures she had glimpsed from time to time: whales and dolphins and the cold-eyed sharks. Could these have Royal-kind?

Now was not the time for such questions. At times like this when her curiosity led her off the trail, Firekeeper knew the bittersweet truth that as much as she was wolf, she was human too.

"We watch the omens as well," Grey Thunder said, and Firekeeper was surprised to see a hint of tension touch him again, and wondered why. Neither she nor Blind Seer had argued against the efficacy of talents. "To this day, no omen has occurred to show that the deities warn us that our enemies are about to return."

Ah, Firekeeper thought. *I forgot. We think of divination as simply another talent, but to these Wise Wolves it is communication from the deities. I wonder if Derian's people think that what comes from divination is communication from the ancestors his people revere? I must ask someday.*

But Grey Thunder's tension did not ebb when neither of his listeners questioned whether or not the deities might be responsible for omens. Firekeeper found herself leaning slightly forward, as if to make sure she did not miss some subtle sign on a nearly obliterated game trail.

"Now, remember that you yourselves admitted that talents could be useful," Grey Thunder said, "and remember that in the days of which I speak the Old Country rulers were not creatures departed and vanished for well more than a hundred winters. In those days, the fear was acute that the Fire Plague would run its course, the sorcerers rebuild their power, and the Old Country rulers return in a few seasons. Even as a bitch digs her den in anticipation of the pups she carries, so the yarimaimalom of those days took actions to prepare themselves against their enemies' return."

Cricket added, "The choice we had made to place a good number of ourselves on these islands added to the dread of the sorcerers' return. For all that the islands gave protection from those who lived on the mainland, should the Old Country magics return, many of us would be trapped and so more easily hunted."

Firekeeper felt her spine tingle at the image this conjured.

"You did have kin on the mainland, didn't you?"

"We did and do," Cricket replied, "but the deaths of those here would have been no less real for that the yarimaimalom would not be destroyed all at once."

Blind Seer chewed the pad of his paw a bit nervously, as if the entrapment were about to begin at this very instant.

"The choice to isolate yourselves here seems strange," he said, "but you must have had your reasons."

"We had them," Cricket said sharply, "and hold to them still. Remember what Grey Thunder has told you about those days."

In a sharp instant, like the striking of a bolt of lightning through the blackness of a midnight storm, Firekeeper was sure they were not being told all of the story. She quieted herself, waiting to hear what the rest of Grey Thunder's account would be. It might be that by the time he wended his way to the end, she would have her answers.

In response to the waiting silence, Grey Thunder glanced at Cricket, saw the senior wolf had nothing more to add, and went on.

"The course of action of which I am about to tell you," Grey Thunder said, "was further precipitated by omens that indicated that someday the Old World would once again cast a shadow on the New. Our forebears felt that something must be done to prepare against that day."

He paused as if awaiting a challenge that did not come.

"Although the yarimaimalom are strong and clever, the equal at least of humans, in the days when the Old World sought to dominate the New, those qualities did us little good. Magic was what gave our enemies the advantage, and though we did not wish to follow in their ways, we thought to increase the occurrence of the divinely given talents—the fragments of Magic in each individual—among ourselves. We did not so much see this as trying to seize more than the deities had given to us, but as tending what had been given and encouraging it to grow."

"As humans do their gardens," Firekeeper murmured.

"Or as strong hunters do the herds," Grey Thunder agreed. "Even the Wise Elk and Deer, while not liking being hunted, agree that without the culling given by hunters they would suffer."

Firekeeper thought of the Story of the Songbirds, a tale even older than that which Grey Thunder related, and knew the wolf's assessment was correct.

Despite the lack of disagreement, Grey Thunder's stiffness returned as he resumed his account, and Firekeeper knew they were reaching the core of the tale.

"So it was that the yarimaimalom of those days began to choose their mates not in the traditional ways, but by seeking out certain talents and attempting to encourage their appearance. Wolf mated with wolf not for the betterment of the individual pack, but for what was hoped to be the salvation of all packs—indeed of all those living who would choose to resist the great magics if the Old Country rulers returned.

"In pursuit of this plan, many rules of common sense were repeatedly broken. Brother mated with sister, father with daughter, mother with son, all in an attempt to concentrate the talents that lay within us. For a time, it seemed that we had succeeded. Then we saw the price that must be paid for carrying too much of Magic's potency within a single body. It is a price we still pay, though such behavior has been outlawed for generations now."

Grey Thunder's gaze rested on the malformed pups, his expression holding affection laced with pity—and with guilt.

"Not only are good things concentrated," Grey Thunder continued, "but bad things as well. Weakness within the bone or within the mind came forth, emerging alongside the talents we had sought—but so focused were we on those talents that we ignored the evidence of what we were creating, though we had ample examples."

Cricket pricked her ears when Grey Thunder said this and again Firekeeper had the sense of something being withheld.

Blind Seer shifted uneasily. Thumping his ear with one foot as if after a persistent flea, he asked, "But weak pups do not often live. Isn't that so?"

Grey Thunder's eyes grew stormy with sorrow.

"It is indeed so. Did you realize that the borderland pack which first welcomed you to Misheemnekuru had more pups this season than those you met? One was too weak to see more than a few faces of the Moon. Those little ones down there are in many cases the remnants of larger litters."

"But in protecting them so they live and breed," Blind Seer said hesitantly, "isn't the problem they represent also given opportunity to breed?"

Cricket answered when Grey Thunder's only reply was an inarticulate growl.

"We forbid the damaged ones to breed, even if the only evidence of damage is something like a bit of missing tail. However, we do not kill our own children. Did your parents kill you when they thought you might have been born blind? Of course they didn't. Neither do we. Our problem is enhanced by our island situation. Hardly any of those who now live here do not carry within their blood the concentration from those old days. When we mix, even without intent of causing Magic to concentrate, the problems arise."

Blind Seer humbled himself in apology for his thoughtlessness. Licking his ear in acceptance of that apology, Cricket went on.

"We have reasons even greater than love for letting our damaged ones live. There remains the chance that one or more will show some strong talent when they mature, for such talents grow as the pup grows. As not even the most doting parent cannot tell which in a newborn litter will be a great hunter until after stumbling puppy days have passed, so no one can tell which pup may grow into the ability to clearly see divine will."

Vaguely remembering some of Derian and Edlin's discussions on breeding dogs and horses, Firekeeper carefully framed what she hoped would not be an offensive question. Both Cricket and Grey Thunder were visibly tense now and an angry wolf pressed too hard resorts to something far more painful than shouting.

"You say that this island living makes the problem live on, even after you have abandoned the course of action that led to it. Why not leave the island and blend with the packs to the west? Or, if you are reluctant to leave your watch post, why not invite some other wolves to join you? Trade out into the larger world."

"You think we have not thought of that?" Cricket asked scornfully. "Puppies always think they are the first to kill a mouse."

The fact that this last was a proverbial expression did nothing to ease its sting, but Firekeeper, proud of the status she had gained, did not snap back as she might have a few days before.

Cricket, perhaps aware that she had been rude, perhaps merely too angry for continued discourse, rose from where she had lain on the rock and stalked off into the gathering dusk.

Grey Thunder watched the elder go, then turned his perpetually mournful gaze onto the two outliers.

"She has raw wounds on that matter. It is a thing on which I have no firsthand knowledge, but I will do my best."

Firekeeper and Blind Seer waited quietly while Grey Thunder organized his thoughts.

"We will not leave Misheemnekuru," he began, "but we are not forbidden to do so. From time to time, some of our number do go to the mainland. More rarely, one of the mainland yarimaimalom comes here—and that one is more likely to be of the wingéd or swimming folk. Others would need to arrange for the humans to carry them on a boat.

"Thus, especially between the land dwellers, two communities have grown up, each with their own legends and codes. Sad as it is to say, each of us scorn the other just a little. We of the islands think of the mainlanders as those who have abandoned the watch. They think of us as inbred fanatics. Such attitudes make blending difficult."

"I see," Firekeeper said, "and Cricket?"

"During a wolf year long ago, she was among those chosen to go to the mainland and advise the seetadisdu. She enjoyed the honor, but I understand she was less than pleased with the mainland wolves. Once her year was over, Cricket returned to Misheemnekuru, and has not only expressed a desire never to return to the mainland, she has refused to take part in choosing other representatives for the duty. She says it is a hunt she could not wish on any she loved."

"That explains her anger at my question, then," Firekeeper said. "If you will forgive the old angers my curiosity has stirred up, I would still like to watch the little ones with you. I am not so unlike them, you know. My shape can hardly be said to be that of the ideal wolf."

Grey Thunder looked at Firekeeper, at first confused, then vastly entertained. His tail stirred the dust on the rock.

"Go get to know the pups, then," he said, making clear that his invitation included Blind Seer as well as Firekeeper. "But mind your fingers. They are eager to try their new teeth on everything."

"We will remember," Blind Seer said, "and tonight I myself will carry back from the hunt a haunch with meat and hide attached so the pups can try their teeth on something more challenging than Firekeeper's fingers."

Firekeeper punched Blind Seer gently on one shoulder, then together they joined Rascal down among the pups. Only once did Firekeeper look up, and then she saw that Cricket had rejoined Grey Thunder. That they were disagreeing was obvious, but Firekeeper turned away quickly, lest by her awareness she bury further the secrets she knew must be there, and that she felt with a desperate certainty that she must somehow learn.

XXI

THEY SAT OUT IN THE WARM, horse-scented night while Varjuna explained the various tensions that had been arising within the community of disdum since the arrival of Firekeeper and the clear evidence of her ability not just to communicate but to converse with the yarimaimalom.

Just a few years before, Derian would have found much of what Varjuna was saying nearly incomprehensible. Religious practices within his own family were relaxed to the point of nonexistence. The family shrine was kept clean and the ancestors appealed to at all the appropriate times, but other than that the family of Vernita and Colby Carter relied on hard work and common sense to get along.

Derian knew that there were families that viewed things differently, families that started every day by invoking the aid and guidance of the ancestors, but " 'Prayer won't shovel any manure,' as my daddy always said" was one of Colby's own favorite sayings. Derian had always taken this to mean that the ancestors, and the vague supernatural powers they communicated with, would be happier if shown more and asked for less.

His horizons had broadened considerably since he had gone west with Earl Kestrel, but oddly it wasn't his exposure to the customs of several foreign lands that helped him understand what Varjuna was explaining. It was his exposure to various levels of political manipulation.

Here in Liglim, beneath the phrases about the will of the deities and appropriate omens, Derian recognized once again the struggle of those who were in power to retain power while those who were without sought the means to gain it. Caught between were the rare creatures like Varjuna who seemed to care little for power except that their positions enabled them to continue doing what they liked best.

An interesting variation was that Ahmyndisdu Tiridanti, who as the supreme representative of Fire and leader in this jaguar year should have been unassailable, was being challenged because she was seen as the instrument of potentially heretical change. Those who actually sought what Derian thought was a more dramatic change—the undermining of an ordained member of u-Liall—could represent themselves as faithful followers of traditional ways.

"I can see," Derian said when Varjuna had finished his explanations, "why you said you hoped that Firekeeper wouldn't return too soon. Just her existence creates problems. If she were here and doing things, saying things, giving one side or another more arrows for their quivers, things could come to a head."

"I fear so," Varjuna agreed. "However, as much as some of my colleagues would like to think otherwise, there is no turning back from the problems her existence has raised. You may be able to reteach a badly trained colt, but there is no stuffing him back into the mare and wishing for another."

Derian let himself smile, for he knew the expression would be lost in the gathering darkness. He had always thought his family was horse-crazy, but by contrast with Varjuna they were only mildly interested in the animals.

His smile faded as he thought about the situation. He liked at least some of the Liglimom and didn't want to see them hurt, but as Varjuna had said, there was no way to change what had happened. What might help would be moderating what would come, and the best way to do that would be to speak with Firekeeper.

"Varjuna, do you think I can go to Misheemnekuru?"

"Possibly. What do you intend to do there? You know we cannot let you go any further than the outpost."

"I know," Derian said, "but I want to talk with Firekeeper and I have no way to get a message to her. Even if some raven arrived and offered to carry a note, I wouldn't know what Firekeeper can read. The few symbols she sent wouldn't do for what I need to tell her."

"You could talk to a Wise Raven and it would carry the message," Varjuna said, the mildest note of reproach in his tone, as if he thought Derian might have forgotten that the yarimaimalom were intelligent. "If one so offered, of course."

"I could," Derian said. He wondered how honest he should be, then decided to plunge in. "The thing is, Varjuna, I don't know what side the yarimaimalom are on in this issue. All I know is that Firekeeper is alive, but troubled. Her being alive means that she is being tolerated, but it doesn't mean she has made friends or allies."

"True," Varjuna said. "You demonstrate wisdom in realizing this. I think many of the disdum assume she has been accepted as a co-equal, maybe as a ruler."

"Human arrogance," Derian laughed, "or maybe just human fear. I've listened to Firekeeper talk about her place among the wolves. She's definitely low-ranking, even among those who love her. From what she's said, even Royal Wolves respect strength and the ability to dominate. I can't see why the wolves on Misheemnekuru would be any different. What status she gains, she'll need to earn, and that earning is going to be tough."

"I believe I understand," Varjuna said. "Because of our deep respect for the wisdom of the beasts, we elevate Firekeeper in our estimation, for she seems to have been accepted as a beast by the beasts. However, within the community of the beasts, she may have no status at all."

"That's about it," Derian said. "I figure she must have gained some or the ravens wouldn't have carried that message for her, but I won't even guess beyond that."

"You wish to tell her what I have told you?"

"That's right," Derian said. "If she realizes what's stirring here, she may moderate her own actions. One thing Firekeeper seems to understand instinctively—probably part of growing up a wolf—is that it isn't a good idea to make enemies of those with power."

Unless, he thought, *you have power to counter them in return and I don't know what power she may have—or think she has.*

He didn't want to go into this with Varjuna, so only said, "I also want to know whatever it is that made her write 'Must Talk,' in her own message. That could throw another handful of rice in the pot."

Varjuna chuckled at Derian's use of the local idiom.

"All good things to consider," he said. "There is only one difficulty as I see it. How will you find Lady Blysse if you go to the outpost? As I said, you cannot leave the area given to us by the yarimaimalom."

"I figure that the yarimaimalom will know right off that I'm coming," Derian said. "If they know, they'll probably tell Firekeeper. I'm going to have to rely on her from that point on. However, if she doesn't show up, then I'll ask for someone to sail me around the islands and see what happens. I'll ask any animal I see to tell her I'm here to see her."

"And if she doesn't come?"

"Then I start worrying." Derian shrugged. "If Firekeeper were here she'd be fidgeting about our planning for things that might not happen. As I see it, the first stage is getting permission for me to go to the outpost. Would it be better if you asked or I asked?"

"Let me," the ikidisdu of the Horse said. "Best for Ahmyndisdu Tiridanti that she not be seen as too liberal with the northerners. My request is within the community, for a guest of my nahal. It will be taken better that way, and those within u-Liall who vie with her for influence will not be as interested in blocking me."

"Is the Temple of the Horse so important then?" Derian asked.

"All nahalm are important," Varjuna said, his note of gentle reproof melding into a chuckle, "but not all provide the beasts upon whose backs we must travel."

Politics again, Derian thought. *Be good to the kind old man or find yourself learning that the omens have ordained you are to ride a swaybacked old nag. I don't think Varjuna would do anything so irreverent, but that doesn't mean that his less reverent colleagues wouldn't think he would.*

RAHNISEETA HAPPENED TO BE WORKING over at u-Nahal when Varjuna arrived to make a special request of u-Liall.

"Happened" was perhaps not a precisely accurate way of explaining her presence. Ever since Harjeedian had told her of the varying degrees of unhappiness and unrest within the disdum, Rahniseeta had resolved that she needed to keep an ear pressed to the ground for any developments that might harm her brother.

The Temple of the Cold Bloods had rallied in support of Harjeedian and his actions in securing Lady Blysse, not so much because Harjeedian was popular—though he was widely viewed as talented and divinely gifted—but because to not do so would have meant justifying why they had permitted one of their own to be the leading agent responsible for acquiring Lady Blysse.

The heads of the temple might have justified their participation—as they had at the time—on the grounds that Harjeedian had shown a singular ability to learn Pellish. They might have reminded everyone that the omens had all indicated that the expedition was the will of the deities. However, rather than justifying, the Temple of the Cold Bloods had taken the position that there was nothing to justify—at least outside of private discussions within the green-and-gold walls of the temple complex.

Therefore, since Rahniseeta felt she would learn nothing constructive within the Temple of the Cold Bloods, she offered her services within u-Nahal. As she frequently worked there in the capacity of scribe or secretary, no one looked too closely at her offer—and those who did either approved her perceived motives or felt she could do nothing that would endanger their own goals.

Rahniseeta was sitting at a desk in the scriptorium, one of several clerks busily transcribing documents that would eventually be sent to the disdum in u-Vreeheera, when Ikidisdu Varjuna arrived. The word of his arrival buzzed up from below, where the five members of u-Liall each had private audience chambers. Varjuna, though, had gone to none of these. He had gone to the larger chamber used for full conclaves of u-Liall. U-Liall had joined him soon thereafter, as had the jaguar Truth.

"Didn't he send a message ahead?" Rahniseeta asked.

"Of course, he did," the senior clerk replied with the snobbish gossipiness of one who is an insider and delights in being so. "However, he followed hard on the heels of his own message."

"I hope nothing has happened to Derian Counselor," Rahniseeta said, almost to herself.

She remembered the distant, hurt expression on the red-haired northerner's face when last they had met. She'd tried hard not to think about it, but she knew in her eagerness to learn whether or not he was maimalodalu she had hurt his feelings.

"That's right," the clerk said, snapping his fingers as if he should have been privy to secret omens. "One of the northerners was given into Varjuna's care—the red-haired one."

"Derian Counselor," Rahniseeta said, suddenly indignant to hear the young man described so superficially. "Or Derian Carter, to give him his other name. He was honored by the Wise Horse Eshinarvash, remember."

She knew her sentence didn't make much sense, but it served her purpose. The clerk snapped his lips tightly shut, his offended dignity warring with his curiosity. He doubtless would have condescended to ask something more about Derian as soon as he had opportunity to work out a way to be suitably snide about it, but a messenger came to the door.

"Rahniseeta, sister of Aridisdu Harjeedian of the Temple of the Cold Bloods," he asked in the general way people do when asking for someone they do not know by sight.

"I am she," Rahniseeta said, rising from her desk.

"Please follow me," the messenger said. "U-Liall desires your presence."

Rahniseeta set her quill carefully down where the ink would not blot on the document she had been working on, and without further word to any of the several clerks who had stopped their own writing to stare, followed the messenger from the room.

"Don't be afraid," the messenger reassured her as they hurried down the stairs, heading for one of the back doors into the conclave chamber.

"Do you know what they want me for?" Rahniseeta asked.

"I do not," the messenger admitted. "I was waiting outside the conclave chamber. However, the one who told me to find you did not seem unduly agitated."

Rahniseeta would have liked to ask if this person seemed agitated at all, but they had reached the doorway to the chamber. The messenger pulled the admittance rope, and the door was opened from within. This was not the formal entrance through with the Rahniseeta had brought Lady Blysse and Blind Seer, but one of the entries used by those who worked within u-Nahal.

"Go directly in," the messenger said, "and stand along the wall on the right side behind the screens until you are called upon. Then go and stand directly in the center, where all u-Liall can view you with equal ease."

Rahniseeta knew the procedure, but she was glad for the reminder. She had to fight to keep her knees from trembling as she stepped into the conclave chamber and leaned back against the wall.

Voices were raised in discussion, but she was so nervous that it took a moment before she could register what was being said, and then it was to hear her own name being spoken.

"Has the woman Rahniseeta arrived yet?" came the clear, young voice of Ahmyndisdu Tiridanti.

"She has," replied someone Rahniseeta knew was a senior clerk.

"Have her come forward, then, so we can resolve this quickly."

The clerk stepped back and motioned to Rahniseeta. She lifted her head high and walked forward as if she stood before u-Liall every day of her life.

U-Liall were not dressed for ceremony as they had been on the day that they received the northerners, nor were they seated in the elaborately jeweled thrones.

More comfortable chairs had been set around a table cut in a horseshoe shape. There they sat in the same positions as before, Ahmyndisdu Tiridanti at the curve. The jaguar Truth lounged on her pedestal near the right end of the table and Ikidisdu Varjuna was seated at the left end of the table.

As she had been instructed, Rahniseeta stood where all of u-Liall could see her, and waited to be addressed.

Tiridanti gave a familiar nod.

"I remember seeing you," she said. "You were here the day we interviewed Lady Blysse, were you not?"

"I was, Ahmyndisdu."

"Very good. Ikidisdu Varjuna here has come with a request from Derian Counselor that this Derian be permitted to go to the outpost on Misheemnekuru, there to meet with Lady Blysse. We were wondering if the aridisdu Harjeedian would be available to act as escort. We were about to send word to the Temple of the Cold Bloods when someone recalled seeing you here in u-Nahal and thought you might know your brother's whereabouts and schedule."

So that's all it is, Rahniseeta thought, resisting the urge to sag in relief. *They're just saving time.*

Aloud she said, "Aridisdu Harjeedian is not currently at the Temple of the Cold Bloods, but is in u-Seeheera proper—or so I believe, based on what he said to me this morning. However, he has nothing on his schedule that would keep him from being of service to u-Liall."

"Good then." Tiridanti turned to look at Varjuna. "How soon does this Derian wish to make the voyage to Misheemnekuru?"

"As soon as possible," Varjuna replied, "for the reasons I have already explained. However, I am certain that he will wait on the will of the deities."

"The omens are that tomorrow's weather should be good for sailing," said Dantarahma, the junjaldisdu, with a warm, affable smile. "Can he leave then? We will make all efforts to assist him."

Varjuna smiled in return. "I believe Derian is attempting to finish his tutoring sessions so that he will be readily available. Shall I have him ride from u-Bishinti tonight or tomorrow morning?"

"Tomorrow will be soon enough," Dantarahma said. "Let the early harbor traffic thin. Derian doesn't need to go too far or go without his breakfast."

Tiridanti took back control of the meeting once more—a thing she frequently must do, so Rahniseeta had heard. Last year had been a dolphin year, and the junjaldisdu could not seem to grow accustomed to relinquishing control—especially to the ahmyndisdu.

"Rahniseeta," Tiridanti said, "I understand that you are somewhat fluent in this Pellish."

"A little, Ahmyndisdu, nothing like my brother."

"Continue your studies," the ahmyndisdu said. "The omens say this will be a useful skill."

"I will do as is commanded."

"Good. Now, if you can leave what you were working on upstairs, go and find Harjeedian and tell him that he is to make himself available to Derian Counselor at the harbor tomorrow. My clerk will send a note to the Temple of the Cold Bloods with further details."

Rahniseeta knew formalities would be out of place here, so she offered her respects in silence, and hurried out. Her heart was pounding hard in relief as she hurried down into u-Seeheera to find Harjeedian.

FIREKEEPER FELT AWASH WITH GUILT now that she understood what the tainted blood of the Wise Wolves meant to them and for their future.

Now she realized how much Blind Seer—his own blood uncorrupted—would mean to these inbred wolves. He would be a strong sire, one these Wise Wolves needed as an isolated pond needs a fresh inflow to flush away the stagnant water. The wolf-woman's guilt came from her awareness that she did not want Blind Seer to stay here—and from her awareness that this might be the place he would not only be most needed, but most appreciated.

During her introduction to the puppies, Firekeeper had learned that the Wise Wolves kept genealogies rather like those she had seen among humans—although the genealogies of the Wise Wolves were oral, not written. Rascal's introduction had included not only each puppies' pack, but who their parents were within that pack, and who those parents' parents had been, and those parents' parents' parents. Rascal's recitation did not go any further back than those three generations, but Firekeeper learned, when she asked Rascal if he knew his own heritage as thoroughly, that Rascal could recite the litany of his forebears for ten generations.

Among the Royal Wolves this type of recordkeeping was not necessary. As Blind Seer explained, scent alone was sufficient to distinguish close relations, and there were strong taboos against mating with one who shared either parent or grandparent. He couldn't say whether the taboos were taught or interwoven into the blood, only that this was so.

If there was an instinctive revulsion against mating with a close family member, the Wise Wolves had bred it from themselves in those long-ago days of which Grey Thunder had spoken. In any case, throughout the Sanctuary Islands the bloodlines had been bred so closely that—as their physical similarities showed—wolves proved to be close kin even when their parents were, ostensibly, unrelated.

Even those like Dark Death, who had come a fair distance, were—so Blind Seer assured Firekeeper—marked by a similarity of scent. Even to one as nose-dead as Firekeeper, the proof of this relationship emerged with the damaged puppies that, as she had been told, still appeared in almost every litter, even when care had been taken to try and make certain that the breeding pair was unrelated.

From the genealogies Rascal recited with such blithe ease, Firekeeper deduced another dirty little secret of the Wise Wolves: the Ones of a pack were not necessarily both—or even either—the parents of the litter the pack reared as its own.

"Secret" was perhaps not the best word for what she learned, for the truth was there, solid and implacable. Pups were presented first as the product of their pack, just as if the One Female had properly born them to the One Male, but in some cases the recitation of the pup's parentage showed differently.

Quite frequently, the litter was said to be "born for" their pack by the intercession of some male with some female. Almost always either the One Male or the One Female of the pack was one of the parents, but the other parent might be a lesser-ranked member of the pack—or an interloper from another pack entirely.

Rascal was young enough that Firekeeper's questions did not trouble him. He knew the way such matters were arranged by his own people. Since he hadn't really thought it could be different elsewhere, he answered Firekeeper's questions without hesitation. Indeed, like young creatures of any species, Rascal enjoyed showing off how much he knew.

"It's obvious that the most important thing for a pack is that the Ones be strong and in harmony with each other," Rascal explained, chasing after a fat little pup who was determined to climb out of the sheltered nursery hollow. "From that harmony comes everything we value: successful hunts, fair judgment in disputes, wise decisions regarding who will do what. Haven't you seen the same among your own people?"

Firekeeper agreed that she had.

Rascal went on, assured that the wolf-woman was sane, "When the Ones are strong together, it hardly matters who actually bred the puppies. What matters is that there is a strong pack to care for them and make certain that as many as possible grow to maturity."

Although she grasped the sense of this, Firekeeper felt odd as she tried to superimpose it over the customs she knew. So much of her upbringing had been founded on the concept that the privilege to breed was one of the rewards for the burden of being the Ones that she had to think her way carefully through to Rascal's way of thinking. The conclusion she reached was that this was indeed the right way for the Wise Wolves to work, but she reached another conclusion that was tantalizing—even if a little frightening.

If she lived among the Wise Wolves, would it matter that Firekeeper was human in body and therefore could not bear puppies to her chosen mate? If she lived among the Wise Wolves, would some female carry Blind Seer's pups and not try to claim him as her own? In this way, Firekeeper could almost be a wolf, but not restrict Blind Seer's choices.

These thoughts both enticed and troubled the wolf-woman. It troubled her that these Wise Wolves—who otherwise made her so uncomfortable through their adoption of human religion—might have a place for her, a place denied to her by those who had reared her and whose values she accepted.

Already the Wise Wolves accepted her as an adult as the Royal Wolves never had. Now there rose this tempting hint that among the Wise Wolves Firekeeper might rise to the pinnacle of personal authority. She could be a One and have Blind Seer as her mate of record if not in fact.

With the knowledge she had gained from Rascal, certain changes that had occurred since Firekeeper won her fight against Moon Frost now took on a new light—especially the actions of the unmated males. Firekeeper had thought their behavior simply reflected a greater welcome and ease with her. She had shown herself strong, not weak, adult, not pup. Thus, knowing her place, they knew how to deal with her and, being like all wolves, creatures who valued order, they were more at ease.

Now Firekeeper wondered if she had understood fully enough. Were some of the young males considering her as a possible One Female to their One Male? It would be a grand situation for them, for although Firekeeper could not run into the hunt as a wolf would do, she had already proven how skillful she was with her bow. She had shown she understood the value wolves placed on mercy as well as strength, and that she could uphold those values even when her life was at risk.

The thought that she might be seen as valuable rather than a burden was both heady and fraught with confusion. She loved Blind Seer no less, but for the first time understood the desire to flirt, to show herself as desirable. She restrained herself from what might be unacceptable behavior, but longed for someone—maybe Elise—with whom she could discuss these matters.

Unhappily, as there was no one to whom Firekeeper could ask the questions she could barely formulate, even in her own mind, confusion and uneasiness came to dominate her mind, diluting the pleasure she had taken in her new adult status.

"Like knows like best," the proverb said, but in this Firekeeper knew she had no "like," and so found herself feeling even more alone than she had when she had thought Blind Seer might abandon her for Moon Frost.

Bitter and Lovable, the ravens, came to Firekeeper as she was meditating over such things.

"We have news for you, two-legged wolf," Bitter said, perching on a nearby maple sapling that bent and bobbed beneath his weight. "Your fox-haired friend is coming to Misheemnekuru. The jaguar Truth sends the message so you may more easily meet him at the outpost. Derian will be there midday tomorrow if Air and Water permit, and the omens say they will."

Firekeeper felt her face light with a smile. In her current mood, this announcement of Derian's coming was a huge relief. There was no way Firekeeper would discuss these personal matters with him, but there was much she could tell him, including some of what she and Blind Seer had seen in the ruins.

She leapt to her feet, bowing in a hybrid of human and wolf fashions to express her thanks.

"But I have something nice for you," she said, addressing Lovable, for thus far Bitter had disdained her offered gifts. "Blind Seer found it when we were digging through one of the ruined denning sites of the Old Country rulers."

She shinnied up the apple tree and drew the sapphire and diamond pendant from where she'd cached it in the crotch of two large branches. Even cupped in her hand, it sparkled, and when she dangled it from the thong on which she'd strung it, it shone like sunlight captured in frozen dewdrops.

"Humans hang these around their necks," Firekeeper said. "They serve no purpose but to catch the light and look pretty. I thought you might like this one."

Lovable hopped eagerly along the branch where she had perched, flapping her wings enough that Bitter puffed out his neck feathers in disgust.

"Give me! Give me!" she squawked, taking the thong in her beak. "Pretty! Pretty!"

Bitter sleaked his feathers. "You are as stupid about sparkling things as if you were a lesser beast."

Firekeeper couldn't help but smiling. The comparison was apt, but she also suspected that Lovable rather enjoyed annoying Bitter.

"I would give you a gift as well," Firekeeper said, "but I fear nothing but my most sincere thanks would satisfy a connoisseur like yourself."

Bitter sleaked his feathers again, and Firekeeper knew she had pleased him more than if she had offered him the largest gem in all the world.

"Please thank the jaguar Truth for granting me this information," Firekeeper continued. In the largely propertyless world of the yarimaimalom, she knew words counted for much—though actions for more. "She must have sent word as soon as the decision was made."

Bitter hacked a raven's laugh.

"Oh, she sent it long before the humans had decided. Remember, Truth is gifted with foresight. She knew what they would decide, even as they worked their way to a decision."

Firekeeper felt a bit uncomfortable about this, but she had decided that much of this talk of foresight must be symbolic rather than literal. Hadn't Truth admitted she could not see clearly where Firekeeper was concerned?

"Even with Truth's forewarning," Firekeeper said, "I should begin my run with little delay. I have a fair way to go."

"Run then," Bitter said. "We shall fly and let Lovable cache this shining thing."

Firekeeper held up a hand. "If you will let me," she said to Lovable, "I can loop that around your neck much as we did the message capsule. It will be heavier and may unbalance you . . ."

Lovable hopped over. "Do it! Do it!"

Firekeeper did, and when the ravens launched themselves into flight, she saw the gemstones gleaming against the dark feathers as Lovable made her slightly lopsided flight.

Blind Seer had seen the ravens' arrival, but had politely waited until they were gone to come over and learn the reason for their visit.

"Derian comes," Firekeeper explained, removing her bow and arrows from their cache in the tree. "I go to the outpost to speak with him. Will you come with me or shall I find you here?"

"I'll run with you," the blue-eyed wolf replied. "I'd hear what Fox Hair says, and remind you of all we have to tell him."

Firekeeper leapt lightly down.

"I am glad to have you with me," she said. "Shall we tell the others where we go? We owe them no deference, but they have been good hosts."

"We will tell them," Blind Seer said. "We are no newly made hunters to prop up our achievements with rudeness."

Firekeeper glowed inside at this reflection of his opinion of her. She knew too well how new-made her own status was—it was good to know that for him she had never been less.

Cricket and Neck Breaker were easiest to locate, and so to them Firekeeper and Blind Seer made their explanations.

"Will you return?" Cricket asked.

"If we are welcome," Firekeeper replied. "I understand the joined packs will soon split again, but we have much yet that you could teach us."

Neck Breaker thumped his tail in approval.

"You are welcome to return to our pack," he said, "and I think I do not take too much on myself to say that I believe you are welcome in any of these packs."

Cricket agreed. "The ocean fish have ended much of their run, and soon summer hunting begins, but we will make certain all the wolves know where you go and that you hope to return."

There was no need for more to be said, and no empty wishes for luck along the trail.

That's the way of wolves, Firekeeper thought with satisfaction as she and Blind Seer fell into the jog that would carry them for great distances without much fatigue. *Humans wish each other luck as if it comes from outside, but wolves make their own luck.*

She knew she was being smug, but with the wind kissing her hair, and Blind Seer running beside her through the coolness of the shaded forest understory, she didn't care.

XXII

HE'D FORGOTTEN HOW strange she was. Derian hadn't thought this was possible. He knew he'd gotten used to the wolf-woman, but at the moment when Firekeeper stepped out of the forest's edge and came to greet him, he realized he'd been expecting someone else—someone other . . .

Her hair needed a good combing. Her clothing—trousers and blouse after the style worn by the Liglimom—was definitely the worse for wear. It needed a wash, and the cotton fabric had never been intended for the hard use to which she had put it. But it wasn't just that Firekeeper needed grooming to bring her image into harmony with the person Derian expected. He'd forgotten the barely suppressed wildness in her every step, the assessing darkness in her eyes, the hundred and one little characteristics that made Firekeeper somehow other than human.

In contrast, Blind Seer, padding with his usual contained swagger at her left, looked positively familiar.

Harjeedian and Derian had discussed the various problems at length on the voyage over to Misheemnekuru, but once they had docked, the aridisdu had left Derian.

"I'm going to visit with the residents of the outpost," Harjeedian said. "Lady Blysse holds no liking for me, and I will not complicate an already too complicated matter with my presence. If she does not appear, you are welcome in the outpost. I know from my fellows' letters that she has not hesitated to come there."

Derian had agreed that he would do better to wait for Firekeeper alone. He didn't know if he'd ever like Harjeedian, but the more he learned of the reasons that had led to the aridisdu's role in their kidnapping, the more he didn't actively dislike him. Harjeedian was another person who seemed to be transforming under his eyes the longer Derian knew him. Was that the problem with this strangeness he now saw in Firekeeper—that Derian had thought he knew her and now must face how little he did know?

Doing his best not to show his disquiet, Derian moved to meet Firekeeper halfway between the forest's edge and the dock.

"I thought someone might tell you I was coming," he said, knowing the wolf-woman's disdain for empty conversation. "Nice to know you've made some friends."

"Some," Firekeeper replied with a slight smile, the monosyllable saying more than sentences would have done. "We speak nearer forest? Blind Seer hot in this sun."

Derian had noticed the wolf was panting. Indeed, his own shirt was sticking to his back.

"I'd be glad to go into the forest, as long as I don't trespass over any boundaries. I promised not to violate any of the agreements between the yarimaimalom and the Liglimom."

"I keep you safe," Firekeeper replied, and without another word she turned and led the way into the green-shaded coolness.

A double handful of paces within the curtain of larger trees they came upon a camp in whose compact design Derian recognized Firekeeper's mark. There was a stone circle in which banked coals glowed. Over these a spitted rabbit was slowly roasting, fat dripping intermittently to sizzle in the embers.

"We eat along the trail," Firekeeper said, "but then there was a stupid rabbit. . . . We have berries, too, and fresh water."

She indicated a pottery jar with a toss of her head.

"That and water I take from well. I even ask."

A major concession on her part, for Derian knew that Firekeeper ascribed to a wolfish view that the strong took and the rest put up with the taking. She must have some reason for wanting to keep the Liglimom sweet. He was interested in what might have moderated her outlook, but explanations might come out without his pressing her with questions.

The camp was set up in an area obviously intended for such—another sign of her accommodation. Whatever the reason Firekeeper had elected to use it, Derian was glad for the table and benches already in place. He really didn't feel like sitting on a rock.

"So, wondering why I came?" Derian asked, teasingly.

"I think, maybe, I say I want to talk and you is kind," Firekeeper said, "but I then think must be more for Liglimom to let you come here so easy."

"Good thoughts," Derian replied. Firekeeper had slid across the table a leaf cup filled with a handful of sweet-tart wild blueberries, and he ate a few of these while he organized his thoughts. "Firekeeper, are you willing to listen to a very long story? I want to know what has been happening with you, the things that you wanted to talk with me about, but I want your promise that you'll give me a chance to tell you some things—important things—before you go running off again."

Firekeeper nodded. "I listen. Even you go first."

Derian realized that part of the reason for this courtesy was that his telling might save the wolf-woman the need to articulate some information that she might have received from another source.

"I'll go first," he said, "but promise you'll ask questions. This gets really complicated."

Firekeeper agreed with another nod. Blind Seer had withdrawn from the fire to a patch of damp ground and his panting had slowed. A dog might have finished cooling off by going to sleep, but the wolf lay watching with intelligent eyes.

Derian began explaining the complicated tangle of fears and accusations, threats of heresy and impiety that had grown from the very small seed of Firekeeper's arrival and the realization that she could without a doubt speak to the yarimaimalom. The wolf-woman listened with astonishing patience, asking occasional questions, and not even being offended when Derian mistook her silence for inattention.

"I listen," she said. "These yarimaimalom do listen to and work with humans. If the humans think strange, so may beasts and so I must know."

"You should also know," Derian said, "because one of these days someone is going to insist—or at least try to insist—on your coming back and playing teacher. I don't know if anyone could put pressure on the yarimaimalom to make you come back, but if and when you do, all of this is going to boil forth."

Firekeeper made a sharp gesture filled with contained energy. She and Derian had been picking at the rabbit during his long recital. Now she snapped one of the bones between her fingers and sucked out the marrow as a child might the honey from a sweet.

"I know," she said. "What I not know is if I can teach this thing—even if they decide that the learning is good. What happens if I cannot teach?"

"Some people will be relieved," Derian said, "and some will be disappointed. Unhappily, the basic question of whether your ability and apparent acceptance by the Wise Beasts makes you the equivalent of one of the five most powerful people in u-Seeheera—I think in the entire land—will remain. The yarimaimalom do seem to have accepted you as one of their own."

Without his intending such, Derian's voice turned the last into a question and Fire-keeper answered it as such.

"The wolves accepted Blind Seer first, and Blind Seer claimed me as one of his pack. Later, I win my place. It is a little place, but, yes, I am accepted by these wolves. Some ravens, too, speak with me—the ones who carried the messages to you and their flock. Whether this is accepting of yarimaimalom or only of some yarimaimalom, I do not know."

"I think," Derian said, "that in this case—at least unless the humans received omens indicating otherwise—some is as good as all. What matters is that the yarimaimalom have not killed you as a trespasser. That makes you at the very least a human with priv-ileges granted to no other—and I, for one, think it makes you a Beast."

He had seen Firekeeper bristle slightly when he referred to her as a privileged human, but she eased as soon as she understood his point.

"And," she said, "if you see me so, so will many others and these problems will become more than words. Very well. If and when I come to mainland again, I be very careful how I act."

That was a greater concession than Derian had expected, and he found himself ask-ing, "What has happened since you've been here?"

Firekeeper tossed the rabbit bone into the embers and stared at the little tongues of flame that licked up in response.

"Blind Seer and I have talked with many Wise Wolves, from many packs. They come for a hunting, but also for a looking over. We learn many things in this time. These Wise Wolves is not like my Royal Wolves—in both body and mind, they are different. I not know what humans know of this, so tell none, but I wish you to know. Speak of it only if humans tell first."

Derian promised, touched and frightened as once before when Firekeeper had confided in him things the powerful Beasts might not want known by humans. There were times when her trust in his discretion was a rather greater burden than he desired.

When Firekeeper finished the long account of how the yarimaimalom had bred for talents and ended up with monstrosities, Firekeeper shrugged as if to say "Now you figure it out." For Derian, who had grown to adulthood in a culture that tolerated inborn talents only because no one could do anything about them, and because many of them were admittedly useful, the idea of breeding for talents was almost as disquieting as the practice of magic.

"You're right," Derian said. "These Wise Wolves are nothing like your Royal Wolves, not in mind or—it seems—in body. The ravens told you that these differences have alienated the yarimaimalom from the Royal?"

"Yes," Firekeeper agreed. "I think it is with all. I have not yet talked with a member of the water folk, though I think some of the otters who hunted among the salmon must have been Wise."

"And probably looking you over as well," Derian chuckled. "You haven't had an easy time of it, have you? I wonder if they're trying to figure out if you're one of the maimalodalum, just like Rahniseeta was doing with me and Barnet."

Firekeeper tilted her head at him in mute inquiry. Derian responded with the story, flavoring it as best he could in Barnet's style. He had expected Firekeeper to be amused, but he had not expected her to seize on it with more intense attention than she had given his account of mainland politics.

"Rahniseeta believe these maimalodalum are real?" Firekeeper asked, her dark eyes burning. "Animals with human shape, humans with animal shape?"

Too late Derian realized what he had done. To him and Barnet the story of the maimalodalum was after the fashion of a fireside tale, amusing, but too fantastic to be believed. For Firekeeper, forever trapped between two worlds, it was tantalizing hint of a dream that somehow might come true.

"It's just a story, Firekeeper," he replied lamely.

"So for humans," the wolf-woman replied, looking over at Blind Seer, "were the Royal Beasts."

WHEN WALN HEARD THAT DERIAN COUNSELOR was being taken to Misheem-nekuru, he smiled—not because he like the idea, but because he knew this violation of procedure was what he needed to bring Shivadtmon firmly over to his side.

Without a word spoken between them, Waln knew that young Carter's admission onto those sacred isles would make Shivadtmon eager to challenge those who had permitted the visit. After all, being posted there was an honor reserved for the best and brightest—an honor of which Shivadtmon had boasted. What had Derian Carter done to deserve being given an equal privilege?

Waln knew he could use Shivadtmon's certain irritation to his own advantage, and made a private bet with himself that he could do so without ever even speaking Derian's name.

As Waln had told Tedgewinn, his first goal was to gain the shipwreck survivors a bit more freedom of movement. Without that, anything else they might hope to achieve would be completely impossible. Now, while Shivadtmon had to be burning with a desire to get even for imagined wrongs, was the time to strike.

After reflecting on various tactics and discarding them all as flawed—basically because Waln just didn't know enough about the way the Liglimom thought—the merchant decided on the direct approach. Therefore, when Shivadtmon arrived for his lesson, the aridisdu found the door to the suite open and Waln staring out of one of the narrow slit windows in the direction of the open water.

Waln let the aridisdu tap once for admission, then a second time before turning to face him. He kept his movements lethargic and made his smile of greeting a bit wan.

"Are you unwell?" Shivadtmon asked, obviously concerned, though Waln thought rather cynically he was probably more worried about infection to himself than ill health in his tutor. "I heard one of the other tutors was ill."

"No, I'm fine," Waln said, motioning Shivadtmon to the table where they usually sat for lessons. He poured them both tumblers of cool water flavored with mint, moving slowly as he did so, pausing once as if distracted.

"You do not seem well," Shivadtmon objected.

"It's not anything you can do anything about," Waln said, deliberately provoking Shivadtmon's pride. "It's being shut up in this cursed building all the time, especially in this stifling heat. I'm a sailor and an islander. I like to see a long ways off. Being closed in . . ."

Waln shrugged. What he really wanted to do was grab Shivadtmon by the collar of his shirt and yell, "Get me out of here, you idiot!" That, however, would be less than productive, and, like any man who had ruled by strength, Waln knew how to pick his battles.

As Waln had hoped, Shivadtmon did not like being told there was something he could do nothing about—especially at a time when he was doubtlessly feeling rather impotent. He bristled, and it was out of anger rather than compassion that he shot forth his next question.

"Being closed in does what to you? I understand that sailors live very tightly packed when on shipboard. I should think you would be well prepared to live like this.

That you would even find the spacious quarters provided for you comfortable beyond imagination."

Waln essayed another weak smile.

"I suppose it would seem that way," he said, "to one who has never been on a long voyage. The difference is that although shipboard quarters may be tight, topside there's open space as far as the eye can see. There's shore leave, too. A merchant vessel like those me and most of my mates served on didn't spend too long out from shore. We went from port to port. The mainland was a longer run, of course, but even that wasn't too bad."

"I see. . . ."

Shivadtmon fell into a tense, thoughtful silence. Waln would have bet anything he owned that the aridisdu was trying to decide whether allying himself with the northerners and their concerns would be to his advantage or not.

"Do your fellows—your mates—feel this way, too?" Shivadtmon asked.

"They do," Waln said promptly. "Thing is, they're just deckhands mostly, and so are a bit nervous about speaking out. They don't quite buy the bit about us being guests rather than prisoners, and are scared they'll end up in a dungeon somewhere if they complain."

"And you do not share their fear?" Shivadtmon asked.

"Of course not," Waln said stiffly. "I believe we are guests and are being treated as such."

Waln wondered if the aridisdu had heard how Waln had agitated to see Tiridanti soon after their arrival. Best to add that first—and if he could tweak Shivadtmon's nose while he did it, all the better.

"Aridisdu Harjeedian came to me as a direct emissary from Ahmyndisdu Tiridanti," Waln said.

He didn't mention that at the time he'd felt like he was being fobbed off on a junior disdu as a direct slight from the ahmyndisdu. He'd noticed before that Shivadtmon resented the prominence into which Harjeedian had come of late.

"Aridisdu Harjeedian explained that our current living quarters were meant to protect us from the general populace. Apparently there is fear that they will take us as some sort of legendary demons?"

Waln turned the last into a question.

"We do have such creatures in our folktales," Shivadtmon said, "but I hardly think the local populace would be so credulous."

"Then we are prisoners?" Waln asked. He was pleased that he managed to sound quite shocked.

Shivadtmon found himself in the position of defending someone who he resented. It didn't improve his mood—but his irritation was not directed toward Waln.

"I do not think you are prisoners," Shivadtmon said in a reasonable tone of voice that confirmed to Waln that he thought the exact opposite. "Rather I think Aridisdu Harjeedian overstepped himself in his explanation. Certainly there are some members of our common folk who would be shocked by your appearance, but not to the point of violence against you. More likely they would run into their houses and bar the doors."

"Could you ask Harjeedian what's going on then?" Waln asked, sounding as pathetic as possible. "We're going stir-crazy in here—all but Nolan, who may well be sickening for lack of fresh air and exercise."

Waln decided to throw caution to the winds. To the bottom with his private bet. He paused as if remembering something.

"Oh, but you can't ask Harjeedian, can you?" he went on, squaring his shoulders bravely against disappointment. "I forgot. Aridisdu Harjeedian has gone to Misheem-nekuru with Derian Counselor. Even when he returns, he will certainly be too busy for such a minor matter."

"I do not need to be granted an audience from Aridisdu Harjeedian," Shivadtmon said frostily. "I can speak to a member of u-Liall myself. I am quite good friends with Junjaldisdu Dantarahma. He was one of my teachers before his elevation."

Waln looked appropriately impressed, but decided it couldn't hurt to twist the knife a bit more.

"If you could speak to the junjaldisdu that would be wonderful," he said. Then with innocent concern etched all over his face, he went on, "But will Junjaldisdu Dantarahma be able to overrule something Ahmyndisdu Tiridanti has ordained? I have heard so much about this being a jaguar year, and how Fire's influence dominates the other four elements."

Shivadtmon's jaw tightened.

"It may be a jaguar year, but that does not mean Ahmyndisdu Tiridanti is the only one who can take omens. Nor is she greater than the other members of u-Liall. A jaguar year gives Fire some importance, but it remains one among the five elements—and a child of Water and Air as well."

Waln was tempted to push even harder, but he knew that he had Shivadtmon ready to go agitate for the shipwreck survivor's freedom. There was nothing else to be gained here—and besides, Waln was pretending to feel unwell. Pushing would be out of character.

"Well," Waln said, reaching for the book in which he kept his teaching notes, "let us get on with your lesson. I apologize for keeping you from your studies with my minor concerns."

Shivadtmon, however, had risen and was gathering up his materials.

"I beg your forgiveness," the aridisdu said, "but though you properly seek not to press your appeal, this is an important matter. We cannot have our guests growing ill from lack of exercise and fresh air. It would be an insult to the deities who brought you to us."

Waln, hearing points of debate evolving, had the wisdom not to delay Shivadtmon. Instead, after the aridisdu had departed, and having some time before his next student would arrive, Waln wandered to the common area on the ground floor. He found Shelby and Rarby there before him, absorbed in a game of Navy versus the Pirates.

Rarby was playing the pirates and, judging from Shelby's scowl, was winning. Waln wasn't surprised. Even among Islanders who had never sailed a pirate venture in their lives, the pirates were figures of romance, and most players concentrated their skills on learning those tactics.

"Done with classes for the day?" Waln asked jovially.

"Not begun," Shelby replied, obviously glad for a distraction. "Saw your first student leave early. Piss him off by criticizing his accent?"

Waln grinned. "Nope. Aridisdu Shivadtmon and I are good buddies, such good buddies that he's gone off to talk with Junjaldisdu Dantarahma about getting us shore leave."

"Shore leave?" Rarby asked, then grinned. "You mean we could go out to the market? I think I know every brick in this courtyard. I'd love a stroll—and maybe a visit to some accommodating lady."

Waln hadn't thought of this angle. The Liglimom had offered a variety of entertainment, but had stopped short of bringing in prostitutes—probably because it would make the shipwreck survivors' true status apparent.

"Better be careful with that," he warned. "We don't know how the Liglimom feel about such things."

"You might not," Shelby scoffed, "but we didn't bunk belowdecks with the hands on *Fayonejunjal* without hearing plenty of stories. Problem will be getting our hands on solid money. I doubt temple association will do."

Waln nodded. "I'll see what I can do, but let's be tactful about it. You've gone longer without, shipboard."

"Shipboard," Shelby said bluntly, "we were a hell of a lot more tired. Does things to a sailor's drive when he's hauling line in the wet."

Waln gave up. He didn't want the northerners to be seen as rutting animals, but maybe it would be best if Rarby and Shelby came across as less than sophisticated. It would make the Liglimom more willing to work with Waln, rather than negotiating separately with each of them.

Waln spent a little more time extolling the attractions of getting out of their prison—though he was careful not to call it such with these two, lest they remember their earlier fears—and wandered off to find Tedgewinn.

The carpenter's mate was busy with a student, so Waln stopped in to visit Nolan, dropping in his ears a hint or two about the possibility that his illness might have been brought on by confinement. Then Waln retired to his own suite and picked up a book one of his other students had given him. It was a children's book about the settlement days, and Waln was translating it word by painful word.

The Old Country rulers had come prepared to settle. Once they had settled they had not hesitated to indulge themselves. That was clear even in this simple primer. After a while Waln ceased reading, his imagination captivated by what treasures might be awaiting him amid the tangled forests and crumbling ruins of Misheemnekuru.

"SO FIREKEEPER HAS HEARD about maimalodalum," Truth said to Bitter. "You know what that means."

The raven had found her drowsing in the gardens surrounding u-Nahal and reported eavesdropping on the long conversation between Derian Carter and Fire-keeper that had taken place the afternoon before. Normally, Truth would have resented being awakened, but her dreams had been so troubled that she was glad.

"I don't have your gift for divination," the raven replied, "but I don't need it for this. Firekeeper is going to want to learn more about them. The question is, how much do we tell her?"

Truth licked her paw. She had prayed very hard on this matter and the deities had vouchsafed her the clearest reply she'd gotten on any matter having to do with Firekeeper. Oddly, the jaguar found this clarity unsettling rather than otherwise. Why did the deities grant visions on this matter when they were mute on so many others?

Truth could not divine the reason for this, but she did know she wasn't going to tell Bitter about her growing feeling that she was being played with by the deific forces she served. It was for cats to toy, not to be the toys of others—not even if those others were divinities.

"We will tell Firekeeper about the maimalodalum," Truth replied, "but we don't tell her everything."

"Like what don't we tell her?" Bitter asked. "Already Rahniseeta has told Derian about the wearing of skins or carrying of a token. We could deny that, I suppose. . . ."

"No. If she already knows that, we do not deny her. We simply will not tell her about the cost to gain that token, at least not right away."

"Why not? Surely Firekeeper should know about that, and about . . ." The raven paused and preened the feathers of one wing, uncharacteristically nervous. "And about the other things."

Truth licked one paw and groomed behind her ear. The rhythmic motion soothed her, and she could answer calmly though her brain was burning with flashes of uncer-tainty.

"Because it is important that she know about those other things we cannot risk her refusing to see them. If she refuses to see them, to witness them with her own eyes, she may be able to disbelieve. She is from the north and those northerners have a deep aversion to the things of the Old World. There is a chance that she will shy away if she learns everything all at once—and the deities have made it very clear that she must go to the central island."

"There?" Bitter puffed out his feathers as against the cold. "Most of our own do not go there."

"A few go there," Truth corrected. "Didn't you mention a wolf called Dark Death has recently come to the large island? He is born of the pack that guards the central island. I do not think his coming at this time is coincidence."

Actually, Truth wasn't sure whether it was coincidence or not, but Truth was not above aiding her visions with more deductive insights. The visions were so often like dreams remembered just after waking—clear enough that one could remember the logic that had functioned within them and even suspect what had inspired them. Later, when the dreams had faded, it was necessary to make the connections for others.

Truth knew that this making of connections was her weak point. It was not simply chance that associated felines and Fire. Like Fire, cats great and small excelled at tearing apart rather than connecting. Nest builders like birds and rodents made better interpreters, but the predators usually were sharper at receiving the initial images—and the solitary hunters, like the great cats, sharpest of all.

"Perhaps Dark Death's arrival is not coincidence," Bitter replied. The raven sounded as if he doubted this. "However, wolves do roam great distances when the mating urge is on them, and the central-island wolves need go further than most to avoid mating their close kin."

Truth extended the claws of one raised paw, saying in effect, "You question my vision?"

Bitter flapped, the motion containing refusal to either admit questioning Truth's divinations or to apologize.

Truth knew Bitter had flown back and forth between Misheemnekuru and the mainland several times. Doubtless he was tired and his temper, never bright, even from the egg, must be frayed. Therefore, she decided to let the matter rest.

"Will you or one of your wingéd kin fly to Misheemnekuru and inform the wolves of the deities' will in this matter?" Truth asked. "Firekeeper will visit with her human friend, then return to the wolves, full of questions. The wolves should be prepared both for those questions and for what they should not say."

"I will have an osprey carry the message," Bitter replied. "My wings are weary of the buffeting of salt winds."

"Done, then," Truth said. "Take my thanks for making these arrangements. Tell the wolves—indeed any who question—that their own diviners may test my vision against theirs. I think they will agree this course follows the divine will."

Bitter flapped as if about to depart, then he folded his wings.

"Truth, do you know why it is so important that Firekeeper go to the central island?"

Truth hesitated, uncertain how much to say. Eventually, she decided that honesty would only help her with this gloomy black bird. He would not take commands as would a doe or other fearful prey animal.

"I have had visions," Truth said, "repeated visions of Firekeeper being there. These are the only visions I have had of her in any place. Her very presence muddles the future, but perhaps because of the fact that she is certain to be interested in the maimalodalum, this one thing is clear. If she is not scared away, Firekeeper will go to the central island. There is nothing in the visions to indicate that the deities do not want her there. Indeed, I sense that were we to try and prevent her going, they would be displeased. That is all I have, but since it is all I have, I assign importance to it."

Bitter flapped up to the top of the wall enclosing the garden.

"I think I understand. I will speak to the osprey. The osprey will speak to the wolves and the wolves to Firekeeper. You do not wish the osprey to carry the message directly to her?"

"No. She is suspicious of our divinely blessed visions and might balk. She is also most pleased when she believes she follows her own will . . ."

"And if she thinks otherwise," Bitter said, "again she may balk."

"Let Firekeeper believe she coaxes the information from the wolves. If Dark Death offers to guide her, all to the good. If he does not, make certain some other puts her on a clear trail."

"You give orders I cannot assure will be obeyed," Bitter protested.

"It is a jaguar year," Truth said confidently. "Fire will drive them on. I am sure of this."

"Pray then," Bitter said, and without further comment took to the air, "for Fire's help clearing the way."

As Bitter moved out of sight, Truth heard the glad cries of the raven's rather silly mate. Lovable had come by earlier, dangling a bit of jewelry from a thong about her neck. She had not stayed through Bitter's report, but had gone to show off her prize to her friends. The jaguar seriously wondered about those species that mated for life. It seemed a form of insanity.

Sleepy now, as if she had been divining rather than merely reporting divinations, Truth curled into a ball, part in sunlight, part in shade, even as her fur was part of each.

"Divine Fire," the jaguar prayed, "guide my dreams. Give me true visions. Take from me the confusion in my mind. Burn away the evil that I fear is stalking us. Make of Firekeeper a light to illuminate those dangers we can hardly see, never hear until the moment when they fall upon us and begin to bite and rend."

For when the leap was made, the fangs sunk into the flesh, as the jaguar knew all too well, it would be too late.

XXIII

THEY HAD TALKED WELL INTO EVENING, what with Derian keeping thinking of things he wanted to tell Firekeeper about—including his new horse, Prahini—and Firekeeper telling him about the Wise Wolves. This often meant telling him about the Royal Wolves, since she had to keep explaining why the Wise Wolves were so different.

Derian and Harjeedian had ended up staying overnight at the outpost. Firekeeper had even gone in with them, since Derian had made the very sensible argument that if she was going to learn to write, why didn't she memorize a few more symbols so she could send him complete messages?

Firekeeper had drawn the line at sleeping at the outpost, what with the night so warm and lovely. She'd awakened early and seen Derian off at the dock, promising him that she would find some way to keep in touch.

Then she and Blind Seer had started running back to the meeting meadows, and every beat of her foot contained a syllable of the same wonderful word: Mai-mal-o-da-lu. Beast-souled. Humans who could take the shape of animals. Animals who could take the shape of humans.

Firekeeper would ask Neck Breaker and Cricket if they knew of any such stories. If they did not, then she would try and dismiss the maimalodalu as one of those crazy stories humans told, but if the Wise Wolves did know something . . .

Mai-ma-lo-da-lu. Beast-souled. Humans who could be animals. . . .

She had heard such legends before, but never from a source that spoke with anything like authority. There had been that ring in New Kelvin. Stories Queen Elexa had told her. Dragons had proven to be true—even if nothing like the stories. Mai-ma-lo-da-lu.

Firekeeper didn't talk about the beast-souled to Blind Seer. She didn't need to. He knew better than most her frustration regarding her wolf's heart and human form. Sometimes she wondered if he shared her frustration. She'd never asked. It would be rude to ask the wolf if he'd like her better if she were really a wolf—and it would force issues she didn't want to even talk about.

It would be even ruder to ask Blind Seer if he ever wished he were a human. She'd heard Doc say once something about a time when Blind Seer must have been wishing he had hands. She thought she might miss her own hands, but if giving up hands was the price she had to pay for being a wolf, she'd pay it gladly.

There would be compensations. . . . Firekeeper glanced over at the blue-eyed wolf who ran sometimes beside her, sometimes in front of her, sometimes behind her—always with her.

THEY ARRIVED AT THE MEETING MEADOWS a day and a half later to find the air smelling of departures. Two of the packs had already returned to their home territories, but that of Hard Biter and Tangler remained, as did the one to which Cricket belonged. Dark Death was also there, as handsome and dominating as ever.

Firekeeper experienced a wash of awkward shyness she had never before felt when in the presence of wolves. This wasn't the familiar sensation of being part-blind that she always felt in the company of these who "saw" as much with their sense of smell as with their eyes, nor was it the newer sensation of being demoted to a very junior status after being treated with admiration—and even awe—by humans.

This was something completely beyond her experience. For the first time she understood Derian's discomfort at being accepted almost as an equal by the nobility. Before the day King Tedric had made Derian a king's counselor, Derian had been a young man of good family and even of fortune, but for all this he had been viewed as one who served rather than one who ruled. With the visible sign of King Tedric's favor, a few blocks from that invisible wall had been removed and Derian had been granted the right to step across the wall, to advise his superiors as if he was one of them.

Now the story of the maimalodalum had given Firekeeper the means to lower the wall that separated her from those she loved best—and she found herself trembling in both anticipation and sudden, unexpected fear.

Blind Seer bumped his head against her.

"You've frozen like a rabbit who hears the eagle's scream," he said. "Have we run all this way only to turn around in the end?"

Firekeeper shook—not just her head as a human would, but her body as well, as a wolf shakes off shedding fur.

"Wise as ever, sweet hunter," she said. "Do I reek of fear?"

"Only to a nose that knows you well," Blind Seer assured her. "The ripest scent blends eagerness and excitement."

That relaxed Firekeeper some. She strode toward the gathered wolves, her head high and her hand just touching Blind Seer's fur.

"You have made a swift trail of it," Tangler greeted them approvingly. "We thought we might meet you along the trail back to our hunting grounds."

"I am glad to have arrived before the dispersal was complete," Firekeeper replied politely. "I am only sorry we didn't get to give our thanks to the other packs. I, at least, learned much from them."

"And I," Blind Seer agreed, "did as well."

"They will hear your thanks in the moon song," Hard Biter assured them. "Was your visit with your fox-furred friend pleasant?"

"Very," Firekeeper assured them. "He told me much of what is happening on the mainland. Not all of it makes sense to one such as myself, but I have struggled to hold it in my head so that I might ask for your advice and clarification."

The gathered packs were now returning to the relaxation that usually occupied the wolves during the heat of the afternoon. All the adults, however, seemed interested in hearing what Firekeeper and Blind Seer had to say. The new arrivals took comfortable places in the shade, and Firekeeper tried to decide where to begin. She wanted to launch immediately into the tale of the maimalodalum, but thought this might be starting the prey before she had closed to a distance where she could make a kill.

"Why not," Blind Seer said, obviously running along a similar trail as herself, "begin with telling them of the changes in the mood of the human herd? These are many and confusing, but these wise ones, so much more accustomed to how their humans think, may be able to untangle them for us."

So Firekeeper began, starting with the mixture of fear and anticipation that greeted her ability to speak with the beasts, and moving to the complications that were evolving among various factions. Blind Seer helped her, and between them she thought they were making a fairly clear report of the twisted mess.

Once or twice, Firekeeper thought she detected a motion from one or the other of the listeners that indicated that what she and Blind Seer had to report was not wholly new to their listeners.

These wolves have allies among the wingéd folk, even as my home pack does. Firekeeper thought. *Doubtless they have been offered some small bites and wait to see how what Derian knows of these events compares in flavor and texture.*

Therefore, although the wolf-woman longed to reach what to her was the matter of real interest, Firekeeper went on, knowing that snappishness would garner her no respect among these hunters. When she had finished, the Wise Wolves seemed thoughtful, but not startled.

"It is easy to see why you value your fox-haired friend," Neck Breaker said. "He has taken great risks to make certain you will be safe from those who fear or resent you."

"Risks?" Firekeeper asked, dismissing any danger to herself as stale scent. "Derian?"

"There will be many who will resent his being permitted to come to Misheemnekuru."

"But he abided by the law. He did not leave the human areas!"

"Even those areas are considered places of privilege by the humans. Of all those who train to become disdum, only a small amount are granted the opportunity to train at the outpost."

"Such restrictions must be made," explained Half-Snarl, the One Female of the pack to which Cricket belonged. "Otherwise we should be overwhelmed with humans. Since the number who may come here is limited, the humans have made it a posting of honor."

"I think," said Moon Frost, "that making it an honor is a way for the humans to assure that those who are sent to the outpost do not chafe at the restrictions. Might that not be so, Firekeeper?"

It was the first time Moon Frost had spoken to Firekeeper since their battle without having been spoken to first. Firekeeper checked the cant of the wolf's ears and the speed of her breathing for any indication of challenge, but found none—unless this assumption that Firekeeper would know how humans would react to any circumstance could be seen as a challenge to Firekeeper's wolfishness. The wolf-woman chose not to see it as such.

"I think you may be right, Moon Frost," Firekeeper replied. "For all that humans build enormous stone dens, I have met few who like the idea of being locked within them. They honor their freedom, even if they do little with it."

"Freedom not to do," Neck Breaker said, "is a freedom in itself. Are these arguments over doctrine and procedure all your friend had to tell you about?"

Firekeeper hesitated, uncertain now that an opening had been given that she could speak of the maimalodalum without revealing the tremendous desire that pushed like a physical ache within her breast.

"Derian told us he has been given a new horse," she offered. "This is good, for there was tremendous anger in him at the killing of his mare, Roanne."

Blind Seer picked up the trail when Firekeeper hesitated.

"In telling us of this new horse, Derian also told us an interesting tale. It seems that one of the humans—Rahniseeta, sister of Harjeedian—learned that Derian belongs to the Horse Society."

There was a general head-tilting of puzzlement, and Blind Seer explained, "These societies are common in the human lands from which we have come. They are something like the temples here, but without the connection to deities: each is instead associated with a specific animal."

"And one of these animals is the horse, then?" Neck Breaker asked.

"That is so," Blind Seer agreed. "The horses are not worshipped, but they are admired and the humans seek to emulate their better traits: support of the herd, responsible leadership by those who lead, faithful following by those who follow, that sort of thing."

Firekeeper was amazed at all Blind Seer knew. She'd never bothered to learn much about the societies. Wendee Jay, who belonged to the Wolf Society, had asked Firekeeper about wolf ways and compared the reality to the ideal her society espoused. This had taught Firekeeper something, but Blind Seer had made an effort to learn much more.

Rascal asked eagerly, "Do the humans in this Horse Society eat grass, then? That's one of the things horses do best."

Blind Seer thumped his tail in amusement.

"I don't think so, Rascal. They emulate an ideal, not imitate the real."

"But what does this have to do with Derian?" Cricket asked.

Firekeeper sensed in Cricket some of the same impatience the old wolf had expressed when Grey Thunder was telling the sad tale of the long-ago attempt to breed for specific talents. Again Firekeeper wondered just how much these wolves already had been told. The thought that she and Blind Seer might be sneaking up on game that already knew they were coming did not make her bolder.

Blind Seer, however, seemed perfectly at ease.

"It seems that Rahniseeta added the knowledge that Derian belonged to the Horse Society to things she already knew about him—that he has a talent for working with horses, that Eshinarvash the Wise Horse granted him a ride on his back, that Derian's slain mare had hair similar in shade to Derian's own, even that he was friends with Firekeeper and myself. She drew a conclusion that to her fit the facts."

"What?" asked Rascal.

As certainly as if I walk on two legs, Firekeeper thought, *if there has been information brought from elsewhere, it has not been shared with all. The yearling pants along the trail.*

"Rahniseeta concluded," Firekeeper said, accepting Blind Seer's silent invitation that she take a share in the narration, "that Derian must be one of what she called the maimalodalum. Derian says the word means something like 'beast-souled.' He says it refers to humans who could, by means of sorcery, take on the shape and senses of a beast."

There. It was said. Would the Wise Wolves force her to ask the next question—to ask if there was any truth in this tale? They did not, and their answer made her nearly tremble with joy.

"Is he then maimalodalu?" Neck Breaker asked. "I had thought the art of taking another's shape belonged to the Old Country that came here, but not to any other."

"I thought Derian's people abhorred magic," Cricket snapped. "Is this not true? How could he be both maimalodalu and hate magic? The one goes with the other as marrow fills a bone."

"Derian is not maimalodalu," Firekeeper said, her heart singing in her. "He does have a talent for horses—though I think he is unaware of this—but otherwise he is as human as human can be."

"Are you saying," Blind Seer asked, "that these maimalodalum actually exist?"

"They have existed," Hard Biter said. He looked off into the distance. "They have. As Cricket said, the taking of another's form was achieved by magic—human magic."

"Rahniseeta told Derian there was a token," Firekeeper said eagerly. "A token worn or carried by the maimalodalu that enabled the change."

"That's right," Hard Biter agreed. "So it is said."

Firekeeper stiffened, scenting evasion.

"Are there any maimalodalum remaining?"

To her surprise, Dark Death, silent as a night dark shadow to this point, rose and shook.

"The ones who can answer those questions are not here, Firekeeper."

"Where are they?"

"They live on islands further within Misheemnekuru," Dark Death replied. "They are members of the pack that gave me birth. I went from them seeking a mate. I could guide you back."

"Me and Blind Seer," Firekeeper said firmly, though Dark Death's inflection made clear he had meant her alone. That she could be alone with another wolf was somehow a heady thought.

"By all means, Blind Seer, too," Dark Death replied. "He is a strong hunter and your close kin as well."

Firekeeper recalled that the Wise Wolves cared not to breed close kin, but shrugged this aside. Whatever else bound them, she and Blind Seer were not literally born of the same parents.

"Anyone else wish to run with us?" Dark Death asked. "It is a long trail, but a fair one."

Moon Frost rose. "I will go, if my pack can spare me."

"This is the easy hunting time," Tangler assured her. "Go. Howl your news home. That is the only hold we put upon you."

Moon Frost assented with a wag of her tail.

"I will tell you what I see and do," she promised. "If I cannot help feed the puppies' bodies, I can feed their minds."

So it was settled. The four might have left that night, but Firekeeper and Blind Seer had just completed a long run, and this one promised to be longer. Therefore, they all settled to hunt and rest.

"Everything will still be there," Dark Death assured her, sensing Firekeeper's impatience. "It has been there a long, long time."

Firekeeper knew he was right, but nonetheless impatience spurred her on.

"Rest," Blind Seer said. "What good the flesh of a fat buck to one without fangs?"

Firekeeper grinned and punched him.

"You make those up."

"Never."

The blue-eyed wolf knocked her over and pinned her.

"Now sleep."

Firekeeper obeyed, but though her body rested, her mind was afire with dreams of what could be.

THE RELEASE OF THE SIX SHIPWRECK survivors from what had been at least a quasi-imprisonment had a result that Waln Endbrook did not anticipate.

There are several things that sailors ashore do almost automatically. First what Waln defined as basic urges needed to be satisfied. Waln's delicacy regarding the matter was unnecessary, for a people does not live as closely to animals as did the Liglimom without accepting sexual impulses as natural. However, as a whoreson bastard, Waln had always believed that what he thought of as "better people" didn't talk about such things—or at least not as openly as Honey Endbrook had done.

The sailors, including Waln, made their visits and paid their money. Then there was the city to explore, often with language students as guides. This was an ideal arrangement for all involved. The sailors saw their fill of the elaborately enameled architecture, visited markets, tailors, and taverns, while their students had an opportunity to exercise their language skills in a practical setting. Questions that never would have been asked in the mannered seclusion of the classroom were addressed, and everyone was aware of the improvement.

However, after these things had been done, one pleasure remained to be satisfied—the pleasure of visiting with friends. As Waln had explained to Shivadtmon, the venture of the *Explorer* had been nearly unique in post-Plague history in that it was a voyage into the unknown. The busy shipping trade in the Isles was from port to port, within the Isles themselves and—before the exile of Queen Valora—to numerous ports in Bright Bay. Merchant sailors might be away for long periods of time, but for all but the greenest, every port was, in a sense, a home port containing friends and family.

Some sailors took this last to extremes, having more than one spouse and set of children. However, as long as the arrangement suited all the parties involved, the law did not get involved. Only sailors who abandoned their families could expect reprimand, and this whether they had one family or three.

The convivial aspect of shore leave, then, was what the shipwreck survivors found themselves missing as soon as several days of relative freedom had blunted their initial excitement. Thus when Lucky Elwyn came wandering into the common area of the building where they still maintained their quarters and stated, "Let's go visit Barnet Lobster. I bet he's lonely!," he found a willing audience.

Teaching sessions were finished for the day, and so all seven spruced up their attire, braided their hair, and tramped up the hill to Heeranenahalm. They had all visited the temple city repeatedly by now. The disdum who made up the majority of their students delighted in showing off their particular temple complexes. Waln had, of course, been into Heeranenahalm numerous times when working on convincing u-Liall of the wisdom of the voyage north to "acquire" Lady Blysse, but even then he had always had an escort.

This was the first time any of them had gone through the elaborate gates unescorted, and most of them fell a little quieter than was usual.

Elwyn, however, maintained a blithe and relaxed spirit. He'd packed a basket with some of Wiatt's northern-style cooking and swung it from his right hand. His walk was heavy. His feet tended to slap the ground, but there was such joyful animation in his bearing that the local citizenry—now repeatedly assured that the fair-haired, fair-skinned northerners were not demons—tended to smile in response.

Waln thought about telling Elwyn to calm down, that they were going into an important place, but reassured by the Liglimom's reaction, he held his tongue. It was very important that he be in control—and very important that the others not suspect how great that control was.

They arrived at the Temple of the Cold Bloods unchallenged and unimpeded. Elwyn banged the bronze knocker—shaped, predictably, like a coiled snake—while the others stepped back and waited.

The porter opened his hatch immediately.

"Yes?"

"We're here to see Barnet Lobster," Elwyn said in careful Liglimosh. "We're from the north, just like him."

Waln thought the last completely unnecessary, but nothing was to be served by reprimanding Elwyn here.

"I shall send a runner to see if Barnet is in his suite," the porter said. "While you wait, please step inside."

At least they weren't being kept hanging about like petitioners, Waln thought with satisfaction. Indeed, they were treated rather like the guests the Liglimom had always claimed they were. Cool drinks were brought and they were offered seats on a bench in a pleasantly shaded area. True, the porter didn't make conversation, but he was probably a servant and careful to keep his place.

The runner returned just as they were finishing their drinks.

"Barnet Lobster would be happy to see you," he said. "Please, follow me."

They did so, Elwyn marveling aloud at the sheer number of reptiles—snakes, lizards, alligators, and like creatures sunning themselves on just about any flat surface. Where the living creatures were not, they were depicted in art: twining up pillars, hanging from gateways, clinging to walls.

Once Rarby reached to touch what he thought was a lovely jeweled figure only to have it hiss at him. Although their guide assured him the reptile wasn't poisonous, after that everyone kept their hands close to their sides—and watched where they stepped.

The infestation was worse than in any of the other temples Waln had visited, but then he supposed that one could not have bears or wildcats roaming around in the same fashion. Shivadtmon's temple had numerous pools for his damp charges and even places where the walls opened to the sea, but mostly it had to make do with artistic depictions rather than the real thing.

At last they arrived at Barnet's suite. The outer gate was open, but Waln's cynical eye saw how easily this comfortable set of living quarters could be converted to a prison. This made him feel better about his own prolonged captivity. Barnet might have been living in Heeranenahalm, but he hadn't been given free run.

They heard the music before they turned the corner, flute and some stringed instrument playing in counterpoint to each other. The melody was not one with which Waln was familiar. Indeed, it had a similarity to pieces played by the entertainers who had been brought in to play for them at their "guest quarters."

As soon as their guide came to the door, the music stopped.

"Visitors for Barnet Lobster," the man intoned, then stepped back to let them walk in.

Barnet's quarters included a small courtyard, complete with fish pond, slender trees planted in pots, and other elegant flourishes. Two doors at one end indicated the presence of other rooms. One of these stood ajar. The other was tightly closed.

As Waln walked in, he saw Barnet setting aside a guitar of some sort and rising to greet them. He also saw who had been the minstrel's accompanist.

She was a lovely woman with shining black hair like wet ink. Although slender, she had lovely curves, and Waln felt a momentary stab of disappointment that the loose blouses and trousers so practical in this hot, damp climate didn't show them off to better advantage. A gown such as had been popular at court in the Isles would have done her far more justice.

Waln realized he had seen the woman before, though not frequently. However, he had long learned that knowing people's names and something about them could be used to his advantage. In a moment he remembered, and when he crossed the courtyard in a few long steps meant to emphasize his height and build, he had it ready.

"Barnet!" he said, putting out his hand in greeting. "We thought we'd come calling, now that our duties permit us some freedom. I believe I remember your companion. Rahniseeta, isn't it, sister of Harjeedian?"

The young woman had also risen and stood, still holding her flute. She dipped her head in the local equivalent of a polite bow, but did not offer her hand. Waln might have been disappointed by this, but then he realized that what he had taken for a bracelet about one firm and shapely upper arm was in fact a living snake. It raised its head and looked at him curiously.

"Waln Endbrook," Rahniseeta said. "My brother has spoken of you and your companions frequently. I know names. Let me see if I can match them to the right person."

Waln, always sensitive to nuances in the game of one-upmanship, allowed Rahniseeta a point. She had taken his remembering her and matched it with the information that she not only remembered him but knew of his companions as well. That she had also made clear that she was her brother's confidante—and perhaps informant as well—protected her from any indecent behavior. Very clever. . . .

But Waln doubted that the other men were admiring Rahniseeta's intelligence as she moved with supple grace to where she could see them more clearly.

"Two brothers," she said. "Rarby and Shelby. That would be you two gentlemen. . . ."

She put two fingers to her jaw in a pretty gesture of concentration.

"I think you," she said, indicating Rarby with an inclination of her head, "are Rarby, and this one is Shelby."

The men beamed and nodded. Like most siblings who bore a close resemblance to each other, they both liked and hated being taken for each other. Rahniseeta's correct identification had pleased them mightily.

"You must be Wiatt," Rahniseeta said to the cook, "and you Tedgewinn. The chef and the carpenter. Harjeedian has spoken many good things about both of your skills."

"Thank you, good lady," Wiatt said. "I'd be more than happy to cook you a northern-style fish stew if you're interested. Thought Barnet might like a taste of home, too."

Barnet grinned. "That would be wonderful. I like the local dishes just fine, but you have a way of getting the most out of a fish."

Tedgewinn, who was staring at the snake coiled on Rahniseeta's arm, blinked as if coming out of a dream. Waln was willing to bet that his next carving would be of a woman similarly adorned.

Better take care that Wiatt and Tedgewinn don't get flattered into thinking they might do better staying here, Waln thought. *I need every able sailor I can get if I'm to get to Misheemnekuru—and home again with what I find there.*

Rahniseeta didn't press Tedgewinn into speech, but turned to Nolan and Elwyn.

These two will be easy, Waln thought sardonically. *How many of us have suffered a prolonged illness, and Elwyn . . . well, he's easy enough to identify.*

Waln found himself wondering if Rahniseeta had actually handled her identifications by some process of elimination. Two who look like brothers, one sick, one awkward; two remaining then to identify. Telling a cook from a carpenter wasn't hard. And, of course, Rahniseeta would know who Waln was. Harjeedian had to have spoken of him—probably frequently.

Introductions completed, Rahniseeta stepped out and ordered drinks and refreshments. Sufficient chairs were found so that everyone could have a seat. This permitted Waln to learn that there were two other rooms to the setup, both bedrooms, one of which would have been used for Derian Carter had he not gone to u-Bishinti.

"Lady Blysse, of course, preferred to sleep out-of-doors," Barnet said with a laugh.

"Probably both of them wanted to get as far as possible from your snoring," Rarby said.

This brought on a general bout of laughter at the minstrel's expense. Then everyone was talking at once, sharing tales of what they'd been doing in the days since *Fayonejunjal* had come into port.

"Hard to believe we've only ended one moon and begun the next," Wiatt said. "Maybe it's all the teaching, but I feel like I've been here most of my life."

"I think it's the heat," Tedgewinn said. "Makes it feel like summer is farther along than it is. What is it, after all, Bear Moon? I feel like it's at least Fox Moon."

"How do your people name the moons, Rahniseeta?" asked Nolan. "One of my students tried to tell me, but we couldn't find enough words between us."

"They are named for various important events in the history of the deities," Rahniseeta said, "at least formally. Informally, they are often simply numbered."

"You mean First Moon, Second Moon, like that?" asked Elwyn.

"In the cities, yes," Rahniseeta said. "Farming people call them after what they must do then: Planting Moon, Thinning Moon, Weeding Moon. Things like that."

Nolan looked relieved. "No wonder I couldn't understand what Kidisdu Paliama was saying. I feel much better. I'd thought it was my fever making me think oddly, but if he was trying to tell me legend lore. . . ."

Barnet looked interested.

"Your months are formally named for stories?" he asked. "I'd like to learn those stories."

"I can teach you them," Rahniseeta said. "Or maybe you should ask some of your advanced students."

"I can do both," Barnet said. "Variations are always interesting."

"What were you playing, Barnet?" Elwyn asked. "It sounded like a variation."

Barnet looked both surprised and pleased.

"It was, Elwyn," he said, "but I didn't think anyone would notice. I'm working on adapting 'The Tail of the Silver Whale,' to the scales more commonly used in Liglimosh music. Rahinseeta has been helping me."

" 'Bang! Down came the whale's tail, shattering the deck,' " Elwyn sang, his voice so off key that everyone winced. " 'Bang! Down it came again. Now the ship was a wreck.' "

Barnet interrupted quickly by strumming a chord on his guitar.

"Here. I'll play it for you. First the familiar way, then how I've adapted it."

Waln watched the men's faces as they settled into the familiar ritual of letting Barnet entertain them. Contentment was the dominant emotion, though Waln caught Shelby sneaking a glance or three at Rahniseeta.

Guess he's forgetting the girl back home who broke his heart fast enough, Waln thought. *Better be careful how I use that.*

Tedgewinn had pulled a small block of hardwood from one pocket and his whittling knife from another. Hands fell to work shaping out what looked as if it might be a lizard, the sharpened blade cutting into the wood almost as if unguided, the carver's foot tapping along with the music, his lips shaping the lyrics.

After Barnet and Rahniseeta had finished their performance, Shelby and Rarby agitated for some dancing music. Most of the sailors were good dancers, but their figures bore only the slightest of resemblances to the elegant line dances favored in the cities. Although there was a similar interplay between partners, there was no flirtation, and the action was vigorous—almost combative—when compared with the formal styles.

Barnet switched to a flute for this, while Rahniseeta took up the guitar and chorded improvised—and slightly odd to Waln's ear—accompaniment. None of the sailors minded, and soon the little courtyard was crowded with the stamp of booted feet and loud laughter.

Waln took part, but when a break came, he excused himself. He had other things to do than idle about dancing. There were maps available for anyone's use in a library shared by the various temples. He thought he'd go take a look. There must be some of

Misheemnekuru showing the location of various buildings. Time to start thinking about his target.

He wanted a place where hopefully more than one building remained standing. His sailors would balk at clearing away too much rock. Then too he wanted a place away from the shore, especially the western shore that faced the mainland. They'd be spotted too easily there. Best follow one of the waterways in a bit—even if that was forbidden turf.

Waln fully expected the yarimaimalom to show their displeasure, but he didn't intend to go unarmed. A few shots from a crossbow in the hands of humans who didn't share the prevalent awe of the beasts, and the Beasties would be deciding to let the humans be, especially since the humans would not be staying. Waln planned to tell the yarimaimalom so; he'd been working out the speech in Liglimosh.

Even if the Beasts decided to fight, the sailors were good with crossbows, and most could handle a longbow as well. Rarby and Shelby had done time on a whaler, and were dab hands with a harpoon. Waln figured that if they were going to acquire a vessel capable of taking them all the way back to the Isles, they'd be able to acquire weapons as well. He'd just tell Shivadtmon or whoever about the threat of pirates once they got farther north.

But that would wait. First he needed to study some maps.

The librarian on duty didn't question Waln's request. Waln had been all prepared to tell the librarian it had something to do with his teaching duties, and was actually disappointed to find the excuse wasted. The man even helped Waln carry the maps over to a secluded table where a big window provided ample light.

Waln unrolled several so a casual observer wouldn't be sure what he was looking at. Then he pulled out his dictionary and notebook.

First, someplace not too visible from shore. Next, someplace that listed a cluster of buildings. Waln found himself humming quietly to himself as he worked.

" 'Bang! Down came the whale's tail, shattering the deck . . . ' "

XXIV

EVEN KNOWING THAT MISHEEMNEKURU was made up of a cluster of islands hadn't prepared Firekeeper for the amount of swimming that would be involved in getting from the island where they had first arrived to their destination.

Wolves can be strong swimmers when the situation requires. However, neither Firekeeper nor Blind Seer had done much more swimming than was required for crossing small rivers or cooling off in lakes. Fortunately, the route Dark Death chose did not require them to swim any distance longer than they would have undertaken by choice.

What was odd about this swimming was how strongly the water tasted of salt, and the peculiar, persistent tugging of the current. Then there were the amazing things the tides did to the shoreline. Many times they were forced to wait until the waters lowered and gave them grudging passage between sections of the archipelago.

"Why do the ocean waters rise and fall like this?" Firekeeper asked during one such wait. "Often I have heard sailors talk about the need to wait on the tide, but never before this have I understood why."

"It is the doing of my namesake, the Moon," Moon Frost replied. "You have heard how she is the child of Water. Even now she calls to her father to make her whole. When she cries loudest, then he reaches to her and the waters recede."

Firekeeper wanted to snort in disbelief, but already she knew this would be more than merely impolite. It would offend. Therefore she asked another question, hoping to turn away from these explanations based on the almost comprehensible actions of divine forces.

"Is Misheemnekuru then all one land?" Firekeeper asked. "If the tide was low enough, would the divisions between the islands vanish?"

"No," Dark Death replied. "Some of the islands are far enough apart that they always remain separated from the whole. In the interior, though, this may be the case. When the waters drop, walking between the islands is like walking through valleys to reach the opposite hill. Except in the seasons of storm most of the animals can swim between the major pieces of land. The outer islands become nesting places for the birds and seals. It works out quite well for all."

"Well for all of us," Firekeeper agreed, finger-combing out the tangles in her drying hair. "Swimming in this salt water leaves my skin feeling tight, but at least my stomach remains my friend."

Blind Seer panted laughter. Firekeeper knew he was thinking about their eventual journey home and how there must come a time when she would commit herself once more to the discomfort of a shipboard voyage. However, it was easy for her not to think about such distant events. Too many interesting thoughts crowded all but the immediate present from her mind.

"I notice," she said, removing her Fang from its Mouth and scrupulously cleaning off every drop of water, "that as we move farther away from the edges where the ocean beats, we see more signs of the humans who once lived here. From what Blind Seer and I had seen, I had thought they dwelt on these islands in scant numbers, but now I see this is not true."

Dark Death rose and waded into the inlet, testing the depth.

"Not yet shallow enough," he said, then shook the water from his coat. "From what I have been told the humans never clustered as thickly on Misheemnekuru as they do now in u-Seeheera. These islands were where the great and powerful made their dwellings. However, many lesser ones lived here as well."

Firekeeper weighed this against what she had learned about how the powerful among humankind lived.

"From what I have seen elsewhere," she said, a hint of scorn in her voice, "among humans those who have nothing must do everything for themselves, but those who have wealth or power are waited on as if they were nursing mothers or young pups. In a wolf pack, the Ones lead and take their share. They give the most and so get the most."

Blind Seer snorted.

"Firekeeper, you make the matter too simple. From what I have seen, sometimes there is good reason for the fashion in which humans organize their packs. Do you think that King Tedric could find hours enough in both day and night to do all that he must do to keep his kingdom running smoothly if he must also cook his own meals or keep his own lair fresh?"

Firekeeper immediately knew Blind Seer was correct, though she felt curiously uncomfortable at this realization. After a moment she realized why. Blind Seer had frequently chastened her when she had overstated the superiority of the wolf way over that followed by humans. However, this was the first time that others had witnessed her chastisement. She resented it, but knew she could not fail to acknowledge his point without opening herself to even greater criticism.

"I suppose a king's hunts are different hunts," she replied a trace sullenly, "his kills different kills." She brightened then, having thought of something that would save her from completely conceding. "Still, you must admit that many of those humans who are waited upon do nothing to earn this privilege."

"There are many idle ones among the nobility," Blind Seer agreed, without any sense of having been shamed. "But you spoke of how the Ones earn their privileges by leading. All I wished to clarify was that the human Ones worked for their keep, even if it might not seem so to a casual observer."

"I have never lived among humans," Moon Frost said. "How do these do-nothing-get-everythings exert their will?"

Firekeeper and Blind Seer went on to explain about money, inheritance, and titles. The wolf-woman had the feeling that their explanations were less than completely successful. Neither Dark Death nor Moon Frost had gone among humans, and the human culture they did know placed less weight on inheritance than on divine selection.

As they struggled to answer the Wise Wolves' questions, Firekeeper realized that Blind Seer actually had a better grasp of the intricacies of human culture than she did, for all that she was human born and he was not. While she had mostly been content to superimpose the order and rules she had learned from the wolves onto the various human cultures they had encountered, the blue-eyed wolf had attempted to learn some of the reasons—or at least rationalizations—behind the customs practiced by the humans.

The discussion filled long hours of running after they had swum across the inlet, and continued during the rest that filled the heat of the afternoon.

"It seems to me," Moon Frost said, "that much of your northern humans' strange behavior must come from their having no knowledge of the deities. Instead they set their own families up as little deities. They then pile up wealth in worship of these deities."

"That is too simple," Blind Seer protested. "Wealth is the means for meat and drink for these human packs. Moreover, they seek to emulate the best qualities of their ancestors—to live up to their heritage."

Moon Frost was not convinced.

"As I see the situation, each lineage can only be as strong or as weak as those who came before them. From what you have said, it seems that many of these families weaken over time as they accumulate useless members who draw on the family for support, but give nothing in return."

Firekeeper didn't know how to answer this. She herself had yet to understand why someone graced with nothing more than a title should automatically be considered the better of someone like Derian. On the other hand, she felt a desire to defend the people of Hawk Haven and Bright Bay. No matter how confusing they were, they were the stock from which she had been bred.

And who would I put in my ancestors' shrine? she asked herself. *Prince Barden and Sweet Eirene? Someone else whose face and voice I cannot recall? Dry bones all.*

Yet Firekeeper felt uncomfortable with this dismissal. She was greatly relieved when Blind Seer responded directly to Moon Frost's comment.

"I know nothing of deities, and only a little more of those who worship them, but it seems to me that belief in deities could be as restrictive as trust in ancestors. Where your system is very strong is that in addition to old lore there is a constant flow of new lore—these omens and divinations in which humans and beasts alike place such trust. What will happen if trust in those is lost?"

Moon Frost replied with confidence. "Trust will not be lost. The deities will guide us through even this difficult time."

Dark Death rose and shook the bracken from his fur.

"The worst of the heat is gone. Let us continue. Would you hunt now or when it is cooler?"

"As the trail brings us game," Firekeeper replied. She knew the question applied to her. The wolves ate more heavily with each meal and consequently could go longer without eating. "Will we come to another place where we must wait before swimming across?"

"Likely so. Moon's face is coming full."

"If something does not strike our trail before, then," Firekeeper said. "I can always fish or forage then. Summer brings many opportunities."

Although the trail was not completely without opportunities for foraging, especially in the form of berries and early summer fruit, Firekeeper was ravenous by the time they reached their next stopping point. She was not so hungry, however, that she failed to carefully examine their surroundings.

"Humans lived here once," she said, knowing from past inspections what lay beneath the tangled vines and clusters of young trees. Here the vines were predominantly honeysuckle, which granted the cooler night air a delicious perfume.

"Many humans," Dark Death replied. "We are nearing the central island, and that was a place where many humans lived."

Firekeeper puzzled over this. Why would wolves—and she was certain that Dark Death had said he was taking her to his birth pack—choose to live near human ruins? Bats would favor the artificial caves. Hawks might choose to nest at the top of some ruined tower. Small animals like mice and rabbits might den among fallen rocks, but neither bats nor hawks nor the little diggers were a wolf pack's chosen prey. Perhaps deer grazed in the meadows?

Dark Death sensed her confusion and clarified.

"You asked about the maimalodalum. From what you and Blind Seer have told us, the humans who colonized this land and those who colonized further north were alike in one thing at least. They relied upon arts that permitted them to manipulate Magic's power, but they did not teach those arts lightly to those born in their colonies. Nor did they wish their subordinates to easily observe the inner workings of their craft. The place to which we are going, where you will find those who can answer your questions about the maimalodalum, is the primary place in Liglim where the magical arts were done."

Despite herself, Firekeeper felt awe and a surge of fear. She had been suppressing that fear ever since she had learned of the maimalodalum and knew they achieved their goal through magic. Even more than their human neighbors, the Royal Beasts had reason to hate and fear magic, and Firekeeper had been suckled on their tales. More recent events had done nothing to quell her fears, but she could not give in to them without giving up her hopes.

"That follows as certainly as fresh eggshells mean fledglings," Firekeeper replied. "I simply had not thought the matter through."

Her belly rumbled loudly, reminding her that magic or not, she needed food.

"No wonder," laughed Dark Death. "I could not think clearly if my belly was shouting so loudly. Will you catch fish?"

Firekeeper glanced at her surroundings. There was willow aplenty.

"I'll make a fish trap," she said, "and while I see if the fish are fooled, I'll forage. If humans lived here once, their crops may have reseeded. Then, too, some fruit trees live a long time."

"I scent fresh water," Blind Seer said. "While you make your trap, I'll find a source free of salt. There must be many if humans made a village here."

Moon Frost hadn't decided whether she envied Firekeeper for her omnivorous habits or despised her just a little. However, though she had teased Firekeeper, she had always kept her teasing just this side of good manners. So she spoke now.

"And in case the fish aren't to be fooled by traps, and the trees will not give fruit, I will sniff out a rabbit or so. These humps of vine and stone must hold as many warrens as the sky does stars. It would not do for Firekeeper to dine on crickets."

"I'll join you, Moon Frost," Dark Death said. "Even if Firekeeper's hunting is successful, I would not turn away a hot mouthful or so."

They went their separate ways. Firekeeper wove a crude fish trap in very little time. She stilled the worst of her belly rumblings with a few handfuls of fresh watercress, then climbed a tree to see if she could locate in the rise and fall of the tree line where there might have been an orchard. Even her superior night vision could see little more than dark against darkness, but she had learned how to understand what she was seeing.

Despite her hunger, Firekeeper felt very relaxed. The warm air was a caress and the calls of Dark Death to Moon Frost as they harried the rabbits she found as comforting as Derian did the rumble of carriage wheels over city streets. Then a sharp, shrill cry, more yap than howl, broke the easy pattern of night sounds. It cut off far too abruptly.

Firekeeper was down from the tree almost before the sound stopped echoing against the air. She knew that voice. It was Blind Seer's.

Swift as the wolf-woman was, the other two wolves were swifter. They came from different directions, for they had been seeking to drive the game from hiding. Firekeeper saw them leaping over the broken remnants of walls, heard them crashing through bracken and vines, sacrificing stealth for speed.

There was good reason for their choice. Other than that one sharp cry, there had been no further sound from Blind Seer. Wolves, like humans, are very vocal. Unlike humans, wolves suffer beneath no burden of false pride when it comes to asking for aid. Blind Seer should have been crying for help. The only reason he would not were if he were being prevented—or if he were unable.

While Dark Death oriented on the sound, Moon Frost dropped her nose to the ground, casting about for Blind Seer's trail. As this slowed her some, it was Moon Frost that Firekeeper caught up with first.

They exchanged no comments, none of the "What happened?" or "Did you hear what I heard?" that might have colored a human meeting under similar circumstances. Moon Frost followed the scent trail while Firekeeper followed Moon Frost. At the same time, Firekeeper kept an eye in the direction from which the cry had come. Dark Death had stopped and head-raised, was sniffing the air, his golden eyes still and unfocused as he used this much more reliable sense.

Moon Frost slowed as she drew near, pausing with a tangle of vines between her and Dark Death.

"Freshly turned earth," Moon Frost reported, "broken stone, torn plants, and water. Blind Seer's scent is mingled with these, but fainter."

"I smell it this way also," Dark Death said, moving to join them.

Too late Firekeeper recognized what the nose-oriented wolves had missed. As Dark Death stepped forward, the tangle of vines between them bowed beneath his weight. He scrabbled, but the springy vegetation gave him no purchase—and there was nothing beneath the vines that could hold his weight. He fell, giving forth an abbreviated yap far too similar to that which had been the last sound from Blind Seer.

Firekeeper attempted to leap back, but the force of Dark Death's weight had been sufficient to tear loose the already precariously balanced earth beneath her feet. She felt the dirt shift as the rock it rested upon gave. Then she was falling. The last thing she did was make herself limp so that the landing might be easier.

After that, there was only darkness.

FIREKEEPER CAME TO HERSELF with a throbbing head, a sharp ache in her backside, and a lesser one in her shoulders. She heard motion in the darkness around her and took some small hope from it.

"Who's there?" she asked.

Dark Death replied, "I am. I can smell the others, but I have not heard them move. I smell blood as well."

"Hot blood or cold?" Firekeeper asked.

"Cold and hot both," Dark Death assured her. "I hear two breathing, though the note is ragged."

"Hold, hunter," Firekeeper said. "I will try to make a light so that we can move without harming ourselves."

"Firekeeper," came the reply, the notes colored with honest admiration. "I had forgotten."

Normally, Firekeeper would have felt some pleasure at this, for Dark Death was guide, but not really friend. Now all she felt was worry for Blind Seer. She didn't know for how long she had been knocked out, but she knew that however long that had been, Blind Seer had been unconscious longer. Dark Death's report was slim comfort in this situation.

Firekeeper opened the drawstring bag she wore about her neck, locating flint, steel, and tinder by touch. She had made many fires in the dark, but rarely with so little idea of whether once she had the flame would there be anything for her to burn. She could feel bracken all about her, but all nearest to her felt green and flexible.

She tugged off her cotton shirt, wincing at the pain in her upper back. When she had fallen, she must have hit first on her rump, then her shoulders, and lastly her head. The back of this was tender, but there was no blood.

When she had the shirt off and placed to one side, Firekeeper set to work striking sparks. At last a few began smoldering in the tinder. Then a pale flame arose. She fed it with strips torn from one sleeve. Using that increased light, she found drier pieces of wood within the litter of vegetation surrounding her.

Her entire world became that hungry little flame. Her breath existed only to fan it, her reason for being keeping it fed, making it grow. In the surrounding blackness, Dark Death sneezed as the smoke trickled upward, but he had watched her make fires before and knew a little of what she needed. He carried over twigs and hanks of dried vine, augmenting her supply before she ran low.

Firekeeper accepted these offerings automatically, never speaking, saving her breath for nursing the single flame into many. Eventually, the fire was strong enough that she could mix greener material into the fuel. This made for more smoke, but slowed the fire's consumption, made it chew its food rather than swallow it whole. Finally, there came the moment when she could raise her head and see what the darkness had hidden.

Broken slabs of stone canted up from heaps of dirt and vines. Bracken was sprinkled over the whole. On one side, water seeped from a segment of wall. Near this lay Blind Seer, half buried in stone and dirt. Moon Frost was closer to Firekeeper, also partially buried in material that had fallen with them, but it was to Blind Seer that Firekeeper went.

"Don't move anything," she cautioned Dark Death, for the wolf had moved to sniff Moon Frost. "We must look carefully else more may fall on us."

"Remember your own warnings" was the other's reply.

Smoky firelight proved to be enough to reassure Firekeeper that Blind Seer did indeed breathe. She bent her head and smelled his breath. Once she had assured herself that it carried the odor of neither bowel nor blood, she relaxed slightly.

The fire needed feeding, so reluctantly Firekeeper moved back. Once she had it burning brightly, she moved to Moon Frost.

Dark Death crowded next to her.

"What are you doing?" he asked, his nose snuffling next to hers.

"A friend who is a healer taught me something of his art," Firekeeper said. "Smelling the breath tells you if bowel or lung has been broken."

"And what good will this do?" Dark Death asked. "If something is broken, it is broken. Lungs and bowel are both beyond hope, unless one of the talented is near."

Firekeeper held herself from striking him. She knew Dark Death wasn't callous. His way was the practical—even fatalistic—one of the wolf.

"Then you may be pleased to know that neither Moon Frost nor Blind Seer seem to be so harmed. We must uncover them carefully, though, for I cannot tell merely by sniffing if bones are broken or bent. We may do damage if we are not cautious."

"I thought," Dark Death said, "to seize them by the scruff and pull them free."

"No," Firekeeper insisted. "That might cause further injury—or cause further falling of things from above."

Again she moved to tend the fire, thinking over what she had learned from Doc. Perforated bowel was indeed almost certainly fatal. This was because the bowel carried shit out of the body. If the bowel was broken and the shit contaminated what was within, nothing short of a miracle could save the victim.

Lungs were not as bad, for they might mend without spreading contamination, but if they were too badly broken they would collapse and refuse to carry air. Firekeeper did not think any damage had been done to either Blind Seer's or Moon Frost's lungs, but Doc had warned her that sometimes a wound to the lungs was temporarily closed by the very thing—such as a bit of rib—that had made it. This then was one reason for moving the injured ones slowly.

Another was the possibility of broken bones or deep cuts. These also might be concealed or temporarily bandaged by the fallen dirt and stone. Better to be ready to treat them before they were found.

"Are you injured?" she asked Dark Death.

"I ache," the wolf replied, "but the vines held me in their grasp for a moment and I fell more lightly for that. Even so, I hit hard enough that there is a confused space in my memory."

"I am glad you were not more severely hurt," Firekeeper said. "I, too, knew I was falling and so saved myself from the worst. I broke nothing, but I think I will be well bruised."

She began ripping her shirt into bandages, hoping there would be enough fabric. It was fortunate that the Liglimom liked loose clothing.

"Can you scent dawn?" she asked.

"Not from here," Dark Death replied. "My nose is full of dirt."

"Then we had better not await light to move them," Firekeeper said. "I go to get the dirt off of Blind Seer. Can you do the same for Moon Frost?"

"Let me watch you," Dark Death replied. "As I said, I would simply have grasped her by the scruff and hauled her free. You seem to follow other trails."

Using a flat piece of stone, Firekeeper moved a portion of fire nearer to Blind Seer. Once this was settled and fed, she began scooping dirt away, checking as she did so for signs of fresh blood. In several places flat segments of stone or tile—most not much larger than the span of her two hands—had also landed on him. These she removed carefully.

In the few places where she found bleeding, she wiped the blood away and checked to make sure its source was nothing worse than a scrape.

In time, Dark Death moved away and began uncovering Moon Frost. Several times, he called Firekeeper over to inspect the nature of a wound. None were fatal, though it was clear the lower long bone in one of Moon Frost's forelegs had been snapped in two.

Blind Seer was stirring by the time this discovery was made, and Firekeeper whispered in his ear.

"I am here, dear heart. Moon Frost has broken a leg and I must go set it. Wait. Be still."

He raised his head sufficiently to lick her face, then laid it down again as if that had been the greatest effort he had ever made. Somewhat reassured by his understanding her, Firekeeper went to help Moon Frost.

She, too, was coming conscious. Crazed from the pain in her leg, she tried to bite Firekeeper when the wolf-woman moved to touch the injured member.

"Sit on her head," Firekeeper ordered Dark Death. "We have assured there is nothing broken there, and she will hurt herself if she struggles."

Dark Death obeyed, and Firekeeper straightened and splinted the leg, wrapping it with what remained of her shirt. She had thought she might need to sacrifice some of her arrows for the splint, but the debris that had fallen among them included numerous pieces of wood.

At long last, the injured ones were freed. Blind Seer had taken a blow to the head, probably from a falling rock. Firekeeper could feel no broken bones, but the blue-eyed wolf was weak and confused. Whenever he fell asleep, he had to be reminded upon waking where he was and what had happened.

Moon Frost's broken leg was the worst of her injuries. She recalled feeling the ground going out under her and trying to leap. She had hit with legs extended and had felt one bone snap at the impact. Then she recalled nothing but the sensation of being buried alive.

Both wolves were lucky in that they had landed in such a fashion that their heads were not unduly close to the surrounding walls. Had they not, they would have probably suffocated under the wealth of dirt that had fallen with them.

Once she had finished doing what she could for the injured, Firekeeper rigged a torch and inspected their surroundings. They were not encouraging. The hole was very deep and still partially curtained above with fragments of vine. These grew along a few heavy beams that still stretched the breadth of the pit. She also discovered that much of what she had taken for slabs of stone were, in fact, tile.

"We are in a cellar," Firekeeper said, settling next to the fire. "I think that the room above must have been floored in tile over wood. Whether it was broken before Blind Seer stepped on it or whether his weight was enough to break the weakened beams that held up the floor I cannot say."

She paused and studied her surroundings once more.

"What I can say is that I'm not at all certain how we are going to get out of here."

৵⊛

FOR SEVERAL DAYS FOLLOWING HIS RETURN from Misheemnekuru, Derian was permitted to entertain the hope that everything would remain unchanged. No one at u-Bishinti treated him any differently—or at least Varjuna didn't, and Varjuna's people took their lead from him.

Derian did his best to live up to Varjuna's belief in him. He wasn't much good at speeches, and, anyhow, Colby Carter had always said that it wasn't the words that dribbled out of a man's mouth that showed who he was, it was how long he spent settling in his horse after a long ride in bad weather.

Vernita had added that how promptly he paid his bills said something, too.

So despite the treasure of a fine horse and freedom to ride just about anywhere, Derian stayed near u-Bishinti. Unless it was absolutely necessary, he combined his language lessons with some other activity. Sometimes it was something as mundane as helping muck out the infinity of stalls. Other times he offered his assistance with whatever chores would normally have filled his student's day. In this way Derian didn't add to the students' burdens but helped lighten them.

Particularly memorable was the night he spent helping walk a promising young filly who'd gotten into a barrel of apples and given herself a nasty attack of colic. Derian and Poshtuvanu stayed up all night, walking the filly back and forth, back and forth, eventually teaching each other the most creative obscenities either could come up with in either language.

They'd both been punch-drunk come morning, but the filly had pulled through, and Poshtuvanu claimed that he was starting to think in Pellish.

Had it not been for his awareness of how far away his family was and his worry about what Firekeeper might be up to off on Misheemnekuru, Derian would have been completely content.

Then came the morning that Derian rode up to the hill for his customary look at the Wise Horses and found Eshinarvash waiting for him.

Derian's first reaction was to blush so deeply that he felt as if his hair might just crisp and fall right out of his head. Poshtuvanu had told him that only children spied on the Wise Horses, and now Derian had so pushed their patience that Eshinarvash had come to tell him off.

He slid from Prahini's saddle and gripped the mare firmly by the reins. She was sidling back and forth, caught between her awareness that here was a stallion to end all stallions, and an uneasy awareness that though he might smell like a stallion and look like a stallion, Eshinarvash was something Else, something Other.

"Easy, girl, easy," Derian murmured, tightening his grip.

The black-and-white paint rolled an eye and snorted, emphasizing whatever he meant with a stamp of one striped front hoof.

Prahini froze, then dropped her head. A few moments later, she was lipping at the grass in apparent unconcern.

"Well, that told her, didn't it," Derian said, speaking Liglimosh on the assumption that Eshinarvash would be more likely to understand it. "I've seen Firekeeper tell horses off. I bet you said something other than 'Be good or my friend and I will eat you.'"

Eshinarvash didn't reply—nor did Derian expect him to do so.

"Is this about my coming up here?" Derian asked. "If so, I'm sorry. Poshtuvanu told me watching the Wise Horses was in bad taste, but I've never seen anything as beautiful as . . ."

He stopped speaking, for Eshinarvash was shaking his head. The gesture wasn't too like a human head shake, but it was obvious what the stallion meant. Happily, the Liglimom used the same gestures for "yes" and "no" as did the Hawk Havenese, and Derian figured the Wise Horse—like Blind Seer—had learned these gestures to facilitate his communication with humans.

"Not that then," Derian said, thinking aloud. "What then . . ."

Eshinarvash's ears flicked back, just for a moment, but enough to indicate that he was annoyed.

Almost too late, Derian remembered the respect in which the Liglimom held the yarimaimalom. He was in awe of the Wise Horses, but not overwhelmingly so. Moreover, his reaction to Wise—or Royal—Beasts had been colored by Firekeeper's relationship with Blind Seer. Clearly she adored the wolf, but she didn't worship him. These Liglimom, though, how they felt came pretty close. . . .

"How may I be of service?" Derian asked, giving the words the most formal inflection he could.

Eshinarvash cupped his ears forward, then shook his mane and raised his head, pointed up and slightly northward with his nose. For the first time, Derian noticed the osprey perched on a tree branch. From its size and composure, it was obviously Wise.

"Another message from Firekeeper?" Derian guessed.

Eshinarvash shook his skin in frustration; then he knelt as he had the one time he offered Derian a ride.

"You want me to come somewhere with you," Derian said. "What should I do about Prahini? Varjuna will worry if she just comes back and I'm missing."

Eshinarvash looked over his shoulder, renewing his invitation. Derian made a quick decision.

"Wait just a moment."

He went to his saddlebags and removed some of the notepaper he carried with him in case something came up that would assist him in his teaching. On this, he scrawled a quick note.

> Varjuna,
> I have been called away by Eshinarvash. My tack is up on the hill west of u-Bishinti where I take my morning ride. If you could, have someone retrieve it. If

Prahini doesn't make it back to the stables on her own, please have someone look for her.

I wish I could say more, but Eshinarvash isn't a great conversationalist.

Derian made two copies of this unsatisfactory missive and tied one into Prahini's mane. Then he quickly unsaddled and unbridled the mare, putting the tack on the ground in the shade of a small tree. He hoped it wouldn't get ruined. It was just about the nicest set he'd ever had. Then he slapped the mare on her rump.

"Go on with you," he said. "Back to the stables and breakfast."

Prahini stared at him in confusion and astonishment, but when Eshinarvash rose and did another round of the wicker-and-stamp routine, the mare fled at a speed that made Derian fear for her legs.

Derian looked between the Wise Osprey and Eshinarvash.

"Now, I'm not going anywhere without at least trying to send this to Varjuna. Will you carry it to him, Mister Fish Eagle? He's the ikidisdu of the Horse. If you don't know him, I'm sure Eshinarvash can tell you what you need to know. All I'm telling you is that I'm not going anywhere if it will leave my hosts to worry."

Derian was feeling manic and a little light-headed. He kept expecting someone to leap out of the shrubbery and laugh at him for falling for such a trick, but no one appeared. What did happen was that the fish eagle gave a few flaps of his wings and glided rather than flew over near Derian.

Derian secured the note to the osprey's leg, glad for the practice he'd had handling raptors when Edlin Norwood had insisted on taking him hawking during the winters he'd spent in the North Woods. He was gladder still for his friendship with another Royal Raptor, the peregrine falcon Elation. The former might have given him some skill in tying things onto bird's legs, but the latter gave him the confidence he needed to bring his fingers near that deadly beak and those punishing talons.

"Right," Derian said when he was finished. "My thanks to you, Mister Fish Eagle. Now, Eshinarvash, I am yours to command."

The Wise Horse knelt again, and within moments Derian was astride the broad back, hoping he would keep his seat without saddle or stirrups.

The osprey departed in a blur of wings and shrill shriek. Eshinarvash rose, and began picking his way down the hillside, into the lands given as a preserve solely for the use of the yarimaimalom.

I'm in for it this time. Derian thought. *First Misheemnekuru, now this.*

Then Eshinarvash was shifting from a walk into a canter, then into a powerful gallop. Wind ripping through his hair and making his eyes tear, Derian could focus on nothing more complicated than keeping his seat.

XXV

THE DENIZENS OF THE TEMPLE of the Cold Bloods had not anticipated that the release of the shipwrecked sailors would mean their corridors would be receiving regular visits from the northerners. Although Rarby and Shelby professed to be disgusted by the proliferation of reptiles, they did not stay entirely away. The sight of Nolan, Tedgewinn, and Elwyn became so familiar that whoever was on door duty would send a runner to Barnet's quarters as soon as they were seen approaching.

Sometimes the sailors came together, sometimes singly. Rahniseeta, asked by the iaridisdu of the temple to make certain none of the visitors did anything sacrilegious or offensive, quickly caught onto what to expect from each visitor. Nolan had taken seriously the concerns about his health and found the arduous walk up the hill a good constitutional—especially since he could get in a long rest at the top.

Wiatt came more often than Tedgewinn, but both came for the same reason. They wanted to learn what they could about the Liglimom and their culture in order to advance their own prospects. Both had skills to offer—one as a cook, the other as a carver—but lacked comfort with the different culture and trusted the minstrel's instincts.

Rahniseeta found it interesting that Wiatt and Tedgewinn preferred to ask Barnet's advice rather than Waln Endbrook's—especially since Waln was a prosperous merchant. She wondered how much of their profit had he requested in return for his advice.

Elwyn—who seemed to be called "Lucky" as often as by his proper name—simply was a social soul who enjoyed visiting Barnet, and was honestly worried that the minstrel might be lonely. He was the most frequent caller, and for all that his flat-footed awkwardness should have led to disaster after disaster, he alone never touched the wrong thing or turned into a restricted area. Rahniseeta began to believe that he was indeed blessed with luck by the deities.

She was embarrassed to realize that Shelby and Rarby came as much to see her as to see Barnet. For all his surface roughness, Shelby proved to have a streak of romance. A few times he borrowed one of Barnet's guitars and sang. His voice was neither good nor bad, but the subjects of his songs were so sentimental that Rahniseeta found herself blushing.

Rarby's attentions were cruder. He rarely said anything, only stared as if he might see right through her clothing if he tried. Despite the ikidisdu's request, Rahniseeta found herself avoiding Barnet's suite on the occasions the brothers came calling. Happily, they were the least likely of the lot to make the climb to Heeranenahalm.

If she was in when the other sailors called, Rahniseeta asked the doorkeeper to notify her. If she wasn't in, the doorkeeper was instructed to make certain someone brought refreshments—anything to keep the foreigners from being given an excuse to wander the temple. Guards could not be assigned, but if servants "just happened" to be in the vicinity of Barnet's suite when he had visitors, so much the better.

Even within the Temple of the Cold Bloods, which continued to present a veneer of uniform support for what was coming to be called "Tiridanti's Venture"—as if all of u-Liall had not fully supported sending Fayonejunjal forth—factions were forming.

"They are much the same as those put forth more publicly," Harjeedian said to Rahniseeta. "There are those who long for the ability to speak directly with the beasts, those who fear it and wish such study to be banned, those who dread seeing Lady Blysse elevated and the Five transformed to the Six. There's a new faction forming as well."

"What?" Rahniseeta asked.

"Let's not talk here," Harjeedian said. "Derian Carter did not arrive to give lessons this morning as scheduled. I have been asked to drive down to u-Bishinti and make discreet inquiries."

"I'd be glad to get away," Rahniseeta said. She glanced at the list of Barnet's lessons. "Barnet will be at the Temple of Flyers much of the day. He is very popular there and usually stays beyond his lessons. Therefore, he is unlikely to have visitors today. The northerners have made an effort to learn each other's schedules."

Harjeedian looked pleased, and actually took her arm as he escorted her to where the light gig was harnessed and waiting. He climbed into the driver's seat and shook the reins. The bay between the shafts was a livelier creature than the horse Rahniseeta had been given to drive and they left at a fine clip.

As soon as he had a feel for the bay's temper, Harjeedian returned to the subject of Barnet.

"Any popularity any of the northerners can gain—even if for nothing more than a pleasant voice—is to our advantage. I assume it is his musical ability that has won Barnet friends at the Temple of Flyers?"

Rahniseeta fought to keep from coloring, glad that she was sitting to one side, rather than across a table from her brother's discerning gaze.

"I have heard that his voice is among the things that make him popular. One of my friends who sings in the choir there says that Barnet is appreciated for other than his voice—especially by some of the unattached disdum."

Harjeedian laughed, then frowned.

"I hope Barnet is careful with what alliances he makes—and who he risks offending. The Temple of Flyers people can have some rather rigid ideas regarding monogamy. I think it comes from the fact that many bird species mate for life. We don't need further complications."

"No," Rahniseeta agreed. "You were going to tell me about a new faction?"

Harjeedian nodded. He waited until the gig had passed a heavily laden wagon carrying fresh produce into market and they were alone on the road again. Rahniseeta swallowed a sigh. Sometimes it seemed to her that Harjeedian took precautions where none were needed. Then again, she was probably being unfair and Harjeedian was only organizing his thoughts.

"So far," Harjeedian began, "all the factions have been arranged around what we should do—or not do—with the complicated possibilities represented by Lady Blysse's ability and apparent acceptance into the company of the yarimaimalom. However, a new group is arising—one that simply does not want to deal with the matter at all."

Rahniseeta frowned. "I don't see how that could be done."

"Oh, there have been numerous suggestions," Harjeedian said. "The simplest is that we gather up the lot of them and ship them back north. This becomes less simple when people start arguing about what we do with the knowledge they will bring home with them."

"You mean, do we welcome trade or not and on what terms?" Rahniseeta asked. She hadn't spent many hours in the company of the northern sailors without grasping some sense of their priorities.

"Precisely," Harjeedian replied approvingly. "Some want to send a message that we're open to trade. Others want to say essentially, 'You've done fine this long without us. Leave us alone.' Others say, 'Trade is fine. Keep Lady Blysse out of here, though.'"

"I get the picture," Rahniseeta said. "It's already as complicated as a nest of hibernating alligators."

"And about as nice," Harjeedian agreed. "That very complexity has created another faction, one of the most dangerous so far—at least to our northern guests, but I fear to any of us who made that voyage."

"What do you mean?" Rahniseeta said, though she thought she knew. Hadn't she entertained rather ugly thoughts in her own despair?

"Kill them all," Harjeedian said bluntly. "They'll end up listed as missing, but who will know? A bunch of sailors and three wanderers—all of whom have enemies. It may cause some ugliness, but that ugliness won't land here."

"You mentioned danger to those who went on the voyage." Rahniseeta said, not quite making it a question, knowing that this was because she feared the answer.

"That's right," Harjeedian said. "If we take that course, there are going to be those who will worry about someone letting the rest of the snakes out of the bag. They're going to think, 'But those sailors know the way . . . our sailors, true, but they're merchants. Harjeedian isn't a merchant, true, but for the good of the land, for keeping faith with the deities, he'd understand if the deities required his death.'"

"Would you?" Rahniseeta gasped.

"Not unless I read the omens myself," Harjeedian said tersely.

The bay sensed his tension along the reins and craned her neck to glance back at him. Harjeedian shook the reins and she trotted on, content.

"Good," Rahniseeta replied. "And I hope you'd insist on choosing the snake."

"I would," he said. "We all know there are tricks one can use, especially with the lesser beasts. . . ."

He trailed off.

"I sound like one of the blasphemers, don't I? Doubting that the omens come from divine sources."

"You sound like an observant man who knows everyone isn't as devout as himself," Rahniseeta said.

She tried to sound staunch and loyal, but her stomach was twisting. She'd never imagined that Harjeedian would be in danger of losing his life. All he'd done was put his gift for languages at the service of u-Liall. He didn't deserve this.

The gig picked up pace and she realized that the bay mare had quickened in anticipation of home. They said nothing more on the matter.

It's as if we think the horses might be listening, Rahniseeta thought. *We're growing afraid of our own breath.*

She admired Harjeedian's poise as he reined in the mare in the designated area and handed her down from the gig.

To the young woman who came hurrying up, Harjeedian said, "Could you tend the mare for us and tell us where we might find Ikidisdu Varjuna?"

"I would be happy to see to the mare," the woman said. "Varjuna is up at his house. He has been there all day."

For the first time, Rahniseeta realized something was wrong. The woman was tense. She hadn't made the usual show-off gesture of naming the mare and her lineage—a thing those stationed at u-Bishinti often did, as if to show they never forgot a single one of the animals in their care.

Harjeedian sensed the mood as well.

"We need not trouble Varjuna," he said with as much courtesy as if he were addressing u-Liall. "I simply wished to pay my respects. I am actually here to see the northerner, Derian Carter."

The woman's hands stopped in midmotion.

"See Varjuna. He will know where Derian is."

There was dismissal in her tone, not rude, but more as if she had forgotten her manners. Rahniseeta walked with Harjeedian in the direction of the ikidisdu's residence. Zira herself answered the door.

"We are looking for Derian Carter," Harjeedian said after greetings were exchanged. "He did not arrive for the lessons he usually teaches in Heeranenahalm on this day."

Zira motioned them in. "Come with me. Varjuna will wish to see you."

Rahniseeta knew that the iaridisdu of the Horse had her residence in Heeranena-halm, so she was surprised to find her sitting with Varjuna in a comfortably shabby office. The iaridisdu of the Horse was quite old, old enough to have given up riding. Everyone knew that Varjuna usually called on her rather than the other way around. Yet here the old woman sat, looking quite exhausted.

Harjeedian and Rahniseeta said all the correct formal things, and then Harjeedian asked again.

"Might it be possible for us to see Derian Carter? He did not arrive to teach today, as would be usual, and I was asked to make certain he was well."

Varjuna glanced at the iaridisdu. She nodded.

"You might as well know," Varjuna said, "but we'd prefer you'd keep it quiet. As of yet the matter seems exclusively one for our temple."

Harjeedian responded quickly, "I will keep silence—although I beg leave to tell my superiors."

"I can leave," Rahniseeta put in.

Varjuna shook his head. "Stay, child. Derian has always spoken well of you and I know you will keep silence if asked. The fact is, Derian vanished this morning. He went out for a ride in the early morning as he usually does. His mare returned without him, but with a note tied into her forelock. Later, I found a rather tattered copy of the same note lying in the middle of my desk."

Varjuna handed a piece of paper to Harjeedian, and the aridisdu held it so Rahniseeta might read it with him.

"Eshinarvash is the Wise Horse who honored Derian by letting him ride on his back," Harjeedian said. "It does not sound as if Derian was frightened—confused maybe, but not frightened."

"We're taking some hope in that, too," Harjeedian said, "and in the fact he had energy to worry about his tack. The thing is, the Wise Horses will offer nothing further. The liaison—not Eshinarvash this time—came forth but was politely noncommittal when I asked after Derian. The iaridisdu had no greater luck."

Rahniseeta now understood why the old woman was there. Aridisdum read omens and divined the will of the deities. This silence was disturbing—especially since there was no doubt that the Wise Horses themselves were directly involved.

"We've searched the grounds for Derian, but there is no sign of him. One of my younger sons is good at tracking, and he says it does seem as if a Wise Horse climbed up to where Derian typically rode. Derian had a child's passion for the Wise Horses and they did not seem to take offense. There even seems to be some sign that Eshinarvash knelt."

"As he would to take on a rider?" Rahniseeta heard herself ask. Derian had related his marvelous ride on the Wise Horse several times, and this detail had stayed with her.

"That's right," Varjuna said.

"In brief then," Harjeedian said, "one of the northerners is gone—possibly taken away by one of the Wise Horses—and we don't know where or why."

"Or even," Varjuna added somberly, "if he's still alive."

"HOW ARE YOU DOING with Waln Endbrook?" asked the master.

He always began these private meetings with Shivadtmon in this fashion. The repeated words infused the routine meetings with a note of ritual, and the master was very aware of how important ritual could be—important and powerful.

"Very well, Master," Shivadtmon replied. "Waln has become very interested in Misheemnekuru. I am making certain he receives access to written material about the islands."

"Have you guided him toward the interior?"

"It was hardly necessary, Master. As you have already noted, Waln Endbrook is not a stupid man. He realizes that raiding an area that is within full view of the mainland would be extremely foolish. Moreover, he has noted that one of the interior islands is recorded as possessing a cluster of buildings."

"And buildings, of course," the master said, "would be very good places to search for treasure. What are the northerners doing with the freedom you so kindly acquired for them?"

"They have reestablished their social contacts with Barnet Lobster. Waln has visited the library in Heeranenahalm. He concentrated on old maps."

"Very good. Now you must help him to move his plan along. However, it is essential that he not move on Misheemnekuru until Lady Blysse returns. Is that understood? Even if you must manufacture some reason for the sailors to be put under house arrest once more, they must not leave for Misheemnekuru while Lady Blysse is there."

"The omens are that bad?" Shivadtmon asked.

"The omens splinter into chaos," the master said. "They are much clearer when she is not present at the time set for sailing."

"I understand," Shivadtmon said solemnly.

The master nodded, colleague to colleague, but he doubted that Shivadtmon had the faintest idea how heady were the currents the master had tasted of late. How could he? That was a secret the master was keeping to himself—and would continue to keep until what he had sensed dwelling in the heart of Misheemnekuru was destroyed.

DAWN CAME SLOWLY to those trapped in the cellar, filtering pale light through the lacework of broken vines that still clung to the beams overhead. One by one, Firekeeper let her fires go out, glad for relief from the smoke.

In the pale light, she inspected their situation and found it no more encouraging in daylight than it had been in darkness. If anything, it was more discouraging. In darkness there had been hope. In daylight, there was none.

Firekeeper paced the perimeter of the cellar, inspecting the walls with minute care.

"What are you looking for, Firekeeper?" asked Dark Death.

He was the only one awake. The other two slept as only injured animals slept, seeking healing in dreams.

She didn't pause in her restless circuit.

"This was once a cellar—a room beneath the ground," she explained. "Humans built it, so they must have had a way to get into it. I had hoped to find a staircase, but I think they must have used ladders."

"Ladders?"

"Stairs are like this." Firekeeper built a rough model with some segments of broken tile. "You climb them as you would a rock, each stair a foothold. Ladders are more like leaning trees. They have footholds, too, but more shallow. Staircases are fixed. Ladders can or cannot be. I see no place where a staircase would have been, so I guess they must have used a ladder."

She inspected the cellar further. The hole they were in was very deep. The walls looked to have once been sheathed in stone. It was odd to think that people would have gone to so much trouble and then gone up and down via ladders. Then again, a stairwell could be concealed behind one of the enormous piles of dirt and debris that had fallen with them.

We could dig, she thought, *but that would just make us tired and hungry. There is no promise that even if we found a staircase it would still be solid. If the builders made the treads of wood, they would have rotted long ago.*

Dark Death rose and padded over to the seep. The water from it was fresh, probably from the same source Blind Seer had been tracking when he fell. The sound of Dark Death's lapping was the loudest sound in the enclosed space. In contrast, the morning songs of the birds without was distant and unreal.

Firekeeper continued her inspection. The task before her was almost impossibly difficult. She must get not only herself but three wolves out of this deep hole. Normally, the wolves' size was to their advantage, but down here, where vibrations might cause further landslides, it added to the difficulty. Moreover, two of the wolves were injured and could not be expected to move with their usual strength and grace.

She paused before a mound of dirt and debris, the one under which Moon Frost had been trapped. It reached halfway to the edge of the pit, but the material that made it up was loose and compacted under Firekeeper's weight. She could not climb here, nor could she climb even if she moved all the dirt and made a great heap. It would still be too soft to bear her weight.

Before Firekeeper had left the mainland, Harjeedian had urged several items of camping gear on her. She had accepted the canteen and medical kit with alacrity. Now she wished she had taken his offer of a length of strong line.

You could have carried it wrapped around your waist, Little Two-legs, she thought, calling herself by her puppy name as she often did when angry with herself, *but you did not wish to be encumbered. Still, maybe there will be a way.*

One thing there was in quantity was vines. Generations of the plants must have snaked across the cellar, gradually creating the impression of solidity that had fooled Blind Seer. The vine mat might even have been dense enough to bear the weight of a small creature like a mouse or rabbit.

Especially if it grew across remnants of the floor—or should I think of it as a ceiling, since I am now below? I felt something give before Moon Frost and I fell. I suspect the ceiling had held until then.

With a methodical patience that would have surprised those of her human friends who thought her impulsive, Firekeeper sorted through the tangle of twisting vines. Moon Frost awoke while she was doing so and lay watching for a time.

"What are you doing, Firekeeper? Are you finding what you can eat and what you cannot? Remember that wolves cannot eat vines. We eat meat."

Firekeeper knew the wolf was in pain from her broken leg. There had been nothing in the medical kit Harjeedian had given her that would dull pain in something the size of the wolf. For this reason, Firekeeper excused Moon Frost's rudeness—and even the threat implicit in her final statement.

"I cannot eat vines either," she said, "or at least not to get nourishment from them. I am hoping to make a rope from the greenest and longest lengths. The small dry pieces I set aside for kindling, so if night finds us here again, I can make a fire."

"Rope?" Moon Frost asked, tilting her head to one side. "I have seen rope, but how will it help us here?"

"If I can make a rope strong enough to bear my weight, I hope to get it over one of those beams above. I have been studying them, and that central one looks sturdier than the rest. It may have been protected from the worst of the weather by the flooring above it."

"So then you are out," Moon Frost snapped. "I have seen you climb like a squirrel. The rest of us cannot climb so."

"No, but from above I may be able to get help. Would your kin not come?"

Dark Death replied. "Closest kin are my pack, across the inlet we would have crossed last night, but Firekeeper, what good would they do? All they could do is drop in food and sing dirges when at last we die. They cannot change the nature of this trap. I do not think any Beast could do so."

Firekeeper was startled. She had already thought of several ways they might get out of the hole. True, they were adaptations of things she had learned from humans, but didn't the Wise Wolves know human ways?

She didn't wish to anger the wolves by questioning their abilities. It hadn't taken

Moon Frost's words to make her aware that she was trapped in a hole with three large carnivores. Blind Seer would not eat her—at least not unless she was already dead and he was truly hungry—but these other two might feel differently, especially if starvation was chewing out their bellies.

Nor did she think Blind Seer could protect her. He was stronger than he had been the night before, but the blow to his head had made him disoriented. This was not a condition in which she would wish a fight on him.

To turn the conversation away from this, Firekeeper asked something that had been much in her thoughts.

"Do your people ever call on the humans for help? Let us say in a circumstance like this one where they might be of assistance or in a time of flood or storm?"

"Never," Dark Death replied. "The ban against humans coming to Misheemnekuru is absolute. If we cannot help ourselves, we die."

Moon Frost agreed.

"Even those of us who guard the territories closest to where the humans dwell observe this. Our stories tell of times long past when the occasional heavily armed human violated our sanctuary. We dealt with them ourselves, even when the humans offered aid."

Firekeeper had enough long lengths of strong, green vine by now and started plaiting a rope. It was tedious work, and more than once she had to start over when a section proved too brittle. After a time, she learned which vines would handle the strain of being worked without breaking and the process moved along more quickly.

Silence had followed the discussion of whether aid could come to them, but now Dark Death snuffled at her handiwork.

"What are you doing, Firekeeper? Why do you twist the pieces that way?"

"I make them stronger," she said. "It is like a wolf pack. Three are stronger than one, and if there is one that finds itself a bit weak, then the other two will keep it from breaking. Even before I knew humans, I did a little of this, but humans have taught me a better way. I would prefer lengths of hide, but these should do."

"Will these bits of vine hold you?"

"There is only one way to know," Firekeeper replied levelly, "and that will be in the testing."

By the time she finished her rope, the sun was high enough to make them glad for the shadows cast from above.

Firekeeper took up her bow; she had carried it in her hand when she fell and it had not been damaged. To the shaft of an arrow she attached the vine rope, then put the arrow to the string.

"This will be easier than throwing," she explained, seeing Moon Frost struggling not to cringe at the proximity of the weapon. The wolves knew well how deadly an arrow could be. "All of you come away from the walls and back from that central beam. If anything collapses further, we should be safe."

Blind Seer was awake enough to understand this and staggered away from where he had lain close to the seep, both so that he might drink without effort and to cool himself. It hurt Firekeeper to see him so, his fur matted with wet and moving as if he were older than Neck Breaker and Cricket combined. Still, she said nothing. Weakness was not coddled among wolves, and she knew he would not appreciate her hovering over him.

Instead, Firekeeper got the rope over the beam with her first try. The rope hung over the beam, and with a few jumps, Firekeeper grasped the arrow and pulled the end down where she could reach it. Then she secured the rope to the beam, holding her breath while she did so. This was the critical point. The vines could more easily bear weight than they could take further twisting, but still they might break. To her great relief, they held.

"Watch lest my climbing makes something fall," she warned.

"Firekeeper," Blind Seer said, "make good your boast."

Climbing rope was not like climbing trees or rocks, but the fight to take Smuggler's Light had taught Firekeeper a few things. She climbed mostly with the strength in her arms, using her feet when necessary. Her shoulders ached where they had struck the ground in her fall, protesting this continued hard use, but she ignored them.

As it took her weight, the beam creaked. Dirt pattered around the edges into the cellar. She heard one of the wolves sneeze.

Then she was at the top and must switch her grip from rope to beam. Firekeeper thought about climbing on top of the beam and walking along it, but dreaded that the jolt as her weight landed on top might cause the old wood to crack. Instead, laboriously, hand over hand, she made her way along the length.

Beneath her fingers the beam was rough and splintery in some places, slippery with rot in others, but Firekeeper maintained her grip. She could feel the hot breath of the wolves as they paced her from below, but could not spare the breath to warn them away. When at last she reached the edge, she saw the beam was set into mortar. It looked secure, so she heaved herself up and onto the solid ground above. Little crumbs of greyish stone trickled down, but the old wood held.

A slide of dirt and bits of stone followed the impact of her landing, but the wolves were prepared for the possibility and took no worse injury than a patina of dirt on their fur. She heard further sneezing.

Firekeeper stood, careful to keep back from that treacherous edge, and heard the wolves howl their pleasure when they saw her rise.

"Bravely done," Dark Death said. "Now that you are up, what plans have you for us?"

Firekeeper shook the dirt from herself and dabbed at a few scrapes on her mostly unprotected skin. Her shirt and much of her trousers had gone for kindling, bandages, and wash rags.

"Remember what I told you of stairs and ladders?" she replied. "I will make you such. We will test where the edge is sound and you will come up that way. First, though, I think I will hunt for you. Even strong wolves need food if they are to mend."

Her fish trap yielded several slim silvery fish, each as long as her forearm. Firekeeper kept one for herself, then tossed the others down, making sure one landed near Blind Seer. She was pleased to see that—contrary to usual wolfish manners—neither Moon Frost nor Dark Death crowded him out of his meal.

Of course, they know he is my pack mate, and they need me to get them out of that hole.
Firekeeper kindled herself a small fire and set her chosen fish to cook above it.

Howling wolves and strange vibrations in the earth had made the rabbits skittish, but nonetheless Firekeeper set snares. A yearling buck, uneducated as to the reach of a long bow, proved less cautious than the rabbits and Firekeeper was able to kill it with two well-placed arrows. Venison was better food for wolves, and adequately fed, they settled to wait for her to tell them what to do.

This is a good thing about wolves, Firekeeper thought. *Humans would worry and fuss, ask many questions, and waste my time with the need to answer them.*

But she couldn't help but think that perhaps just such human worrying had been what created ladders, staircases, and the other tools she was coming to appreciate.

There is something to be said for both ways. Perhaps Blind Seer is right and there is some value even in things that seem useless.

After finishing her fish, several handfuls of watercress, and a rather tart apple, Firekeeper went back to the problem of how to get the wolves out of the cellar. First she established which edge was most stable. This done, she used a length of vine to measure the depth she needed to bridge.

Dark Death gripped it in his teeth, saving her the need to weight it, and cooperatively moving back and forth so Firekeeper could judge the added distance needed to deal with angles, since the wolves could not be expected to climb straight up. Blind Seer had managed in the tunnels beneath Thendulla Lypella, but Moon Frost's foreleg was broken and Dark Death had never even seen a ladder in use. Had Blind Seer not been injured, he might have demonstrated, but Firekeeper was leaving nothing to chance.

A stairway would have been best, but Firekeeper knew that it would take days to haul rocks of large enough size to be of use. Then, too, she was not sure she could build a staircase. She tried a few in miniature, but they did not seem stable.

A ladder, then, must answer. She had saved the hide and sinews from the yearling buck so there would be no need to fuss with brittle vines. Her camping gear included a small but very solid hatchet. She'd already learned the usefulness of axes, but had never had one of her one. During this venture she had come to love the hatchet almost as much as she did her Fang.

The wolves remained patient as she cut and trimmed two solid young trees for the side supports, then made the rungs from thick sections of branch on which she left the bark for better traction. It was a very long process, made more so by several false starts before Firekeeper worked out the best ways to tie things together.

She resolved to make a better study of tying knots. Hadn't the sailors aboard *Fayonejunjal* always been tying things together? Perhaps if she could keep her stomach from troubling her, she could learn from them.

By midafternoon, the rabbits had grown less cautious and Firekeeper found several in her snares. All but one she tossed down to the wolves, and once again neither of the others denied Blind Seer his share. The blue-eyed wolf showed signs of recovery, and when Firekeeper at last completed the ladder, he volunteered to test it.

"Let me see if it bears my weight, first," Firekeeper said. "Then we will see about the rest of you."

As before, everyone stood back from the edge while she placed the ladder, but the earth seemed to have stabilized and only token bits fell. Firekeeper clambered down the ladder, noting where the rungs needed tightening. After she had done so, she ran up and down it a few times until it did not shift in the least.

Blind Seer shouldered her back.

"Now it is my time," he said. "I have climbed these before."

Firekeeper braced the base of the ladder as Blind Seer went up. He moved steadily, but to she who knew him there was a trace of hesitation on a few steps. After he was up, there was no stopping the others from trying. Dark Death made a few false starts before understanding how he must balance, but with her broken foreleg Moon Frost could not manage.

"I can tuck it beneath me on the flat," she said, "but here I fall to the side."

"I have thought on this," Firekeeper said. "I must carry you to the top. I will need my arms, so you must drape yourself over my back and let my arms and legs serve as your own. We will bind your leg so that it will not be jarred."

She made this suggestion calmly enough and hoped her scent would not give away her fear. After all, not so long ago Moon Frost had tried to kill her. It seemed that Moon Frost, too, thought of their battle, but in a different way.

"I understand. I will ride your back as you rode mine. It will be awkward, but I have seen how strong you are."

Firekeeper had been long enough among humans that she was astonished by the wolf's trust, but after a moment she accepted it. In the wolf way the beaten one knew her place. Someday Moon Frost might challenge Firekeeper again, but not here and not now.

Indeed, that I help her when she is injured makes me even more her senior. I had forgotten. The strong assist the weak, not the weak the strong.

Even with Moon Frost cooperating as best she could, the climb was arduous. Firekeeper's shoulder throbbed and every bruise in her body shouted its complaint. Moreover, wolves grow hot when they are frightened and Moon Frost could not have helped being afraid, especially since the movement had to hurt her broken leg. She panted alongside Firekeeper's face as the wolf-woman carried her upward, and Firekeeper thought she would smother in the hot moist air.

As she climbed, the wolf-woman paused to rest several times. Just as she was thinking she could not do more, that they must find another way, the weight across her back grew less. At first Firekeeper thought Moon Frost was losing her hold. Then she realized that the wolf was sliding upward. It was a strange sensation, but Firekeeper held herself steady and when Moon Frost's tail dragged over her head, she looked up.

Dark Death was looking down, panting laughter.

"I dragged her by the scruff of her neck as a mother does a puppy. She weighs a bit more, but we got her up without harming her."

Firekeeper mounted to the top of the ladder and punched Dark Death in the shoulder.

"Clever," she said. "Now cool water for me. When does your tide lower enough for us to swim across?"

"Later tonight," Dark Death said. "Rest this afternoon. I will hunt for all of you."

"Stay away from the ruins," Firekeeper said. "I don't know if I'm up to getting anyone else out of a pit."

"Of course you are," Dark Death said, wagging his tail in admiration. "You know how to build ladders."

XXVI

WALN HAD FEARED THAT A DOSE of freedom would diminish Tedgewinn's enthusiasm for his plan to raid a ruin or two on Misheemnekuru and then return home in triumph. Nor was he comforted when he learned that both Tedgewinn and Wiatt were making inquiries into the possibilities of doing business with the Liglimom.

Relief came when Waln realized that Tedgewinn and Wiatt were looking into business opportunities not because they didn't plan to go home but precisely because they did. They wanted to return to Liglim with ships loaded with goods that would sell. Wiatt was even toying with the idea of an inn that would provide northern-style meals and comforts for what he thought would be a steady stream of business.

"And once I get it running well," Wiatt said, daydreaming aloud, "I can go home during the worst of these summers and come back in time to spend the winter here."

For Waln, whose dreams included an order of knighthood, his title restored, and his wife and daughters waiting on the queen, inns and curios seemed small beer, but he was glad enough to encourage such if it kept the sailors working with him.

Then Shivadtmon came with an interesting rumor.

"There is talk a ship is being outfitted to take you people back north before the worst of winter," he said.

"How certain is this rumor?" Waln asked.

Shivadtmon gave a quietly superior smile.

"So certain that I should not call it rumor. You know how closely our temple is associated with the sea. Who else would be asked if the omens favor such a venture? Then, too, we own several of the best vessels. *Fayonejunjal* is partly owned by our temple."

"I didn't know that," Waln said, feeling that he had been given another piece of the puzzle.

He had always wondered why Shivadtmon so strongly disliked Harjeedian. Now he realized that Shivadtmon—and indeed all his temple—must have been offended at having an aridisdu of the Temple of the Cold Bloods chosen over one of their number to serve aboard *Fayonejunjal*.

"It is so," Shivadtmon said smugly. "We have many good shipbuilders among us."

"So a ship is actually being outfitted?" Waln asked. "Are we being sent home?"

Shivadtmon shook his head. "The matter is not that settled. However, there are those who think that your return to your homelands would be a good thing. To make these content, the ship is being readied, so if a decision is reached there will be less delay in taking action."

"Wise, wise," Waln mused aloud. "The heart of winter is a nasty time for sailing, as is early spring. If a ship wasn't ready, we might be forced to remain until later spring."

Waln couldn't believe his luck. He was almost inclined to believe in the deities. One of the weak spots in his plan had been exactly how they would acquire the necessary vessel to carry them home. The Liglimom had ample fishing vessels, and Waln had thought he would need to beg, buy, or steal one of these. Indeed, he had already taken to walking the docks in the evening so he might inspect the ships as they came in.

If a ship is being readied for the purpose of taking us home, Waln thought, *we'll hardly even be stealing it. I must find out who the crew members are to be. Certainly some of them will be those who have made the voyage before. I can sway them to serve under me—especially if I have wealth with which I can pay them.*

Aloud, Waln said, "I wonder who the disdu for the voyage will be? Have you thought of asking for the post? I would so enjoy having the opportunity to show you my homeland as you have shown me yours."

Shivadtmon smiled a tight-lipped smile.

"I have offered my services," he said, "but the iaridisdu of my temple reminded me that the voyage is far from a certainty—and that in any case, who will serve if there is a voyage will be chosen by the will of the deities."

"So true," Waln said. He made a great show of pulling out his chair and readying his books.

"Well then, be seated. I know a busy man like yourself doesn't have all day. Let us apply ourselves to Pellish. After all, a gift for languages was all Harjeedian had going for him when he was chosen. With a little hard work, we can make the deities' choice obvious."

Shivadtmon's face grew tight. For a moment Waln thought he might have pushed too hard. Then the aridisdu relaxed.

"You have an odd way of stating things, Waln Endbrook, but I believe your desire to help me is sincere. By all means, let us study Pellish. However, would you care to tour the harbor with me this evening? Several ships are being considered for the journey, and I would like the opinions of a talented sailor like yourself as to which might best serve."

Fighting an urge to drag the man to the harbor that very moment, Waln nodded.

"I would be delighted," he said with a smile. "Delighted to be of service."

ESHINARVASH SLOWED TO A CANTER when u-Bishinti was well behind them.

I wonder if Eshinarvash put on the burst of speed to make sure I'd be out of range for any easy retreat? Derian thought. *Does this mean I've been kidnapped again? Or is he just showing off?*

Now that they had slowed, Derian felt more comfortable taking a look at their surroundings. They were moving through an open valley, the green fields interspersed with clumps of deciduous trees. In the distance he saw a small lake spreading like a mirror to catch the sun.

There was no sign of any of the Wise Horse herds, but he glimpsed a doe and fawn watching them from one of the clumps of trees. Another time he caught a flash of red that had to be a fox. Birds were present in countless numbers, from little seed eaters to the occasional wind-riding hawk circling lazily above.

The whole area had a managed look, and Derian wondered if the Wise Horses permitted periodic human incursion. Elsewhere untended land rapidly went over to young forests intertwined with vines and scrub growth. Then Derian had a startling thought.

What if the Wise Horses manage it themselves—they and the other yarimaimalom? Saplings that sprout where they are not wanted could be trimmed by browsers and grazers. Beaver are always cutting down trees for their dams. Overgrazing is only a problem when the animals are penned and too stupid to move on. What if the herds discipline themselves?

It was an interesting theory. Derian found himself looking for indications that he might be correct, but Eshinarvash was moving too swiftly for easy inspection. This forced Derian back on his own thoughts for company.

Why am I out here? Varjuna told me about the different factions, and most of them don't seem to like us much. What if the yarimaimalom have factions, too? They've run the shop here for a long time. There have got to be those who don't like the idea of changing the way things work. If there's one thing Firekeeper has let slip, it's that the Beasts— call them Wise or call them Royal—are no more perfect than we are.

Unlike the night of his first ride with Eshinarvash, Derian found it hard to nurse such apprehensions. If the Wise Horse wanted him dead, he could have thrown and trampled him long before. Moreover, though the summer day was hot, Derian was washed with a cooling breeze. The surrounding landscape was lovely, and, perhaps most important for Derian Carter, he was riding the most magnificent horse he had ever seen.

After a time, Derian realized that they were closing on a clump of trees large enough to be termed a small forest. Eshinarvash was slowing, confirming that this was their destination. A stream meandered out of the shadowy coolness, and at the sound of running water Derian realized that he was thirsty—hungry, too. He usually took his morning ride before eating breakfast and the handful of sugared nuts he had snagged on his way out the door had long since been burned away.

When Eshinarvash stopped, Derian didn't need the slight shivering of the horse's skin to tell him to dismount. He slid to the ground, noting as he did so that both he and the horse were rather sweaty. He was also quite stiff. Riding bareback used different muscles than did riding with a saddle, nor did the shape of a horse's spine agree with a human backside.

He stretched up, then out, trying to work out the kinks.

"If you drink there," Derian said, pointing to a small pool, "I'll take my water from above. Don't worry. I won't muddy it."

But though Eshinarvash must have been thirsty, he did not move to drink. Instead he walked slowly back and forth in the shade.

He's walking himself cool! Derian thought in astonishment. *I guess I never thought about it, but even a Wise Horse would be subject to colic. I wonder what they do about stones in their hooves?*

Derian resolved that, if Eshinarvash would permit, he'd check him over just as he would any other riding horse before they went any farther. Meanwhile, he'd tend to his own needs.

He had been forced to leave without much more than he kept hanging on his belt, but that meant he had a knife and the belt wallet in which he kept various useful sundries. None of these included a cup, but his hands served. He splashed off the worst of the horse and man sweat, then set about considering possibilities for breakfast.

A blackberry bramble supplied several handfuls of tart fruit, but this made him rather more hungry than otherwise.

If I had fishhooks, I could try for fish, but I don't, and anyhow, I don't know for how long Eshinarvash plans to stop here. I'm sure both of us have frightened off any small game—even if I had the means for catching it. I'm no Firekeeper to make a snare from a few bent twigs. Maybe I should have paid better attention to Race and Edlin.

Derian compromised by eating some young sassafras leaves. They were slimy when chewed, but tasted nice and gave the impression that he had something in his stomach. When he returned from his foraging to find Eshinarvash grazing on the thick grass closest to the stream, Derian felt positively jealous.

He resolved not to show it, but rounded out his repast with several more handfuls of water.

"Let me take a look at your feet," Derian said to the horse. "You've done a lot of running."

Eshinarvash nickered in what seemed a conversational fashion. He didn't say "yes," but then he didn't shake his head "no" either. Derian walked over and lifted the near front hoof. With a few minutes' inspection, he learned a great deal more about the Wise Horses.

They differed from domesticated horses in more ways than their intelligence and wildly patterned coats. The walls of their hooves were thicker, the frog less vulnerable. Cracks and splits wouldn't be common, nor would strains.

Derian ran his hand along Eshinarvash's foreleg and could feel the strength of the bone. Somehow he could sense the density. The weight of the bone was what he would have expected in a much larger horse. Whatever the Wise Horses' origin, they were well adapted to their lives.

"I bet you have a better digestion, too," Derian said, "at least more tolerant of change."

He finished his inspection of Eshinarvash's feet and wandered over to a small heap of dung. He kicked a horse apple open with one boot toe and inspected it. He couldn't tell for certain, but the contents seemed to prove his conjecture.

"You people don't fit the picture," Derian said aloud. "Wolves, jaguars, deer, all the rest are animals we think of as wild. Horses, though . . . All the wild ones I've seen are more like strays, feral—descendants of horses let loose at some time. It's hard to judge based on one horse, but it seems to me you're a separate breed. Did you come about it naturally, like a jaguar does her spots, or did something else happen?"

Eshinarvash's ears flickered as he listened, but he did not comment, nor did Derian expect him to do so.

"Is it safe for me to go past the fringes of the trees?" Derian asked. "I'm still hungry."

Eshinarvash raised his head and then carefully nodded.

"I can go into the forest?"

Nod.

"Right."

Damn, that was weird. I mean, I should be used to it by now, but no matter how I try, it still gets me. I know Roanne understood me well. Prahini is learning, but Eshinarvash understands me as well as Varjuna does. I'll take his word that the forest is safe, but I don't think I'll go too far. He might not think about how vulnerable an unarmed human is. I don't have his strength or ability to trample.

Rather than risking getting lost, Derian stayed close to the stream. As he walked, he tried to remember the type of things Firekeeper had brought to augment his meals when they had traveled together. This helped, as did judicious sampling of likely looking leaves. His best find was a beech tree with nuts beginning to ripen. Before this he had thought the little nut meats too small to merit the labor needed to extract them, but now they were welcome.

No longer hungry, if not precisely full, Derian returned to where Eshinarvash had made great inroads into the grass along the stream. The horse was still grazing, but more idly.

Derian glanced up at the sun.

"I've filled the worst of the holes," he said, then clarified when the horse twitched his ears back and forth. "That is, I'm fed. If there's somewhere you need to take us, just let me know."

In reply, Eshinarvash walked over next to a large rock that would do quite nicely for a mounting block.

"We're off, then?" Derian said. "Right."

He mounted with ease. Although he preferred a saddle, he'd been on and off horses as long as he could remember, and many times he'd pulled himself up onto old Hauler or one of the other quieter horses rather than walk. His rear end protested the abuse, but Derian ignored it. He had other things to think about.

Eshinarvash's original course had taken them west, but slowly he was angling north. U-Bishinti was south of u-Seeheera, and Derian wondered just how close to the city they would come.

Taking me west could have been a means of getting me out of sight of u-Bishinti. I wonder if this forest connects up with the one we rode through on our first trip back to u-Seeheera from u-Bishinti? But if he only needed to take me to the city, why all this fuss? Why not just come out and get me? Why do it so early?

The most logical reason was because the Wise Horse did not wish all of u-Bishinti to be buzzing with gossip regarding Derian's departure.

I hope I didn't mess things up with the note I sent Varjuna, but Eshinarvash let me send it. Maybe he trusts Varjuna to keep a close tongue where the affairs of the Wise Horses are concerned. I'll bet anything he does. But why take me to the city, then?

By late afternoon, Derian was certain that they were not going to u-Seeheera. Beneath the cover of the foliage it was hard for him to keep track of directions, but he caught frequent enough glimpses of the sun to be sure that they weren't moving in circles. Although Eshinarvash had indeed brought them back east somewhat, they must have long ago passed the city.

Eshinarvash had also taken some steps to assure Derian's comfort. They stopped repeatedly so both could stretch, cool, and drink. At the third or fourth of these stops, Derian was delighted to find an injured fish swimming in one of the shallow pools. There was no sign of disease; rather, it looked as if it had escaped fatally injured from the clutches of some predator.

Derian hadn't grown up on the banks of a major river without learning how to clean and cook fish. His wallet contained flint and steel, and though he didn't have Firekeeper's gift for kindling a fire, he did well enough.

When a fish in similar condition was waiting at their next stop, Derian stopped believing in luck.

"You have someone helping us," he said to Eshinarvash.

The Wise Horse blew out his breath as if to say, "Of course!"

"Thank whoever it is for me," Derian said. "This would have been a hard ride on an empty stomach."

The horse's ears twitched and flattened at the idiomatic expression. Derian laughed.

"You know perfectly well that I wasn't calling you an empty stomach. Poshtuvanu told me that the expression is very similar in Liglimosh. What I was saying was that I would have found it hard to go so long without something substantial to eat."

Toward evening, they stopped again and Derian had the impression that this stop would be for a longer period of time. This time, the fish catchers were waiting to get a look at him. They proved to be a pair of otters, slender, shining brown, and as self-possessed as cats. They did not seem markedly larger than the otters Derian had glimpsed in the Flin River, but then size would not be a great advantage to a creature who lived in streams and must snake easily through small gaps when the waters ran low.

One of the otters nosed a fish across to Derian, and though by this time Derian would have been ready for a change of diet, he accepted it gratefully. When he cleaned it, he started to bury the guts, then remembered that Firekeeper always offered them to Blind Seer or Elation.

"Would you like these?" he asked the otters.

The bolder of the pair made as if to move closer, but hesitated. Derian understood.

"Stand clear," he said, and tossed them over using an underhand motion he hoped would not seem threatening.

Derian was aware of Eshinarvash standing by, slowly chewing a mouthful of grass, and wondered if he was somehow translating—or at least clarifying what Derian said. Did all the yarimaimalom speak Liglimosh? Somehow Derian didn't think so. Fire-keeper had once told him that at the time of their first meeting the falcon Elation had understood Pellish far better than Firekeeper herself had. Indeed, Firekeeper had needed to be taught the language. By implication, Blind Seer had not understood it at all, though he had most certainly learned.

I wonder if I'm here as some sort of substitute for Firekeeper. She understands them, but she's off running and howling with the wolves on Misheemnekuru. What could there be that couldn't wait for her return?

He didn't like that thought much, but by now he was completely confident that whatever the reason Eshinarvash wanted him, at least some of the yarimaimalom didn't mean him any harm. Washed and filled with fish, Derian made himself as comfortable as possible on the grass.

"Wake me if you need me," he said to Eshinarvash, and despite various aches he had been certain would keep him awake, he dropped instantly off to sleep.

WHEN HE WOKE, it was full dark and markedly cooler. Eshinarvash was nosing him, his breath warm and smelling of chewed grass. Derian hadn't put out his last fire, but had banked it down as low as he could, hoping to use the coals to start a new one.

To his surprise, the fire was already burning fairly strongly and what he glimpsed in the firelight was more astonishing than the fire.

A contingent of yarimaimalom sat just visible in the glow. Derian recognized the otters—or at least two very like them. He was less comfortable with the two great cats who sat there. One was a jaguar, the other a puma. There was an owl as well, a great horned barn owl that kept twisting its head away from the light, then twisting it back to get another look at Derian.

They don't look like they're planning to eat me, he thought slightly hysterically. He took a second look at the two great cats. *I don't think I'd make much of a meal for them anyhow. They'd do better with venison. Right? Right.*

"Good evening," Derian said aloud, then repeated the greeting in Liglimosh. In his nervousness, he'd spoken Pellish.

Animal heads inclined in reply—all but that of the owl, who had been looking the other way. He spun his around with a swiftness that made Derian's neck ache. Derian licked his lips.

Eshinarvash wouldn't have brought you all this way just to let somebody eat you. He's standing there calm as can be. The otters brought you fish. They're waiting, too. Thing is, they can't talk except maybe to manage a "yes" or "no." You've got to do the talking for all of you.

"Do you need me to go somewhere? Do something for you?"

The jaguar—not Truth, Derian felt fairly certain; this one was heavier—stepped into the firelight. Moving with the sort of deliberate caution a human uses when approaching a dog he isn't sure is friendly, the jaguar came over to Derian and with incredible delicacy bumped his head against Derian's arm.

"I'm going to take that as 'yes'," Derian said, rising to his feet. "I'd like a drink of water, then I'll go wherever you want."

The jaguar looked at the fire and made a rasping noise—sort of an alley-cat yowl spoken softly. He raised a paw and scraped at the dirt.

"You want me to put the fire out," Derian said. "I can do that. I'm going to have trouble seeing without it, though. I'm not Firekeeper."

The jaguar came and put his shoulder next to Derian's hand, inviting him to touch. The fur felt like the finest plush velvet, and Derian had the guilty thought that with her red hair, his mother would look magnificent in a coat made from this fur.

Keep those thoughts to yourself, Derian, my lad, he thought. Aloud, he added, "You're going to guide me this way, by touch?"

The jaguar bumped against him again. Derian turned to Eshinarvash.

"You're not coming?"

The Wise Horse shook his head. Derian wished the Wise Horse could explain why.

Really, I can see why there are those who are eager to learn how to talk with the yari-maimalom as Firekeeper does. Even with whatever elaborate gimmicks they've worked out over the years, communication has to be frustratingly slow—and complicated ideas probably get reduced to simplistic forms.

With nothing in which he could carry water, Derian had to resort to using dirt to smother the fire. A large flat piece of rock made an adequate shovel, though he wouldn't have wanted to use it as such if the ground were harder.

Derian then crossed over to Eshinarvash, stumbling just a bit now that there was no light.

"Thank you for the honor of letting me ride you," he said softly, reaching to stroke the horse's neck. "I hope I'll see you again."

Eshinarvash blew on him in what Derian thought was a friendly manner. When Derian turned to thank the otters, they had vanished. All that was left were the puma, the jaguar, and the owl.

Three night creatures, Derian thought. *I hope they're patient with me.*

They were more than patient. The two great cats flanked him when the path was wide enough. When it was narrow they walked one in front, one behind, assuring he would neither stray nor bump into anything. The owl flew off, but returned periodically, and after one such visit, Derian noticed that the puma—who was walking in front—had picked up the pace. By this time, Derian's eyes had adjusted somewhat, and in the light of the full moon he was able to avoid stumbling.

Then just as suddenly as he had increased the pace, the puma halted.

"What's wrong?" Derian asked, when the great cat didn't move.

The puma craned his neck around and hissed at Derian. At the sight of those enormous fangs revealed in their glory and the moonlight glinting off of slitted golden eyes, Derian couldn't have made a sound if he had wanted to—but if he could have made a sound, he would have screamed.

The jaguar came to stand beside the puma, and together they stood watchfully, their ears pricked forward and even their whiskers seeming to curve ahead. Derian strained his own hearing to see if he could catch what had caused this alteration in attitude.

For a long time he heard nothing. Even the crickets and night peepers had fallen silent. Then he realized that what he'd taken for the croaking of a bullfrog couldn't be. The timbre was wrong, as was the tempo. In a moment, Derian placed it. Someone was beating on a drum.

It was a low, repetitious thudding, not overly loud, but paced to match the beating of a human heart at rest. The sound made Derian's skin crawl.

Side by side, jaguar and puma lowered themselves and began to creep forward. Derian took a step forward, but at a glare from the jaguar dropped as well. Going on all fours took most of his concentration, especially since it was becoming increasingly clear that his feline companions desired not only that he not be seen, but that he not be heard as well.

Still, as they did not move with any great speed, Derian was able to trail them. He did his best, knowing as he did so the inferiority that Firekeeper had lived with all her life, the sense that his body was the wrong shape with which to do anything useful, that his senses were not only weak but had lousy priorities.

Right now, Derian would have given everything he had to be able to see in the dark or figure out what was going on by smell. As it was, all he could do was smell the slightly rank scent of cat and see well enough to be absolutely certain that the two cats in front of him were both definitely male.

But the drumming was becoming louder, and that heartbeat rhythm was a guide of its own. Derian heard other things, too. Someone had set up a wind harp. No other instrument made that wispy, ethereal sound. There was a blowing snort that had to come from a horse, a sharp bark that sounded like a dog or fox, a strangled squawk.

He smelled smoke, not the stale smoke that still clung to his clothing, but smoke from a big fire. When he looked up from his concentration on the ground in front of him, Derian thought he saw a faint glow ahead.

A bonfire, but built lower than we are. I'll bet anything that whoever it is we're sneaking up on is down in some sort of hollow where they're pretty much out of sight. Late at night, hidden in a hollow somewhere in the middle of nowhere. Whoever's up to whatever, they don't want anyone to know. They don't figure anyone does know, either, or they wouldn't risk the fire and the music. The yarimaimalom know, though, and they wanted me to see whatever this is. They probably wanted Firekeeper, but she's not available, so they settled for me. Let's not disgrace the species, Derian Carter.

With that admonition, Derian crept forward. The jaguar and puma had been lying side by side for several moments now and a space just the right size for Derian had been left pointedly open between them. Trembling despite the fact that they had not offered him the least harm, Derian crept into the space. He wanted a drink, and that of something stronger than water. Then he looked through the screening branches and forgot about everything but what he saw.

He'd been right about the hollow. What he hadn't expected was the temple. It had the step-pyramid shape that still capped the buildings in Heeranenahalm. In this case, the step pyramid was the entire temple. There were no buildings around it or beneath it, no meeting rooms or apartments or rooms in which to keep the various animals that seemed indispensable in the Liglimom's religion.

It wasn't a very high pyramid, either. If Derian had been standing next to it, another of himself standing on his shoulders would have been able to see the top. It rose from a squat base with the careful gradations that testified that the builders had been working not from plans, but from necessity. They'd made the base as wide as was needed to support the top, and the top had to be wide because it was where all the activity would happen. From what Derian could see, there needed to be room enough for at least two humans to move around the shining black stone altar at the very top.

At first, Derian had thought this must be a very old temple. Then he realized that the reverse was what was true. This was a very new temple, probably not more than a decade old. That probably explained its roughness. The temples in u-Seeheera had been built before the Plague. Their builders had used magic to help them along. If they hadn't used magic, they'd at least had experience on their side. This temple had been built without magic, with trial and error as an architect, and—again Derian was sure he was right—on the sly.

His skin began to creep, and this time the sensation wasn't due to the proximity of the two carnivores who lay on either side of him. If anything, they were a comfort.

Why did they bring me here? Why didn't they bring someone like Varjuna or Tiridanti or even that rather silly woman who likes the bears? Why me? Why now?

Derian couldn't ask, though he longed to do so with almost a physical pain. Instead, he settled himself and resolved to figure out the answers through observation.

A ritual of some sort was under way. Derian had the feeling that they were just warming into it. He tried to count how many people were down there and to see how many there were. Two disdum fussing about on top. The fellow on the drums. A woman playing very softly on a flute. Then there were what Derian figured was the congregation, a couple dozen men and women settled in prayerful attitudes far enough back from the pyramid that they could see the top.

There wasn't a single bonfire as he had thought originally, but smaller fires set along the steps, so that what was going on at the top could be clearly seen. The centrality of the firelight cast everything else into shadow, so it was a while before Derian saw the group on the far side managing the animals. To be honest, he didn't focus in on them until a woman in the formal garb of a kidisdu of birds started climbing to the top. She was holding a snowy white cockerel in one hand. The bird was hanging limply, as birds that have had their eyes covered usually do.

The congregation started singing something low but fervent. Derian struggled to get a clearer look at the group clustered with the animals. They were on the far side of the pyramid from him, and that made seeing difficult. Then suddenly, he realized that what was important wasn't how many there were, but why they were here.

The woman holding the cockerel had surrendered it to one of the men at the top and then dropped to her knees one step shy of the top. She bent her head. The singing rose in intensity. The man now holding the cockerel raised his voice in triumphant song. The bird struggled just a little as if suddenly sharing Derian's feeling that something wasn't right.

Then the disdu holding the cockerel nodded to his subordinate. The other brought up a gleaming knife and slashed. Blood went everywhere, splattering the stone and the robes of the three disdum atop the pyramid.

The cockerel was set down on the cloth that topped the altar, and when the blood had run through it, the dyed cloth was held up for inspection.

Derian continued to watch, but although he registered detail after detail, his thoughts were in a whirl of confusion and horror. Hadn't Rahniseeta or someone told them that animal sacrifice had been stopped as part of the treaty with the yarimaimalom? Sacrifice of any animal, he was sure, not just the yarimaimalom. Yet here in this hollow in the woods, he'd witnessed it. He recognized the man who held the cockerel up before the congregation, too.

It was Dantarahma, the junjaldisdu, a member of u-Liall—and apparently, a man willing to break with what his people believed was the will of the deities.

•

XXVII

THE SWIM ACROSS the inlet posed a challenge nearly as great as getting the wolves out of the cellar. Moon Frost was already learning to run and even hunt with her broken foreleg, but swimming would remain beyond her.

"I could remain on this side," Moon Frost said, but it was clear from the cant of her ears that she didn't want to do so.

"I could see if there are any water folk who would carry you across," Dark Death offered, "but we would miss this tide."

His comment gave Firekeeper an idea.

"Moon Frost, your hind legs are strong enough," she said, thinking aloud, "but without both of your forelegs your head will go under—and this is too long a swim for any of us to support you. But I have an idea. Dark Death, do we have time before we must set out?"

"We do," the wolf replied. "I awoke everyone early in case difficulties arose."

He didn't say more, but Firekeeper suspected Dark Death had anticipated Moon Frost's problem—and had probably been wondering if Blind Seer would be strong enough as well.

Blind Seer privately confided to Firekeeper that his head continued to hurt and that he had moments of double vision, but that otherwise he was doing well. He had assured her that he could manage the swim. She took him at his word, privately resolving to swim close, just in case he needed aid.

Keeping these worries to herself, Firekeeper turned her attention to how to assist Moon Frost in her swim. She found the answer in a piece of driftwood, so dry that it was extremely buoyant.

"I'll need your help," she explained to Moon Frost, "in order to get the measurements right."

"What are you going to do?" Moon Frost asked.

"Have you seen rafts?" Firekeeper asked. When Moon Frost indicated she had, Firekeeper went on, "I am going to make a little raft that we will set under the sound bone of your upper leg. The broken portion will hang over the edge and into the water. The raft will keep your upper body above the water, but you will need to work hard to pull yourself along."

"I will try," Moon Frost said, obviously feeling some doubt, "but I hope I am strong enough. I remember how the current can pull."

Firekeeper hadn't considered this, but Dark Death came up with an answer.

"Is the rope you made still good?" he asked Firekeeper.

"It should be," she replied. "I don't think it has had time to dry out."

"Then we will attach one end of that rope to the raft, the other to me. I have made this swim numerous times and know I have strength to spare. I will lend that strength to Moon Frost."

It took some experimentation to get everything right and the tide was beginning to turn when they set out.

"We should still have ample time," Dark Death assured them.

The pull of the current was strong now that the tide was on the rise, but Firekeeper found she could manage. She had experimented with adapting her swimming style, using her legs more than she had before and changing her arm stroke. Blind Seer had learned a few tricks from Dark Death and was so obviously up to the challenge that Firekeeper positioned herself downcurrent from Moon Frost, where she could help keep the injured wolf on course.

All were bedraggled and exhausted when they arrived on the farther shore, but despite this, Firekeeper had to fight down an urge to start running toward the towers Dark Death had indicated were their destination. She could see a few of the tallest through breaks in the trees, and thought she could easily find her way.

Mai-mal-o-da-lu once again beat in her head as a refrain, drumming so loudly that Firekeeper was almost surprised that the others could not hear her thoughts.

However, despite her urge to rush off, Firekeeper made herself rest. Dark Death located a reliable source of fresh water and she rinsed the salt from her skin. As she did so, she looked about. There was evidence of human habitation here as well and she wondered if this might have been a landing area used to cross to the larger island in the days when humans had lived in this place.

"We will rest for a bit," Dark Death decided, "and even so I think we will arrive at the towers before the worst of the heat. Is anyone hungry?"

Moon Frost admitted rather shamedly that she was. Firekeeper could tell that this reduction to puppyhood was hard for the proud hunter.

"I am hungry, too," Firekeeper said, lying just a little. In reality her feelings were so roiled that she could hardly swallow water. Still, she knew she should eat, even if she didn't wish to do so.

Dark Death wagged his tail slightly.

"If you would check Moon Frost's leg," he said, "I will hunt for all of you."

Blind Seer pulled himself to his feet.

"I will come with you."

"Rest," Dark Death said. "Your head may not be broken as is Moon Frost's leg, but still it has been given little time to mend."

Blind Seer surrendered so easily that Firekeeper knew he must feel terrible. She wondered if the willow tea Doc had taught her to make would work on a wolf. There were ample trees about and she resolved to find some way to make a brew. Perhaps she could find a cup or bottle mostly unbroken among the ruined buildings.

First, though, she kindled a fire and when it was burning unwrapped Moon Frost's leg just enough that she might check for signs of infection.

"I miss Doc," she said to Blind Seer. "He could set this right in a few days."

"Doc?" asked Moon Frost.

They had mentioned the human healer before, but Firekeeper suspected that Moon Frost was looking for distraction from the pain she was certainly feeling. The raft had kept her afloat, but even with Dark Death's help, the swim had been hard on Moon Frost.

Firekeeper and Blind Seer told tales of their earlier ventures, emphasizing how Doc had saved each of their lives more than once. When Moon Frost drifted off into an uneasy doze, Firekeeper rose.

"I am going to look in the ruins for something in which I might mix you some willow tea," she told Blind Seer. She saw him start to rise and pressed him back, pausing to kiss him on top of his head. "Don't worry. I will be very careful. Stay here and watch Moon Frost. Right now she's so tired an ambitious ant would be able to carry her off."

Blind Seer panted laughter as he settled himself to rest again. Cheered, Firekeeper went searching for a pot or pan. What she found was a glass bottle. The sides were thick enough that she decided it would work, especially if she kept the glass from direct heat. Then she found a battered metal cup and knew this would serve even better.

I'm not jealous of Moon Frost anymore, Firekeeper thought as she brewed the willow tea, *but I know I would be if she started sniffing around Blind Seer again. Maimalodalu. Is that the answer? Can I really have everything I want?*

Firekeeper was young enough to hope, and old enough to doubt. The uncertainty kept her from resting. It did not keep her from falling asleep and dreaming.

She is at a ball, an extravaganza the like of which she has never imagined. Music plays its seductive patterns, and though she longs to join the dancing, she waits and watches.

The skins of the dancers are dark and light, soft browns, dark browns, peach, red, golden brown, and even the multihued painted patterns of the New Kelvinese. Some of the dancers wear the styles of the Gildcrest colonies: floor-length sweeping gowns for the women, elaborate multipiece suits for the men. Others wear the billowing blouses and trousers of the Liglimom, the fabric stiff and glittering with embroidered patterns. Still others wear the long robes of the New Kelvinese, the dancers graceful despite their curly-toed slippers, long-braided queues interwoven with strands of sparkling gems.

Firekeeper watches the gaudy throng, searching for someone in particular, someone who is not there. Man after man emerges from the crowd, begging her for a dance. Some are rich, some are young and strong, some are handsome. Her dance card is growing full, but her heart remains restless, curiously dead to the admiration of those who surround her. She inspects face after face, not finding the one she seeks, despair flat and sour in her mouth.

Her temperament is not one that waits. She is a hunter. She goes looking, uncertain who is her prey.

She is pushing through tangled growth, raising curtains of vine, feeling the hem of her gown knotting around her feet. Satin slippers bind her toes. She kicks them off, feels the yielding dampness of the duff beneath her feet. This is better.

She pushes aside the vines, steps around heaps of stone that are the ruins of buildings that once made trees seem small. She hears new music, comes upon another ball. Here the dancers are cranes dancing two by two, their long legs curiously human in their stilted steps, their long feathers as elegant as any silk dress. Now they intermingle with the human dancers, the ballroom's garlands are flowering vines, the candlelight the flickering glow of fireflies.

All at once, there is a pause in the music. Heads turn to see who is entering. He is tall and lean, his bearing graceful. His attire is that of Hawk Haven: knee-britches, waistcoat in patterned silk, white shirt closed at the throat with a flowing cravat. His feet, though, are bare, and the legs that extend below the gather of the trousers are grey-furred and wolf-pawed.

When he turns so that his gaze might sweep the crowd, she sees the bushy tail that balances his height. He turns further, and now it is clear that the face beneath the tricorn hat and the tidy formal wig has a long muzzle, a wolf's face with wolf's fangs, but the eyes that meet hers are blue.

He strides across the room to her. She tears her dance card in half. Tossing it to the polished boards of the floor, she steps with light eagerness to meet him. She lets him take her into his arms, feeling there the thrill she had not at the approach of any of the many human suitors. Together they are dancing, grace and motion wedding them into one. But those who have crowded the sidelines are not smiling; there is no approval on any face. Now she sees that there are beasts among the crowd, and they look no happier than the humans. Hackles are raised, claws extended, lips curled back from shining fangs.

"Impossible!" comes the cry from every throat. "Impossible!" And her partner is dropping onto all fours, his finery shredding about him. Hands are pulling her back, and her struggles mean nothing against that one word: Impossible.

Firekeeper sat bolt upright, finding her hand wrapped around her Fang. She had fallen asleep with her head upon Blind Seer's flank. When the blue-eyed wolf turned his head and looked at her, his gaze that of the handsome swain in her dream, she felt her heart twist with pain.

Dark Death had just entered the clearing. Doubtless the sound of his return was what had wakened her. He was dragging behind him the carcass of a young wild boar, hardly more than a piglet and fat with its mother's milk. The wolf wagged his tail in greeting, obviously hoping for her approval.

With dream-born insight, Firekeeper realized that Dark Death's attitude toward her had changed, that she was no longer a human intruder or useless weakling. Dark Death now saw her strength and usefulness. Wolf-like, he strove to impress her—to win her?

A thrill of mingled excitement and fear washed through Firekeeper, leaving her weak. She gripped dirt in the curled fingers of her free hand, fighting not to let any of her companions know how confusion threatened to overwhelm her.

After several ragged breaths, Firekeeper rose from Blind Seer's side and moved to help Dark Death carry the meat. When she easily lifted what he had been forced to drag, the wolf breathed his approval.

"You are very strong," Dark Death said. "I had not known humans could be so strong."

The wolf's praise thrilled Firekeeper, a thrill she had never felt in response to praise from any human male, though there had been men who had admired her—even those who claimed to love her.

Firekeeper's nightmare haunted her and she ripped her Fang through the young boar's hide, gutting it and throwing the offal savagely away. The wolves swarmed after it, snapping at each other in not quite playful competition.

Impossible.

DERIAN CLUNG TO THE DIRT as a dog was killed, then a lamb, then a calf.

At least they're domestic animals, right? he thought frantically. *The rules don't forbid butchering, do they? No. Just animal sacrifice. How is this different?*

He knew he had arrived at the justification the disdum below were using. As such, he could recognize the portents when the white mare was led forth.

She was a beautiful animal. Without looking at her teeth Derian couldn't be sure, but he was willing to bet she was no more than three years old. Her coat was as pale as sea foam, her mane and tail combed out so they shone, giving back the firelight with hints of silver.

She wasn't led to the top of the pyramid, so at first Derian hoped they didn't intend to kill her. Then he realized that the clean sand being spread around the base would serve the same purpose as the cloths placed on the altar above. He started to pull himself upright. A huge paw placed directly between his shoulder blades forced him down.

Although the air below must reek of blood from the animals that had been slaughtered before, the white mare was almost impossibly docile. When they led her between two flaming brazers she only glanced at the fire with mild interest. Derian recognized the symptoms.

Drugged. They've doped her with something. It wouldn't do to have your sacrifice bucking and pulling and trying to save her life, not when the whole thing is supposed to be a way for the deities to tell you their will. I wonder how many of those people realize what's going on? How many of them realize that if that horse is killed they're moving into new territory?

During his time in u-Bishinti, Derian had learned that the Liglimom did not typically eat horse meat. An old horse might be killed and its meat then used for animal feed, but horses were not raised to be eaten.

Any more than dogs are, Derian thought. *I should have seen it before. These sacrifices aren't some new thing, triggered by our coming. This has been going on for a while. Probably at first they killed a chicken or a rabbit—hardly anything more than any farmer does for the pot. Then they needed something more dramatic, more enticing, more worthy. I wonder how long before they move on to wild animals? I wonder how long before someone thinks to try again with the yarimaimalom?*

His thoughts thundered in his head, beating back against the horror he felt as incantations were spoken. As before, the culmination was when the knife wielder slit the animal's throat, but here there was a new horror.

Before the animal had been killed quickly and cleanly, but the mare's throat was only cut open. She shook her head as if feeling the sting, but otherwise remained docile. Blood splattered from the wound, splashing onto the clean sand. Dantarahma looked at the patterns it made in the sand and therein read portents.

Maybe they won't kill her, Derian thought, trying to raise himself up and feeling the paw push him back down. This time there was a prickling of claws and he lay very still. *She's a fine animal, a valuable horse. Certainly someone would miss her.*

But the drumming grew louder, its heartbeat rhythm increasing in intensity, and Derian knew the mare was doomed. At the crescendo, when the drumbeats had become so rapid that one blended into the other in a horrible pulsing of sound, Dantarahma took the knife from his colleague and tore it through the red-splattered whiteness of the shining throat.

Blood fountained everywhere, and to Derian's horror the worshippers, even the musicians, rushed forward, seeking to be showered beneath the life fountain. They never stopped singing. When the mare's body thudded to the earth and the knives came out, Derian felt the paw lifted from his back.

They left before the feast really began.

DERIAN FELT SICK TO HIS STOMACH, but the cool appraising gazes of the jaguar and the puma helped him regain control. After taking Derian far enough that he, at least, could no longer hear the sounds from the hidden temple, they guided him to a stream.

Derian not only drank, he washed himself, splashing the cool water over his face and upper body as if he could somehow rinse away the horrible scene he had witnessed. When he ceased his frenzied bathing, he looked around. The two great cats had vanished, but Eshinarvash had returned.

The young man's eyes had once again adjusted to moonlight, but now they played a curious trick on him. Eshinarvash no longer looked like a black-and-white horse, but rather like fragments of a white horse floating independent of any body against the darkness. For a moment it seemed as if the uneaten portions of the white mare stood before him in mute reproach. Then Eshinarvash shook and the illusion vanished.

Staggering slightly, Derian walked over to the Wise Horse.

"Did you know what they were taking me to see?"

Eshinarvash nodded.

"Have you shown this to any other people?"

The horse shook his head.

"Why not? Wouldn't Varjuna or someone like that be better?"

Eshinarvash shook his head again, but, of course, he could say nothing more. Instead he nuzzled Derian, than looked back over his own shoulder, toward his back.

"You want me to ride now?"

Nod.

"I think I can. I want to get as far away from this place as possible."

Once Derian was astride and the horse had begun walking—no galloping now in the darkness—he tried to work out why the yarimaimalom would have shown him the ritual. He knew Varjuna would have been as horrified as he had been. He was sure that most of the other disdum would have been as well.

"But that's the problem, isn't it?" he said aloud. When Eshinarvash gave no signal that he should be quiet, Derian continued. "You think you know who you can trust, but you can't be sure. If Dantarahma himself is leading the sacrifices, who might he have converted to his cause? With all the fires burning there, it would be impossible to identify most of those people by scent, and even if you did, what could you do?"

Eshinarvash gave what Derian was certain was an encouraging nicker.

"You can't accuse someone—not without some elaborate ritual, and then you'd have to hope that someone understood. Even if you spelled it out letter by letter, it's a long tale. How could you be certain that the person to whom it was told wasn't in on it or wouldn't tell it to someone who was or wouldn't have an accident before anything could be done?

"What Dantarahma and his cronies were doing was worse than killing a few domestic animals. They were sacrificing them and reading the omens—and finding them good. I wonder what they decided their deities told them to do tonight? I bet you really wished Firekeeper had been here."

To his surprise, Derian felt Eshinarvash shake his head.

"You don't?" Then, again, understanding came. "She's considered a threat, isn't she? An accusation from her would look like a rival trying to upset the established order, but coming from me, especially with her out of touch there across the water, it's something else. The disdum at the outpost can witness how limitedly she can write.

There is no way Firekeeper could send such an elaborate plot—even if she thought that way, which she doesn't. If she wanted to take over, she'd probably challenge each of u-Liall to a fight—or maybe take them on all at once."

He laughed and heard the nervous note in it.

"So not only don't you want her to tell about this, I've got to do something before she decides to come back. Given what I told her about the maimalodalum, that's probably not going to be for a while, but still . . ."

Derian fell silent, trying to decide in whom he could confide. He liked Rahniseeta and she certainly seemed to understand the inner workings of the interlocking temples without really being part of them, but in the end she'd probably just advise him to tell Harjeedian.

Right now Derian was feeling even less friendly than usual toward the aridisdu. He kept thinking of how Harjeedian had ordered Roanne and the pack horse killed, and then coolly had their meat set aside as feed for Blind Seer. Was this simply efficiency, as Derian had thought, or was this the callous calculation of one who approved of animal sacrifice and who might have read a few omens in the spilled blood before having his comparatively ignorant sailors mop it up?

No, Derian would definitely not trust Harjeedian, at least not until he had proof the man had not been among those gathered below. Derian hadn't seen Harjeedian, but he and the great cats had watched from above, and from a distance. Only the fact that Dantarahma had been at the top of the step pyramid, in the center of the light, had made that identification certain. Derian hadn't even recognized the other two he'd seen clearly: the assistant in the rites and the woman who had carried the various smaller animals to the top.

He might know them if he saw them again, but then again he might not. The Liglimom all had dark hair, skin, and eyes. He was learning to recognize the many differences in facial structure and build, but he hadn't exactly been studying to remember. He'd been too busy realizing what all of this meant.

Eshinarvash carried him for some time, then stopped and shivered his skin.

"Rest break?" Derian asked, sliding to the ground. "It must be getting on for dawn."

Eshinarvash nickered, nosing at something at about nose height. Derian made his way over—certain now that it was getting lighter. He found a pair of recently killed rabbits cached in a crotch of a tree.

"Out of reach of the bugs," he said, fighting down nausea at the sight of the dead animals. Their limp forms reminded him of the sacrificed animals. Then he remembered how Firekeeper would think. "Someone brought me breakfast, and I shouldn't let it go to waste. Thank you."

He wasn't sure, but he thought he heard a faint hoot in reply.

As always, Eshinarvash had stopped where there was grass and fresh water. Derian made a fire, set the rabbits on a spit above the fire, and did a bit of foraging while waiting for them to cook. When he finished eating, he looked at the Wise Horse.

"It's well into day now. Do we head back right away or wait until later?"

Eshinarvash stared at him, chewing slowly, his liquid brown gaze seeming mildly reproachful. Derian realized he'd asked a question that couldn't be answered with either yes or no.

"Are we going back immediately?"

Eshinarvash shook his head.

Derian decided he might as well get some sleep. He was making himself as comfortable as possible on a mat of oak leaves when a thought occurred to him.

"Will we be going back?"

Eshinarvash nodded.

"Soon?"

Nod.

Derian decided to try something. "I'm going to make some suggestions as to when we might leave. Just nod if I get close."

Eshinarvash snorted in a fashion that reminded Derian rather oddly of how Firekeeper reacted to human inquisitiveness.

"Look," he said, "I'm not arguing, I just want to know. Humans are herd animals only to a point."

Another snort. This one sounded more amused than annoyed.

"Right. It's morning now. Will we leave this morning? Noon? After noon?"

This last elicited a nod.

"Soon after noon? Midafternoon?"

Nod.

"So you're looking to bring me back after dark," Derian guessed. Probably don't want anyone to see me come back with you."

Nod.

"Any ideas what I should tell them to explain my vanishing?"

He hadn't expected an answer, but to his astonishment Eshinarvash looked at him, then rather dramatically limped a few paces. Then he lifted his foot as he had learned to do when Derian wanted to check his hoof for a stone.

"You're suggesting I tell them that you came to get me because you . . ."

Snort. Violent shaking of head.

"Because one of the Wise Horses had something wrong—maybe with his leg?"

Nod.

Derian thought for a moment.

"That could work—especially if no one asks too many questions. A leg or hoof injury would explain why the horse wouldn't come on his own. Why me? Well, I'm the idiot who goes out every morning in hopes of seeing the Wise Horses. I was available. And if anyone pushes too hard, I can tell them that I think you horses wanted a closer look at me as much as I did at you. I think I can seem appropriately embarrassed."

Derian sighed. He didn't like lying, but knew perfectly well that there were times when only a lie would protect the innocent. He'd lied to protect considerably less honorable enterprises, now that he came to think about it.

"I can pull it off," he assured Eshinarvash, "but I'm going to need to confide in someone. There's simply no way I can accuse one of u-Liall without some support."

Eshinarvash nodded and then went back to grazing. Derian had the feeling that the horse was tired of talking. Fine. He could wait, at least for a while. He couldn't help but think it would be nice to talk to someone who could answer more than yes or no.

DERIAN WALKED UP to the ikidisdu's residence at u-Bishinti at dusk, near the hour that would usually find Varjuna's family scattered to their own activities. The two younger sons would be occupied with their studies. If Poshtuvanu had come to have dinner with his parents, he would have long ago returned to the dormitory where he lived with other newly made kidisdu. Unless some emergency called them away, Varjuna and Zira would be sitting together on the east-facing porch, where they could enjoy the breeze off the ocean.

With this in mind, Derian planned to find his hosts on the porch, make his apologies, and reserve explanations until they could speak in some place more secure from the chance of being overheard. When he approached the sprawling house, he immediately abandoned this plan. Lights burning in areas of the house that would usually be dark at this hour told him that the normal patterns had been broken.

Although he was weary and aching from the better part of two days spent riding bareback, Derian quickened his pace. He had a feeling that the reason for this unexpected disruption was his own absence, and the sooner he assured his hosts of his safety, the sooner everyone could relax.

Though they'll relax only to face a worse problem than a wandering northerner, Derian thought ruefully, *but there's no helping that.*

He had almost reached the front door of the house when a voice spoke out of the darkness.

"Derian? Is that you?" Poshtuvanu called softly, his voice pulled tense between hope and dread.

"It's me," Derian assured him. "Sorry to have caused such trouble."

Poshtuvanu hurried to meet him.

"If the Wise Horse came for you, you had no choice. Earth and Air be praised that you are safe. The omens were anything but clear—even when old Meiyal did the readings herself."

Derian had been introduced to the iaridisdu of the Horse and knew all too well the importance that had been attached to his disappearance if Meiyal herself had done the reading. Not only was the iaridisdu physically fragile, but in anticipation of an honorable retirement she had begun to delegate all but the ceremonies of highest consequence over to her subordinates.

Poshtuvanu went on, "They're all in my father's study. I was about to walk back to my dormitory when I thought I saw someone coming up the path. It's rather dark to tell, but it looked like you. Didn't walk like you, quite, so I didn't say anything."

All the time he'd been talking, Poshtuvanu had been leading the way into the house and down the wide corridors to Varjuna's office. Now he flung open the door.

"Father, Derian's come back."

With those words, Poshtuvanu ushered Derian in, then followed after. There was a general hubbub of greetings and exclamations over which Zira's voice rang clearest.

"You look exhausted, Derian. Sit down. Have something to drink and eat—or would you prefer a bath first?"

Derian wanted a bath and a change of clothes, but he wouldn't leave his hosts waiting and wondering—especially not after he noticed old Meiyal sitting huddled in one of the high-backed chairs. She, Varjuna, Zira, and Poshtuvanu were the only ones present.

"Something to drink would be welcome," he said, "and to eat, eventually. I can make do with sugared nuts, even. I was taken good care of."

"Taken care of?" asked Varjuna. "By the Wise Horses?"

"By them," Derian said, "and others."

A cool drink redolent of mint and fruit nectar was pressed into his hand and he drank thirstily before continuing.

"It's a long story," he warned, "and not one for all ears."

"Our younger sons were scheduled to go on a packing trip to u-Vreeheera," Zira replied, "and we encouraged them to go as planned. They wanted to stay, but we told them that we were certain you were fine, and that the story of where Eshinarvash had taken you would only get better for the wait."

Derian was relieved. He knew that Varjuna and Zira usually dispensed with servants after the evening meal had been cleaned up, so except for whatever servants Iaridisdu Meiyal had brought with her, the house should be empty. He had already decided to trust the iaridisdu with his tale. Not only could she have not been among the number at the temple last night—the ride would have been far too taxing for her—he knew Varjuna respected her deeply and would want to consult her before taking any action.

"You got my message, then," he said. "Prahini's well?"

Varjuna nodded. "She came down to the stables just as you thought she would. The kidisdu who saw her wandering about delivered your message directly to me. He was so determined to be discreet he clipped it from her forelock."

"The hair will grow again," Derian said, absently, his thoughts elsewhere. "Did you receive any other copy of the message? I sent two."

Varjuna nodded, his expression heavy with puzzlement.

"I found a second copy on my desk. It was rather mutilated, but readable."

"When you did not come back by afternoon," Zira said, "and the Wise Horses were being singularly uncommunicative, we decided to consult Meiyal. She consulted the resident horses in Heeranenahalm and was concerned when the omens were ambiguous, so she came here to see if the Wise Horses would say more to her."

Meiyal spoke, her voice as dry as a cricket's chirp, but just as musical.

"They were quite difficult," she said with a chuckle, "and so I remained. I am glad I did so, for now I can hear your tale—that is if you trust me with it."

"I do," Derian said, coloring. "I didn't mean to imply otherwise. However, once you've heard what I have to say, I think you'll understand why careful consideration needs to be taken before it goes any farther. In fact, can we be overheard from here?"

Zira shook her head. "Not unless someone is prowling out in the dark."

Poshtuvanu had been leaning against a wall, listening with interest.

"I can take a look," he said, "and then maybe I had better leave. Clearly these are matters beyond a mere kidisdu."

Meiyal waved her hand. "If Derian has no problem with Poshtuvanu remaining, I certainly have none."

Varjuna looked at Derian. "Nor do I, but the decision as to who stays and who goes is Derian's."

Derian hated what he had to do, but he had to be certain. Poshtuvanu was young and strong enough to have made the trip to the ceremony last night and to have gotten back in time to not be missed at his duties. Moreover, he stayed with his parents just frequently enough that if he were not at the dormitory he would be assumed to be at the ikidisdu's residence.

"Where were you last night?" he asked.

Poshtuvanu looked startled. "Here, actually. My father asked me to stay in case news about you turned up and he needed another pair of hands."

"I'm not as young as I once was," Varjuna said, "and the younger boys were gone."

"Good, then," Derian said. "Take that look around outside, then come back and hear what I have to say. You'll hear soon enough why I had to ask, and I apologize in advance for doing so."

While they were still sorting out that strange statement, Derian took a moment to go rinse his face with cool water. Then, when Poshtuvanu returned and assured them that all was quiet, Derian launched into his account. He moved quickly through the first part, but skipped nothing, including how the various yarimaimalom had cooperated to provide him with food, and how the great cats had escorted him to the ceremony. When he reached the point where he must describe what he had seen, he paused.

"Now comes the hard part," he said. "I'm going to try and tell it without saying what I thought about it—just what I saw. When I'm done, well, then I've some questions for you."

Derian had never had a better audience. They listened attentively, not asking even a single question, though from the way Zira folded down the fingers in one hand as if counting, she, at least, would have a few. When he finished, though, it was Meiyal who spoke first.

"You are certain it was Dantarahma you saw?"

"I am."

Meiyal sighed. "I wish I were surprised, but for many years Dantarahma has been eager for reform. I think he believed that when the former ahmyndisdu died, one who thought as he did would be appointed to u-Liall, for the omens indicated great changes were upon us. Then Tiridanti was anointed. She and Dantarahma were, well, like Fire and Water. They can hardly bear to be in the same room together. I thought—as I think many thought—that Dantarahma had accepted the omens. Now I see he has not."

Varjuna rose and began pacing the long end of the room.

"What are we to do?"

Zira interrupted before Meiyal could reply.

"We can do nothing tonight," she said firmly, "and will do less than nothing if we exhaust ourselves. Let us sleep on this matter and speak of it to no one."

"I won't," Poshtuvanu said. "Do you want me to stay here or go down to the dormitory?"

"Enough people heard about Prahini returning without her rider," Varjuna said, "that I think it would be wise for them to hear he has returned well and safe. Derian, have you given any thought to how we might explain your absence?"

Derian sketched out the tale he and Eshinarvash had worked out regarding a Wise Horse with an injured hoof.

"It will do," Varjuna said. "Poshtuvanu, go to your dormitory and pass that on to any who ask—and a few who do not ask. Gossip travels on galloping hooves. The tale will be to those who care to know in Heeranenahalm with the morning milk. If I have not contacted you otherwise, come back when your morning tasks are completed. We may well need you."

Meiyal nodded her agreement.

"Lack of sleep will make us take poor counsel. I will go to my rooms and pray for guidance." She pushed herself to her feet using the arms of the chair and looked up at Derian. "Sleep well, young man. You've had a rough time. I only wish I believed that the worst was behind you."

XXVIII

AFTER EATING HER SHARE of the young boar, Moon Frost collapsed into a sleep so deep that once or twice Firekeeper rose to make certain she still breathed.

"It is the healing sleep," Blind Seer assured Firekeeper when she returned to his side. "That swim was hard enough with two sound forelegs. That Moon Frost did it with one, even assisted . . ."

Firekeeper knew he was right. She knew, too, that her restlessness was keeping the blue-eyed wolf from the sleep he needed at least as much as Moon Frost did. Although in the past Blind Seer had frequently chided her impatience with the proverb "Hunt when hungry, sleep when not, for hunger always returns," this time he did not, nor did he settle back into sleep.

"Let Dark Death call the trail," Blind Seer said softly, "but follow him with care."

"Why? He has led us fair this far."

"Didn't you notice what he did when he went hunting—or rather what he didn't do?" Firekeeper indicated puzzlement and Blind Seer continued. "Use your mind as something other than a den for dreams, sweet Firekeeper. We are in another pack's territory, but did you hear Dark Death howl?"

"I didn't," she admitted, "but this is no stranger's hunting grounds. This is the land held by his own birth pack—or so I understood."

"More reason for him to howl, then," Blind Seer replied. "Would you swallow your voice if we were within cry of home?"

"No," Firekeeper said promptly. "Not unless . . . Not unless something dangerous followed me and I did not wish to lead it to the others."

"At last you think. Now, I do not think Dark Death thinks us a danger. I smell no such apprehension from him. Indeed, I think he rather likes you, at least. Me he tolerates, but that is well. We are of an age to be rivals."

Firekeeper didn't want to follow that thought, so she asked rather quickly, "If he does not think us a danger, then why not howl?"

"Give me back the answer," Blind Seer said. "You know it if you would but think."

"Because," Firekeeper reasoned, "he wished opportunity to speak with his Ones without our hearing."

"So I think also," Blind Seer said. "We have heard this island is a sanctuary within a sanctuary. Best Dark Death warn his Ones about us. I think his Ones may have had warnings already."

"Oh?"

"I think of the ravens. They are great talebearers and have taken an interest in you."

"Yes. I see that, but even so, Dark Death would wish to tell what he has learned during these days' running."

"So I see it, dear heart."

"Thank you. I will follow Dark Death with care, but who knows how the ruling of his Ones will have changed the trail."

"Good. Sleep now. You do neither of us any favors if you appear before these Ones draggle-tailed from lack of sleep."

Firekeeper obediently settled herself down, and forcing herself to breathe slowly and deeply, fooled her body into rest.

Dark Death roused them all shortly after dawn.

"I know we had a hard night," he said without apology, "but this time of year the day grows hot almost before the sun is high. Our trail is through thick forests, but why exhaust ourselves needlessly when we might lie up cool at our destination?"

No one argued against his reasoning. Breaking camp was as easily done as digging dirt over the coals of Firekeeper's fire. She tied the metal cup onto her belt next to the wallet. Blind Seer claimed to have little pain now, and while the tea might not have helped, it was good to have something in which she might heat water.

As Dark Death had promised, their trail was beneath tall forest giants that shaded the way along which the four wolves moved in the steady distance-eating trot that can be kept up for hours. Moon Frost had adapted to her tripod gait, and though she panted somewhat more heavily than did the others, she did not ask for favors.

Firekeeper noticed that their route seemed to be along what had once been a human road. Where rains had scoured away the dirt, fragments of paving showed. Occasionally there were small ruins. Once they crossed on a low-arched stone bridge, as sound as on the day its last piece was laid, but for where moss and rain had chewed a bit on the stone.

The wolf-woman noticed these things, but did not comment. She had no desire for anything but to reach their destination and learn at last the answers to her questions. Yet Blind Seer's rebuke of the night before stayed with her and Firekeeper did not let herself become lost in dreams.

So it was that she easily spotted the first sentinel, though the wolf watched from shadow and might easily have been mistaken for a section of the fallen tree trunk that lay nearby. Dark Death did not acknowledge the watcher, so neither did Firekeeper, but she knew from how Blind Seer flicked his ear when she glanced his way that he, too, had taken note. As they ran on, Firekeeper spotted at least one other watcher, and thought she glimpsed a third.

The ground was rising beneath them and the forest giants were thinning. As they had seen at the first ruin that they had visited together, the winds were not friendly toward those who challenged their might, but here, as had not been the case in that other place, there was evidence that efforts had been made to move the fallen trees so that the hilltop would remain clear.

Wolves could not do that, Firekeeper thought. *There are beaver marks on that section of trunk, though there is no water on this hill such as beavers like. Yet they have been here. I wonder why they would care?*

Dark Death was slowing now, and at last he gave the searching howl Firekeeper knew she should have been listening for last night. It was answered immediately, and from close by.

This is like one of those plays about which Wendee told me, Firekeeper thought. *This is no true greeting, but a pretend. Moon Frost gives no indication that she has noticed the oddness of this. Blind Seer does not either, so I will be guided by their manners.*

A wolf came forth to greet them almost before Dark Death's howl had quavered to silence on the hot late-morning air. She was not a lovely creature, not sleek and silvery as was Moon Frost. She moved easily enough, but with an odd drag to her step. This, Firekeeper realized, was because her right forepaw was gifted with twice as many toes as were usual and these were all of different sizes and shapes.

The wolf's coat was almost the same shade as Dark Death's, but the fur was coarser and lay less evenly. Her ears were a trifle too large, and one flank bore a large, ragged scar. Yet there was an aura of power about her, a sense of contained purpose that made Firekeeper certain beyond the slightest doubt that this was a One fit to lead.

Firekeeper thought that the One was less old than Cricket or Neck Breaker. There was a compact confidence as yet unweakened by the advance of years. She had also borne puppies this year, and had not quite recovered from the demands of nursing.

"I am Integrity, the One Female of this island," the wolf said as greeting. "Dark Death I know, but name yourselves."

Again Firekeeper had that sensation of being in a play. She accepted the role, and let Blind Seer lead. He introduced himself, and then Firekeeper, much as he had to the first pack they had met. He left Moon Frost to name herself, in that way making clear that she was an outlier, not a member of his pack.

Firekeeper was amazed at the relief she felt at this little gesture. She knew Blind Seer would never claim what was not his. Indeed, Moon Frost could be said to belong to Firekeeper more than to either of the males, for Firekeeper was the one who had fought and bested her. But Firekeeper was not so proud as to make such a claim, and Blind Seer did not do it for her.

After Moon Frost had named herself and her lineage as was the way of the Wise Wolves, Integrity led them to a shaded place near to a cool stream. It was a good place for escaping the afternoon heat that so plagued the thick-furred wolves, and there they met Integrity's mate, Tenacity, and the two pups of this year.

Like Integrity, Tenacity bore marks of physical deformity. His skull was broader between the ears, and he carried his head as if it was rather heavy for his neck. The pups, as far as Firekeeper could tell on sight, were completely normal.

"The rest of our pack is elsewhere," Integrity explained. "This time of year is good for ranging abroad. Though this island is not as large as the largest, it offers space in which to roam."

"Our people also go their own ways," Blind Seer said, "once the pups are eating solid food. It is good to run in ones or twos, and test oneself."

"But you have not come here to compare how we raise our families," Integrity said. "I hear that a specific legend drove you here."

"Maimalodalum," Firekeeper replied, tiring all at once of this playing as if these wolves did not know precisely why they had come, and probably everything about them that could be observed. "Maimalodalu. The beast-souled. That is the tale that brought us to your island. When I asked the wolves of the largest island they sent me here. Can you tell me more?"

"Tell you, yes," Integrity said. "It is a tale best related here, for reasons I think you will understand in time. I scent your impatience, Firekeeper, and will not ask why one from a land that so hates magic is interested in magic. It is obvious that you feel yourself born into the wrong shape for your soul. True?"

"As you say it," Firekeeper replied. "All I know is being a wolf, but my human form does not match what I feel."

"And you wish to change this," Integrity said. "Wishing is not enough. For anything there is a cost."

Firekeeper knew she was being tested and schooled herself to patience.

After all, she thought, settling herself, *they are right to test me. We talk of serious matters here.*

"Speak to me of cost," Firekeeper said. "Speak to me of the maimalodalum. Tell me everything I must know. My ears are yours, my stomach will go empty if you so will. I am here to be taught."

Integrity's tail thumped once in approval, and though her gaze was on a pup that was wandering beyond limits, her attention was for Firekeeper.

"To tell the tale, I must go back in time," she said.

"I am learning that most tales begin back in time," Firekeeper replied, and she tried to sound pleased. "How far does this one go?"

"It goes back before those who founded this colony came from the Old Country," Integrity said. "Have you been told that our religion was brought from that place?"

"Yes."

"Well then, we are well along already. Now in the Old Country, there were no creatures like the yarimaimalom. All the beasts were Cousins. Even so, as here, the Cousins could act as liaisons between the deities and those who desire to abide by their will.

Then, as now, the problem was that of communication. No matter how elaborate were the charts drawn up by the aridisdum, no matter how complex and complete the volumes of lore, still there were many times when the will of the deities was less than clear.

"The humans bred their beasts for ability to hear the will of the gods, hoping that the breeding of one who was a good diviner to one who was a good diviner would create a lineage of such. Soon it became clear that the deities were capricious. The progeny of such lines sometimes were quite gifted. Other times a wild creature trapped by chance would serve as well.

"Thus other efforts were made to bridge the gap. Since these Cousins could not be taught to communicate more precisely with humans, so the next thought was to create humans who could communicate more fully with beasts."

Firekeeper could see where this was heading and longed to urge Integrity to greater speed, but she remembered that this was not only a tale but a test and resolved to listen carefully.

"You know of human talents," Integrity said. "Indeed, I think if one who has the gift for scenting talents took a sniff of you they would discover that you are among the talented."

Firekeeper felt no surprise at this. She had heard the theory before, and dismissed it as irrelevant. If she had talents they were not like Doc's, hers to use at will. They were more like Derian's, a background to all she did, but no more hers to control than she controlled her sense of touch.

Integrity paused as if to give Firekeeper a chance to confirm or deny the existence of her talents, but when she did not, the wolf went on with her tale.

"The sorcerers from the Old Country experimented with creating a means of letting a human borrow the form of a beast. I will not weary you with tales of how long they worked or how many times they failed. At last they learned what they needed to know. Magic could be worked that would let a human take on the shape of a specific animal. It would not work for every human. Only those who had the talent for relating to that specific animal could achieve the transition."

Firekeeper wanted to make certain she understood, so she asked, "By 'relating' you mean those who understand a specific type of animal more deeply than is usual, is this correct? My friend Fox Hair is like this with horses. Are you saying, then, that he would be a candidate for the magical transformation?"

"Yes," Integrity said. "If he desired to sometimes have a horse's shape. He could not, however, become an otter, say, or an eagle. The sorcerers of long ago were not pleased when they learned the exchanges would be so limited. However, they rejoiced that they could be done."

"Thank you," Firekeeper said. "I understand. I think, however, there is more to your story than this."

"Definitely so," Integrity replied. "There was great celebration over this achievement, but soon after humans began taking beast form, limitations were discovered. One was minor and easily overcome. In beast form the maimalodalum must keep by them some token of their human self or be unable to reverse the change. When in human form the maimalodalum must keep some token of their animal self or the entire ritual would need to be repeated from start to finish. As this was time consuming and expensive, no one wished to do this.

"Soon tokens were made containing both of these elements and the maimalodalum wore them always. Even today stories have survived in which the central element is a maimalodalu who has lost his or her token—usually when in animal form—and must hurry to regain it."

I suppose I might hurry, Firekeeper thought, *but being a wolf forever and always would not trouble me too greatly.*

Integrity went on. "Now, this matter of tokens was the lesser limitation. There was an even greater one. Cousins are all well and good, and we are blessed that the deities have set them upon Earth's surface with us. However, in comparison to humans—or yarimaimalom—they are very limited in how they think. They are not precisely stupid, but they are not creative or versatile.

"Some of the maimalodalum loved their beast forms so much that they rarely changed back into their human one. In this way it was learned that when a maimalo-dalum does not return to the human form from time to time and remains that way, the beast soul consumes the human. The maimalodalu simply becomes a beast. So the matter stood when those from the Old Country crossed the oceans and discovered the yarimaimalom."

Moon Frost had been listening with perked ears. Now she interupted, eager, but with her ears flat to her head as if facing a dreaded enemy.

"Yarimaimalom are as smart as humans," Moon Frost said. "If these maimalodalum sacrificed a yarimaimalom rather than a Cousin when they did their magic, there would not be the problem of becoming stupid when in beast shape. Is that what they thought?"

"That is what they thought," Integrity replied. "Remember, these were humans who thought the deities were pleased with the killing of beasts. They did not see any wrong in what they did as long as they profited from it."

Tenacity interjected, "Much as we might like to think otherwise, Moon Frost, we are not so different from those long-ago sorcerers. We do not hesitate to kill to feed ourselves and our young. These human sorcerers did not shy from killing when they needed to feed their magic—magic they thought reflected the will of the deities."

Firekeeper felt a tendril of uneasiness at what she was hearing, but she had schooled herself to obedient listening and did not wish the thread of the unwinding story to be lost in questions. After a moment Moon Frost's ears rose and her hackles lowered, but she licked the exposed paw beneath her broken foreleg over and over, until Firekeeper worried she would rub the fur away and leave the skin raw.

"Now," Integrity went on, "although the Cousins had been given no say in the mat-ter, the yarimaimalom did not care for the use to which the sorcerers would put them. When captured and set within the spell chambers, their spirits struggled against the spell and sometimes they won. More often the sorcerers won. Sometimes neither won, and from these undecided battle were born creatures neither human nor beast."

"Wait," Firekeeper said, for the tendril of worry had grown into an entire thicket. "What do you mean? What does say in the matter have to do with anything? I can see that the yarimaimalom would not like to have their shapes copied, but could they defy the spell? Beasts have never practiced magic."

Integrity looked at her, real pity in her amber eyes.

"I forget how much your people hate magic, Firekeeper. They hate it so much that they forget why."

"Why we hate it?" Firekeeper retorted. "Because great magics were used to beat us back from our lands. Had humans not had great magic, we would have beaten them away. This would still be our land and the humans would remain in the Old Country."

"Is that all they tell you, then?"

Blind Seer replied, "That is what we have been told. There are little snippets here and there that hint at other reasons, but nothing that has been woven into a web."

"Hold those snippets," Integrity said, "I would hear them later. First I must emphasize one point. The great magics were all cruel magics. Unlike the talents which are born into a person, the great magics stole power from other things."

Firekeeper froze, not wanting to hear, knowing she must.

"Firekeeper." Integrity said the name as if it was a charm, holding the wolf-woman with the command of her presence. "In the creation of a maimalodalu the yarimaimalo could fight the sorcerers, because in order to create a maimalodalu the animal—Wise or lesser—must die. Its soul is subsumed by the one who would become 'beast-souled.' That is where the fight occurred, between soul and soul. And Firekeeper, even if the yarimaimalo won and kept its soul, still it died."

"WE NEED WEAPONS," Waln said, "and to get into practice with them."

He had joined Rarby and Shelby down in the coolness of the interior courtyard. They were playing Navy versus Pirates again, but from what Waln had seen from the upper gallery, not even Shelby, who had drawn the pirates, seemed too keenly interested.

At this time of day, none of them had lessons to teach. As the summer days had grown longer and hotter, the Liglimom had informed the northerners that a midday hiatus was customary.

Waln had taken to the concept of a rest period with great enthusiasm. Even within the shaded gardens and the thick-walled buildings, sleep or quiet meditation seemed the most reasonable way to employ oneself. Even thinking seemed to take extra effort, but ever since Waln had toured the harbor with Shivadtmon the day before, his mind had been alive with possibilities.

"Weapons?" Rarby echoed, setting down the miniature ship he had been about to move. "As in bows and swords and stuff?"

"Maybe not those precisely," Waln said, "but the like. We'll definitely need bows."

Shelby stretched lazily, popping the joints in his shoulders as he did so.

"Slow down," he suggested, "and tell us what we're going to need weapons for."

"You don't think," Waln said with a trace of sarcasm, "that the animals on Misheemnekuru are going to take our trespassing lightly, do you?"

A few days before, Shelby might have looked at Waln like he was crazy, but freedom to roam around u-Seeheera and the public areas of Heeranenahalm had pretty much made certain that everyone would have encountered at least a few yarimaimalom. These moved about the city with the arrogance of spoiled pets, but there was that in their manner that made clear they belonged to no one but themselves.

"You've a point," Shelby said without rancor. "Those won't be scared off by a few loud noises or a fire circle. I'm not sure . . ."

Waln cut Shelby off before he could frame his thought. It was much easier to argue when the other party had not stated a position.

"We have a tremendous advantage over these animals," he said, deliberately avoiding calling them either "Wise Beasts" or "yarimaimalom." "They've lived without being hunted since the plague years, when they made this deal with the locals. They may know about crossbows and such, but they've never had to deal with them. I figure a few shots home and they're going to be more scared of us than any dumb wild animal would be."

"I don't quite get it," Rarby said. "Wouldn't they just figure out how the weapons work and stay out of range?"

"Good for us if they do," Waln said. "Out of range is where we want them."

Shelby didn't seem convinced.

"I don't know," he said. "Why would they end up being more scared of us than a wild animal would? I've heard some stories about bears and boars and like that charging hunters. Don't boars attack even after they've been speared?"

"They might," Waln said, deliberately shrugging this off, "but don't you see? That type of behavior is precisely because they're dumb animals."

"What?" the brothers said, speaking almost as one.

"Imagination," Waln said. "The same thing that's getting you into a twist right now. You're imagining what could happen. You're imagining dangers. That's good, because it lets us make our plans in advance."

"Won't it be good for them, too?" Shelby said.

Rarby chortled. "No, stupid, because they won't have time to plan. We're going in there armed for bear—or wolf or boar or whatever. We'll hit them hard, and while they're still trying to figure out what happened, we'll grab the treasure, hop a boat, and get out of there neat as can be."

Shelby flared. "Don't call me stupid, Rarby. I may be younger than you, but I'm not stupid."

Waln stepped in before fraternal bickering could ruin his presentation.

"You're both right," he said firmly. "Rarby figures it like I do. Imagination is going to work against the animals. We'll have speed on our side, but, Shelby, you're right, too. We can't risk giving them time to work out plans and contingency plans and alliances and all."

"Alliances?" Shelby frowned, and Waln gave himself a mental kick. "With the humans?"

"Maybe," Waln said, "or with other animals. I don't know how they work things over there, but I get the impression that being smarter doesn't make them suddenly less animals. Those that need packs or herds continue to live that way. Those that are solitary by nature don't start liking crowds. But none of this will matter if we can work quickly. Fear will keep them back for a while, and while they're bickering, we'll finish up and be on our way."

At that moment, the two brothers were all too aware of how even the closest associates can disagree, so neither pressed Waln.

"You said practice," Rarby said, seizing on a nonconfrontational point. "We need weapons if we are to practice, right?"

Waln nodded. "I think I can get us the basics. Yesterday, Shivadtmon told me something rather interesting."

He gave them an edited version of his long discussion with Shivadtmon regarding vessels to carry them back north. He focused on the ships he'd seen and his own recommendations.

"Shivadtmon seems inclined to listen to me," Waln said. "They're not accustomed to having enemies here, and I told him all about not only Bright Bay and Waterland, but pirates, too. *Fayonejunjal* carried weapons. It isn't going to be hard to convince Shivadtmon to make sure we have some, too. From there to pointing out that weapons are of little use unless you are in practice shouldn't be hard."

Both Rarby and Shelby looked quite pleased at this, then Shelby frowned again. Waln swallowed a sigh. The brothers were the most inclined to use force of any of the shipwreck survivors. That had been why he'd chosen them to assist in taking Lady Blysse. Unfortunately, Shelby was a worrier.

"We can't take a ship into those islands," he said. "And won't the humans wonder what we're doing if we take a smaller vessel and vanish for a couple days?"

"I'm working on that," Waln promised. "I told Shivadtmon that several of you had expressed a desire to do a bit of sailing in the bay. He told me we'd be welcome to two or three of the vessels his temple keeps. I figure we start taking little jaunts right away. They'll get used to it. By the time we're ready to head for Misheemnekuru, I'll have figured out an excuse to cover our absence."

Shelby still didn't look convinced, and Waln had to resist an urge to hit him.

"Anyhow," Waln said, "what will they do if we do disappear and they think we've landed on Misheemnekuru? From what I've heard, they're forbidden by treaty not only to land on the islands, but even to sail the inner waterways. Once we're in, they won't know for certain where we are."

Unless the yarimaimalom tell them, Waln thought, *and I'll be beggared if I volunteer that. I'm not even certain the animals could communicate something that complicated.*

Rarby, eager to show he was both game and smarter than his brother, spoke up.

"We could tell them that we sailed a bit further south and had something break, that we had to go to shore to mend it. There are villages that way, but plenty of empty coast, too. When we come limping back all on our own, who's to say where we've been?"

Maybe the animals, Waln thought, *but I've said all I'm going to about them. Enough that I've introduced the idea that they need to get in practice with their weapons of choice. If these two agree, the others will follow.*

"Good idea," Waln said aloud. "I've been collecting what maps I can, and I'll look for one that gives details of the coast south of here. Maybe we'll even do a little scouting."

Shelby brightened. "That's a good idea. Our original voyage was supposed to be one of exploration. We're just doing our job. That'll make those who are eager to send us home see we'll be happy to go."

Waln nodded.

"Now," he said, "if you're interested, let me show you a map I copied the other day. It shows the area I'm considering for our target."

They unrolled the map on the table, weighing down the corners with bits from the Navy and Pirates set. A raven flying overhead dismissed their activity as just another game and flew off to enjoy how her sapphire-and-diamond pendant glittered in the afternoon sun.

DERIAN WOKE EARLY the next morning, but found the rest of Varjuna's household up before him.

"We suggest you follow your usual routine," Zira said. "Take Prahini out, visit with a few people, be seen being as normal as possible."

"That makes sense," Derian said.

"And stop looking so worried," Zira scolded. "Glow."

"Glow?"

"Glow. Look happy. Look elevated. You're the crazy foreigner who kept sneaking off to look at the Wise Horses. You've been honored with yet another ride. You've been taken into their lands. Glow."

"But don't gloat." Derian laughed, understanding. "I'm happy, thrilled, and honored, but not too full of myself."

"Exactly."

Derian paused, thoughtfully spreading honey on a thick slice of bread.

"Actually that shouldn't be too hard," he said. "I am awed and honored. I'm just terrified about what comes with the honor. It reminds me of how I felt when King Tedric gave me the counselor's ring. Everyone around me was going on about the honor and all I could think of was the responsibility."

Zira patted him on the shoulder. "You'll do just fine. Poshtuvanu said you two are scheduled for a Pellish lesson midmorning before the break. We're going to meet then and discuss matters further. Meiyal can't stay away from Heeranenahalm too much longer, but it makes sense that she not return until the cool of the day."

When they met at midmorning, Derian was immediately certain that Varjuna and Meiyal had already been working on the problem. To those who had observed them, doubtless it had seemed that the iaridisdu was being given a slow and decorous tour of the new foals, but Derian had no doubt that the topics under discussion had been more than conformation and pedigree.

Kept them in plain sight, he thought, *and if Zira just happens to work with the foals and eliminate the need for anyone else to be in earshot most of the time, and if they look very serious—well, to horse breeders, foals are a serious matter.*

Now they retired to Varjuna's office once more, and Zira had made certain of their privacy by sending the servants home early for their midday break.

"We have decided," Varjuna began, "that the best thing we could do is find outside confirmation for what Derian saw. This is not because we do not believe you, son," he said, seeing Derian begin to speak, "but because there will be those who will not be inclined to take the word of a foreigner—especially over that of one of u-Liall."

"There's the problem of your hair as well," Meiyal said.

"My hair?"

"It is so red. You look to be a natural ally of Fire, and Fire and Water have always been rivals. Moreover, you came here in the company of one called 'the Firekeeper,' and though some have argued that this name portends a desire to control Fire, others say it indicates an alliance with that deity."

Derian's head swam as he tried to twist his thoughts into this pattern, but he knew he had to try and see the world as these people did. Therefore, he didn't protest that this was all ridiculous, only nodded.

"So we need confirmation," he said. "I wish I could identify someone other than Dantarahma. If I saw them again, I might be able to identify the man who helped him with the sacrifices, or the woman who relayed most of the victims to the top of the pyramid, but I can't be sure."

"Nor will we rely on you for that," Varjuna said comfortingly. "We have some other avenues to investigate. One is the question of white animals. You said all the animals sacrificed were white?"

Derian nodded.

"Chickens and lambs are common enough, but a pure white dog, calf, or horse would have been harder to find. We can do some checking there, try to learn who made those purchases."

Zira cleared her throat.

"We can check the matter of the mare from two angles," she said. "There is a chance the poor animal was born in a stable supervised by our temple. Pure white horses that young are uncommon—the greys take time to fade. It is possible that even if the mare was born elsewhere, its owner offered it to the temple at some point."

"I'm only guessing the mare was young," Derian reminded her anxiously.

"You have a good eye for horseflesh," Zira said. "I'll take your word. If we trace the mare, then trace her ownership, we may find out something useful."

"You do this, Zira," Meiyal said. "You handle many of our breeding projects, and it would not be unlikely if you or one of those who work with you were looking for a promising mare. We also need to check into who Dantarahma has been associating with of late. I can ask a few questions, but not too many."

"Nor can I," Varjuna said. "Dantarahma has always preferred travel by boat whenever possible. We have little in common."

"Why not," Derian asked hesitantly, "ask Rahniseeta, sister of Harjeedian, to see what she can learn? From what I can tell, she does a little bit of everything for many people, but because she isn't really anyone, no one notices her."

Varjuna smiled. "That's a very good idea. I know she clerks at u-Nahal from time to time, and I've seen her helping set up for various festivals and ceremonies."

Meiyal was a trifle less certain.

"But she is associated with her brother, isn't she?"

"True," Derian said, "but that's for the good. Harjeedian isn't likely to be on Dantarahma's side. He's put too much on the line with the trip north. That means it's unlikely that Rahniseeta is associated with them either."

He remembered his own momentary suspicion of Harjeedian and put it from him. Harjeedian might be coolly practical, but he didn't seem like a heretic.

"Anyhow," Derian went on, "if anyone thinks anything about Rahniseeta nosing around, they're going to figure she's trying to help her brother. My understanding is that the Temple of the Cold Bloods is standing firmly behind Harjeedian right now, but that doesn't mean there haven't been any rumbles of discontent."

"You have a good point, there," Meiyal said. "I will ask a few discreet questions of my own. Harjeedian and Rahniseeta were among the few who knew where you were. If I find no evidence that they said anything out of line, then I shall call her to me."

Meiyal gave a thin smile.

"I understand the young woman writes a fine hand. Most assuredly, an old woman like myself can always use a scribe."

"HOW ARE YOU DOING with Waln Endbrook?" asked the master.

"Very well, Master. He was quite excited by the news that a boat was being equipped for a possible voyage north. He has also showed an interest in obtaining weapons for his men, and in having opportunity for them to hone their skills. The excuse he gives is that the waters to the north are alive with pirates and raiders. I have pretended to agree, and have supplied them with weapons and ammunition. They also have repeatedly taken out a small sailing vessel. I am certain that this is to accustom those who live and work near the harbor to the sight so there will be no comment when they make their actual venture."

"Have you found a way to suggest that they not go to Misheemnekuru until Lady Blysse returns?"

"This is more difficult, Master," Shivadtmon said unhappily. "To do so, I would need to indicate that I am aware of what they plan. I have managed not to do so to this point."

"The omens indicate that the time has come for you to break your reticence on this matter," the master said.

"Master?" Shivadtmon was too obedient to question directly, but he made the single word express his doubts.

"Do you fear that you would be committing sacrilege?" the master asked. He smiled gentle reassurance. "If so, then be at peace. The isolation of Misheemnekuru, its exclusive use by the yarimaimalom, was a secular arrangement, not a sacred one. Moreover, the yarimaimalom themselves have already broken the agreement."

Shivadtmon was again the student showing his cleverness to the teacher.

"By admitting Lady Blysse?"

"That is right, by admitting Lady Blysse. No matter how some of the disdum choose to interpret her acceptance by the yarimaimalom, I analyze the matter with a mind unclouded by their wistful romanticism. Lady Blysse is a woman, nothing more. A woman with a strong rapport with wolves, yes, but her spirit dwells within a human body. She thinks with a human mind. Even her provenance is known. She is the child either of that northern prince or of one of his lackeys. There is no mystery about her. She is human. So I will argue before u-Liall, so I present the matter to you here. Do not fear you commit sacrilege in going to Misheemnekuru, for it is not a sacred place. Do not fear that your going will break the secular agreement, for the yarimaimalom themselves have already done so."

At the conclusion of this explanation Shivadtmon looked rather stunned—as he should. The master had delivered it with the eloquence he usually reserved for a full conclave.

"Do you understand?" the master asked more gently.

"I do, Master. I do."

"Then go forth. Create an opportunity for Waln to 'discover' your desire to accompany him. Lead him into seeing the advantages of your participation in the venture. Never for an instant let him think he is not leading the expedition."

"I understand, Master."

Shivadtmon bowed himself from the room, and Dantarahma, his master from the young man's earliest days as a servant of Water, watched him go, his attitude one of quiet sorrow.

Although the aridisdu did not know it, Dantarahma had felt forced to lay the groundwork for denying any knowledge of Shivadtmon's betrayal of the beliefs the aridisdu professed. There were documents that would be found in Shivadtmon's room, a record of indebtedness, some writings on heretical topics.

Their frequent visits, if anyone had noticed, would be explained as a maintaining of a long association. Dantarahma sincerely felt the sorrowful guilt with which he would confess that he had suspected Shivadtmon's straying into heresy, that he had entertained Shivadtmon so often in the hope of keeping him faithful to the orthodox way.

It would be in the best service to the deities if Shivadtmon died during the attack on the central islands. Then only the planted documents would speak for his "true" character. If Shivadtmon lived, however, he would still be condemned. Even when he heard Dantarahma speak against him, Shivadtmon would never dare betray his connection to Dantarahma's private religious circle. All the participants had sworn never to reveal the holy rites in which they partook, and Shivadtmon was unlikely to break this oath. As an added means to assure his silence, Shivadtmon would receive communications indicating that if he only kept true to his vows, he would be spirited away to begin life anew.

But the omens indicated that Shivadtmon would die.

And these omens had been communicated in living blood as it streamed from the victim. They had been heard by the soul of one glorying in the power to be taken along with a life.

Years before, in his investigations into the sacrificial rites common in the days before what the ignorant called the Divine Retribution, Dantarahma had felt the tingling force that was ancient sorcery. Although that first encounter had been accidental and he might have withdrawn with nothing more than a scar on the tissue of his faith, Dantarahma felt no desire to retreat.

To retreat would have been to open himself to the suspicion that had touched him with the first burn of magic along his nerves—that the faith he had inherited from his ancestors was nothing more than an excuse to legitimize the uglier elements of sorcery.

Over years of increasingly bloody rituals, the dark side of Magic had become the goddess Dantarahma adored. As his long life drew toward its close, all he desired was to give her blood in the prayerful hope she would in return grant him life.

XXIX

ALTHOUGH THE SUN CONTINUED BRIGHT in the summer sky when Integrity finished telling of the creation of the maimalodalum, for Firekeeper it was as if darkness had fallen. She sat blinking at the gathered wolves, and even the romping of the two puppies could not awaken gladness in her heart.

I wonder how many of their littermates were born too disfigured to live? she thought bitterly. *I wonder if it would have been better if I had died in the fire that killed my parents? Certainly the kindness of the Royal Wolves has disfigured me for life.*

Without a sound, Firekeeper rose from where she had seated herself with such anxious eagerness when the sun had been bright and the air cool. She turned back into the forest and was gone before the wolves realized her intent.

Firekeeper was very good at hiding her trail from wolves. Such games had been the hide and seek of her childhood. Now she waded into a stream and went directly from the waters into the branches of an overhanging maple. Maple carried her to beech, beech to oak, all without her feet touching the ground.

Tree to tree Firekeeper went until she found one about whose base grew a tangle of honeysuckle and wild rose that she knew would mask her scent. Then she settled into the shelter of the broad-leafed branches, vanishing into stillness and despair.

Even Blind Seer's howls, high-pitched and increasingly anxious, were not enough to call her back.

Why should I go to him? I am better gone from him and from all people. I cannot be one or the other, and he would do far better with a mate who can be his true partner.

It did not help Firekeeper's mood to hear Moon Frost's voice raised along Blind Seer's, nor Dark Death's mingling with theirs. As for Integrity and Tenacity—their howls were the voices of despair and dark mockery. Firekeeper shrank from them as she shrank from no other.

One by one the wolf howls stilled. The cry that persisted the longest was Blind Seer's, but eventually even that voice grew quiet. Firekeeper noticed only to use that silence to pad the substance of her sorrow. She felt neither hunger nor thirst, only hopelessness.

The sun had been nearing its zenith when Integrity had completed her tale. It sank slowly into the long twilight of evening and still Firekeeper sat in her tree. Her muscles grew cramped, then eventually gave up their complaint and settled into stiffness. Her stomach tried a rumble or two, but stilled when it knew it would be unheeded.

Firekeeper sat as darkness fell and the stars began to twinkle. Eventually, she even ceased to grieve, forgot why she had taken to her perch. All she knew was that she had no reason to come down. She shifted a little to make herself more comfortable, but other than this accommodation, she didn't move. Motion in the forest below meant nothing to her, nor did the renewal of the wolf howls.

". . . if only a wolf may live, then you must be one. Strange wolf you may be, but if only a wolf may live, then you must be one. Strange wolf you may be, but if only a wolf may live, then you must be one."

The words rose from the drifts of memory, but Firekeeper could not remember where she had heard them. They were forgotten as soon as formed, yet they chased through her mind, filling all the spaces where she refused to think about the things that hurt. They repeated themselves, carving channels into her mind, and continuing to repeat even as Firekeeper drifted into an uneasy sleep.

She is very small, very sick. The wolves she loves have fought to save her life, but they are losing the struggle. They take her somewhere. Someone she cannot remember helps the wolves to care for her. However, she cannot make herself eat as the wolves do. Inexorably she is melting into death.

Anger shades the voice that urges her to drink hot blood and to gorge on hot flesh as the wolves do. The child chokes at the idea, retching up even the little she has swallowed. At last the voice says in anger, "If wolves are to live, then I name you a wolf. Be a wolf. Forget that you ever were human. Your heart is a wolf's, your appetite a wolf's, your memory a wolf's. Strange wolf you may be, but if only a wolf may live, then you must be one."

Child becomes woman and woman becomes knowledge. Bitter knowledge confronts the unseen speaker.

"But I am not a wolf. I am a human. I have two arms, two legs. I have hands, not paws. I have no tail. My nose is dead. My eyes see differently. I hear but poorly. My naked skin breaks and leaks at the least scrape. I am not a wolf."

"Strange wolf you may be."

"I am no wolf. I am human."

"Only a wolf may live."

"I am no wolf."

"Then you must be one."

"How can I be one? Twice I have come close to that which I thought might make me wolf. Twice I have found only hatefulness. I cannot be a wolf. I am human."

"Strange wolf you may be."

"I tell you, I am no wolf! I am human."

"Only a wolf may live."

"If only a wolf may live, then I must die."

"You must be one."

"How?"

"Strange wolf you may be."

It is like shouting at an echo. Firekeeper howls in frustration and hears the frustration turn into a human scream, a scream that rips into her ears and forces her . . .

Awake.

Firekeeper found herself awake, and awake found herself falling. Somehow she had let herself drift deeply enough off to sleep that she had lost her balance. This was a thing that had never happened to her before, not in countless nights spent asleep in the relative safety above the ground.

She grabbed at the branches as she fell, managed to slow her descent, twisting to orient so that she would land as the squirrels do. When she hit, the thick cushion of honeysuckle and rose caught her. Even so, she hit hard enough that the breath was knocked from her, but there was no sharp cracking of bone, no loss of consciousness.

She had stepped clear of the torn vines and was shaking her limbs, making sure that each would obey her, when Blind Seer burst through the underbrush. His breath came hard and ragged. From the sound she knew he had run fast, summoned by her scream. Blind Seer did not stop to catch his breath. Instead, he knocked Firekeeper from her feet and pinned her to the ground.

"Hey! That hurts!"

That was the human sense of the yelp he forced from her. Blind Seer returned neither pity nor amusement.

"I've worried about you, bitch. You're lucky if all I do is knock the breath from you. You're lucky I don't break your legs so you can't run away again."

Firekeeper lay back, surrendering, mutely begging for mercy she knew she did not deserve. An angry human might have refused that surrender so sincerely offered, but Blind Seer was a wolf and after a long moment he released her from his weight.

"Why did you run?" he asked. "Why didn't you answer me?"

Firekeeper trembled, a shadow of her earlier despair touching her as she forced her shaken body to sit upright. She leaned back against a tree and looked up from beneath her lashes at the blocky shadow that was the blue-eyed wolf.

"I thought you would do better without me. I've seen how you looked at Moon Frost. I've heard how the Wise Wolves need new blood. I am no help, only impediment. As long as you must watch for me . . ."

"Firekeeper . . ."

The sound Blind Seer made was a soft moan, a cry from the heart.

"Firekeeper, I never meant to hurt you. It is so hard sometimes being only with the humans. You have not had time to play. I admit, I enjoyed the romps with Moon Frost, but I never meant to make you jealous."

There was a long pause.

"Well, maybe a little jealous."

Firekeeper held out her hand. Blind Seer came and lay alongside her. The touch of his fur should have been too hot to bear on this sultry night, but it was not.

"You did?"

"Umm . . ."

That was all the sound, but it carried within itself a wealth of information. It was a declaration of love and devotion, of desperation, of awareness of futility.

"Firekeeper, don't give up."

"Give up?"

"Give me up. Give up trying to find a way for our worlds to meet. When we left our pack, you were my favorite sister. I don't know when or how things changed, but they did. You are my partner. Your heart beats with mine. I don't know why we're the wrong shapes, but somewhere there must be the means to make a bridge between us."

"Must there be?" she said.

Her hand rested on Blind Seer's back, and he bent around to lick it.

"There must be," he said. "Think, dear heart. We have only been out in the world for a bit more than two years. Twice in that time we have come across what seems to be an answer."

"If Melina guessed right about that ring," Firekeeper said, but her mind was struggling to capture a memory. Something about "twice." "Twice I have come close . . ." Who had said that?

"I did," she said aloud, and her belly grew cold.

She had long known that she dreamed at night, dreams that held fragments of her past, but never before had she remembered one of her dreams so clearly.

"Eh?" Blind Seer said. "What is it, Firekeeper? You did what?"

Firekeeper curled her fingers tightly in his fur.

"I dreamed, Blind Seer, about when I was very small, when the wolves first took me in."

"I thought you remembered nothing of that time," he said, and she heard something that she realized after a moment was jealousy.

"Blind Seer, I think it was a true dream, not a memory. A voice saying odd things to me, about my being a wolf."

"Of course you are a wolf!" Blind Seer said emphatically. "A strange wolf, but no less a wolf for the strangeness."

The dream was fading now, but she heard it again in Blind Seer's words. "Strange wolf you may be, but if only a wolf may live, then you must be one." She might forget the rest of the dream, but those words she would remember.

"Firekeeper," Blind Seer said, "if you can bear it, Integrity told me that there are things she would show us, things rooted in the Old World magic. I begin to think that the Royal Wolves are unwise to court ignorance of such things."

Firekeeper longed to say "Why? Such things are gone. They have no place in our world," but with the voice of memory still pounding in her head, she could not.

"Even if the Old World sorcerers are gone," she agreed, "their heritage remains. It shapes the people who are descended from them and has left traces wherever they gathered thickly."

"There is that," Blind Seer agreed, "but as I see it, there is another matter to consider."

"Oh?"

"It seems to me that the Royal Wolves are as puppies regarding this matter. They are torn by thorns and so kick dirt over the bush until it is buried, saying to themselves, 'There are no more thorns, now. I will never be scratched.'"

Firekeeper nodded, not liking this thinking at all, but seeing the wisdom in it.

"But the bush grows out from beneath the dirt or casts seeds, and soon there are as many thorns as ever," she said. "And in reality, the thorns were never gone. The pup simply could not see them."

"Exactly," Blind Seer said. "We have seen several of these hidden thorns already. Now Integrity offers us a chance to see others, but she can offer us what no one else could—some understanding of how they grow."

Firekeeper grunted her agreement.

"I will listen and try to learn," she said. "I think that magic and the avoidance of magic touches us deeply."

Me more so than you, she thought, *or so I am beginning to suspect. I hardly know what words to use.*

"Blind Seer," she said aloud, "would you believe me if I said I think that my running away was more than bad temper?"

"I would believe it more easily than I believe you are capable of such an extended snit," he said. "You have your moods, but rarely are you so ungracious."

His sides huffed in amusement. "And I have never before even heard of you falling from a tree."

Firekeeper thumped his flank. Slowly and carefully, she related what she recalled of her dream. When she finished, Blind Seer was very still.

"Do you know of any such as I recall? Someone who could give an order to a mind and make it think itself other than it was?" she asked.

"Only Melina," Blind Seer recalled. "This has something of the same flavor to it. Remember, though, I was hardly a pack leader when we left. There may have been secrets our parents did not confide in me."

"True. Or maybe they did not know. Rip and Shining Coat were not the One Male and One Female in my youngest days. Do you know what I think happened to me when Integrity told the story of the maimalodalum?"

"I can guess, but tell me and I will listen."

"I think I was truly in a very bad temper, like a puppy who has for the first time been refused choice meat from the kill. I despaired of ever being a wolf, and somehow touched on this long-ago working in my mind."

Firekeeper could not go on, so Blind Seer did for her.

"Despair made you consider yourself human, not wolf, and somewhere in your mind was this trap—a wolf could live, but a human could not. You warred with yourself and might have done worse damage than a fall but for that one phrase, 'Strange wolf you may be.' It gave you permission to live, though in order to do so you must accept your strangeness—and your wolfishness."

He rose and licked her face.

"Can you accept that strangeness, dear heart? I am very afraid of your refusing to live."

Firekeeper hugged his head close.

"I can accept it," she said. "After all, my own strangeness is the thing I know best. Come. We dwell on such matters too long and too seriously. Perhaps in the end, they are nothing more than phantasms. Let us go to Integrity and see what she has to show us. Things preserved this long are certain to be more solid."

Blind Seer looked Firekeeper up and down.

"You might want to stop and wash. Falling from a tree has done you no good. We could feed you, too. I heard your stomach rumbling protest while we spoke."

"I will wash," Firekeeper said, feeling the tangles and mats in her hair.

"While you do so," Blind Seer said. "I will hunt for you—and howl to our hosts that you are found and we will be to them by the cool time of evening."

"Will that be polite?" Firekeeper asked. "I have already been rude enough."

"Who wants to discuss serious matters in the heat of the day?" Blind Seer replied reasonably. "Whatever they wished to tell us has waited this long. It can wait a bit longer. Besides, not only are you dirty and unfed, you look as if you need sleep."

Firekeeper shivered. "I'm not sure I want to sleep. I'm afraid of what I might dream."

RAHNISEETA RECEIVED THE INVITATION to call on Meiyal, iaridisdu of the Horse, without too much surprise. Rumors were already circulating that Derian Carter had returned from wherever the Wise Horse had taken him.

Of course, for most of those relating the story, the return was the first they had heard of the adventure. Rahniseeta and Harjeedian had kept their word to say nothing of the matter. She assumed Harjeedian had made some report to the iaridisdu and ikidisdu of the Temple of the Cold Bloods, but they had been politic enough not to say anything further.

Now, I suppose, we are being offered a more complete version of the tale as a reward for our cooperation, and I, rather than Harjeedian, am being given the report because no one cares where I go, while Harjeedian is rising in importance.

Despite the sour taint to her thoughts, Rahniseeta felt good about the summons. Varjuna had praised her discretion and she had not been found wanting. Now once again that quality was being rewarded in the only way possible—with further confidences.

Rahniseeta was escorted into Meiyal's private office immediately upon her arrival. The Horse Temple complex was much smaller than that of the Temple of the Cold Bloods, because so many of the disdum resided in u-Bishinti. Elaborate statuary, paintings, and tile murals representing the patron animals provided ample reminder of to whom the temple was dedicated.

Meiyal did not rise when Rahniseeta entered, but the young man sitting in a chair near her desk did so with alacrity marred only slightly by a certain stiffness.

"Derian!" Rahniseeta said. At the sight of him well and strong, a worry she hadn't known was with her unclenched itself from around her heart. "You look well."

"I am," he said, "and so do you."

He grinned at her, and Rahniseeta was both pleased and slightly discomfited to hear a compliment in his words. She was more accustomed to tongue-tied silence from the northerner.

Meiyal motioned Rahniseeta to a chair. The clerk who had escorted Rahniseeta in offered refreshments, then stood by the iaridisdu's side, ready to be of service but offering nothing but a very correct smile by way of greeting. Unlike Rahniseeta, Cishanol was training to become a disdu. Clerking for the iaridisdu meant he was considered promising. In a moment, Rahniseeta would realize that his remaining meant that Cishanol also had Meiyal's complete trust.

"Rahniseeta, we have summoned you here to show you Derian alive and well," Meiyal said. "As the Temple of the Cold Bloods where you reside has actively supported the project to bring us into contact with the northerners, we felt we owed this unofficial courtesy."

"Support the project," Rahniseeta thought. *That's a polite way of saying the Temple of the Cold Bloods is in over its head, but isn't abandoning Harjeedian now that Firekeeper has proven nothing like what anyone expected. But there's something odd here. Why shouldn't Derian simply come over and visit? He's done that often enough.*

Meiyal's wrinkled lips shaped a slight smile.

"I see you have questions you are too polite to ask. Derian, tell Rahniseeta why Eshinarvash came for you."

Derian did so, and as he spoke Rahniseeta could tell this was a polished account, but for all of that she did not think Derian was leaving anything out.

After Derian reached the point where he revealed Dantarahma's involvement, Rahniseeta was certain. If ever there had been an item to omit, this would be the one. Catching a glimpse of the emotions that flickered across the face of Meiyal's clerk as he listened, Rahniseeta felt certain Cishanol had not heard this before either and she experienced a curious sensation that their mutual shock was a bond between them.

"Do you wish me to report this to the i-disdum of the Temple of the Cold Bloods?" Rahniseeta asked, and she heard the quaver in her voice but felt no shame.

What Dantarahma had done went beyond sacrilege; it broke the treaty with the yarimaimalom—and the Beasts knew it. For their own mysterious reasons, they had chosen to act in this fashion. Rahniseeta hoped it was because they valued the Liglimom as much as the majority of the Liglimom valued the yarimaimalom.

"No, Rahniseeta, I do not wish you to confide this information to the i-disdum. Although I trust they are faithful to their vows, there may be those close to them who are not. I confide in you, and in you, Cishanol, because before this tale can go any further, we must have confirmation."

Cishanol spoke and there was relief in his voice. "Then this may not be true?"

"Oh, no," Meiyal said. "I believe it is true. However, the further we ride from those who either know horses or this northerner, the harder it will be to convince them. Best we have all the horses between the shafts and ready to pull before we set out on a journey."

"I see," Cishanol replied, "and am, as ever, at your service."

"I know you are," Meiyal said, "and I know you are completely worthy of trust. Rahniseeta has also proven herself faithful."

Meiyal sighed deeply. "And I have made what inquiries I could, and it seems that you both were within Heeranenahalm on the night Derian witnessed the ceremony."

Rahniseeta blinked. Where had she been? Playing music with Barnet? Copying letters? No, there had been a special service that night, an anointing of some new candidates. Both she and Harjeedian had attended, he to serve, she because a girl she had known for several years was among the candidates.

The clerk looked as if he, too, was trying to remember where he had been, and smiled slightly.

"A good thing that I was the one who drove you to u-Bishinti, I think. However, iaridisdu, that is not enough proof. I might have intended to attend a service, but had to cancel because you called upon me."

Meiyal waggled a finger at him.

"That quibbling is what will delay and delay again your ordination, Cishanol. There are other proofs. I have seen how well cooked you take your meat—if you eat it at all. I cannot see you rushing to eat life hot flesh from a slain mare, or delighting in the shedding of blood."

Cishanol paled a trace.

"You have a point, Meiyal. I only raised the question because . . ."

"Because you are cautious, as Rahniseeta has proven herself to be cautious. Caution is what we will need in this matter, caution and discretion. Varjuna and myself cannot run about asking questions without raising suspicions. This is a bad time for the temples. Too many issues have been raised. Even if none suspected why we were curious, some clever mind might make the wrong deduction and a new argument be raised.

"Look at this matter of whether or not to ship the foreigners back north," Meiyal continued. "Some days ago it was nothing. The questions were whether or not learning to directly speak to the yarimaimalom would please or anger the deities. Now that matter has fallen to the wayside and this new one taken its place—though the first is certainly not resolved. This is a touchy time, and we will do our best to start no rumors."

Cishanol bent his head in acquiescence. Rahniseeta sat with her hands folded, awaiting orders. She had thought she disliked being undervalued. Now she was finding that having a value brought its own problems.

"Cishanol, you are to be my research assistant," Meiyal went on. "Derian's account raises some interesting points. One of these is that all the animals slain were white. It seems to me that in my studies long ago I came across a reference to the old ceremonies and that different animals were considered appropriate sacrifices at different times and for different needs. Dantarahma may have needed to adapt these rituals because of his need for secrecy, but even so, we may learn something useful."

The clerk nodded. "It occurs to me that one of the things I may be able to find out is the sequence of rituals, and the frequency at which they were held. We may be able to anticipate when the next one will be."

"Or what," Derian added thoughtfully, "animals they will need. Then we can trace who is collecting what and perhaps get some names."

"Good thinking," Meiyal agreed. "Another thing you may find, Cishanol, especially if you must go from our temple library to the larger one, is that certain texts have been used recently. Try and learn who has used them, but be very careful. The wrong questions could give our suspicions away. It is best that the heretics go on believing themselves undetected or they may take actions that will make it impossible for us to find them."

Cishanol nodded. Rahniseeta had the feeling the clerk was itching to take notes, but was smart enough to realize that while no one could read what he thought, someone might stumble on a written note.

"Rahniseeta," Meiyal said, and the young woman tried to sit up even straighter, "your task is similar to Cishanol's but much less easy to define. As with him, you will be trying to find things that will enable us to tell who other than Dantarahma is involved in this. Derian saw no effort being made to conceal the worshipper's faces from each other, so they know each other.

"As a member of u-Liall, Dantarahma is a member of no temple, but originally he was an aridisdu of the Water Beasts. Even more than most of u-Liall, he continues to associate with his former temple. It is likely that several of his worshippers are drawn from their numbers. Fortunately, the Temple of the Cold Bloods has its aquatic element. See what you can learn about who are Dantarahma's associates. Your brother may be of help in this."

"Then I may tell Harjeedian?" Rahniseeta said with some relief.

Meiyal gave a tight smile. "He was attending the same initiation you were on the night of the blood sacrifice, so we know he was not among the worshippers. Moreover, I do not think he is at all inclined that way. I know that restraint is admired by those who work with reptiles, but Harjeedian has never struck me as uncaring."

Rahniseeta thought of the attention that Harjeedian gave those serpents that were given into his charge and nodded.

"However," Meiyal went on, "you may confide in Harjeedian only if he will swear by whatever he holds most dear that he will not confide in anyone, even in the i-disdum of his order. If you do not think he could do this, make up some excuse for your interest. Say you wondered because of something the foreigners said. Be creative."

Rahniseeta blinked. She wondered if she could manage to fool Harjeedian, but if it was a matter of protecting him from being torn between allegiances, she would find a way. This was too important to do otherwise.

"I understand, Iaridisdu. I really do."

"I thought you would," Meiyal said. "Dantarahma's intimates are not the only ones who may be involved in this heretical movement. Indeed, I doubt that he has drawn his support from so limited a group. If he had, the absence of so many at a given time could not help but be noted before now.

"Therefore, we are looking for links between people intimately associated with Dantarahma to others—others they might not normally be expected to befriend. One possibility is an antiquarian interest. Another is dissatisfaction with current trends. Another might be some resentment of the yarimaimalom. There have always been those who feel that the omens are purer when they come from the lesser beasts."

Rahniseeta resisted an urge to press her hands to her head. She knew now why Cishanol had wanted to take notes. There was so much here, and while Meiyal had clearly given much thought to the matter, it was all new to Rahniseeta.

Meiyal went on relentlessly, "In a way, we are divinely blessed that this matter has been uncovered during a time of general unrest. People are speaking their minds. In another the unrest is not in our favor, for many who otherwise would be content are speaking out."

"I can only try," Rahniseeta said relentlessly, "but I think I would rather look for white calves."

"Zira is investigating the pedigree of the white horse," Meiyal said. "We will go from there. We may also look into builders, for Derian thought the structure he saw was of relatively modern manufacture. Although the step pyramid was truncated, stone had to be hauled for the building."

"Do you know where the temple is?" Rahniseeta asked.

"Not precisely," Meiyal replied, "but Derian kept good track of directions and we have an idea. Unhappily, riding out to take a look is the last thing we should do. I doubt there is a custodian. The place is certainly deserted when not in use."

"And we don't want to give anything away," Rahniseeta said. "I understand. I'll begin right away—by doing nothing out of the ordinary."

Meiyal beamed. "Precisely. Perhaps you could give Derian a tour of u-Seeheera. I understand this has been planned for some time, but you've all been kept too busy."

Derian looked for a moment as if he was about to protest that he was still too busy, then smiled.

"I'd be pleased—if Rahniseeta has the time."

Rahniseeta felt she owed Derian countless apologies for how she'd treated him. She'd refused to see him as a person—only as a puzzle piece, something to be solved and worked with. The Wise Horses had seen his worth from the start. The yari-maimalom had confided in him. It was time to start making amends.

"You've seen much of Heeranenahalm," Rahniseeta said when they had taken their leave of Meiyal and left the Horse Temple.

"Bits and pieces," Derian agreed.

"Would you like to see more," Rahniseeta asked, "or to go down to u-Seeheera?"

"U-Seeheera," Derian replied promptly. "It's still something of a ghost city in my mind, empty streets and no one at any of the windows."

"That's right," Rahniseeta said. "They cleared the processional way when you arrived, didn't they?"

"Uh-huh. I like u-Bishinti just fine," Derian went on, "but it's artificial in its own way. There are no markets, no shops, no taverns—unless you count the place I took you when you came there with Barnet. How is Barnet, anyhow?"

"He is doing well," Rahniseeta said. "Like you he has begun to make friends. His collection of stories is growing, too. Sometimes he tries one out on me. He can be very good—or completely miss the point."

She went on to relate how Barnet had retold a story from the Temple of Flyers in a fashion that would have horrified the originator of that religious tale. For a moment she thought about telling Derian the rumors that Barnet was gathering more than stories in the Temple of Flyers, but decided against it.

"I think, though, that he longs to return north," Rahniseeta said. "Do you?"

"Definitely," Derian said. "My family is there, as well as friends, and lots of unfinished business. Remember, I didn't choose to take this trip."

The words hung between them, and Rahniseeta could think of nothing to say. She settled for changing the subject, talking rapidly about the techniques used to make the elaborate tile murals that adorned the buildings along the processional way.

The street was busy today. Its width invited use by carts and wagons hauling much more prosaic materials than the flower-trimmed floats and elegantly caparisoned beasts that it had been designed to accommodate. Children chased each other up and down the median, playing hide-and-seek around the planters.

"This is more like it," Derian said, looking around with pleasure. "Eagle's Nest could use a road like this one. It's getting to the point that there's talk about barring commercial traffic except at night."

"This is nothing," Rahniseeta said. "Come this way. I will show you where the farmers come to trade. In summer the stalls are brighter even than the festival parades."

In the market, Derian walked alongside her, making animated comparisons between what was sold here, in his home city, and in the markets in New Kelvin. Although the northerners were hardly a common sight, the others had been out and about enough that they no longer drew a crowd merely by walking along a public way. Derian's red hair attracted some attention, but only a few small children actually tried to touch.

Derian was very tolerant, and that toleration bred courtesy in return. Soon the pair was able to go their way amid the stalls deliberately unheeded. Derian began to enjoy himself, and asked for her help buying a few small presents for his family. Rahniseeta had prepared for this, and had with her a liberal supply of the tokens which vendors could exchange for services at the various temples and related facilities. The vendors were at least as happy to take these as they were to receive the more usual currency offered by shoppers unassociated with the temples.

Derian talked about his parents and siblings as he selected gifts, about his lovely but practical mother, about his father. "Varjuna rather reminds me of him." About his younger sister and brother, the one still trying to find an orientation for her various gifts, the other so fixated on horses "that he makes me seem only mildly interested. I'd love to bring him a horse like Prahini, but he'll have to settle for some models."

Rahniseeta had the impression that Derian was torn between renewed homesickness and anticipation of the pleasure he would bring to his family as he related tales of yet another fantastic land.

She remembered Harjeedian's telling her that some factions were agitating to have the northerners not merely imprisoned or sent back where they had come from, but killed.

We will not permit that. Rahniseeta thought fiercely. *No matter how eloquently the disdum speak of omens and revelations, Derian, Lady Blysse, and Blind Seer were taken from their homeland by force. I have no idea why they haven't escaped. Perhaps it is because they have nowhere to run? Perhaps because we have entangled them in our affairs?*

She was startled from her thoughts by Derian laying a hand on her arm and pulling her back into one of the many narrow streets that bordered the market.

"Sorry," he apologized in a low voice, "but I'll not speak with that man. If we stay here a moment, we can avoid him. He seems pretty engrossed in whatever he's discussing with his companion."

Rahniseeta looked in the direction Derian indicated with a stiff toss of his head and saw Waln Endbrook walking along with one of the aridisdu from the Temple of Sea Beasts. She struggled for a moment to remember his name, then had it. Shivadtmon. Harjeedian had mentioned him in connection with the selection of the disdu for the voyage of *Fayonejunjal.*

"I'd prefer not to see them, either," she admitted, leading the way into a weaver's shop, where the two men were unlikely to come by chance. "Waln makes me uncomfortable, and Shivadtmon dislikes Harjeedian."

Judging by the look on Derian's face, he wouldn't cut anyone off his social calendar just for disliking Harjeedian.

He said almost as much aloud.

"Well, I can't say anything about liking or disliking Harjeedian, but anyone who will get that chummy with Waln Endbrook is either a fool or playing some game."

"What do you mean?" Rahniseeta said, turning over a swatch of tightly woven wool cloth dyed a soft jade green.

"I mean Waln Endbrook is as nasty a bit of goods as there is," Derian said, his voice tight with the anger he was trying hard not to show. "He sold us, didn't he? Would u-Liall have gone after Firekeeper if Waln hadn't come telling tales of wonder? That's not the worst he's done either. Waln Endbrook didn't get what he wanted from that gambit, but that won't stop him from trying another."

There was such a hard, angry light in the young man's hazel eyes that Rahniseeta feared to ask what else Waln Endbrook had done. She gave the shopkeeper a few tokens for some of the green cloth. By the time the transaction was completed Waln and Shivadtmon had gone off in the direction of the harbor.

"Well," she said, "Shivadtmon is not a fool. One of the reasons he dislikes Harjeedian is that he felt he should be given the berth as disdu on *Fayonejunjal*. Harjeedian won it, not only because of his skill with languages, but because many of the disdum felt that Water already had honor enough in supplying the ship, her captain, and much of her crew."

Derian looked at her.

"Water did? As in the Temple of Water? I had the impression that this was Fire's project."

Rahniseeta could see Derian was no longer interested in shopping, so led the way into a pleasant park where they could sit and talk in relative privacy. She bought them chilled drinks from a vendor, and led the way to a bench surrounded by roses. Anyone watching them would think they were courting, not conspiring—or so she hoped.

"The project was begun under the aegis of Fire," Rahniseeta said, "but Water is the patron of most things related to the sea. It only makes sense. Air has some say when sailing vessels are concerned, but Earth and Fire are distinctly in second place."

"And Magic?" Derian asked. "Where does Magic fit in?"

"Magic is in a strange position," Rahniseeta said. "We do not abhor her, as your people do, because it is her touch that enables us to communicate with the deities. However, sorcery carries with it the taint of the Old Country rulers. Therefore, though all acknowledge Magic, none practice her arts except to reach the divine."

"I think I understand," Derian said. "So Shivadtmon doesn't like Harjeedian because he thinks Harjeedian got his berth. This sounds awful, but is Shivadtmon associated with Dantarahma? I mean, other than their having started out in the same temple."

Rahniseeta had been having similar thoughts, but they sounded somehow harsher and more final coming from Derian.

"He might be," she said. "He well might. Harjeedian said the level of Shivadtmon's disappointment at not being chosen was inordinate, 'As if he had been promised the post in advance.'"

"I think," Derian said slowly, "it would be very good if you could find out more about Shivadtmon. Even if he isn't part of Dantarahma's group, anger and resentment are good tools for getting people to do what you want."

Rahniseeta nodded. "You are very right."

Derian glanced up at the sky.

"I've a bit of a ride back to u-Bishinti," he said. "May I walk you home?"

Rahniseeta blinked but found nothing forward in Derian's expression, only kindness and courtesy.

"And if Barnet's in, I can at least stop to say a few words," Derian went on.

Rahniseeta wondered why this further proof of the young man's good-mannered thoughtfulness should leave her feeling so very disappointed.

XXX

NOT ONE OF THE WOLVES asked Firekeeper about what had precipitated her flight when she and Blind Seer returned. Perhaps the blue-eyed wolf had taken advantage of leaving to hunt to give them some explanation. Perhaps the Wise Wolves respected her privacy—certainly they had secrets enough of their own. Whatever the reason, Firekeeper was grateful.

That the pack had already eaten was evident in the rounded bellies of the two puppies. These fought a mock battle over a strip of hide, invigorated, as were all their kind, by the cooler air of night and the exciting scents carried in the breezes off of the water.

Integrity came closest to prying into the reasons behind Firekeeper's reactions, but even she was circumspect.

"We had thought you might not believe our tale," Integrity said, "but it seems rather that you believed it all too well."

"What you told me spoke to something deep within my heart," Firekeeper replied. "Perhaps I knew all too well that something as wonderful as the ability to adopt another's shape could not be had easily. Even more, I have seen some strange things these past two years. Tales of magic are not as strange to me as they would be to most northerners."

"So Blind Seer has told us," Integrity replied.

Integrity licked between the many toes of her deformed paw, and Firekeeper found herself wondering whether those members of the pack she had not yet seen also bore some stigmata. Were the Wise Wolves of this central island recruited from puppies such as she had seen in Grey Thunder's pack? Was this island a home to those who could not be permitted even the chance of being seen by humans—but who were still treasured by their pack members?

But Integrity was speaking, and that demanded Firekeeper's attention, for reason of good manners if nothing else.

"There are things we would show you," Integrity said, "things that are intertwined with the maimalodalum. Will you look or would you prefer to rest further upon what you now know before . . ."

The One Female trailed off, and Firekeeper knew she was being offered an opportunity to further calm herself. Therefore, whatever it was Integrity and Tenacity wished to show her was likely to be upsetting.

The night before, Firekeeper had slept where she could reach out and touch Blind Seer; it would have been cruel to sleep as she so often did with her head pillowed on his flank in this damp, sticky heat. Her sleep had been dreamless, but several times she had shaken herself awake rather than let the dreams rise. Despite a growing sense of dread, Firekeeper knew what her answer must be.

"I am willing, Integrity, and I thank you for the honor. Am I right in guessing that these things which you are about to show us are among those things of which one does not speak?"

Integrity twitched her overlarge ears, almost as a human would have chuckled.

"See for yourself. Then tell me what you think."

With that, Integrity rose, and her mate and pups rose with her. The pups seemed to have some idea where they were going, and took pleasure in it. For the first time, Firekeeper realized that Moon Frost and Dark Death were not present.

She asked after them and Tenacity replied, "Moon Frost's broken leg was well set. No wolf could have done for her what you did. Even so, the injury is giving her pain. One of our pack has a talent for healing. Dark Death is arranging a meeting."

Firekeeper grunted her thanks. She was just as glad not to have the others along. Moon Frost was positively humble these days, but there was threat lurking beneath her surrender. Wolves took advantage of weakness in their rivals, and Firekeeper knew how weakened she had been by the truth about the maimalodalum.

Dark Death was another matter. His changed attitude toward her had initially amused and pleased her, but having embraced her own feelings toward Blind Seer with greater honesty than ever before, Firekeeper realized that Dark Death's admiration for her was a threat to Blind Seer.

These thoughts kept her from worrying about where they were going as they climbed the slope to where clustered stone towers blocked out the stars with their height. Blind Seer raised his head to better catch some errant scent, but made no other comment. Nor did the other wolves—who must have noticed the motion and its implicit question—offer anything in reply.

Firekeeper dropped one hand to her Fang, but did not draw it. She wondered if she should ask for the wolves to permit her to make a light. What good would it do to show her whatever it was by moonlight? Her night vision was far better than that of any human she had met, but even so . . .

She was about to ask Integrity to wait when a door swung open in the base of the centermost of the towers and warm golden light flooded out. It illuminated a long rectangle of paved courtyard in front of the door, and in that light Firekeeper pinned down something that had been bothering her.

.The area here was too well maintained for ruins. Her feet had met none of the rolling crumbles of stone, or the unevenness caused by weeds and grass thrusting their way between slabs that she had subconsciously expected. The towers she had seen outlined against the sky showed no broken battlements, no collapsed roofs. The buildings had been maintained. Why would even the yarimaimalom bother to do that?

Firekeeper wanted to stop, wanted to grind in her heels and demand explanations, but the two puppies were running eagerly ahead. Neither of their watchful parents made any move to stop them, and so Firekeeper went toward the spreading light, trying very hard to remain unafraid.

Blind Seer pressed close to her.

"Odd smells," he said softly, "but there is no tang here of fear or hate. Nor do the Wise Wolves smell of anything other than the mildest concern. Come along. Haven't we fought our way out of worse?"

Firekeeper actually wasn't sure that they had. Fighting their way out of things didn't happen very often, and it always seemed that one of them ended up severely injured. Still, she understood the spirit of Blind Seer's brag and resolved to live up to his confidence in her—or rather, to his confidence in them.

Puppies before them, Integrity and Tenacity behind, Firekeeper and Blind Seer walked through the golden-lit door. The portal was wide enough that they could pass through side by side, and Firekeeper wondered if the humans who had built the place had been larger than the humans today, or had only wished to give the impression that they were giants.

The room they entered was rounded, comprising the entire base of the tower. The only interruptions in the vast space were regularly spaced pillars whose purpose might have been to support the beams of the floor above, but which might have been purely ornamental. Even Firekeeper, usually indifferent to art as she was to most things that were not strictly useful, saw the beauty in the shaping of these columns and was impressed.

But even the elegant pillars with their fanciful shapes could not hold her attention beyond a flickering instant. Gathered at the far side of the large chamber, as if to emphasize by their position that they would not stand between their visitors and the door, were a doubled hand of the strangest creatures Firekeeper had ever seen.

Not one was a creature that Firekeeper could name, but in their making were elements she recognized. Horns like those on a bull. Feathers. Shining iridescent scales. Antlers that would have been the pride of any buck. Stripes identical to those running down the tail of a skunk.

Even in the clear light within the chamber Firekeeper could hardly make her eyes see sense. Not even the costumed creations of New Kelvin rivaled this lot for variety and strangeness. Those costumes mimicked monstrosities through the clever use of fabric or fur or tanned hides. These before her were living bodies that held within their shapes impossible combinations of form.

Firekeeper stared. Then she pressed her hands over her eyes and, after releasing them, stared again. The assembly remained. The monstrosities studied her and Blind Seer. In those many eyes Firekeeper found a focus and sought to find individuals.

Integrity broke the silence that had dominated the encounter to this point.

"These," said the One Female, "are the maimalodalum."

"Maimalodalum?" Blind Seer repeated, his voice thickening to a barely suppressed growl. "Are they immortal then?"

"No."

The answer came from a figure that was shaped somewhat like a human, but a human with bluish grey feathers sprouting out all over her body. The feathers were short over her torso and trunk, longer on her arms, as if some force had sought to shape the arms into wings and halted midway in frustration. The bird-woman's face was human, but her eyes were bird's eyes, and her nose was short, sharp, and very narrow.

"We are the descendants of the maimalodalum of whom Integrity has told you—the ones in whom the battle between beast soul and human soul pressed the body into conflict, so that rather than gaining the ability to change into one form or the other the soul was trapped within a body that was neither."

Firekeeper swallowed hard. This bird-woman reminded her somewhat of a shape Blind Seer had taken in a dream forgotten until this moment. Yet if the bird-woman was unsettling as a dream, many of those clustered behind her were nightmares. This creature at least wed two recognizable forms but most of the others borrowed from four or five sources, merging them into function without harmony.

So there were wolf's ears on a mostly human head, this head attached via a long neck to a body crafted in hybrid of wolf and jaguar, the whole overfurred with spots akin to those on a jaguar's coat though colored in shades of grey, not gold and black.

Another creature possessed an eagle's head on a snake's body. The sleek scaled torso sprouted very human arms and legs, though these were patterned over with scales to match the whole rather than naked as human limbs should be. The latter portion of the snake torso trailed behind the creature's legs as if it were the tail on an upright lizard.

Yet another of these maimalodalum bore a superficial resemblance to a hirsute man or a brown bear standing on its hind legs. Then she noticed the maimalodalu's hands and feet ended in heavy, rounded claws. She looked at its face, expecting to meet the small fierce eyes of a bear, and found instead the slit pupils of a snake. The tongue that lashed out as the creature inspected them was a snake's as well.

And these were the creatures easily parsed. The others possessed such an incomprehensible blending of limbs furred, scaled, and naked, of bodies defended by fangs, claws, stingers, that Firekeeper found herself studying details. Her mind simply refused to grasp the whole.

Only one thing was constant in all the maimalodalum. Whatever their shape, color, or size, the eyes that studied Firekeeper in return held intelligence. The weirdly shaped bodies bore themselves with rational control. The Royal Beasts who had raised Firekeeper had divided the spectrum of living things between Royal Kin and

Cousins, and in the maimalodalum Firekeeper could not deny that what stood before her were kin.

At her side where his fur brushed lightly against her, Firekeeper felt Blind Seer tremble. She knew that at the least excuse he would flee. She, too, wanted to run, but after her earlier panic she was done with running. Run as fast as she would, the puzzle offered by these strange creatures would remain, and though she might swim all the way back to Port Haven, and from there run west into the mountains, and there hide beneath her mother's belly, still the question would remain.

"You are the descendants of the maimalodalum," Firekeeper said, forcing her voice not to quaver. "Yet I thought the beast-souled were one and one. Your shapes hold many."

The bear-snake-man growled, "Your eyes are not impaired, at least."

Firekeeper flared, "But how? How has that happened? Did the spells go amiss? Did the plague heat twist you so?"

The bear-snake-man replied, "Yes, but not as you mean it. We are the descendants of the maimalodalum who survived the Fire Plague. Those who bore us came here for safety—and for other reasons—and so we have remained."

"Those who bore you?" Firekeeper tried to stifle the distaste in her voice, but the bear-snake-man heard it nonetheless.

"So are love and children only for the beautiful, Firekeeper? Are they only for those who resemble each other? I thought you would better understand—given your own inclinations."

Firekeeper flushed hot with shame.

"I . . . am stupid. The Wise Wolves told me of how the yarimaimalom once bred for talents and tainted their blood. I thought . . . I am a fool and very confused. Forgive me."

The bird-woman spoke. "Our blood is not tainted from overbreeding as is that of our Wise kin. We are children of the yarimaimalom who won their struggle against the sorcerers, yet that battle is one that cannot really be won. Many who defeated the attempt to take their forms and kill their will died. Those who lived found themselves trapped in bodies that were neither one creature nor the other. These fled into the wilds, knowing the sorcerers would destroy them. The yarimaimalom, however repulsed they might have been, at least felt pity."

The human-wolf-jaguar spoke, and at the sound of that voice Firekeeper felt a strange thrill, though the voice was rough and not at all musical.

"There were three compensations given to those who survived what the sorcerers would have done to them. First, although some were sterile, most could have children—if they could find a mate." The too-human lips curved. "I believe wolves have a saying 'Like knows like best.' We have no 'like' but ourselves, and our greatest likeness is that we are all unlike."

Firekeeper nodded understanding, but was still too ashamed to speak.

The human-wolf-jaguar went on, "The second compensation was that though many of our ancestors fell ill during the Fire Plague, very few died. The third compensation is related to this. Just as we inherited spots or fangs or claws from the Beast portion of our pairing, so we inherited traits from the human side. Only sorcerers could attempt to become maimalodalum, and the ability to do magic is a talent, not merely a skill."

Blind Seer spoke as one who thinks aloud: "So all of you are sorcerers?"

"Not quite, Blind Seer. Rather all of us have a latent sensitivity to sorcery—a sense rather than an ability."

"I do not understand," Blind Seer confessed.

"Nor I," Firekeeper said.

"Think of any of your senses," the human-wolf-jaguar said. "Vision, perhaps. You can see what is in your line of sight, but you cannot take out your eyes and throw them away from you and still see what they gaze upon. So it is with us. We can sense sorcery, look upon it as it were, hear its call, feel its vibrations, taste its tang in the air, smell its taint—but we cannot work original magic any more than you can manipulate an item merely by looking upon it or hearing the sounds it makes."

Firekeeper blinked. "That is a very good explanation."

"We have had," the bear-snake-man said, his earlier irritability dampened now, "a long time to work on it. Generations, in fact."

Firekeeper felt a blush rising again, but tried to answer calmly, "Then you have spent your time well."

The bird-woman gave a dry little laugh. "We are glad you think so."

"I stumble over my feet again," Firekeeper said, "but then where these things are concerned I am a pup beginning to walk. I will make no excuses, but try to remember my manners. I am called Firekeeper. This is Blind Seer. May we ask what to call you?"

"She reminds us of our manners," shrieked the eagle-headed maimalodalu, the one with the snake's body and human limbs.

To Firekeeper's surprise, this one's language was that of the yarimaimalom, though those with human mouths had spoken Liglimosh—a thing she had not thought about until now. She said nothing of this contrast, for the eagle-headed one was continuing.

"Prettily done, Firekeeper. We have had warning of your coming, but you have had little warning of us. Perhaps you are not the only one who should be shamed."

The eagle head turned to look at Firekeeper sideways, after the manner of birds. "I am called Sky-Dreaming-Earth-Bound, but Sky is enough."

One by one the others introduced themselves, and Firekeeper realized that she could understand them all, no matter their manner of speech. Moreover, they could all understand each other and those with human facial features could, like Firekeeper herself, speak the language of the yarimaimalom.

It seems, Firekeeper thought, *that the Liglimom could have found the translator they desired closer to home, but I do not think they would have welcomed these creatures. The maimalodalum are too great a reminder of what their ancestors were willing to do to gain power.*

Introductions completed, all settled comfortably onto the clean stone floor of the tower. Integrity and Tenacity also remained, and their two puppies ran out and about, calling everyone "aunt" or "uncle" with joyful lack of discrimination as to species. Firekeeper decided that this was the guide to follow and again felt ashamed.

I have long shouted my wolf's heart is trapped in a human body. How could I have been so quick to judge by appearances? The maimalodalum all have thinking minds and faithful hearts—though perhaps some are more pleasant than others.

She looked to where the puppies played tag around the gathered creatures, to where Tenacity and Integrity lay side by side.

And I think the Wise Wolves did not tell me all the truth. Here is proof that their tainted do still breed, but these pups show this can be done safely. Perhaps this island is where custom ends and something else rules.

The human-wolf-jaguar turned out to be named something like Defier-of-the-Deities. Firekeeper could not quite make sense of the term, for neither the Royal Beasts nor the humans she knew best had deities who could be defied. She decided that "Questioner" or "Challenger" might have been this creature's name had he not been born where gods were believed in, and the maimalodalu agreed.

"Call me Questioner, if that is easier for your mind," he said. "I have been called worse."

There was a smattering of what, despite the many different-shaped throats and noses that shaped it, was clearly laughter.

"Once we learned that you had been told the tale of the maimalodalum," Questioner said, "we knew you would ask the Wise Wolves if the tale held any truth."

"We?" Firekeeper asked. "Who is this 'we'?"

Questioner's ears flattened in annoyance.

"Little Two-legs, do you think you have gone hither and yon unwatched, unobserved? Even as the Liglimom find you unsettling, so do we. Truth the jaguar is nearly mad from her inability to read anything of the future where you are concerned. When she learned—a raven bore her the tale—that you had been told of the maimalodalum, for once her visions were clear. You were to be told the truth of the tale, but only in the right place, where you could not deny the uglier realities. You accepted those realities far more immediately than any of us had thought one so filled with hope and desire could, but still we felt you must see us."

Firekeeper's mind was trying to hold on to a handful of thoughts at once, each as confusing as the other. She spoke the simplest.

"Raven told her?"

"The ravens are interested in you," Questioner replied. "They rather like you, in fact. They knew Derian would bring you news from the mainland and worried it would trouble you. They thought to offer counsel and so listened to your conversation in order to know what to say."

Firekeeper doubted this altruism, but didn't press for another explanation. The yarimaimalom had permitted her to come into their sanctuary, but they had protected themselves from possible betrayal by spying on her. Very well. It was a wise precaution.

"I trouble Truth's visions?" Firekeeper asked. "Just me or all three of us newcomers?"

"You mostly," Questioner replied, "as I understand it. However, the more closely anything is connected to you, the more muddled the visions become. Therefore, Blind Seer is as hard to read as you are. Unless the matter deals with horses, so is Derian."

Firekeeper felt a touch of longing to see Derian; then she thought of her current company and was glad he was spared this shock. At least she and Blind Seer could understand what was said here. Derian would be at least half deaf.

Almost unbidden the next words came to her lips.

"Questioner, you called me 'Little Two-legs.' No one calls me that but my close kin, and few enough among them have used the name these last years since I am grown. Your voice troubles me. I think I know it, but I could not."

Questioner looked at her, his ears speaking wolf, his eyes wholly human. His eyes were blue, Firekeeper suddenly noticed. The realization made her feel very strange.

"Many years ago," Questioner said, his tone detached, "a maimalodalu thought he could do what no other had done since the days when yarimaimalom made treaty with humans and so exiled themselves from others of their kind. He thought he could explain our customs, reopen contact. He thought because he questioned, he could answer questions. He was wrong."

"You?" Firekeeper said. "You came north?"

"It was a long journey and a hard one. I found little welcome and less liking for the message I carried, but there were exceptions. One of these was in a place you and Blind Seer know well, a territory west of the Iron Mountains where the wolves watch against the coming of humans."

Blind Seer said gape-jawed, "Our home territory?"

"Just so," Questioner replied. "Chance was with me when I came to that place— chance or the will of the deities. I arrived soon after humans had made the crossing from the lands to the east. The Royal Wolves were crazed with fear, dredging up from half-remembered legends what little they knew about humankind. They might have slain the humans out of hand, but I convinced them to do otherwise. I told them how to the south we lived peacefully, even profitably with humans. My words blended with the Royal Wolves' own reluctance to kill for no reason, and so the humans lived."

"None still reside within that pack who can give lie to your tale," Blind Seer said, his hackles rising. "Though I do recall we have met one who was of the pack in those days."

"Speak with this one," Questioner said. "The tale will be the same."

Firekeeper stroked Blind Seer along his back as if she could smooth away his worries along with the roughness in his fur.

"Dear heart, I have memories . . . dreams all but forgotten until we came to this place. I cannot say the truth of the dreams, but I feel I have heard this voice before."

"These maimalodalum want something of you," Blind Seer rumbled. "I smell it on them. Always others want something from you. Always they give nothing back."

Firekeeper shook her head. "I will not argue that thanks have been slender and grudging, but the Royal Wolves have always given me life and home. The humans gave me life. I owe for that."

"For how long?" came the frustrated growl.

Questioner interrupted with understanding gentleness, "For as long as she cares to pay the debt, Blind Seer. I will not deny that we here have our hopes for Firekeeper, yet I will hold back any account of my tie to her past if you think that all I do is seek to put her in my debt."

Blind Seer replied, "That is something only Firekeeper can decide."

"Then I must know," Firekeeper said. "As for debts, Questioner is right. I pay, but I choose to pay. Wolves make a pack and grudge nothing, not even life, to the pack. I would be a wolf in this at least, so tell me what you can, Questioner."

Blind Seer turn his head to lick her hand.

"As you will, Firekeeper. Only I would hear more howling of your praises when you have run hard on another's hunt, that is all."

Firekeeper said nothing to this, for she had no answer.

"Tell on, Questioner," she said. "Please."

Fur over the human face, even fur short like that of a cat rather than long as on a wolf, made expressions harder to read, but Firekeeper thought Questioner looked a little wistful as he cast himself into memory's stream.

"The stay with your pack was a good time for me," he said, "among the best in my journeys. The humans had many among them with talents, and I taught the wolves and the other Royal Beasts how this might facilitate communication between ourselves and them. This group of humans were very determined to have nothing to do with those to the east, at least until they could treat with them as something other than petitioners. Then, too, it was clear that beyond talents these human settlers had no magic among them. Thus the Royal Beasts were assured that the humans could be chased away—or slain—if they violated the treaties made between them and the Royal Beasts.

"I have no idea how the fire that destroyed the settlement started. The humans had built many fires within their homes and these homes were constructed mostly of wood, rather than of clay and stone as is the case here. At the time of the fire, I had gone further west, hoping to build upon my success with your home pack. When news of the fire reached me, I returned only to find all but one small girl-child dead."

"Me," Firekeeper said.

"You. Your mother had rescued you, then she died trying to rescue your father, but not before she begged the wolves to care for you."

"My parents," Firekeeper said. "I don't remember them. Do you . . ."

"Their names were Donal Hunter and Sarena Gardener," Questioner said. "Donal had the talent for understanding animals. It is a great talent, for usually a mind can only understand a single type."

"As with Derian and horses," Blind Seer said.

The blue-eyed wolf leaned closer to Firekeeper and she knew he could feel her fighting down tears. To the best of her knowledge she had never felt more than the most abstract interest in these humans. Her mothers and fathers were all wolves, but now the tears were welling in her eyes, sobs choking at her breathing.

Questioner politely pretended not to notice, but went on with his gentle telling.

"Sarena had the talent for making plants grow. Apparently, this talent ran very strong in her family, and in her own way she was as special as Donal. They were among the first the wolves approached, for Donal had already sensed that there was something odd about the territory.

"Donal might have stumbled on some version of the truth," Questioner went on, "for he was sensitive to animals, but he was—as his name states—a hunter. Wolves, bear, and puma may all live in the same forest, but this does not mean they don't squabble when their interests overlap. If not informed that his competition was different from what he was accustomed to, Donal would probably have felt that what existed was a structure in which he and his could have competed as pumas and wolves compete. He would have, of course, been wrong."

Firekeeper knew the old tales of how humans and Royal Beasts had clashed. Tears rolled down her face as she struggled to balance this sudden, shocking grief against the need to learn more. Only if she learned more might she glimpse the past from which she had been so long isolated.

The heartrending pain of sorrow seemed a high price to pay for something she had done without so long and so well.

Or did you? Firekeeper asked herself. *Haven't others commented about the violence of your nightmares? Those are not usual, nor are these holes in memory. Walk forward into the tangle. If the underbrush has thorns, pull them out and clean the wound.*

Questioner went on. "Donal Hunter didn't like learning he was not the greatest predator of them all. He'd been spoiled by hunting Cousin-kind, and among them had taken his share of wolves, bears, and wild cats. However, Donal also was no fool. He knew the difference between true rivals and false, and so made his peace. It didn't hurt that Sarena encouraged him in this course, or that while Donal felt pride in his kills, he did not need to kill in order to have pride.

"But we never had the chance to learn what we might have built through our association with the settlers. Fire took them and their dreams, leaving only ashes and one small child. The wolves were determined to honor their promise to Sarena that they would care for you, but though they struggled to feed you, your injured body would not thrive.

"They brought you to me, for though I am as you see me, to their eyes I was closer to a human than any other they knew. Moreover, I had gained at least some knowledge of humans from observing the Liglimom. I examined you, and knew as the wolves had done that you were dying. You had swallowed smoke. You were weakened from hunger, for your throat was raw.

"Sarena had liked to hear about Liglim, and in return had taught me much about plants she used for healing. Combining her knowledge with what I already knew, I made medicines for you. I also fed you on sweet, soft things from which you could take nourishment. A wolverine, oddly blessed with a talent for healing, came and aided you further.

"However, you would not thrive. Autumn passed into winter, winter into spring, and still you would not live. The wolves brought you the best kills from their spring hunting, but you would not eat. Your heart was sick with pain and your soul cried out to be permitted to follow those you loved. In the end, I had two choices. I could let you die, or I could make you forget."

Questioner sat back on his haunches and for the first time Firekeeper realized that his forepaws were—like the rest of him—hybrids. They possessed pads and claws, but the toes were long and one stuck out to the side. It must take skill to run on those hand-paws without harming the fingers, but not only had Questioner done so, he had gone upon them to what must have seemed the ends of the earth—and come back once more.

"I wanted you to live, Little Two-legs, at first because in you I saw one who might bridge the world of the beasts and the world of humans. We cannot remain separate forever, no matter what many of both types think. Later, though, after I had spent long moons nursing you, I grew to care for you. A soul who could love as deeply as you could deserved a greater reward for love than death.

"We told you how we can sense magic but not do it ourselves. This is true, but this does not mean we are without talents ourselves." At this Questioner gestured, and Firekeeper noticed how the golden yellow light that illuminated the room came from translucent blocks set in the wall. "Sky can sense energy and awakened the power that exists in those blocks both to gather light from the sun and hold it, and to release it again when darkness comes.

"I have a small gift for persuasion. I used this gift on you. I took great care not to change you from what you were, but instead took you down a trail that might twist around itself and lead you into life. You see, Firekeeper, you were not bitter in your grief. You did not begrudge any others life—only denied your own right to live. I merely invited you to see yourself as that other—to become a wolf, for the wolves wanted you for their own and you already loved them."

Firekeeper felt her lips move, almost involuntarily, quoting words heard in a dream. " 'If the wolves are to live, then I name you a wolf. Be a wolf. Forget that you ever were human. Your heart is a wolf's, your appetites a wolf's, your memory a wolf's. Strange wolf you may be, but if only a wolf may live, then you must be one.' "

Questioner gave a slow smile. "Are those the words? It has been many years. I had forgotten them."

"Those are the words," Firekeeper replied. Her voice grew tight. "Does that make all my life since a lie? You made me think I am a wolf when I am really human."

Sky turned that overlarge eagle head and stared at her. "A life is not some abstract thing, Firekeeper. A life is a mosaic, crafted from the tiny pieces of what you do each day, every day. You have lived as a wolf, followed the codes and creeds of a wolf, honored wolves and sought to do them honor. Were those actions lies?"

"No!" Blind Seer half rose in indignation. "Firekeeper knows so little of lies that they shock her when she realizes how easily others use them. Nothing she has ever done was less than truth."

"Put down your hackles, wolf," Sky replied mildly. "I offer no threat to your loved one."

At Sky's words, and even more at Blind Seer's defense, Firekeeper felt a wash of relief, yet despite this she knew that she would continue to be haunted by a sense that she should belong to one world or other—that this living in between was somehow a defilement of the natural order.

Yet, silly pup, Firekeeper chided herself, *how can you think so with the maimalodalum gathered before you. If ever there was proof that a life can be lived outside the forms you have known, it is here. Sky speaks wisdom. You are a puppy fighting your reflection in a puddle, but the water from which your enemy shines back is nothing other than your own fears.*

Blind Seer let his hackles fall smooth, but Firekeeper could tell he remained unsettled as he turned to the human-jaguar-wolf.

"Questioner, you did not stay in the north," Blind Seer growled. "You came back to Misheemnekuru. Why?"

Questioner's snort was human. "Was I thrown out by your forebears, is that what you mean? No. I left of my own will. I could see that except in a few places I did more harm than good. Firekeeper was alive and learning to live. She no longer needed me.

"Before I left, I taught the wolves a few skills I thought might benefit her as she grew—something of tanning, of the use of a knife, of how to explain striking fire from flint and steel. I was not very good at these skills, but Donal had enjoyed showing me the tricks of the human hunter, and I had often spoken with him while he worked. He was more at ease with me when his hands were busy."

"And then you left?" Blind Seer persisted. "Why not go further north into New Kelvin? I think you might have found welcome there—among the humans, if not among the Beasts."

Questioner looked at the wolf, blue eyes meeting blue.

"I should give you my name, Blind Seer. You chase after a problem as if it were fresh game and you winter-starved for meat. Very well. I left because I was weak and tired and desperately homesick. I longed to go where my shape would not arouse loathing, my every word awaken fear. Do you think me a coward?"

Blind Seer lowered his head onto his paws, surrendering the anger that had motivated his queries.

"You forget, Questioner, I too have gone where my size and shape have made people fear me. I know some small taste of what you faced. Far from thinking you a coward for returning home, I honor you for your courage in setting out. I followed Firekeeper west in ignorance of what we would find. You went with full awareness."

Questioner's human face held astonishment while his tail, feathered like that of a wolf rather than smooth like a jaguar's, wagged.

"I think for a people who knew nothing of divination, your parents named you well. You see where others are blind."

"I try," said Blind Seer. "I try."

XXXI

TRUTH WADED CHEST-DEEP THROUGH TIME, trying to feel the strongest current, the one that flowed into probability.

Finding probability was something at which she excelled, and had even when she was a small, blind kitten. Her mother had noticed how the still nameless kitten unerringly found a nipple without fumbling, without snuffling or wasting effort crawling where milk was not to be found. Before long, this kitten was the strongest of her litter, and with strength that internal vision grew.

True, their lineage ran to diviners, but this kitten's powers were unnerving. Usually, training didn't even begin until the kitten had passed the chaotic insanity of youth. With this kitten the training began before she had learned to kill. Teaching her to see the currents of probability was the only way to save her from starvation.

Truth, as she was called in an effort to fix her on finding the true path among all the other currents, was plagued with possibilities. Every leap she essayed she saw not only completed a thousand times, but the hundreds of times she fell short, the tens of times she was injured, the one time she twisted, broke her back or neck, and died.

She saw the dying, too. The slow deaths where she lay trapped by paralysis while starvation claimed her. The tortured deaths, eaten by ants and small birds. The quick, burning deaths where a white-hot flash of pain heralded only darkness.

The same ability that had brought Truth into strength before her time now threatened to make her wither away from fear. She could not kill without seeing all the consequences of that death. Never mind that most were nothing more than a fat, sated jaguar licking herself clean—she dreaded the possibilities that showed fires destroying forests or famine spreading through the land all for the lack of a single deer or beaver or fat woodchuck.

So the teaching began.

First, Truth learned to imagine time as a broad ocean, an ocean filled with currents most never saw, currents that separated, intertwined, and went their own ways once more, someday, perhaps, to touch and intertwine again. More important, Truth learned to ignore the tug of the lesser currents, to block them from flooding her mind, their backwash granting them inordinate importance all out of proportion with the probability of their occurrence.

Later yet, Truth learned to focus on a limited segment of that ocean, to block out the futures affecting places that came to her mind only as a sparkling medley of colors and strong scents, cryptic icons for things for which she lacked a point of reference within her very limited experience.

With that lesson learned, Truth began to become an effective diviner. Even so, there were more years of training while she learned the cumbersome methods used for communicating visions to the humans. Sometimes, when frustrated by the complexity and rote memorization, Truth swam down currents that led her to a probability where some injury caused her ability to diminish so that she became merely an extraordinarily lucky hunter.

A few currents showed the complicated series of events that led her to lose her ability entirely. She swam this way only once. The jaguar she met and merged with was as one deaf, blind, and nose dead. Far from possessing the peace Truth had sought, this jaguar was trapped with no means of testing her actions.

Truth had torn herself free from that horrifying vision and resolved never to test those waters again.

Yet now she found herself almost as badly off as she had been that day. The currents were sluggish; their motions hardly perceptible. Whereas formerly Truth had been able to glance into that metaphorical ocean and note a tiny ripple here, a greater ripple there, and make her assessments with little effort, now, even when she submerged herself into the time stream, she could feel only the strongest currents.

What frightened her most was that all these currents reeked of destruction, of utter devestation to all she loved.

Had Truth not been a jaguar, she would have had someone to whom she could turn. Wolves served in packs, horses in herds, birds in flocks or pairs according to their nature.

Jaguars, even the Wise, did not share their territories willingly. They mated and parted, coming together for the occasional discussion or romp, then gladly going their ways again. Truth had no kittens she was rearing, no inclination to seek out any of the other felines who resided in Heeranenahalm. A wolf would have howled to another. It simply was not in the jaguar's nature.

Thus Truth swam alone through the ocean of time. The scent of bloody destruction permeated her brain and slowly began to drive her mad.

AFTER THE TUMBLING cascade of events that had filled the days from the moment Eshinarvash had taken Derian from the hilltop outside of u-Bishinti, the deliberate and contained quiet of the days that immediately followed provided a peculiar contrast.

Peculiar, Derian thought as he rode Prahini along the coast road to u-Seeheera, *because I know all the activity boiling underneath.*

Indeed, his own trip to u-Seeheera was part of that activity, for he had been nominated that day's liaison between those working from u-Bishinti and those who remained in the city.

"Two good reasons why you should do it," Zira had said. "One, you're already scheduled to go up there and assume some of the burden of teaching. Varjuna has had complaints from the disdum that u-Bishinti has grooms and trainers enough without stealing you as well. Secondly, you can dart in and out of the Temple of the Cold Bloods and ask to see young Rahniseeta, and no one is going to wonder why."

Zira grinned wickedly at this, and Derian felt himself blush. Moving down to u-Bishinti had helped him rein in his initial wild attraction to Rahniseeta. Reacquaintance wasn't only reawakening his earlier interest, it was intensifying it. Derian was learning that there was a lot more to Rahniseeta than her curves. What was equally fascinating was that she seemed to only just have discovered confidence in herself.

As Derian's road brought him alongside the green bulk of Misheemnekuru, he raised an arm and waved as if Firekeeper might really be watching. He'd had a note from her a few days before. Best as he could make out from the terse symbols, she was doing well, learning things, and missed him. As this note was followed by no urgent summons to meet her at the outpost, Derian decided that the note was a formality and grinned at the idea of his wolf-woman learning to write bread-and-butter notes.

In Heeranenahalm, Derian first dropped by the Horse Temple; then he met with a kidisdu of Bears who had apparently exhausted either the patience or the ability of her previous teacher. Then he went to meet Rahniseeta.

As arranged, she was waiting for him by one of the fountains outside of u-Nahal. A light basket rested on the turf near her feet, and she looked glowingly pretty. Her hair had been elaborately braided and piled up on her head, the dark mass intertwined with ribbons the same saffron yellow as her outfit. Even the smudges of ink on her fingers couldn't mar her perfection.

"Ready for our picnic?" Rahniseeta greeted him, her dark eyes twinkling. "I've brought some things that will surprise you."

Derian bent to pick up the basket.

"This is certainly heavy enough to hold any number of surprises. Where would you like to go?"

Rahniseeta draped a light cotton blanket over one arm.

"There's a nice shady park out the gate and up the hills," she said, gesturing with a toss of her head that gave Derian proof—if he'd needed it—that she had a lovely neck. "We can see the water from there."

Derian found he had to swallow hard before he could make his voice come out something like normally.

"Sounds great," he said. "Lead on."

She did, chattering pleasantly about various items of interest as they passed them. A statue of Air creating the skunk as a joke, a tableau of Earth teaching the first diviners, a mural portraying the fractioning of Magic. Her explanations were so lively that a group of children started trailing them to listen—until Rahniseeta shooed them off with a reminder that their teachers would be looking for them.

Derian listened attentively, but realized he was taken far more by the music of her voice than by the stories she was relating.

Horse apples! he thought. *I'd better take care or this playing at courting couple is going to get too real—for me at least—and that wouldn't be fair to her, not with my planning on going home and all.*

Rahniseeta chose a spot for them in the spreading shade of a maple tree where they could, indeed, see the bay. The waters sparkled in the sunlight, giving diamonds to the sky. It was a lovely place, but Derian found himself wishing it were a trifle more private. Some lacy bushes provided token screening, but . . .

Rahniseeta said, her voice low and conspiratorial, "I chose this place because while it seems private, we can actually see around us for a good distance. No one will be able to sneak into hearing distance without our knowing—no human, at least, and I think the yarimaimalom are on our side."

Derian wasn't sure he liked the possibility that even the birds and rabbits couldn't be trusted, and found himself eyeing a robin suspiciously. Then he remembered that Firekeeper had told him that the Royal Beasts, at least, didn't include the smaller songbirds and little animals, and decided to relax.

Rahniseeta took the picnic basket from him and began fishing out cloth-wrapped packages.

"Most of what I brought are things I could get from the temple kitchen," she said, "but I really do have some surprises for you. One of the sailors—Wiatt—is a cook and has been trying to find out which of your foods we might like. He left a plate of meat pastries this morning. The spicing is good, but strange, so I was able to steal away only a few before they were all gone."

Derian was genuinely pleased, especially by her thoughtfulness. He took a bite and savored both the taste and the piquancy of hope. Then he realized that it was probably all part of the charade for Rahniseeta. The young lady walking out with a fellow, bringing him a few treats.

He sighed and stared at the pastry.

"Is it bad?" she asked worriedly.

"Oh, no." He bit into it again to prove his words and chewed quickly. "Wonderful. I was just . . . thinking about my mother. She'd like these, want the recipe for our cook. Then Cook would get all offended because she'd think Mother was implying that we didn't like her cooking and she'd threaten to quit and . . ."

He started laughing and Rahniseeta was laughing with him. Then she sobered far too quickly.

"You do miss your home. Well, we will do what we can to return you safely and with honor. Just this morning Harjeedian was saying that the sooner the disdum resolve their debates, the better for you. He says that ocean travel is more safe in some seasons than others and if we are not careful you could end up stranded until spring—and that is when the year changes."

"And it wouldn't be a good year at all," Derian said, understanding, "if it turned out to be a Water year, would it?"

"That is what I fear," Rahniseeta said. "The deities mean us well, but even they have difficulties if their servants become corrupt. I sometimes wonder how much of the worry over how our ability to talk to the yarimaimalom might lead to corruption comes from the hearts of those who have already tasted that temptation."

"Takes one to know one?" Derian asked. "Maybe. Probably for some of them, but I'm sure there are more good disdum than otherwise. Varjuna's wonderful, and I think Poshtuvanu shows signs of being just as devoted. It must be the same for all the other temples."

"I know," Rahniseeta sighed. "I have been looking into shadows so much these last several days that I am starting to see nothing but darkness."

Derian reached over and took her hand.

"Well, there's lots of light, Rahniseeta. Look out in the bay. How would you say it? 'Fire's home is casting gemstones on his brother's breast'?"

Rahniseeta smiled and removed her hand from his, but only because she needed to pull more things out of the picnic basket.

"I've never heard it put quite that way before, but I like it."

She unwrapped a dark loaf, a crock of already melting butter, and a jar of honey.

"We should start with these before the butter turns to oil," she said. "I don't know what I was thinking when I chose it. I have water infused with mint and also wine."

"Not white wine with honey," Derian said, glancing at the bottle. "Maybe after I've eaten and it won't go to my head."

Rahniseeta poured them both mint water.

"Do you wish to begin, or shall I?"

Derian swallowed the rest of his meat pastry and started cutting bread.

"I'll start. I'm already ahead of you when it comes to eating."

Rahniseeta nodded, her gaze drifted across the sparkling waters, then began smearing a thick slice of bread with soft butter and adding a thin bead of honey. Derian watched her hands move, but otherwise forced himself to concentrate.

"Zira is making progress on the matter of the white mare," he began. "She was right when she guessed there wouldn't be too many candidates. None born at u-Bishinti in the last several years are unaccounted for. She's sent letters to various private owners who offered u-Bishinti a white filly in the last five years, specifically asking not only if the mare is still available, but if it is not, where she might locate it. So far, there have been no replies, but there should be, maybe even by the time I've gotten back."

"That's good," Rahniseeta said. "Zira's researches may lead nowhere, but at least she has started something."

"I stopped in and saw Meiyal before going to my lesson," Derian continued, "on the excuse of dropping off some records on the most promising of this year's foals. Her clerk has been busy, and all I can say is that I can see why the yarimaimalom moved to have animal sacrifice banned."

"Oh?" Rahniseeta said, and from her tone Derian couldn't tell whether or not he had offended her, then she added, "I really don't know much about sacrifices. It is something the disdum learn about in the course of their training, but Harjeedian said it was an ugly part of our past and while best not forgotten, shouldn't be dwelled on either."

"I can see his point," Derian said. "However, we're rather beyond the 'not dwelling on' part. By the way, have you told him what I saw?"

"Not so far," Rahniseeta said. "I've been able to make excuses for the questions I've asked him. He has enough worries right now without this."

"So doesn't he wonder," Derian asked, feeling himself flushing and hoping that Rahniseeta would think he was reacting to the heat, "about your suddenly spending so much time with me? We've gone out nearly every day since that walk in the market."

Rahniseeta grinned. "Big Brother is quite pleased. He asked me to make certain the Temple of the Cold Bloods did not lose touch with you when you went to u-Bishinti. I told him quite roundly that I wouldn't play his games—but this is my game and if he thinks I've repented and am being dutiful, all the better."

Derian blinked at this convoluted but logical evaluation, and decided his pride could take it. After all, Rahniseeta had refused to play up to him just because Harjeedian told her to do so.

"Good," Derian said. "I think. No, really. Good."

He frowned, bit into a piece of buttered bread, and reorganized his thoughts.

"I was telling you about what Meiyal's clerk has learned. Well, it seems that not only were there regular rituals to commemorate major events—harvest, the first sailing of the fishing fleet, that sort of thing—there were rituals for routine divination."

Rahniseeta looked puzzled. "But that's how it is today."

"With one major difference," Derian said. "You people don't splatter blood all over the place for every one of these rituals. Before the treaty with the yarimaimalom it seems that practically no one did any rite without spilling at least a bit of blood. There's a whole area outside of Heeranenahalm that's now a nice little produce-and-flower market, but that Cishanol says once was where you went and bought your sacrificial animals. Common people had to settle for chickens or lambs, but the disdum were into wild animals—the harder to catch or more exotic the better, and if you could get a Wise Beast, well . . ."

Rahniseeta looked a bit sick, and put down her bread and honey. Derian decided he'd made his point.

"The thing is, Cishanol has had to wade through all of this to find what we need—the earlier sacrifices when lives were offered only on really important occasions. Cishanol's smart, and he cross-referenced with dates hoping to find that white animals were offered at a particular season. Well, that led him astray, but eventually he got back on track."

"Yes?"

"White animals were used for initiation," Derian said. "It's likely that what I saw was Dantarahma initiating a batch of new recruits. That means we have to be careful before eliminating someone who wasn't there because we can't be sure if the old hands were needed there."

Rahniseeta, who had been about to raise the bread and honey again, set it down.

"This is terrible!" she said. "Who can we trust?"

"Our core group, so far," Derian said. "We've all known for several days and no one has had an accident or a threatening letter or a mysterious summons from Dantarahma. We need to be careful, but on the other hand, I think it's likely that at least most of Dantarahma's acolytes were there. It stands to reason that his cult can't be a large group or someone would have gotten wind of it already."

"Fair," Rahniseeta said, and this time she determinedly finished her slice of bread. "Anything else?"

"Cishanol has come up with the names of some possible members of Dantarahma's cult. I had to write them down because my accent's not good enough that I might not accuse the wrong person by saying 'puh' for 'buh' or something like that. Meiyal said very seriously that you were to read, memorize, and destroy the list."

With due solemnity, Derian handed over the slip he'd hidden in his wallet. Rahniseeta read it. Her eyebrows shot up once; then, after scanning the list several more times, she tore the paper into tiny scraps of confetti and dropped them into the dregs of her glass of water.

"That should make them unreadable," she said, watching as the ink muddied the water. "However, I shall need to switch to wine."

"Seemed like you knew at least one of the names," Derian said.

"I came across the third one down when I was asking in the markets after white calves. It seems he had been making similar inquiries not long ago. As he is a member of the Temple of Flyers, this raised some comment. I presented myself as on a similar shopping expedition, and was asked what the Temple of Flyers and Temple of the Cold Bloods needed white calves for. I had an excuse ready having to do with a request from a farmer who gathers wild specimens for us. Apparently, this fellow was less subtle. He told the drover to mind his own business."

"Guaranteeing," Derian said, "that his business would never be forgotten. What an idiot."

"That's why I was ready to discount the story, but his name appearing on this list does make me wonder."

"I'll pass on the information," Derian said, "or rather Poshtuvanu will. I'm reporting to him, and he's going to relay to the Temple of the Horse. I hadn't been in the habit of visiting there too often, but he regularly makes the run."

"We are being careful," Rahniseeta said amused, "but then we know we may be checked after. They thought no one knew they existed."

"Makes all the difference," Derian agreed. "What else do you have?"

Rahniseeta pretended to look affronted. "Isn't that about the calf enough?"

Derian only grinned. "I'll pour the wine. You talk."

She did, reporting rather less success in her quests after white dogs, especially since she hadn't wanted to be too obvious. She'd also had an opportunity to sneak a look at Dantarahma's schedule of appointments.

"It isn't that hard, really," she said, when Derian expressed surprise. "Each of u-Liall has an enormous slate board on which their appointments for weeks in advance are listed. I simply waited until no one was there and made a list of the names. There are a few interesting repetitions. I made a list with notes as to which ones are interesting and why. Do I give it to you or do you memorize it?"

"I'd better pass it to Poshtuvanu," Derian said. "This is more than I can keep straight, especially the explanations."

"It will make more sense to Meiyal or Varjuna," Rahniseeta assured him. "They know what's usual—a member of u-Liall is simply a glorified iaridisdu/ikidisdu, after all."

"If you say so," Derian said. "I wish we could simply all meet and discuss these things, but as Meiyal said, even if no one guessed the truth, conspiracy would be suspected."

Rahniseeta nodded.

"My last item of interest is out there on the bay," she said.

She pointed, and Derian looked along the line of her arm.

"That little boat?" he said, impulsively grabbing her hand and kissing it before letting her reclaim it.

She raised an eyebrow.

"I thought I was supposed to be flirting with you," Derian said, keeping his face very straight.

Rahniseeta sighed, but she didn't complain. She didn't give him her hand again, either, though.

"That little boat," she said, "is a light sailing vessel, one of many of the type owned by the Temple of Sea Beasts, and used for regular trips around the bay. Except in bad weather, it can be crewed by only two sailors."

"Interesting," Derian said. "I guess."

"What is interesting," Rahniseeta said, "is that boat is currently being used by Waln Endbrook and the other sailors who were shipwrecked last year."

"They have a lot of freedom all of a sudden," Derian said. "Don't get me wrong, but I sort of had the impression that they were under restriction."

"Those restrictions were recently raised," Rahniseeta said, "on the same grounds for protest that you yourself used—that either they were prisoners or guests, and if they were guests they deserved more freedom to come and go."

"Ah," Derian said. "Did Waln make the appeal?"

"It was made for him by Aridisdu Shivadtmon," Rahniseeta replied. "The same Shivadtmon who later got them use of the boat. Lucky Elwyn told Barnet that when he invited Barnet to join them sailing."

"That's the same Shivadtmon we saw with Waln in the market, isn't it?" Derian asked.

"The same Shivadtmon," Rahniseeta said, "who was with Waln in the market, and who regularly visits Dantarahma. I've seen him there myself."

Derian frowned. "That's odd. I don't remember seeing Shivadtmon's name on that list of appointments."

"It isn't there," Rahniseeta said with smug smile. "Interesting, isn't it?"

※

FIREKEEPER WAS SO OVERWHELMED by everything Questioner had told her that it took her several days before the obvious occurred to her.

She and Blind Seer found Questioner on the observation platform at the top of one of the towers. He was lying with his forepaws in front of him, his face turned to the east.

"That's the direction they will come from," he said, flicking one wolf ear in their direction. "The Old World has always come from the east, never from the west. It's very strange, when you think about it."

Firekeeper leaned against the parapet and looked at him. She was very aware both of the maimalodalu and of Blind Seer, seated in the narrow band of shade cast by the wall, watching the maimalodalu with silent, guarded intensity.

"So you sit up here in the sun and watch?" Firekeeper said. "You'll see Old World ships coming sure enough. If they don't come, the sun will make them in your head."

"The sun isn't that hot at this time of day," Questioner said dismissively. "What is it you want?"

Firekeeper replied without the verbal fencing a human surely would have used. "You say you have been north, even to Blind Seer and my own home territory."

"Yes, I did."

"Did you travel over land or sea?"

"Land."

Firekeeper struggled to contain her rising excitement.

"Then it is possible to travel safely by land? I had heard there is a sea that eats into the land to the north. I thought it might make the land route impassable."

"The land route is possible, but you must go far west in order to reach a point where the inlet is narrow enough to cross on foot. Even then many rivers converge there on their journey to the ocean. A foot traveler must ford or swim each one."

"Could a horse go that way?"

"I think so, but it wouldn't be an easy journey, nor a particularly swift one. Going by sea would be faster."

There was a trace of a chuckle in Questioner's voice and Firekeeper was willing to bet that someone—probably one of the ravens—had told him of her tendency toward seasickness.

"But it is possible to travel by land," Firekeeper said, "even if the way is long—and the travelers could take a horse. That is very good to know."

"Oh?"

Firekeeper flared at the maimalodalu's blandness. All this time Questioner had not even turned his head to look at her, but had kept his gaze fixedly toward the east.

"Oh?" Firekeeper echoed mockingly. "Yes, it is good to know. Maybe you have forgotten, but Blind Seer, Derian, and I were brought to Liglim against our will, as prisoners in a ship. I would have run away a long time ago but I did not know if there was somewhere to run. Now I do."

"And so you will run?"

Firekeeper shrugged. "First I will talk to Derian. I will tell him what you say."

"Will you tell him who said it?"

Firekeeper looked at him. "Would you prefer I do not?"

The ugly face with its wolf's ears and grey-spotted fur turned on the long neck and the blue eyes looked at her with a mixture of exasperation and sorrow.

"What do you think?"

"I think," Firekeeper said, "I will tell Derian that I learned of this land route from a wolf who was adventurous in his youth. I think I will tell him that the tale of the maimalodalu was just a story. I think that version of the truth would serve better for everyone."

"For one who does not lie easily, Firekeeper," Questioner said, glancing at Blind Seer, "you certainly came up with that lie easily enough."

Firekeeper stared levelly at the maimalodalu, her dark eyes unreadable for a long moment while she tried to decide whether this was insult or compliment—or perhaps a little of both. Unable to decide, she answered from the heart.

"I do not think calling you a wolf would be a lie," she said, indicating the maimalodalu's wolf's ears, feathered tail, and body that borrowed details equally from wolf and jaguar. "You are at least as much wolf as I am."

Questioner's lips moved in what should have been a smile, but was not. "Then that would be a good answer to give your friend, Firekeeper. Do you leave for the mainland immediately?"

"Soon," Firekeeper said. "It would not be fair to leave Derian alone and wondering when at last I have something to tell him."

"I think it would be good for you to go to the mainland, Firekeeper," Questioner said. "But I want you to think about something as you run to the outpost. Kidnapping you was wrong, but because of what was done to you, you learned things you might never have otherwise known."

"I met you," Firekeeper said bluntly. "That is the good thing. Now I know who other than the wolves I owe for saving my life. Otherwise, I am still trying to decide if this knowing is good—there is too much there, and too confusing."

"Do you regret, then, knowing you are not a princess?"

Firekeeper looked at him in astonishment.

"You mean that my parents were not Prince Barden and Sweet Eirene?"

"Yes."

"Not a bit. It seems to me these other two you named—Donal and Sarena—were every bit as useful and strong. What is 'princess' but a shaping of air into a hissing sound? Only when a princess works to be a princess—like Sapphire is learning—only then is the word something to be proud of, but just as a word, a title?"

Firekeeper laughed in scornful dismissal. "I remember what Sky said. Life is what you live. I want to live a wolf, not a princess. How close I came to losing that wolf part of me is what makes me afraid and uncertain. Whatever you did to my mind is fraying, and I wonder if I can remake that certainty."

Questioner smiled, this time with a hint of honest amusement.

"Somehow, I don't think you will stay uncertain about how very wolf you are, not with your own stubborn will and Blind Seer to remind you. Go then to the mainland. Being among humans again will be good for you."

Firekeeper suspected that it would be. Among wolves she had always been aware of her weaknesses. Humans reminded her of her strengths.

Questioner shifted, rising at last from his couched position and facing Firekeeper and Blind Seer.

"I hope that before you decide to leave for the north you will find an opportunity to return to Misheemnekuru and say good-bye. I have spent a dozen long years wondering if you had lived or died. It sorrows me that our acquaintance will be so short."

"If you ask for me to come back," Firekeeper replied with sincerity, "then I will do so even if I have to swim here."

Blind Seer panted laughter and looked at the maimalodalu relaxing the guarded manner that had informed every line of his body throughout the interview.

"Actually," the blue-eyed wolf said, "I think Firekeeper would actually prefer to swim if her only other choice was getting on a boat."

DARK DEATH ONCE AGAIN SERVED as their guide when they headed back to the outpost. He led them via a shorter route this time, for they did not need to go back in the direction of the elk meadows. They ran by night and lay up in the heat of the day, hunting in the cool portions of morning and evening. Dark Death carefully set their trail to avoid ruins. The memories of past disasters were too acute for curiosity to outweigh caution.

At the outpost, the disdum were eager to ready a boat to take Firekeeper and Blind Seer to the mainland. The oldest aridisdu politely but firmly insisted on exchanging what remained of Firekeeper's torn and ragged clothing for a fresh outfit. She thanked him politely, glad for the chance to discard the old clothes. Cotton had great advantages over leather when one wished to avoid becoming too hot, but it did tear and stain very easily.

As once again they must wait on some vagary of the tide, Firekeeper also accepted the opportunity to bathe in hot water and wash her hair. Consequently, she felt quite eager to reencounter humanity by the time they boarded the boat. The swaying of the deck beneath her feet reminded her of the ordeal to come.

"Did you enjoy your time with the Wise Wolves?" asked the young woman minding the wheel once the boat was under way.

"Yes," Firekeeper said tersely, her knuckles white on a railing, tensing as the boat chopped across a wave.

The young woman, though her eyes were bright with questions, saw Firekeeper's misery and kept her peace.

Upon landing, Firekeeper went to a public fountain and rinsed her mouth several times, then she turned to Blind Seer.

"Now to find Derian," she said. "Do we go to the place of horses—this u-Bishinti we have heard so much about—or do we ask for him elsewhere?"

"Ask," Blind Seer said promptly. "Many days have passed since last we saw Derian. He may have shifted his lair, or gone on a long journey for all we know."

"True," Firekeeper said. "Let us start at the Temple of the Cold Bloods. If Derian is not there, Barnet or Rahniseeta or Harjeedian may know where we might find him."

"Or we could ask the jaguar, Truth, to divine his location," Blind Seer said with a panting laugh. "I have my doubts as to just how good these diviners are."

Firekeeper grinned at him. "You have a wicked streak. That jaguar is too full of herself for my liking. Let us start with the humans, and turn to Truth only at the last."

They walked up the processional way and the humans parted right and left to let them pass. Even the children playing some chasing game along the median paused to watch their passage. Firekeeper was aware of the many eyes on her, but she kept herself from panic with the awareness that the many gazes held awe, admiration, and a trace of fear, none of these emotions uncongenial to a wolf.

HARJEEDIAN WAS AT THE TEMPLE of the Cold Bloods, and proved quite willing to direct Firekeeper to where she might find Derian.

"He has been coming up from u-Bishinti most days, lately," Harjeedian said, "and often calls on Rahniseeta. I believe they frequently go walking either in the city or in the park to the north of Heeranenahalm."

Firekeeper thanked Harjeedian and hurried outside once more.

"Let's try the park," she said to Blind Seer. "We've just come up through the city and didn't see him there."

"We hardly saw all of the city," Blind Seer replied, deceptively mild, "only the processional way."

Firekeeper knew she was being teased. Although she had grown more comfortable in urban areas, she still preferred the wild lands. As usual, spending time away from cities had done nothing for her tolerance of crowds, noise, and stench.

"Even so," Firekeeper said, refusing to respond directly to Blind Seer's gibe, "we are closer to this park. I recall seeing a gate into greenery in the northern wall. That must be what Harjeedian was referring to."

They found things as Firekeeper had remembered and they stepped through onto thick sheep-mowed turf that merged without any rigid borders into open forest. After the tangled undergrowth of Misheemnekuru the artifice of the place was evident, but that made it no less pleasant to Firekeeper's eyes.

They stepped around a group of children playing some game involving a ball and a great deal of running, and moved deeper into the cool greenery.

"I've Derian's scent," Blind Seer reported, "and Rahniseeta's—and that of fresh bread and sharp cheese."

"Today's scent?" Firekeeper asked.

"Definitely." The wolf raised his massive head and pointed with a toss of his nose. "They went along this trail."

Were they seeking wolves, the pair would have howled, but humans didn't welcome being shouted after except in emergencies, and, in any case, this park was no one person's territory. Blind Seer encountered numerous scent trails, though these grew thinner the farther the pair went from the gate.

"Quite a long walk just to eat bread and cheese," Blind Seer commented, "but then this carries them deeper into the forest where it will definitely be cooler."

"We are still on their trail?"

"Certainly," the wolf huffed a trace indignantly. "Had you my nose, it would be as if they walked along before us, that's how strong the scent is."

Firekeeper rubbed behind his ears in mute apology, and companionably they strolled on. So quiet were they that the little birds resumed singing in the trees. A squirrel dared scold, brave in his certainty that nothing so large could reach the dancing ends of the long tree limbs where he took up his station.

"There," Firekeeper said softly, "ahead. I see a basket. The grass is flattened as well, but there is no sign of our quarry."

"I would swear they haven't backed the trail," Blind Seer said, "and I hear no conversation."

"Then let us go on," Firekeeper said. "They may have finished eating and gone for a walk."

They walked within a few paces of where the picnic basket sat, a mostly empty wine bottle alongside. Firekeeper was about to ask Blind Seer to track when her gaze fastened on a glint of paler color back in the greenery.

Frowning, she motioned Blind Seer to silence and ghosted forward. In the shelter of a thick clump of trees, invisible but to one who came upon them as she had just done, Firekeeper found Derian and Rahniseeta.

They lay close together on the cotton blanket whose trailing pale blue had been what had first caught Firekeeper's eye. Although fully dressed, they were closely intertwined. Derian held Rahniseeta, his mouth pressed closely against hers in what was far more intimate than the chaste kisses Firekeeper had more usually witnessed. His shirt was open at the top, and Rahniseeta had one hand splayed out against the skin of his chest. Both of them had their eyes closed, as if better to savor the pleasures of touch.

Firekeeper drew back in silence motioning Blind Seer to come away with her.

Although she felt a trace of embarrassment at seeing what Derian had so clearly wished to go unseen, her dominant emotion was confusion and apprehension. She been so very certain that Derian would be excited to learn that she had found them a way home.

Now, remembering how the young man had cradled Rahniseeta in his arms and the intensity with which he had kissed her, Firekeeper wondered if Derian would ever want to leave the land of the Liglimom.

XXXII

"RAHNISEETA SISTER OF HARJEEDIAN?" the voice came as Rahniseeta was hurrying along a corridor past some of the administrative offices within u-Nahal. "Ahmyndisdu Tiridanti would like to speak with you."

Earth, Air, Fire, Water, Magic! Rahniseeta thought. *Somehow Ahmyndisdu Tiridanti's discovered the snooping I've been doing! What am I going to say to her when she asks me about it? Oh, it's nothing, great lady. Some friends of mine and I—well, and some of the yarimaimalom as well—we suspect your fellow within u-Liall, Junjaldisdu Dantarahma, of reverting to blood sacrifice?*

Rahniseeta halted and stared wildly at the speaker, a minor aridisdu from one of the Earth-related orders, she thought. A kind enough man, comfortable in the middle ranks in which his talent had set him, content to be a clerk to a seventeen-year-old girl if that was how he could best serve the deities.

"Oh!" was all Rahniseeta could manage to say.

"Is this a bad time?" the aridisdu asked kindly. "Are you perhaps expected elsewhere?"

"Only in the scribes' hall," Rahniseeta said. "I've been doing some copying."

And some reading of recent accounting records when no one is looking, she confessed silently.

She went on quickly, "I would be very happy to place myself at the ahmyndisdu's service if she wishes to see me."

"Thank you," the aridisdu said with gentle courtesy. "Please follow me."

Rahniseeta did so. Her mind feverishly rehearsed a series of excuses, so that when she was led into the ahmyndisdu's private chambers and the clerk had left, pulling the door shut behind him with a firmness that said as clearly as words "I will guarantee your privacy," she hardly heard what Tiridanti said.

"Thank you for coming so promptly, Rahniseeta. I am worried about truth."

Truth? Rahniseeta thought in a panic. *I'm sure she is worried about the truth. Anyone who knew the truth would be worried about it.*

Then she saw the jaguar pacing restlessly back and forth, back and forth at the far end of the room, and the meaning of what Tiridanti had said came clear to her.

"Truth?" Rahniseeta said aloud.

"Yes," Tiridanti said.

The ahmyndisdu was not wearing any of her formal costumes today. In loose blouse and trousers in Fire's favorite red and orange, the cuffs and collars trimmed in brilliant yellow, Tiridanti looked very young, the coltish lines of her still maturing body very evident.

"Truth has been behaving strangely for some time now," Tiridanti went on, looking over at the jaguar. "Divination has become a struggle for her—enough that I have been calling on some of the others when I must do a reading. Lately, however—within the past four or five days—Truth has seemed to completely lose touch with reality. She is not violent or temperamental in the least, but all she does is pace."

"Has she eaten?" Rahniseeta asked.

She didn't know how often the great cats needed to eat, but knew their metabolisms were faster than those of the snakes she and Harjeedian tended.

"A little," Tiridanti replied, "but the food must be set directly before her for her to notice it. Even then she only eats a few mouthfuls before starting to pace again."

Why did you ask me here? Rahniseeta thought. *I'm no kidisdu. I certainly know nothing of any type of cat. They're not exactly welcome in the Temple of the Cold Bloods.*

But whatever else she was, Tiridanti was no mind reader. She interpreted Rahniseeta's concern as for the jaguar.

"Truth is in no immediate danger," Tiridanti assured Rahniseeta. "To be completely honest, she was having too much fun being waited on and had put on a little extra weight. Even so, I would very much like to know what is troubling her—and the omens are completely silent on the matter."

Rahniseeta was appalled, but she still didn't know why she had been summoned, and although Tiridanti was not standing on formalities, Rahniseeta could not forget that the young woman was the ahmyndisdu.

"I had heard," Tiridanti went on, "that Lady Blysse has returned to the mainland."

"Yes, Ahmyndisdu," Rahniseeta said. "She arrived yesterday."

Rahniseeta felt very glad that her skin was not as fair as Derian's, for at the memory of her first meeting with the traveler she felt her skin grow hot.

She and Derian had encountered Lady Blysse upon returning from one of their picnic outings. The wolf-woman and her blue-eyed companion were resting near the wall that separated the park from Heeranenahalm. Something in Lady Blysse's guarded expression made Rahniseeta think that the wolf-woman had been deeper into the park, and then had politely retreated.

Rahniseeta still wasn't quite certain just when or how she and Derian had graduated from pretend flirtation to something rather more intimate, but this hadn't been the first time they'd taken the blanket into the shrubbery, out of sight of casual passersby.

They hadn't progressed beyond kissing and a certain amount of mutual exploration, but the interest in learning more was definitely there.

Freckles had been a revelation.

Rahniseeta forced herself to focus on what Tiridanti was saying.

"I was hoping that Lady Blysse would come and speak with Truth," Tiridanti said hesitantly. "However, I did not know how to locate her, and I did not wish to issue a formal summons. I believe it would be best if the disdum at large did not know about Truth's difficulties."

"I will say nothing," Rahniseeta assured her. "Do you want me to try and find Lady Blysse for you?"

"Please. I will be leaving u-Nahal in a short while, so it would be best if she called on me at my residence. You are welcome to escort her."

"Thank you, Ahmyndisdu."

"Do you know where Lady Blysse is staying?"

"I do not," Rahniseeta admitted, "but I know a few places to check and a few people who I can ask. Unfortunately, Derian Counselor is not due in Heeranenahalm until quite late or I could ask him. If anyone human knows where Lady Blysse is, it is he."

Tiridanti nodded, but Rahniseeta had a distinct impression that the ahmyndisdu was having difficulty focusing. With a chill, Rahniseeta wondered if this was the usual distraction of one who fears for a loved one or something more sinister. What if whatever was wrong with Truth was spreading to the ahmyndisdu?

Rahniseeta waited for a formal dismissal, but one did not come, so somewhat awkwardly she said, "I will go seek Lady Blysse now."

Tiridanti looked at her and gave a wan smile.

"Make all haste," she said, her gaze returning to where the jaguar continued her restless pacing. "I am worried about Truth."

"THE YARIMAIMALOM KNOW what this Dantarahma has done," Firekeeper said to Blind Seer. "Why do they not make their displeasure clear?"

Blind Seer stretched, then rolled over on his back so she could scratch his chest. The park in which they had found Rahniseeta and Derian intertwined had proven a good place for more innocent resting as well. The wolf and woman had taken refuge from the day's heat in a grove canopied by broad-leafed young maples, but though their chosen place was comfortable and the humid heat argued that sleep was the best way in which to spend the daylight hours, Firekeeper's mind would not let go of all Derian and Rahniseeta had reported.

"I think," Blind Seer replied, "that the yarimaimalom have made their displeasure clear. They used Derian to inform more trustworthy humans than Dantarahma of that betrayal."

Firekeeper frowned. "They could have killed Dantarahma as easily—and no one the wiser."

"I am not as sure of that as you are," Blind Seer replied. "However, even if the yarimaimalom did slay Dantarahma, who is to say that the one who would succeed him would be any better? Do you truly believe that deities ordain the chosen rulers?"

"I don't know," Firekeeper admitted. "One of the Wise Wolves said that their diviners have felt a presence guiding their searches. Who am I to call them liars? It would be like claiming that there was no scent on a trail simply because I cannot smell as well as you."

"That's one way of looking at it," Blind Seer admitted. "Another would be to say that these Liglimom—human and yarimaimalom alike—credit to divine intervention what someone like Doc would explain as an inborn talent."

"You are always," Firekeeper said, not quite able to hide her exasperation, "so very reasonable."

"Someone has to be. You are always so certain that the best way to deal with a problem is to eliminate the most obvious source."

Firekeeper moved her hand up under the wolf's jaw, rhythmically scratching.

"And sometimes it is," she said defiantly.

"And sometimes it isn't," Blind Seer replied, angling his head slightly so as to bring an itchy spot under those strong fingers. "I think in matters of humans in intrigue, the simplest solution is not the best."

Firekeeper was about to pursue this further when in one strong, lithe motion Blind Seer had rolled out from beneath her hand and onto his feet. He stood, ears pricked, nose up to catch the breeze, alert to signals that even her keen hearing had not detected.

"Someone comes," he said after a few deep breaths. "Rahniseeta. Alone. Agitated. I scent uncertainty as well."

"She doesn't know we are here then," Firekeeper said. "Do you think she seeks us or someone else?"

"Do you mean Derian?" Blind Seer gaped his jaws in a laughing grin. "That is not in the scent I catch. Moreover, didn't Derian tell us that he might not come to Heeranenahalm today—something to do with a white mare?"

"That's right," Firekeeper said. "Let us go learn if Rahniseeta seeks us."

With no further delay, the pair ghosted from their shaded refuge and toward the trail where they would intersect Rahniseeta. They saw her before she did them, and Firekeeper noticed how the woman twice opened her mouth as if to call, then stopped.

"Do you think she fears seeming foolish?" Firekeeper asked Blind Seer. *"Or is there something more here?"*

"More," the wolf immediately replied.

"Then let us ease her apprehension," Firekeeper said, and wedding thought to action, stepped out onto the trail a handful of paces in front of Rahniseeta.

The Liglimo woman drew up short, admirably concealing a cry of astonishment. Even so, the breath she swallowed meant that she must pause before greeting them. Despite this, Rahniseeta addressed the reason for her being there with what Firekeeper thought was almost wolf-like directness.

"Ahmyndisdu Tiridanti wishes your help," Rahniseeta said, addressing herself to Firekeeper, though her body language made clear that she did not exclude Blind Seer. "The jaguar Truth has been acting strangely and Tiridanti hopes you can speak to Truth and discover the source of her distress."

Firekeeper remembered the ahmyndisdu from their earlier meetings. Once the wolf-woman might have dismissed Tiridanti as a girl holding her post through titles and luck rather than skill. Now, though her opinion of the other had not changed, Firekeeper understood the mystic power humans attached to the idea of rulers. She also remembered that Dantarahma was the representative of Water, as Tiridanti was of Fire, and wondered if this sickness in Fire's representative Beast was coincidence.

She said as much aloud to Rahniseeta, and saw the other woman's face tighten.

"I wish I could say that you are the first to put this thought into my mind," Rahniseeta confessed, "but from the moment I left Tiridanti's side, I found myself wondering if there might be a connection."

"How to do?" Firekeeper asked.

"You mean how would Dantarahma harm Truth?"

Firekeeper grunted agreement.

"I don't know. As we told you, we have been trying to discover who Dantarahma's allies might be. We have a few sound guesses, and from them have concluded that though Dantarahma has drawn heavily from those he knew when he served in the Temple of Sea Beasts, he has cast his nets more widely. Strangely, another grouping seems to come from those closely associated with Fire."

"Fire? Tiridanti's people?"

"That's right," Rahniseeta said. "We were puzzled at first. Then Varjuna recalled the resentment when Tiridanti was chosen to represent Fire in u-Liall. Everyone thought that matter resolved and forgotten—that those who had resented her appointment were resigned if not glad, and that, indeed, most were glad."

"Because," Firekeeper said, remembering something said in a discussion that seemed long ago, back when she was still a prisoner in the Temple of the Cold Bloods with nothing to do but drowse and listen to interminable human chatter, "Tiridanti will rule for life and a life is a long time to gather favors to oneself as a squirrel does nuts."

"Exactly."

They were close to the gate into Heeranenahalm now, and Rahniseeta signaled that the matter should be spoken of no further.

"Tell me," Rahniseeta said, stopping her hand halfway to the gate, "do you know how to find Tiridanti's residence on your own?"

Firekeeper did, having made certain of the territory as any wolf would.

"A house shaped like this," she said, tracing a rough teardrop in the air. "Has wall. Stinks of cat."

Rahniseeta's formerly serious expression melted into a grin.

"That's right. Do you think you could meet me there, and make an effort to be seen by as few people as possible? Tiridanti didn't wish Truth's difficulty to become common knowledge."

"I can," Firekeeper said. "Warn them of our coming."

"I shall."

They parted then. Firekeeper and Blind Seer spent an enjoyable time working out a route that took them to the residence of the ahmyndisdu, as they flattered themselves, undetected. They were helped in that most of the Liglimom had retired indoors from the heat, the business of the temple city suspended until late afternoon should bring relative coolness.

When Firekeeper made as if to climb over a wall near a small door and so to admit the wolf into the compound, a somewhat sarcastic voice commented from amid the vines atop the wall.

"Why not try the latch?"

Firekeeper looked up to meet the yellow gaze of a bobcat lying stretched amid the cooling vines. Its tawny fur with undertones of rust and pattern of spots provided admirable concealment—until the tufted ears twitched in amusement.

The wolf-woman glanced at Blind Seer and the wolf muttered defensively: "The entire place reeks of cat. Who am I to scent one more?"

Firekeeper grinned at him, then, without exchanging further words with the bobcat, put her thumb to the latch and pressed down. It rose easily and, except for a slight click of metal against metal, without a sound. She pushed open the door and stepped through.

The bobcat was waiting for them, poised lightly on what seemed to Firekeeper rather oversized paws, its short tail held stiffly in what might have been an attitude of wariness.

"Come this way. The ahmyndisdu awaits."

The wolves followed, and were taken along curving paths overhung with scented greenery and flowering vines to a structure that had eschewed the usual walls for tightly stretched fabric suspended in metal frames. The roof was solid, plated over in enameled metal that gave the sky back its blue.

"Two humans," Blind Seer said. *"Tiridanti and Rahniseeta. The jaguar Truth. No others, not even in the garden. Tiridanti's will rules here, that much seems certain. What she wishes kept secret is kept so."*

Firekeeper nodded. She was certain, however, that though the potentially gossipy humans were kept away, the yarimaimalom were not. Did Tiridanti trust them more, or was this another indication that in the land of the Liglimom the yarimaimalom did indeed outrank even the most highly ranked humans?

She shrugged the matter from her, and when the bobcat had led them into the screened house, the wolf-woman stood still and silent, her gaze fastened on where the jaguar Truth paced.

The great cat's motion was not like that of the great cats Firekeeper had seen kept caged in New Kelvin. Theirs was a restless back and forth, back and forth, a tracing of the limits of the cage as if each pass held the hopeless hope that something might have altered, some way into freedom been revealed.

Truth's pacing was a drunken thing, weaving steps probing one paw in front of the other as if the jaguar were feeling her way over uneven ground. Periodically, she paused, raising her head as if listening, but to whatever sounds she heard, Firekeeper was deaf.

Firekeeper glanced at Blind Seer, but though the wolf's ears pricked forward, he indicated that he heard nothing.

"Has Truth been poisoned?" Firekeeper asked, hearing her own voice hoarse against a quiet broken only by the pad of velvet paws against stone.

Tiridanti looked at her, and shook her head.

"I do not think so. I was kidisdu before I became ahmyndisdu, and we learned how to check for such things." Tiridanti gave an apologetic smile, as if confessing to personally committing some great crime. "In the countryside, herders sometimes set out tainted baits when they suspect their flocks are being preyed upon."

"Truth looks poisoned," Firekeeper said. "Or drunk."

"For days now, Truth has had no food but that which I have prepared for her with my own hands," Tiridanti replied. "I have selected the meat myself, while the beast that grew it still lived and breathed. I myself have cut the animal's throat and drained away the blood. Moreover, none of the other great cats are so ill, though some of those from lines known to be gifted in divination have shown something of the same . . . drunkenness."

The ahmyndisdu frowned and tapped her chin with a forefinger on which the chewed nail revealed the anxiety she would not let enter her voice.

"That is an interesting comparison, Lady Blysse. Drunkenness. I had not thought of it. But what could Truth be drunk upon? She has drunk nothing but blood from freshly killed game and water from the same pitcher from which I myself have eased my thirst."

Firekeeper felt pity for the ahmyndisdu—an emotion she was not accustomed to experiencing for one who was, after all, nearly a stranger. Yet it was clear that Tiridanti was tremendously worried about Truth—and for the cat's own sake. Never once had the ahmyndisdu expressed an awareness that the great cat's illness might be a symptom of some greater attack on the human with whom she was most closely identified.

"Rahniseeta say you wish me talk to Truth," Firekeeper said. "I will do this, but I ask one thing. You will not be able to understand how I talk, and I not wish to stop to tell."

Tiridanti had not practiced divination for several years now without learning something about interpreting cryptic statements.

"You mean we should listen quietly, and not ask you to translate."

"As I say," Firekeeper agreed, knowing she was being perhaps a trace brusque.

Although Firekeeper would never admit it to anyone save Blind Seer, the great cats rather intimidated her. In her childhood, Firekeeper had encountered pumas and bobcats both, but wandering wolf pups are fair game to other predators, so Firekeeper had never lingered to extend the encounter. More recently, she had spoken with great cats both Royal and Wise, but never without a lingering sense that the cats were luxuriating in a sense of self-importance.

Tiridanti nodded. "You will be attempting something very difficult. The least I can do is keep silence. Do you wish us to leave?"

Firekeeper shook her head and found a thin smile.

"I think you here is good, in case Truth is unhappy with me."

"I understand."

Tiridanti looked at Rahniseeta.

"I am not certain how to explain your extended stay here, especially when I am asking everyone else to stay away—and with keeping Lady Blysse's presence rather quiet. I can, of course, simply say that I divined it needed to be so, but . . ."

Rahniseeta was already rising.

"I had been thinking much the same myself, Ahmyndisdu. I will leave and make my own excuses."

"Thank you, Rahniseeta."

After Harjeedian's sister had left, Firekeeper lowered herself to where she would be at eye level with the jaguar. The burnt-orange eyes looked through her as if she were not there.

"*Truth,*" Firekeeper said. "*Guhuarr.*"

As so frequently since they had come to Liglim, Firekeeper was aware that this manner of speaking contained elements that she did not know how she would explain to another person. There were sounds, yes, and gestures, true, but there was a third element . . .

Firekeeper shook her head as if she could physically clear these random thoughts. With Truth before her this was certainly not the time to let her mind wander.

The jaguar's gaze was muddy with confusion, yet the eyes were not blank. They moved and shifted as if the jaguar sought to keep in view some rapidly moving thing none of the rest of them could see.

Firekeeper slowly moved one hand in front of the jaguar's apparent field of vision, but Truth's eyes did not move.

"*Guhuarr,*" Firekeeper repeated. "*Truth. Can you hear me?*"

The jaguar's black-rimmed ears flicked back and forth, as if Truth was trying to catch an elusive sound, not one spoken within a few fingers' breadth of her head.

Again Firekeeper waved her hand in front of the jaguar's eyes. This time she was rewarded by the faintest shifting of the unfocused orbs in the direction of the motion, but it was nothing more than what might be granted by a butterfly fluttering on the periphery at a moment when the great cat was focused on more substantial prey.

"Firekeeper," Blind Seer said from where he was lying to one side of the screened shelter. *"You have tried eyes and ears. There are other senses."*

"I certainly am not going to touch her!" Firekeeper said. *"No matter how distracted Truth may be, she is still a hunter. I would lose my hand—or more."*

"Quite likely," Blind Seer agreed, *"but what about appealing to her sense of smell?"*

Firekeeper nodded. It was a good suggestion, and one she might have thought of on her own but for the human request that she talk to the jaguar. She cast around the screened room, looking for something that might break through the jaguar's isolation. She knew Tiridanti had been able to get Truth to eat, but that food alone had not been sufficient to break the firm grip of whatever held the jaguar's mind.

She rose and turned toward where Tiridanti sat.

"Have you spoken with Truth?" Tiridanti asked eagerly.

"Not really," Firekeeper said with bare honesty. "I think she hears, but as if I call from across a vast distance. Do you have perfume?"

Tiridanti blinked at Firekeeper in surprise.

"Perfume?" she asked, saying the Liglimosh word very carefully, as if she thought Firekeeper might have meant something else. "Scented oil?"

"That would do," Firekeeper agreed. "Or something that smells very strongly. Brandy, maybe, or even a foul scent like skunk. No food scent, though. I not want to make Truth hungry—not when I so close."

The ahmyndisdu nodded. "I can see why you wouldn't want that. I do not have any perfume with me here, but I have some in my chambers. Let me go fetch it. I will attempt to return as swiftly as possible, but I may be delayed."

Firekeeper nodded absently. "While you go, I will still try."

Reassured, Tiridanti left quickly, and soon even the sound of her sandal-clad feet against the brick-paved path was lost to hearing.

Blind Seer yawned.

"Perfume was a good idea," he said. *"I had thought about pissing on the jaguar's nose, but I think Tiridanti would have been offended."*

"As doubtless would have been the jaguar," Firekeeper said. *"Drink deeply. We may still come to that."*

She resumed her place on the floor near the jaguar, watching as the great cat paced, continuing her attempts to break through Truth's distraction. Her success in this was slight, but she became certain of one thing. Truth was aware of what was said and done in her vicinity, but she was more aware of whatever other reality it was she saw in her visions.

"It is as if," Firekeeper said to Blind Seer, *"dreams and reality have changed places. Have you ever been dreaming and something has happened in the waking world and your mind has been so reluctant to leave the dream that it has taken the element of reality and woven it into the dream?"*

Blind Seer wrinkled his brow in confusion.

"Not often," he said, *"and then only little things, like dreaming the weather is hot*

because some two-legs is sprawled on top of me. Are you saying you can sleep through dis-
turbances? Isn't that dangerous?"

Firekeeper nodded. *"Yes and yes. I have done it, and it is dangerous. Mostly for me it*
is as with you. A minor physical thing—like some four-legs' tail tickling me—weaves
itself into my dreams so that I am not awakened. However, sometimes a sound such as
distant thunder has woven itself into my dreams, so that I have dreamed of thunder."

Blind Seer was clearly disconcerted.

"Do not take offense, Firekeeper, but is this a human thing?"

"I think so," Firekeeper admitted somewhat ashamedly. *"But this is not important,*
not now. What I was trying to explain is that I think that for Truth the place of dreams
and the place of waking have been exchanged. She hears and sees, but then translates
these into her dreaming."

"That makes sense," Blind Seer said. *"When we were in Misheemnekuru, I spoke with*
several of the Wise Wolves about divination. They thought my name might indicate that I
came from a diviner line. I had to disappoint them, but in the discussions I learned about
the many forms of divination as practiced by the yarimaimalom. Apparently, divination
of the future is often likened to a sort of dream, one that foretells the various might-be's. A
skilled diviner can sort these from each other, and offer advice based upon them."

"So Truth," Firekeeper said, *"may have set off to track a future and lost herself. Didn't*
one of the ravens say Truth had difficulty reading the future where I was concerned?"

"It was Questioner who said this," Blind Seer replied, *"but ravens were tied up in it.*
I wonder just how much those great gossips know?"

"Worry about that later," Firekeeper said. *"Right now I want you to worry about how*
you will keep my skin relatively whole as I try to bring Truth out of her dreams."

Tiridanti returned shortly thereafter, bearing with her several flasks of perfume.
The bottles were tightly corked and sealed with wax, but even so, strongly mingled flo-
ral odors flooded their vicinity.

Firekeeper accepted a flask that smelled as if it contained every rose that had ever
lived. The other smelled equally strongly of some southern flower, the name of which
the wolf-woman did not know, though she had seen the small white blossoms starlike
against the night.

Blind Seer sneezed, and backed away involuntarily.

"I brought better than perfume," Tiridanti said with a smile. "These hold pure
essences such as would be used to blend perfumes and incense for our temple. The
stillroom keeper gave them over but reluctantly."

Firekeeper accepted the flask that smelled of roses, motioning for the other to be set
aside.

"If this work," she said, breaking the wax seal, "the keeper will have these back
unspilled."

"What are you going to do?"

"Truth walks in dreams," Firekeeper said without explanation. "I try and lead her
back."

Tiridanti frowned. "With roses?"

"With roses to wake her," Firekeeper said. "Something you say help me—that Truth would eat if food is before her. I do not think she see it. She smell it."

"I should have thought of that," Tiridanti replied, dismayed. "I've fed enough kittens. They suckle best after they can smell the milk."

"Humans are nose-dead," Firekeeper said. "Blind Seer remind me of this. Now, stay to side and quiet. I not know if this work, but I know Truth has sharp claws."

"She does," Tiridanti agreed. "She does."

Without further comment, the ahmyndisdu carried a lightweight woven chair to a corner from which she could watch without being in the way. Firekeeper forgot her immediately. Her attention was wholly upon the jaguar. Truth's nostrils had flared slightly when the perfumes were brought into her vicinity, but that had been her only reaction. Was she already lost in a dream wherein inexplicably flowers were now blooming in profusion?

Firekeeper knelt where Truth's pacing would bring the jaguar slightly to one side. As Truth was padding past, Firekeeper unstopped the bottle and held it directly beneath the tawny pink of the jaguar's nose leather.

Truth stopped in midstride as if she had been physically struck. Her haunches bunched beneath her as her forequarters suddenly reared back. Her tail puffed to twice its size. She tried to roar, but what should have been an intimidating sound tapered off into a whine of pain.

From the corner of her eye, Firekeeper was aware of Tiridanti starting to her feet, of Blind Seer's admonishing growl, but she could not spare attention for either. Truth's eyes had lost their focus on elsewhere, but Firekeeper could not be certain whether those potent dreams would claim her once more.

"Truth!" Firekeeper said. *"Listen to me."*

The jaguar lashed out at the perfume bottle with one paw. The claws were extended, each curled length sharp and cleanly polished. Firekeeper jerked back the flask, sloshing out a few drops of the aromatic liquid in her haste, but she need not have been so quick. The jaguar's blow was clumsy, lacking the eye-blurring speed that is the birthright of a hunting cat.

So Truth is yet half in the dream, Firekeeper thought. *Then I must draw her out.*

Thinking that too much more of the pungent scent might drive the jaguar away, Firekeeper stoppered the flask and put it away from her. Then she again moved her hand in front of the burnt-orange eyes. This time Truth tracked the motion more alertly, raising one paw as if to strike, then pausing, blinking bleary-eyed, striving to focus.

"Truth," Firekeeper called, seasoning the note with the notes of a wolf's howl. *"Truth, look over here. Here I am. Firekeeper. Remember me?"*

"Wolfling." The reply came faintly, as if Truth was struggling to recall speech. *"I cannot see you."*

Firekeeper was both pleased and frustrated. She recalled how Questioner had said that Truth had been frustrated by her inability to predict Firekeeper's actions. If this was indeed true, and if Truth turned once again to the world of dreams, Firekeeper might lose the ability to reach her. Truth would simply incorporate Firekeeper's presence into her dreams and there deny her existence.

"*That's right,*" Firekeeper said. "*The wolfling. The northerner. The one you cannot see. I'm here now, right beside you. Look and you will see.*"

But already the glazed look was occluding the jaguar's eyes. In frustration, Firekeeper did what she would not have dared had she not been fairly certain Truth's reflexes were far slower than usual. Darting out one hand, Firekeeper grabbed the end of the jaguar's tail and twisted. She didn't twist hard enough to break the bones, only hard enough to hurt.

Truth yowled. She pivoted, balancing on her hind paws, striking out with her fore. Firekeeper let go immediately, rolling back and out of the way, but even so a claw traced a line of blood across her upper arm.

"*Hah! There!*" Firekeeper shouted, and to Tiridanti's ears it sounded like a wolf's howl, short and sharp. "*Here I am, kitten. Can you see me now? Look with the eyes in your head. I am here. Here in front of you. You can't find me in the dream, but can you find me here?*"

Truth roared, a harsh staccato sound, strident and alarming.

"*I see you!*"

She leapt, but her muscles were still not wholly under her control, and Firekeeper danced clear.

"*Do you still see me, kitten?*" Firekeeper taunted. "*Come after me if you do.*"

Truth sprang, burnt-orange eyes flaring brighter and clearer, and Firekeeper leapt so that a table was between them. Truth cleared the table easily, but now Blind Seer had joined the game. Coming around behind, he nipped at the jaguar's flank, darting away so that her striking paw met only fur.

Truth roared in frustration.

"*I see you!*" Then she faltered, one paw landing as if the jaguar had misjudged the location of the floor.

"*See with the eyes in your head!*" Firekeeper said, desperation turning what had been meant as a command into a plea. "*The other eyes are no good. They will lead you astray. Use the eyes in your head!*"

Blind Seer dealt in more direct persuasion. He struck three times, snapping painfully at flank and shoulder, always avoiding the retaliating claws—though once Truth hit and blood beaded in a thin line across his nose.

Truth's paws darted and dashed, making crazy patterns all around her. It was as if she batted at moths or gnats—or at a dozen images, only one of which was real. Her frustration was growing, her growls and roars becoming bestial and incoherent.

Firekeeper seized up the pottery water jar from the floor and emptied its contents over the jaguar's head. The jar was large and still mostly filled. The contents sluiced through Truth's thick fur and onto the tiled floor. The jaguar snarled, reared to strike, and then, in midmotion, froze.

For a long moment, Firekeeper thought she had pressed too hard, that this final stimulus had been too much. Then she saw the last of the glazed look melt from the jaguar's eyes, saw the burnt-orange light again with the translucent glow of gold, and saw Truth steady herself, holding still for an eternal moment of calculation before methodically shaking the wetness from her fur.

Firekeeper drew her arm across her face to wipe away the fine spray and noticed for the first time since it had happened the thin score where the jaguar's claws had sliced her. The wound was bleeding cleanly, so she as immediately dismissed it.

"Truth?" she asked. *"Can you hear me?"*

The jaguar turned a baleful gaze on her.

"I can and I do. The real question is whether you will be glad for it."

XXXIII

"SO YOU'VE ALREADY SOLD THE MARE?" Poshtuvanu's disappointment sounded genuine, even though he was quite aware the mare was no longer in the farmer's keeping. "Oh, well . . ."

The farmer's evident unhappiness at disappointing a representative of u-Bishinti was not without an element of self-defense.

"I notified u-Bishinti when the mare was foaled," the farmer said in a voice as thin and reedy as his build. "I even asked if the name Freshwater Pearl met with the disdum's approval. However, I never received any indication that I should hold on to her—and horses are expensive to keep, true white horses more than most, as I see it, what with their fair skin and the problems of dealing with stains."

He didn't so much stop speaking as trail off into a rather insect-like whine. Derian glanced at Poshtuvanu, and saw from the other's slight nod that it was his turn to speak.

"Can you tell me to whom Freshwater Pearl was sold?" he said. "White horses are very greatly valued in my homeland. I would pay much for her."

Zira had suggested this approach.

"If representatives of u-Bishinti ask too many questions," she had said, "it may create suspicions—especially since we didn't snatch up the mare when she was a foal. However, who knows what a foreigner will fasten on as important? Derian can press and pry. All that will do is make him seem different—and there's nothing anyone can do about that."

Remembering the grin Zira had given him, and how she'd leaned across to tug a trailing lock of red hair that had slipped from his queue, Derian had to suppress a grin.

Although Derian's request had been rather more usual than not, the farmer seemed hesitant to reply. Although Derian found himself wondering if this meant the farmer had been told to keep silent about the transaction, he realized there was a much simpler motivation.

"And lest you suffer a loss for your kindness," Derian went on, "I could arrange for you to be paid for your trouble. I realize you do not wish to annoy a valued client—even if it may be to his advantage."

And especially since it would not be to your advantage at all. Who wants an associate bragging that they sold the beast you sold them for a hefty profit? It's the type of thing that can rankle for years.

Poshtuvanu interjected smoothly. "I have some tokens here that can be redeemed for services at u-Bishinti. Medical care, divinations, a loan of skilled labor . . ."

The farmer's hesitancy vanished at once. Apparently, what Poshtuvanu offered was more valuable than mere money. If he wondered why u-Bishinti should offer to pay for information given to a foreigner, he probably thought it was because the disdum stood to make a hefty profit when trade with the northern lands became more common.

"I can check my records," the farmer said, accepting the three baked-clay tokens Poshtuvanu slipped into his hand. "Will you come inside? My wife was churning this morning, and her sweet butter is excellent. I believe we have berry muffins as well."

The repast they were given was much more extensive than mere bread and butter. Indeed, Derian had the impression that the farmer was due for a tongue-lashing from his wife about the importance of treating representatives from u-Bishinti with more courtesy than one gave the usual buyer.

Am I reading too much into his reluctance to talk to us? Derian thought. *He did seem to clam up when Poshtuvanu mentioned Freshwater Pearl. No way of knowing—or even confirming suspicions—until we find out if Freshwater Pearl has indeed vanished or if she is happily eating her head off in some field somewhere. After all, this was not the only white mare Zira located. We've been disappointed already.*

But confirmation that they were on the right track came as soon as the farmer brought out his records. The buyer's name matched one on the list compiled by Meiyal's clerk, that of a kidisdu specializing in water birds.

The excellent muffin went dry and hard in Derian's throat as he realized the difficulties that could arise if the farmer decided to try and buy back Freshwater Pearl so that he could be the one who profited.

"You won't tell your client we've been asking?" Derian said, balancing a friendly expression against a tone that said "I've been a horse trader since I could walk. I know the tricks and I won't think kindly if you try them on me."

"Of course he won't," snapped the farmer's wife. The manner in which she glowered at her husband made Derian think he'd guessed right about the man's character. "We understand you'll want a fair deal, and telling the kidisdu in advance that you're very eager to buy the horse might raise the price."

I should have thought of that, Derian thought ruefully, *and of course the farmer would get a cut of the sale price.*

He grinned at the farmer's wife.

"I'm sure you're honest folk, a credit to your deities. We'll burn incense for you in Heeranenahalm."

That seemed to make even the farmer happy, and when Poshtuvanu and Derian took their leave it was with wishes of good fortune all around.

Poshtuvanu waited until they were out on the road and well out of sight of the farmer's property before turning in his saddle to give Derian a triumphant grin.

"That's the one," he said. "I'd bet my best saddle on it."

"You won't find a taker here," Derian said with a laugh. "Tell me, is it common for a kidisdu to own his own horse?"

"Not one assigned to u-Seeheera as this one is—not unless he was already horse-crazy, and then it's quite likely we'd already know of his interest."

"Because he'd stable his horses with you?"

"That's right. Neither the Temple of Flyers nor the Temple of Sea Beasts maintain separate stables so close to u-Bishinti. It's easier to let us do the work."

Derian's momentary glee faded slightly as a thought occurred to him.

"He could have bought the horse as a gift for someone."

"Without coming to us first?" Poshtuvanu scoffed. "Oh, he wanted the mare as a gift, a gift to the deities, given in blood. If he just wanted to please a lover or someone in her family, he would have come to us."

The mention of love gifts brought heat to Derian's face. He'd been meaning to ask Poshtuvanu what was appropriate, but he didn't quite know how to go about it. Part of his problem was that he didn't quite know what the relationship between himself and Rahniseeta was.

Despite some interesting afternoons, they weren't lovers—at least not yet. He wasn't even sure if they were courting. What would his parents think if he brought home a foreign bride? He tried to imagine exotic and lovely Rahniseeta with her golden-brown skin and ink-black hair in the Carter family house. It wasn't easy.

Oddly enough, it was easier to imagine her at court. She'd look lovely in a flowing gown of New Kelvinese silk, her hair twisted up in some elaborate fashion and interwoven with gems or, maybe, pearls . . . No, gems. Nothing large and gaudy. Topazes, perhaps, or garnets. He didn't think he could afford rubies, though they would look fine, too.

He sighed and decided that for now he'd need to settle for flowers, probably wild ones gathered along the road, since he still went around rather short on pocket money and he'd feel the fool walking through u-Seeheera clutching a bouquet.

"Hey, Derian!"

Poshtuvanu leaned over in his saddle and poked Derian in the ribs. The action caused his deceptively understated bay to crowd Prahini and Derian found himself struggling to keep his seat.

"Why'd you do that?" Derian asked indignantly.

"I'd asked you three times if you thought it would be a good idea if one of us went straight to u-Bishinti and the other to Heeranenahalm. As it is, we won't be able to arrive at either place until evening, but I thought this might be important enough to report without delay."

"Sorry," Derian said. "I was thinking."

"About the importance of our news, no doubt," Poshtuvanu said with a twinkle in his eye that reminded Derian rather too much of Zira.

"That," Derian said, "certainly. Why don't I go to Heeranenahalm? I'm the one who's supposed to be interested in buying this horse, and the kidisdu the farmer mentioned is posted there. Do you think I'll find him at the Temple of Flyers or the Temple of Sea Beasts?"

"Flyers, probably," Poshtuvanu said. "You can ask someone to check a listing, though. The temples offer courtesy accommodations when the boundaries between types of animals aren't clear."

"I think I'd heard that," Derian said. "So, will you take u-Bishinti?"

"Most certainly," Poshtuvanu agreed, "and when you go to Heeranenahalm don't forget to tell Rahniseeta what we've learned."

This time his twinkle spread into a broad grin that Derian could not pretend to ignore.

"Is there anything wrong with my liking Rahniseeta?" he said, his own snappishness reminding him of the farmer's wife. He immediately softened. "I mean, Rahniseeta doesn't seem to mind, but I don't know if I'm doing anything wrong."

Poshtuvanu looked instantly serious.

"I don't think anything is wrong unless you're misleading Rahniseeta in some way. She doesn't exactly run screaming when you come into sight. However, if you've promised her something you can't give . . . or you have a wife at home or something . . ."

"No wife," Derian said promptly. "The girl I was walking out with a few years ago unceremoniously dumped me when Earl Kestrel assigned me to Firekeeper."

Derian had already explained something of how he'd come into his current position and responsibilities, so now Poshtuvanu nodded that he understood.

"How about Lady Blysse?" he said. "Does she have any claim on you?"

"Friendship," Derian said. "I'd do just about anything for her, but I don't love her like you should love a wife, and she certainly doesn't love me that way. I once thought she might be starting to, but I think I was wrong."

"Yet she was willing to let herself be taken prisoner rather than see you harmed," Poshtuvanu said.

"And I'd do the same for her," Derian replied. "I might even die if my death would assure her life, but I can't imagine marrying her."

Derian frowned.

"But we're talking about marriage awfully fast here. What constitutes a promise among you people? If holding hands and a bit of kissing . . ." Derian felt himself growing red but forged on determinedly, "If that constitutes a promise of marriage, then I'm in over my head."

Poshtuvanu's words were only somewhat reassuring.

"If a girl lets you close because she thought you were promising marriage—and could provide some proof . . ."

"Proof?"

"Like an expensive gift or taking her to some function where you'd normally only escort a member of your family—a religious ceremony, for example."

Derian sagged a little in relief.

"Go on."

"Anyhow, if Rahniseeta could give proof that you led her on, then you might be in trouble. Her brother, as her closest family member, could extract some penalty from you—even force a marriage if she were carrying a child. Otherwise, it's fair game, and the only thing on the line are broken hearts."

"I'd hate to hurt Rahniseeta even that way," Derian admitted, "but it's a big jump from a bit of playing around in the woods to bringing home a bride."

"I understand," Poshtuvanu said. "The important thing is making sure that Rahniseeta understands, too."

"HOW ARE YOU DOING with Waln Endbrook?" asked Dantarahma.

"Very well," replied Shivadtmon, with an almost piratical grin. "I have him, and have him convinced he has me."

"Good. The time has come to let our bird fly."

Shivadtmon's grin lost some of its boldness.

"So soon?"

"Rather," Dantarahma replied, "let us pray we are not too late. Moreover, the chief reason for my wishing for you to delay him is taken care of. Report has come to me that Lady Blysse has returned from Misheemnekuru to the mainland."

"Two days ago," Shivadtmon agreed, "and seasick all the way, or so I heard it from the captain of the vessel that carried her back."

"Have you also heard where Lady Blysse went earlier this very day?"

"No, Master."

"She went to the House of Fire where Tiridanti has for several days been acting very strangely."

Dantarahma knew something of the reasons behind Tiridanti's strange behavior, but he judged it best that Shivadtmon not know all. Best the aridisdu run swiftly, if in ignorance, to do his master's bidding.

Fear, quickly concealed, now lit Shivadtmon's eyes as a banked ember still holds the potential for fire.

"But why would Lady Blysse go there? For what reason?"

Dantarahma decided to blow gently on the coals of Shivadtmon's fear.

"All I know is that during the afternoon rest time, one of our congregation saw Lady Blysse and the wolf, Blind Seer, moving swiftly down one of the side streets toward the House of Fire. They were not precisely sneaking, but they did not go to the main door. Instead they went to a side door and let themselves in. I have asked some judicious questions. Earlier today Tiridanti left u-Nahal and returned to the House of Fire. Since then, she has been alone in the gardens but for the jaguar, Truth."

Shivadtmon looked as if he would give anything he owned to have reassurance that Lady Blysse's business had not been with the ahmyndisdu, but Dantarahma was not going to grant him that. He needed Shivadtmon tense and ready to act.

"Do you know who had been the ahmyndisdu's previous caller?" Dantarahma asked. He went on without waiting for Shivadtmon to essay a reply: "Rahniseeta, sister of Harjeedian, the same Rahniseeta who has been keeping company of late with the human who is quite probably Lady Blysse's closest friend. Although most callers have been asked to leave Tiridanti to her prayers, Rahniseeta remained a long while. I do not know for certain if she was admitted to Tiridanti's presence, but it is a likelihood."

Shivadtmon looked very nervous now, and for good reason. Although Dantarahma had convinced most of his followers that their private worship was neither immoral or illegal, those like Shivadtmon were well aware that to most of their fellows the return of blood sacrifice was anathema. It was easy to justify oneself in the company of like-minded individuals, much harder when it seemed the secret might get out.

Dantarahma decided that he had wound Shivadtmon about as tightly as was profitable. Any tighter and the string would snap and be useless. When Shivadtmon seemed about to voice a question, Dantarahma interrupted him.

"We have no time for questions, my son, not if you are to sail tonight."

"Tonight?" Shivadtmon's voice broke.

"Certainly." Dantarahma reached out with a fatherly hand and patted the aridisdu's shoulder. "Haven't you been complaining that you've been having trouble holding the northern sailors back? Go now and be confident that in serving me you serve divine Water and all his family. Go now and the deities go with you."

Shivadtmon bowed low and left. Dantarahma made a mental note to check with the agent he had watching Waln Endbrook and his comrades as to how long it took the aridisdu to arrive. Although Dantarahma had commanded Shivadtmon to arrange for the Endbrook group to leave tonight, he would settle for any time in the next several days. The important thing was that they leave before the debate could resume in force as to whether to send the northerners back with apologies or to keep them.

Dantarahma had no desire to keep the foreigners overlong in Liglim, but before he was rid of them, he had several uses for them. Shivadtmon was aware of only one of these uses—to discredit Tiridanti by having the northerners who had arrived here under her aegis do something outrageous.

Whimsically, Dantarahma thought of this as committing sacrilege by proxy. In the general air of outrage that would certainly follow the invasion of Misheemnekuru by the northerners, Dantarahma should find it easy to increase desire for isolationism and religious reform among the Liglimom. From there, reintroducing traditional religious practices should be much easier.

However, Dantarahma had other reasons for wanting Misheemnekuru in particular to be the target of this invasion. Some years after he had first felt the caress of divine magic touch his soul during a sacrifice, he had also become aware of entities somehow sensitive to those magical emanations. Their outcry of astonishment had been so loud that he had immediately ceased what he was doing—rather shocking his congregation.

Research into many an old tome, and patient practice of the rites recorded within, had taught Dantarahma two very important techniques. First, he had learned how to conceal those emanations so that he was fairly certain that he had gone undetected for many years now. He rather fancied that whoever the listeners had been—and he was certain there had been more than one—they had by now decided either that they had erred or that the magical surge they had "heard" had been a random event, perhaps connected to some item left by the Liglimom's former rulers.

The second thing Dantarahma had learned had been a refined form of augury. This enabled him to narrow down the possible location of the listeners, and test after test had pinpointed the central reaches of Misheemnekuru. The procedure had raised him in the estimation of the disdu, who hailed him as one who would reform the church by introducing new ways of divining the will of the deities. As Dantarahma's greatest desire was to bring the church back to its earliest roots, he found this extremely ironic.

However, whatever the reasons behind his skills, Dantarahma knew himself to be one of the greatest augurers to grace Heeranenahalm since the days of the Old Country rulers. Soon he hoped to also be acknowledged as the first sorcerer to grace these shores since the last vestiges of Old Country magic had vanished from the land.

Yes, thought Dantarahma after the departing Shivadtmon. *Go with the deities, and, if I am lucky, go to them as well.*

❧

AFTER LEAVING TIRIDANTI, Rahniseeta went back to the Hall of Scribes, but she had trouble concentrating on the intricate calligraphy she had been working on. After spoiling a perfectly good page two fingers' breadth from the bottom she set her work aside.

"Water and Earth clearly do not favor my completing this today," she said to the disdu in charge. "Best I set aside my quill."

"Best," the disdu agreed rather sourly, looking at the spoiled sheet. "The omens are against your success."

Returning to the Temple of the Cold Bloods, Rahniseeta resolved to take the rest she'd missed by waiting on Tiridanti. She had thought she'd been too anxious to sleep, but almost as soon has she'd stripped off her outwear and given herself over to the coolness of her sheets, she was asleep.

She awoke to find the early edge of dusk visible outside of the window and a delicious coolness in the air that suggested that Water had granted his mother respite from the heat in the form of rain. Rising and dressing in clean blouse and trousers, Rahniseeta felt rejuvenated, and went out into the center room she shared with Harjeedian feeling lighthearted, temporarily relieved of the responsibilities that had weighted her down for so many days.

How the divine elements must laugh at human antics and ambitions, she thought. *Not long ago I was bemoaning being nothing but Harjeedian's useful sister. Now that I have been given responsibilities because there were those who saw my worth, I am relieved to have a respite.*

Harjeedian had, as was his custom, left her a note indicating that he would be gone through the dinner hour. Rahniseeta decided that she would dine in the public area rather than bring a tray back to her room. It would be nice to see some of the friends she had been forced to neglect of late.

She was just finishing a dish of spiced rice noodles garnished with thin slices of marinated saltwater bass when one of the porter's messengers came up to her. He waited politely until Rahniseeta's dinner companion—a kidisdu who specialized in incubation—finished the anecdote she was telling, then said politely:

"Knowing that you were in, the porter thought you would like to be informed that one of the northerners—the clumsy one—has come to visit Barnet Lobster."

Rahniseeta swallowed a sigh. She'd been enjoying her respite, but all her companions knew the pull of duty.

"And is Barnet in?"

"Yes. He returned at the afternoon break and has not since left his suite."

Rahniseeta, who knew that the northerners found the damp, sticky summer heat oppressive, was not surprised. She rose and excused herself to her friends.

"Save me one of those fruit crisps," she said after accepting their sympathy. "That is, if you're really sorry for me."

The kidisdu laughed, but Rahniseeta saw her slide a pastry to one side of the serving plate as a reminder.

Still in good spirits, Rahniseeta made her leisurely way down the storm-cooled corridors. A slim green snake glided across her path, then coiled up a pillar, freezing among the vines that grew there like a stem returned to its parent plant.

There was a legend about just that, and she thought Barnet would like it. Elwyn, too, had a childish eagerness for stories. After Derian, these two had become her favorites among the foreigners.

Thinking of Derian made Rahniseeta's cheeks warm, but it was not at all an unpleasant heat. With a smile on her face and her feet light, she turned down the corridor that led to the suite that Barnet continued to occupy alone, except on those rare nights Derian chose not to ride back to u-Bishinti.

What she heard as she drew closer to the gate made her stop, still as the snake among the vines, and listen.

Elwyn's voice, unmusical against the accompaniment of Barnet's fingers playing something idle and intricate on one of his stringed instruments, spoke eagerly.

". . . and so we're sailing out tonight."

Barnet replied, laughter underlying his words, "Going to get lost again?"

Rahniseeta remembered the incident to which Barnet referred. The northerners had broken a line or something, and had ended up staying away all night. The event had been something of a sensation, for even those disdum who wanted to be rid of the foreigners wanted to do so on their own terms. The thought that they might have simply left had been unsettling.

The disdum of the Temple of Sea Beasts had been quick to reassure everyone that the boat on which the northerners had been sailing lacked the size and capacity to sail outside of the relatively sheltered bay, so even if the northerners had attempted to leave without permission, they were unlikely to get far. It had been distinctly anticlimactic when the small vessel had limped into the harbor the next morning.

"We didn't get lost then," Elwyn said, laughing in return, clearly aware he was being teased. "We won't tonight either. We know just where we're going. Want to know?"

Rahniseeta had started to move again, but once again she froze.

"Sure," Barnet said, "especially since I'm being invited to come along. Where?"

"To Misheemnekuru," Elwyn said, dropping his voice almost to a whisper. "Those islands in the bay. Waln's been saying there's treasure there, enough to set us all up as fine gentlemen back in the Isles."

"Enough to buy Waln Queen Valora's forgiveness," Barnet mused. "I wonder."

His tone changed.

"But, Elwyn, you know we're not to go to those islands. They're restricted, even to the Liglimom themselves."

"Oh, that's all right," Elwyn said dismissively. "We've got permission."

"Permission? Like Lady Blysse had permission?"

"I think so. Waln has talked about it to an aridisdu who's really important and knows all this stuff."

"And the aridisdu gave permission?" Barnet sounded distinctly disbelieving.

"Sort of," Elwyn admitted. This was clearly getting beyond what his rather simple intellect could handle, but he was obviously eager to convince Barnet. "It's like this. The islands were animals-only, no people, right up until Lady Blysse went there. No matter how strange she is, there's no doubting she's human, so the animals must not mind humans coming there anymore."

"And this is what the aridisdu told you?" Barnet did not sound convinced.

"Pretty much," Elwyn said. "Anyhow, he must believe it himself, because he's coming with us."

"He is?"

"Yep. And he's done more than that. I bet you wonder how we're going to get out of here with our loot."

"I can't say I had."

"Waln has. He's arranged with this aridisdu to have that ship they're getting ready in case they're going to send us home all set. The crew that's on board is friendly to Waln's aridisdu and will go with us. So it's up anchor and to home. That's why we really want you to come with us. You'll get treasure and home with honor. That's why we went out exploring, isn't it?"

It was a long speech for Elwyn and gave Rahniseeta a good idea just how carefully Waln Endbrook had been preparing for this moment. She also had no doubt who this aridisdu was. It had to be Shivadtmon—and would the crew he had prepared be members of Dantarahma's cabal? How would the rulers of the northern lands view Liglim if their first encounter with her people was with a group given to blood sacrifice?

Rahniseeta didn't dare let her mind wander to the possible ramifications of this, but she remembered Derian's tales of the century of war between his people and Barnet's—peoples who differed only in who their ruler was. How would they act toward people who looked and thought so differently?

She shivered, longing to run with this information to Harjeedian or Meiyal, to pass on the responsibility to anyone else, but she must risk remaining long enough to hear what Barnet decided.

Barnet had paused, even his fingers on the strings stilling as he thought. Now the music resumed, but the tune was no longer light.

"We did go out for those reasons," Barnet said slowly, "but I don't think this is the way to get honor and treasure. It just doesn't feel right. I've been living up here among the disdum, and while lots of them are unhappy with Lady Blysse's visit to Misheemnekuru, not many talk like this aridisdu."

"But Barnet . . ." Elwyn whined like a child. "You've gotta come with us. Waln says we'll need the extra hands."

Rahniseeta heard the instrument put aside, a chair being pushed back.

"I'll come with you," Barnet said, "though I'm not promising to take part in this mad venture. Maybe I can talk some sense into Waln Endbrook's head. At the least I'll learn if this aridisdu really thinks going to Misheemnekuru isn't sacrilege. Bide a moment while I get myself ready."

Rahniseeta did not dare wait any longer. Moving with great care to stay silent, she fled.

RAHNISEETA'S FIRST THOUGHT was to confide in Harjeedian, but then she remembered that her brother was away and might not be back for hours. Although she had served them, she was not close to either the ikidisdu or iaridisdu of the Temple of the Cold Bloods. Moreover, her head spinning with what she had just learned, blending with warnings not to confide what she knew about Dantarahma's cabal to anyone lest that person be a secret member, she had begun to see enemies in even the most familiar faces.

She went to her suite, but it was indeed empty. As she changed into darker clothing, hardly knowing why she was doing so, she laid her plans.

Harjeedian was away. Derian had not yet returned from inquiring after the white mare—and might not return until tomorrow. Lady Blysse was either with Tiridanti and Truth or vanished somewhere. She was a great wanderer by night, and in any case, Rahniseeta did not fancy trying to explain this to the strange woman.

That left Meiyal, iaridisdu of the Horse, and her clerk as the only ones privy to the secret who might be reached. However, it would look very odd if Rahniseeta went to the Temple of the Horse at this hour. Looking odd was not a good thing.

Moving into the suite, Rahniseeta took writing implements and began writing letters. One was to Harjeedian and gave an account of what she had heard but nothing more. The second was to Derian, and included her suppositions that this newest development might somehow be connected to Dantarahma. She had to be rather cryptic about this last, omitting names other than that of Shivadtmon. Derian was smart. He'd work it out. The third was to Meiyal and included much the same information.

Rahniseeta left the note to Harjeedian in the usual place and prayed for Earth to grant him wisdom in his actions. The note for Derian she sealed multiple times and, as an afterthought, sprinkled with a bit of scent. The one to Meiyal she bound into a package with several sheets of blank paper. Then she took both with her to the front gate.

"Derian Counselor may come calling tonight," Rahniseeta said to the porter on duty, with a smile she hoped did not look too forced. "If he does, can you give this to him?"

"Gladly," said the porter, who had noticed Derian escorting Rahniseeta a time or two and thought he knew what made the lady look so strained.

"And I found I carried home some papers I was working on for Iaridisdu Meiyal. Could one of your messengers carry this packet to her residence? I fear she may need them early tomorrow."

The porter nodded. "It's a quiet evening. I'm sure one of the youngsters will be glad of a chance to stretch."

"Thank you," Rahniseeta said gratefully.

She waited until she was outside the door to pull her shawl over her head, hoping thus to conceal her features. Then, with a pounding heart, she hurried down side streets in the direction of the harbor, there to keep watch where the boat Waln and his crew had been using was usually docked.

I cannot stop them by myself. That kind of thing is for a minstrel tale such as Barnet loves to tell. But I can watch, and listen, and see how many go out and how well equipped

they are, and whether they are equipped for fighting or merely for robbery. That will cer-
tainly be useful and help will not be too far behind me. Meiyal, at least, will be in and she
will act when she reads my message.

But what Rahniseeta could not know was that when the runner from the Temple of the Cold Bloods arrived at the Temple of the Horse, the porter there saw no reason to trouble his mistress for something that was not an emergency. Thus Rahniseeta's packet to Meiyal was placed squarely in the center of the iaridisdu's desk, waiting for morning.

XXXIV

THE THUNDERSTORM SOME HOURS EARLIER had spent every drop of
moisture in the air, and so the stars showed clear and bright against the silent
blackness of the night sky. Waln could almost believe that, as Shivadtmon had
said, the omens were in favor of this expedition.

But he wasn't going to rely on omens for the success of a venture on which so
much rested. Ever since he'd won the last of the shipwrecked sailors over to his
cause, Waln had been drilling them on what they should do when the time finally
came. Waln had known for some hands of days now that they would not have a long
time to prepare, nor would they likely be able to set the date themselves. That would
be up to Shivadtmon, for Shivadtmon would be the one who could arrange for a sympathetic—or at least malleable—crew aboard the larger vessel they must take in order
to make their escape when they were finished on Misheemnekuru.

Waln hadn't been precisely pleased at just how little lead time Shivadtmon had
given them, but when he weighed that inconvenience against the increasing restlessness evidenced by Rarby and Shelby—and a few signs that Wiatt, at least, was beginning to change his mind—he had decided that little lead time or not, they must move.

He had set the sailors to their various tasks, reminding them as he did so, "We won't
leave until well after dark, so don't rush; don't look anxious. If you have a student to
teach, by all means, give the lesson, but don't let anything slip."

As far as Waln could tell, no one had, but some time after the dinner things had
been cleared away, the first complication arose. It came in the person of Barnet Lobster, escorted by a worried and yet excited Elwyn. By the worry on the half-wit's face
Waln guessed that Barnet had raised some doubts, but by the excitement Waln felt
fairly certain that those doubts had not been sufficient to unset the twin hooks of
buried treasure and a voyage home that he'd used to land this particular fish.

Barnet had about him a touch of what Waln thought of as his "court manner," by
which Waln guessed that the minstrel was more nervous than he might seem to a less
insightful observer.

"Waln, may I speak with you—privately?"

"Certainly," Waln said, glad that the others would not be witness to the undoubted eloquence Barnet would bring to his position. "My suite is just up the stairs."

As soon as they were inside and the door firmly shut, Barnet looked squarely at Waln.

"I don't think you should go to Misheemnekuru, Waln," he said without preamble. "If you must, by all means take the waiting ship and sail her north. Along with the information you'll bring back with you, she's prize enough to reestablish your fortune. Queen Valora has been seeking allies outside of those lands we already know. She'll find excuse to swallow her pride if you bring news of a possibility. You might even smooth things with Hawk Haven by bearing word of where the king's favorite and his counselor have gone."

Waln smiled sardonically.

"And you really think the Liglimom will ally with the Isles after I steal one of their ships?"

"I think they, too, will find a way to work around their pride, especially since you can always argue you were misled by that aridisdu of yours—Shivadtmon's his name, isn't it?—into believing that you were on another diplomatic voyage. From what Elwyn told me, the ship's crew already are of Shivadtmon's party."

Waln was momentarily tempted. Then he recalled the probable treasures of Misheemnekuru, of his dream of returning to the Isles dripping with wealth and hinting at power. No, he wouldn't be swayed, but Barnet must be put off gently. Having that facile tongue at his side when he returned to put his case to Queen Valora would be invaluable.

"Shivadtmon tells me," Waln said, "that there will be no difficulty with our landing on Misheemnekuru. He says that the dominant view is that this would no longer be sacrilege. Besides, I have promised the others wealth with which to pull themselves from their low stations. It will be harder to keep their cooperation without that."

"Elwyn related some of what Shivadtmon had told you," Barnet said, "and I wonder at his motivations. I've talked to a good many disdum, and few seem as certain on this matter as he is. As for treasure, you were a wealthy man in the Isles. You will certainly be so again. Use that to promise the others their reward."

Again, Waln was momentarily tempted. Then he shook his head.

"No. There is no question as to what course of action I am taking. The only question that remains is whether you are with us or against us."

Waln let a note of threat fill his voice at this last. It would be good for Barnet to remember where he was and that his court relations did not count here. Here Barnet Lobster was only a smaller man facing a much larger one—and the larger one had allies within call.

But Barnet neither wilted at the implied threat nor resumed his argument. Instead, he fell silent, as if weighing what he wished to say—or whether he should even say it. At last, Barnet cleared his throat and said:

"Waln, I'm with you, but only on conditions. I'll not set foot on Misheemnekuru. I don't believe the truce or treaty or whatever it is between the yarimaimalom and the Liglimom has been broken. I won't be party to breaking it."

Waln started to speak, but Barnet held up a hand.

"Hear me out. I won't land on Misheemnekuru, but I'll help you take the ship and sail her north. I'll even help you sail whatever smaller vessel you plan to take to Misheemnekuru. I just won't go ashore and dig for treasure."

He stopped, but again signaled he was not finished.

"You'll want to know my reasons for this—and, flatly, much as I would like to see my family again, it isn't homesickness or anything like that. Are you aware I have a lover among the disdum of the Temple of Flyers?"

Waln nodded. Shelby, half-envious, half-amused, had brought that salacious bit of gossip back one day.

"Well," Barnet went on. "Ours was no great lovers' tryst, but she liked me for more than my voice and the novelty of my pale skin. From time to time, she dropped little bits of gossip about the debates among the various factions of the disdum. One of these, told in all seriousness, was that I should take care before I boarded any ship to take me home—at least unless I was very certain about the captain's orders."

Waln chuckled. "Did she mean to keep you here?"

Barnet's mouth shaped a half-grin.

"At first I thought something similar—that her warning was nothing more than sweet talk. I pressed her, though, and she said she'd heard rumors that the vessel being prepared had no other course than to carry its passengers to their deaths. She gave proof enough to make me worried. That's why I'd sail home on a ship with you as captain and men I knew as crew."

"I've heard similar rumors," Waln said, "and not only from Shivadtmon. These Liglimom can argue a problem into more threads than you'd find in a piece of tight-woven silk. It comes from having no monarch to tell them what to do. Every person's a little monarch in his own head—trying to sway the others and stay in good with their deities as well."

"You may be right," Barnet said, "but whether or not those who end up in charge are those who want my death or not, I'd rather assure myself by sailing home before the disdum make up their minds. That's why I'd go with you—but on my terms."

"And if I don't accept them?"

"I think you will," Barnet said easily. "You wouldn't have sent Elwyn after me if you didn't have use for me. Otherwise, I'm one more with whom you have to split your treasure. Think of it this way. I'm not asking for the treasure. All I'm asking for is a working passage. My being along will even spare you another hand to treasure-hunt, for I won't leave the boat."

Waln made up his mind instantly. Bluster and fuss hardly made sense when, after all, as Barnet said, Waln wanted the minstrel along and cooperative.

"I'll sign you on then," Waln said, thrusting out his hand. "On your terms with my word on it that I'll not ask you to change your mind."

"Done, then," Barnet said, returning the clasp. "I only wish we could get Derian and Lady Blysse away as well."

Waln shook his head. "That's not possible. Not only can't they be reached, honestly, they both hate me. They'd accept you, me, and all the rest dead before they accepted my command."

"Possibly," Barnet said, but his tone changed the word to "Definitely." "In any case, they are the least likely to be murdered out of hand. Both have been favored by the yarimaimalom, and that complicates matters."

"For the Liglimom, perhaps," Waln said, "but not at all for me."

He smiled hard, thinking of the crossbow with which he'd been practicing until he'd regained skills he'd had long ago.

"Definitely, not at all for me."

WHEN WALN AND HIS ALLIES went down to the harbor, the streets had stilled even of the late-evening traffic that came when the lowering sun brought a relief from the worst of the heat. The shadowy figures they passed here and there were not the type to trouble a large group of men. Indeed, several moved away rather hurriedly when the group approached.

Waln told his party to make no effort to hide themselves. They were going out for a bit of night fishing, that was all, but even so the sailors spoke infrequently, and when they did they kept their voices low.

Most personal property had been transferred aboard already. There wasn't much of this, as Shivadtmon had promised that the oceangoing vessel would carry stores of clothing as well as food and water. Barnet, though, had insisted on taking a small trunk of musical instruments. Tedgewinn had his carvings. Elwyn had a sack of what to Waln's eyes was nothing more than junk, but Elwyn seemed sure would find ready buyers in the Isles.

They had left clothing and routine items in their rooms so as not to alert suspicion if any visitors came to call or if the servants were poking around come morning. The longer they had without questions being asked the better, for no matter how optimistically Elwyn spoke of them "hopping ashore and grabbing the treasures," Waln knew they might be two or three days on Misheemnekuru before they found what they wanted.

But that doesn't matter, he reminded himself. *Shivadtmon says that the ship's crew doesn't get rotated for several days—that's why he wanted us to start as soon as possible. We're set.*

They'd informally renamed the little sailing vessel they'd adopted for their own *Islander*, a name that certainly seemed nothing but patriotism to those who heard it, but for Waln was ironically significant. It was not just a boat sailed by Islanders, but one that would be going to the Sanctuary Islands—and that would be the means of making him an Islander once more.

They were making ready to cast off when a man came hurrying up the wharves and spoke urgently in Shivadtmon's ear. Waln frowned and hurried over. He'd seen the man a time or two before, and had thought he might have been watching them for one or more of the disdum factions, but Shivadtmon not only appeared to know him, he was listening intently.

"What's going on?" Waln asked, snapping in a note of command although he kept his voice low.

"This man," Shivadtmon said, "tells me that someone is watching us from that alley across the way."

The man nodded.

"I've been set to watch you northerners," he said, admitting to spying without prevarication, "by those who value your lives. I came down here after you and was searching for a nice place from which I could see you off without myself being seen. That's when I realized there was a snoop here before me."

"Were you seen?" Waln asked.

"Not until I stepped down here," the spy said confidently. "The snoop might still be there."

"Can we grab him?" Waln asked.

"If he's there," the spy said, "I can slip around back. I'll take my leave as if I had some message for the aridisdu, then go. Give me a count of a hundred, then move from this end. It's the alley between the fishmongers' clearinghouse and the warehouse."

Waln remembered the buildings, so he didn't turn to look.

"You have a count of a hundred," he said.

"And the blessings of our good master," Shivadtmon added. "I'm sure they will be made tangible when you report. Now, go!"

Waln frowned a little at this last, but it was far too late to wonder just which faction Shivadtmon belonged to. It didn't really matter, for obviously their desires ran alongside each other.

He strolled down to the pier and, hissing for Rarby and Shelby, briefed them on this new twist. Happily, they were already three-quarters into the discipline required at sea and accepted his commands as if he were already striding the captain's deck.

"We'll have him," Rarby promised. "Quick and quiet."

"Go now," Waln said. "Shivadtmon's man should be in place."

The brothers crossed the open space between the pier and the buildings, moving with quick purpose, not bothering to hide, for the hidden watcher would have no place to run. There was a scuffle and a yelp as if someone had taken a blow, and then the brothers were returning, hauling someone between them.

"Look who we found," Rarby announced in a hushed voice that was far more menacing than any crowing.

He tilted back their prisoner's head, revealing the high-cheekboned features of Rahniseeta, sister of Harjeedian.

"We aren't going to kill her, are we?" Shelby asked anxiously.

Waln remembered the looks Shelby had been giving the girl and smiled silkily.

"Oh, no, we'll take her along with us—as a hostage. I think her brother would appreciate that tactic, don't you?"

OTHER THAN EVENTUAL NIGHTFALL, there was no real reason to press the horses. Derian and Poshtuvanu had already ridden a fair distance, and with the long summer afternoon before them, there would be light for traveling awhile. So the young men took the road back from the farm at a fast walk, stopping to refresh themselves and the horses when a late-afternoon thunderstorm blew through, and riding on through the considerably cooler afternoon when it had passed.

They went their separate ways as planned, Derian heading on to Heeranenahalm and Poshtuvanu for u-Bishinti. Even without Poshtuvanu's pleasant company to ease the journey, Derian felt no need to press Prahini. The information as to who had bought Freshwater Pearl confirmed some of their suspicions, but it was not as if Dantarahma himself had been seen buying the mare.

Dantarahma.

Derian shook his head in disbelief. Even having himself been the witness to Dantarahma's involvement, it was hard to imagine the kind and gentle junjaldisdu as the wielder of the knife. In a way, it was harder now than it had been. Before, Dantarahma had been a distant figure, certainly one he'd seen well enough to recognize without a question, but not well known.

In the days since Eshinarvash had carried him back, Derian had become very aware of Dantarahma. It seemed that whenever people mentioned him, they mentioned his kindness and gentleness in the same breath. Breaking that illusion was not going to be easy—and probably could only be done with the complicity of at least one of his followers.

Despite the fact that Derian had told himself that there was no need to hurry, he found himself urging Prahini along, resenting the occasional, inevitable delays. When he found himself begrudging a stop to relieve his bladder, Derian forced himself to face his impatience.

It's Rahniseeta, he thought. *Why not be honest with yourself, Derian Carter? You're hoping to get there before it's unreasonably late to call on her. Is that fair? You're behaving like you're courting—calling at all hours, planning long walks, and longer halts. Why not look at it directly. Are you interested in courting the girl?*

The answer came almost immediately.

If she's interested in being courted by a red-haired, sunburned, freckled northerner . . . well, yes. I think I am.

The thought made him smile, and he rode on, alternating singing and whistling, much to Prahini's swivel-eared consternation.

However, in spite of his new honesty with himself—or perhaps because of it—Derian didn't go directly to the Temple of the Cold Bloods. After leaving Prahini at the facility that was flippantly referred to as u-Bishinti North, Derian cleaned off the worst of the road dirt and went to call on Meiyal.

The iaridisdu was pleased to see him, and invited him to a latish supper while he told his tale. She politely offered him the use of a washroom while dinner was being set, and Derian, knowing he still reeked of horse sweat, gladly accepted.

He briefed her over an excellent meal of sweet and spicy chicken over rice, washed down with many glasses of cold mint tea, and followed by fresh peaches in thick cream.

"We'll turn this information to our use," Meiyal promised when Derian had concluded with his own doubts that this information would be of much use. "I think it's getting to be time to involve one of the other members of u-Liall."

"Tiridanti?"

"Perhaps. I was thinking of Bibimalenu of Air. He's a good man, and gentle."

"They say the same of Dantarahma."

"But Dantarahma has also long evinced an interest in religious reform—in the most literal sense. He wants us to return to the oldest forms. He doesn't quite come out and say blood sacrifice, but those who think beyond his talk of reinstituting some of the old prayer forms have wondered. Bibimalenu is the opposite. Indeed, some of what Dantarahma would call 'new' forms came into use early in Bibi's tenure—and that would be twenty years ago, now."

Derian, full now, fairly clean, and definitely rested, tried not to fidget, but though Meiyal's eyes might be old, her vision was keen.

"But you must be moving on. Are you intending to ride to u-Bishinti tonight?"

Derian shook his head. "That would be unfair to Prahini. Barnet Lobster has told me to make myself free of the spare room in his suite, so I'll go over to the Temple of the Cold Bloods."

Meiyal didn't bother to hide her smile.

"And if you happen to get a word alone with Rahniseeta, do brief her. She has been as useful in this matter as you promised she would be."

"I'll do that," Derian promised, then decided he was tired of blushing. "I'm hoping it's not too late to call on her."

Meiyal glanced out the window and the darkening sky.

"Almost, but not quite. Thank you for speaking with me. I will notify you before I speak with Bibimalenu."

Derian thanked her and, as soon as he was politely away, almost ran to the Temple of the Cold Bloods. He fleetingly wondered where Firekeeper might be, but at this hour she could be anywhere. It was always easier to find her when the day was hot and Blind Seer wanted to sleep.

The porter at the gate of the Temple of the Cold Bloods admitted Derian with a cordial nod.

"Had you noticed if Barnet Lobster is in?" Derian asked. "I thought to avail myself of his hospitality tonight."

"Actually," the porter replied, "he went out some time ago and I don't think he has returned, but I'm sure he wouldn't mind if you went to check yourself."

"Thank you." Derian tried hard to sound casual. "And Rahniseeta sister of Harjeedian?"

The porter turned away so that Derian wondered if he was hiding one of those damned knowing smiles, but when he turned back he had a folded note in his hand.

"She went out some time ago, but left this in case you called."

Derian accepted the note, savoring the perfume that drifted from it. Then a thought shook him from his momentary revery.

"Did she go out with Barnet?"

"Why, no. She went out alone sometime not long after dinner. He went out about the same time, but with another of the northerners—the clumsy one."

"Elwyn," Derian supplied automatically. "Well, I'll just go along to Barnet's suite then."

"Do that," the porter said amiably, sitting back in his chair against the wall and reaching for the mug of beer he'd put by to answer Derian's knock. "And if Rahniseeta comes in, I'll let her know you were asking after her, and that you're staying the night."

Derian didn't doubt that he would. In his experience, porters came in two types: the utterly taciturn and the complete gossips. This man was definitely one of the latter.

He found Barnet's suite empty, and dithered for a moment as to whether he wanted to read Rahniseeta's note out by the pond or in the privacy of the spare room. He decided on the spare room. After getting a lamp lit, he settled in the solid carved wooden chair near the desk and began breaking seals.

There were several, as if Rahinseeta had not wished anyone else to get even a glimpse of the contents. This, along with the perfume, set Derian's hopes soaring. Had she been thinking along the same lines as he had? In Hawk Haven, the forms of courtship placed much of the burden on the male, but—as Derian's friend Elise had found—if the woman was higher-ranked socially or in some other way advantaged, it was her responsibility to make interest clear.

Fleetingly, Derian wondered if Doc and Elise had resolved their complicated romance, but even as he wondered, his fingers were busy and his eyes were scanning the first lines of Rahinseeta's elegant writing.

She had written in Liglimosh, but had kept her words simple and had eschewed the elaborate calligraphic flourishes that Derian knew were prized. This was a letter meant for him, and to be understood by him. It also was not a love letter, and the contents drove almost all thoughts of love from his mind.

Waln Endbrook and Shivadtmon in conspiracy? That was within expectation, but a raid on Misheemnekuru? Piracy? At least Barnet hadn't been part of this, but if he hadn't returned, did that mean he'd failed in persuading Waln not to do anything?

Derian pressed his fingers to his temples, trying hard to think what to do. He wanted to run down to the wharves, but they were extensive. Even if he went there, he'd have no idea how to check whether one boat out of the many anchored there was gone. He needed someone who knew more.

Harjeedian. Whatever else Derian thought of the man, he knew Harjeedian's affection for his sister was sincere. Rahniseeta had spoken of him with occasional exasperation, but had always tempered that by recalling how Harjeedian had not abandoned her in his rise to power.

Harjeedian, then, and if after he read Rahniseeta's note Derian had to explain the whole damn conspiracy or religious reformation or whatever you wanted to call it, well, then he would . . . as long as he could do it on the move.

Derian was out of the bedroom and through the courtyard before the thoughts were fully formed in his mind. He remembered the route to the suite sister and brother shared, and arrived to find Harjeedian seated at the table in the center room. The aridisdu had a lamp lit and was poring over a stack of papers, one of the omnipresent snakes coiled about his forearm. There was a tumbler near at hand, and over those impossibly high cheekbones, Harjeedian's eyes looked very tired.

"Derian!" Harjeedian said, when Derian entered. His tone made the word more exclamation than greeting.

"Have you seen Rahniseeta?" Derian asked.

"Why, no. I only arrived a short time ago. Her door was closed, and I thought she might have gone to bed. I didn't wish to disturb her."

"Check if she's there," Derian said, "and when you have, I need to talk to you—and show you something."

Harjeedian rose, not so much obediently but as one humors a child or madman. His expression when he knocked, received no response, then investigated and found Rahniseeta's room empty changed from bemused puzzlement to apprehension.

Derian, meanwhile, had checked the spot where he knew Rahniseeta typically left messages for her brother and had located what he had hoped to find.

"Read this," he said, thrusting a note—folded, rather than sealed as his own had been—at Harjeedian.

Harjeedian unfolded the note, and Derian watched with growing tension as the man's gaze flitted over the written characters. Just how much had Rahniseeta told her brother?

Finishing, Harjeedian bent his fingers around the note, unconsciously crushing the paper.

"What is this? A raid on Misheemnekuru? Is this some sort of joke?"

"May I see what she wrote you, Harjeedian?" Derian countered.

Harjeedian handed it over, his slim, strong build held tense. The snake on his arm, responding to that tension, lifted the upper length of its body from Harjeedian's warmth, its tongue nervously tasting the air.

Once Derian had confirmed that Rahniseeta had not told her brother anything other than what she had overheard being said in Barnet's room, he shaped his reply, giving it force by the simple expedient of starting to leave the suite.

"This is much of what was contained in the note she left me," Derian said. "I came here for your help, because I have no idea where to start looking along the wharves. Are you with me or not?"

Harjeedian uncoiled the snake from his arm, and set it gently amid some of the plants that grew about the suite.

"I am with you," he said, "but why would Rahniseeta go there herself? This could be dangerous. Why wouldn't she get assistance?"

"Aren't all of us northerners rather politically charged right now?" Derian said, leading the way out. "Rahniseeta may not have wished to start anything until she was certain that Elwyn was not talking fancy—he's not among the brightest, you know. Or she may have hoped that Barnet would succeed in dissuading Waln. Either way, a major scandal would be averted."

Derian was almost amazed at how easily he made up excuses that held just enough of the truth to be convincing, without giving away those things he still thought best to conceal.

Two years of conspiracy and intrigue have evidently taught me something, he thought, but the thought was devoid of amusement.

Nor was he certain that Harjeedian did not suspect that Derian was holding back something. However, as the aridisdu was willing to wait for explanations until they had found Rahniseeta, Derian was grateful for the respite.

Once they left Heeranenahalm, Harjeedian took the lead. He stayed off the processional way, taking them through side streets that snaked toward the southern end of the wharves. They did not talk, saving breath for moving as quickly as possible. In contrast, the sounds that came from the open windows—a baby fretfully crying, drunken laughter, a woman's voice intoning a prayer—seemed surreal, as if these hints that even late at night human lives went on were eddying through from another world.

"This is the part of the wharves where Waln's people have kept their *Islander,*" Harjeedian said. In response to Derian's puzzled look, he answered, "That is what they call their boat."

"Ah."

Derian looked at the rows of tarped vessels bobbing at anchor. Their masts were bare, those lines left in place hummed in the breeze, the metal fittings ringing faintly against each other. To Derian's eyes the sailboats were indistinguishable. Yet, tied as they were bow and stern so the shifting currents would not cause them to bump into each other, they rather reminded him of stabled horses—and there was an unsettling gap in the line.

"One seems to be missing," he said softly.

"And I think it may be the *Islander*," Harjeedian said. "Let us look more closely, and if Rahniseeta is still watching, she may come out to meet us."

The wooden pier bore some interesting marks, visible even in lantern light.

"Fresh mud," Derian said, kneeling to inspect it. "Damp. Someone was here, perhaps with mud on his boots from the storm earlier."

"And a sailboat is definitely missing," Harjeedian said. "We must assume then that the northerners have indeed gone out—the question is whether they went to Misheemnekuru."

As one the two men scanned the dark expanse of water, but there was no telltale light to give testimony.

There wouldn't be, Derian thought. *Waln is mean and dangerous, but he's not dumb.*

He glanced back at the shadowy bulk of the buildings set back along the wharves. There was no sign of anyone coming out to meet them. His heart beat uncomfortably fast.

"No Rahniseeta," he said uneasily.

Harjeedian's expression, glimpsed in the light of the lantern he shifted in his grip, was also uneasy, but he did not let that uneasiness touch his voice.

"She may have gone to Heeranenahalm by a different route than the one we took and be waiting for us—wondering where we have gone, and we forgot to leave her a note. Why don't you go up there and look for her? I will meet you, but first I want to go by the building where the shipwrecked sailors were quartered and see if they are still there."

Derian nodded. "I can do that. It's a good idea if you check. We'd look pretty stupid if we raised an alarm and they were sleeping soundly in their beds."

"My thought exactly," Harjeedian said. "Rahniseeta may have even had a similar thought and gone there to see. As you said, Lucky Elwyn is not the best witness."

"We'll meet in your suite," Derian said, "and decide what to do."

Harjeedian nodded, and together they began to walk quickly down the pier.

"There is one other thing you can do," Harjeedian said as they walked.

"Name it."

"If you do not find Rahniseeta—or Barnet Lobster—where they should be, you might see if Lady Blysse is easily found."

"Firekeeper at night?" Derian snorted. "As easy as pinning down the wind."

"Our stories say that was done once," Harjeedian said. "Don't go far, but if you can find her, it might be a good thing."

"Fine, I'll do it, but why?"

"Because," Harjeedian said, "if this rumor is indeed correct, and Waln and his men have gone to Misheemnekuru, Lady Blysse is likely the only one among us who the yarimaimalom will not view merely as the second wave of an invasion."

XXXV

FIREKEEPER RAN ALONGSIDE TRUTH, with Blind Seer on her other side. They had left the House of Fire some hours after Firekeeper had finally broken through the jaguar's abstraction. Although the great cat's mind could now interact with what Firekeeper rather stubbornly insisted on defining as "reality," Truth demonstrated an alarming tendency to slip in and out of focus.

A thunderstorm in early evening did much to clear both the air and the jaguar's head. When Truth demonstrated a desire to leave the screened house and go hunting, Tiridanti, who was well aware she had too long neglected her own duties, was glad to facilitate this wish.

"But would you go with Truth, Lady Blysse?" asked the ahmyndisdu. "She may think herself strong, but I know better than she how little she has eaten these last days."

Firekeeper, who had already been invited by the jaguar, and who had only hesitated lest this apparent mark of favoritism make her an enemy she could ill afford, went happily.

Now, free of the city, the oddly sorted trio ran beneath the dripping foliage, hunting nothing so much as an escape from the constraints that had bound them all. When they were wearied, they collapsed upon a mat of thick, damp moss near a streambed.

Firekeeper, always the quickest to grow hungry, for the great predators often go days between meals, found a stand of sturdy yet flexible reeds and began to weave a fish trap.

"Tracking through probability," said Truth, "is not unlike what you are doing there."

"What do you mean?" Firekeeper asked.

"Humans often talk as if divining the future is like divining for water or ore," the jaguar replied. "There is a source and one scents it. When seeking what course the future may follow, one must twist over and under the various currents, seeing which is strongest, which fade into nothing, which—given the right stimulus—might become reality."

Blind Seer, who Firekeeper knew had been wondering a great deal about divination, sneezed as if the jaguar's description had tickled his nose.

"It sounds complicated," he said.

"It is," Truth said, bending in a curious arc to wash between the toes of one hind paw. "But I was very good at it."

Something in the statement lacked the jaguar's usual easy self-satisfaction, and Blind Seer sprang on it as he might have upon a running deer.

" 'Was'?" he asked.

Truth contorted to groom the underside of her tail.

"I do not know," she admitted, "if I will ever again dare look into the currents of time and possibility. I am afraid . . ."

A pause came, as if she awaited mockery for admitting to fear. When the wolves remained listeningly still, Truth continued.

"I am afraid I will become trapped there again."

Firekeeper, leaning on her belly, close to the water so she could see if the fish trap moved, agreed.

"I can see why. It was very hard to get you out, and you were far from pleasant when we succeeded."

"If you had seen what I had seen," Truth replied, "your mood would have been less than sweet."

"Can you recall what it was you saw?" Blind Seer asked.

"A little. I had become trapped while trying to discover why I could see so little about Firekeeper and what she will do to us. At first I thought it was only some indecisiveness in her own character that hid her from me, but eventually I became aware of a . . . I don't know how to describe it. It was like deafness but not of the ears, blindness but not of the eyes. It was a little like the way a fawn's spots make your eyes slide over where the little morsel lies, even when your nose proclaims it must be near. In short, something other than Firekeeper herself was keeping me from seeing her.

"I did what I could to dig through this obstruction, and that is when I became trapped in the ripples of possibility. I cannot say it any better than that. Rather as the fawn's spots fool the eyes, so this fooled my ability to divine by splitting possibility into finer and finer ripples. I came away with one certainty, though. It was not Firekeeper who was being hidden from me, but rather that her fate was intertwined with some other—and that other was hiding . . . or being hidden."

The jaguar shook her head as if flicking water from her ears. "I cannot think of it any more. Even now my head is spinning."

"Let us tell tales, then," Firekeeper suggested. "Let us tell you of our venture to Misheemnekuru and what we did there. Doubtless the ravens have already told you much, but there are things we learned upon our return that you may not have heard."

Truth seemed grateful for this respite. She listened for a long while, holding herself with such stillness that only the flicker of gold in the burnt-orange eyes betrayed how carefully she listened. She listened with the same motionlessness even when Firekeeper kindled a fire and cooked some fish, even when Blind Seer finished off the guts. Only when Firekeeper and Blind Seer had finished relating Derian's report did Truth move, stretch, and yawn.

"I knew pieces of this," Truth said, "but it is good to hear how you saw events."

Firekeeper waited to see if the jaguar would say more, and when she didn't, asked a question that had been troubling her for some time.

"Truth, from what Derian and the others have discovered, this cabal of Dantarahma's is no newly hatched fledgling. Why did the yarimaimalom wait for our coming to ask for help?"

Truth stretched, her rear end rising, her tail curving over her back as if to remove silence from her limbs. Then she sat with her paws before her, her eyes giving back the light from the fading embers of Firekeeper's cook fire.

"You speak of yarimaimalom as if we were one beast with one mind," the jaguar replied at last. "Are you not yet old enough to realize that the very intelligence that makes us different from the Cousins assures that we will not all think the same way? But, I forget, you are wolves, and wolves follow the rule of the pack, not their own minds."

Had she possessed fur, Firekeeper would have bristled, but Blind Seer's hackles remained smooth.

"We have seen," he said, "differences even between wolves. We can accept that, but Firekeeper and I are not your prey that you may toy with us. Can you answer her?"

Truth's feline arrogance did not quite admit an apology, but there was a softening about the angle of her whiskers that said she was amused at being challenged, even—or especially—so mildly.

"I can and will," Truth said. "The answer is like the progress of time, simple and complex. The simple answer first. The yarimaimalom have indeed been aware of Dantarahma's desire for what he thinks of as 'religious reform.' How could we not be aware when we move in and out of the humans' lives so that they hardly notice us? Indeed—and this is no taunt—the birds are difficult to tell from their Cousin kin unless upon close inspection."

"True," Blind Seer said, making his response sound like a proverb. "Who can tell the size of a raven on the rooftops?"

"Or a hawk in the trees," Truth agreed. "So we knew, and initially we did not worry. Dantarahma began by using older forms of prayers. He restricted these to small groups worshipping in private, and if these prayers spoke of blood and death rather more than seems tasteful—especially given that these humans are well fed—we did not worry much about it. Surely you have noticed how humans speak. They often say things they do not mean—not literally."

" 'I'll kill him,' " Firekeeper agreed, "or 'I hate his guts' or 'I love him more than life itself.' These puzzled me for a long time. So you thought these prayers were more of the same."

"Exactly," Truth said. "The blood sacrifices are a recent development, and even then we were not too worried. What difference does a chicken or rabbit make? The worshippers were even eating what they killed—though raw, which is unusual for humans."

"Very," Firekeeper said, remembering how many times her taste for undercooked meat had aroused revulsion in her human friends. "Here it would be even odder than in Hawk Haven, I think. The cooking favors heavy sauces and long stewing."

"I hadn't thought of that," Truth admitted, "but you are right. It does make this eating of raw meat even odder. Now, the large sacrifices, such as your friend Derian witnessed, these are very new—the first was reported soon after Tiridanti came into office. An owl brought the news—to me, as it was the beginning of a jaguar year. I tasted the omens, and found nothing immediately dangerous if we waited, and some rather unsettling possibilities if we acted. Therefore, we agreed to wait."

"For how long?" Firekeeper asked.

Truth's tail switched in annoyance.

"For as long as we needed," she replied. "But it seems that what I thought not too long a wait seemed too long to Eshinarvash. Perhaps someone in his herd saw more clearly than I. Perhaps they allowed for Derian's participation, and this shifted our chances for success. To be honest, I don't know. I was born on Misheemnekuru, and am not in the confidence of those of the mainland."

She licked her paw complacently. "And horses are rarely comfortable around the great cats."

"And," Blind Seer said, not to be diverted, "I think your mind was even then not entirely your own. We were told that you were having trouble reading the future regarding Firekeeper even then. Perhaps you were reluctant to hunt in those currents you mentioned."

Firekeeper expected the Wise Jaguar to growl or snarl, but Truth only laid her head on her paws in surrender.

"That is so," she admitted. "Perhaps it would have been better if this had not been a jaguar year, and some more cooperative beast walked in my place."

Seeing the great cat humbled gave Firekeeper no pleasure.

"Your deities said it was a year for fire," she said, "and fire burns as well as warms, destroys as well as clearing the way for new growth. Serving fire is a complicated matter."

Truth raised her head and looked with unblinking eyes at Firekeeper, but seeing nothing but sincerity, her tail did not twitch.

"Maybe this is somehow part of Fire's clearing," the jaguar said, "but such wildfires are rarely pleasant for those caught within them."

"As I know all too well," Firekeeper said with a shiver. "Ever since we spoke with Questioner, my dreams have been fire-haunted. Now that Eshinarvash and those like-minded have acted, will you support them?"

"I will," Truth said. "You and Blind Seer have done well in relating what dangers may follow Dantarahma's rise. This is yet a jaguar year, but nothing is more certain than that summer will pass into winter, winter into spring once more—and if the deities listen to Dantarahma's prayers, he may sit in Tiridanti's place among u-Liall."

"But what are we to do?" Firekeeper said. "Already there is word that we will be sent north again, and though I hate sailing, I hate being a prisoner even more. Although I could go home afoot, the journey would be long and, at least for Derian, very dangerous."

"That decision is not yet made," Truth said, her tail lashing, "and after what you have done for me, you have a strong ally in your desire to come and go as you wish. Let us leave that, and concentrate on how Dantarahma might be undone."

She licked her forepaws, one then the other, with nervous, anxious strokes of her tongue, the action so violent that Firekeeper could easily hear the rasp of tongue against fur.

Blind Seer thumped his tail reassuringly.

"You are wondering whether it would be wise to look again into the currents of time and see what we might best do," he said to Truth. "You are thinking you know so much new now that what was unclear, might become clearer."

Truth jerked up her head to stare at him.

"Are you a diviner then? Truly a seer where others are blind?"

"No more than any who listens with heart and mind," Blind Seer said. "I am not very old, but I have learned to recognize the signs of indecision and of fear."

Truth did not relax, but she lowered her gaze to where the cook fire had died to smoky embers.

"I think I should try," she admitted, "and I fear that trying. I hardly know how to think without divination to guide me. It is not that it told me how to think or what to do, but that it provided me with options more rapidly. Now I feel as if I am trying to hunt without scenting the wind."

Firekeeper laughed a trace harshly.

"I must do that nearly all the time," she said. "You have my sympathy."

Truth's claws slipped from their sheaths, but only to savage the moss.

"A quick dip," she said, "concentrating hard as I did when I was first learning. Shaping the question tightly in my mind, then diving in."

"And knowing," Blind Seer said, "that you have friends on the bank ready to pull you out. Try it, otherwise the dread of attempting will cloud your thoughts as efficiently as whatever caught you there before."

Again Truth gave him an appraising look.

"Whatever gifts you have, Blue-Eyes, divination or not, your parents named you well. I will look and trust your strong jaws to haul me out."

Firekeeper felt warmed, for Truth clearly referred to them both, but she said nothing, only sat ready and waited alert for any sign, no matter how small, that Truth was in difficulty.

The jaguar did not lie down, or close her eyes, but the inner lid did droop, opaquing the gemstone brightness of the ember-lit eyes. Truth grew still, her breathing deeper yet more rapid, as she took scent on something neither wolf could detect.

Her tail tapped on the moss; then she stiffened and jumped up, fur standing out from her body as if she were a startled house cat of impossible size.

"All the currents stream in one direction," she snarled, leaping to her feet. "They move toward Misheemnekuru. Something terrible is going to happen there, something that at best will lead to the rise of Dantarahma, at worst could lead to the destruction of all we hold dear."

Firekeeper was already scooping dirt over the embers, pulling up the fish trap and breaking it so no fish would die without serving as food first.

"Is there anything that we can do to stop it?"

Truth was beginning to run in the direction of Heeranenahalm, but her answer came back on the notes of a jaguar's roar.

"You must be there. Only if you are there is there a chance of stopping what will come. Only then! I have known! How could I be so blind!"

Firekeeper stared at Blind Seer; then, without discussion, they began running, following in the now silent wake of Truth.

"I DON'T SEE HOW we can go after them before dawn," Harjeedian said.

He'd returned from checking the building where Waln and the others had been quartered, and told Derian that although some care had been taken to make it seem as if the northern sailors were still in residence, he was certain they had departed with no intention of returning.

"We can, however," Harjeedian continued, "do something about their plans to take the ship upon their return."

Derian's head was pounding with an unpleasant mixture of apprehension and exhaustion as he listened, but he managed a coherent reply.

"Nothing too obvious," he said. "Until we know for certain what is going on. You don't want to start something unnecessary."

Harjeedian nodded. "Good point. Then again, we cannot go after them until dawn."

"What about Rahniseeta?" Derian asked. "I'm not happy she hasn't returned—and that you haven't found her."

"Neither am I," Harjeedian admitted.

Derian said what he knew the other must be thinking.

"Do you think Waln caught her watching and . . . did something?"

Harjeedian's brows came together and his mouth twisted with worry.

"I don't know what to think," he admitted, "but I know what I fear. I wish we could find Lady Blysse. She might have answers."

"I've done my best," Derian said, "but finding her—especially at night—is impossible unless she wants to be found. If Elation were here, I might have a chance, but without that sort of help . . ."

He trailed off and Harjeedian, who had already heard this and knew well who Elation was, nodded.

"I know. Why don't you get some sleep? You rode most of the day and the night isn't getting any younger."

Derian hated to admit how much he needed that sleep. His craving for rest felt heartless when Rahniseeta was who knew where, but the reality of his body's need could not be ignored.

"I'll try," he said. "Would you mind if I stretched out here? I don't want to go even as far as Barnet's room in case something happens."

"Take my room," the aridisdu replied. "I'll take the divan out here in case Rahniseeta returns."

"Fair," Derian said.

He staggered off to collapse on Harjeedian's bed, and even the lidless stare of the watching snakes was not enough to keep him from sleep.

DERIAN AWOKE TO THE SOUND of voices in the next room, and to the awareness that they had not spoken more than a few words. As he struggled into consciousness and onto his feet, he managed to reconstruct what he'd heard.

"Truth see something, but she not tell, only lead us here. Fast."

"Let me get you something to drink," Harjeedian said, "and I'll wake Derian Counselor. Then you can relate your tale only once."

Derian made his way to the doorway at that moment to be confronted by a remarkable sight. He was accustomed to Firekeeper and Blind Seer, but the addition of the jaguar Truth to the company added an indefinable note of wildness to the scene. The owl and raven that flapped into the room a moment later did nothing to reduce the strangeness of the scene—especially as the raven wore around its neck a sapphire-and-diamond pendant depending from a fine gold chain.

"Derian," Harjeedian said. "You're awake."

The completely unnecessary statement made Derian sure that for all his apparent poise, Harjeedian was rattled by this strange visitation.

Though I wonder what's strange to him, Derian thought, accepting the glass of water Harjeedian handed to him. *The Beasts or Firekeeper?*

The animals were drinking from bowls Harjeedian set on the floor, their thirst testimony to Firekeeper's claim that they'd come at a run. Firekeeper looked sweaty and disheveled, but no worse than Derian had seen many other times. She set her tumbler aside, and began speaking with unconscious arrogance:

"Truth say to tell you, something bad is happening, going to happen at Misheem-nekuru. She say it be worse if I am not there. You must get me there."

Harjeedian nodded.

"We have had some inkling of this. Waln Endbrook and his people are gone, and according to a missive left by my sister, Rahniseeta, their destination was Misheem-nekuru."

"So," Firekeeper replied impatiently, "I say. Bad thing. Can we go now?"

Derian knew it was time to insert himself into the conversation. When Firekeeper got into one of these moods, she was an impediment to her own wishes.

"Firekeeper," he said. "Ask Truth if it can wait until morning. Harjeedian was telling me that sailing by night is a thing best left to those who know the waters—and no one knows the inland waters of Misheemnekuru."

"No," came the blunt reply. "Truth say more time goes, more chance even me being there cannot fix. We go tonight."

Harjeedian asked, his tone far more hesitant than was usual.

"Can Truth tell if my sister is with those who have gone to Misheemnekuru?"

Firekeeper glanced at the jaguar, then nodded her head once, abruptly.

"She is. Truth says time eddies around her. I not know what this means, but Truth thinks is important."

Harjeedian drummed his fingertips on the table in three sharp tattoos. Then he stood, his mind made up.

"I learned to be a fair sailor, during my time at the outpost. There are those in this temple who can sail as well, but explanations would need to be made."

Firekeeper shook her head.

"Must go fast. Derian can help you. No explanations."

Truth's very audible growl seemed to second this.

"Fine," Harjeedian said. "Derian?"

"I'm with you," Derian said, eyeing the jaguar and wondering what she would do if he continued to delay. Blind Seer seemed to guess his thoughts and panted laughter.

Firekeeper was halfway out the door before she paused.

"Harjeedian, do you have that seasick medicine?"

The aridisdu nodded.

"Please bring some," the wolf-woman went on. "I not think I be good for Truth or for myself if my stomach is my head."

FRIGHTENED AS SHE WAS, even through the haze of pain from where someone had struck her on the head, Rahniseeta had to admire the competence of the northern sailors.

Under the guise of sailing around the bay, the northerners had charted their course to Misheemnekuru, and now, with those observations augmented by maps Waln had copied from the library in Heeranenahalm, they were taking the sailboat along as confidently as if it had been full daylight.

At first their only light had been a dark lantern, but when the *Islander* was well away from shore, Waln permitted a bow lantern as well. The moon had waned to a sliver, but as their eyes adjusted to the available light, the lantern was quite enough for Rahniseeta to easily view the expressions of her captors.

Waln looked so completely relaxed and in control that Rahniseeta was startled until she recalled that the role of ship's captain, if not this particular venture, must be like a homecoming to him after the uncertainties of the past year or more. In contrast, Shivadtmon, the aridisdu from the Temple of Sea Beasts, looked edgy, almost sick. No matter what excuses he had made to Waln, Rahniseeta was willing to bet Shivadtmon was far from certain about the religious rightness of this venture.

Barnet Lobster looked tense and concerned, but he took Waln's commands right along with the other sailors, so readily, in fact, that Rahniseeta was finding it hard to believe that this was the same man with whom she had traded stories and songs. Once again, he seemed alien and unpredictable.

In time she noted that two of the sailors pulled line far less than the others. Instead, Rarby and Shelby stood amidships on opposite sides of the vessel. As Rahniseeta's night vision improved she realized the blocky items near them that she had taken for some part of the sailboat were in fact an array of weapons.

Did Waln then fear a mutiny? Or were Rarby and Shelby alert to some other danger, and did that alertness explain some of Shivadtmon's unhappiness?

Rahniseeta would have liked to work through these possibilities and arrive at some conclusion that would help her plan some practical course of action, but over and over again her aching head kept returning to the very real danger of her situation. She was the prisoner of men who thought nothing of sacrilege and piracy if such would advance their desires. For now she had a value as a potential hostage, but if she caused too much trouble, they might well decide that prospective value was not reason enough for keeping her alive. After all, their initial plans had not included a hostage.

So she huddled where she'd been placed so that whoever was manning the wheel could keep an eye on her. So motionless and meek was she that she was spared the indignity of having her hands bound or indeed of any other form of restraint. As the hours passed, Rahniseeta rather came to despise herself for offering so little threat. Lady Blysse would not have been given such freedom.

Rahniseeta thought of the wolf-woman as last she had seen her, crouching alongside the strangely maddened jaguar, and wondered, as she might have about a story she'd heard told long ago, how that had resolved. Her memories of Derian, of the dinner she'd eaten not all that long ago in the Temple of the Cold Bloods, of the documents she had been copying, all seemed distant and unreal. The only thing that mattered was the rise and fall of the boat's deck, and the increasing frequency with which Shelby made excuses to stroll near her and brush against her as he passed.

In this strangely focused state, Rahniseeta was very aware when the feeling of the water beneath the hull altered, becoming smoother and less choppy. The movement of the air was less vigorous as well, and the salt scent of the open water was now mitigated with that of damp vegetation and dead fish.

Land smells, she thought. *Misheemnekuru? The thunderstorm must have hit here as well. Harder than on the mainland.*

Waln, who had not spoken for a long time except to order a sail hauled in or a line loosened, now spoke.

"This is far enough for now. We'd be fools to try and land in the dark. We'll drop anchors bow and stern, and keep to the middle of the channel until we have light. Rarby, you, Nolan, Wiatt, and Elwyn get some sleep. The rest, stand by to fend off shore if we've misjudged."

But his voice held confidence that they would not have misjudged, and it dropped to a conversational level as Waln turned to Shivadtmon.

"You can sleep if you wish, Aridisdu, but maybe you'd like to luxuriate in being where none of your people have dared go for well over a hundred years."

Shivadtmon did not look as if this honor pleased him; nonetheless, he did not move to where the off watch were rolling out blankets and making themselves comfortable with the ease of long practice.

"I will remain awake," the aridisdu said. "I am not in the least weary. If you wish to rest . . ."

"I'm fine," Waln said. "Done longer watches than this since I was a boy."

Rahniseeta thought they might talk more, but silence fell. She drifted off just a little, but never so much that she wasn't aware of the quiet circuit of the sailors about the deck. She woke to full knowledge of herself and her surroundings when she felt a hand on her shoulder, a hand that slid to her breast and squeezed once, then twice, in a confidently familiar manner.

"Wake up, sweetheart," Shelby said softly into her ear. "I've brought you some water."

Indeed, he pressed a cool leather bottle into her hand, but he didn't remove the hand that was casually exploring her curves, now dropping from her waist to caress her hip, then down to squeeze one buttock.

"Nice," he said, and he might have been talking about the water.

Footsteps on the deck announced Waln's return to his post by the wheel. He looked down at the tableau, but made no effort to interfere.

"How's she doing, Shelby?"

"Nice," the sailor said. "Real nice."

"Sitting up here on deck can't be too comfortable," Waln began. "Why don't you take her below and make her . . ."

What he was about to suggest was interrupted by a thumping from below the waterline.

"Have we swung and hit a rock?" Shelby asked, leaping to his feet and forgetting Rahniseeta in an instant.

"Doesn't sound quite like . . ." Waln said. "Wrong feel. Grab a lantern and look over starboard. Tedgewinn, do the same over port."

He was obeyed without delay or question.

"Movement down there," Shelby reported almost immediately. "In the water. Do they have sea monsters here?"

"Looks like animals of some sort," Tedgewinn corrected. "Seals, I think."

"Shivadtmon," Waln ordered. "Take a look. Tedgewinn, show him what you've spotted. Shelby, wake Rarby. Get someone to take over watch on your side."

"Aye, sir."

Rahniseeta came fully awake as the sailors sprang into action. She rose and went to look over the rail, but made no move to jump.

She had come to respect Waln Endbrook too well to think that he might have forgotten her. In any case, even if he did, what could she do? If she went over the side and swam for land, would the yarimaimalom know her from any other human? And what if those weren't seals down in the water? What if there were sharks?

Rahniseeta wondered if the seals Tedgewinn thought he had seen were yari-maimalom, if this was some sort of warning that the boat had strayed into forbidden waters. In a moment, Shivadtmon confirmed her guess.

"Seals, definitely," he said, "and from the size I'd guess Wise Seals. They're not try-ing to upset the boat, but they definitely want our attention."

"I'll give them attention," Rarby growled, lifting what Rahniseeta now realized was a nasty-looking harpoon.

Shivadtmon was shocked.

"No!" he said. "They're not attacking."

Rarby looked at Waln.

"Do we have to wait for them to stave in a couple of planks before we hit? It's gonna be hard to get back with a busted boat."

"Wait," Waln said, "and if they try to damage the boat, then by all means use your harpoon. Dawn isn't long away. Once we're on shore, and pull the boat into more shal-low waters, the seals—if they're wise—are going to think twice about attacking us."

He laughed at his pun, and Lucky Elwyn laughed shrilly with him. Rahniseeta felt sick, and thought she saw a similar nausea in Shivadtmon's eyes.

"We won't have to deal with seals ashore," Barnet said, his voice too even. "Just wolves, wildcats, and who knows what else."

"They," Waln replied confidently, "can't do anything to the boat. We've come with enough quarrels to make their mothers think they've turned into porcupines. You have any problem with that?"

He looked at Barnet as he spoke, but Rahniseeta had a feeling that the statement was made for Shivadtmon. Neither man said anything, and Waln went on with the same raw confidence filling his words.

"We'll explain really careful to these yarimaimalom what we're about. They don't want what we want to take—that's sure enough. We'll explain. When they know we're going to leave as soon as we've done a little digging, why I don't think they'll risk their pretty hides."

"And if they do," said Wiatt the cook, a man Rahniseeta had always thought more gentle than not, "we'll take them with us. Can you imagine the crowds that would come to see the hide of a giant wolf or jaguar? It would make a tavern back home, it would."

"Maybe so," Waln said equably. "Shivadtmon, maybe it wouldn't hurt if you started the explaining right now. Just lean over the edge and talk. Explain to the beasties that we're here and we're going as soon as we get what we came for. They can be good hosts and let us visit, or be rude and get what we've got for them. Pretty it up any way you like, but make clear we're not bluffing."

"I'll show 'em," Rarby said, obviously itching to use his harpoon on one of the shining backs that surfaced from time to time as the seals rose to breathe.

"Patience," Waln advised. "Patience. Save your harpoon for those that deserve it. Unless these animals are a lot wiser than I think, someone's going to have to test if we're serious."

Rahniseeta heard his words with horror, not so much that Waln spoke so of killing the yarimaimalom, but because from the manner in which he spoke it was evident that—unlike Wiatt, who still seemed to think of them just as merely giant animals—Waln Endbrook thought of the yarimaimalom as people. They weren't even people he particularly disliked, but they were people he wouldn't hesitate to kill if they got between him and his goals.

Rahniseeta listened to the urgent note in Shivadtmon's voice as he spoke over the rail to the splashing pod of seals, and knew that he, too, had awakened to the viciousness of his allies. Dantarahma and his associates might contemplate offering a life to the deities, but that sacrifice in itself was a twisted way of expressing respect for life.

Waln had no such respect, and he had put weapons into the hands of those of his men he knew for certain shared that lack of respect.

For the first time, Rahniseeta faced her own fate squarely. As long as she was useful as a hostage, she would live, but in the end, she would die. She might be used to reward Shelby and some of the others, but in the end Waln would make sure she would die. She had seen too much, could give lie to whatever excuses and justification he thought he could make.

She was doomed and Shivadtmon was doomed. The only difference between them was that she knew, while from the desperation in his voice, Rahniseeta could tell that the aridisdu still twisted after the cruel lure of hope.

XXXVI

DESPITE FIREKEEPER'S BEST efforts to get the humans moving, dawn was pinking the horizon to the east by the time Harjeedian loosed the sailboat from its moorings and set course for Misheemnekuru.

Although the wolf-woman would not admit it lest the humans be given further excuse for dallying, the time spent preparing for the venture had not been completely wasted. A few owls and other night birds had methodically surveyed the various inlets throughout Misheemnekuru and located where the *Islander* was anchored.

Staying as high as was practical, an osprey now circled overhead, keeping watch over the ship and the humans aboard her, ready to relay through others of her kind any significant developments.

When Truth told Firekeeper that one of the islands near to where the *Islander* was anchored was the one upon which resided the maimalodalum, Firekeeper was deeply troubled. Although humans might believe otherwise, on most of the islands the yarimaimalom would simply flee if humans violated their territory. There would be time enough after careful reconnaissance to decide how to deal with them with the least risk of injury to the yarimaimalom.

But, for all their animal characteristics, the maimalodalum were very human in their attachment to the towers in which they dwelt.

"They will not leave them—and least not to permit them to be looted," Truth said with certainty. "Not only are the maimalodalum as territorial as nesting birds, in the towers are stored records of the days before Divine Retribution drove the Old Country rulers from our land. The maimalodalum have guarded these for generations, and will not likely relinquish that trust now."

Firekeeper thought there were other things the maimalodalum would be reluctant to give up. She remembered the softly glowing panels of light, so superior to any lantern or candle. She wondered, too, what other little comforts the maimalodalum retained from the days before the practice of more complex magics had all but vanished from the New World. She did not think the maimalodalum would surrender these lightly.

Nor should they, she thought, *not when the victor would be one like Waln Endbrook.*

Nor could she forget the links that bound Waln to Dantarahma. That Shivadtmon sailed with Waln could not be coincidental, and Firekeeper wondered just how much the junjaldisdu knew of this venture—and what he hoped to gain from it.

The owls had also confirmed that Rahniseeta was among the humans. They reported that although she was alive, unbound, and apparently uninjured, the young woman moved about very little. Word had been passed back via the owls to the seals who were watching the *Islander* that—although the seals must be the final judges—if they could keep Rahinseeta alive, it would be appreciated.

One of the younger seals had come out himself to offer assurances.

"We shook the boat in the night," he said, the liquid velvet of his eyes wide, his nostrils flared as he caught his breath—and relived his excitement, "but stopped when the humans offered threat. We saw the girl then, looking over the side, but she seemed subdued and made no effort to come away, though as far as any could tell she was unbound."

"There are things," Firekeeper said, her hand twined in Blind Seer's fur, "that can bind one as tightly as any rope. Fear may hold her there."

"Or a desire to escape notice," the blue-eyed wolf added. "A fawn or rabbit huddles not merely from terror, but from a wisdom that knows how motion catches the eye."

The seal, a creature of the ever-moving waters, did not appear to understand, but was too polite to say so. His report given, he occupied himself catching fish, splashing ahead as he guided them toward the fastest route to their destination.

Firekeeper scratched the long hairs along one of Blind Seer's ears, wholly in agreement with him. Whatever the reasons Rahinseeta did not act to free herself, Firekeeper did not think the less of her. However, the wolf-woman could do nothing to change the situation until the boat brought them closer. For now, she stilled her impatience by rejoicing that Harjeedian's medicine spared her the worst of the seasickness—and that the passage between mainland and islands was not so very long.

"Soon," Firekeeper said to the wolf, "soon we will once again run on the central island. Then we shall see how clearly Truth reads the future—or whether we are too late to do anything but mourn lost opportunities."

"And friends," added Blind Seer somberly.

BY THE TIME Waln realized that he had overstepped himself, he realized that there was no turning back.

I should have killed the girl there on the docks, he thought desperately. *There might have been questions as to how she came to be there, but with any luck, blame would have been laid at Derian Carter's feet.*

Yet even as Waln delighted in the image of one who had helped lay him low there at Smuggler's Light laid low in turn, Waln knew such puerile fantasies would not change the situation in which he found himself.

Now Rahniseeta is gone, and by morning, if not before, there will be a search. Will that search also lead to our being found gone? Quite possibly. If they come to suspect that the two disappearances are connected, then the search will be for us as well. Even if all they think is that we have gone sailing and took the girl along, they will be looking. They will not look here in these sacrosanct waters, but the fact of their looking will make our taking the ship and getting home aboard her all the more difficult.

Waln dared not even think that the goal might now be impossible. So much had depended on quickness, and no one worrying overmuch about the northerners going sailing.

Can I order the men to turn around?

He shook his head as if to an actual interrogator.

No. They've come this far on promise of homecoming and treasure. They'll not return meekly to accept whatever penalties will be brought upon us for trespass and kidnapping. It is forward or not at all.

Immediately, Waln began to consider what actions might best secure their survival—even the chance of their success.

We are eight men, well armed and well trained. We have much to gain, little to lose. I think I can make even Elwyn see that. Shivadtmon will side with us without a doubt, making us nine. Moreover, he has hinted that the crew of the ship are somehow indebted to him. If we can make it aboard and away . . . Yes. There is still a chance.

Despite the thick tangle of forest growth surrounding them on all sides, there was no doubt when darkness gave way to damp, grey predawn light. Waln took the long glass and scanned the shore methodically, looking for the best possible place to bring the *Islander* to shore.

Based on his readings among the old charts, Waln had gathered that this particular island had been liberally equipped with landings that would take boats that drew far more than the *Islander*. Indeed, stone for the towers whose highest points were just visible above the trees had been quarried here, assuring clear waterways that—if he was any judge—the strong ocean currents would have kept scoured clean.

"Ready tow," he said. "Rarby and Tedgewinn, take soundings over there by those large rocks."

The men obeyed, readying the two rowboats that did duty whenever taking the sailing vessel in would be awkward or uncertain.

"We can do it," Rarby called back. "We may need to raise the rudder, just to be safe, but I think we're fine."

"Let's be at it then," Waln said. "Shivadtmon, these are your lands. Why don't you join Elwyn and Barnet in one of the tow boats? Wiatt, when Rarby brings his boat over, help them make fast, then drop down and pull an oar."

The operation went smoothly, all the more so for Waln in that the two he was least certain about—Barnet and Shivadtmon, along with the unpredictable Elwyn—were down in one of the small boats where they were unlikely to cause trouble. As if they were coming into a familiar harbor, they brought the *Islander* in, then made her fast bow and stern so that the changing of the tide would not rattle her about.

This close to shore, the tower tops were no longer easily visible, but Waln had taken his readings with great care and felt confident they would easily find their way. How hard could it be to find high ground after all? The island was large enough, but not so huge that a man in good condition couldn't walk end to end in a few hours.

"Right," Waln said. "Now, Barnet, you've vowed not to go ashore, and I'll not try to force you. We'll leave you anchor watch. Maybe you can sing to the seals if they come back around. That should keep you from getting lonely."

Much as I hate leaving you, Waln added silently, *I'd rather have you here than armed and at my back. As there is no way you can manage the* Islander *alone, you might as well serve a useful purpose.*

Waln rather thought from the look in Barnet's eyes that the minstrel understood what he was thinking, but that hardly mattered now, did it?

"Rahniseeta is coming with us," Waln went on in response to the mute question on the girl's face. "I don't want anything happening to her where I can't see it."

Shelby's expression said that, unlike his brother and Tedgewinn, he hadn't caught the implicit threat in Waln's comment. All he cared was that Rahniseeta would not be left alone with Barnet. Shelby went over to her and helped her rise. Then he escorted her to one of the rowboats. If he was rather free with his hands while assisting her, Waln chose to overlook it. Rahniseeta remained mute, her high spirit apparently broken.

And no wonder, Waln thought. *How much spirit can a people who let themselves be ordered about by animals really have?*

The thought comforted him. It was with more confidence that he doled out weapons, sacks, rope, and digging tools. If some sailors were given rather more gear than weapons, everyone was well enough armed that no one protested.

Waln made certain that the bows he left for Barnet's use had markedly less range than those carried by his best archers. Barnet would be able to protect the *Islander*, but he would be putting himself in grave danger if he tried to hold the vessel against them when they returned.

And who was to say he would? Barnet had already indicated that he feared treachery from the Liglimom and that he was willing to work for passage home. So far he had done nothing to indicate he had changed his mind, but from time to time Waln had seen something in his eyes that made taking precautions only wise.

They landed and pulled the rowboats up well beyond the high-tide mark.

"Do we start digging for treasure now?" asked Elwyn eagerly. He pointed with the handle of the shovel he held loosely in one hand. "I see a bit of wall right over there, and another bit there. There might be treasure right here."

Waln shook his head and adopted a parental tone.

"If there is, Elwyn, storm and sea will have done their part to bury it more deeply. You know how it is close to the water's edge. I'm for the towers up on the hill. They're likely to have stood sound, and maybe even have vaults in which things stored long ago remain untouched."

Elwyn immediately brightened.

"Look!" he said, his voice still bright with excitement. "Is that a road going up?"

It was not so much a road as a trail, but it went in the right direction, and as they mounted there was ample evidence that at some point there might well have been a road here.

"If we walk steadily," Waln said, "we should be to the towers before the sun is truly risen. Everyone up to it?"

The response was a general quickening of pace. The lust for treasure was on them now, running through their veins like gold fire. These were men who were accustomed to standing long watches at sea when storms would not allow the luxury of rest. They had been well cared for by the Liglimom, and even Nolan was now in sound health. Anticipation was all they needed to make them hurry.

Waln wondered what might be watching them from the woods. From the surreptitious glances cast side to side by his companions they were wondering so as well.

But nothing came forth. Though at times the birds and little frogs let their songs fade into startled silence, the humans still heard nothing.

Stalked by nothing, they climbed.

THEY ARRIVED AT the top of the hill before the morning was old, but the air was no longer cool. By common consent, they moved to where a section of crumbling wall still cast a band of shade and seated themselves. Water bottles were passed back and forth, while the cluster of towers was subjected to silent scrutiny.

"Those towers are where we should start," Waln said. "We'll start by figuring which one is least likely to come down on our heads and go from there."

"They all look really good," Elwyn said happily. "They're not falling down at all—well, not much."

Waln looked more carefully and realized the idiot was right. They'd passed a number of crumbling walls and foundations on the way up, some recognizable because the bulky shapes covered in vines could only be ruins. In comparison, these were in excellent condition.

Each of the five towers was a different shape: one cylindrical, one square, one octagonal, one star-shaped, and the one in the center a half-moon. All the towers were grown over with climbing tendrils of vines, sometimes intertwining through the crenellations that uniformly bordered the top. Random stones within these uneven borders had fallen away, making for a gape-toothed grin.

This relatively high standard of preservation might be credited to superior magical construction, but surely magic could not explain why the ground between the structures was free from the more usual vegetative clutter. Yet not a sapling split a flagstone, nor did grass grow where the mortar between the stones had eroded away.

Deer, Waln thought. *Elk. Rabbits. There might even be feral sheep. Sheep can shave a field down to bedrock if there are enough of them. On an island like this it's a wonder anything is still growing with the animals all trapped.*

But Waln couldn't convince even himself of the likelihood of roaming flocks of feral sheep. He was relieved that no one else seemed to have noticed the relative tidiness of the area. Sailors might not notice anything to do with plants, of course, but was Shivadtmon too quiet?

"What do you think, Aridisdu?" Waln asked, partly because he wanted to know, partly because it would be better if Shivadtmon offered any worries in response to Waln's query rather than on his own initiative. "Do your studies give any insights as to where we should begin?"

"The high places were preferred for sacrifices," Shivadtmon said, his voice a trace unsteady, "but I cannot think those who abandoned this place would have stored their goods where the breaking of a window or shutter would have left their valuables vulnerable."

"My thoughts precisely," Waln said, though he knew little and cared less about the religious aspects. All he wanted was confirmation of his gut feeling that valuables would be stored underground.

Waln heaved himself to his feet, carefully hiding that his muscles had stiffened during the short rest. These men were like wolves. Show them weakness and they would be upon him—one less to share the treasure.

At the thought of wolves, Waln scanned the green curtain of the forest's edge, but nothing moved unless at the lazy caress of the wind.

"It's getting hot," Tedgewinn said impatiently, hefting his shovel. "Let's get on with it. Bound to be cooler inside."

As they crossed toward the cluster of buildings, the group bunched close, though by instinct rather than by order. Rahniseeta was set in the middle, circled by her captors as a herd might encircle a calf. Rarby and Shelby, their crossbows loaded, flanked the group, bulls with their horns lowered. Nothing challenged them, but Waln felt increasingly sure something must be out there.

Where is the rubble? Waln thought. *Where are the little bits of grass thrusting between the pavers? If rabbits and deer have nibbled them away, where are their droppings? Surely the wind doesn't politely roll them away to feed the earth, no matter what Shivadtmon might blather.*

Waln wanted to command the men to clear out, to get away from this place before something bad happened, but he had known for hours now that the time for turning back was long past. He strode forward, schooling his gait to the same easy confidence he would use if he were walking across his own courtyard at home.

Elwyn bounced beside Waln, his motions ridiculously childlike for such a hulking fellow.

"Five," Elwyn crowed. "I count five towers. One in the middle, four set around."

"That's a traditional arrangement for sorcery," Shivadtmon said, and he now had his voice under control. He might have been giving a lecture to a group of new acolytes. "The tower in the center—the one shaped like a half-moon—represents Magic. She stands, balanced between her potentialities, supported by her family all around her."

"I'm betting," Tedgewinn said, "that the best treasure will be in the Earth tower, then. After all, riches come from under the earth, right?"

Shivadtmon gave a short laugh that wasn't quite condescending, merely patronizing.

"Our cosmology is not nearly so simplistic. Each metal and gem is associated with one of the elements—and sometimes the reasons for association are fairly abstruse. Since this complex was dedicated to the use of Magic, if I were betting on where the most valuable things were stored, I would choose the center tower."

Although he walked ahead, Waln could hear the frown in Nolan's voice when the ropemaker spoke.

"Waln, you never said anything about taking us to some place where magic had been practiced."

Actually, Waln hadn't realized the type of place this was any more than Nolan had. His surging apprehensions, born from a hundred different tales in which sorcerers were the villains, made him speak harshly.

"I didn't say anything," Waln echoed mockingly. "Only because I didn't think I'd need to say something so obvious. Didn't I tell you that we were going to a place where the Old Country rulers had lived? Doesn't every child old enough to listen to bedtime stories know that the Old Country rulers were all sorcerers?"

"Still . . ." Nolan began tightly, but he bit off the words before saying more.

Waln knew that none of the others would add anything either, lest they seem as stupid as Elwyn. Like Waln, their pride committed them to moving forward, even thought their best judgment told them to retreat.

"The center tower, then, Shivadtmon," Waln said. "So it shall be."

The center tower was crafted from a light cream-colored stone glittering with tiny flakes of imprisoned mica. From its top rose a step pyramid, similar to those atop the temples they had already seen. Waln found himself wondering just how closely magic and religion had been associated by the Liglimom's ancestors. If symbols said anything, the relationship had been at least cousinly.

The pyramid was embellished with a device that vaguely recalled a weather vane, though the directions were not marked nor was the shape one that would easily provide a pointer. Instead it was a rendering of the full moon. When the wind blew, the corroded metal spun, creating the illusion of a complete globe, but it was long since the works had been oiled and the motion was far from smooth.

Temple or not. Place of sorcery or not, Waln thought as once again he examined the solidity of the towers, *these Old Country rulers built for defense as well as for height. It was much the same in Hawk Haven and Bright Bay, as I recall. New Kelvin is too insane to be sure what their founders built for. I wonder what the Old World rulers feared? Each other, perhaps? Harjeedian did say that we northerners had become demons in their legends.*

At the thought of Harjeedian, Waln found himself wondering if any on the mainland had missed them yet. Probably so. Not only did the fisher folk rise early, but many of the temples had services soon after sunrise. Even if none of the servants who tended to their residence had noticed, someone would have seen that the *Islander* was no longer in her slip.

However, missed or not, certainly no one had the least idea where to seek them. They would notice the *Islander* gone and check up and down the coast, first. No one would even consider looking into the forbidden interior of Misheemnekuru.

Waln felt a momentary uneasiness as he considered the possibility that the seals might give them away. Then he shook the thought from him. What could a bunch of lolling water bears do? Wasn't the whole reason for the eagerness to kidnap Lady Blysse because, for all they reverenced them, the Liglimom couldn't really communicate with their "wise" beasts?

Still, anxiety nibbled at the edges of Waln's soul, and he picked up his pace. Perhaps, if there was a stair intact within one of the towers, it wouldn't hurt to send someone up to take a look. Elwyn, maybe, though he'd probably just call down something about how pretty the water looked. Maybe Nolan. A little job to quell the incipient spirit of mutiny.

That decided, pleased with himself, Waln halted before the double door that marked the way into the tower. The door was set in the exact middle of the flat side, its core sheathed in a dark metal. The sheathing was pitted in places from the salt air, but otherwise in remarkably good condition.

Around the edges, the door's surface was embossed with intricate patterns. A large illustration dominated the center section, bridging the two panels so skillfully that Waln had to look twice to confirm that this was indeed a door.

The illustration depicted the tower before them. Men and animals alike marched in the air around the half-moon, their mouths open, though whether in song or screams Waln really couldn't tell. Some of the marching figures had reached the top of the tower, and at least one lay draped across the apex of the pyramid. Stylized rays ending in what might have been raindrops or stars burst from the tower, more thickly at the top than at the bottom. Waln, remembering how the Liglimom believed Magic fragmented and those fragments had lodged in various people and things, couldn't escape the feeling that in this picture Magic was somehow being dislodged.

The thought made Waln's flesh creep, and he hurried to open the door before any of those who followed him could get too long a look at the picture.

"I wonder if it's locked," Waln said, keeping his tone jovial.

He placed his hands on the broad, wide latches and lifted. He had expected them to stick, but they snapped out of their groove with an obedient metallic click.

"They pull open," Shivadtmon said from beside him. "Most ceremonial doors do. It saves space within."

Waln resented being told what he could have worked out from a look at the hinges, but he did not stay Shivadtmon's hand when the other made as if to open one of the doors. Better to get them open and that alarming picture out of view.

"Ready?" he asked, and Shivadtmon nodded.

Together they pulled open the massive metal-bound doors. These swung lightly on their hinges without a creak or hint of sticking. Again Waln felt his flesh creep. He'd come prepared for broken ruins, wild animals, spiders, snakes, and other filth. This was too easy, too quiet.

Shivadtmon, however, was clearly uplifted. The nervousness had vanished from his voice. His eyes shone with religious transformation.

"She welcomes us!" he said reverently. "She welcomes us!"

He spoke so softly that Waln's men, all of whom had dropped back and readied crossbows in case something came rushing out when the doors were opened, didn't hear him. Waln was relieved. Shivadtmon might be delighted at what he took for evidence of divine welcome, but tell these northern sailors that Magic was making them welcome and they'd be down to the *Islander* as fast as they could run.

For a jealous moment, Waln wondered if this was exactly what Shivadtmon intended. After all, that would leave all the treasure for him. Then Waln took a second look at that transfigured face and doubt left him. Shivadtmon had found a treasure here already in this confirmation that among his deities, Magic, at least, did not resent his intrusion.

The aridisdu was already stepping inside, and Waln hurried to catch up with him. He didn't know what they would find, but he knew for certain that he did not want Shivadtmon to find it first.

INITIALLY, Rahniseeta had been too stunned both physically and emotionally to do anything but go mutely where she was told. The last of her headache had dissipated on the voyage over and by now she had certainly had more rest than any of her captors.

The lethargy and depression that had sought to claim her had ebbed, replaced by fear of the sacrilege she was being forced to commit. The arrival of the seal the night before had seemed an omen, a promise that rescue was coming, that she had not been forgotten. Would the yarimaimalom feel the same now that she had trespassed—no matter how unwillingly—on their preserve?

Rahniseeta might try and explain how she had no choice but to do as Waln directed or the foreigner would kill her. Would the yarimaimalom accept this, or would they feel she should have died rather than break a sacred trust?

No, Rahniseeta certainly should not wait to be rescued. Not only could she not be sure that the yarimaimalom would rescue her, but waiting would also mean she could be used as a hostage against her friends. Rahniseeta wasn't sure if threat to her safety would stop Lady Blysse from doing whatever the wolf-woman felt was right, but she was certain that neither Harjeedian nor Derian would act if their actions would bring injury to her.

Therefore, Rahniseeta must escape, preferably long before rescue arrived. She considered fleeing into the forest, shouting as loudly as she could that she was a friend of the Firekeeper. Rahniseeta knew few details about the wolf-woman's visit to Misheemnekuru. She didn't even know if Lady Blysse had come to this particular island, but she was certain that the yarimaimalom were at least as devoted to gossip as were humans. Whoever lived here would have heard of Firekeeper.

Then, if the yarimaimalom let her live, Rahniseeta could beg their forgiveness and hopefully redeem her life by telling in detail about the weapons the sailors carried with them, and their willingness to kill.

Rahniseeta discarded that plan almost as quickly as it shaped in her mind. The area between her and the forest's edge was wide and open. The well-groomed cobbles would make for easy running, but the lack of obstruction would mean that a crossbow bolt would reach her all too easily.

Shelby's groping caresses had left no doubt about his interest in her, and she'd caught an appreciative glance from a few of the others. Yet, despite this admiration, she had no illusions that if ordered to shoot her, any one of them—even Shelby—would not hesitate. Hesitation would raise doubts as to where loyalties lay, and Waln Endbrook was not a man to take disloyalty lightly.

Rahniseeta was certain that not one man here particularly liked Waln Endbrook—Elwyn excepted, since Elwyn seemed to like just about everyone. However, liking was not the issue—getting home was, and Waln Endbrook had offered the northerners a way they could get home with honor and maybe fortune.

During the voyage over from the mainland, Rahniseeta had heard doubts expressed that they'd ever see that home except by their own efforts. She wished she could be indignant at this lack of trust, but she had seen enough now of the intrigues and factions among the disdum that she knew the northerners had reason for their fear.

She recalled that Barnet had been the one to introduce the subject, and wondered if he had been indirectly offering an excuse for his own action in joining Waln's party—something he might see as a betrayal of a sort, given how long he had resided in the Temple of the Cold Bloods and acted as if he thought her a friend.

But Barnet and his possible guilt were not here on this island hilltop. Waln Endbrook and his associates were—along with Shivadtmon, an aridisdu who had returned to the way of blood sacrifice. Rahniseeta didn't think Shivadtmon would hesitate if

Waln threatened to cut her throat. He might even volunteer to perform the act himself and make her blood an offering to the divine five.

Yes. Definitely, she had to get away from here, but if running into the forest was out of the question, what remained?

As she was herded toward the five towers and noted their relatively good condition, an idea came to her. If she could not run away, perhaps she could run into one of the buildings. Waln and Shivadtmon both seemed to believe that treasure would be found below. That would be where their attention would be fixed.

So I, thought Rahniseeta, *must find a door and get it between them and me. A strong door. Maybe I can even find a stairway up. From above I could call warning to the others when they arrive. And maybe, maybe, Waln will not even bother to come after me. I'll be locked up where he can get me later, after all, and he won't want to waste time to chase me down when I can be retrieved easily enough.*

As Shivadtmon, closely followed by Waln, took a few steps into the tower, the filtered sunlight that came in with them illuminated an area in far less good repair than the outer precincts. Blown leaves had accumulated on the floor, along with a liberal scattering of dirt and grit. A shaft of light from a window set high in the wall revealed the likely source of this intrusion.

"Shutter must have broken," Waln said, glancing up. "Clearing away this crap is going to have to come first if we're going to find a way down."

Shivadtmon nodded.

"Reasonable. However, we should test the floor as we go along. The same window that admitted dirt and leaves may have let in enough water to encourage rot. If there is a cellar beneath . . ."

Waln nodded and sent Tedgewinn out to cut some saplings to use as probes.

"See if you can cobble a broom or two while you're at it," he called after.

Rahniseeta heard the carpenter's reply only absently. Her attention was fully occupied scanning the room. This particular chamber took up only about the front third of the tower, and another set of double doors stood resolutely shut along the back wall. She noted these as possible escape routes, but even more interesting was a door set on the left side of the room. From her knowledge of architecture from before the deities visited their retribution upon the Old Country sorcerers—a style of building she saw daily in Heeranenahalm—she guessed there was a staircase behind that door.

Shivadtmon reached the same conclusion a few minutes later. Carefully testing every step, he made his way across to the door. It was slightly stuck in its frame, but Elwyn's muscular arms worked it loose without much effort.

"What's there?" Waln asked eagerly.

"Stair," Shivadtmon said, "going up."

It said something about the level of trust between the men that Waln came over and inspected the stairwell himself.

Rahniseeta longed to join them, but knew she dared not show too much interest. Even though she had continued to act beaten and vague long after she had formed her resolve to get away, someone always seemed to be watching her—Shelby most often. There was a proprietary edge to his watchfulness that she did not want to challenge until she had some hope of escaping.

"Nolan," Waln said, "run up those stairs and see if there's any sign we're being followed."

Nolan shook his head decisively, the first real defiance of Waln's will that Rahniseeta had witnessed.

"With Shivadtmon warning us to watch the floor in case it breaks under us?" Nolan retorted. "I don't think so. Let's see how sound the building is before we go running up stairs."

At Nolan's words, a thrill of mingled anticipation and fear touched Rahniseeta's heart. She hadn't thought about the possibility that the stairway might be unsound, but now that Nolan had voiced his fear, the others would be slower to pursue. She'd have to risk it when the time came.

If the time came.

"The stair looks sound enough to me," Waln said, "but if you don't want to go . . ."

"I don't," Nolan interrupted sharply, "and don't you think your calling me a coward will make me do your bidding, neither. If you're so eager, go yourself."

Shivadtmon stepped in, making himself peacemaker.

"No need to quarrel. It's unlikely in any case that we could see much. The forests have grown thick since the days when the Old Country ruled, arching over many of the channels between the islands. As for ships at sea, how could we tell whether one pursued us or not? The bay is a busy place. In any case, I think pursuit unlikely."

Waln let himself be persuaded without further argument. Indeed his gaze was already on the doors in the back wall.

"Fine. We should get these doors open. Possibly there's a matching staircase to this one on the other side of the wall—a staircase leading down."

The sailors, already tired of clearing away leaves and rubble with their hands and the makeshift brooms Tedgewinn had put together, were more than happy to take his suggestion.

Once the floor in the first room had been tested and declared fairly sound, everyone crowded into the building. Rahniseeta let herself be herded along, but took care not to press forward, edging herself toward the side of the room where the staircase was. Now all she needed was a distraction of some sort.

She contemplated how she might create a distraction while Waln and his men forced open the two interior doors. These led to another larger, deeper room with remnants of fine tile work on the walls. There was no convenient door to a cellar stair, however, and the debris that covered the floor was deeper than in the outer room.

Waln set the now grumbling sailors to work clearing away the leaves, bracken, and bits of broken tile, but he didn't forget to post guards. Rarby was set on the outer door, and Shelby just inside. No one stated that Shelby was to guard Rahniseeta, but Shelby clearly found her at least as interesting to watch as the work going on in the inner room.

Rather than meet Shelby's eyes and accidentally do anything that could possibly be interpreted as invitation, Rahinseeta kept her gaze fastened on the work inside. It was sickly fascinating to mark the progress, for unlike those who hoped for riches, she could only anticipate disaster. She distracted herself from visions of being carried off to sea as just another piece of loot by inspecting the room.

Here, too, a window shutter had broken against the pummeling of time. By the light it admitted, rather than by that of the lanterns Waln had ordered lit, Rahniseeta inspected the beams that held the floor above. Some were solid, as were the sections of floor they supported, but others were seamed with slips and cracks. One was so far gone that it hung in a distorted V, bits of flooring gathered in a mass at its tip. The beam might hold for another hundred years, but to Rahniseeta it looked as if a robin's weight would be more than it could bear.

It was while Rahinseeta was scanning the ceiling and wondering if she should offer some sort of warning that she noticed motion near the broken shutter. At first she thought it might be her rescuers, and imagined them sneaking up on the far side, where Rarby—jealous of missing anything—only reluctantly patrolled. Then she realized the motion was a raven, a raven moving with considerable stealth and purpose.

Unnoticed by any but her, the raven squeezed in through the broken shutter. It stood for a long moment on the sill, bobbing up and down as it inspected the activity below. Then its head turned and Rahniseeta could have sworn the bright gaze fastened on her directly.

The raven held her gaze for a long moment, then dipped its beak toward its own breast. When it lifted its head again, Rahniseeta saw it held something that shot rainbows in the light.

The raven made an odd tossing gesture of its head, and Rahniseeta realized that it had been wearing a pendant of some sort. With this in its beak, it flew silently to where Elwyn and Wiatt were clearing away debris. The raven let the pendant fall onto the nearest heap. Then, still unnoticed by the men whose attention was fixed so resolutely down, it flew out again through the window.

Rahniseeta realized the raven had—deliberately or not—created the diversion she needed, but that the sailors had not noticed. Seizing the opportunity, she raised her voice and called out in a voice in which the note of excitement was not in the least feigned.

"I see something glittering! Over there, by Elwyn. Is it gold?"

As Rahniseeta expected, her words caused a general scrabbling toward Elwyn and Wiatt. Even Shelby turned his attention that way. When Elwyn's atonal voice blatted out "It's gem! Gems on a golden chain! Finders keepers, fart faces!" Shelby forgot he'd ever been on guard.

Not waiting to see if Rarby had responded to the commotion, Rahniseeta turned for the stairwell. Shivadtmon had left the door ajar, and she pulled it closed as soon as she had slipped inside. The bolt had rusted into place and defied her efforts to pull it, so she left it and she ran up, praying to Magic, to whom this building had been dedicated, that the old stone stairs would not give beneath her.

She felt creaks beneath her feet and one ominous crack, but Magic answered her prayer.

As in u-Nahal, the stair ran along the wall, and at the first landing there was a door. Rahniseeta pressed up the latch and pushed her shoulder against the wood, but the door was swollen tightly into place. She abandoned it and ran up to the next landing. Here again there was a door, and this time the latch rose to her touch and the door moved.

Rahniseeta pushed the door open, then closed it solidly behind her. There was another bolt here, and unlike below, this one could be forced into place. Ancient brackets awaited a bar, and Rahniseeta cast around for something that might fit. She found a length of hardwood where it might have been left over a century before.

She did not wonder at this, but picked the bar up and shoved it into place. Her precautions might not help for long, but she was looking for time, not to withstand a long siege.

A shout below announced her flight had been noticed, and Rahniseeta pivoted around to inspect this refuge she had found—and see if it held anything she might turn into a weapon. For several long, ragged breaths her eyes refused to comprehend what stood among the old furnishing and remnants of carpeting, framed by the fragmenting mosaic work that adorned the walls.

The room was filled with monsters.

Rahniseeta froze in terror. Then, in a voice so shrill and piercing she hardly knew it for her own, she began to scream.

XXXVII

DERIAN WON A FEW new blisters helping Harjeedian sail the smaller sailboat they'd commandeered. Firekeeper crouched in the bows calling back navigational instructions, relayed—presumably—from the seal.

"We're fortunate that the seal will help us at all," Harjeedian said. "There must be those among the yarimaimalom who consider that the treaty between our people has now been broken."

Derian wiped his sweaty forehead on the back of his arm.

"Surely the yarimaimalom realize that this is the act of several renegades, not a change of your government's policies?"

"Do they?" Harjeedian said. "Do even yarimaimalom think that way?"

Firekeeper, the only one who might have answered that question, remained noticeably silent. Other than when she must repeat the seal's instructions, she said nothing. From the way Blind Seer hovered close, Derian guessed that the wolf-woman's seasickness had returned.

The jaguar Truth was indifferent to the human's discomfort, but sat crouched in the widest part of the boat. Occasionally Truth shook off the spray that beaded on the plush black and gold of her coat, but otherwise she remained so still and watchful that Derian could have once again mistaken a living creature for a statue.

With the seal to guide them, finding where the *Islander* had tied up was simplicity itself. Harjeedian stood the vessel off outside of crossbow range and hailed her. In this, as in navigation, they were better informed than they would have been without the cooperation of the yarimaimalom. A raven Firekeeper called Bitter had reported that except for Barnet Lobster, the *Islander* was empty.

"Ho, the *Islander*!" called Harjeedian. "Barnet Lobster, are you there?"

He repeated the question in Pellish, and by the time he had completed the last phrase, Barnet's fair head was visible coming up the companionway from below.

"I am here," he replied in Liglimosh.

"Will you surrender to us?" Harjeedian said.

Barnet, now moving to the rail, made a gesture to show that he carried no weapons of any sort.

"On the same terms that I came here with Waln," he said. "I don't set foot on any of the islands."

Harjeedian had begun to bring their own sailboat closer, but he paused long enough to ask, "Why won't you go ashore?"

"Because I don't agree with Shivadtmon's interpretation of events," Barnet replied easily. "He may say that Lady Blysse's visit to Misheemnekuru means the yarimaimalom no longer wish sanctuary here, but I'm not going to bet my life on it."

The minstrel looked down into the water where now numerous seals could be glimpsed swirling just below the surface.

"I think those fellows," he went on with a toss of his head, "might have had something to say about our venturing this way at all, but Waln threatened them and they backed off."

"Threatened?" Firekeeper asked, her voice hoarser than usual.

"Crossbow and harpoon," Barnet replied. "And men who are very good at using them. Guess the Wise Seals didn't want to lose a friend or family member."

"Yes," Firekeeper said.

Barnet addressed Harjeedian again. "He's got something worse than a crossbow bolt to hold you off, Aridisdu. He's got your sister."

"We know," Harjeedian replied shortly. "Rahniseeta left a note after she overheard your discussion with Elwyn. When we couldn't find her, and discovered all of you gone . . ."

"You guessed," Barnet said.

"And the yarimaimalom have confirmed it," Derian added.

Derian knew his voice was tight, but he couldn't help it. All night he'd been trying hard not to think about what Rahniseeta might be going through. Now to have Barnet talking so calmly about her. There'd even been a teasing note in his voice when he'd told Harjeedian that Waln had Rahniseeta.

The small sailboat was near shore now and Barnet bent down from the *Islander* to help them secure her.

"Waln and the rest have gone up the hill, to where those towers are," the minstrel volunteered. "I'll mind your boat for you, but I won't be forsworn, not even if the jaguar invites me to come along and speaks fine Pellish to do so."

Firekeeper had leapt down and waded through the shallows to shore. Now she stood wringing the water out of her trouser legs and making sure her knife blade was dry. Her impulsiveness was typical and unnecessary—Derian and Harjeedian disembarked dry-shod, their gear dry with them.

"If Truth invite you," Firekeeper said to Barnet, "you come, but she not asking. Is all of them there, and how armed?"

Barnet blinked at the wolf-woman's blunt rudeness, but answered calmly enough.

"There are nine of them—counting Rahniseeta. Everyone has crossbows, knives and such, but Shelby and Rarby are the only real killers among them."

"And Waln," Derian said, "and Shivadtmon, too, I suspect."

"I won't argue with your judgment," Barnet said, "but I will add that all of them will fight if they believe their lives are in danger—and Waln will make sure they think that's the case."

Truth and Blind Seer were casting about, doubtless collecting the scent. They started up a faint trail into the woods. Firekeeper made as if to follow them, then paused.

"Come," she ordered sharply. "We know the way. Blind Seer and I comed here before."

"Came," Derian corrected as he accepted the weapons Harjeedian handed him from the store they'd put on the boat.

The local style of bow was shorter and more compact than the one he'd learned, but Derian thought he could manage to hit a man-sized target. The sword and knife were like enough to what he was accustomed, but as he belted them on, Derian repeated what he had said to Harjeedian the night before.

"I'm trained. I've been blooded, but I'm no killer."

Harjeedian nodded, checking the hang of his own gear as he began walking after their guides.

"I know. I am much the same. Somehow I don't think we'll be fighting, but it's best to be prepared."

"Good luck," Barnet called after them, sounding rather wistful now that he was being left.

"Thanks," Derian called back, but he forgot the minstrel completely as soon as the boats were out of sight.

They trudged up the trail behind Firekeeper, Blind Seer, and Truth. The yari-maimalom set a fair pace, but Derian had love and worry to keep him going. Whatever motivated Harjeedian made him grim and relentless as death.

They walked steadily, the humans watching their footing on the uneven trail, while around them the morning grew warmer. They spoke little. What use was speculation when sooner or later some osprey or raven was likely to show up and give Firekeeper a briefing?

"I wonder if they know we're coming?" Derian asked after a while.

Firekeeper gave him a strange look.

"Some know, I think, but not Waln."

That was when Derian realized that neither Truth or Blind Seer walked alongside her. He'd been too busy watching his feet to notice when they had slipped away.

"Where're the others?"

"They go and make quiet howl," Firekeeper said. "Not wish Waln to know we have friends."

Eventually, both wolf and jaguar returned. Soon after they did, Derian thought that from time to time he glimpsed motion in the surrounding greenery. It wasn't much: a flash of golden brown, a glitter of amber eyes, a branch or bit of shrubbery moving rather more vigorously than the breeze alone could explain.

I guess the howl worked, Derian thought, *and I guess that like the seals, these yari-maimalom have accepted our presence as a necessary evil.*

He wished he felt better about this.

Then, just as he was adjusting to life as a rhythm consisting of steady motion that was almost, but not quite, demanding enough to keep him from worrying about Rahniseeta, Truth emitted a horrible choked roar and began to weave drunkenly.

Firekeeper dropped to her knees at the jaguar's side, putting her arms around the great cat's neck and shaking her violently. When Derian saw the proximity of the young woman's face to the jaguar's fangs, his heart nearly stopped beating. He glanced over at Blind Seer, counting on the wolf's reaction to tell him at least whether the situation was as odd and potentially dangerous as it seemed.

That Blind Seer had angled his ears flat against his skull didn't ease Derian one bit. He started forward, not certain what he would do, but certain he should do something. Then Firekeeper leapt to her feet.

"We go," she said to Derian. "Truth seed. We go now—or better we not come at all."

Derian wanted more explanation than this, but he knew he wasn't going to get it. The jaguar was already running up the trail, her stocky body opening up into a run far faster than anything Derian had thought she could achieve. Firekeeper and Blind Seer bolted after, the young woman's long legs reminding Derian of a deer in full flight.

But what he would remember ever after was what followed the pair.

Out of the forest's edge came streaming all who had been following so silently. Most were wolves, but there were puma, red fox, another jaguar, and a bear. Intermingled with these were herbivores—elk and deer—demonstrating as they ran the speed with which they managed to outdistance the terrible hunters who, on a more usual day, would pursue them.

Derian stopped in midstride, too overwhelmed to move. He saw the bear, loping with considerable speed on all fours, come alongside Firekeeper, saw the wolf-woman grab the thick fur at the bear's neck, then leap astride in one lithe motion. She clung there, riding far more easily than she had ever ridden a horse.

Then the furred horde vanished around a twisting in the trail, and but for the swath they had torn through the greenery, Derian might have been able to convince himself that the entire incredible thing had never happened.

HAD IT NOT BEEN for the door she herself had barred and bolted, Rahniseeta would have fled from that terrible gathering. However, the bar stuck in the brackets, and she was not about to turn her back on the horrors in the room in order to pry it loose.

Now that she was forced to pause, she realized that her initial impression had not been completely accurate. The room was not full of monsters. There were only three, but that these were monsters could not be doubted.

Two were bipedal, but that was where any likeness between them ended. One might have passed for human, if any human had ever been covered head to foot in blue-grey feathers, and possessed a nose that somehow evoked a beak. The other could never have passed as human, not with his white eagle's head, snake's torso, and human—though scaled—limbs.

The quadruped was all the more horrid in that his head was human, though no human had ever had wolf's ears. For that matter, no human had ever had a body covered in a jaguar's fur in shades of black and grey, nor a wolf's tail, nor those disturbing front paws with what were clearly fingers.

Rahniseeta fumbled behind her for the bar, hoping to pull it loose, but all her efforts brought were crumbling bits of iron and an increased sense of desperation.

Then the quadrupedal monster said, "Have we done you any harm, Rahniseeta, sister of Harjeedian? Think on that before you race back into the arms of those who have done you harm."

Rahniseeta froze in place, pushing back against the door so hard that both bar and bolt dug into her flesh.

"You talk?"

"We do," the quadruped said, "though you will not be able to understand Sky's speech. Human talk does not come easily from an eagle's beak."

"Sky?" Rahinseeta tried desperately to answer politeness with politeness, though head and heart were both pounding so hard she could barely think. "And you? You are?"

"Questioner is as good a name as any," came the reply. "Firekeeper, whom I believe you know, called me that. This one beside me is called Hope."

"Hope," Rahinseeta repeated.

From below she could hear smatterings of what sounded like argument. Shelby's voice was loudest. It seemed he was demanding the right to go to her rescue. The others seemed less certain this was a good idea.

"Firekeeper," Rahniseeta said, what Questioner had said coming clear now. "You know Firekeeper."

"Indirectly, you are the one who sent her to us," Hope replied. Her voice was very rich, the words coming from deep in her chest, not pinched by that thin little nose. "Are you not the one who told Derian Carter of the maimalodalum?"

"I did," Rahniseeta began. "I thought he might be one, come to . . ."

She stopped, drew in a few deep breaths. Below the arguing had resolved to three voices: Rarby's, Shelby's, and Waln's.

"Sent her to you? Then you are maimalodalum?"

"Such as remain," Hope said. "Rather we are descended from those upon whom the enchantment failed to work as those who cast it intended. It is a long story, one we do not have time for now."

"I suppose not," Rahniseeta agreed. "Though I think it must be fascinating. What happens next?"

"That depends largely on the men below." Questioner moved his wolf ears to better catch the sounds. "They cannot decide whether coming after you is a good idea. The one called Shelby is determined, but someone called Rarby is trying to dissuade them."

"They are brothers," Rahniseeta said, aware this was rather inconsequential.

"And Shelby thinks you are a great enough prize to risk his neck," Questioner said.

He grinned, and Rahinseeta saw that not all his teeth were human. His eyes were blue, a darker shade than Barnet's. She realized with mild shock that they were only the third pair of blue eyes she had ever noticed.

"Why are you here?" she asked.

"This is where we live," said Hope. "Not in this tower specifically. It is less sound than many of the others. We consider ourselves custodians of what remains here. When the yarimaimalom brought word that the northerners were coming here, we sorted ourselves into groups and took up station within the towers. Our plan was not to interfere unless necessary."

"And have I made it necessary?" Rahniseeta asked, feeling shy and awkward.

"That depends," Questioner said, "rather on you. We do not want that door opened, you see, not now that any who come through it will expect trouble."

Recalling her own frozen shock, Rahniseeta could understand.

"What were you going to do before I messed things up?" she asked bitterly.

"Wait for those who are coming to take away the invaders," Hope replied, "but though the yarimaimalom argued otherwise, we would not abandon our trust."

"Well," Rahniseeta said, "if you'll forgive my screams from a few moments ago, I'd like to stay with you. I've seen real monsters now—you three are only maimalodalum."

NEVER AGAIN, Waln thought, *will I hire a romantic—if I have the chance to learn of that failing in advance, that is, or,* he added with wry self-awareness of how little control he'd had of much of this situation, *if I even get to pick my crew.*

Rarby and Shelby had resumed their posts on guard, but that hadn't stopped them from arguing over whether or not Shelby should go after Rahniseeta.

The others had returned to searching the back room, but Elwyn's find had not been duplicated, nor had they found any sign of a door that might lead into a cellar.

"The bitch must have thrown it over there," Nolan said sourly. "Threw the bauble and made a run for it."

"Lots of good it did her then," said Wiatt. "That scream!"

"Probably just twisted her ankle," Tedgewinn said. "She'll be glad enough to have Shelby fetch her down when the time comes—be properly grateful, too, I'll bet."

Waln saw he had to stop this line of thought before he had the whole lot of them vying to go after Rahniseeta.

"I was thinking," he said, "the entrance to the underground might be concealed somehow—a good idea if they kept treasure. Why don't a couple of you start checking the walls? Shivadtmon, you can read the old writing. Why don't you see if there's anything written somewhere that'll help us out?"

In reality, Waln was losing any hope that there was treasure here to find, but the next stage in his plan was taking the ship and that would have to be done well after dark. Best to keep the men busy a while more—and a hidden entrance to a treasure vault wasn't a bad idea.

The men dispersed to their new tasks and there was even a joke or two as hope rose anew. Waln made himself busy checking the side of the front room directly opposite the staircase up on the theory that architects liked order and balance.

Rarby volunteered to see if there was anything odd about the building that could be seen from the outside. He stepped out and in again almost at once.

"Captain," he said, his voice low, "I think you need to see this."

Waln frowned. There was something in Rarby's tone that didn't seem to indicate that he'd found a cellar door. Shelby was already crossing to where Rarby stood by the open double doors.

"What you . . ."

Shelby's words trailed off, but his crossbow came up into a firing position. As soon as Waln reached the doorway—instinctively careful to keep his bulk behind the other two men—he saw why.

Lady Blysse stood at the far end of the flagstone yard that filled the area between the five towers. She stood near one point of the star-shaped Tower of Air, her enormous wolf beside her. She carried a long bow after the local design, strung and ready, but was, Waln noted, neatly outside the range of the crossbows they carried. Whether Waln and his men were outside her range was a matter of question.

Two large black ravens perched nearby. One stood cheekily on the wolf's back, the other amid the vines growing up the stonework of the tower. They looked as watchful as did the woman and wolf, and Waln guessed them to be yarimaimalom.

"Waln Endbrook," Lady Blysse called, her odd, husky voice carrying easily. "Surrender, you and your men. Come quiet and no one will be harmed."

Waln knew he could not surrender. Whether the Liglimom would treat what he and his fellows had done as sacrilege or merely theft hardly mattered. For over a year he had been little better than a prisoner. He was not going back to that.

He was framing his reply when Rarby gave an arrogant laugh.

"We're to surrender? To you and your dog? I fancy you're good with that bow, but we're good with ours—and we're eight to your one."

"I no one," Lady Blysse—no, Waln could not think of her as other than Fire-keeper—replied. "Look."

She waved her hand and it was like a conjuring trick. From around the corners of every tower, even from the one in which they sheltered, from against stone and behind low walls that Waln would have sworn would not have hidden anything, emerged a horde of beasts. Black, grey, tawny brown, russet red, and gaudy golden adorned with spots, they showed themselves to the three at the doorway of the tower and then as silently vanished.

Worse almost were the winged forms—ospreys, hawks, eagles, and ravens—that rose in a feathered cloud and then dropped again to the stony heights where they had taken refuge.

"I am not one," Firekeeper called, "not even with my 'dog' and these 'birdies' you see. I am many. Come though, and for me they will let you go."

Waln didn't believe her. The yarimaimalom were clever. Shivadtmon had told him this. They were using the girl as a mouthpiece—with her knowing or not. They would never let the northerners escape.

Behind him, the other men had gathered, peering around and sinking back in consternation.

"We going to surrender, Captain?" asked Nolan, always the weak stick.

"To be torn to shreds?" Rarby spat. "You really believe her?"

Waln was glad Rarby had spared him the rebuttal. He hadn't been certain he could keep the panic from his voice. Now he very carefully schooled it into a sneer.

"Surrender? I don't think so. I've been prisoner long enough—and have you forgotten? We have Shelby's lady love upstairs, just waiting to be our shield. We'll get away yet."

"Upstairs has another advantage," Rarby said. "They won't slip back and forth so easily when we've got the drop on them. Shel, help me wrestle these doors shut."

There was no protest from without as the doors were closed, and Tedgewinn brought over a couple of the wooden probes he'd cut earlier.

"We can use these to shim the door tight," he said. "Better than a bar, because pushing will jam them tighter. Elwyn, lend me a hand."

Waln didn't worry about these minor usurpations of his authority. The men were acting as might sailors in a storm, each tending to his own department, thus freeing him to plan and judge the larger picture. The stair up first.

"Shivadtmon," Waln said, "you were over inspecting the staircase. Will it take us? Some of us are much heavier than Rahniseeta."

"Should," Shivadtmon said. "They were good builders. The supports are anchored in the outer wall. Still, be wisest if we didn't go up all at once."

"Fine," Waln said. "Shelby, you've been panting to go after the girl. You first. When you get up, we'll anchor a line so if the stair can't take repeated use we'll have another way up and down."

After arguing for just this chance, Shelby could hardly refuse. He even looked eager and anxious as he coiled the length of rope about his waist, leaving his arms free to carry bow—and knife, if necessary.

No one was saying anything about whatever had made Rahinseeta scream, for no one wanted to do anything to make Shelby change his mind now that someone had to lead the way up. Of course Elwyn stopped pounding shims under the door to bleat loudly:

"Be careful, Shel. I bet Rahniseeta saw one of those big birds. They'd like it up there. They'd rip out your eyes faster than I fart after eating beans."

Shelby glowered at the fool, but his pride was too entangled with the venture now for him to stop.

"Thanks," he said, securing the last of the line, and checking his bow. "I'll remember to shoot high."

He went up the stairs one at a time, and to Waln, watching with Shivadtmon from the foot of the stair, it was evident he was testing every block.

"Creaks a bit," Shelby called down, "but I think it's sound."

He tried the first door he came to. The latch wouldn't budge, but when he pounded his shoulder against the old wood, something snapped and the door creaked open.

"I'm not going in there," Shelby announced. "The floor is rotted. Looks like a mouse's weight would make it give. No way Rahniseeta went in there."

Leaving the door open behind him, Shelby mounted the stair. There was something in how he took the steps that made Waln guess the sailor was thinking about turning around, but he kept going until he came to the next landing.

Once again, the door wouldn't move, but the latch lifted easily beneath the pressure of his thumb.

"Something's holding the door fast," Shelby called down. "Rahniseeta would have had time to throw a bolt, and presence of mind to do it, too. She's a clever lass. Have someone bring me an axe. The door's only wood. We can cut through."

"Tedgewinn, bring Shelby an axe," Waln called.

The carpenter not only did so, he braved the stair to help with the chopping. Wiatt, speaking from where he was looking out through a narrow slit left between the front door and jamb by weather warping, gave impetus for this boldness.

"Can't see clearly," the cook reported, "but there's motion out there. Those giant wolves are sniffing around, sure as yeast makes the bread dough rise."

"They'll be sniffing back blood when we get up there," Rarby said confidently. "Stop dragging your feet, Shelby!"

Shelby ignored his brother. Tedgewinn had broken a hole through one of the door panels, and Shelby had stuck his hand through and was working it about. His head was thrown back slightly and his eyes were closed as if this would give his hand the use of the vision he wasn't using.

Idiocy, Waln thought.

He drifted over to where Wiatt was still peering out through the crack. "Anything?"

"Nothing," Wiatt said. "Guess they figured they can't get through the door. Maybe they're figuring on starving us out."

The cook sounded rather anxious at the prospect, but Waln just laughed.

"We carried water with us, and food enough. We'll have convinced them a siege would be too costly long before we're feeling any hunger."

Wiatt didn't ask just how this miracle would be achieved, and Waln didn't offer details. He paced back to where Shelby was still working at the door.

"Any sign of the girl?" he asked.

"No," Shelby said. "Nothing but some sticks of old furniture. I've got the bolt open, but there's a bar, too, and that's harder to lift. . . ."

He was twisting about as he spoke, obviously working to get an angle on the bar.

"There," he grunted, satisfaction evident in the sound. "Be just a minute now."

He pulled himself away from the door, and glanced at Tedgewinn. The carpenter had a crossbow in one hand, a hatchet in his belt. Shelby retrieved his own crossbow from where he'd set it.

"Be ready to follow us up," he said.

Then, taking cover behind the doorjamb, Shelby gave the door a push. It swung inward, but from beneath Waln could see nothing.

"What's there?" he called.

"Nothing," Shelby said, "just furniture, but from the marks on the floor someone's been in here recently enough to mark up the dust. There's another door. I'm going to check it."

Tedgewinn stood in the open doorway watching. A moment later he called down, "The other door is locked, too. Why don't you start coming up? Someone else can see where the stair goes above while we work here."

Waln nodded.

"Wiatt, you see where the stair goes. Rarby, you keep watch where Wiatt was. The rest of you, follow up but try and keep no more than two on the stair at a time. I'll stay with Rarby in case Lady Blysse and her critters try to break through."

The reminder moved them along nicely, and though the old staircase creaked and the occasional shower of mortar dust fell as the more heavy-footed made their way up, the old building proved solid.

Waln heard rhythmic thumping as Shelby put a hatchet to work on the inner door. The blows sounded heavy and angry. Waln smiled to himself.

Are you there behind the door, Rahniseeta? I hope you're scared, because I think Shelby wants to speak with you about running away—and somehow I don't think he's much a man of many words. He's so much more comfortable with using his hands.

❀

WHEN THE SOUND of booted feet coming up the stone stairs reverberated dully into the room where Rahniseeta waited with the maimalodalum, she was surprised by the course of action her new allies chose.

Questioner crossed to one of the narrow windows and, standing on his hind legs, looked outside through a break in the shutter. He dropped then and said something Rahniseeta could not follow to his two companions. Sky immediately crossed to a door in the inner wall and opened it. Hope and Questioner turned to follow.

"Are you still with us?" Hope asked when Rahniseeta didn't move to accompany them.

"Shouldn't," Rahniseeta asked hesitantly, "someone stay and make sure they don't get through?"

"There is no stopping that," Hope said. "You yourself pulled the bolt and set the bar we had put by for our own use in just such an eventuality, but surely you can see the door itself is very old. If those men are determined—as they have every reason to be— they will break through."

"But we could do something as they came through," Rahniseeta protested. "They couldn't get through more than one at a time."

"True," Hope said, "but we are largely unarmed. We had hoped to be out of here before this."

Her statement puzzled Rahniseeta, but something else the bird-woman had said demanded more immediate attention.

"Reason?" Rahniseeta said, moving somewhat reluctantly to follow. "You mean me?"

"Don't sound so guilty," Hope said briskly. "You are certainly one reason the men will come this way, but a greater one is that Firekeeper has shown herself to the men. She has offered them opportunity to surrender to her and the yarimaimalom. They have refused. As this tower is now their fortress, they must investigate it."

"Firekeeper? How do you know all of this?" Rahniseeta asked. "By magic?"

"Hardly," Questioner replied, and his dry laugh sounded more like a bark. "When I went to the window just now, Bitter the raven told me the newest developments. His mate, Lovable, has been listening from just outside one of the open windows on the first floor. She's quick with languages, and has picked up Pellish quite nicely."

"How?"

"Listening to the classes the northerners have been teaching. She prefers someone named Barnet Lobster, I believe."

Shaking her head in mild astonishment, Rahniseeta passed through the door and helped Questioner draw the bolt and set the bar. Then she turned to examine the room.

The wall to her left was curved, the plaster that had once covered the stone fallen away except for a few patches randomly placed. The area around a large window about halfway into the room was uniformly devoid of plaster, and pale green-tinted light came through the vines that grew directly over the broken glass.

The room was minimally furnished, with a few broken sticks of what might have been furniture resting on what once must have been magnificent glazed tiles. The tiles were now cracked and their glaze dimmed, whatever patterns that had once been painted on them obscured.

At the far end of the room a door stood open, apparently stuck that way. Through the opening Rahniseeta could see a room that was even less hospitable, for the floor bowed near the center. Recalling the weakened beams she had noted below, Rahniseeta thought she knew the reason for this.

"Walk close to the outer wall," Hope said from where she stood with Sky near the window. "We do not trust the soundness of the floor near the center."

Rahniseeta's only problem in obeying was that even with ample evidence that the edge of the floor remained sound, her knees trembled when she thought of moving. Not wishing to seem a coward, she bit her inner lip and forced her feet to move. Once they were doing so and nothing collapsed beneath her, she regained her confidence.

"What next?" she asked.

"Before you arrived," Questioner said, "we were salvaging the last of what we think may be important. Since this tower began deteriorating beyond our ability to effect repairs, we have been slowly removing things, but you know how it is."

The jaguar-wolf body gave a very human shrug. "You always think you have time to finish an unpleasant and rather dull job. There were a few things remaining. Had we had a few more hours, this tower would have stood empty."

Sky turned from where he had been leaning half out the window and Rahniseeta saw he held a rope in his hand. The eagle head gave a shrill but distinctly conversational shriek.

"That's the . . ." Questioner was beginning when a loud crash from the other room announced that the door had been broken through.

Shelby's voice could be clearly heard, though what he said was—to Rahniseeta's hearing—dulled by the intervening wall and the fact that he was shouting to those below. Questioner's wolf ears were by no means so limited.

"They're going to be moving more quickly now," he said, helping Sky haul in a length of fairly heavy rope. "We've lowered down the last of the salvage. Rahniseeta, you down first."

"No," she said. "They have reason not to shoot me. They'll have none not to go for you. Someone else go first and I'll stand where I'll be the first thing they see when they come through the door."

"That's risky," Questioner said—not as if he was doubting the wisdom of her plan, just as one states a fact.

"I know," Rahniseeta said, "but it makes sense. Get to it."

She moved away from the window, and the maimalodalum did not move to stop her.

"Fine," Questioner said. "You next, Hope."

The bird-woman did not argue, and Rahniseeta wondered fleetingly at the rationale for choosing her as the first to be gotten away. Where they protecting her because she was female? Or because if it came to a fight she was the least naturally equipped for violence? Or some other reason that made sense only if you were a maimalodalu?

Certainly, Sky's eagle's beak was a nasty weapon and his scaled fingers ended in what looked rather like talons. Questioner's paws ended in something like fingers, but his teeth didn't look wholly human. He might wield a weapon and bite as well. And, frankly, either of the males was more dangerous-looking, more purely monstrous, than the bird-woman. Hope, if looked at without the element of shock coloring one's opinion, was actually rather pretty.

Rahniseeta searched among the broken furniture bits for something she might turn into a club. Though she carefully kept from the center of the room, she imagined she felt the beams beneath her groan, and as soon as she found a solid table leg she scooted back toward the edge.

She listened intently as someone tried the door. There was a rattle as the latch was worked, than a few dull thuds as if someone was trying to ram it with his shoulder. Then Shelby's voice, distinct though muffled, said:

"Probably bolted again. Give me the hatchet, Tedge."

Rahniseeta skittered closer as the first blows hit the old wood, splintering it easily. The doors had been well made, but the maimalodalum had been right. Over a hundred years of damp, of summer heat and winter cold, had not been kind to the stuff. Apparently, the maimalodalum had made some efforts to maintain the towers, but when this one had deteriorated beyond their abilities, they'd given it back to the elements.

Rahniseeta hefted her club, inching closer to the opening as the hatchet widened it to permit questing fingers. She stayed out of direct line of sight, knowing how limited the scope would be. Whoever looked through might glimpse a little motion from over by the window, but probably not even that if he was accustomed to light other than the dim green-filtered sunlight.

As she had expected, a hand—Shelby's most certainly, she was all too well acquainted with his hands—came through, feeling for the bolt. Rahniseeta took a deep breath and swung her table leg, aiming carefully for the fingers.

She hit, and felt an atavistic thrill of pride as she heard Shelby howl in pain.

She heard Tedgewinn laugh very unkindly.

"I guess the lady doesn't want to be rescued," he said. "At least not by you, Shel."

No one had taught Rahniseeta the string of Pellish words with which Shelby responded, but Rahniseeta didn't need a translator to know they were profane. She grinned to herself, and readied the table leg for another strike.

From overhead there came a dull thumping and bits of dirt rained down. Worried, she spared a glance for Questioner and Sky. The human face with its wolfish ears gave her an encouraging smile, and Sky looked up from watching Hope make her descent and pointed with his beak toward the ceiling.

Rahniseeta looked where he had pointed and saw that the beams above were reassuringly solid. She also understood the maimalodalum's silence. Best that Shelby and those with him didn't realize she wasn't alone.

But although they were in no danger from the roof caving in on them, the man above—Wiatt, so it proved—offered another danger. They heard him give an excited yell, which was followed almost immediately by a wolf's howl from without. Before the wolf's howl stopped vibrating in the afternoon heat, Wiatt's voice shouted excitedly.

"I saw one of them! I saw one of the bastards! I got off an arrow! Don't know if I hit anyone, but I think I might. Did you hear the bastard yell?"

Questioner dropped to all fours—he'd been leaning with his upper body on the windowsill helping Sky lower Hope—and padded over.

"No one was hit," he said very softly to Rahniseeta, "but we're going to have to wait to lower anyone else. We'd just be trapped at the base."

"Hope?"

"She's skirting the base under the vines and should get away. The northerners won't have it all their own way. Firekeeper will do something."

Questioner spoke with almost parental pride, and Rahniseeta wondered with a trace of jealousy at the relationship that had grown with such apparent speed between the maimalodalum and the wolf-woman. Not long ago Firekeeper hadn't even known them as legends. Now, apparently, she was their general.

But Rahniseeta fought back this unkind thought. Firekeeper had come to Misheem-nekuru very quickly—probably as soon as she had learned of Rahniseeta's message. That meant that Derian and probably Harjeedian were near, too.

Rahniseeta felt very strange as she realized that she had not so much as thought of any of them for what seemed like a lifetime. Her universe had collapsed into a sphere in which the only realities had been herself, her captors, and now the maimalodalum. It was almost as if she had not dared think of those she had left behind, of the messages she had left, for fear that somehow what she had done would be discovered and undermined.

Now, though, she thought of it, and felt a thrill of relief. She and the maimalodalum need only hold out and rescue would come. She shifted her table leg in her hand and watched for motion coming through the hole in the door, determined to do her part.

There had been lots of shouting in response to Wiatt's announcement, much pounding up and down the stairs. Apparently, Rahniseeta had been forgotten in the greater excitement, but she did not believe for a moment that they would continue to forget. Shelby would want revenge for what she'd done to his hand, and if he was in no condition to get it, Rarby would take great delight in roughing her up on his brother's behalf.

She waited, listening intently, but glancing from time to time over at Questioner, for she'd already learned the maimalodalu would hear anything significant long before she did.

Still, the sound of renewed footsteps into the room came to all of them at once. They were heavy, as if weighted down, and when the door vibrated in its frame, Rahniseeta understood.

From somewhere they'd scavenged something to make a ram. She stepped back nearer to the window, knowing this was not a threat she could stop with a blow to the fingers.

"Got it, Elwyn?" she heard Tedgewinn say. "On three. You can count it off."

"I got it!" Elwyn replied brightly, happy as always to be part of the team. "One, two, three!"

The old door shuddered beneath the first several blows, each hit prefaced by Elwyn's cheerful count. Inevitably, the old wood shattered into splinters and the two men came barreling through.

Momentum carried them into the middle of the room at a hard, stamping run. Their weight, combined with that of the heavy chunk of wood they had used for a ram, was too great for the damaged beams supporting the floor. With a shriek and a sound of tearing, several of the old support beams sagged, then snapped. Without them to rest upon, the floor gave out, planks breaking and twisting as they tore free. Elwyn and Tedgewinn fell with the rest of the litter.

Around the falling bodies, tile fell like hard rain.

XXXVIII

"I DON'T KNOW WHAT GOOD my sitting here does," Firekeeper said. "Waln is secure in his lair, and so we have rushed here for nothing."

Truth looked at the wolf-woman from those unsettling orange-gold eyes. The jaguar was clearly struggling not to be dragged back into the depths from which Firekeeper had dragged her, and the battle had not improved her temper.

"Are you now a swimmer in Time's rivers to tell me this with such confidence?"

"No," Firekeeper said. She struggled not to sound like a sulky child. "But I have done nothing but say a few words to Waln and he do nothing."

"You mean," Blind Seer said before Truth could frame a suitably caustic reply, "that he did not do what you desired. Why does this surprise you?"

"It does not," Firekeeper admitted, "but when Truth say we must run hard and fast to get here or all chance of stopping them would be gone. . . . I thought more would happen."

Truth met Firekeeper's gaze and the wolf-woman noted uneasily that the jaguar was struggling to keep her in focus.

"Let me tell you things that would have happened had we not been here," Truth purred. "First, a young wolf of your acquaintance, one Dark Death, would have seen the man you name Rarby walking patrol around the tower. Thinking to impress you, Dark Death would have seized Rarby and killed him.

"In one deep current, Dark Death succeeds, but in some way Rarby's death makes the others fight more fiercely. In another deep current, Rarby kills Dark Death before—usually—dying himself. Dark Death's dying, witnessed by his pack members, moves them to fury. They attack the humans and many on both sides are slain including—I may add—one who must be taken from here alive if we are to claim victory."

Firekeeper did not doubt that those unfocused eyes saw realities that had not happened. She tried to ignore her own pleased embarrassment that Dark Death would think her worth impressing.

"And my being here stopped this?" she asked.

"Yes. Dark Death saw that you did not wish the humans slaughtered, so his thought to impress you in that fashion died before he could act on it. Had we taken more time getting here. . . ."

Firekeeper nodded.

"I stand humbled, Truth."

"You have done more than stand," Truth said, and to Firekeeper's relief her gaze flickered to follow a butterfly dancing on a flower head. "You have been a good teacher."

"Me?"

"Don't you recall how the first thing you did upon arriving here was warn all the yarimaimalom that the humans carried crossbows?"

"But they knew that!"

"But they did not know just how deadly those bows are, or how far they can strike. You—and Blind Seer—made this clear."

Blind Seer laughed softly.

"Bows and the danger they pose were among the first things I studied when I resolved to stay with my Firekeeper."

"Although we have lived close to humans," Truth said, "only those of us who delight in hunting in company—such as wolves—have seen bows in use. The Water Folk know something of harpoons, for humans cannot tell Wise from Simple when they are hunting and the humans here rely much on oil taken from whales and their kin."

Normally, Firekeeper would have asked questions about the Water Folk, but nothing could distract her from the matter at hand.

"Do you yet see how long we wait?" she asked, trying to sound humble rather than impatient.

Truth licked her front paw, worrying at the sheath of a claw.

"Not too much longer," she said. "Listen to the ravens!"

Firekeeper did and heard reported how the humans were moving about the tower, then the warning that they had reached high enough that those waiting on the forest's edge might not be so well hidden as before.

Firekeeper howled reply, pleased to be a One in this matter of hunting humans. It was a minor promotion, one that would not last beyond the hunt, but it was new to her and thrilled her blood.

She listened as Bitter reported the bird-woman maimalodalu, Hope, safely down, and the resolution of the others to remain inside until the humans could be distracted from their watching over the tower's edge.

"I do not like that we have our own in there," Firekeeper admitted. "Waln knows this taking of hostages. I do not wish them to be taken so."

"You might find yourself wishing otherwise," Truth said enigmatically, "in not too long."

Before Firekeeper could make herself ask the arrogant cat to clarify her comment, a rhythmic thudding came from the tower. Firekeeper surged to her feet, waiting to hear the raven's report. Her bow stave was in her hand, and she held it ready to bend and string.

When the horrible cracking noise came, confusedly, Firekeeper thought her bow had broken as she bent it to fit the string, but the stave remained in her hand, the string loose. Then she realized that the cracking noise was only one of many.

Oddly, impossibly, the tower of Magic was shaking, the stonework seeming to ripple as did the scales on a snake when the snake was hurried. Mortar showered loose and stones fell. The flat side of the half-moon suddenly showed gaping holes where patches had been ripped loose. More stone fell and what glass remained in the windows broke, scattering rainbows as it fell.

Firekeeper ran to close the distance, the difference between enemies and friends vanished in the face of this larger disaster. The raven Lovable swept out of the sky and winged alongside her.

"The beams holding the third floor above those below were weak and broke when weight was put upon them," Lovable reported. "The force of that breaking has weakened still more. For now parts still stand, but I do not know how much longer."

"And those within?"

"Some are blood upon stone," Lovable said, "but some still live. The two maimalodalum and the human woman with them were near the side, and still cling. Bitter is checking the rest. We need not fear crossbows now."

This last was said matter-of-factly, but with a certain relief as well. Firekeeper realized how unsettling it must have been for these Wise Wingéd Folk to face being shot at when in Liglim humans held their arrows lest they injure a divine messenger.

"Lead us," Firekeeper said, "to where Rahniseeta and the maimalodalum wait. Tell your kin to find where others may need rescue."

Lovable gave the necessary guidance, then caught an updraft and sailed off, her hoarse voice shouting Firekeeper's orders even as her beating wings carried her higher.

Firekeeper felt no pride of leadership now, only the fearful awareness that except possibly for a few of the maimalodalum, she alone could help those stranded above.

"I understand now what Truth meant," Blind Seer said, "when she spoke of wishing differently. I could accept the tiresome necessity of a siege as an alternative to this."

Firekeeper grunted agreement, letting her feet slow as she closed with the dangerous zone near the tower. Loose stones fell only occasionally, but there was a sense that the entirety of the structure was unstable.

"Find Derian," she said, "and Harjeedian. Bring them here. This is a time for human hands and human voices—and the maimalodalum will frighten Waln and his people, if any are still alive."

"Several yet live," said the raven, Bitter, landing near Firekeeper. "They were close to a stair and the old humans built well. Much of the stair still clings to the wall. Others had reached a higher section and as the beams there were sounder, some still hold. They will not for long, not with the wall that holds them threatening to fall."

Firekeeper nodded her thanks.

She threw her head back, wishing for wings so she might see the situation as the ravens did, but when she considered the consequences of wishes, she resolved to stop wasting time and focus instead on what she might do.

Rahniseeta's dark head appeared at what had once been a window opening. Her lovely face was smudged with dirt and her eyes wild. Despite this there was about her the tense stability of one who knows that there is room for nothing other than strength.

"Up here! We need help. Sky was hit by something falling and Questioner's . . . caught."

Firekeeper didn't waste time asking for more details.

"Can you lower one or other? We guide or catch?"

Rahniseeta shook her head. "They're too heavy for me. I've tried."

Something in how she moved alerted Firekeeper.

"You are hurt, too?"

Rahniseeta nodded. "Something hit me. My right arm and shoulder are numb."

"I come up," Firekeeper said.

Firekeeper looked around and noticed a length of rope trailing through the debris. She tugged at it, but too much of it was buried beneath the rubble for her to take time digging it out.

She cast around and located Integrity and Dark Death, both newly arrived, and looking up apprehensively.

"I am going to climb up," Firekeeper said. "Find the maimalodalum and tell them I need hands."

Blind Seer came loping up at that moment.

"I found Derian and Harjeedian," he reported. "They follow close behind."

"Have them dig that rope out," Firekeeper said. "We may need it. Also, don't let them go far. I will need help when I bring those above down."

Blind Seer pressed close.

"You are going up there?"

"They need help. I have hands and feet for climbing this as no beast does. The maimalodalum are mostly larger than I."

Firekeeper shrugged. There was no time for further explanation.

"I only hope," she said, picking her way through the rubble to the vine-wreathed base, "I will not cause it to fall."

She set her hands and feet to the first of the stones, finding rough holds. As she began to climb, Truth spoke from behind her.

"Keep an ear to my voice. If I dip into Time's river, I may be able to guide you."

Firekeeper knew how risky this was for the jaguar, but was it any worse than what she herself was willing to do? She accepted without debate and continued to climb, head tilted up and back to find the next handholds, feet guided by feel alone. She tugged at the vines to see if they would hold her, but their roots were shallow and would not bear any weight.

Several times Truth warned Firekeeper away from a handhold just as she would have rested her weight upon it. Other times the jaguar's coughing roar guided her to set her foot slightly to one side or another. It was painstaking, tedious work, and had the distance been farther, she might not have managed it.

Eventually, nails broken and bloody, the cotton of blouse and trousers torn, her skin scraped and oozing in countless places, Firekeeper hauled herself over the window ledge into what had once been a room.

Many of the crossbeams and braces had broken, but some—built strong by those who wished them to bear the weight of tile in addition to more usual burdens—had survived. Two of these supported a narrow catwalk beneath the window, and on this Rahniseeta knelt next to Sky.

The white feathers on the maimalodalu's eagle head were bloodied, but a rough bandage had been tied around the source of the injury. Sky's other hurts were such that Firekeeper immediately ceased to feel her own aches and scrapes, but he continued to breathe, the sound shallow and painful, but without the bubbling that would announce a punctured lung.

"He spread his wings," Rahniseeta said, looking up from where she had clearly been attending to Sky's wounds, "to shelter me. I almost have him free. Can you get Questioner?"

Firekeeper turned to look and understood at once why Rahniseeta had said nothing more. Where Sky rested on the catwalk beneath the window, Questioner was caught within an interweave of splintered wood, rubble, and less definable detritus. He hung out over the void, and Firekeeper dreaded that his body was integral to whatever web-work supported their tenuous walkway.

She leaned to touch his human face and his blue eyes fluttered open, looked at her from a world of pain, then closed again.

"Rope," Firekeeper said, not voicing her despair.

She rose and went to the window.

"Rope!" she shouted down. "We must have rope."

The scene below had changed while she climbed. Derian was there, as was Harjeedian. Several of the maimalodalum had come out as well. All with hands were working to clear a path through the rubble. There was another cluster around the jaguar Truth, and Firekeeper fleetingly wondered if once again the jaguar was lost in possibility.

Derian looked up at her, his expression filled with confusion, and Firekeeper realized that she had howled rather than spoken.

"I need rope," she said, "to get hurt ones down. Have you some?"

"We've freed up most of a line," Derian said. "But how to get it to you . . ."

Bitter croaked sardonically and plopped himself down in front of the human, answering the question quite effectively. Derian, accustomed to the ways of the peregrine falcon Elation, extended one end. Bitter took it, adjusted to the weight, and began flapping up while Derian played out the line so it would not become tangled.

As she reeled in the rope, Firekeeper noted that Derian actually seemed relieved at the comparative normality of being ordered around by a bird. Doubtless he had not yet adjusted to his first sight of the maimalodalum.

"How with others?" she asked.

"Harjeedian's trying to get them to calm down," Derian said. "They're a floor or so up from you, but back around the corner, not directly above. I think there are four alive."

Firekeeper didn't bother to ask which ones. Frankly, until these who had a greater claim on her loyalty and skill were safe, she didn't care.

RAHNISEETA COULDN'T FEEL her right arm below the shoulder, and from the way it flopped when she moved, she was actually glad. With Firekeeper's help, she bound the useless limb close to her torso, and then concentrated on taking orders.

"We lift Sky," Firekeeper said, "you under lower legs. Me upper body. First to window, then over. Lower slowly until those below can catch."

They had rigged a sort of harness around the maimalodalu's upper body. His scales were tougher than those of a snake and Rahniseeta hoped they might protect him some. However, there was no way the constriction about his torso would do him any good.

But what is our choice? Rahniseeta thought. *Leave him here until the building falls?*

Before Firekeeper had reached the top, Rahniseeta had taken a chunk of rock and smashed away the slivers of glass that remained in the windowframe. Even so, as they lifted Sky she noted smears of blood on the stone.

"Move legs over edge," Firekeeper ordered, her voice showing no strain, though she held most of Sky's weight. "Hurry. Floor moves."

Rahniseeta hurried, moving Sky's long, scaled legs to dangle over the edge.

"Now move more," Firekeeper said. "I have rope."

The wolf-woman did, too, wrapped around her body to leave her arms free. They hadn't trusted the stonework to provide a solid anchor.

Rahniseeta felt as if she was pushing Sky out of the window, but the rope slowed his descent, and as she leaned out to grab hold and help steady, she saw that an enormous maimalodalu who resembled a bear as much as anything was standing directly below. They felt the change as soon as he had hold of Sky.

"Get rope," Firekeeper ordered, releasing it from her body as soon as they knew Sky was supported from below. "I check Questioner. Yell. See if they can help you down."

"And leave you and Questioner?"

Firekeeper shrugged.

"Less weight on floor."

Rahniseeta didn't think the wolf-woman could manage alone, so although she retrieved the rope and coiled it ready for use, she did not attempt to descend. Instead, moving as carefully as possible, she went to help Firekeeper.

"Is he alive?"

Firekeeper snorted, and Rahniseeta translated the sound as meaning "Do you think I'd bother if he wasn't?"

Instead of asking anything else, Rahniseeta busied herself helping Firekeeper free the maimalodalu from the wreckage. Questioner looked worse than Sky had, but Rahniseeta took some hope from two things. One, a large piece of planking had fallen over his torso, effectively making a lean-to that protected that vulnerable area from greater injury. Two, from time to time, blue eyes opened, watching for a moment with painful clarity.

One by one they freed the dangling legs, and in another demonstration that he was aware, Questioner drew them close to his body—all but the left foreleg, which he tried to move and then stopped with an involuntary moan of pain. Firekeeper ripped a strip from her already ragged trouser and tied his leg to Questioner's body.

"I'm sorry," she said softly in Pellish. Rahniseeta had never imagined the wolf-woman capable of such pain over something that, after all, had to be done.

There was a tense moment where it seemed that they might not be able to get Questioner's tail free. Firekeeper drew her knife to cut it off, then in an apparent fit of temper smashed the plank that pinned it. This precipitated a minor avalanche, but the tail came free.

"Rope," Firekeeper said at last. "When we have him harnessed, you get on that windowsill or I put you there. I think he holding up that—" She indicated the "lean-to" board with a toss of her head. "And when we move him, it drop, and when it drop . . ."

Rahniseeta understood.

"What are you going to do?"

"I slide him slowly, then lift him, and we lower like Sky."

"And if the floor breaks?"

"That is why you on windowsill."

Throughout the long process, Rahniseeta had been periodically aware of sounds from outside. There had been voices, human and otherwise, shouting orders, occasionally calling up to them for reports on their progress. She gathered there were several different crews at work: trying to rescue the northerners, treating the wounded, and shoring up the tower as best as possible.

Now a clear shrill howl cut through all of this, and at its call, Firekeeper's head snapped up.

She howled in return.

Rahniseeta watched in amazement as Firekeeper's hands tied the final knots on the harness, moving as if unaware of what they did. Periodically the wolf-woman howled, the sounds high and keening, occasionally interspersed with argumentative growls.

The last growl, though, came from Questioner, and at the sound of it, Firekeeper rose stiffly and turned toward the window.

Questioner had said nothing all the while they worked over him, but that growl was clearly no moan of pain. It was an order, and Firekeeper had obeyed.

"Tell me what's going on!" Rahniseeta said sharply.

Firekeeper didn't stop moving.

"Truth say I must get Shivadtmon. I trust Questioner to you. He is my father, and I would not leave."

The wolf-woman's face was alive with grief and fear.

"Do what I say before and maybe it work. Truth say it might."

And on that enigmatic note, Firekeeper climbed heavily onto the windowsill and began groping her way up the side of the tower.

IN THE COOL LITTLE CORNER of his mind that never stopped looking for the advantage, Waln assessed the different ways men faced death.

Four remained of the nine who had gone in. Tedgewinn and Elwyn were presumably buried beneath the collapse their foolishness had started, and as Waln saw it, the only pity was that they'd have such a large monument to mark their graves.

Rarby was somewhere down there, too. He'd been mounting the stairs when the crash came and had vanished in a cloud of dirt and stone. Nolan had been standing a few steps from the top, and had lost his balance. His raw scream as he fell still echoed distractingly in Waln's imagination, though it had long since vanished from the air. He had no idea where Rahniseeta was, nor did he care.

The survivors—Waln, Shivadtmon, Wiatt, and Shelby—crouched on an island where the two sides of the half-moon-shaped building met. The stairs had broken off beneath them, cascading down, each hitting the ones beneath until just stubs of stonework remained. The portion of the staircase that remained was nowhere near them—even if any of them had felt the impulse to climb up to the teetering remains of the stepped top.

Down wasn't that attractive either—not now that what had been hiding in the forest and the other towers had come out. Gigantic beasts prowled among the scattered stones—for not all the detritus had fallen into the shell of the tower—and here and there among them monsters could be seen. Moreover, not one of them was uninjured, and while the injuries were far from fatal, the pain reminded them of the risks they would be taking.

Yes. It was interesting to study the different ways men faced death.

Shelby was obviously shattered by the death of his older brother, so shocked that he felt neither anger nor regret. Indeed, Waln would be surprised if he felt much of anything at all. Shelby sat at the point where two corners of the wall met, the crossbow he'd somehow retained unloaded and resting idly between his knees. There was a nasty cut on his forehead, but the blood had mostly stopped flowing, leaving Shelby's features bordered in dried blood.

Looks like we have a new nominee for ship's fool now that Elwyn's dead, Waln thought, but despite the jocular cast he tried to give his thoughts, Shelby made him uneasy. There was no telling what his mood would be when he emerged from the shock, and Waln depended on having some idea how those he led would react.

Wiatt had proven equally unpredictable. He'd come close to falling—indeed, if one wanted to be perfectly technical about it, he had fallen, but he had caught the jutting edge of a broken beam and laboriously pulled himself to the relative safety of this aerie. In the process, he'd banged his right knee badly, and even wrapping it hadn't stopped it from ballooning up to twice its size. However, even with the pain from his knee, Wiatt's biggest worry seemed to be how the yarimaimalom would react when he reached the ground.

"You don't think they know I'm the one who shot that arrow?" he kept asking. "They couldn't have seen it was me, right? I was behind a wall then. Do you think they could smell me on the bolt? Surely they can't. I only handled it for a moment."

This, or variations thereof, spilled from his lips so continuously that Waln was rapidly able to ignore the sound as he ignored the sound of the wind when he was at sea. What bothered him more was that Wiatt had dropped his crossbow and bolts down among the wreckage.

But neither Shelby's brooding silence nor Wiatt's nervous nattering bothered Waln as much as how Shivadtmon was treating the situation. Initially, Waln had thought the aridisdu both composed and uninjured. He had been grateful for that composure while he had inspected the other men for injuries and inventoried what gear was left to them. That hadn't proved to be much. Most of what they had carried up from the *Islander* either had been left below or had been stacked on a floor that was now indistinguishable from rubble.

When Waln had asked Shivadtmon if the other had, by chance, held on to one of the bundles of rope, the aridisdu had looked at him calmly.

"I don't understand how this could happen. She invited me. The door opened. Why would she let this happen?"

"Maybe it wasn't her that opened the door," Waln said, "maybe it was one of those monstrosities. You saw them coming out of the other towers. They live here."

But Shivadtmon had responded to this sensible statement with a small shake of his head.

"Magic invited me. I am sure of it. Somehow I have missed something crucial."

"Well, if you think of a way we can get down," Waln said, "intact and alive, that is—the other way is easy enough—let me know."

Shivadtmon had granted Waln a distant and bemused nod, and gone back to staring at the ruined stonework.

All three of them driven mad, Waln thought, *and so no help to me, but it would be best if we all got down. We've been through a lot, wouldn't look good at all if I left them. Of course, if Shivadtmon took a tumble, then we could claim he put us up to this—he did really—and it would only be his word against ours.*

But then Waln remembered cursed Barnet Lobster, presumably alive and comfortable on the *Islander*, and knew he couldn't make that work.

Waln had tried to see if he could climb down the outside, but two things prevented him. A wrist he'd twisted somehow in the crash wouldn't bear his weight—but more important, he couldn't make himself take that step over the edge without so much as a line to cling to. He didn't like how the stone shifted and grated, how the mortar crumbed and crumbled. Give him honest rigging and he could still climb with the best, but on stone, with unforgiving ground beneath him, he might as well be a landsman.

Waln pulled himself back onto the relative solidity of what was seeming more and more like an island in the sky, and wondered why no one was getting around to rescuing them. He knew how his own people would react in a similar situation. All hands would struggle to rescue a sailor from drowning even if he was due for flogging as soon as he got out of sick bay.

Maybe these Liglimom didn't see things that way. Maybe—like Shivadtmon—they saw this all as a punishment sent by their deities, and it would be up to Waln and the others to get themselves out. That was an ugly thought, and Waln was still considering it when he glimpsed the fiery red hair of Derian Carter down below. He was walking with a large wolf Waln thought might be Lady Blysse's companion.

"Hey, Derian Counselor!" Waln shouted as loudly as if he were in a storm at sea, not thirty or so feet off the ground.

"Hey, Waln Endbrook," Derian replied, looking up. The wolf beside him looked up as well, his jaws gaping apart and showing a wealth of teeth. "Didn't you know Misheemnekuru is off-limits to humans?"

Waln ignored this banter, thinking it in rather bad taste.

"Tell me. Is anyone going to help us down from here? Even a line would be useful."

"There was only one rope here," Derian said, "and it's in use. We've sent runners to the boats, and then we'll see what can be done."

Waln didn't bother to ask what the other rope was being used for. He'd heard noise around the other side of the structure and assumed that someone—Rahniseeta most likely—was being gotten down.

"Runners will take a while" was all he said.

"These less than most," Derian replied. "They sent a couple of white-tail bucks. I wrote a note for Barnet. Hopefully, he'll figure things out."

Waln nodded. He'd wondered why Derian hadn't asked the obvious questions, like how many were alive, and how badly injured and all that. Then he'd realized that there must be those among the birds who could report to Lady Blysse. The thought made his skin crawl, even as he was grateful.

"You have water?" Derian asked.

"Some."

"Then stay as still as possible. You can't see it from there, I guess, but whenever you go pacing about, things start crumbling. They're working on shoring up things, but nobody has a lot of experience with this. Can your carpenter advise?"

"He's one of the ones who created this mess," Waln replied bitterly.

"Ah."

There wasn't a lot to say after that. Waln passed on the warning about keeping still, but Wiatt insisted on going close to the edge and calling down his interminable litany to Derian.

Derian seemed amused rather than otherwise.

"If they didn't know before," he said, "they do now. However, I think they're willing to leave you to the authorities."

Wiatt seemed relieved by this, and Waln didn't bother to point out that here the authorities were likely to be animals—or worse, one of those monsters. He'd kept shying away from looking too closely at them, but what he'd seen . . . Well, he'd been to New Kelvin, and he didn't think those were costumes.

Forbidden to pace in body, Waln did so in spirit, his mind swinging back and forth, trying to find the best way to deal with this once they were down. There was no question that they'd violated their host's laws. Could they claim they'd been bewitched? It had been an acceptable defense in Bright Bay until fifty years after the Plague. Would it work here?

"Shivadtmon," he called softly. "Do your people have tales of magic being used to influence how others think?"

The aridisdu looked at him curiously.

"We call it divine inspiration."

"No. I don't mean divine magic. I mean the human type—like that woman Melina I told you about."

Shivadtmon's eyes narrowed. "All magic is divine. Humans may misuse it, but Magic is one of the divinities."

"Forget it," Waln said, but Shivadtmon was looking at him very strangely.

"Magic invited me," the aridisdu said. "The master sent me. How can this wrongness have happened? Is Magic testing me? Is she seeing if I am faithful?"

Waln shrugged, trying hard to say the right thing.

"You're the aridisdu. Can you read the omens? Does Magic want something from you?"

Shivadtmon's eyes brightened with alarming intensity.

"Something of me . . . and the master has taught us what the deities want, what has been withheld from them for too long."

"Well, then pray to Magic," Waln said, hoping he didn't sound exasperated. "Promise her you'll give her whatever it is when you're down from here."

"Better," Shivadtmon said, rising to his feet and pulling his knife from its sheath. "I'll give it to her right now."

XXXIX

FIREKEEPER FELT THE INSTABILITY in the stonework as she climbed, but by now she trusted Truth—or at least the jaguar's ability to see what was important.

This time her climb was as much horizontal as vertical, going along the rounded edge of the tower before pushing upward. Here she did not have as far up to go. At this point, the fourth-story walls had almost completely collapsed, and rather than climbing to a window ledge, she simply went through a hole in what had been the outer wall. A few smaller stones crashed down in her wake, but she didn't have time to worry about that.

Her ears had not been closed as she climbed, so she knew she was coming into trouble. What she hadn't realized was how much.

To her left, Shivadtmon had backed Waln Endbrook against a stand of lath and plaster that was all that remained of an interior wall. Firekeeper could easily envision what had happened. Shivadtmon had come at Waln with the knife that still was in his hand, and Waln, unprepared, had backed away, only to discover too late that he had made his situation worse. He had his hands out in front of him as if by that alone he could keep the aridisdu back.

"Shivadtmon, in the name of all the ancestors, what's gotten into you? Someone stop him! He'll be for you if you don't do something. Do something!"

The other two sailors had not ignored Waln's pleas. Firekeeper heard Wiatt shouting something about not acting crazy, that they'd have the whole rest of the mess down about their ears if they weren't careful. He'd thrown away his own bow, she recalled, so doubtless shouting was all he could do. No harm in that.

Shelby was another matter. Firekeeper had heard the wingéd folk's report that since he had learned of his brother's death Shelby had done nothing but sit staring off into space. Shivadtmon's action, however, had penetrated his despair. Now he had risen and was slotting a bolt into place. Firekeeper recalled that Shelby, like his brother, was skilled in arms and didn't think that he would miss.

She finished pulling herself onto the level, then rose to her knees, grasping blindly for something she might throw, for she was reluctant to relinquish her Fang. Waln's frantic chatter provided ample distraction. Indeed, she wondered if any had noticed her arrival, so focused were all on Shivadtmon and Waln.

Waln yammered on, "Shivadtmon, Magic doesn't want me. You've misread the omens, I think. That door wasn't an invitation . . ."

Firekeeper's fingers found a stone of throwing size. Normally, she would have leapt to her feet and thrown in one motion, but she remembered the warnings about how unstable this area was and settled for raising herself to one knee.

Shelby had loaded his bow and was aiming carefully, his task made more difficult because although Waln had nowhere to run, he was ducking back and forth, trying to evade the blade with which Shivadtmon was tracing patterns in the air an arm's length from his body.

Shivadtmon was muttering something, too, but Firekeeper hadn't learned Liglimosh well enough to grasp the meaning in his elaborate wording. She'd seen magic being done before, and recognized the signs. For a moment she paused, uncertain who her target should be. Then she remembered Truth's warning and threw.

Her rock caught Shelby in the stomach just as he was about to fire. The crossbow went off, but the bolt did not find its mark. Instead of hitting Shivadtmon, it impacted squarely in the main beam supporting the section of wall against which Waln had been backed.

The beam, already abused, could not take the added strain. It snapped with a sharp, almost metallic sound, and the fragile construction that relied upon it went with it.

Waln staggered, but reflexes trained on the pitching decks and swaying riggings of oceangoing ships would not let him fall. He compensated, swaying forward, and met the knife Shivadtmon had been about to plunge into the vicinity of his heart.

The long blade met Waln's gut instead, ripping in and up, tearing through muscle and intestines with not only the force of Shivadtmon's blow, but with all Waln's own desperate attempt to keep from falling.

Firekeeper saw the blood wash forth, smelled the stink of bowel, and knew there was no saving him—but then saving Waln Endbrook had never been part of her plan. She picked up another rock and surged to her feet. To her left Shivadtmon was shrieking something, the only part of which she understood was the beginning:

"You have heard me! Lady who is the Moon, give your servant . . ."

Over to the right, Shelby, dually unbalanced by the recoil of his bow and the rock Firekeeper had thrown, was swaying back and forth, trying to regain his balance. Firekeeper didn't care if he did this, but didn't think he should be permitted to keep the bow. Having it aimed at her would make rescuing Shivadtmon even more difficult than it was already turning out to be.

She hefted her new rock and looked over at Wiatt.

"Help Shelby, but no bow or my people not forget you shot at them, understand?"

Wiatt quite clearly did. It probably helped that he was used to taking orders and that her orders fit neatly in with his own personal mania. Firekeeper heard him calling to Shelby, and put those two from her mind. Even if Shelby didn't listen to Wiatt, he was going to have trouble shooting Shivadtmon around the cook, and if he shot Wiatt, Firekeeper would hear.

She took careful aim and threw her rock. She didn't dare put too much strength behind the throw lest she knock Shivadtmon forward and into the collapsed interior of the tower. What she wanted was to turn his attention away from whatever he was screaming over Waln's corpse and toward her.

Her rock caught Shivadtmon right where she had aimed, squarely on his right shoulder blade. The aridisdu's incantation halted in a gulp of surprise and pain, but he started again almost immediately.

Firekeeper heard a raven's croak from somewhere immediately above her, recognized Bitter's voice.

"Truth says the tower will not hold much longer. Get Shivadtmon and yourself down."

Firekeeper did not waste breath or motion replying, but some small part of her wanted to wring the raven's neck. Didn't he see she was already doing everything she could? The aridisdu had a knife and he'd already shown himself all too willing to use it on behalf of this weird divinity.

Eschewing safety now, she moved forward, her Fang drawn and ready.

"Shivadtmon!" she shouted. "The tower falls. Come away!"

Shivadtmon wheeled and stared at her in incomprehension, his eyes filled with such intensity that Firekeeper felt scorched.

"Magic herself will bear me away," he said grandly. "I called upon her, and she says the sacrifice is good."

Firekeeper darted out her knife hand and struck the blade from Shivadtmon's own.

"I am to bear you away," she growled. "Truth say. Come."

Shivadtmon looked down where her Fang had scored a thin line across the back of his hand, then raised the hand to his mouth and licked away the blood.

"Perhaps Magic has sent you," he said with insane mildness. "Lead on."

Firekeeper didn't trust the aridisdu to follow, but grabbed him by one wrist and, with her blade pricking reminder at his back, hustled him along to the outer edge of the tower. She wondered how she could carry him down, but resolved to face that problem once they were there. The stones were vibrating under her bare feet and she knew she didn't have time even to worry.

Wiatt had succeeded in steadying Shelby and in getting him to drop his bow. Now both were looking over the edge. Derian's voice came up from below.

"Jump, you idiots. It's your only chance!"

Firekeeper wondered what sort of chance anyone had in a jump from so high onto paved ground, but she understood when she came to her own edge. Harjeedian stood below, and when he saw them, he snapped a command.

Instantly, a wide sheet of something pulled tight, held around the edges by Harjeedian, some of the maimalodalum, a bear, and several wolves.

"Jump!" Harjeedian yelled. "Jump!"

Firekeeper didn't give Shivadtmon time to think. She pushed him, and saw him go over, too astonished to even draw himself tight. Limp was the best way to fall, she reminded herself as she waited for the aridisdu to be gotten off the canvas and it to be drawn tight again.

She glanced over to Shelby and Wiatt. Wiatt was vacillating, but the crumbling of the edge beneath his feet made up his mind for him. He went over the outer edge, his scream of terror high and shrill. Shelby watched him fall, then stood for a moment in contemplation.

He looked at Firekeeper.

"I don't want to explain to the folks about Rarby," he said. "It's all my fault he was here." Turning toward the interior, Shelby jumped into the pit that had already claimed his brother's life.

Firekeeper felt the bile rise to her mouth and incomprehension paralyze her. Blind Seer's howl, deep and filled with desperation, broke into her daze.

"Beloved! Jump! The tower falls! Jump!"

And Firekeeper grabbed on to his voice as if it were a lifeline and threw herself out into space.

"BARNET SENT UP THE CANVAS," Derian explained as he sponged Firekeeper's scrapes. "He thought, well, he thought we might need it to wrap bodies. That's what they do at sea."

Firekeeper, bruised everywhere she wasn't scraped or cut, and sometimes both, hardly cared what anyone did anywhere, but after all the strangeness, she appreciated the familiarity of Derian's very human way of supplying unneeded information.

Humans might be kin to ravens, she thought. *That would explain a great deal.*

"Tell me," Firekeeper said, "who lives, and who not."

Derian looked as if he'd rather continue talking about burial customs at sea, but he looked at where Blind Seer was licking some of the worst of Firekeeper's scrapes and seemed to realize that if he didn't tell, the wolf would stop his first aid and do so.

"Sky," Derian began, "the first one you sent down, he didn't make it. His head was too badly broken. Wiatt's knee was already a mess, I understand, and he broke a couple bones falling—and when the rocks that fell with him hit him. Still, he should make it. None of the other sailors have been found alive, but some of the yarimaimalom are sniffing around to make sure. The tower's down now, and there's not much danger."

"Rahniseeta? Questioner?"

"Alive, but . . ." Derian swallowed hard. "Firekeeper, it's still not certain if they'll pull through. Race had shown me how to make a tree-trunk ladder and one of the maimalodalu helped me. I got up that way and Rahniseeta and I got Questioner down. Then I helped her down, but the wall didn't like all that weight leaning against it. That's probably part of what pushed it on its way."

"It would go anyway," Firekeeper said. "Truth say."

"Truth is another problem," Derian said. "She's gone again wherever she went before, and this time no perfume is going to pull her back."

Firekeeper was astonished enough by this bit of knowledge on his part to be momentarily distracted from her fear for Questioner and Rahniseeta.

"How you know this?"

"Blind Seer told Hope. Hope told me. Firekeeper, you didn't tell me about the maimalodalum. They're . . . incredible. I thought I'd lose my breakfast when Harjee-dian and I followed Blind Seer over here and saw, but it's true what they say about need clearing away differences. After a while, all I could see was that they had hands—some of them did, anyhow—and we needed hands more than anything."

Firekeeper remembered hands, the hands that had saved her when she was dying.

"I must see Questioner."

Derian helped her to her feet without comment. Blind Seer gave a long scrape on one leg a final lick and said, *"Follow me."*

Derian came with them.

"Firekeeper, Rahniseeta said you said something about Questioner being your father?"

"No and yes, not like Colby yours, but I would not live if not for him. Later, I tell all."

Derian nodded.

They found Questioner, Rahniseeta, and Wiatt all on pallets in a ground-floor room of the eight-sided Tower of Fire. Questioner wasn't moving, but a wolf Fire-keeper did not know lay beside him holding one of his hand-paws in her mouth, so Firekeeper took hope that he was not dead. Wolves were singularly unsentimental about dead meat.

Wiatt was moaning softly, but seemed to be asleep. Rahniseeta also was asleep, but she made not a sound and her breathing was shallow. Harjeedian sat beside her, look-ing very worried.

"I gave her something to make her sleep," he said. "She was frantic."

"She was more than frantic," Hope said, coming forth from another room with a pitcher in her hands. "She is burning alive with fever, but refused any treatment until Questioner was helped. He wanted the wolf to tend to her, but she refused and would not accept even what help her brother could give her until we promised all our efforts would go to save Questioner."

Firekeeper understood.

"This wolf—I think Integrity told me of her—she has healing talent?"

"That's right," Hope said.

She poured the contents of the pitcher into a basin and a scent of herbs, among which Firekeeper immediately identified lemon balm, lavender, and chamomile, touched the air. Harjeedian took a cloth and started sponging Rahniseeta's fevered skin.

"Questioner made clear he knew his wounds were severe and that the healer's talents were to go to Rahniseeta, but she refused. She said she'd put him and Sky at risk, and, well, she was making herself worse, so we promised her we'd do as she wished."

Firekeeper realized that one name had been omitted from Derian's account.

"Shivadtmon. Does he live?"

Hope gave her a strange look.

"He does, and we have him under guard in the Tower of Air. Do you realize. . . ."

She stopped. Firekeeper, who had been moving to get a better look at Questioner and reassure herself that Questioner was indeed breathing, stared at her.

"I not realize anything except I do what Truth say and get him down alive. What?"

"Shivadtmon doesn't have a mark on him, Firekeeper," the bird-woman said softly. "Not a scrape or a bruise, not a scratch or a nick. He's not even dirty. His clothing is a complete wreck, like you'd expect, but his person is unmarred. He keeps going on about Magic taking him under her protection—and it looks as if he may be right."

DANTARAHMA AND THE OTHER MEMBERS of u-Liall were briefed as to the departure of the northerners to Misheemnekuru soon after the earliest services were completed. The news was brought by the iaridisdu and ikidisdu of the Temple of the Cold Bloods, and in their eyes he saw omens that something else was coming. However, they said nothing but that one of their own, the aridisdu Harjeedian, had taken a small boat and was delivering Lady Blysse and several of the yarimaimalom to Misheemnekuru. Derian Carter was sailing with them, but it was left unsaid whether the humans actually intended to go ashore.

As soon as the conclave was adjourned, Dantarahma shut himself in his office and netted a fish from the aquarium he kept there—ostensibly for ornamentation. Such little creatures were not the best for blood auguries, but Dantarahma had become very skilled. He spilled the swimmer's guts onto a clean sheet of vellum, and the manner in which they swirled and the patterns cast by the droplets of blood told him all he needed to know.

Events were not progressing precisely as Dantarahma might have wished. All his planning had depended on no one knowing the intimacy of the link between Shivadtmon and himself. The augury showed that some knew far more than they should—and when the news of the violation of Misheemnekuru became general knowledge, these would share what they knew.

Dantarahma did not have to spill another fish's blood to know that things would not go well for him then. At the very least he would lose his position. He might lose his freedom as well, and there was a possibility that he might lose his life.

But Dantarahma had not been a scholar of omens and probabilities for over half a century without learning to plan for contingencies. The rulers of the little city states to the south included some he counted as friends and allies. He would go to them. There were boats ready in the harbor, and none would question the junjaldisdu taking out the one reserved for him, especially when such a crisis had arisen on Misheemnekuru.

Dantarahma went to his office door and spoke to the clerk on duty. That this one was also an initiate into the mysteries of blood, Dantarahma took as a sign that the deities favored him.

He favored the clerk with a gentle smile.

"Send word to the harbor to have my vessel readied for me. I also wish two other boats of the same class to accompany me. The sails on all must be blue-green, but take care that there are white ones in my vessel's locker as well. If you wish to sail with me, you are welcome. If those who also have celebrated the mysteries make up the crew of my vessel, well and good."

The clerk, a minor aridisdu with a greater talent for administration than for augury, understood.

"All shall be readied, Dantarahma." The clerk glanced at the tide tables pinned to the wall alongside the calendar. "The tides will be favorable for some hours yet."

"Good. I will be in my chambers, preparing the appropriate accoutrements."

As much as Dantarahma longed to leave instantly, he could not. The city-states would welcome him with much more gentility if he did not come empty-handed. Then, too, there were books and papers he would need to continue his work. However, this too he had prepared ahead, for the omens had always been that in this matter he danced on the curve of the moon.

And Dantarahma knew he had time. Those who would oppose him would not confront him without first explaining matters to the other members of u-Liall. These, already distracted by the news about Misheemnekuru, would not welcome further trouble—or not all of them would. He fancied Tiridanti would jump at the chance to bring him down, but neither Noonafaruma nor Feeshaguyu would be so eager. Old Bibimalenu was in his dotage and half deaf besides.

No. He would have time. He prepared fully, and no summons came for him from u-Liall. When the word came that the ordered ships were ready, Dantarahma left for the harbor without haste and with all due decorum.

The divinities had been with him on the matter of finding a crew. Shivadtmon had already assigned many of their allies to the ship that was to carry them north. Dantarahma's clerk had merely reassigned the most devout of these sailors to Dantarahma's smaller vessel.

Dantarahma boarded his chosen vessel in all state.

"Sail for Misheemnekuru," he ordered the captain, "but keep to the southern side. When we are out of clear sight of land, we will change sails and head south."

The ship's captain, long in Dantarahma's confidence regarding these plans, nodded.

"Very good, sir. Winds are fresh and we should be easily away."

Dantarahma smiled and went to the bow, standing proud despite his years, so the people on shore could see him. Spray kissed his face, and he knew the deities were with him.

ELWYN'S EMERGING FROM the cellar beneath the tower the next morning, battered but not severely injured, his arms overburdened with a rotting sack of jewel-encrusted chains, should have been the most amazing event following the defeat of Waln and the capture of Shivadtmon, but to Derian's way of seeing things, it was not.

Far more astonishing was finding himself seated within the pentagon-shaped center room of the star-shaped Tower of Air taking part in a council that consisted of yarimaimalom, maimalodalum, himself, Harjeedian, and, of course, Firekeeper and Blind Seer.

Rahniseeta was still deep in a drugged sleep, but the wolf with the healing talent—called, with wolfish directness, Healer—was reported as guardedly hopeful regarding her recovery. Rahniseeta's arm was badly broken, and whether or not she would regain full use of it remained in doubt, but all that could be done for her had been done.

Now Healer reclined with her paws before her alongside Questioner. The maimalodalu looked weak, but he had apparently insisted on being present for this meeting. Healer's side touched Questioner's, and Derian wondered whether she was giving him more than physical support.

He wondered a good many things, actually, and had been promised that a few would be clarified here.

Since everyone present understood Liglimosh, the meeting was conducted in that language. The two humans had been assured that whatever the yarimaimalom said would be translated by Hope.

Harjeedian had looked more rueful than Derian had thought possible upon learning that the maimalodalum could translate for the yarimaimalom.

"To think I went north and to all that trouble thinking I would be bringing something new to our land."

Derian was surprised to find himself comforting a man he'd thought he'd always dislike.

"You did bring back something new—I assure you, you won't find more than one Firekeeper anywhere."

Harjeedian nodded. Firekeeper was sitting surrounded by wolves. Blind Seer was at her right, an enormous one Derian had learned was named Dark Death pressed close at her left. A silvery grey female with a splinted leg hovered to the side of Dark

Death. It looked as if Firekeeper had a pack of her own, and Derian wondered uneasily if the wolf-woman would be staying here on Misheemnekuru.

Harjeedian was thinking about a matter closer to his own heart.

"The maimalodalum will not commit to saying they will let their existence be known. I think they have grown used to this life. However, they did confirm that the yarimaimalom who have acted as diviners no more willingly led us astray than did any aridisdu."

Derian grinned. Harjeedian hadn't said so, but that answer clearly meant that there had been times when diviners had skewed the answers to their advantage, but on the whole, they were probably honest. That made him think of Truth. The jaguar was not present as far as he could tell, though to him one jaguar still looked much like another. He started to ask Harjeedian if he knew, when Powerful Tenderness, the maimalodalu who blended the qualities of a human and a bear with a touch of reptile, opened the meeting.

"First," Powerful Tenderness said, his voice gruff, "a few matters some of you already know. Last night one of the ospreys carried a missive to Meiyal, iaridisdu of the Horse. In it, Harjeedian reported fairly truthfully the events that had occurred. Omitted were specific mention of the maimalodalum and the role they played. Stressed instead were that the northerners and Shivadtmon had been captured, and that while Derian, Harjeedian, and Rahniseeta were being given leave to stay on the island, that this in no way should be seen as waiving the yarimaimalom's exclusive claim to Misheemnekuru.

"Meiyal sent a message in return. Yesterday morning, fairly early, Dantarahma, the junjaldisdu, took to sea in a boat capable of limited ocean sailing. He was accompanied by two other boats. All flew colored sails, but when the vessel carrying Dantarahma was out of sight of land, it changed its sails to the more usual white. Then, according to the captains of the two boats that were his escort, they were ordered to sail north, cutting in and out of sight from shore among the islands, while Dantarahma's vessel went south. Essentially, Dantarahma has fled. This is being taken as a confirmation of the accusations brought against him by Meiyal on behalf of Derian, who in turn spoke on behalf of Eshinarvash and other of the mainland-dwelling yarimaimalom."

For a long moment, Derian found himself the focus of any number of inhuman eyes. He was uncomfortable in a way he had not been during the numerous crises of the afternoon and evening before, but shook the feeling from him. He'd seen how some of the Liglimom had shied from his red hair and, by their standards, light eyes. Rahniseeta had been inordinately fascinated by his freckles; they didn't happen on her darker-skinned people.

He recalled how she had laughed, confessing that had she known about them she would have been even more certain he was one of the maimalodalum, for the Wise Horses were very often paints or spotted.

I wonder if she'd had any idea what the real thing was like would she have been so eager to find one? Derian thought. *I wish I could tease her about it.*

He forced himself to listen as Powerful Tenderness reported on Truth's condition.

"Truth is far gone into possibility," Powerful Tenderness began, "so far gone that there is doubt she will ever be drawn forth again. Even if she does come back to us, there will be no alternative but to attempt to keep her from divining, or risk losing her again. Therefore, it has been divined that Bright-Eyes-Fast-Paws will take her place representing the island jaguars at the court of Tiridanti for the remainder of this jaguar year. We thank the deities for their firm guidance on this matter."

There was a prayerful muttering to acknowledge this statement, and Derian realized that only he, Firekeeper, and Blind Seer had not automatically reacted.

Shape doesn't seem to matter, he thought. *In this, at least, Blind Seer is closer kin to me than Harjeedian would be—or Rahniseeta?*

The thought made him very uncomfortable, as if he'd somehow been unfaithful to her.

"We now must address the matter of Shivadtmon," Powerful Tenderness went on, "and come to a conclusion as to how to deal with what he represents. We must deal with Elwyn and Wiatt, the surviving northerners. However, as will be seen, their crime is merely one of trespass and willingness to do violence in order to steal. Shivadtmon's is far more serious."

Next, the bear-human-reptile summarized what had occurred, including Shivadtmon's role as Dantarahma's tool, his deliberate misleading of Waln and his followers regarding Misheemnekuru, and, finally, in greatest detail, what had happened atop Magic's tower.

"Are you saying," Hope asked, interpreting for a wolf called Integrity, "that the evidence is that Shivadtmon actually performed magic?"

Powerful Tenderness looked at the wolf as he replied, "Yes. As you know, we of the maimalodalum can sense magic as you hear sound. The ability varies among us, but at the moment the wingéd folk report that Shivadtmon's knife took Waln Endbrook's life, each and every one of us felt something. Those of you who were working beside us may recall the moment."

There was a general stirring among the yarimaimalom and Derian did not need a translator to know this was confirmation. Harjeedian looked very uncomfortable.

"I was working with Healer over Questioner at that time, and saw the reaction mentioned. I was called out almost immediately after, however, to hold the canvas onto which Shivadtmon and Firekeeper jumped. When he landed, I distinctly heard what Shivadtmon said: 'I prayed to Magic and she answered my prayers.' Are you saying that he believed he prayed, but what he did was sorcery?"

Questioner stirred, and Derian instinctively knew that this was why he had insisted on being present.

"Harjeedian," Questioner said, "what I am saying—and not all my kin agree—is that where blood is involved, there is no difference between sorcery and prayer. The rituals involved may be called prayer, but they are sorcery. I think one grew from the other."

Harjeedian looked offended, as well he might.

"But, Questioner—though I understand your divined name is Defier-of-the-Deities, and now I have some idea why—that is blasphemy. Our records show that blood sacrifice was involved in the earliest rites of prayer. We evolved away from it over time, especially as the lore of the aridisdu devolved to provide other ways of knowing the divine will, but it was not until the time of Divine Retribution that the practice was relinquished—and then, so many argue, it was as much a secular decision, meant to ease our relations with the yarimaimalom, as one willed by the deities."

"So argued Dantarahma," Questioner said.

A fit of coughing forced the wounded maimalodalu to stop, and Powerful Tenderness took up the account.

"Harjeedian, the most sensitive of us—the ones with the best 'hearing' for matters of magic—have long sensed something awry on the mainland. We think that Dantarahma also was aware of us. We believe he took actions to prevent us from sensing what he and his fellows did. Therefore, we were uncertain whether we were sensing something more than an unusually powerful talent or some minor artifact sporadically at work.

"We do not think it was chance that Dantarahma sent his minion not merely to Misheemnekuru, but precisely to this island. If the matter was merely, as Shivadtmon says, to weaken the yarimaimalom's claim to exclusive use of these islands, then touching ground anywhere would do, but Shivadtmon was steered—and Waln Endbrook through him—to this one island out of so many, to the very place where those who could sense Dantarahma's actions lived.

"The northerners as a whole view anything magical as an abomination. They might make an exception for a beautiful piece of jewelry that might or might not be magical in nature, but for a maimalodalu? Waln was a violent man, as were many of his followers. I think Dantarahma expected—perhaps he had even divined—the likelihood of our paths crossing, and of our being destroyed or so severely weakened that we would no longer offer a threat to him. At the very least, he would receive confirmation as to our existence, learn whether he was threatened by a peculiarly talented yarimaimalo or—as I think he divined—something else."

Harjeedian had remained silent through all this long speech, but anguish remained on his face as he spoke.

"Are you saying that the miracles we credit to the intervention of the deities in our lives are instead the foulest of sorcerous practices?"

Questioner was blunt, but not unkind.

"That is the very question I asked myself when my travels took me into lands that did not know the deities as we do. You call me blasphemous, but I think of myself as one who would sort truth from the fraud. Only when that is done will I look upon the face of the divine unshrouded by confusion."

"And have you done so?" Harjeedian asked harshly.

"I came home again," Questioner replied, "and it remains my home. Find your answer in that."

The pain it caused Questioner to speak was obvious, but Derian rather thought it was how Healer bared her fangs that made Harjeedian cease his inquiry.

"Returning to the immediate problem of Shivadtmon," Powerful Tenderness said, "Truth averred that saving his life was essential, but she is gone to where she cannot tell us why."

Hope spoke for the jaguar Bright-Eyes-Fast-Paws.

"I do not have Truth's ability, but this much is clear. Shivadtmon must live because through Shivadtmon's testimony Dantarahma will be completely discredited. Moreover, Shivadtmon can identify others who shared worship with Dantarahma. Right now, Shivadtmon is still exhilarated from what he believes is a showing of divine favor, but when that elevation leaves him, there are several ways to convince him to assist us. I will be pleased to advise."

Derian swallowed hard, noticing now the jaguar had raised a paw from which claws extended, but he did not think physical violence would be the first resort. Shivadtmon's vanity might be appealed to, or it could be pointed out to him how he had been used and then abandoned. Derian would make sure these suggestions got to someone, just in case they needed advice on the workings of the human mind.

"And after?" Hope asked, speaking for the raven Bitter. "What do we do then? Has Shivadtmon been blessed or is he our curse?"

This led to a considerable amount of debate, and although Hope did her best to translate, Derian lost some of it. The end result was that if at all possible the fact that Shivadtmon had done magic must be concealed, lest intelligent listeners draw appropriate conclusions—and some ambitious ones chose to act on it.

"The fact is," said a maimalodalu whose name Derian had missed, "Shivadtmon was in a very good place for sorcery and had what may be the ideal sacrifice. It has been suggested that taking the life of one of one's own kind—thus symbolically slaying the self—is a powerful magical conduit."

"So," Hope said, speaking for herself this time, "I suggest we do not give any of the details. Harjeedian's report told that most of the northerners were killed when the tower fell. When Shivadtmon calms, I think he will not wish to boast of killing another human. Murder is not looked upon highly even in the civil courts. It is punished far more severely in sacred law."

Harjeedian smiled one of his thin-lipped, snaky smiles.

"I think that I can say a thing or two to lead Shivadtmon's thoughts in the right direction. I believe I can be subtle enough that he will not see himself led."

His offer was accepted, and the discussion moved on to the matter of Elwyn and Wiatt.

To Derian's relief, neither sailor was to be executed, but equally, neither would be permitted to leave Misheemnekuru.

"They will be our prisoners," Powerful Tenderness said. "Frankly, I would not like to be the one who tries to harm Elwyn. His luck is incredibly powerful. His nature is crude, but his intelligence childlike. I think, in time, he could be happy here. Wiatt may be less so, but although he was strongly led, still, he made his own decisions."

"One thing more," Powerful Tenderness said. "The humans have sent boats after Dantarahma, but, perhaps out of shame, they have not asked for our assistance. A seal or dolphin could do a great deal to limit the search—so could seagulls or ospreys. What are the omens?"

"We help," said Bright-Eyes-Fast-Paws the jaguar. "Even were I not a diviner, I would know this. Dantarahma must be stopped, lest he spread his blood cult to other susceptible minds. Moreover, the humans must know he is dead so they can name another to his place without hesitation."

"And those who sailed with him?" asked Questioner. "What of them?"

"Boats sink," said the jaguar with finality, and no one disagreed.

XL

FIREKEEPER HAD SAID NOTHING during the long conference, for she felt this was not her place. However, overall she approved of the course chosen by the yarimaimalom and the maimalodalum.

"Or perhaps," she said to Blind Seer as they left the star-shaped tower, "I should simply think of them all as Liglimom, for they are alike beneath their shapes, different as all beasts are different, but alike in their worship of these deities they rely upon for guidance."

"And you?" Blind Seer asked. "Have you decided what you are?"

Firekeeper would have answered, for recently she had thought a great deal on the matter, but Dark Death, who had been as her shadow since her return to Misheem-nekuru, sometimes forcing himself very rudely into her company, now snarled at Blind Seer.

"You can ask Firekeeper that? You who claim to love her? She is a wolf, a marvelous wolf, and if you were not such a coward, she could have all she desires."

"Are you as lost to reality as Truth?" Blind Seer snapped. "What are you saying?"

"I know a way that Firekeeper can have her dream," Dark Death replied, and there was no hiding the menace beneath what he said. "Fight me, Blind Seer. Fight me, and if you win, Firekeeper can have my life and take my shape. We have heard today how magic works, and know what is the most powerful sacrifice, do we not? Magic's tower may have fallen, but we know that she listens to those who give her worship."

Blind Seer growled, his ears flattening against his skull, his eyes narrowing.

"And if you beat me?"

"Then you promise the same," Dark Death replied evenly. "I thought you treasured Firekeeper. Do you treasure her so little that you will not help her gain what she most desires? She is a marvel of strength and courage. Her human shape lets her climb and use weapons. What might she achieve if she possessed a wolf's shape as well?"

"Stop!" Firekeeper ordered. "I will have nothing of this. I have already said this making of maimalodalum is a foul practice."

Neither of the males heard her, so concentrated were they on each other, locked in a conflict as old as time.

"I love Firekeeper," Blind Seer snarled. "None will question that."

"Then you fear me, fear losing to me," Dark Death taunted. "That is why you will not fight me."

"I do not fear you, nor any wolf," Blind Seer retorted.

"Stop it!" Firekeeper shouted.

The males were circling now, deaf to any sound. Those who had been leaving the area now that the meeting was complete were drawn to the snarling, but tellingly, no one but Derian even tried to interfere.

The red-haired man ran over to Firekeeper.

"What's wrong with them? Can't you stop them?"

Firekeeper spared him a glance.

"Would you step between those? I would not and they claim to fight for love of me."

Derian's expression of shock became one of understanding.

"Still," he said weakly. "Maybe a bucket of cold water?"

"That would work for dogs," Firekeeper said, "but these do not fight on impulse. The matter has been long building."

Derian accepted this without argument, but Firekeeper had no attention to spare on surprise. Her universe had narrowed to the snapping, snarling pair. Dark Death had all the apparent advantage. He had been spared the injury that had laid Blind Seer low not that long before. He was also the larger, and probably the stronger, but Firekeeper placed her hopes on the knowledge Blind Seer had gained in their travels—and then she realized how unwise she was to do this.

For two years now, Blind Seer had run with her rather than with wolves. He had missed the daily sparring that defined the hierarchy within even the best-run packs. His opponents had been other than wolves—mostly humans and their dogs. With a sudden rush of panic, Firekeeper began to fear for him, and her hand dropped to her Fang.

"Don't," Derian said softly. "Take it from another man. Blind Seer would prefer to lose than to win only because you fought at his side. In any other fight, he would welcome you, but unless wolves are far different from what you have led me to believe, Blind Seer would not welcome you here."

Firekeeper looked at him, but the very stillness of the wolves who stood watching gave proof to Derian's wisdom. Dark Death's entire birth pack was present, and even when a well-timed slash from Blind Seer brought the blood welling up through the fur along one shoulder, not a one moved except where ears and tails flickered in comment to those who stood near.

So Firekeeper dug the tips of her broken fingernails into her palms, and struggled not to move, not to cry out, lest word or sound from her distract Blind Seer at a time when he needed every iota of his concentration.

Both wolves were bleeding now, Dark Death from shoulder and flank, Blind Seer from hip and throat. Both were trapped within the white heat of fury and would not feel anything other than a crippling wound—and that not until the limb crumpled and refused to respond.

Was Dark Death flagging? No, that had been a feint, but Blind Seer had not fallen for it. Dark Death might have hoped to lure the blue-eyed wolf close, but Blind Seer had kept his distance, and Dark Death was forced to make up momentum lost.

Blind Seer did not make this easy for him. By preference a wolf goes for throat and belly, but even a tail feels pain and it is hard to concentrate when lightning quick strikes hit everywhere. Dark Death grew confused, while Blind Seer became more and more concentrated. There was an attacker now and a defender, but Dark Death was not surrendering, and his defensive stance was enabling him to catch his breath.

Losing fury's white heat had also enabled Dark Death to think more clearly. When he resumed the attack, he went for Blind Seer's head, striking from the rear when he could, but eschewing several easy holds on neck and ruff to bite at Blind Seer's skull. Blind Seer kept his ears flattened back, and did his best to force Dark Death to attack from the front, where he would be exposing his throat, but it was evident he was disconcerted.

There was a stir of interest among the wolves. A yearling elk stomped his foreleg in excitement. The ravens set up a chatter, and an eagle shrieked.

Derian muttered almost to himself, "What's Dark Death about?"

Firekeeper answered tensely. "Blind Seer was hit in head soon before we first come to this island. He was much in pain. Dark Death has remembered and sees if old wound can be made new."

"That's nasty!"

"Yes," Firekeeper said softly. "Very good fighting to go for weak and old."

Had her climb up the tower walls not broken every fingernail she possessed, Firekeeper's palms would have been slick with blood. As it was, her fingertips ached in complaint, and Firekeeper forced herself to ease the pressure. What good would she be to Blind Seer if she bruised her hands beyond use?

With shock, she realized that she was anticipating him losing this battle, already planning how she could save him if he preferred death to surrender. She didn't care what Derian said. She wasn't going to let Blind Seer die from pride.

Bite and slash. Dark Death rearing up onto his hindquarters to get the elevation he needed to hit from above. Blind Seer rearing back in return, chests crashing together bringing both so close that—lacking a jaguar's claws—they could do each other little injury so they must fall back again, circle, and strike.

Then Blind Seer failed to make the answering rise. Instead, as Dark Death reared up, he dove down and under. In a move almost too blindingly fast to see, Blind Seer clamped his jaws tight onto Dark Death's left hind leg, high above the joint. He pulled back, jerking his unbalanced opponent hard onto his back.

Releasing the leg, which was bleeding heavily, Blind Seer straddled Dark Death and grabbed his throat in his jaws. He shook once, threatening. Knowing there would be no second warning, Dark Death went limp, his tail curling between his legs and every line of his body signaling absolute surrender.

Instantly, Blind Seer stepped back, and scraped contemptuous dirt over his fallen opponent.

"*Someone,*" he sniffed, "*might look to this fool's wounds.*"

Limping slightly, Blind Seer went over to Firekeeper, his head held high with a triumph that left no room for pain. Kneeling, she gave him an exuberant hug; then she began inspecting his injuries. There were a good number. Derian went without being asked to bring a bucket of the boiled water being kept for cleaning Rahniseeta's, Questioner's, and Wiatt's injuries. Derian then excused himself to go sit with Rahniseeta for a while.

Blind Seer huffed a bit at being cleaned and medicated at a time he clearly wanted to strut around, but he submitted with the wisdom of one who has survived his share of battles and knows the value of the physician's arts.

Firekeeper was no healer, but she had learned everything she could from those who were, and even had the skill to shave and stitch the longest of Blind Seer's slashes.

"My work may rob you of a scar or two," she told the wincing wolf, "but we both have enough of those that none may doubt our courage."

By the time she had finished, Hope brought report of Dark Death's condition.

"He lives and will walk again, but he'll do so without that hind leg for a good while to come. Healer used a bit of her power to knit the worst tears, and has asked any other duelists to hold their challenges until she has had time to recover."

Firekeeper looked up in shock, appalled at the thought there might be others, but saw that Hope was joking about this last.

"From what I have heard, both of you have made your preferences clear enough that none here will challenge you," the bird-woman said reassuringly. "Dark Death wishes to speak with you. Will you come?"

Firekeeper didn't want to do so, but she knew her manners and, with Blind Seer as entourage, went.

She found Dark Death stretched out on his side, his ribs rising and falling steadily. He was attended by Integrity and Moon Frost, but he had eyes for none but the two who approached.

"I made an offer when I challenged Blind Seer," Dark Death said proudly, "and I would offer it again rather than have you doubt my sincerity."

"I never accepted those terms," Firekeeper said, but Dark Death went on as if he had not heard her.

"When I said you were marvelous, I meant it. Yours is a wolf's heart, imprisoned in a human body. I would give you the means to set it free—and yet to allow you the freedom to return to the human shape that, as we saw today, grants you abilities wolves do not have."

Firekeeper met Dark Death's gaze, not to dominate as might a wolf, but with the frankness humans so valued.

"Dark Death, I never accepted your offer. Once I heard how the first maimalodalum came to be, I thought the practice foul. Even were you to offer your life willingly—as those sacrificed to the ambitions of the Old Country sorcerers did not—I would not accept. Blood magic seems to have a dangerous taste. I think one swallow would only make one hunger for more."

Dark Death growled.

"My life is yours to use. Take it! Let me at least give you what you desire. If I cannot have you, let me have that."

"No."

"Then when I can stand, I will throw myself into the ocean or from a cliff. These breaths I draw are an illusion, for from the moment I surrendered, I gave myself to death. Since I will die anyhow, can you not at least make my death worth something?"

Firekeeper stared at him in incredulity.

"Dark Death, I thought you a wolf, but now I realize you are naught but a pup. Ask Sky if he would have thrown away his life for nothing more than bruised pride. Ask those who are buried beneath the stone."

She wheeled away, disturbed and somehow disgusted, and Moon Frost limped after.

"Firekeeper," the silvery wolf said hesitantly. "If you have relinquished your claim . . ."

Firekeeper put a hand on Moon Frost's head.

"Win him for life, sister," she said softly. "There has been too much death."

She looked to the star-shaped tower where one alone had not emerged after the conference—but into which the maimalodalum had been unobtrusively slipping for some time now.

"And I fear there will be more."

TRUTH PACED, SHOULDER DEEP in the rivers of possibility. She was in so deep, she could hardly see where the streams split, but could only go where the strongest currents carried her. She was beyond choosing now. The drifting was almost restful, but for the concern that she would be carried in over her head.

The currents carried her through the collapse of the tower of Magic, streamlets flowing from many into one as Firekeeper resolved to save Shivadtmon rather than let him die. Truth felt a certain abstract pride that it was the wolf-woman's faith in Truth's own wisdom and goodwill that guided her actions, but this was not enough to pull her from immersion within the myriad ways time could split, to drag her back onto the relative dryness of contemplation.

Other currents flowed into one as Elwyn emerged from the ruins and was accepted, not killed, as the conference met and resolved how they would act on various matters. There was a great tangle where Dark Death challenged Blind Seer, varying from the blue-eyed wolf's refusing the challenge to the many ways the battle might end, and through Firekeeper's final decision. When these were resolved, a single current began to dig a deeper course than all that surrounded it. In the way of water, a deep river begins to flood its banks, flowing wide and slowing without losing power.

Truth found herself merely submerged to her knees now, but she would not get out and search for higher ground. From higher ground she might see—and in seeing try to choose and in choosing see and so go back in beyond her ability to control.

Even so, she felt when the swift swimming dolphins caught up to the boat that carried Dantarahma and his adherents south. There were twisted deltas here as lives lost meant lives touched more ways than the mind is fit to contemplate, but Truth was within the river, not above it, and she let the probabilities wash over her until resolution was reached.

Dantarahma's body was being pushed back to the harbor of u-Seeheera. When it arrived there would be another storm of questions. Each answer, each conclusion would create its own currents, some doubling back into the main, others cutting potential courses of their own.

Truth lowered her head and swam in the broadening stream, refusing to look.

BLIND SEER WALKED BESIDE FIREKEEPER as the wolf-woman made her way to the star-shaped tower. She laid her hand lightly on the wolf's neck, taking strength from his presence, forcing herself to walk toward when all she wanted to do was to run away.

In the pale light of a few lit stone panels, Questioner lay, and Firekeeper did not need a wolf's nose to know he was dying. She pressed her lips together tightly, fighting back sobs, but the tears came anyway, and she made the last few steps to the maimalodalu's side guided by Blind Seer.

She collapsed to her knees and found the strangely furred but very human face by touch.

"Is there anything that will save you?" she asked in desperation. "Only name it, even if it is my own life, and I will give it to you. I only have this life because of what you did for me, and I would give it back."

"No, child," Questioner replied, his voice wispy but distinct. "I said twelve years past that we would need you. We have only begun that need. In any case, why do you think I would accept the blood magic you yourself reject?"

Firekeeper hung her head, accepting, but the tears still fell and she dashed them away so she might see Questioner more clearly.

"This life has not been without its pleasures," Questioner said, "and I will be sad to leave it, but the deities have been kind to me. They let me see you, grown to all and more than what I dreamed."

"And I have seen you, and been given back my human father and mother as well," Firekeeper managed, "but I would have had more time. I wish I had not gone back to the mainland so quickly!"

"We make our best choices," Questioner said, his voice so soft Firekeeper had to bend to hear him. "Knowing too much only drives us mad as Truth."

He didn't say anything for a long time after, and Firekeeper drew back slightly. The maimalodalum had already lost Sky, but they didn't run from this new death in their small circle. There was courage in this that she could emulate, so Firekeeper wrapped one arm around Blind Seer and rested her free hand lightly on Questioner's flank, and waited.

Time passed in breaths. Some of the maimalodalum wept, others remained stoic. A few talked softly to Questioner, telling him how they valued his courage, his willingness to look beyond their own borders, and even to doubt when that doubting might lead to deeper understanding. They promised him they would not forget his example, and this would be his heritage.

But Questioner did not answer, only breathed, each breath becoming more laborious. Water dribbled from his mouth and matted his fur. Firekeeper wiped it away as gently as she could.

A shiver ran through Questioner's spotted flanks, a shiver that shook him from head to foot. He drew a ragged breath, and though they waited, no breath followed. They waited, and not even Firekeeper's sensitive hand resting on his flank could feel a rise or fall.

"He is gone," said Powerful Tenderness, and the massive, blocky bear body bent and lifted the other as if with the release of spirit, Questioner had suddenly become light.

Then Firekeeper could take no more. Rising to her feet, she ran before the tears could blind her step. She ran into the light, and when she could run no more, she threw back her head and howled.

The sound of her grief was so terrible that—as the maimalodalum told it after—had the Moon not already been broken, it would have shattered at the sound.

XLI

FIREKEEPER HAD VANISHED into the forest almost immediately after Questioner had died. Over a day had passed and she hadn't returned, but Derian was resigned to not worrying about her. Given her dislike of boats, he doubted she'd left Misheemnekuru, and the yarimaimalom had shown themselves quite adept at keeping track of what was going on throughout Misheemnekuru.

Derian and Harjeedian had been encouraged to remain in Misheemnekuru until Rahniseeta was ready to be moved, and they had accepted. Full reports had been sent back to the mainland, along with Shivadtmon and Barnet Lobster. The aridisdu was more than willing to redeem himself with his deities—and their earthly representatives—by talking. As had been predicted, Shivadtmon was already less inclined to boast about being chosen by Magic, and more pragmatically interested in keeping his life.

The remaining members of u-Liall were prepared for Dantarahma's eventual return—and were making plans for the selection of his successor. These apparently involved a variety of rituals and invocations, followed by a yarimaimalo representative of the year in question guiding the members of u-Liall to the chosen new member. Harjeedian was quite ready to speculate regarding who this would be, but Derian couldn't make himself care.

He suspected that Harjeedian cared less than he seemed, but lectured on about past successions to keep from expressing what he—and Derian—were both worried about to the point of distraction.

Rahniseeta was not doing well at all. She had not come around until a day after Questioner's death. When she had learned what had happened she had sunk into such a deep depression that even Healer the wolf was obviously worried about her. The mind could have a powerful influence on the body's ability to heal, but as long as Rahniseeta did not try to heal, complications from her injury that she otherwise would have easily thrown off would continue to plague her.

"Rahniseeta blames herself," Harjeedian explained pedantically, "not just for what happened to Questioner, but for everything. She says none of it—the deaths of the northerners, the collapse of the tower, Sky and Questioner's deaths—would have happened if she hadn't meddled."

Derian nodded. He'd sat his share of vigils alongside Rahniseeta's sickbed, had heard what she murmured in the periods between drugged sleep and dazed waking.

"And Rahniseeta doesn't see how events might have turned out worse if she hadn't gotten involved?" Derian asked, knowing the answer already.

"No one has been able to convince her so," Harjeedian said. "Perhaps if the jaguar Truth was able—and if Rahniseeta would believe a translator—Truth might convince her, but Rahniseeta knows Truth is gone again into madness, and blames herself for that as well."

"How can she?" Derian said, mostly to himself, but Harjeedian chose to answer.

"Rahniseeta feels that if she had not been captured, the yarimaimalom would probably have subdued the northerners long before they reached the towers."

"And how would they would have managed this without anyone getting hurt?" Derian asked.

"That isn't the point," Harjeedian said. "Rahniseeta has convinced herself this would be so—and although Hope has explained that the yarimaimalom would likely have suffered grave injuries and many deaths in such a battle, Rahniseeta will not permit herself to be convinced."

Derian shook his head, but deep down inside he understood.

"Have you had a chance to tell Rahniseeta she'll probably keep her arm?" he asked hopefully.

Harjeedian nodded. "But the news didn't do much to help her state of mind. All Rahniseeta said was that she'd have been glad to lose the arm if one of the others could have been saved."

"Who's with her now?" Derian asked.

"Powerful Tenderness," Harjeedian replied. "I'm sure he wouldn't mind if you wanted to take over. I'm going to check the tinctures I have brewing in the maimalodalum's stillroom. Rahni's getting some feeling back in her arm, and she's going to be in a lot of pain."

Derian nodded. He'd done his share of sitting with the wounded, and it had always seemed rather cruel that there were times when pain must accompany healing.

"I'll let Rahniseeta know where you are," he said.

After Powerful Tenderness had lumbered away, Derian sat watching Rahniseeta sleep. His hands moved automatically, shelling a large basket of beans intended as part of the evening meal.

Outside he could hear the buzzing of insects complaining about the heat. An occasional raven called, and in the middle distance, Elwyn's odd, flat voice droned happily as he sang. He'd been assigned to carrying stones to build a cottage for himself and Wiatt. Wiatt was also at work, but unlike Elwyn, he didn't sing.

Otherwise, the area was quiet. One never would have guessed a thriving community lived here. Most of the yarimaimalom slept through the heat of the day. The maimalodalum seemed to have adapted to their wild cousins' habits. Only humans, dependent on the sun for light, paid tithe in sweat.

"I wanted to be something other than Harjeedian's sister," Rahniseeta said, speaking as if they were in the middle of a conversation.

Derian started and dropped an unshelled pod into the pot between his feet. Rahniseeta gave a thin smile as he ducked to pull it out.

"I seem to bring disaster whenever I open my mouth," she said.

"Don't say that," Derian replied. "It's just a bean pod."

Rahniseeta's smile faded.

"Are all the rest just bean pods?"

"No, but I think you're taking too much on yourself. You didn't make Waln and the others sail here. You didn't take up watch in a tower you knew was unstable. You didn't make all those choices. Might as well blame the storm that first shipwrecked the *Explorer* as yourself."

"But if I hadn't run up there," Rahniseeta said, her tone torn between anger and pleading, "Shelby and the rest wouldn't have followed me."

"They would have gone up there anyhow," Derian said, "once Firekeeper and the yarimaimalom let them know they were trapped."

"But they would never have gotten up there," Rahniseeta said. "The yarimaimalom would have stopped them."

"The yarimaimalom would have been arrow-stuck," Derian said with brutal bluntness. "That much I've learned from what Truth said. Leave it alone, Rahniseeta. Why do you think Truth went mad? Seeing what would have happened, what might happen, is too complicated. Leave it alone and concentrate on what you can do."

"Which is?"

"Get well. Give us something to celebrate. Give me back a girl I can hold without worrying that I'll break her. Give me . . ." Derian faltered, heard himself go on as if he were listening to a stranger, "Give me back the girl I fell in love with, Rahniseeta."

"She's gone," Rahniseeta said, and Derian even wondered if she'd heard him. "That innocent who thought she wanted to make a difference—to be someone outside of her brother's shadow. She started dying at about the time she woke up aboard the *Islander* and realized that all she'd brought was trouble."

"The girl you're talking about isn't the girl I fell in love with," Derian said. "I fell in love with the one who was already making a difference—the one who could find the things no one else could, who made strangers feel at home. Sure, later you were willing to go against a member of u-Liall and that made me love you more, but I already loved and admired you."

"Loved?"

Rahniseeta stared at him as if she'd finally heard what he was saying.

"Love. Do I have the wrong word?" Derian asked. "What I mean is I like you. I admire you. I enjoy spending time with you. I don't want to leave you behind. I want to take you home to meet my family. I'd like to marry you."

He swallowed hard. Rahniseeta's expression flickered through a course of emotions revealing disbelief, wonder, even anger—but any of these was better than the dull indifference mingled with self-hatred she'd shown to this point.

Derian put out his hand and took hers. They were very different, his heavy freckled horseman's paw engulfing her slim, brown, long-fingered hand. His fingers were slightly green from the bean pods. Her fingers were still dirty under the nails, but despite the differences, they fit together surprisingly well.

"What do you think, Rahniseeta? Is there someone other than you I should ask for permission to marry you? We could get married twice, once here, once in Hawk Haven. It seems to be the way it's done when the bride and groom come from different countries—I have this on royal authority."

"There's no one whose permission you would need to ask," Rahinseeta said. "I'm an adult. But, I . . . I don't want your pity, Derian Carter."

"Rahniseeta, I'm not proposing out of pity! If you don't believe me, hop on a boat and visit Poshtuvanu. Ask him. Ask Zira. She's been teasing me about you practically since I moved to u-Bishinti. Horse! I think you're half the reason I went to u-Bishinti."

"What?"

"I was going crazy being so close to you, but separated by the fact that—no matter how prettily your bosses insisted we northerners were guests—I was a prisoner and you were my jailer. That made anything between us just plain impossible. In u-Bishinti I really felt like a guest—and an honored guest. That made it possible for me to start thinking about you—and did I ever. . . ."

Derian grinned at her, and Rahniseeta managed a wan smile in return.

"Do you really want to take me to meet your parents? Like this?" She flopped her broken arm for emphasis.

"Healer and Harjeedian both say that the arm is likely to mend with minimal long-term damage—if you work at it. I've heard that sea voyages are good for the health." Derian found himself grinning again. She hadn't said no—not yet. "There certainly isn't much to do at sea unless you're a sailor. You'd have plenty of time to let the arm heal and to exercise it when it's sound. I know one of the best healers in Hawk Haven—maybe the best. Doc would set you right."

"You've mentioned him. He's the one who's in love with the future baroness."

"And she with him," Derian said, "and the rest of us just wishing they'd get on and see sense. Maybe I've learned something from them. Forget the agony of long drawn-out courtships. Rahniseeta, my darling, I've seen you in leisure, in adversity, and now injured in body and soul. I love you more for knowing the strength beneath the beauty. Be my wife, Rahniseeta. Please?"

Rahniseeta let her eyes meet Derian's, and this time her smile was warm and relaxed.

"I never knew you could be so eloquent, Derian Counselor."

"I didn't either," he admitted. "See what you do to me?"

"I thought I had," she said, and this time her smile was definitely flirtatious. "I like what I'm seeing now."

He bent his head to kiss her, and she returned the caress with warmth.

"So," Derian said, and his voice was husky. "Will you marry me?"

Rahniseeta touched his cheek with her one sound hand, and Derian knew she was tracing a pattern amid the freckles.

"Yes," she said softly, "I will."

RAHNISEETA FEARED HARJEEDIAN would disapprove of her engagement to Derian, but instead of disapproving, the aridisdu was enthusiastic.

"This is marvelous, Rahni! I am certain that u-Liall will want to send some sort of embassy to Hawk Haven, Bright Bay, and possibly the Isles as well. You might well find yourself made ambassador to Hawk Haven. Your marriage to Derian Counselor is certain to soften any feelings of hostility that our . . . ill-planned venture may arouse once King Tedric learns of it. You may even be able to convince Derian to present the matter from our point of view—show that we meant no harm."

Harjeedian stopped for breath, and Rahniseeta inserted, "And it doesn't hurt that Derian is a king's counselor and can claim some favors from his heirs."

"Not in the least," Harjeedian agreed. "How can they react aggressively toward a land where one of their honored advisors has found a wife?"

Fleetingly, Rahniseeta found herself thinking of Derian's mare, Prahini. Was that all Harjeedian considered her, a consolation prize of some sort? When next she spoke, the thought gave her tone an ironical edge.

"And it doesn't hurt that Derian says he loves me?" she said. "Or that I love him?"

"Not in the least," Harjeedian assured her. "It's better that way. It will add a certain degree of sincerity and romanticism. From the tales I've heard Barnet Lobster sing, the northerners place a high value on romantic gestures."

Harjeedian was about to say more, but suddenly became aware of the tightness that had come over his sister's expression.

"Rahni . . ." he said, faltering. "I . . . I've made a complete fool of myself, haven't I?"

She only stared at him, not trusting her voice.

Harjeedian sank down on his knees next to her bed, and took her hand in his, much as Derian had done not long before.

"Rahni . . . I'm sorry. I do care that Derian treasures you. I suppose I've simply spent too much time looking at omens and portents. Nearly since the moment I had Firekeeper and Derian aboard *Fayonejunjal* I've been plagued with doubts regarding the rightness of what I did. The deities don't accept acting on orders as an excuse for unwise actions—especially from an aridisdu. I'm a selfish clod. Forgive me?"

"I'll think about it," Rahniseeta replied frostily, but she also managed a smile.

"Thank you." Harjeedian rose. "I'll go find Derian and let him know that I would welcome him into our family."

"And you will not mention the possible political advantages for us all," Rahniseeta said, her tone making this an order.

Harjeedian had the grace to looked shamed.

"I won't," he promised, and took his leave.

A FEW DAYS LATER, Healer and Harjeedian both agreed that Rahniseeta was strong enough to make the descent to where a boat would take them back to the mainland. She wasn't as certain. Her arm still throbbed when it was joggled, and lying in bed had done nothing for the stiffness of her torn muscles and bruised flesh.

However, Healer's talent had done a great deal to keep complications from arising. Rahniseeta was free from both infection and fever, and the others were eager to return to the mainland. Even Firekeeper had reappeared, explaining that she and Blind Seer had gone to the other island to thank those wolves who had been their first hosts. Rahniseeta also gathered the wolf-woman had arrived at some conclusion or other, for Derian reported that the tension that had haunted Firekeeper since their capture back in Hawk Haven had vanished.

Firekeeper even made a point of coming to tell Rahniseeta that she approved of the engagement.

"Derian is my first human friend," the wolf-woman said, "and always be my friend. I am glad to see him like this. Happy."

Rahniseeta found herself inordinately pleased by the wolf-woman's support. Firekeeper's disapproval would not have changed Rahniseeta's mind, but it would have created unpleasantness.

The maimalodalum had arranged to have two Wise Elk carry a litter suspended between them so Rahniseeta would not need to make the long walk. The elk's gait was deliberate and smooth, even on the steepest inclines, and Rahniseeta was deeply honored by their aid. She knew full well that even the Wise Horses did not permit themselves to be harnessed except upon the greatest need, and as far as she knew, the Wise Elk never did.

Except for Firekeeper becoming mildly seasick, the voyage back to the mainland was as pleasant as a holiday outing. Dantarahma's body had "washed ashore" a few days before, and the matter of his treachery—though not the details—had been made public. They knew they were all regarded as heroes, and that made for a degree of giddiness. Even Harjeedian, usually so careful of his dignity, was merry.

Barnet Lobster was an honorary member of the crew that came to bring them back, and had news of his own.

"U-Liall is willing to let me go home to the Isles, in order that I might speak to the queen on their behalf. It's in the way of being my reward for refusing to go ashore on Misheemnekuru. I've agreed to publicly represent myself as the only survivor of the shipwrecked *Explorer*. To be honest, given how the others behaved in the end, I'm just as happy with that. Queen Valora, however, will be told the full truth."

Harjeedian smiled sardonically, "Honesty is best, especially as if trade does begin between our peoples, some may hear rumors otherwise—though u-Liall will certainly declaim this an inauspicious matter for discussion."

Barnet nodded. "That's what I suggested as well. I'm not even really telling a lie. Except for those here, no one knows the precise truth, and I've already found that most of the disdum do not care to contemplate how narrowly disaster has been averted."

Rahniseeta listened carefully. She'd seen how both Firekeeper and Derian had tensed at the mention of Queen Valora, and thought it sad that Barnet, who had been Derian's friend, would now be—at least politically—his adversary. Being an ambassador was going to be more complicated than she had imagined—but she reassured herself that she would hardly be given the honor herself. More likely she would be advisor to some aridisdu appointed to the task.

Derian's voice interrupted her thoughts.

"That's quite a crowd on the wharf," he said. "How are they going to keep what happened quiet if they give us such a public welcome?"

"Say that the omens favored it," Harjeedian said, but his tone was absent, and he borrowed a long-glass from one of the sailors and scanned the shore.

After a moment, he lowered it, speculation dominating his expression.

"Very interesting," he said. "I'm not sure that the crowd is for us specifically."

"What do you mean?" Rahniseeta asked.

"Can you look through this?" Harjeedian said by way of answer. "Tell me what you think."

Handling the glass one-handed was awkward, but Rahniseeta managed.

"It reminds me," she said, "of the processions a few years ago when Ahmyndisdu Tiridanti was chosen for u-Liall. The robing is the same, as is the order of precedence. There's a jaguar to the fore, just as the doe was then."

"With Truth in retirement," Harjeedian said almost absently, "omens dictated that the mainland representative take over. A new jaguar will come over from Misheemnekuru in a few days."

Rahniseeta offered him a return of the glass. Harjeedian immediately raised it to his eye.

"Do you think we'll be in time to see who is going to be chosen?" Rahniseeta asked. "I suppose that they're heading for the Temple of Sea Beasts. The new junjaldisdu must be of that order."

"Perhaps," Harjeedian said, and his voice had tightened with excitement. "Perhaps, but they don't seem to be moving. They seem to be waiting."

He lowered the glass and Rahniseeta could see that his eyes were shining.

"Waiting," he said with emphasis, "for this boat . . . or more precisely, for someone on this boat."

Rahniseeta understood Harjeedian's excitement. Although in the past members of u-Liall had been chosen from the general populace, most commonly they came from the ranks of the disdum. Moreover, as the crew had left shore earlier that day, it was unlikely that the jaguar sought one of their number. That meant the one being waited for was among the four returning humans: Firekeeper, Harjeedian, Derian, and Rahniseeta herself.

The former two were the most likely. Ever since her arrival, there had been debate that Firekeeper's ability to speak directly with the yarimaimalom made her a logical member of u-Liall. Selecting her to take Dantarahma's place would give her the honor without forcing the creation of a new post. Firekeeper's tendency toward seasickness did make Rahniseeta wonder how good a representative she would be. Perhaps the deities would free her from that susceptibility.

A far more likely choice would be Harjeedian. The Temple of the Cold Bloods had its associations with water. Indeed, the majority of the yarimaimalom associated with the temple were at least part-time water dwellers. Harjeedian also had made a historic sea voyage, and was one of the few Liglimom who possessed intimate knowledge of lands that would certainly be of great concern in the coming years.

Glancing over at her brother, Rahniseeta could tell that his thoughts were similar to her own. He had straightened, his merriment giving way to dignified gravity. He was even trying to surreptitiously tidy his clothing, which was rather worse for wear after several days on Misheemnekuru.

Derian had taken up the long-glass and was examining the crowd on shore.

"Eshinarvash is there!" he said, his voice warming with pleased excitement. "And Varjuna and Zira and Meiyal . . ."

Harjeedian interrupted. "It is not uncommon for various members of the yarimaimalom to accompany the procession. Of course, the temple heads do so as well."

Rahniseeta wondered if anyone else could hear the excitement vibrating below Harjeedian's deliberate lecture. From the soft smile on Firekeeper's face, and Blind Seer's much broader panting laughter, she thought at least two did so, very clearly.

"Maybe," Rahniseeta said, hoping to soften Harjeedian's disappointment if they had misread the omens, "the procession is merely waiting for us. They may wish Firekeeper to offer direct verbal interpretation for the jaguar. It would be a nice touch and an honor for one whom our people have so misused."

Harjeedian frowned at this reminder of Firekeeper's privileged position, but nodded crisply.

"Good thought, Rahniseeta. In any case, it means we won't miss the choosing."

His voice still held that anticipatory vibration. Visualizing her brother's disappointment, Rahniseeta found herself hoping that he, and not Firekeeper, would be the one the deities had chosen.

The sailboat glided into its dock, handled with more than usual expertise by a captain and crew all too aware that they were the center of attention. They did credit to their training, and the gangplank was lowered with quite unnecessary ceremony.

Despite her seasickness, Firekeeper—Blind Seer at her side—managed to be the first onto solid land. They paused, waiting to assist Rahniseeta, but she waved them back.

"My arm's broken," she said, feeling all too much the center of attention, "not my leg."

Nevertheless, Derian insisted on giving her some support, for which she was grateful. Her balance wasn't everything she would like. Harjeedian hovered behind, and Rahniseeta fought down giggles at the idea of her dignified aridisdu brother diving into the water to haul her out if she slipped.

But all the passengers made it to shore without incident. Before the captain and crew could begin the jangling routine of taking down sails and getting the sailboat ready for dock, an enormous male jaguar strode forward. Tiridanti and the other three members of u-Liall walked behind him.

Fortunately the crowd dropped politely back, so there was room for those who had just arrived to walk forward and meet them on a broader section of the wharf. Otherwise, someone would quite likely have ended up inadvertently shoved into the water.

When the jaguar paused to sniff noses with Blind Seer, Rahniseeta heard Harjeedian's swift, sharp intake of breath, but he said nothing, and if he sighed in relief when the jaguar passed on after this exchange of politenesses, he did so so softly that Rahniseeta didn't hear.

It was evident that the jaguar was coming their way, and Rahniseeta made to move to one side so it could pass and get to Harjeedian. To her utmost astonishment, the jaguar stopped in front of her. It looked her up and down, heavy head moving with thoughtful deliberation, eyes more golden than Truth's intently focused. Then, aligning both paws directly in front of its chest, the jaguar gave a deep bow.

The motion was deliberate and calculated. No one could mistake it for a stretch. Rahniseeta's ears began to hum, and she thought she might faint. As from a great distance, Rahniseeta heard Tiridanti's high, young voice raised to carry to the waiting multitude.

"A choice has been made! The deities have spoken. The new junjaldisdu is named Rahniseeta."

The jaguar stepped back. Feeling as if she were being tugged by an invisible thread, Rahniseeta stepped forward. Cheers rose from the excited multitude, and if the faces of a few of the disdum were less joyful, Rahniseeta couldn't blame them. Twice in as many elections, the deities had chosen one from outside of the usual order—first Tiridanti, so young for her post, now Rahniseeta, who wasn't even a disdu.

I wonder what the deities are trying to tell us? Rahniseeta thought. Then she saw Derian's expression.

The red-haired northerner was standing only a few steps away, but clearly he was aware of the gulf that so suddenly gaped between them. Rahniseeta knew Derian didn't believe in the deities, but he would have respected her beliefs. In a private person, this would have been enough. Indeed, Rahniseeta suspected there were many who went through the forms of belief without holding belief, but such charades would not be enough for the spouse of a member of u-Liall.

Unable to look at Derian, Rahniseeta sought Harjeedian. She found him looking differently stunned, but even as she watched, Harjeedian's disappointment was changing into delight. He did believe that the deities directed this choice, and accepted the miracle that the younger sister he had done so much to care for had been chosen to represent Water. This choosing was validation of all the favors Harjeedian had begged on Rahniseeta's behalf, all the little sacrifices he had made on her behalf, all his pleasure was evident.

A heavy clopping sounded above the human voices, and Rahniseeta turned to see the Wise Horse Eshinarvash coming through the crowd. The throng parted before him, all the excited chatter falling silent. Eshinarvash had come to carry Rahniseeta to Heeranenahalm, to grant her a perch high above the crowd so that everyone could see her. If she accepted his offer, Rahniseeta knew there would be no changing her mind.

She turned to the man who, until moments before, she had thought would be her husband. Rahniseeta forced herself to look him squarely in those strange hazel eyes, and saw their greenish brown overwashed with unshed tears.

"I'm sorry, Derian," she said, then turned away.

Eshinarvash knelt, and despite her broken arm, Rahniseeta had no difficulty mounting. Then she felt herself rising, being carried upward in triumph.

Though she looked side to side, acknowledging the cheers of those who lined the processional way, she never looked back.

FIREKEEPER KNEW HER news would do little to alleviate Derian's pain, but she went to tell him anyhow. She found him in one of the suites of the building that had housed Waln and his people. It was nearly empty now, and had been given over to the remaining northerners.

Derian had been invited to return to u-Bishinti, but he had delayed, wanting to resolve the questions that remained regarding the northerners' status, and the likelihood of their returning home. Perhaps, too, he had not wanted to put himself where the pity of his friends and Zira's all too knowing gaze would not let him forget his loss.

Padding in soft-foot, Firekeeper found Derian lounging in a chair, apparently listening to Barnet strumming something on one of his string instruments. That Derian's thoughts were far away became evident from how he started when Firekeeper spoke.

"The Wise wingéd folk have agreed to carry messages home to our people," she said without preamble. "They know it is dangerous—the Royal Beasts have no love of them—but I have told them to use my name and maybe some will manage."

"Told," Derian said automatically. Then he sat up straight in his chair. "Are you saying that the letters I've been writing home might not have gotten there?"

Firekeeper shrugged. "How do they? The Liglimom have no trade to the north."

"I guess I . . ." Derian trailed off, frowning. "I guess I did think the yarimaimalom would have had something to do with it. Harjeedian did rather lead us to think that."

"Harjeedian," Firekeeper said, "does not so much lie as let you think and not say. I have guessed for some time, but I not see that this will help you."

Derian nodded. "I can see that."

He made as if to get up and search for paper and pen, then slumped into his chair. "What does it matter? How can I write my parents about any of this?"

Barnet set his instrument aside.

"You can let them know you're alive. It's been two moonspans and more since you disappeared. It's going to be at least another before you can be in Port Haven. One of the yarimaimalo will get there a lot sooner."

Derian looked at the minstrel, his expression guarded as it had been since he had learned Barnet would be returning to the Isles.

"Do you have family back north?"

"I do," the minstrel replied.

"You've been gone a lot longer than I have," Derian said, almost accusingly. "Doesn't it bother you? Didn't you want to jump ship rather than go kidnapping?"

Barnet gave a humorless smile.

"Of course I did, but you know we weren't given much more choice than you were. I thought about jumping ship in Hawk Haven, but, well . . . I had my reasons for going along with what Harjeedian wanted."

"Like wanting revenge against Hawk Haven," Firekeeper said to Blind Seer. *"I wonder how Barnet finds that taste now."*

"Sour," the wolf replied. *"You can smell it on him."*

"But I'm not the louse you think me," Barnet went on. "In Port Haven I managed to get a letter out to my family. I said I was on secret business for the queen and they weren't to worry—I'd make them proud when I came home."

"And the rest of the sailors?" Derian asked. "Did you send messages to their families, too?"

"I didn't," Barnet admitted, "but I'll go home and make sure due honor will be given to those who died—especially those who died in the original shipwreck and so are guiltless of all that followed."

"Where do lies end and stories begin?" Derian asked softly, but to Firekeeper's satisfaction he rose and located letter-writing materials.

"Write small," she reminded him. "It must go with a seagull or osprey."

"I'll remember," Derian said.

"Then when you write family, write King Tedric, too," Firekeeper said. "The Wise wingéd folk say they take to him, too. This way he know before sweet speaking ambassadors come.'"

Derian grinned, the first such expression Firekeeper had seen since Rahniseeta had ridden away.

Later that evening, when Barnet had gone to visit his lover, the other three went for a walk along the wharves. The locals watched them with polite fascination, but none obstructed them. Versions of what Dantarahma and his allies had been about were being circulated. In those stories, the northerners were being represented as divine agents, brought to set things right.

Firekeeper doubted this, but she didn't mind the respect with which the Liglimom viewed her. Blind Seer strolled along with such arrogance that Firekeeper teasingly told him he must have cat blood. The blue-eyed wolf laughed, then grew serious.

"It's not so funny," he said, *"when one knows of the maimalodalum."*

Across the waters, Misheemnekuru lay, dark green, hiding more mysteries than her mainland neighbors could imagine. Now, with the elevation of Rahniseeta, the maimalodalum knew there was one in power who knew of their existence. Would they welcome this or fear it?

Firekeeper didn't know.

Derian's voice broke what to him had been silence.

"So, the disdum have accepted that you cannot teach anyone how to speak to the yarimaimalom. You're free to go wherever you want. Are you going back to Misheemnekuru?"

Though he was obviously making an effort to speak smoothly, Firekeeper heard the catch in his voice.

"Yes." She shook as if to rid herself of flies and concentrated on making her meaning clear. "The yarimaimalom and the maimalodalum all have much to teach."

"I thought," Derian said, "you might make a home on Misheemnekuru. Those there don't seem to draw many lines between human and otherwise—and there were those who admired you."

"No," Firekeeper said, and her hand rested on Blind Seer's shoulder. "We not make a forever home there, only for a little."

Derian relaxed, and Firekeeper knew he had felt himself rather universally abandoned. He would recover, she thought, though his heart would stay sore for a time. Firekeeper knew she would always mourn Questioner. A short acquaintance was no guarantee against grief at parting.

Firekeeper wished she had the words to explain to Derian what she had learned, but in this, as in so many other things, she struggled to be human.

Free as she was to go anywhere her feet would carry her, Firekeeper knew herself to still be a captive, but thanks to Questioner and the others, she knew at last who held her so.

Her captor was not the Liglimom nor the wolves nor any to whom she felt love or duty. Firekeeper knew her ultimate captor was none other than herself. She had chosen to walk a way between worlds, to be neither human nor wolf nor anything other than Firekeeper.

Meeting Blind Seer's gaze, Firekeeper knew he too had made choices that set him apart from his people. They both were captives—or perhaps in openly admitting what bound them, they both were truly free.

GLOSSARY OF CHARACTERS

Agneta¹ Norwood: (H.H.) daughter of Norvin Norwood and Luella Stanbrook; sister of Edlin, Tait, and Lillis Norwood; adopted sister of Blysse Norwood (Firekeeper).

Aksel Trueheart: (Lord, H.H.) scholar of Hawk Haven; spouse of Zorana Archer; father of Purcel, Nydia, Deste, and Kenre Trueheart.²

Alben Eagle: (H.H.) son of Princess Marras and Lorimer Stanbrook. In keeping with principles of Zorana I, given no title as died in infancy.

Alin Brave: (H.H.) husband of Grace Trueheart; father of Baxter Trueheart.

Allister I: (King, B.B.) called King Allister of the Pledge, sometimes the Pledge Child; formerly Allister Seagleam. Son of Tavis Seagleam (B.B.) and Caryl Eagle (H.H.); spouse of Pearl Oyster; father of Shad, Tavis, Anemone, and Minnow.

Alt Rosen: (Opulence, Waterland) ambassador to Bright Bay.

Amery Pelican: (King, B.B.) Spouse of Gustin II; father of Basil, Seastar, and Tavis Seagleam. Deceased.

Anemone: (Princess, B.B.) formerly Anemone Oyster. Daughter of Allister I and Pearl Oyster; sister of Shad and Tavis; twin of Minnow.

Apheros: (Dragon Speaker, N.K.) long-time elected official of New Kelvin, effectively head of government.

Aurella Wellward: (Lady, H.H.) confidante of Queen Elexa; spouse of Ivon Archer; mother of Elise Archer.

Barden Eagle: (Prince, H.H.) third son of Tedric I and Elexa Wellward. Disowned. Spouse of Eirene

Norwood; father of Blysse Eagle. Presumed deceased.

Barnet Lobster: (Isles) sailor on the *Explorer.*

Basil Seagleam: see Gustin III.

Baxter Trueheart: (Earl, H.H.) infant son of Grace Trueheart and Alin Brave. Technically not a title holder until he has safely survived his first two years.

Beachcomber: a Wise Wolf.

Bee Biter: Royal Kestrel; guide and messenger.

Bevan Seal: see Calico.

Bibimalenu: (L.) member of u-Liall, representative for Air.

Bitter: a Wise Raven.

Blind Seer: Royal Wolf; companion to Firekeeper.

Blysse Eagle: (Lady, H.H.) daughter of Prince Barden and Eirene Kestrel.

Blysse Kestrel: see Firekeeper.

Bold: Royal Crow; eastern agent; sometime companion to Firekeeper.

Bright-Eyes-Fast-Paws: a Wise Jaguar.

Brina Dolphin: (Lady or Queen, B.B.) first spouse of Gustin III, divorced as barren.

Brock Carter: (H.H.) son of Colby and Vernita Carter; brother of Derian and Damita Carter.

Brotius: (N.K., Captain) soldier in New Kelvin.

---

¹Characters are detailed under first name or best-known name. The initials B.B. (Bright Bay), H.H. (Hawk Haven), N.K. (New Kelvin), or L. (Liglim) in parenthesis following a character's name indicate nationality. Titles are indicated in parenthesis.

²Hawk Haven and Bright Bay noble houses both follow a naming system where the children take the surname of the higher-ranking parent, with the exception that only the immediate royal family bear the name of that house. If the parents are of the same rank, then rank is designated from the birth house, greater over lesser, lesser by seniority. The Great Houses are ranked in the following order: Eagle, Shield, Wellward, Trueheart, Redbriar, Stanbrook, Norwood.

Calico: (B.B.) proper name, Bevan Seal. Confidential secretary to Allister I. Member of a cadet branch of House Seal.

Caryl Eagle: (Princess, H.H.) daughter of King Chalmer I; married to Prince Tavis Seagleam; mother of Allister Seagleam. Deceased.

Ceece Dolphin: (Lady, B.B.) sister to current Duke Dolphin.

Chalmer I: (King, H.H.) born Chalmer Elkwood; son of Queen Zorana the Great; spouse of Rose Rosewood; father of Marras, Tedric, Caryl Gadman, and Rosene Eagle. Deceased.

Chalmer Eagle: (Crown Prince, H.H.) son of Tedric Eagle and Elexa Wellward. Deceased.

Chutia: (N.K.) Illuminator. Wife of Grateful Peace. Deceased.

Cishanol: (L.) assistant to Meiyal, disdu in training.

Citrine Shield: (H.H.) daughter of Melina Shield and Rolfston Redbriar; sister of Sapphire, Jet, Opal, and Ruby Shield.

Colby Carter: (H.H.) livery stable owner and carter; spouse of Vernita Carter; father of Derian, Damita, and Brock.

Columi: (N.K.) retired Prime of the Sodality of Lapidaries.

Cricket: a Wise Wolf.

Culver Pelican: (Lord, B.B.) son of Seastar Seagleam; brother of Dillon Pelican. Merchant ship captain.

Daisy: (H.H.) steward of West Keep, in employ of Earl Kestrel.

Damita Carter: (H.H.) daughter of Colby and Vernita Carter; sister of Derian and Brock Carter.

Dantarahma: (L.) member of u-Liall, representative for Water.

Dark Death: a Wise Wolf.

Dawn Brooks: (H.H.) wife of Ewen Brooks, mother of several small children. Deceased.

Dayle: (H.H.) steward for the Archer Manse in Eagle's Nest.

Derian Carter: (H.H.) also called Derian Counselor; assistant to Norvin Norwood; son of Colby and Vernita Carter; brother of Damita and Brock Carter.

Deste Trueheart: (H.H.) daughter of Aksel Trueheart and Zorana Archer; sister of Purcel, Nydia, and Kenre Trueheart.

Dia Trueheart: see Nydia Trueheart.

Dillon Pelican: (Lord, B.B.) son of Seastar Seagleam; brother of Culver Pelican.

Dimiria: (N.K.) Prime, Sodality of Stargazers.

Dirkin Eastbranch: (knight, H.H.) King Tedric's personal bodyguard.

Donal Hunter: (H.H.) member of Barden Eagle's expedition; spouse of Sarena; father of Tamara. Deceased.

Edlin Norwood: (Lord, H.H.) son of Norvin Norwood and Luella Kite; brother of Tait, Lillis, and Agneta Norwood; adopted brother of Blysse Norwood (Firekeeper).

Eirene Norwood: (Lady, H.H.) spouse of Barden Eagle; mother of Blysse Eagle; sister of Norvin Norwood. Presumed deceased.

Elation: Royal Falcon, companion to Firekeeper.

Elexa Wellward: (Queen, H.H.) spouse of Tedric I; mother of Chalmer, Lovella, and Barden.

Elise Archer: (Lady, H.H.) daughter of Ivon Archer and Aurella Wellward; heir to Archer Grant.

Elwyn: (Isles) also called "Lucky Elwyn"; a sailor on the *Explorer.*

Eshinarvash: a Wise Horse.

Evaglayn: (N.K.) senior apprentice in the Beast Lore sodality.

Evie Cook: (H.H.) servant in the Carter household.

Ewen Brooks: (N.K.) spouse of Dawn Brooks, father of several children.

Faelene Lobster: (Duchess, B.B.) head of House Lobster; sister of Marek, Duke of Half-Moon Island; aunt of King Harwill.

Farand Briarcott: (Lady, H.H.) assistant to Tedric I, former military commander.

Feeshaguyu: (L.) member of u-Liall; representative for Earth.

Fess Bones: a pirate with some medical skills.

Firekeeper: (Lady, H.H.) feral child raised by wolves, adopted by Norvin Norwood and given the name Blysse Kestrel.

Fleet Herald: a pirate messenger.

Fox Driver: (H.H.) given name, Orin. Skilled driver in the employ of Waln Endbrook. Deceased.

Freckles: a Wise Wolf.

Gadman Eagle: (Grand Duke, H.H.) fourth child of King Chalmer and Queen Rose; brother to Marras, Caryl, Tedric, Rosene; spouse of Riki Redbriar; father of Rolfston and Nydia.

Garrik Carpenter: (H.H.) a skilled woodworker. Deceased.

Gayl Minter: see Gayl Seagleam.

Gayl Seagleam: (Queen, B.B.) spouse of Gustin I; first queen of Bright Bay; mother of Gustin, Merry (later Gustin II), and Lyra. Note: Gayl was the only queen to assume the name "Seagleam." Later tradition paralleled that of Hawk Haven where the name of the birth house was retained even after marriage to the monarch. Deceased.

Glynn: (H.H.) a soldier.

Grace Trueheart: (Duchess Merlin, H.H.) military commander; spouse of Alin Brave; mother of Baxter.

Grateful Peace: (Dragon's Eye, N.K.) also, Trausholo. Illuminator; Prime of New Kelvin; member of the Dragon's Three. A very influential person. Husband to Chutia; brother of Idalia; uncle of Varcasiol, Kistlio, Linatha, and others.

Grey Thunder: a Wise Wolf.

Gustin I: (King, B.B.) born Gustin Sailor, assumed the name Seagleam upon his coronation; first monarch of Bright Bay; spouse of Gayl Minter, later Gayl Seagleam; father of Gustin, Merry, and Lyra Seagleam. Deceased.

Gustin II: (Queen, B.B.) born Merry Seagleam, assumed the name Gustin upon her coronation; second monarch of Bright Bay; spouse of Amery Pelican; mother of Basil, Seastar, and Tavis Seagleam. Deceased.

Gustin III: (King, B.B.) born Basil Seagleam, assumed the name Gustin upon his coronation; third monarch of Bright Bay; spouse of Brina Dolphin, later of Viona Seal; father of Valora Seagleam. Deceased.

Gustin IV: (Queen, B.B.) see Valora I.

Gustin Sailor: see Gustin I.

Half-Snarl: a Wise Wolf.

Hard Biter: a Wise Wolf.

Harjeedian: (L.) aridisdu serving the Temple of the Cold Bloods; brother of Rahniseeta.

Hart: (H.H.) a young hunter.

Harwill Lobster: (King, the Isles) spouse of Valora I; during her reign as Gustin IV, also king of Bright Bay. Son of Marek.

Hasamemorri: (N.K.) a landlady.

Hazel Healer: (H.H.) apothecary, herbalist, perfumer resident in the town of Hope.

Healer: a Wise Wolf.

Heather Baker: (H.H.) baker in Eagle's Nest; former sweetheart of Derian Carter.

High Howler: a Wise Wolf.

Holly Gardener: (H.H.) former Master Gardener for Eagle's Nest Castle, possessor of the Green Thumb, a talent for the growing of plants. Mother of Timin and Sarena.

Honey Endbrook: (Isles) mother of Waln Endbrook.

Hope: a maimalodalu.

Hya Grimsel: (General, Stonehold) commander of Stonehold troops.

Idalia: (N.K.) assistant to Melina. Sister of Grateful Peace, spouse of Pichero; mother of Kistlio, Varcasiol, Linatha, and others.

Indatius: (N.K.) young member of the Sodality of Artificers.

Integrity: a Wise Wolf.

Ivon Archer: (Baron, H.H.) master of the Archer Grant; son of Purcel Archer and Rosene Eagle; brother of Zorana Archer; spouse of Aurella Wellward; father of Elise Archer.

Ivory Pelican: (Lord, B.B.) Keeper of the Keys, an honored post in Bright Bay.

Jalarios: see Grateful Peace.

Jared Surcliffe: (knight, H.H.) knight of the Order of the White Eagle; possessor of the healing talent; distant cousin of Norvin Norwood who serves as his patron. Widower, no children.

Jem: (B.B.) deserter from Bright Bay's army.

Jet Shield: (H.H.) son of Melina Shield and Rolfston Redbriar; brother of Sapphire, Opal, Ruby, and Citrine. Heir apparent to his parents' properties upon the adoption of his sister Sapphire by Tedric I.

Joy Spinner: (H.H.) scout in the service of Earle Kite. Deceased.

Kalvinia: (Prime, N.K.) thaumaturge, Sodality of Sericulturalists.

Keen: (H.H.) servant to Newell Shield.

Kenre Trueheart: (H.H.) son of Zorana Archer and Aksel Trueheart; brother of Purcel, Nydia, and Deste Trueheart.

Kiero: (N.K.): spy in the service of the Healed One. Deceased.

Kistlio: (N.K.) clerk in Thendulla Lypella; nephew of Grateful Peace; son of Idalia and Pichero; brother of Varcasiol, Linatha, and others. Deceased.

Lillis Norwood: (H.H.) daughter of Norvin Norwood and Luella Stanbrook; sister of Edlin, Tait, and Agneta Norwood; adopted sister of Blysse Norwood (Firekeeper).

Linatha: (N.K.) niece of Grateful Peace; daughter of Idalia and Pichero; sister of Kistlio, Varcasiol, and others.

Longsight Scrounger: pirate, leader of those at Smuggler's Light.

Lorimer Stanbrook: (Lord, H.H.) spouse of Marras Eagle; father of Marigolde and Alben Eagle. Deceased.

Lovella Eagle: (Crown Princess, H.H.) military commander; daughter of Tedric Eagle and Elexa Wellward; spouse of Newell Shield. Deceased.

Lucho: (N.K.) a thug.

Lucky Shortleg: a pirate.

Luella Stanbrook: (Lady, H.H.) spouse of Norvin Norwood; mother of Edlin, Tait, Lillis, and Agneta Norwood.

Marek: (Duke, Half-Moon Island) formerly Duke Lobster of Bright Bay but chose to follow the fate of his son, Harwill. Brother of Faelene, the current Duchess Lobster.

Marigolde Eagle: (H.H.) daughter of Marras Eagle and Lorimer Stanbrook. In keeping with principles of Zorana I, given no title as died in infancy.

Marras Eagle: (Crown Princess, H.H.) daughter of Chalmer Eagle and Rose Rosewood; sister of Tedric, Caryl, Gadman, and Rosene; spouse of Lorimer Stanbrook; mother of Marigolde and Alben Eagle. Deceased.

Meiyal: (L.) iaridisdu of the Horse.

Melina: (H.H.; N.K.) formerly entitled "lady," with affiliation to House Gyrfalcon; reputed sorceress; spouse of Rolfston Redbriar; mother of Sapphire, Jet, Opal, Ruby, and Citrine Shield. Later spouse of Torovico of New Kelvin, given title of Consolor of the Healed One. Deceased.

Merri Jay: (H.H.) daughter of Wendee Jay.

Merry Seagleam: see Gustin II.

Minnow: (Princess, B.B.) formerly Minnow Oyster. Daughter of Allister I and Pearl Oyster; sister of Shad and Tavis; twin of Anemone.

Moon Frost: a Wise Wolf.

Nanny: (H.H.) attendant to Melina Shield.

Neck Breaker: a Wise Wolf.

Nelm: (N.K.) member of the Sodality of Herbalists.

Newell Shield: (Prince, H.H.) commander of marines; spouse of Lovella Eagle; brother of Melina Shield. Deceased.

Ninette Farmer: (H.H.) relative of Ivon Archer; attendant of Elise Archer.

Nipper: a Wise Wolf.

Nolan: (Isles) a sailor on the *Explorer.*

Noonafaruma: (L.) member of u-Liall; representative for Magic.

Northwest: Royal Wolf, not of Firekeeper's pack. Called Sharp Fang by his own pack.

Norvin Norwood: (Earl Kestrel, H.H.) heir to Kestrel Grant; son of Saedee Norwood; brother of Eirene Norwood; spouse of Luella Stanbrook; father of Edlin, Tait, Lillis, and Agneta; adopted father of Blysse (Firekeeper).

Nstasius: (Prime, N.K.) member of the Sodality of Sericulturalists, sympathetic to the Progressive Party.

Nydia Trueheart: (H.H.) often called Dia; daughter of Aksel Trueheart and Zorana Archer; sister of Purcel, Deste, and Kenre Trueheart.

Oculios: (N.K.) apothecary; member of the Sodality of Alchemists.

One Female: also Shining Coat; ruling female wolf of Firekeeper and Blind Seer's pack.

One Male: also Rip; ruling male wolf of Firekeeper and Blind Seer's pack.

Opal Shield: (H.H.) daughter of Melina Shield and Rolfston Redbriar; sister of Sapphire, Jet, Ruby, and Citrine.

Oralia: (Isles) wife of Waln Endbrook; mother of three children.

Ox: (H.H.) born Malvin Hogge; bodyguard to Norvin Norwood; renowned for his strength and good temper.

Paliama: (L.) a kidisdu.

Pearl Oyster: (Queen, B.B.) spouse of Allister I; mother of Shad, Tavis, Anemone, and Minnow.

Perce Potterford: (B.B.) guard to Allister I.

Perr: (H.H.) body servant to Ivon Archer.

Pichero: (N.K.) spouse of Idalia; father of Kistlio, Varcasiol, Linatha, and others.

Polr: (Lord, H.H.) military commander; brother of Tab, Rein, Newell, Melina.

Posa: (Prime, N.K.) member of the Sodality of Illuminators.

Postuvanu: (L.) a kidisdu of the Horse, son of Varjuna and Zira.

Powerful Tenderness: a maimalodalu.

Puma Killer: a Wise Wolf.

Purcel Archer: (Baron Archer, H.H.) first Baron Archer, born Purcel Farmer, elevated to the title for his prowess in battle; spouse of Rosene Eagle; father of Ivon and Zorana. Deceased.

Purcel Trueheart: (H.H.) lieutenant Hawk Haven army; son of Aksel Trueheart and Zorana Archer; brother of Nydia, Deste, and Kenre Trueheart. Deceased.

Questioner: a maimalodalu.

Race Forester: (H.H.) scout under the patronage of Norvin Norwood; regarded by many as one of the best in his calling.

Rafalias: (N.K.) member of the Sodality of Lapidaries.

Rahniseeta: (L.) resident in the Temple of the Cold Bloods; sister of Harjeedian.

Rarby: (Isles) a sailor on the *Explorer.*

Rascal: a Wise Wolf.

Red Stripe: also called Cime; a pirate.

Reed Oyster: (Duke, B.B.) father of Queen Pearl. Among the strongest supporters of Allister I.

Rein Shield: (Lord, H.H.) brother of Tab, Newell, Polr, Melina.

Riki Redbriar: (Lady, H.H.) spouse of Gadman Eagle; mother of Rolfston and Nydia Redbriar. Deceased.

Rillon: (N.K.) a maid in the Cloud Touching Spire; a slave.

Rios: see Citrine Shield.

Rip: see the One Male.

Rolfston Redbriar: (Lord, H.H.) son of Gadman Eagle and Riki Redbriar; spouse of Melina Shield; father of Sapphire, Jet, Opal, Ruby, and Citrine Shield. Deceased.

Rook: (H.H.) servant to Newell Shield.

Rory Seal: (Lord, B.B.) holds the title Royal Physician.

Rose Rosewood: (Queen, H.H.) common-born wife of Chalmer I; also called Rose Dawn; his marriage to her was the reason Hawk Haven Great Houses received what Queen Zorana the Great would doubtless have seen as unnecessary and frivolous titles. Deceased.

Rosene: (Grand Duchess, H.H.) fifth child of King Chalmer and Queen Rose; spouse of Purcel Archer; mother of Ivon and Zorana Archer.

Ruby Shield: (H.H.) daughter of Melina Shield and Rolfston Redbriar; sister of Sapphire, Jet, Opal, and Citrine Shield.

Saedee Norwood: (Duchess Kestrel, H.H.) mother of Norvin and Eirene Norwood.

Sapphire: (Crown Princess, H.H.) adopted daughter of Tedric I; birth daughter of Melina Shield and Rolfston Redbriar; sister of Jet, Opal, Ruby, and Citrine Shield; spouse of Shad.

Sarena Gardener: (H.H.) member of Prince Barden's expedition; spouse of Donal Hunter; mother of Tamara. Deceased.

Seastar Seagleam: (Grand Duchess, B.B.) sister of Gustin III; mother of Culver and Dillon Pelican.

Shad: (Crown Prince, B.B.) son of Allister I and Pearl Oyster; brother of Tavis, Anemone, and Minnow Oyster; spouse of Sapphire.

Sharp Fang: a common name among the Royal Wolves; see Northwest and Whiner.

Shelby: (Isles) a sailor on the *Explorer*.

Shivadtmon: (L.) an aridisdu.

Siyago: (Dragon's Fire, N.K.) a prominent member of the Sodality of Artificers.

Sky: also Sky-Dreaming-Earth-Bound, a maimalodalu

Steady Runner: a Royal Elk.

Steward Silver: (H.H.) long-time steward of Eagle's Nest Castle. Her birth name and origin have been forgotten as no one, not even Silver herself, thinks of her as anything but the steward.

Tab Shield: (Duke Gyrfalcon, H.H.) brother of Rein, Newell, Polr, and Melina.

Tait Norwood: (H.H.) son of Norvin Norwood and Luella Stanbrook; brother of Edlin, Lillis, and Agneta Norwood.

Tallus: (Prime, N.K.) member of the Sodality of Alchemists.

Tangler: a Wise Wolf.

Tavis Oyster: (Prince, B.B.) son of Allister I and Pearl Oyster; brother of Shad, Anemone, and Minnow Oyster.

Tavis Seagleam: (Prince, B.B.) third child of Gustin II and Amery Pelican; spouse of Caryl Eagle; father of Allister Seagleam.

Tedric I: (King, H.H.) third king of Hawk Haven; son of King Chalmer and Queen Rose; spouse of Elexa Wellward; father of Chalmer, Lovella, and Barden; adopted father of Sapphire.

Tedgewinn: (Isles) a sailor on the *Explorer*.

Tenacity: a Wise Wolf.

Tench: (Lord, B.B.) born Tench Clark; right hand to Queen Gustin IV; knighted for his services; later made Lord of the Pen. Deceased.

Thyme: (H.H.) a scout in the service of Hawk Haven.

Timin Gardener: (H.H.) Master Gardener for Eagle's Nest Castle, possessor of the Green Thumb, a talent involving the growing of plants; son of Holly Gardener; brother of Sarena; father of Dan and Robyn.

Tipi: (N.K.) slave, born in Stonehold.

Tiridanti: (L.) member of u-Liall; representative for Fire.

Toad: (H.H.) pensioner of the Carter family.

Tollius: (N.K.) member of the Sodality of Smiths.

Toriovico: (Healed One, N.K.) hereditary ruler of New Kelvin; spouse of Melina; brother to Vanviko (deceased) and several sisters.

Tris Stone: a pirate.

Truth: a Wise Jaguar.

Tymia: (N.K.) a guard.

Ulia: (N.K.) a judge.

Valet: (H.H.) eponymous servant of Norvin Norwood; known for his fidelity and surprising wealth of useful skills.

Valora I: (Queen, Isles) born Valora Seagleam, assumed the name Gustin upon her coronation as fourth monarch of Bright Bay. Resigned her position to Allister I and became queen of the Isles. Spouse of Harwill Lobster.

Valora Seagleam: see Valora I.

Vanviko: (heir to the Healed One, N.K.) elder brother of Toriovico; killed in avalanche.

Varcasiol: (N.K.) nephew of Grateful Peace; son of Idalia and Pichero; brother of Kistlio, Linatha, and others.

Varjuna: (L.) ikidisdu of the Horse; husband of Zira; father of Poshtuvanu and others.

Vernita Carter: (H.H.) born Vernita Painter. An acknowledged beauty of her day, Vernita became associated with the business she and her husband, Colby, transformed from a simple carting business to a group of associated livery stables and carting services; spouse of Colby Carter; mother of Derian, Damita, and Brock Carter.

Violet Redbriar: (Ambassador, H.H.) ambassador from Hawk Haven to New Kelvin; translator and author, with great interest in New Kelvinese culture.

Viona Seal: (Queen, B.B.) second wife of King Gustin III; mother of Valora, later Gustin IV.

Wain Cutter: (H.H.) skilled lapidary and gem cutter working out of the town of Hope.

Waln Endbrook: (Isles) formerly Baron Endbrook; also, Walnut Endbrook. A prosperous merchant, Waln found rapid promotion in the service of Valora I. Spouse of Oralia, father of two daughters and a son.

Wendee Jay: (H.H.) retainer in service of Duchess Kestrel. Lady's maid to Firekeeper. Divorced. Mother of two daughters.

Wheeler: (H.H.) scout captain.

Whiner: a wolf of Blind Seer and Firekeeper's pack, later named Sharp Fang.

Whyte Steel: (knight, B.B.) captain of the guard for Allister I.

Wind Whisper: Royal Wolf, formerly of Firekeeper's pack, now member of another pack.

Xarxius: (Dragon's Claw, N.K.) member of the Dragon's Three; former Stargazer.

Yaree Yuci: (General, Stonehold) commander of Stonehold troops.

Zahlia: (N.K.) member of the Sodality of Smiths. Specialist in silver.

Zira: (L.) kidisdu of the Horse; wife of Varjuna; mother of Poshtuvanu and others.

Zorana I: (Queen, H.H.) also called Zorana the Great, born Zorana Shield. First monarch of Hawk Haven; responsible for a reduction of titles—so associated with this program that over-emphasis of titles is considered "unzoranic." Spouse of Clive Elkwood; mother of Chalmer I.

Zorana Archer: (Lady, H.H.) daughter of Rosene Eagle and Purcel Archer; sister of Ivon Archer; spouse of Aksel Trueheart; mother of Purcel, Nydia, Deste, and Kenre Trueheart.